The Hazards of the Old Ones

Also by Ren Garcia:

The League of Elder: Sygillis of Metatron

Coming Soon from Ren Garcia:

The Temple of the Exploding Head Trilogy:
Lady Sammidoran of Monama
The Machine
The Temple of the Exploding Head

The Belmont Saga:
The Sands of the Solar Empire
The Shadow tech Goddess

For a complete on-line glossary of terms, please visit:

www.theleagueofelder.com

The Hazards of the Old Ones

Ren Garcia

iUniverse, Inc.
New York Bloomington

The Hazards of the Old Ones

title page art and back cover text: Justine Marie Hedman

iUniverse books may be ordered through booksellers or by contacting:
iUniverse
1663 Liberty Drive
Bloomington, IN 47403
www.iuniverse.com
1-800-Authors (1-800-288-4677)

ISBN: 978-1-4502-3883-0 (pbk)
ISBN: 978-1-4502-3884-7 (ebk)
ISBN: 978-1-4502-3885-4 (hbk)

Printed in the United States of America
iUniverse rev. date: 8/5/10

Table of Contents

Part 3—The Shadow tech Conspiracy

List of Illustrations

Map of Kana (*Carol Phillips*)

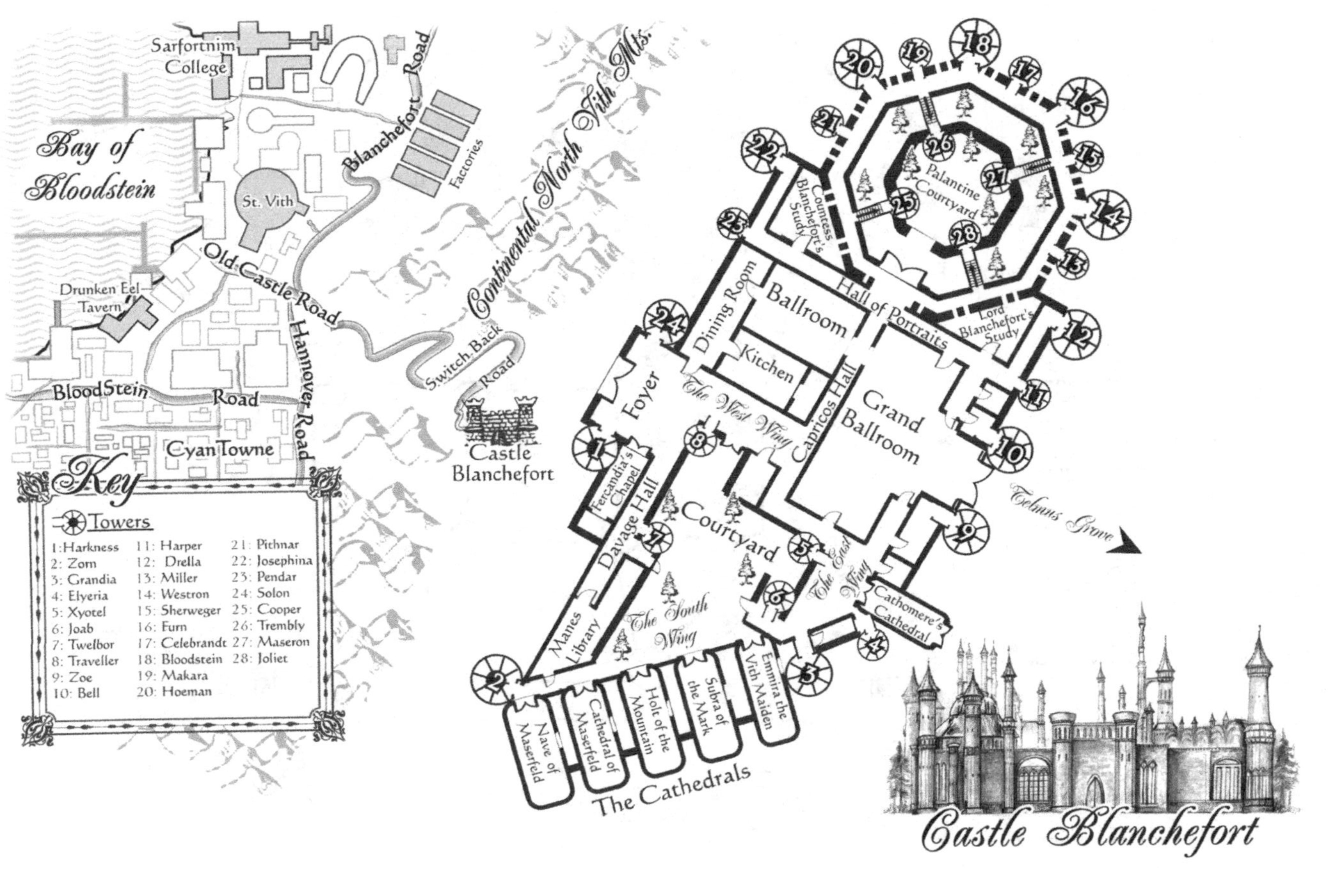

Map of Castle Blanchefort (*Carol Phillips*)

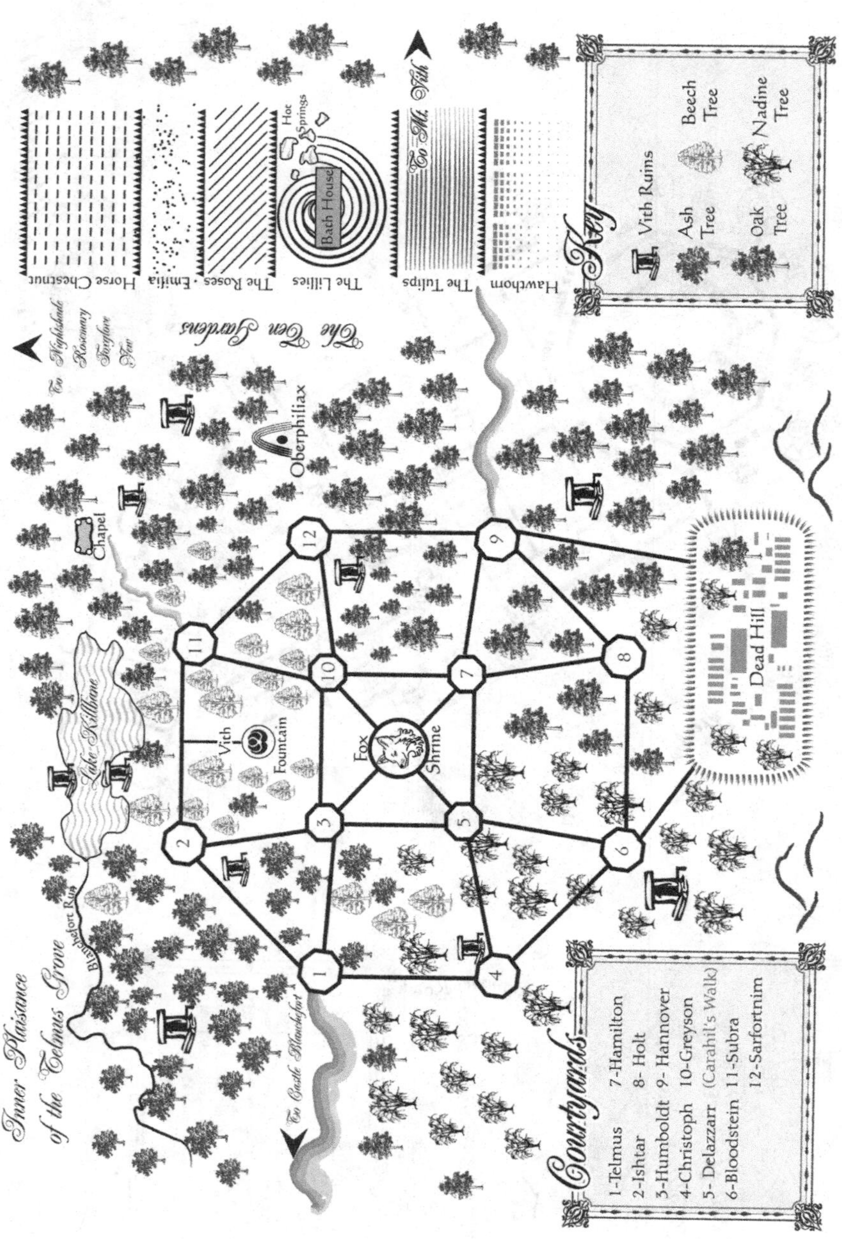

Map of the Telmus Grove (*Carol Phillips*)

Carahil has a Vision (*Justine M. Hedman*)

Forward

-A God's Gambit

How does a young god protect himself from his own best intentions? How to save what needs to be saved without losing one's own soul? In this work, we find the newly formed god, Carahil, going about his daily duties (feed kittens! plan pranks!) when he is beset by a disturbing apparition. A demonic, evil twin of the god appears in his grove, bringing with it a vision of the destruction of a planet's worth of humanity. "You can save them," the demonic twin informs Carahil, adding. "Be a god for them…and set me free."

But Carahil knows better; as young as he may be, his head is filled with information. He understands how the Universe punishes gods who do not adhere to the old rules of Balance, as in the tale of the House of Bodice, whose Elemental Spirit tried only to protect them. In the end, the House of Bodice was lost and their Elemental Spirit protector was stripped of his godhood, turned into a demon and left to suffer as a prisoner of the House of Windage, his power turned towards chaos.

So, how to become the savior of humanity when your heart is filled with love for all small, helpless things and your brain is filled with insane amounts of power but your hands are tied by the laws of the Universe. How to avoid a miscue, a misstep that would lead even the best intended god down the steep, rocky path to damnation? For as we all know "Power tends to corrupt; and absolute power corrupts absolutely."

If this is true of men, then it is true one billion times over of even the most playful, prank-loving god, for all power comes with a price and all actions have consequences, even for the noble of heart. The sad truth that exists in all universes is that good deeds have only a fifty-fifty chance of succeeding. And, the good intentions of a god could prove, with disastrous result, to pave the way to the Windage of Kind.

-Jasmine B. Brennan

San Francisco, CA

Prologue

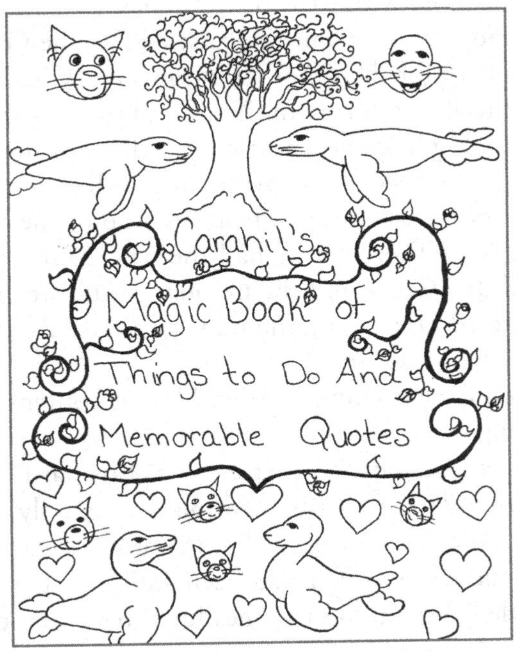

Carahil's Diary (*Justine M. Hedman*)

I—Item 10: Save Planet X!

May all be saved.

He watched the kittens finish their lunch of warm milk lapped up from a saucer. It was a little chilly out in the Grove today, and he heated a few rocks so that they would radiate steady warmth all afternoon. When the kittens, a spry bunch of mackerel tabbies, finished, he removed the saucer from their box and gently nosed them around, situating them for sleep. A few, full from their lunch, were already out. The rest licked his nose with their tiny tongues.

He had found the kittens in the back half of the Grove the other day; hungry, looking for their mother. As always, he gathered the little buggers up and took care of them. He was always on the lookout for lost creatures needing help; he was friend to all tiny things gone astray. He'd rescued a goose with a hurt wing and an Ibex with a bad hoof. The Elemental Spirits called down from the top of the Universal Tree and laughed at him. They said he had the whole universe to play in, why bother with the Grove and the mundane little creatures he found there? They pestered him to join them in the Celestial Arborium. They said that's where he belonged.

Time enough for the Universe later. He was content where he was for the time being.

Like the kittens he watched over, he was also a fairly new creation; a baby. In the mundane counting of time he was only a few months old. His mind, however, was packed with information. He knew the old stories and the wisdom that had been won over the centuries. He possessed knowledge spanning the ages for it had been carefully built into him by his Mother.

When the kittens settled, he got his book out. He had a book that he conjured up whenever he wanted. It was a thick diary entitled *Carahil's Magic Book of Things To-Do and Memorable Quotes.* He created it himself. In it, nuggets of wisdom, lists and notes automatically scratched themselves on the pages. Sometimes, he scribbled things in himself with a marker held in his teeth, for he didn't have hands to write with. Mother certainly picked an odd form for him to inhabit, though, he could have hands if he wanted. He could be anything he wanted; however, he mostly confined himself to the small streamline shape Mother had given him.

He loved writing things down in his book. It helped keep the mind clear, and he liked to be organized.

Today's read:

THOUGHT FOR THE DAY: No hour is too early and no labor is too great for a friend in need.

TO DO:

Item 1)—Feed the kittens. DONE

Item 2)—Heat up a few rocks for the kittens. (Might be chilly today) DONE

Item 3)—Prank Mother. (Hide her favorite hat)

Item 4)—Prank Lord Blanchefort. (Hide his favorite hat too, preferably in a different place where you hid Mother's hat)

Item 5)—Prank Countess Blanchefort. (Undetermined—possibly steal a gown from her wardrobe and hang it from the Josephina Tower pole, where it may be clearly seen from the village) WARNING!!—Countess might still be angry from pie-in-face fiasco last week, and the missing knickers! Tread with caution.

a)—Prank Countess anyway.

Item 6)—Check kitten's box for litter.

That should make for a full day.

The other ones, the lesser creations of murky silver Mother tinkered about with, gathered to watch him fuss with the kittens and write in his book. They were drawn to him as always. But he paid them no mind. They were crude silver automatons. He, on the other hand, was a masterpiece, a one-of-a-kind. To use sporting terms, he considered himself the Cinco Pass, the Royal Flush-draw, or the 7-10 pickup, while *they* were warm-up pitches, a pair of deuces and late gutter balls at best. Mother wasn't going to be outdoing herself anytime soon. Possibly, without realizing it, his Mother, with rolled-up sleeves and torrents of Silver, had created an Elemental Spirit—in essence, a god. He was a god who loved to protect lost kittens and hang gowns from flag poles.

He was going to head out and set to his pranks. He *loved* pranking his Mother and the people in the castle. He meant no harm, and Lord Blanchefort actually pranked him back with a pail full of fish guts the other day. That was good clean fun! He'd been avoiding Countess Blanchefort; her reaction to his thrown pie at the spring ball was rather volcanic and unflattering. Ah well. Perhaps when she returns from the village and sees her gown hanging from the flagpole her demeanor will improve.

He checked the kittens one last time, when his book opened and a fresh entry scratched itself in:

Item 7)—Encounter a demonic version of yourself in the Grove.

That's when *He* came stumping around the green, leafy corner; an image of himself. A backwards, distorted, maniacal image of a sadistic bearing.

They stood there staring at each other. Though the image was evil and somewhat terrifying to behold, he had to admit the brute was devilishly handsome. If he had any flaws or vices, Pride, it must be said, was his. He was a bit of a narcissist.

He knew, from the ancient wisdom, that meeting one's self was a dire omen. Nothing good can happen when confronted with one's twin. And there he was, an exact copy; only his eyes were foreboding and his smiling mouth was prickly with serrated teeth like a shark.

This was an image of himself turned to a demon. Becoming a demon was his greatest fear. Becoming a demon was a punishment for misuse of power and the breaking of Universal rules of balance. Demons were sent to the bottom of the Universal Tree, to the huddled, steam-shot buildings of the Windage of Kind. The sullen windows of the Windage were dark, betraying nothing of the terrors hidden within except for the occasional red eyes peering out.

He'd been to the Windage once, and he didn't like it much; a dirty, noisy place. Every so often, since the time of his birth, his book flipped a page and scratched out an odd recurring entry that perplexed him:

Someone stares out the windows of the Windage of Kind at you. She's not a bad girl, just needs a little love. Maybe a bright smile will make her happy. She hasn't been happy in a long time. You should make it a point to visit her. She'd like that. Demons have feelings too.

Who was this girl the book kept mentioning, and what was she doing in the Windage? Once, he actually decided to take his book's advice and went to the Windage, staring into the windows. He saw huddled shapes within, and blinking red eyes looking out seeking forgiveness. His book interjected:

She's not there, you missed her.

* * * * *

His twin stood there and sniffed. *"I smell sweet morsels. Give them to me."*

He got in front of the box containing his kittens to protect them.

The image laughed. *"I am you, merely unbound …"* his twin said. *"You like to protect the weak, then look at me … I have a rare treat for you. See what is to come. I offer you a vision …"*

His book added another entry:

Item 8)—Witness a horrific vision of the death of billions.

"Look at me and see what is to come …" his twin said again.

He didn't want to look, but his evil twin insisted. *"Look, look. See the dying. Listen to the screaming … Can you hear it?"*

Can you hear it?

He looked into his twin's wide eyes and saw everything. So much death, so much loss under purple skies and upon sandy ground. He listened to dying mouths praying to be saved.

"Save us!"

"Save us! Who will save us?"

"What have we done to deserve this?"

He stood there on his haunches and wept, unable to turn away.

"You can save them," he said. *"None of this has to be. Simply go there and perform a miracle, listen to their praise. They will love you. They will lift their cups and call you a god. Be a god for them … and set me free."*

"I can't—I can't simply save a bunch of people, I'll become a demon! I'll go to the Windage!"

His evil twin faded away. *"Then it's all on your conscience. Save them … and set me free."*

He stood there alone in the Grove, open-mouthed, panting.

Save them?

What was he supposed to do? How could he prevent such a thing?

It's not fair, not fair! Why should he bother? Why was it his responsibility? There are others, there are many gods floating about, let somebody else take care of it.

This was too much for him. Let somebody else save them.

Another entry in his book:

Item 9)—Pretend you didn't see what you saw. Take no action. Think happy thoughts.

He was bound by the old rules of Balance, the mystical bond placed upon all insanely powerful creatures. He could soar the heavens, he could frolic on a star if he wanted, but he couldn't save a life or directly influence fate. There were age-old rules against that.

If he didn't follow the rules, then he was to go to the Windage and become a demon, a horrific image whose power was turned to chaos.

He closed his bright eyes and twitched his whiskers. He continued to see his vision replayed for him with vivid detail, like a sad vid he didn't want to watch but couldn't turn away from; the death and loss, the end of dreams. Unsuspecting eyes, open at present, shall soon be shut … forever. The masses of people going about their lives, oblivious of the deadly wave that is coming for them: waking, dressing, eating their meals, conceiving new life only to soon lay unburied on a vast killing field where any who might weep over their fallen bodies are dead too.

Somebody, anybody, save them! I can't. I can't!

He prayed for guidance. He looked up to the top of the Universe and prayed for one of the Arborium to hear his call and take some sort of action; to do something spectacular while he watched, taking notes as an eager student, ready to learn. Perhaps the next time he had a vision of horrific death and destruction, he'd be more ready to do something about it with the practical knowledge he'd witnessed firsthand from this experience.

I know what to do—I saw a master in action, first-hand. Lemme' at `em!

The bovine, equine, avian, canine and ophidian forms inhabiting the Arborium were quiescent for a change. The silence was telling. He knew that this brutal vision was his alone—if not he, then no one else. No one was coming to save them.

Wind played through the branches of the beech trees. Unseen birds chirped. The kittens rustled in their box. Time moved on toward that coming black moment when it would all end, the Grove unmindful and uncaring.

What would his Mother say? What would she think? She'd probably be quite disappointed, that he saw what was going to happen and did nothing—let it happen, let them all pass into memory, as if they'd never existed at all. He didn't want to fail his Mother, and, more so, with every passing moment, he didn't want to fail these people either; like a mangy stray that had crossed his path, caught his eye, and now was stuck in his heart—like his kittens. The well-being of these doomed people was now his responsibility. Another entry in his book, repeated over and over:

Item 10)—Save Planet! Save them all!

His Pride set aside, his Humanity and the heart his Mother gave him, spoke.

You cannot let them die. You cannot ignore what you saw. You have to save them.

But how? How was he supposed to do this? He had the power to help them—he might have to fortify himself a little bit, to add a touch of magic to his already arcane makeup, and then he should be more than up to this task, easily. But he couldn't simply swoop in and save the day, he wasn't allowed to do that; there were universal rules against such things, and the only thing the Universe cared about was the rules.

Nobody breaks the rules, they said in the Arborium. *We'd have to punish you.*

We don't break the rules.

You don't break the rules either. We'd have to redden your eyes and send you to the Windage.

You want to fix a bad future, then gut it out!

That's why they call it the 'Frustration of the Gods'—because it's frustrating, get it?

The ramifications for ignoring or breaking the rules to both them (the people he wanted to save) and to himself would be terrible. They would simply die another day, and in probably a worse fashion than the first time, and he'd become a demon, just like his evil twin.

Save them … set me free.

Gut it out!

If they were to be saved, then he had to do it the right way—the hard way, by ruse and deception, by manipulation, by getting the Softlings to take action, to willingly risk their own mortal lives in order to save the lives of others; the lives of strangers—the lives of enemies.

The Softlings—that's what the Arborium called them in a rather arrogant fashion: the weak, mortal people, the mundane folk of the universe—yet, it was the Softlings that added weight to the cosmic scales. It was the Softlings who ultimately determined what the gods could and could not do, when miracles could and could not happen.

It was the deeds of the Softlings who gave the gods their arms and filled their quiver with arrows. That's how the Universe wanted it.

Several more entries appeared in his book:

TO DO: Save Planet X

THOUGHT FOR THE DAY: The best way to clean up a mess is to get started.

WARNING!! You cannot directly intervene without upsetting the Universal Balance.

1)—Add weight to scales.

a)—Gather forces you can have faith in.

b)—Move them into place.

c)—Push your forces in the direction you need them to go, regardless of the immediate consequences. (Blackmail and intimidation tactics might be accepted) (See Task 4) Gift giving is applicable. Bribery is also applicable, but not desired.

2)—Players

a)—Who will participate in saving Planet X?

Who will participate? Whose lives was he about to dangle over the abyss? Who was about to get shaken and cast like a pair of dice before the winds of fate? A bit of the demon entered his mind and the diary continued:

b)—Get yourself a whole bunch of expendable low-lifes and zeros, touch pots and pinch-pricks. Drag all you can find to Planet X and force them to participate. Threaten them. Frighten them! Who cares if they want to or not? Who cares if they get killed in the process (nobody will miss them when they're gone). Throw them in like a handful of chopped scallions in a Dutch oven of boiling water and watch `em float!

He shook his head and cleared his mind. What had come over him? He realized how easy it would be to lapse and become a demon after all; to be the cause of a tragedy instead of the preventer of one. There really was no way to do this other than to invest himself completely and take the route closest to his heart; to directly involve the people he loved most. He scratched out the entry and continued:

THOUGHT FOR THE DAY: For best results, use the best ingredients.

b)—Find the most honorable man you can: Lord Blanchefort
c)—Find a lady whom you adore: Countess Blanchefort
d)—Find the most powerful person around: Mother
e)—Find the person with the biggest heart: Lt. Kilos
--to these four people you entrust the fate of billions.
NOTE!!--Must be suitably imperiled for weight to be added.

He thought a bit.

d)—EXTRA WEIGHT FOR REPROBATES!! In addition, I'll need a criminal after all. Just one. Find yourself a scalawag or rootless bravo you can trust or blackmail to help save Planet X. A scalawag—a real rot-gut swilling degenerate—will add lots of weight to scales (if he willingly cooperates). Check prisons, bars, alleys, casinos, cricket huts, bowling alleys and docks for scalawag.

3)—Once weight is added, perform Miracle at Planet X.

4)—Apologize to any whose lives you ruined in the process of saving Planet X.

a)—Flowers are always nice.

REQUIRED MATERIALS:

5)—Will need a bit of magic to touch yourself up. Possible candidates:

a)—Trama-Lana (necklace) REJECTED (not powerful enough)

b)—Moonglow (knife) REJECTED (won't really help)

c)—Oberphilliax (gate) POSSIBLE—if things go bad, can reset.

d)—Brightstone (beryl) Will allow you to be in many places at once. ACCEPTED

6)—Chosen Resource: Brightstone

a)—Brightstones are all registered with Sisterhood of Light. Stealing one will be dangerous.

b)—Brightstones kept in place that is beyond your reach. Will need help fetching one. No Blue may walk there—must have a Brown. A Brown may stand where a Blue cannot.

c)—Enlist help of Lt. Kilos to fetch Brightstone. It MUST be Lt. Kilos.

d)—See, Task 4 regarding Lt. Kilos.

Resigned, he looked around at the vast green of the Grove and put his book away. A whole planet of "kittens" needed saving, and he cannot fail. He must not! And, he must not lose those whom he loved in the process.

He looked at the little kittens in the box, soundly sleeping in the warmth of the nearby rocks he'd heated. A tear rolled down his muzzle and dripped off.

It sizzled on a rock.

II—The Capture

"Who are you?" came a demonic voice over the Duke of Oyln's transponder as he dove his black *Goshawk* ship toward the sloping ground far below. In a steep dive, the sweptback wings of his ship groaned in protest and began flapping slightly in the thickening air. Holding his long pipe in his teeth, he kicked the lateral bar, lined his targets up and pressed the button.

Flashing lances of Sar Beams shot out and blasted the people standing on the ground to steaming pieces.

The survivors below were startled. They were deep in a Painted Cloak, invisible to all. None should be able to detect them. The Duke, however, had a bank of exotic scanners in his *Goshawk* ship. Properly adjusted and carefully tweaked over the last few days of searching, he had them properly tuned and dialed in. He could detect their heat and see them just fine. There they were: the gigantic, unwashed men naked as the day they were born standing guard, and the ragged, bone-thin women shuttling back and forth. All, either through fear or mindless ignorance, served their abhorred master, and many who were alive and well in the morning often didn't live to see the nightfall.

They served a Black Hat of a cruel and deadly note. Sudden, agonized death was something they lived with.

They stood at their posts as the Duke's *Goshawk* roared in on them through the purple clouds. They stood there as the pelting Sar Beams ripped into them. The naked men—the Hulgismen—clearly had no idea what to do. They had no necks to ring, no limbs to rend. Like primates, they beat their fists against the ground in agitation but left their feet planted right where the Black Hat had put them. To move would mean death at her hands.

And to stand there meant death too, as the Duke's weapons mowed them down.

The ragged females, the Adepts who might one day become Black Hats themselves, clambered about. They ran to their emergency posts, manning their Darklights, hoping to catch the Duke's bat-like ship in their sights and send him down in a shapeless pile of blackmetal slag. Casually, he banked, aimed and pressed the button.

Sar Beams.

Adepts dead at their posts, their Darklights shot to pieces. A few more Darklights came on and went skyward. He aimed. The lights went quiet.

And then the star of the show, the Black Hat herself, came out of her tent; the tent the Duke had been carefully avoiding. In an ironic twist, the Black Hat's tent, where many Hulgismen and Adepts died at her hands every day, was, at the moment, the one safe area to be found.

The Duke was not going to shoot at the tent; he might hit the Black Hat, and she was his whole reason for being there.

She threw open the flap and stormed out in her scarlet robe and black, featureless mask. She was, no doubt, used to being in complete control. What was this ruckus? Who was about to die for disturbing her much needed rest? He imagined all sorts of things must be going through her evil, Shadow tech clouded head.

In his scanners, he saw her look up at his ship and, for a moment, she was clearly just as dumbstruck as her Hulgismen guard had been.

How was her contingent discovered under full Painted Cloak—that's what she must be thinking.

"Who are you?" came her thoughts over his transponder in a demonic growl. He banked to the west and slaughtered the remainder of the Black Hat's Adepts and the few Hulgismen who still had a spark of life left in them.

He then turned his black ship to face his prize. The Black Hat was now alone and quite defenseless, for he had picked the time of his attack well. He knew she was drained of her Shadow tech. He knew she was out of her head with exhaustion.

The Duke knew the Black Hat was quite helpless.

She turned and began running to the north, her slender arms and long sleeved scarlet robes swishing at her side. Unused to running, she quickly tired and began stumbling.

She Wafted away in a smoky cloud. He saw her reappear a good ten miles away in his scanners. Not a bad Waft. He adjusted his course and was back on top of her in just a minute or two, his vessel quickly covering the distance.

She Wafted again. Again, he followed. And again, and again, over and over; he could play this game all day, however the Black Hat could not. Eventually, she tired and fell to the ground, unable to Waft any further.

He bore down on her.

"*WHO ARE YOU?*" came her thoughts again as she lay there on all fours, unable to stand.

The Duke closed the distance in his ship and that was that.

III—The Death of the Bodice

Three thousand years ago, in 99989EX ...

They had asked for help for years. They went to the Sisterhood, hats in hand, and told them what they were going through.

"Our land is poisoned, gone bad."

"We see demons in the night—we're afraid for our children," they said.

"And, we hear noises, on the wind, like a furtive drumming."

Lord Porter of Bodice and his folk told the Sisters how their lands were no longer safe. The Sisters listened, thanked them for taking the time to visit, and told him and his contingent that they shall discuss what was told, and decide a suitable course of action.

Relieved, Lord Porter took his people and returned to their farmlands, confident that the Sisterhood will help them.

Unfortunately, the Sisters didn't think twice about Lord Porter and his lot—these people who had come to them for help—the Bodice, a House of simple-minded farmers from the Hala region. The Sisters, thinking the matter was insignificant, did nothing. Surely, if such a thing was truly happening with frequency then they, the Sisterhood of Light, should already know all about it, have investigated and collected reams of documentation on the matter. The Bodice, kind and goodly people, must be mistaken, paranoid or possibly delusional.

The matter will sort itself out. The Bodice will be fine.

Lord Porter and the Bodice, however, were not fine—they were not delusional. They suffered on their poisoned lands by the River Seven, their births becoming tainted with deformity and death. They were indeed seeing demons in the night—horrible, fleshless creatures—and they heard the maddening drums that never stopped.

The demons became bold and knocked on the Bodice's door. They laughed at them, and began trying to take their children. The Bodice, ignored by the Sisters, melted in fear. They tried relocating several times, upping stakes and rebuilding miles away, starting fresh in a new manor, but the demons always followed them. What were they to do?

One night, the demons broke into their manor as they slept and took Lord Porter and his large family.

"*We're going to burn you,*" they said with delight as they carried them out into the night.

A strange creature came from the sky. In a roar, it drove the demons away and released the Bodice. It was huge, elephant-like with tusks that reached up into the sky, and could talk. It loved the Bodice's many children and told them that it could help. It kept the demons at bay and promised it would protect them. For years the elephant stood watch over the Bodice. The demons stayed away—they were afraid of it.

Maiax was his name, and for the Bodice's children, whom he loved, he maintained his vigilance.

One day, the elephant told them that their lands were hopelessly tainted and the demons had placed a stain upon their souls. The only thing to do was leave—and not just leave the area, or Hala, or the whole of Kana for that matter, but to get as far away as they could, to leave the League and the Sisters who had forsaken them. It told them that a vast group of Great Houses were preparing to go to the Xaphans and join with them. The Bodice were followers of Elder religion, and didn't want to go to the Xaphans. The elephant told them there was a green planet, far away, where they could grow their crops beyond the reach of the demons. The green world was a place where their children could play at safety and peace. It took some convincing, but the Bodice agreed. They trusted the elephant, for he had protected them.

They took everything they had and went to the stars. The elephant, all smiles, told them he will be waiting for them on the promised world.

There, he waited and waited in lush fields, but the Bodice never showed.

Unbeknownst to him, the cosmos was moving against the House of Bodice.

* * * * *

Shortly after leaving Kana, they were beset upon by the House of Charn, also leaving the League for the Xaphans. Unlike the Bodice, the House of Charn was mad and savage—eager to go to the Xaphans. The House of Charn was starving as they made their way through space, and they fell upon the Bodice in their slow-moving, defenseless transport. Boarding their ship, they stole their supplies, their guidance controls and stellar compass, drained their tanks of fuel, and left them nothing.

They killed Lord Porter and threw his body out the lock into space.

Desperate and slowly starving now themselves, the Bodice children cried out for the elephant to come and save them, as he had before.

But the Universal Balance was out-of-scale and swinging randomly, forming a wall of chaos between them and the eyes and ears of their protector. Their guardian elephant, so dutiful through the years, couldn't see and hear what was happening to them, couldn't predict the terror that awaited—such was the danger of upsetting Balance. He had upset Balance for years, bending it to his will to protect the Bodice.

Now, the scales of Balance were swinging in the other direction, and there was nothing he could do about it.

The elephant happily awaited their arrival on the green world, slowly becoming worrisome when they failed to show.

The Bodice, out of supplies, out of fuel, leaderless and going hungry, diverted to a dark, smoky world of pits and vapor-filled chasms. There they huddled in their powerless transport and prayed to their guardian elephant for help.

After several days of waiting, there was a knock on the hatch of their transport. The children were happy—they thought the elephant had come at last.

The demons were at the door, clenching their fleshless fists, and this time there was no elephant to come and save them.

First, the children were taken to an unknown fate, and soon the adults were taken as well. They were taken someplace deep, where the beating of drums was loud and terrible. And, one by one, they were burnt alive in basins of fire before a deadly horned god whom the demons worshipped.

Soon, the House of Bodice, cursed and tormented, forsaken by the Sisters, was gone in burnt ash and drifting smoke.

A victim of Balance gone astray.

The elephant, sitting there waiting for them, was punished for his role in this tragedy. His eyes turned red, his power gone to chaos, and he went to the Windage of Kind to stare, red-eyed, out the windows.

Maiax, the Great Elephant, in trying to save the Bodice from the demons, became a demon himself.

Part 1 – The Sister's Program

Countess Sygillis of Blanchefort (From Carahil's Diary)

1—The Countess of Blanchefort

Sygillis, Countess of Blanchefort (formerly of Metatron), had faced many enemies in her long life, but this surely was the most implacable.

She stood there in the vast, semi-darkened room, standing stock still. Sixty feet away in the pooled light, was her enemy; silently mocking her. She was normally a fearless woman, but in this case she was tentative and unsure of herself. She leaned forward a bit, bent down and raised her weapon to her breast, gripping it tight; never once taking her eyes off the foe that had humiliated her time and again but was determined to master. She side-stepped to her left a couple of boards.

She and the enemy were at a standoff. The vast room around her was silent, save for the slight crinkling of her gown. Oh, this blood-gutted gown she was wearing! How was she supposed to do this attired in such a cumbersome garment?

* * * * *

She was a brand new countess and was still assimilating to the complex life at court in the League. She cut a stately, but somewhat comical, figure as she glided about the castle at her lord's side wearing her Blanchefort gown. She wasn't used to such a thing, but, for her lord, she was trying her best. At just a shade over five feet high, she was diminutive when compared to the tall, lean Blancheforts. She was more than a foot shorter than Lord Davage, her husband, though she often wore her wavy red hair "up" in the old Blanchefort style, and that certainly made up for her lack of height. Uncomfortable in a gown, she often lapsed in protocol. At a recent ball she was hosting, she was caught scratching her back behind a potted plant when she thought nobody was looking; her face turning as red as her hair. What might have been a humiliating scandal was dashed away when her lord promptly decreed the space behind the plant a designated scratching area and insisted that all in attendance have a turn (some guests even had a second turn behind the plant, scratching away).

It had been nine months since she had been wed to the tall, blue-haired man whom she adored and became the one thousand, four-hundred and sixty-third Countess of Blanchefort. The Blancheforts, as she had come to know, were notorious throughout history for having "different" sorts of countesses heading up the Household; ladies not of the usual, tea-drinking stock generally populating other Great Houses all over the League. Traces of these old Blanchefort countesses could be found all over the castle, hidden in the unseen places the ancient structure teemed with. She discovered the chapel of Lord Davage's mother, Countess Hermilane. She had been a fierce, pugilistic woman and the icon hanging in her hidden little chapel depicted her carrying a drawn rapier as proof. She discovered another one, of Countess Treiste from centuries ago. From her reading, she had been reputed to breathe water like a fish, and, sure enough, she bore a pair of gill-like slits on her neck. These were Dav's ancestors and she loved them all; since she had none of her own, she cherished his all the more.

Sygillis fell in love with this old castle. She had never had so much in her whole life. For nearly two hundred years she had been a creature known as Sygillis of Metatron, an evil, terrifying Black Hat of Hammer class and enemy of the League. The number of people she had remorselessly killed as a Black Hat was impossible to accurately count. She could do all the things that Black Hats could do: withstand hot and cold, find her way in the dark without error, determine lie from truth and, occasionally, see the future. Like her Black Hat sisters in their dark Shadow tech temples, she was fearless and of long life. Like her Black Hat sisters, she bore the mark—the Shadowmark. It was a twisting intersection of black lines wrapping around her right eye, ending near her cheekbone. It was the only blemish on her otherwise perfect complexion. Its black form was offset by her fierce apple green eyes; eyes that captivated the people. At first rather shy regarding the mark on her face as an evil stigma, she thought to cover it with a demure hand or a veiled hat, however she was moved to tears when, visiting a class of school children in the village one afternoon, she found they all had painted little marks around their eyes in tribute. To be accepted and loved without question or hesitation was something still new to her.

The Shadowmark, with its intricate design, looked like a tattoo, but was actually a birthmark. With it came Shadow tech, that ancient, illegal substance that grew within her body and gave the Black Hats their fearsome power. The Shadowmark was the key to Shadow tech's growth within her, except, in her case, her love for her lord had turned the black Shadow tech to silver: "Silver tech", he had called it.

A captain of the Fleet vessel *Seeker*, occasionally her lord Davage was compelled to away to some stuffy Fleet function or League meeting. His absences were never long, but the countess felt every moment. She was devoted to him body and soul.

She passed the time by removing her regal Blanchefort gown, putting on her black Hospitaler bodysuit, and prowl barefoot through the labyrinthine castle. If she was clumsy in her gowns, she was as agile as a panther in her bodysuit. Using her Black Hat skills, she explored the castle with relish, knowing precisely where she'd previously been, and she never failed to discover more. On her many expeditions she'd discovered lost passageways teeming with ancient treasures, huge forgotten halls plunged in walled-up darkness (one of which was gorgeous and was crying out to be refurbished), hidden courtyards overgrown with ivy, and obscure libraries full of the arcane

As she fared the stars at her lord's side in the *Seeker,* her time in the castle was limited and she made the most out of every moment.

* * * * *

The standoff with her foe was finally over. Ready at last, the countess attacked. With short, pounding steps she glided down the wooden floor; her knees maddeningly slapping against the heavy fabric of her gown. She cranked back with her weapon and let it fly in a graceful arc. The midnight blue ball leapt from her hand, slid down the lane and hit the tenpins with a satisfying commotion.

She stood up straight and inspected the damage. Hmmm … Five pins down. She had gotten the 1, 2, 3, 6 and 10. She returned to the scoring table and looked at her totals. After ten frames, she had scored a 74.

Creation …

Bowling had quickly become a passion for her. In her crawling adventures through the tunnels and hidden spaces of the castle, she had accidentally discovered the Blanchefort's secret bowling alley that nobody had told her existed. She found a tiny chute beneath the stately Palantine Courtyard in the northern wing of the castle and squeezed through it, popping up in the pin pit of lane 3. Seeing the pins lined up in order, she thought this must be some forbidden, pagan temple she'd stumbled into. Pulling herself out of the pit, mouth open with wonder, she walked up the immaculate wooden alley, nearly slipping and breaking her body-suited fanny on the heavily oiled surface.

The jig was up and she confronted her Lord. What was this place? She demanded to know. What sorts of things went on there?

"Bowling," he said, leading her by the hand through the Ten Gardens, "is a common game that we of the Great Houses openly abjure. It's a vulgar sort of thing and we, accordingly, dismiss it as such. However, we all love to bowl, truth be told. That is a common feature of the League, Syg, to openly dismiss a thing while heavily partaking of it in secret. We bowl on Nether Day by tradition. We bowl whenever we can. It is a hidden passion we have—appearances, though, are everything. Blues are not supposed to like bowling. All Great Houses have a hidden bowling alley on their grounds that they do not speak of. And, if you wish to impress other ladies about the League, Syg, your bowling average is an important, if understated, talking point to challenge the ladies with, though I thank Creation you are not heavily concerned with such banal Blue trivialities."

He took her through the secret entrance in the Palantine Courtyard and down the hidden stairwell. And there was the fabulous Blanchefort alley, hidden from all eyes except theirs for centuries. It was pristine and ornate in the Vith style. There was a bar and well-stocked service made of carved marble and other decorative stones. Lit from above by pools of hidden light were three long lanes of compact, yellowish maple-wood boards bordered on either side by a metal depression that she was told was called a "gutter". At the end of the lanes were ten, neatly arranged white clubs called "pins". The Blanchefort coat-of-arms was stamped on each one in bold red. Lining the walls in multi-tiered galleries were life-sized statues of past Blanchefort lords and countesses, tall and proud, dressed in their best and all holding carved stone balls.

Before each lane was a small console with plush chairs where the game was observed and scored. Near to that, was an elevated "hole" where balls appeared. Several brightly colored balls sat on rails near the hole.

"How is it played, love?" she asked, quite intrigued.

He served her a cool summer drink from the bar and seated her at the console of Lane 1. As she sipped her drink, he took a ball, squared himself up, leaned over and trotted down the lane in a slight crouch, his CARG jangling at his hip. He wound back and threw the ball at the pins; she thought he looked ridiculous as he accomplished the action. Small wonder they performed this activity in secret.

His ball spun down the lane with an ominous rumble and then struck the pins, making a great clash of noise that shocked her. He knocked all of the pins down. Some sort of robot or crafted sorcery then gathered and reset them into position.

"Ah," Davage said, smiling. "That is a strike, you see, ha ha! Bravo!"

Seemed simple enough. She set her drink down and stood to give it a try. He gave her a ball (it was rather heavy and smooth), helped her stick her fingers into the small holes and showed her how to hold it.

She then trotted down the lane in her gown and threw the ball, having trouble with her bare feet (the countess hated shoes) sticking on the wooden floor. The ball travelled a bit and then went into the gutter on the right side.

"What is that?" she asked.

"A gutterball, Syg. It's not a good thing."

She surveyed the situation. "May I have another ball, please?"

And that was that. She quickly developed a love/hate relationship with bowling. She loved the sounds of the ball rolling and the pins clashing and the feeling of the hidden place. She loved playing with her lord and his sisters (his sisters were very good). She would sit there at the scoring table in her gown (she was told by Dav's sisters that *ladies* always bowled in their gowns, though it seemed pointless to her. After all, they were doing this in a secret place; who was to know what they were wearing as they bowled?) and tingle with excitement at the whole thing. On days when they were going to go to the alley and play, she found herself thinking about it ahead of time, savoring the thought. Dav's sister Pardock, blue hair drifting about her back and shoulders, played with coiled passion, winding up and clobbering the pins as if they were anathema to her.

The countess *hated* the fact that she was terrible; that she didn't dominate. Therefore, she would practice until she did dominate, come what may be.

* * * * *

Another throw. Nice pin action, though she left the 7. Gods! Why didn't the ball bite more? She simmered in frustration.

Her lord was at a Fleet meeting to the south and Lady Poe was away on an outing. The countess was alone for the day. She'd been bowling for hours. Davage had assumed that she didn't care for League Blue society nonsense like status and gossip. However, the countess was quickly beginning to enjoy such things, regardless of what her husband thought. She wanted a good bowling average to impress the ladies—though hers refused to break 90. And, she had actually spread some gossip around for the first time the other day, pulling some shopkeeper in the village aside and filling his ear with little tidbits that she'd heard. She was turning Bluer by the day and hoped to be a true gossip machine and feared bowler by the end of the year. Oh, what Dav will say about that.

Her hard work in the alley was beginning to pay off. She had perfected her approach, swing and release. She now could determine a good throw from a bad one as soon as the ball left her hand. She had several custom-made balls that she prized very much. She was getting better, bit by bit.

Alone in the private alley, she eventually stripped off her gown and bowled nude—wearing nothing but her bowling shoes. Nude, or in her bodysuit, seemed much better suited for bowling than her blood-gutted gown, which got in the way. Maybe she should suggest it to Davage, that they all bowl nude. Perhaps it might become a tradition. She should insist upon it. She was always amazed at what she could get away with when she insisted on things around the castle.

Standing there naked, her empty gown propped up at the scoring table like some sort of lacy ghost, she kicked at the floor with her right shoe. It didn't feel right. The countess hated shoes of any kind going back to her Black Hat days when she was forced to wear the fearsome Dora shoes, however she could not bowl barefoot; the floor was too grippy on her feet. Several head-over-hips tumbles down the oiled lane proved that to her. Her sister-in-law, Lady Poe, had suggested she be fitted for a good pair of bowling shoes.

Shoes? She was outraged.

Poe lifted the skirt of her gown and showed her hers: an odd, mostly flat shoe that looked like something the factory workers wore. She swore up and down they were quite comfortable. Master Krenshaw had made them for her and she highly recommended the countess summon him to the castle for a fitting.

Dubious but rather desperate as her body was taking quite a beating, she summoned this Master Krenshaw to the castle and, truth be told, was rather rude to him and uncooperative as he patiently tried to fit her. Quickly though, he put her at ease with a calming wit, fitted her, and made a special pair just for her with extra padding and holes for ample breathing. They were wonderful. She could barely feel them. These shoes, allowing her a proper run up and slide, were like a pair of lanterns leading her to bowling glory. Her average immediately jumped up thirty points.

* * * * *

She kicked the floor. After much use, her right shoe was definitely feeling a little soft and was throwing off her approach. The left shoe was very taught to the floor, while the right slid easily by design. But, today it didn't feel normal. Something was wrong with her shoe. Her shoes were starting to get worn.

Oh! She remembered Master Krenshaw promised to have her new pair ready today. She was excited. With those shoes she might stand a chance of staying with Davage's sister, Countess Pardock of Vincent, for a few frames. Pardock was a torrid bowler and she was to arrive for a visit in a few days. Syg had "thrown it down" in a recent letter to her and Pardock was slavering to have at her.

She needed her new shoes in a bad way and was going to the village to fetch them. Her staff did not approve. If she had business with Master Krenshaw, then *he* should make an appointment, be announced and admitted, and conduct the business here in her study as was proper.

Nonsense, the countess loved going to the village and walking around. She was glad to go to him for her shoes.

She left the alley and changed into one of her beloved Hospitaler bodysuits and hit the tunnels. There were untold tunnels under the west wing—the castle and the lush Telmus Grove behind it were shot-through with them. There were dark spaces and crawlways leading this way and that through the old stone, some huge and spacious, others sickeningly small and tight. Some exited in the lush green and stone of the Telmus Grove, some ended in little shrines tucked in the towering mountains, and many ended up in various parts of the village.

She crawled through an easy tunnel that she knew snaked its way down to the central village. The villagers had become used to seeing the countess 'pop up' in the oddest of places from out of nowhere: filthy, smiling, red-headed, green eyed, gownless. Where else in the League or on Kana could such a thing happen? With greetings, they always welcomed her. They'd come to love her just as they did their Lord.

She emerged in a small fox shrine just south of Old Castle Road tucked neatly into the maze of newer and older buildings. She climbed out of the hole at the base of the shrine, popped on a pair of sandals from her pack, and put on her light shawl. She then made her way to the north. Master Krenshaw's shop was just a few blocks away near the college campus. Passing villagers saw her and bowed with respect. She waved, knowing many of them on a first-name basis by now. She'd rather be informal if she could.

As she made her way north, she began to feel uneasy. Though the afternoon was sunny and the environs pleasant, something troubled her more and more with each passing step.

She stopped. Something was wrong.

Her Black Hat instincts warned her of things; warned her of danger. And there was danger about.

Nothing apparent. Nothing readily seen, but it was there certain enough.

* * * * *

There had been strange folk about and an odd feeling in the village for the last few days ever since she and her lord returned in the *Seeker.* Yesterday, right after her lord left for his meetings, she had been informed by her staff that a visitor waited to be seen in her study.

"Who awaits?" she asked her staff.

"A Madame Abyssina-Burmilla of Selkirk."

"Who?"

The countess knew no such House existed in the League. She had access to a small block of Holo-Net that had been shown to her by Lady Poe, and in it she could look up the bowling average of virtually any lady in the League.

There was no Madame Abyssina-Burmilla of Selkirk listed. Her average was therefore 0.

The staff was uneasy—they wanted to either get the magistrate or await the return of Lord Blanchefort. Clearly there was an impostor in the castle.

Ridiculous, Sygillis wasn't afraid. Rolling her sleeves up, her green eyes flashing, she marched into the study, only to find it empty.

Waiting on the desktop was a folded note. It read:

YOU HAVE BEEN SELECTED BY AN
ELEMENTAL SPIRIT. YOU WILL BE PLACED
INTO DANGER. DO NOT INTERFERE. –M

A search of the castle uncovered nothing. She chalked it up to ghosts, as the castle was rank with them, or possibly Carahil, that little silver trickster who loved to torment her and throw pies. Oh, how he was going to pay for that.

But, other things happened as well. In the village, she was certain something was watching her as she made her usual rounds. A Black Hat always knew when unwanted eyes were upon her. She had signed up for a two day self-help course at the college (an unusual step for a countess to take). After one of her classes she found an odd note waiting for her in her satchel. It read:

BEWARE! THEY ARE COMING FOR YOU. –M

* * * * *

Whatever she was sensing, it came from the alley across the street. Something hid within. She squinted, seeing nothing in its depths but shadows. She pumped her fist and readied her Silver tech, should it be needed. She moved across the street to confront whatever it was.

"Who's there?" she asked.

Something boiled in that alley. She felt a coiled-up geyser of ancient emotions pouring out, and having spent a good portion of her life feeling similar things, she was quite familiar with them: anger that was never ending, spitefulness and centuries of bitter rancor. She could also determine that whatever was the source of these emotions didn't start out angry and spiteful as she had; no all those things had been forced upon it by ages of grief and tragedy, leaving no room for anything else. At one time it might very well have been happy and loving, but no more.

For the briefest of moments, the Countess pitied it, however, the creature in the alley was certainly dangerous and she could not allow the villagers to be subjected to it. She had to protect the people.

"I said who is there? Fail to answer me and I shall purge this alley clear with Silver tech."

A crawling voice replied. *"I told you they'd be coming for you."*

"Who are you?"

A low growl, like that from a predatory animal, was the response she received.

Determined to protect the villagers from an unknown danger, she plunged into the cobbled dark hoping to come to grips with the creature.

She found nothing but ash cans and bits of refuse in the depths of the alley, the cans now overturned and rolling about.

As she blundered around trying to right the mess she'd made, she heard the voice a final time: *"The docks, Countess. Look to the docks. You have been warned ..."*

Whatever it was, she felt it depart. It was gone, taking its cyclone of anger with it.

The docks? The voice said to look to the docks. The Cathedral of St. Vith was nearby with its looming dome and lightstand cupola. From up there she would have a commanding view of the entire village. She finished up in the alley, turned and long Wafted to the top of the copper-covered dome with a burst of wind. The breeze blowing in from the bay was stiff and cold, moving her hair around like a red flag.

She looked around. To the south, parked on its submerged pylons, was the *Seeker*, her Lord's Fleet battleship, saddled up to the dock like a great, long-necked beast feeding from a trough. The *Seeker's* hatches and plates were thrown open as the ant-like Fleet craftsmen slowly worked on her, doing things the countess could only speculate on. Once the work was done, she and her lord would set off to the stars once again for a month or two. She was in no hurry. She loved her time in the castle.

So, where was this danger? Nothing she could see, just the huddle of buildings, the long curve of the dock and the *Seeker*. Nothing dangerous about any of that.

Wait!

Coming in from the west over the open water was a single vessel, floating low. It was a small ship, possibly a transport. Using the *Seeker* as a yardstick (as it was the only star-faring vessel she was familiar with) she surveyed the newcomer. It didn't look like the *Seeker* at all. If the *Seeker* was spread out and swan-like in shape, the new ship was rather compact and nautiloid in appearance, being rather roundish and coiled with a confusion of tentacles reaching forward and testing the air and water in front of it in an organic sort of manner. It appeared to be about a fourth of the size of the *Seeker*. She squinted to see. The *Seeker* was white, this newcomer was a stony gray, and, in fact, it looked like stone instead of metal, like a great carving that could fly.

Her Black Hat instincts went off. That ship. The danger was in that ship, she was certain.

She had the feeling it was the Sisters. The Sisterhood of Light.

Being an ex-Black Hat, her relationship with the Sisterhood of Light was always tenuous at best. The Sisterhood was a powerful League sect, and, some said, was its true ruler. As a Xaphan Black Hat, the Sisters had been her mortal enemy. She had openly fought them, met them on various battlefields and killed some of them outright.

But that was a lifetime ago.

That was when her lord, Davage, came into the picture. Dav had nurtured her small, fragile soul and taught her to love. Though cordial, she found the Sisters always unnerving, always probing and watching … waiting for her to screw up somehow and take her from her lord. Waiting to do to her what was always done to Black Hats: kill them.

Let the Sisters just try to take her from Davage. Let them see the fight they'd have on their hands.

Standing in the glowing cupola, she watched the ship land with careful interest. It waded through the water and was secured at dock. Its tentacles retracted into its stony shell.

The hatch opened and out came the Marines in their lovely red uniforms. They quickly secured the dock, ushering away all of the dockhands and the passing curious. Where there were Marines, there were Sisters, and sure enough out they came. There were four of them, white robed, cloaked with their characteristic winged-headdresses shaped like the laminar airfoil of an airship.

As usual, the Marines took up defensive positions around the Sisters. The countess always thought it quaint that the Sisters chose to pretend like they needed Marines to protect them. The Sisters needed no protecting, except from the Black Hat Hulgismen, who were immune to their power. There were no Hulgismen in Blanchefort village, or anywhere else on Kana. The countess guessed they liked to make a show that they needed protecting—that they were simply passing travelers, nothing more. She, however, knew better.

They stepped into two floating litters and disappeared inside. The Marines piled into long, open-float platforms that flanked the litters and off they went. She watched as the procession began its slow, steady way through the village down the Old Castle Road, the people lining up to watch them pass. They did not stop at any of the old Vith chapels and places of worship along the way. They continued on through the maze of streets and alleys moving right past her position atop the cathedral, until they reached the old switchback road that climbed up into the rapidly rising mountains, and made its lonely way to the castle.

The Sisters were coming to the castle! They hadn't announced themselves; this was completely unexpected. The Sisters always made a grand fuss about their visits to various Great Houses across the League, with volumes of messages passed back and forth between their vast PR department at the chapel of Kurtis in the Great Armenelos Forest and her House staff. The countess had a staff member whose only job was to plan and coordinate such things. A pending visit from the Sisters should have been a key topic of conversation for months. Even when she was away on the *Seeker*, the countess Commed-in with her everyday regarding important League functions such as balls, invitations, Perlamum tournaments and visits; especially visits from the bloody Sisters.

But here they were, snaking their way up the mountain road unplanned, unannounced.

Great!! They're coming to get me, she mused. "You're right, 'M', whoever you are," she piped. With that she casually dropped off the cathedral dome and long Wafted away, to the castle to change and great them.

This ought to be interesting. Picking up her bowling shoes would have to wait.

Fallsworth, Duke of Oyln (From Carahil's Diary)

2—The Duke of Oyln

The noise coming from the lowest level of the manor was loud and somewhat frightening. The moaning, the banging ... a miserable demon must certainly be imprisoned down there.

There had been few guests at the manor recently, and those that did come were troubled by the noise. Casual strolls through the manor were disturbing, dinners were impossible. They inquired about it to the staff, and asked when the noise would stop. They were certain a huge, pained animal was locked in the dungeon, wretched and miserable—one that ought to be given peace.

Hershey, Lord of Milton, a stately and gangly gentleman, bewigged, Cloaked to make himself appear like an old man, had stormed into the manor one afternoon after the garden party he'd carefully planned at his giant-sized manor across the green had been disrupted by the cries. His curled wig bouncing with rage, he demanded the thing be silenced—immediately. Milton, of course, knew exactly what was in the dungeon, he simply hadn't thought it was going to be so noisy, so damn inconvenient.

Normally, a demanding and powerful lord, such as Lord Milton, was not to be questioned. Normally such a scene was to be dealt with at once by the House staff, however Lord Milton, important as he was, was not in charge here.

The Duke of Oyln was.

The giant manor was the Duke's. The grounds belonged to the Duke. The wailing thing in the dungeon belonged to the Duke … and so too, for that matter, did Hershey, Lord of Milton.

There were very few Dukes in the modern, enlightened League. There were less than five in standard counting. The League was leaning toward greater freedoms for the various Great Houses, and the concept of a Duke was passé at best. In the traditional vein, a League Duke held sway over two or more Houses, be they of Great or Minor status. There were once many Dukes, with various Great Houses held in fealty to one another for various reasons. Some Houses were held in bond for a debt that was owed, some were defeated in battle and accordingly subjugated, while others had formed a mutual alliance and agreed upon a Duke to rule them.

And so, the Duke of Oyln.

House Oyln was one of the premier Houses stemming from the sturdy, ancient line of Esther located in the marsh-riddled eastern continent, north of Calvert. The ancient Esthers were close allies of the Vith and, through generations of inter-marrying, had incorporated many of the Vith Gifts into their own, though Vith blue hair was unheard of in Esther. Their sandy-blonde hair swamped it out. Clinging to the old ways, the tradition of a League Duke was still practiced in Esther areas, including the large city of Effington. There, House Oyln held fealty over three Houses: House Milton, House Welk, and House Ruthven. Ruthven, traditionally a proud and fierce House Minor of the Calvert line, had been defeated in battle long ago. The relationship was mutually beneficial and the two Houses, though separated in name and standing, co-existed as one. House Welk had voluntarily subjugated itself to the House of Oyln several years back; they went bankrupt and needed ready cash, it was said. Maudlin and uninspired, House Welk kept to itself in the city of Gamboa, living off of a monthly allowance provided by the Duke and did as it was told without fuss or further interest.

And then there was House Milton, a stuffy, complaining, scheming House to be sure. It was a House that chaffed in its situation and yearned loudly to be free. Given the noise they made, the public cries of injustice and subjugation, one couldn't help but think that House Oyln should be glad to be rid of them. But, House Milton was quite useful if properly tempered and kept in check. House Milton was an old line of stuffy accountants known throughout the League for their demonic skills at crunching numbers and burying data. They could either straighten out a client's books with minimal fuss and effort, or "cook" them to order without error or trace. Not needing a pad or computer terminal, the Miltons could perform elephantine mathematical functions without error all in their heads. They never forgot a single list, digit or transaction. Such skill made them highly in demand, despite the fact that they were generally odd and somewhat misshapen in form. Also overlooked was the fact that when a Milton gazed at you, it was as if they were greedily eyeballing a piece of savory meat.

Lord Milton had a grand ancestral manor outside Effington on land that was once a swamp. His manor was big, somehow oversized and out-of-scale, which the Miltons proudly stated was an old architectural tradition that ought to be revived. It was as if his manor was built to accommodate a person or persons twenty-feet tall. There were two grand manors on the Milton's land; the strange big one that Lord Milton resided in, and a normal-sized manor on the grounds to the south which House Oyln had relocated to decades ago.

House Milton was held in bond over a secret that House Oyln had access to. What that secret was, nobody really knew outside of the Duke and the Lord of Milton, and speculation, of course, was rampant. Whatever that secret was, it was potent enough to keep the malcontented, grumbling, wig-wearing Miltons at bay and under wing.

The current Duke of Oyln was Lord Fallsworth, a tall, blonde-headed, pipe-smoking vagabond. He was a unique man to say the least, a man in search of himself; a man who characteristically searched in all the wrong places. He was a man who generated strong feelings one way or the other.

"A brash, neat, slap-hand," some said.

"A rootless mal-content, rogue and privateer," others thought.

"A blood-thirsty pirate, raider, bravo, squatter and peddler of flesh," Lord Milton often said with considerable bile.

The Duke had heard all of this, and, being a mostly-honest man, he couldn't say he wasn't—to at least a small degree—some of those things.

An enigma, even to himself, he satiated his caprices by indulging in endless misadventures and ill-conceived forays. It was as if he couldn't pass by a dark, dangerous alley without plunging into its depths, hoping to find himself somewhere in the darkness. His father, the late Lord Ursul, a taciturn and unsmiling man, had worried about his son. He worried what sort of fellow he would become, what sort of Duke. He had raised his son alone. His duchess, a Lady Potenta of Witherspoon, had died when Fallsworth was just a lad. The most vivid memory he had of his mother was her lying in her sick bed smoking a large pipe; the kind of pipe a man might smoke. That pipe was the only thing of his mother's he wanted after her death, and he kept it with him always, smoking it as she once did. Devoted to her even in death, Ursul never re-married and raised his son alone. It was a tough task, and Lord Ursul watched as his son grew into maturity "missing" something; certainly, his beloved Potenta would have known what to do. He worried for his son. He would be Duke some day, and it wasn't easy being a Duke. The pressure, from both outside and inside, was immense.

Even as the lid to his coffin was slammed shut, Lord Ursul bore a confused look on his dead face that cried out: *"What in the Name of Creation have I left to this world? Who is this boy I raised?"*

For years prior to his death, the Lord Ursul had no idea what to make of his obviously intelligent and capable, yet untamable son, ever restless and wandering. His son seemed to be searching for something elusive, what it was, the Duke didn't know. How could a man who had everything, and was virtually untouchable in League Society, be so lost? Perhaps too much idle time was taking its toll.

Yes, that must be it, Lord Ursul thought. His son needed direction, activity, to occupy his thoughts.

"Join the Fleet, learn a trade, learn some discipline, and become an Admiral some day," he had said, hoping to fill his son's time. And he joined the Fleet as his father asked, only to get drummed out shortly thereafter; unruly, undisciplined, unacceptable, untrainable, uncontrollable the Fleet Admiralty said as they kicked him out. A true disappointment and a serious black eye for House Oyln.

Red-faced, his father prayed at his duchess's tomb, hoping for answers. He tried yet again. "Become a merchant," Lord Ursul said, hoping to teach him thrift, hard work, and enterprise. And Fallsworth dutifully followed his father's advice and became a merchant, though not in the way his father had intended. He became an adventurous privateer, raiding cargos and selling the booty, purchasing contraband from the Xaphans, running Fleet blockades and out-smarting the local regulatory ships sent to stop him; the more illegal and forbidden the goods, the better.

His father on learning of this midnight activity was appalled. What will be said? What will become of the House? His only son and heir had become a common scalawag.

When he saw the massive profits his son was piling up from his illegal, swashbuckling escapades, he changed his tune a bit. After all, his son wasn't really hurting anybody, just swiping off with their goods, and, with Lord Milton available to launder the booty into respectable-looking assets, Lord Ursul couldn't say too much about it. The Oyln fortune quadrupled. He wondered what he would do or say when the authorities came looking for his son, and that was a moment he dreaded. However, Fallsworth proved to be a master at committing these robberies yet leaving no tangible proof that the League authorities could use to arrest him. It wasn't much of a secret, yet what one knows and what one can prove are two separate things all together.

Developing a lip-smacking taste for cosmic adventure and romance, the Duke recruited several of his faithful Ruthven servants, John of Ruthven, Peter of Ruthven and Sage of Ruthven to join him on his adventures—the quartet becoming known by the romantic pirating name: The Black Goshawks. The quartet rarely hurt anyone, save a bruised ego and a black eye or two.

With the Ruthvens at his side, the quartet made a formidable and talented group: John, or "Little Johnnie" as he was known, was the gun-hand and blunt instrument, gentle Peter was a mechanical genius, and Sage, the eldest brother, was the know-it-all.

Dissatisfied with the motley assemblage of ships he and his dashing Ruthven crew had been flying, he determined to mount up in style—Goshawk style. Using a copious amount of shadow money that he had accumulated from his illicit activities, he commissioned a fleet of four custom-built vessels, and they were some sweet-flying ships. The League had strict rules regarding the dimensions, appointments, speed and ordinance of private "yachts", and the Duke's *Goshawk* fleet broke just about every one of them. Should any nosy League inspector or local magistrate catch wind of his fleet, a lengthy stay at Hagthorpe prison and a censuring by the Sisterhood might be in order. Accordingly, he berthed them in Cloaked, camouflaged revetments hidden under the swamps. The ships, it had been said, were designed by none other than Lady Rondo of Probert, the sister of Lord Milos of Probert, the League's brilliant lead engineer. Again, none of that could be proved and Lady Rondo certainly wasn't talking.

With his new Goshawk fleet, the Duke's career as a successful runner and out-and-out pirate was hitting a high note. His home and social status, however, was another matter.

His father had tried to impress upon him over the years that being a Duke wasn't easy. There were pressures coming in from all sides at all times. It never stopped. Flying through space and stealing things was easy. Politics was hard and rather brutal, truth be told.

With his father gone, the Duke quickly found himself under enormous pressure, not only from the various Lords of Effington and Esther who made political demands of him, but from Lord Milton as well, as he had a habit of trying to kill him.

At his father's funeral, Milton laid it out for him as they shook hands. Milton wished it known that, though he was the Duke's vassal, it was *he* who was running things. He wished that made most plain. His father had played ball, knew his place and understood the score. As a reward, he lived a long life. Now, it was Fallsworth's turn to know his place.

As they shook hands, the Duke could feel the soft, yet undeniable strength from Milton's grip. Milton told him his first task would be to take one of his Ruthven servants, it didn't matter which, and kill him as a test of loyalty. He said his father had been similarly tested and passed years earlier. The Duke smiled, summoned his own Gift of Strength and squeezed back, and the two men tested each other for several minutes. Milton's grip, though a bit rubbery, was like a vice.

"You wish to kill somebody," the Duke said, "then have at me."

Then, Milton let go. "Be it so," he said, and walked away in a huff.

That's how it started. Soon, odd little attempts to take his life began rolling in. As he was a good pirate, Milton, was likewise a good master villain. The Duke even found he enjoyed matching wits with Milton, it added a touch of spice to the hum-drum of the day, though his Ruthven associates, Sage especially, were appalled.

He became aware of his mortality as he survived one attempt after another. He decided to take a duchess and have a few sons. That way, should Milton get lucky and put him to the grave, then the dukedom would be secure and the Ruthvens would be taken care of. He arraigned, via his staff, to be wed to some Remnath lady. It didn't really matter who it was, he wasn't planning on being a faithful husband anyway. Too much temptation was floating around out there.

The marriage was a failure, the lady not content to be forgotten. They divorced.

A second woman was found, and then a third, each ending in quick divorce. Apparently, they wanted an actual husband.

He considered fathering a bastard child, but the dukedom couldn't be passed to a bastard. So, wives came and went with greater or lesser frequency; all with the same results. League society began stirring a little. Rumors of the Duke being unable to properly service his duchess began to circulate. Such rumors normally didn't concern him much, however, on one of his pirating runs, his Xaphan contact, a smelly, mustachioed reprobate from the dregs of Vain, brought it up and heckled him over it. That was simply too much.

He had a bit of an epiphany—something that helped bring things into focus. He had to fight a pitched battle to enter his own manor after his tenth wife, Josephina of Jeste, had tried to lock him out and taken arms against him. Now that was a woman.

He found Josephina's sudden resourceful toughness and willingness to do him real bodily harm refreshing ... exciting even. She'd never shown that type of cloth before: not on the town, not in the parlors and certainly not in bed.

But there she was, hoisting gun and burping off clouds of lead, cursing him the entire time.

As he fought his way into the manor, bullets and energy beams flying, he thought, just for a moment, that he'd discovered himself at last—that all he'd have to do is take her hand and perhaps he'd finally become a complete person—the rogue, the playboy, the pirate, the Duke, could all merge together and become a complete man. Josephina had proved herself a lady worthy of respect, and maybe that's what he was looking for all along. Perhaps with her at his side he could set himself and become a proper Duke, a proper husband, tending to the Dukedom and his duchess, and fathering an heir at long last.

All that could have been his as he reached out to Josephina, only to watch her plummet away out the window to her death; gown, weapons and ammo billowing as she fell, gracefully choosing the long fall over the slow burn as his duchess. She jumped out the window rather than continue to be his duchess, and he mused the elusive missing half of himself plummeted to the ground with her.

And Fallsworth continued on as he was, in search of wholeness and toiling under the mounting problems of being a Duke.

Time for a new wife, but this time, he wanted something different. All ten of them so far had been standard League socialites. This time, he wanted someone tough; someone like Josephina, whom he remembered fondly and memorialized with a grand vault.

And Lord Milton, ever the snake, ever the serpent in the grass had the answer … though the obvious connotations were sinister.

As he went through the latest haul of swag, cleverly hiding the booty into respectable and legal outlets, Lord Milton told him that, of all things, Xaphan Black Hats made wonderful wives. They were exciting, loving, intelligent, powerful, and extremely dangerous to boot. Some idiot northern League Lord had broken a Black Hat and turned her, so he said … married her and now roams the skies with her at his side. The precedent had been set, Black Hats were not only welcome in League society, they were quite popular at the moment. Obviously, Lord Milton could not be trusted. Obviously Lord Milton was an old crutch eager to see him dead, but he was a good source of information when properly tempered. He might actually be onto something.

A Black Hat for a wife? He'd not thought of such a thing before, and the idea titillated him. The Duke sat there smoking his pipe and considered the possibilities. The obvious problem with courting a Black Hat was clear: they're evil. Having dealt with Xaphans for as long as he had, he knew they lived in terror of them—a sect of tiny murderesses in red and black scattered about Xaphan space in their foreboding Shadow tech temples. He recalled seeing one once, flying over Moane in his *Goshawk*: a black, sullen, windowless structure, seeped in evil, sticking up like a rotten tooth and given a wide-berth by the other buildings in downtown Moane. The Black Hats weren't just evil, they were mean too, delighting in mayhems and cruelty, in pain and death, and they didn't care who they inflicted their trade upon. Any soul, League or Xaphan, would do. Their temples all featured a huge open door that spewed darkness, and those who happened to wander into the door were never seen again—killed inside like a bug in a web.

So, in order to get to the allegedly sweet center of the Black Hat's heart, the undeniably thorny exterior would first have to be dealt with in earnest. But maybe, just maybe a tamed, in-love Black Hat could answer the life-long question that Josephina nearly had: who am I?

And so, the ululation coming from his dungeon.

The Black Hat he had captured.

It hadn't been easy; it hadn't been easy at all. His usual partners in crime, the Ruthvens weren't much help: Little Johnnie as usual was up for it, Peter, the mechanic and all-around nice-guy, urged extreme caution and Sage, the bookworm, flat stated that it was not possible to turn a Black Hat, it hadn't been done in thousands of years.

"That northern fellow did it," the Duke replied in earnest.

"Propaganda!" Sage fired back. He mused that the northern Lord probably fell in love with some cheap harlot, barfly or undesirable, fungus-infected dirty courtesan, married her, and made up the romantic Black Hat story to cover his shame and gloss his reputation. Black Hats, Sage said again, could not be turned; they were born evil and they would die that way.

That was that, his heart was set on a Black Hat. Somewhere out there, a Black Hat was about to be turned.

But, how to do it? How? He couldn't just go to their temples and charge in, those dark places were their centers of power—there, they will surely kill him and have him trussed up in Shadow tech in no time. If one was to be taken, she will have to be out in the open where she was vulnerable, where she could be had.

He went to his Xaphan contacts, the shadowy figures from whom he ran contraband, and casually inquired where he might find a Black Hat.

The contact he spoke to in the dark city of Midas, most definitely didn't want to talk about Black Hats. They were sinister, evil and eager to inflict pain and death on anyone caught in their grasp—the contact said his own cousin had been horribly killed by a Black Hat from Midas whom the terrified townsfolk called "The Knife". They had also heard stories that just being near a Black Hat was dangerous—if they became interested in you, they could psychically follow you home and invade your dreams, where there they tortured and killed you—contrabulation they called it. The Duke thought such a thing was a lot of nonsense, but the contact insisted he knew a brother of a friend of a friend who had died in such a fashion. The contact was afraid to even discuss the matter.

The Duke, however, wasn't going to let it drop. Shrugging, pulling him aside in whispers and plying him with cash and drink, the contact told him about a Black Hat snaring operation that was under way somewhere on the planet Xandarr and that he had supplied a load of food to it a few days earlier. They said they were pilgrims, but the Black Hat's sinister presence was unmistakable. The contact also said not to bother looking for them, because the Black Hats worked under Painted Cloak and were undetectable, and, even if he did somehow manage to detect it, he would die—horribly.

The Duke, smiling in his black duster, SAPP scarf and black triangle hat, puffed on his pipe and anticipated what was to come. He wasn't going to miss it for anything.

Delivering several cargoes of fine Onaris coffee, a popular underground drink in Xaphan Society, to Xandarr, he discretely poked about, tying to glean some information regarding the whereabouts of this Black Hat snare operation. Nobody seemed to know anything and it was damn frustrating.

This was a chase however, a hunt, and the Duke thrilled at the prospect, not only locating the Black Hat, but of the epic fight he was going to have on his hands once he got her. Sending the Ruthvens off to run some Zirkel spirits back to the League, the Duke stayed in orbit, watching, waiting.

Sage told him, begrudgingly, that Shadow tech tends to be hot, and, if the Duke *really* wanted to locate a Black Hat Snare operation, then to look for heat. One advantage that the Duke of Oyln had over his Fleet counterparts was that his *Goshawk* ships were brimming with scan and sensing equipment, much more so than a standard *Straylight* vessel mounted, falling just short of the equipment on board a Science Ministry *Venera* vessel. Using his gear to the fullest, the Duke combed the surface of Xandarr. He wasn't quite sure what sort of heat he was looking for, but he put his nose to it anyway, tuning his gear. If the Duke was anything, it was patient.

Eventually, his efforts yielded fruit.

Near a small Xandarrian village, he located unusual heat patterns. Adjusting his scopes, he found what he was looking for. There they were, lit up in his thermionic scanner, fifty people busy at work. What they were doing, per se, he couldn't tell, but they were hard at it. There were naked men stationed at various intervals—the Black Hat's dreaded Hulgismen no doubt standing in defense. Others, females, were busy with this and that, and, there, in the middle, was the Black Hat, a small but commanding robed woman, masked, hot Shadow tech pouring out of her like water out of a fountainhead.

The Duke, safe and snug in orbit, watched and waited. He eventually tuned his scanners to the point where he could hear the Black Hat speaking. Her voice was thin and tart, dripping with malice and cruelty—the voice of the woman who will one day love him. Whatever they were doing down there, it was big and part of something much larger. He could see with his tuned scanners a massive cache of Shadow tech, a virtual ocean of it, buried just beneath the surface and the Black Hat was busy Painting an illusion over the top of it. The Duke frankly didn't care what they were doing, it meant nothing to him other than the fact that the Black Hat was bleeding herself dry in the process.

Good, good. He waited, waited for his prize to be at her most vulnerable.

Then, gripping his throttles and kicking the bar, he heard what he was waiting for. The Black Hat, after a long day of covert Painting and casting said: "*I go to rest. I am tired and can do no more. Look to these rabble for I am not to be disturbed on pain of death …*"

Oh, the Duke thought lighting his pipe, she was about to get plenty disturbed. He rolled his *Goshawk* down from orbit and heated his Sar-Beams. Normally, the Duke was not the sort of fellow to go in guns ready, but this was a Black Hat. She was evil and if he was to survive this, he'd have to arrive swinging.

"I'm coming for you, darling!" he roared through clenched teeth, his pipe smoking like an ancient locomotive.

The dark contingent below did nothing at first, as the black winged ship wailed down from the heavens, confident in their Cloak.

When they were in range, he opened up. His Sar-Beams mowed down the standing Hulgismen, and as they began scattering, he concussed the area with illegal fragmentation shot, dismembering the survivors brutally—he showed these Xaphans no mercy. The Black Hat emerged from her tent, enraged, but exhausted, tentative. She watched as the attacking ship finished the rest of her guard and followers.

When they were all dead, the Duke saw her run. She ran toward the country-side at an exhausted crawl, her arms flailing in her robed sleeves as she made painfully slow progress. She began a long series of Wafts, trying to escape him, however, his scanners covered the entire continent and there was no place she could go that he couldn't immediately follow. The Waft took its toll and eventually she fell, exhausted. He settled the ship over her in anticipation of the capture. Suddenly she reached up and shot off part of his starboard wing with a bit of Shadow tech.

There it is, there's the spunk. Josephina of Jeste would have been proud, Elders rest her soul.

"I'm going to make you fix that, baby doll!" he said yawing the *Goshawk t*o keep it in level flight.

He safed the ship, Wafted down, and clocked her square in the face with a left hook. She went down in a heap.

He stood over her for a moment, pipe in hand. Sad really, he'd been eager for a bit more of a fight.

And he took her home to his manor, and, placing her in his dungeon, he began the process of turning the Black Hat. It could be done. The Northern Lord had done it, twice, so too shall the Duke of Oyln.

He shackled her in waft-proof chains, stripped her naked, and surrounded her with herbs and minerals that, according to Sage and the old texts from his libraries, could inhibit the growth of Shadow tech with her. His dungeon stank with clashing smells: salt, stale rosemary, orange blossom and a number of off-world items that had been "trucked in" for this very purpose. Sage also, using red paint, made a strange circle on the floor with her in the middle of it—protection against her Sten and Mass, he said.

Good thinking.

Peter also installed a De-Magulator, a small device that garbled her voice and rendered her Dirge useless. Black Hats certainly had a full range of weapons.

He also wore an arcane amulet that had cost him a huge sum of money—a ward against TK, though he could still feel her "invisible" pincers wrapping around his brain, trying to squash it.

He was pleased. His Black Hat was very beautiful. She was small and fit, with long black hair and bright blue eyes. Nice bone structure. Pretty face. Inviting lips. Her Shadowmark was large and black around her right eye. The Duke wanted to carefully examine it, but couldn't get the Black Hat to sit still long enough.

He had expected her, despite Sage's warning, to take one look at his handsome face and immediately fall in love with him. That's what he expected. That's all it should take.

It did not work out like that at all.

She shrieked with rage, she cursed and uttered obscenities that made even his seasoned ears blush. She jerked at her chains and kicked him. He asked her name. She spat back in response. She was also adept at breaking free from her manacles, always at the worst and most inconvenient of times. Using whatever means were available to her, she was frequently able to free her hands, and there in the dungeon, the Duke found himself in a heated fight, the small, naked Black Hat fully able to kill him with her bare hands had he not fought back roughly. The Duke posted a 28 bell guard around her, to nip her escape attempts in the bud.

And there was her TK, that was the worst of all. Being of Painter class, as Sage earlier pointed out, her TK was extremely potent and developed. She often lifted and threw things at him, hoping to clock him right in the head. He could feel the pincer grip of her TK trying to feel its way through the power of his amulet. She caused the plumbing to back up in the manor, making several toilets explode in a rush of filthy water. Like a house haunted by an insane poltergeist, she opened and closed doors, banged the furniture, broke windows, rocked the chandeliers and threw food about in the pantries and kitchen. Once, she even lifted the Duke out of his bed and threw him out a window into a reflecting pool. Luckily for the Duke, it was a first floor window.

More books, more reading and Sage found another amulet that was supposed to quell her TK. Spending another small fortune, he acquired the amulet, and, in one of the biggest fights with her yet, got it around her tiny neck.

* * * * *

"Let me show you how to warm a lady's heart," John of Ruthven said approaching her one afternoon. Moments later she had nearly strangled "Little Johnnie" to death with her bare legs around his neck, ankles crossed, his eyes nearly popping out of his skull as his laughing brothers watched.

The Duke being the Duke, however, was excited; she was full of the sort of spirit he had hoped for after all, and he'd even learned a few novel Xaphan swear words in the process.

But, as the days went on, he began to grow frustrated. As Sage had said, the Black Hat showed no signs of calming, of turning no matter what he tried. She roared and shrieked until her voice was a hoarse, de-magulated squeak. She kicked and injured herself, breaking both arms several times requiring Hospitaler intervention to mend. Feeding the Black Hat, at first an interesting game, was a fruitless exercise, the Duke having to physically force food down her protesting, swearing throat. Nearly choking to death one evening, the Duke had to finally resort to sedation and feeding her by vein.

Something needed to happen and soon, otherwise he'd have to kill this Black Hat as a rabid animal.

But she was so beautiful …

3—Visit from the Imp

The Duke sat alone in his study, his hat and duster thrown over the arm of a fine Hoban chair along with his usual arsenal of personal weapons: his black SAPP scarf, his trusty FENNESTER whip, a leather brace with five RED HAWS locked in place, his black, gold-capped BAZU stick, and his pistols—a small, high-powered Grenville 40 and a buzzing Hertamer A9 pulse gun. Behind, a huge picture of his father, Duke Ursul, loomed over the fireplace. He looked at his late father for a moment, at the big unsatisfied face that towered over him, and opened a nearby drawer.

He got out a silver medallion and looked at it for a moment.

Press the medallion, Lord Milton had told him, whispering in his ear… *and the Imp will come. The Imp will help you,* he had said.

"AAAAAAAAAAAAAAAAAAAAAAAAAAAAAAAAAAAAAAAA!!" came a muffled cry from far below.

The Duke was all alone in his manor. There were servants rolling around here and there, but, nevertheless, the Duke was alone. His friends, the Ruthvens, were gone. He had heard a secret cargo of good Kanan grain spirits was en route to Hoban. The cargo, hushed in secrecy, was unmarked and unguarded in order to avoid massive duty payments that were otherwise required.

Kanan grain spirits will fetch a healthy price in Xaphan space, where the spirit was highly prized. Though he thought better of it, he bade the Ruthvens, John, Peter and Sage, to go and secure the cargo. There, smiling, with a laugh and a wink, they will board the cargo ship and be off it … the crew of the ship red-faced but otherwise unhurt.

The medallion glinted in the soft light of the study. The Imp will come, Lord Milton had said. Sage would never approve—"An Imp? Come on," he'd surely say. The Imp will tear his soul apart.

"REEEEELEASE ME AT ONCE!! DO YOU HEAR?? DO YOU HEAR!!!" came the screaming voice from below.

The Duke was worried. The Black Hat was in the slow process of dying. The injuries she had racked up were mounting by the day: three broken bones in her left arm and four in her right, a broken femur and a broken foot, a lacerated kidney and a sudden bout of renal failure, along with a case of malnutrition from not eating properly. Finding a decent Hospitaler to care for her injuries was a difficult and expensive chore. What's worse, the Duke became aware of some meddling man in a silver cloak prowling the bars, casinos and bowling alleys looking for a criminal. Must be an Agent from the League. Time to deal with him later.

The constant strain and struggle she put herself through was also wearing on her heart. She was pained in her manacles. She thrashed, wailed, her head on a swivel, seeing things that weren't there, like she was in a daze, in a fog that would not lift. Her complexion, previously a handsome alabaster, had faded to an unhealthy gray.

Just as Sage had said …

She was so beautiful, that black hair, those blue eyes. He wondered what it might be like to have those blue eyes look at him with love. Her mouth that grimaced and howled obscenities—he imagined it smiling and laughing at a joke he'd told her. If only she'd stop, relax and give herself a chance. Anything she wanted was hers.

Stop fighting, stop resisting. You are killing yourself.

And so, the medallion and the Imp it commanded.

All you have to do is press it …

Strange doings. The Duke had found several messages left for him in folded paper throughout the manor since the Ruthvens had left. One message read:

KILL THE BLACK HAT. –M

Another read:

DO NOT MAKE ANY BARGAINS WITH
THOSE YOU CANNOT TRUST. –M

He found three notes of a similar tone that morning.

They said:

BEWARE—DO NOT GO TO XANDARR. –M

XANDARR IS CURSED. –M

YOU WILL FIND NOTHING BUT DEATH ON XANDARR. –M

All notes were signed: "M". They might be from Lord Milton; "M" for "Milton", or they could be from Sage, who went by the call name: Muskrat. They had to be from Sage. Odd advice, but prudent, as planet Xandarr was under the watch of the Fleet this time of year, though Sage was probably being a little dramatic, which was unusual for him. When the Ruthvens return, he would have to ask him about them.

Then, before he could stop himself, he pressed the medallion as he had been told to do by Lord Milton, who had acquired it from persons unknown. The medallion was small and silver. It had an embossed coat-of-arms of some important Great House person on the front side—the Duke didn't know who it might be. He knew enough of heraldry to understand that the coat-of-arms was presented in a lozenge, and, therefore, it belonged to a woman. On the reverse was the big-eyed image of some strange creature: the face of the Imp.

Touch the image, Lord Milton told him, and it will come. It will do what he asked.

Don't do it—he heard Sage's voice in his ear. *Milton wants you dead!! Your soul will be at stake.*

"AAAAAAAAAAAAAAAAAAAAAAAAAAAAAAAA!!"

His soul was at stake, true enough.

He pressed the medallion. He pressed it over and over again until his thumb hurt.

* * * * *

The Imp he was summoning did not appear immediately, as he thought it would. Instead, it took hours, but finally, eyes shining in the dark, the Imp arrived, its body huddled up and obscured in the corner. It emerged from the shadows and the Duke had a good look at it. He called it an "Imp" for lack of better terms. He really didn't know what it was.

"And so, my Lord Duke, I am here at last," the Imp said in a bright, clear voice.

The Duke, sitting there with his pipe, tried to be brash. "Punctuality, Imp, must not be in much favor in whatever fire pit you come from." The Duke paused a moment. Even in his study he could hear the female beast raging in the dungeon far below, wailing and moaning.

"I come at my own good pace," it said. It lifted its silvery head and listened.

"DIEEEEEEEEEEEEE,DIEEEEEEEEE,IKILLYOUDEADEAT YOURHEARTDIEDIEDIEAAAAAAAAAAAAAAAAAAAA AAAAAAAAAAAAA!!!"

The Imp smiled. "And, I suppose that racket issuing up from below is why I am here, yes?"

"Aye," the Duke said. "Are all you Imps as well-informed?"

The creature darkened a bit. "I do not like being called, 'Imp', sir. I am not an Imp. If I were an Imp I would be mangling your flesh by now. Be thankful I am of a kinder cloth. If you wish to toss names about, I am certain I could think of a few for you as well—there's quite a selection to choose from, isn't there: Raider, Brigand, Adulterer, Cut-purse, Fiend, Pirate … *Scalawag* …"

"I think I like Pirate the best."

"Really? I prefer 'scalawag'. You are a scalawag, yes?"

"Aye. I have been called that," the Duke said.

"I've been looking for a scalawag."

"Have you? Well, look no further."

Some sort of tablet or tome appeared next to the creature, and it wrote something into it. The tablet then vanished and it came forward a bit and shone in the light with a silvery glow. It was less than waist high, smooth and metallic, like living mercury. It was some sort of bizarre half slug/half dog quadrupedal animal, standing on strange, bent, somewhat aquatic-looking front legs. Not being an animal lover, he didn't know what kind it might be.

"My time is short, sir. I already know what you want, but I'd like you to spell it out for me anyway … to ensure there is no confusion here today," the creature said.

The Duke ran a hand through his blonde hair, opened his box, stuffed his pipe with fragrant tobacco, and lit it. "I want you to calm that damned Black Hat in my dungeon. We need to commence to having children, and her yowling is impeding progress."

"Really ... children?? Hmmm ... that Black Hat down there doesn't seem to like you much, sir."

"She will, in time."

"AAAAAAAAAAAAAAAAAAAAIKILLYOUIKILL YOUAAAAAAAAAAAAAAAAA!!!"

"Given the standard of your previous marriages, it appears this one is off to your usual start."

The Duke puffed his pipe, un-amused by the creature's attempt at humor. "Can you help me, or can you not?"

"And what have you done so far ... to cheer your 'wife's' sour mood?"

And the Duke told him, he told the creature everything, and it quietly listened, nodding every so often. The Duke found it felt good to talk about the whole thing—to get it off his chest, and the creature, whatever it was, was a good, comforting listener. The Duke even told it that Sage of Ruthven suspected the Northern Lord had made up the Black Hat story and wed a dirty courtesan—which triggered a huge series of open-mouthed belly laughs from the creature. The laugh was infectious, and soon the Duke was laughing too—the first time he'd laughed in days.

Just the Duke and the silvery thing sharing a moment in his study.

"So," the Duke finally said. "Can you help me?"

The silver creature thought a moment and scratched its face with its left front appendage. "It appears that you have done all you can. Yes, of course I can help you. But, as in all things, there is a price, dear Duke."

The Duke recalled the message he received. "What do you wish ... my soul perhaps?"

"That raggedy old thing? No, no, I desire something much more useful and much more immediate."

The Duke sat back in his chair, whitish-gray smoke from his pipe curled up toward the high, ornate ceiling of the study. He thought about it. This creature didn't seem foul or evil. He felt it could be trusted. "I'll give you whatever you want. But help me now. If you get me results, I am yours."

The silver creature twitched its whiskers. Its shining eyes grew large. "Excellent. Then let's proceed, we've wife and best friend to make for you. You going to teach her to bowl?"

The Duke smiled. "We do not speak of bowling."

"But you do bowl, right?"

"Of course, and her average shall be the envy of the whole of Esther."

The creature laughed. "Well, we can't delay that, can we? Shall we to the dungeon?"

The Duke stood and put his black triangle hat on.

"I didn't realize Esthers wore Vith-style clothing," the creature said, noting the hat.

"I fancy Vith hats."

"Ah ..."

Together they exited the study, the Duke slowly walking, the summoned creature loping along in all fours. Actually, as the Duke noted, it didn't have four legs, rather it had two strange front legs, and its rear legs were nearly fused together and dragging behind—three legs. Odd.

"Her name, Duke. Once we break the darkness around her if you can get her to willingly tell you her name, then that appears to speed the process along, though I know not why."

"The Darkness? I believe I've heard of it."

"Yes, the Black Abbess's Clutch. A shell of evil swirling around her ... a darkness that will not break. It must be thrown aside, that's what I am here to do. I shall break it for you, and she will calm. Oh, and if I may offer up a bit of advice?" It said.

The Duke looked at it, pulled on his pipe, and listened.

"You seek a wife in all of this, a woman who will love and bear you many fine sons. This particular Black Hat is at least a hundred and forty years old, yet her soul is as undeveloped as a newborn's. When we enter your dungeon, Duke, and do what needs to be done, we will be, in essence, welcoming a brand new person into the League. All of her feelings, her deepest thoughts, her wants and desires that have been thrust aside, stunted, battered, deprived, hidden and denied her for all these years are about to come flooding to the surface. It will be a remarkable thing to witness.

"You wanted someone to love—you've not seen such love as a freed, reformed Black Hat can offer. She will stand by your side, loyal to the end. She will love you the sum of her days; yet, she will not be your toy, your pet. She will be your foil, your equal, terrible in her power, endless in her devotion. She will argue with you, she will make her thoughts known. She will make you a whole person and you will do the same for her. All these things are very possible, however, love, in any case, is earned—not given. You must be worthy of her love. After ten failed marriages, I should think that you'd have learned that by now."

The Duke pulled on his pipe and thought.

"Additionally, the Lord of Blanchefort—for that is the 'Northern Guy' who tamed the Black Hat Sygillis of Metatron, cracked darkness hovering around her like a walnut shell—which is why I am here, because you lack what he can do. You cannot break the Black Abbess's darkness around her."

"Certainly, I'll wager his Black Hat was nothing of the tempestuous little fiend that mine is."

"AAAAAAAAAAAACOMETOME … LETMEKISSYOU … DEADMANDEADMAN … AAAAAAAAAAAAAAAAAAA!!"

"On the contrary, Sygillis of Metatron was a foul, evil, unrepentant woman … every bit as vile and dangerous as the one shackled below—though, admittedly, not quite as noisy."

The creature nosed the door open. "On a more social note, Duke, the Lord of Blanchefort also possesses a number of additional qualities which you appear to need work on. Kindness, decency, wit, and basic courtesy are just a few. You might be wise to follow his example. Forget being the Duke of Oyln for a bit, forget being the swashbuckling pirate, and try being a man for a change. Perhaps you have as much to learn from her as she does from you."

The Duke shrugged and held his pipe. "It … could be argued so." His previous apprehension had fallen away completely—this creature was not evil, he could feel it. He fancied he even liked it a little. He allowed himself hope—perhaps this silver beast could help him after all.

"AAAAAAAAAAAAAAAAAAAAAAAAAAAAAA!!!!!" came ominously from the bottom of the stairs.

The silver creature looked up at the Duke. "And remember, you, sir, will be in my debt. When the time is correct, I will come a-calling on you, and I will expect you to assist me as I wish."

"AAAAAAAAAAABBESSSABBESSSAVEYOUR DAUGHTER!!!!"

"Silence this woman and open her arms for me," the Duke said moving down the stairs, "and I am yours however you see fit."

The Duke and the silver creature entered the dungeon, and approached the screaming Black Hat. She spat and cursed. She opened and closed her fists, wanting to wrap them around the Duke's neck.

Standing back, the Duke watched as the strange silver creature began its work.

4—Esteemed Guests

The doors to the central hall opened, and out came the Countess of Blanchefort, resplendent and rather tiny in her golden gown.

She looked around. Standing in orderly rank in the cool, half-lit hall were the Marines she'd seen earlier from the cathedral. No Sisters in sight. The countess felt somewhat relieved.

They came to attention. "Sygillis, Countess of Blanchefort, well met!" the squadron officer said. "Lt. Getzen, ma'am, 25th Marines at your service. We are humbled to be in your presence."

Sygillis smiled. "Thank you, Lt., you and your squadron are most welcome here. I have ordered a table set, and a meal prepared. I entreat you to please sit and refresh yourselves at once."

"Your hospitality is most gracious, and heartily appreciated, Great Countess."

"Then come, gentlemen, please eat and drink your fill, and I shall return when you have finished."

With that, the countess led the Marines away to their meal.

She wished her husband was home.

* * * * *

The Marines ate in the Capricos Hall. It was one of the countess's favorites, she and her lord often ate there when they were home. The lofty heights of the stone ceiling were lined with colorful Great House flags. The walls were covered with weapons of all sizes and types, including a few unidentifiable contraptions—the complete family of LosCapricos weapons, one for every House in the League, though most here were non-functional mock-ups. At the end of the hall was a small entryway that led to yet another huge corridor, leading off to the vast north wing of the castle. It was there that she and Dav, and their friends, had engaged and defeated the Fanatics of Nalls some time back.

Dav had always said, since the battle, that he'd seen their ghosts gliding around in the corridor, still wondering how they'd been beaten.

Dav and his Sight …

The staff was bustling about, filling cups and re-filling plates—the Marines certainly had healthy appetites. When Sygillis came in, they all stood and raised their cups to her.

"Great Countess," the Lt. said, "we thank you again for this wonderful meal."

"I am glad you have enjoyed it."

Sygillis sat and made small talk with them for a bit, the Marines being a model of courtesy and manners. She often caught them taking a second glance at her Shadowmark, her Black Hat's mark making a rather P-shape around her right eye. Curiosity was not to be unexpected, and she didn't mind.

The Marines were delighted to find that the countess was a remarkably personable and easy to talk to lady—she freely exchanging wit, debating topics and swapping stories with them, as if she had been an old Marine herself. They could tell that her proper manner and courtly method of speaking was there only because that was expected of her—that she could lay back and speak plainly as a commoner was obvious. There were many Great House countesses who were so stuffy and uninteresting that to sit with them for any length of time was nothing short of unbearable. But this one, this Countess Blanchefort, was not only beautiful, but was completely affable and full of surprises as well—she was, after all, an ex-Black Hat. They'd hoped that she might share a few anecdotes with them regarding her days as a Black Hat, and how her lord came and saved her, but, on that matter, the countess remained mum.

Some of the Marines were quite taken with her and even considered trying the age-old custom of cuckoldry since the lord was not home, Marines being known for accomplishing the occasional countess seduction. But, it soon became clear that the countess's heart belonged completely to her lord, so instead the Marines settled for merely enjoying her company.

"Lt.," the countess said after a time, "though I am greatly honored at your presence, I am understandably curious as to the nature of your visit. It is not often we entertain such a handsome squadron of Marines here at Castle Blanchefort. I am wondering, sir, what it is that I can do for you?"

The Lt. set his cup down and wiped his lips. "Great Countess, I am certain you know that we bear service to the Sisterhood of Light."

"Indeed. And where are the Sisters, perhaps I have been remiss in properly welcoming them."

"Please do not fear, Countess, they have retired to their usual quarters for the evening. The staff here at Castle Blanchefort are well versed in the Sister's visits and have attended to them with all the graciousness and courtesy always afforded throughout the ages."

"I see. And is it a usual practice of the Sisterhood to arrive at a Great Household unannounced with a squadron of Marines in attendance?"

"It is not, Great Countess, however, a remarkable situation has occurred and the Sisters were forced to act quickly, bypassing the usual channels of protocol. I assure you they are planning to offer a rich compensation for this unannounced visit."

"Seeing your contingent coming up the mountain road, I thought I was in trouble."

The Lt. laughed. "Clearly not, Great Countess. Quite the opposite, truth be told. They are here because they cherish the House of Blanchefort and are desperate for assistance."

"Truly? How is it that we here can be of assistance?"

"The Sisters wish to see Lord Blanchefort."

"Lord Blanchefort is out of the province on Fleet business, and there are none who miss his presence more than I. He will not return until tomorrow evening. I will personally attend to the Sisters needs in the morning."

The Lt. looked alarmed. "Great Countess, I …"

"You may speak plainly, Lt."

"Great Countess … they will see none but Lord Blanchefort. They will not emerge from their quarters until he arrives. I am sorry, they will not see you."

The Lt. looked sad and unsettled.

"Lt., the countess said, "you needn't feel uncomfortable, sir, you are not in control of the Sisters actions."

He relaxed a bit.

"Unfortunately, Lord Blanchefort will not be able to see the Sisters tomorrow upon his arrival home. I have greatly missed him, and he will be in attendance with his countess for the rest of the evening—of course his duty to his wife takes precedence over all else. I will attend to the Sisters needs in the morning, and serve them as best I can. Apparently, their need is great and I shan't delay."

The Lt. looked shocked, other Marines appeared eager, as if they were going to see some action in the morning … a fight possibly. They appeared to like this countess's moxie.

The Lt. bowed his head. "I will convey your wishes to them, Great Countess, and bade them to expect you."

* * * * *

The countess was up before dawn. She went out onto her favorite balcony on the tall Elyria Tower and sat in the pre-dawn chill, looking at the cold, mosaic landscape stretching out far below. Far off in the distance, the white, patina-capped spires of Castle Durst rose up between the mountains, just visible. She knew the castle well—part of her soul had grown up there.

She looked to the south for incoming ships, she wanted her husband like nothing else, but the sky was clear. He will not be home until the evening.

She came back inside and dressed in a fine green Blanchefort gown. She always dressed herself, she never felt the need for the staff to help her. As a Black Hat, she had trembling servants dress and feed her … and she killed them, often times at a whim. Free from her Shadow tech nightmare, she determined to always dress herself—to make amends, in a small way, for all she'd so killed.

She went down to the kitchens to instruct the staff to begin preparing a hearty breakfast for the Marines. She figured they were probably already at it; her staff was top-rate. Entering the kitchen, she found Lady Poe addressing her head-of-staff, who was busy bustling about, the smell of cooking food thick in the air.

Lady Poe—Dav's sister.

For a lifetime, she had been infirm, a sufferer of frequent spells that left her drooling and stumbling about. When she wasn't suffering a spell, she felt great pain roaring from within. It was thought throughout the League, that Lady Poe was insane.

Like the countess, Lady Poe had the Shadowmark on her face—she also carried Silver tech within her, though that was unknown to her for a long time. Her condition had been hidden from all, and she'd been defended from the clutches of the Black Hats by her protective father, Lord Sadric, and she had covered her Shadowmark. The countess took her under her wing and taught her how to marshal and control her vast power, freeing her from the spells and the pain. She and the countess became close friends, almost like sisters, and they were once inseparable when Dav was away. Lady Poe's Shadowmark was big and complex—much larger than the countess's and she was always amazed at the remarkable things Poe could create. Incredibly advanced stuff considering Poe had only been working at her Silver tech for a few months. As the countess had already discovered the hidden bowling alley under Palantine courtyard and, therefore, the cat was out of the bag, Poe brought her there to bowl all the time; it was a passion of hers, the two of them throwing the balls around with abandon (though Syg was a real "Gutterball Queen" at first).

As Poe's condition improved, and it was discovered in League Society that she hadn't been "crazy" all those years, she went from being untouchable social poison to a hot commodity—gentlemen from everywhere clamored for her attention. Her time was now literally consumed with those hoping to court her, so her presence around the castle had become scarce. The countess had hoped that Lady Poe might court Lord Milos of Probert, the League's lead engineer. Though nothing to look at, he was a brilliant, witty man and good friend of she and her husband, and the countess had once saved his life, but Poe was coy and silent on the matter, caught up in all the attention she was suddenly receiving.

"Lady Blanchefort," the countess said.

"Countess," Lady Poe said in return.

They smiled at each other for a moment, laughed, and then embraced. Poe, of the Blanchefort line being characteristically tall and thin, towered over the diminutive countess.

"Morning, Poe," the countess said cheerfully, informally.

"Morning, Syg," Poe said addressing the countess with her nickname.

"It's good to see you," Syg said. "Back from your latest romantic trip, I see. Who was it this time—Lord Pitcock, possibly?"

"No, Lord Pitcock was last week. Yesterday, it was Lord Rupe of House Wiln. We went to his northern home in Minz."

"I see." Syg reached up and touched Poe's sallow face. "Minz, hmmmm? Are you going to make time for Lord Probert anytime soon?"

"I think of Milos like a friend, a brother …"

"He's a kind, brilliant man, and I wish you, at least, gave him a moment of your time. He loves you so, and for a lot longer than these new hangers-on."

"You and Dav are so keen on seeing me and Milos court. If you like him so much, why don't you marry him?"

"I think I might do just that. Goodbye Dav—hello Milos!"

"And, Syg, if he really wishes to court me, all he need do is ask."

"He hasn't asked?"

"No, he's always a bundle of nerves."

Syg laughed. "I'll have a talk with him when next I see him. I'm glad you're back, Poe. I understand we have exalted company here today," she said.

"Yes, the Sisters. They often visit the castle. They're wanting to see Dav."

"I'm going to go and see them today. Dav's going to be busy with me when he gets home."

Poe looked shocked. "Is he?"

"Oh yes … What is it, Poe?" Syg asked seeing the odd look on her face. "Everybody seems very put off that I'm going to see the Sisters. I am the countess after all … attending to the various needs of our guests is part of what I'm expected to do, isn't it?"

Poe struggled for words. "Umm, Syg, you're still new here and …"

"And what?"

"The Sisters won't see you. They want Dav. They won't see anybody but Dav: not me, not Pardock if she was still around … and not you either. Don't take it personally, that's just how they do things."

"Nonsense. I am the countess, they should be glad to see me."

Poe went to say something, but then stopped herself. "Listen, Syg, why don't we away for the day. Let's go to the village, and see the shops, perhaps take some lunch. It's been some time since I've been down there; or, why don't we visit the Palantine courtyard for some … you know …"

"You mean *bowling*, Poe? Why won't you just come out and say it? I don't see what the big deal about hiding it is. Perhaps later. I'm curious, are you trying to fill up my time, or possibly make me forget about the Sisters visit?"

They walked outside into the glorious morning, the lengthy green passes of the Telmus Grove steaming with morning haze.

"No, Syg … well, you have to understand, the Sisters operate a little differently than most."

"Yes, I've noticed. They pretty much come and go as they please, do they not? The width and breath of the League throwing itself in front of their cart to grease the wheels."

"They're the Sisters. They have the whole League at their feet."

"And I'm the Countess of Blanchefort, I've this whole castle at mine. Where are they? I'm going to see them, regardless. I need to know what they want. I am determined to know."

"I think I can guess what they want, and you aren't going to like it one little bit. It's better if you don't."

"What do you mean?"

As they walked through the vine covered stone, a large silver seal bounded from around the tree-lined corner. The seal regarded them for a moment with bright, blinking eyes and twitching whiskers, then it bowed.

"Good morning, Mother," the seal said in a clear voice.

"Good morning, Carahil!" Poe said embracing his head and neck and kissing him on the dome. Poe loved to create little Silver tech animals—her skill at creating Silver tech creatures now far outstripped Syg's, who had never made much of a study on creating Silver tech beasts. She'd created a flock of little birds, including a canary familiar named Tweeter that she used to keep herself from getting lost in the huge marketplaces to the south—Poe's sense of direction being notoriously bad, even in her own castle. She'd created fish, deer, horses, dogs, cats and various beasts of myth. To them she had given a body and a heart, and a soul, and she set them loose in the Grove where they wandered around in silver herds.

Her crowning achievement, by far, was a little seal named Carahil. In the dirty wastes of Metatron, her brother, Davage, had met a wonderful, gigantic silver seal named Carahil who could talk and fly. Lady Poe, inspired by the dinner-time stories Dav told of him, re-created Carahil in Silver. He took months to cast and put together, Poe toiling and fretting over every detail, wanting to make him perfect. She had found an ancient dry Vith fountain somewhere in the vast reaches of the Grove, and there she filled it with Silver tech. She bled herself dry in the making several times. She dragged Davage to the fountain and asked him questions, causing him to remember Carahil in detail, and Poe pulled the thoughts from his head as encoded Silver tech and tossed it in. Not content to make him with mere average intelligence, Poe added libraries-worth of knowledge to the Silver tech, mixing in lore and legend, and knowledge of nature and the cosmos. Not stopping there, she added a vast assortment of books to make him well-rounded. She added self-help books, joke books, books of puns and quips, books of magic and the arcane, cook books and several almanacs. She even pulled knowledge out of the dead heads of their deceased ancestors on Dead Hill and threw them in for good measure to give her creation age-old wisdom.

She added one final thing at the last minute. The kitchen staff had a hound dog named Cookie that never wandered far from the bustle and noise of the castle kitchen. Cookie was old, spending much of her time sleeping on her cushions in an out of the way corner. The staff loved her. Cookie was known for her motherly kindness. The staff often found abandoned kittens in the various reaches of the castle, and they would bring them to Cookie, who patiently suckled and cared for them until they got big (assisted by bowls of warm milk from the staff). Poe even heard that Cookie did a similar service for a pair of baby ducks once. One morning, Poe went into the kitchen to get a pot of coffee to take with her into the Grove—she was nearly finished with her newest Silver tech creation—her masterpiece. She'd been laboring for months and he was nearly ready.

The staff was sad. They told Poe that Cookie, their beloved dog, was dying. She was so old. Poe felt a great sense of loss, for she loved Cookie too. She went to the dying dog, hugged her about the neck and left, forgetting the coffee she had come for in the first place.

Poe hurried into the Grove. Held in her hand was a shining ball of Silver tech. In it was Cookie's nature, her kind goodness and patience. The Silver tech was weak and fragile and Poe had to make haste, lest it be lost. She arrived at the fountain and put it in. Of all the great things Poe had mixed into the vast fountain of Silver, the knowledge and wisdom, she thought the little bit of Cookie she added at the last moment was the most important, the most defining.

That evening Carahil emerged from the fountain, smooth and silver, opening his large bright eyes for the first time. Like all Poe's Silver tech creations, he bore her Blanchefort Coat of Arms stamped under his right flipper.

Davage himself remarked at how close Poe had been able to capture the essence, the spirit, the goodness of the original—the biggest difference being this Silver tech Carahil was perhaps a forth of the original's gigantic size, though he could modulate his size on a whim. Like the original, he was kind and brave and wise, but there were a few differences as well. He had a mischievous streak to him—a love of pranks and jokes, never cruel or mean-spirited, but ever-present and inventive. One had to be careful when walking the areas of the Grove that he frequented, the possibility of becoming a victim to a sudden prank or joke was a constant consideration.

Poe loved him like her own child, and he became her confidant, friend, advisor and protector. She created several silver medallions, embossed on one side with Lady Poe's coat-of-arms, and on the other with Carahil's happy, bright-eyed, whiskery face. If his image was touched, he usually appeared from nowhere—always available should he be needed. Poe had given a medallion to Dav and Syg, and to several of her friends, she being so proud of him. Syg wore hers for a time, until she lost it in the village when an alley cat jumped out and startled her, losing the medallion in the process. Davage had his in one of his Fleet coat pockets that he transferred from coat to coat.

"Morning, Carahil," Syg said dryly.

"My countess," he said whiskers twitching, "you are as radiant as ever."

"Yes," she said, "a pie in the face does wonders for the complexion, doesn't it?"

Poe laughed. "Oh, Syg—it wasn't Carahil who hit you with that pie. Honest."

"Really?" she said. "Then who did it? Who is about to face a Black Hat's wrath?"

Poe rolled her eyes and thought. "All right. I'm not sure you're prepared to hear this, but it was Dav who did it."

"Dav did it?" she replied, skeptical.

"Yes. Are you going to blow him away with your Black Hat anger?" Poe asked.

"I just might. And did Dav also hang my favorite green gown from the flagpole for all to see last week?"

Carahil's whiskers drooped.

Syg looked around. "So, Carahil, what do you have planned here?"

"I do not know what you mean."

"You've probably got something stashed in the bushes, some mannequin or foolish prop to waylay us with at your convenience. And, by the by, have you been leaving me a bunch of messages around the castle and in the village?"

"Messages? Would I do such a thing, my countess?"

"Yes … and don't play dumb. They really aren't funny."

"Messages?" He furrowed his brow. "What did they say?"

"Nothing good. They were signed with an 'M'."

"An 'M'?" A silver book appeared in mid-air next to his face and he scribbled in a few notes with a marker held in his teeth.

"Ah-ha!" Syg cried. "What do you have back there stashed in the bushes, Carahil? Probably my stolen knickers."

"Nothing."

Syg marched past him, knelt down, and peered into the bushes. There, safely tucked away, was a small box from the kitchens. Several kittens looked up from within the box with their round, hopeful eyes. They were tucked in with a light blanket and a saucer of milk sat nearby.

"I don't know what happened to their mother," Carahil said. "I've been taking care of them, the poor things. They were half-starved."

Poe took his face into her hands. "You have such a heart, Carahil, I am so proud of you!"

Syg stood and blushed a little. "Well, you should bring them inside, Carahil. It might be a little chilly out here."

"Thank you, my countess, I will do that." He turned back to his book. "Oh, Countess, if I may ask, did any of the messages you received mention the coming of the Sisters?"

"Yes, yes they did, in fact. They mentioned that the Sisters are here to 'get me'."

Carahil was surprised. "Get you?" He added more notes to his book. "No, no … Well, I can promise they are not here for you at all."

"That's a relief," Syg said. "I'm going to see them."

Carahil was clearly shocked. "Are you?" More writing in his book.

Poe chimed in. "Actually, Carahil, I was hoping to take the countess with me to the village today for an outing."

"Oh … oh, the village, yes. An excellent thought!"

Syg was skeptical. "Poe's trying to get me out of here. She doesn't want me talking to the Sisters."

"I see," Carahil said. "That's understandable."

"Do you know where they are?"

"I do."

"Then spill it—your countess requests it of you. Where are they?"

"Don't you dare, Carahil," Poe said.

"He doesn't have a choice, Poe. I demand to know."

Carahil twitched his whiskers. "Well then, I suppose that they're in the Vith Grand Chapel, just over there on the other side of the Grove."

Poe shook her head. "Great going, Carahil."

Carahil's whiskers drooped at the reproach.

Syg craned her neck. Way off in the hazy morning distance, the old chapel loomed, gray and ornate—it was the place where she and Dav were married. She loved the old chapel and liked to often go and sit in it, remembering her wedding day. But now it was infested with Sisters, like it belonged to them.

"What is the big deal, you two? They probably want Dav to donate to some new church or research facility they want to build somewhere. That's fine, I'll be generous. I don't mind throwing our money around. I kind of like it, actually."

"Isn't it fun!" Poe said.

"Yes … I find I like spending huge sums of money and watching Dav roll his eyes."

"They … want a 'donation' … that's for certain," Carahil said. "Though, their timing is a little off."

"Quiet, you!" Poe said, pointing at him. Again, Carahil's whiskers drooped as he scratched more into his book.

"You two are driving me crazy!" Syg yelled. She whipped her gaze to Carahil. "What are you writing in this book of yours?" She reached out and snagged the book out of the air with a rope of Silver tech. "And, don't think for a second, Carahil, that I don't know it was you who hit me with that pie, hung my gown and stole my knickers. You are on my list and then some!"

She glanced at the page. It said:

Item--*Sisters should not be here. Not her time. Why this particular Sister?*

Item—*Odd messages. Who is "M"?*

IMPORTANT—Stall Countess. Do not let her see Sisters. Could create trouble.

The book disappeared in a puff of smoke. Syg's eyes flashed. "Stall Countess, eh?"

Carahil, whiskers twitching and fins flapping, took flight and headed away as fast as he could. He flew in a crazy, zigzag pattern—like an uncorked balloon glinting in the sun.

"Get back here, Carahil, you pie-thrower! I want to know what the Sister's want!" Syg cried. "Carahil!"

He looked back as he flew into the distance. "I cannot hear you, my Countess!" he said swimming effortlessly through the air.

Syg spun around in frustration. "Well, I suppose you're not going to tell me, are you—even if I ordered you, right, Poe?"

"Right."

"Well then, I'm just going to have to march over to the chapel and ask them myself, aren't I?"

Poe watched her for a moment. "Are you sure you want to do this, Syg?"

"Positive."

Sygillis wound her way to the chapel, Poe falling to the rear.

The chapel loomed ahead through the beech trees, oddly sinister.

Something happened.

She was walking, she could feel her legs moving, her feet touching the old cobbles of the path, her heart beating… but she wasn't moving.

She was locked in place, like in her old dreams.

Overhead, the clouds splashed across the northern sky like a spilled drink. The Kanan sun began sprinting, followed by the mid-day rising of the two moons.

The Sisters, what were they doing? They didn't want to see her. They were going to stop her. She was locked in place … locked in time.

They wanted Dav, not her … not her. As always, they were in complete control.

Not here! This was her home, she and Dav's, and they were not going to dictate where she went in her home.

So, the age old fight was on once again: Sisters against the Black Hats. A Black Hat Hammer.

No, no … not a Black Hat.

A Countess of Blanchefort. The Sisters were about to face a Countess of Blanchefort, and they've never seen anything like her before.

Resolute, heart pounding, time spinning, she continued, step by step … inch by inch, willing her feet to move, willing herself forward.

Ahead, through the green, was the chapel and the Sisters within. She thought she heard a soft voice swirling through time.

"*Beware the Sisters …*"

Lord Hershey of Milton (From: Carahil's Diary)

5—Lord Milton

Oh look, there he is!

I can smell him from here!

Let's eat him!

Hershey, the Lord of Milton, held his tea cup and trembled with frustrated rage as he tried to ignore the voices in his head. He sat on his grand marble mezzanine, out in the fine afternoon sunshine, dressed up in his trendy League clothes, his wig, and his old man's Cloak. He loved making himself look old. He appeared withered, gray and bent. He thought it distinguished him from the crowd. Perhaps it will become a fad, he hoped so. Lord Milton liked to be centered around the latest fads. He liked his name mentioned in upscale circles, though, in most of League Society, he was considered a grouchy, unpleasant, insulting and slightly off-putting character. His be-wigged Old Man appearance really didn't help matters, though nobody had the grace to tell him.

He sat at the fine table and drank his tea—the table seemingly too small for his long, skinny arms and legs. He sat ram-rod straight. If he didn't, the confining girdle he was wearing underneath his clothes pained him badly.

The things he had to do for appearances.

We demand the Duke's flesh, cooked up and served.

No! Raw!

A leg! I demand a leg!

The voices again—always the voices. To that point, he pulled a thin gold case from his coat pocket and opened it. Inside was a collection of fragrant leaves resting on a bed of various salts and minerals. He took a leaf and a few grains of salt and put them into his tea, stirring them in with his spoon. The leaf did wonders for him. It helped keep the mind clear and quiet the gaggle of soft voices that had grown loud in the last few years. An unclear mind was a prelude of bad things to come, where the voices won out and got their way.

He drank his tea and soon was alone in his head with his thoughts.

His wonderful, giant-sized manor rose behind him and cast a huge shadow with the sun already peaking past noon. His manor was a provincial Esther design—wonderful, exquisite. The manor was ancient—a veneer of new Esther stone covered the original rough-hewn rock that had stood for centuries in the old swamps that once dominated the landscape. It was, by far, the biggest estate in the Esther region, size-wise. It wasn't really anything more than a two-level hut with several large-sized rooms within; a very large, giant-sized hut.

A distance away, across the green, was House Oyln's manor, that ramshackle den of tyrants and thieves, pinch-pricks and touch-pots. Formerly, it was the South Manor, the squatter's manor, now, it was the home of House Oyln.

The House of his "*master,*" the Duke.

Bah!!

When the Duke is dead, he will personally demolish that damned manor and everything that went with it, and let it become a swamp again, as it was ages ago.

Speaking of the Duke … From his vantage point, he could see the Duke—that charlatan, that walking corpse, that uninformed dead-man—strolling about the green, missing his usual duster, scarf and black hat—his "Attire of Hell", as Lord Milton called it. The Duke had very much taken to his "pirate" persona in recent years, the romantic swashbuckler he had styled himself after, and dressed the part most of the time. To a man with a clear eye for certain things, such as Lord Milton, the Duke never had seemed like a complete person, but rather a composite, a half-person, his bravado and outrageous behavior a mere varnish hiding an insecure wretch struggling to discover himself, struggling to be accepted by a father who could never embrace or understand him as is.

The Duke's late father was a man Lord Milton could deal with and manipulate at his leisure; his son, however, was a stubborn mess.

But now, here he was, his costume thrown aside, his clothes clean and regal, strolling the grounds almost like a responsible gentleman, a respectable fellow.

A small, black-haired woman wearing an expensive-looking violet dress walked closely at his side holding a basket which she was filling with colorful flowers.

They browsed the massive garden, the Duke stopping and pointing out various flowers to the woman, who looked up at him and listened intently as he spoke. Then, the Duke picked a flower and gave it to her. She smelled it and arranged it into her basket. Every so often, she took the flowers he gave her and placed them into her hair.

Bah!—the Duke probably didn't even know the proper names of half those flowers, the ponderous clod.

How had this "*happy*" situation happened?? How … how!!

* * * * *

Lord Milton had tried to kill the Duke many times in the past. House Milton, once the original House of Esther in the East, had been under the thumb of House Oyln for three hundred years:

The Secret, always that damn Secret that was held to their knobby throats as a knife.

If he wasn't so worried about appearances, if he wasn't so mindful of the repercussions, he'd kill the Duke with his own hands ... it should be so easy. He could throttle the Duke to death without half trying, but, he had to control himself, such a display might cost him dearly. There might be no going back from such an action.

If he allowed himself the luxury of savage action and primal pleasures, such as personally tucking the Duke into a nice, long dirt nap, the voices in his head might grow louder and stay loud, struggling for control.

The Secret the Duke had on him wasn't good, it was ruinous, and if it became generally known, then House Milton will be pulled apart at the seams. They will flay the flesh from his bones should the Secret be made known, and so, he sat and chaffed, the ever "faithful" servant of House Oyln ... waiting to kill the Duke though unscrupulous means and silence the Secret forever.

The Duke, in his foppish "with it" demeanor, almost seemed to relish the attempts, to pit his feeble skills against those of a legendary schemer like Milton. It became a matter of pride between the two—Lord Milton setting up some elaborate assassination, and the Duke somehow managing to survive it. The Duke's gaggle of Ruthven lackeys didn't help matters, the four of them usually managing to generate enough brain matter to endure the plot with a hail and a hoist.

Of course, Lord Milton could, if he chose, simply go to the authorities and turn the Duke in ... his pirating activities long suspected and talked about in League Society but never proved, and Milton had reams and reams of evidence in his possession—enough to send the Duke to Hagthorpe Prison for a very long time. Of course, should he do that, Milton himself would then be immediately arrested himself, as he was complicit in the laundering of the Duke's illegal earnings—even skimming off a fair portion for himself. The Duke had reams and reams of evidence in his possession to that fact.

To use the vernacular, the two men "had the goods" on each other.

Lord Milton, despite the persistent voices in his head, was a practical man. The Duke, though a shifting, rootless tongue-toodler and buffoon-supreme, was admirably good at his chosen trade and money poured in. Why ruin a profitable thing? He'd sit there and launder the proceeds and be a good boy.

But, after a time, Lord Milton had amassed so much money that he felt he really didn't need any more. His investments were blooming, his battery of shadow operations were in full tilt, and, as the Duke's incoming stream of money grew less and less important, Lord Milton's assassination attempts grew more and more mean-spirited. Though careful and meticulous at first, Lord Milton found as he tried and failed to put the Duke to the grave time and time again, that he really no longer cared if anyone else got hurt in the process. He wanted Oyln dead … period.

There were, of course, the obligatory pedestrian attempts; the knives to the belly, the aimed shots from afar that never seemed to find their mark and the perfunctory poisoned dishes that rarely made it out of the kitchens. He tried hiring the deadly Erynes, those death-dealing, tongue-twisting courtesans from Planet Fall with their dreaded Red Eye Weed. They wanted too much money, so he backed out. The Erynes were outraged—nobody backed out on them, and they tried to turn their ire toward him personally. Unfortunately, they were in for the shock of their lives. Those screaming, Red-Eyed courtesans never knew what hit them when faced with the naked truth as they tried to ply their trade upon his person. Ah—the memories.

On a lark, he went at the Duke's tenth wife, Josephina of Jeste. He showed the demure, unremarkable woman from Remnath several vids of the Duke philandering around with a batch of dirty courtesans. He'd hoped to enlist her help in poisoning the Duke's coffee, instead the vids seemed to drive her to madness. She demanded revenge, and Milton armed the duchess and her handmaidens with a small arsenal. The lovely lady actually put up a pretty admirable fight, choosing death over defeat in the end.

Josephina gave Lord Milton an idea, and so, his master stroke.

This time Lord Milton was certain the Duke would be trying on a new coffin once and for all. His plan to kill the Duke was perfect, multi-layered … flawless.

First, the opening act: he mercilessly filled the Duke's ear with suicidal thoughts of courting a Black Hat.

Courting Xaphan Black Hats, or "Fighting" them as it was known, was about to become a real trend in the League. The Lord of Blanchefort, that northern celebrity and always reluctant trend-setter, had turned a Black Hat in space, and, in the process, forged for himself a fine and loving countess. He also had introduced the League to Bethrael of Moane; an enchanting, sultry vision whom Lord Milton himself had to admit was much to his liking. He had danced with her at the Nether Ball in Armenelos and felt a connection. He hoped to court her. It seemed Black Hats weren't so bad after all, just look at them. Look what they had to offer. They were usually quite beautiful under their faceless black masks. They were seductive, powerful and full of love and new feelings—feelings previously denied to them, and the League couldn't get enough of them.

Still, Lord Blanchefort's triumph aside, Black Hats were nothing to trifle with. Lord Tillbury of Dexter, he had heard, had tried to turn a Black Hat, and was sent home in several boxes. Tillbury, the great fop, had gone out into Xaphan space with his entourage, as if on an outing, and been horrifically slain and sent back in pieces, except for his head which was said to be kept alive and screaming via arcane means in some rank Black Hat temple.

Seeing a grand opportunity, he slid into the Duke's ear and railed him on how some paltry northern League Lord—some puny Vith—had turned a foul Black Hat and made her his countess. He told him, truthfully, how her evil had transformed into a bounty of love. He shamed the Duke—if some fool Lord from the north, some Vith, could accomplish such a thing, then certainly the mighty Duke of Oyln, the pride of Esther, could do it too. Grinning and sucking on his pipe, the Duke listened and took the bait.

The stage set, Lord Milton sat back and waited …

As "commanded," the Duke took off in his black ship, leaving his Ruthven pets behind in the bars. Lord Milton fully expected the Duke to be killed in the capture, to be likewise sent home in a box as Lord Tillbury had. Certainly a fearsome, well defended Black Hat could kill off a single foolish attacker. If fortune smiled, then the Duke's severed body parts would be arriving any time in the daily post.

If so, his head, if available, shall soon be sitting on his mantel, varnished and forever unhappy.

But, to his infinite shock, not only did the Duke survive, but he actually managed to bring a snarling, writhing Black Hat home to his manor, bound tightly in Waft-proof chains.

How in the Name of Creation …

Shaking his wigged head, Lord Milton sighed. No matter, no matter—the capture was simply the opening salvo in the Duke's Death Cannonade. Many more kill shots were still to follow.

To the interlude. From his reading, Milton knew that the Black Hat's Shadow tech will certainly be the Duke's end. That darkness, that ancient substance which the Black Hats commanded, grew, festered, and would allow her to dispatch the Duke in any number of creative ways. With it, she could simply form it into a weapon of some sort and slice him in two, or she could use it to create a slavering monster and devour the Duke. Or, she could cover him with invisible Shadow tech snares for some spectacular, time-released effect; perhaps his genitals will explode, preferably out in public where the embarrassing spectacle could be properly appreciated.

Shadow tech was formidable and difficult to deal with. But, from his reading, Milton knew that certain herbs, salts and chemicals, heaped in abundance around the Black Hat's naked body will serve to inhibit the growth of Shadow tech and cast it so slow in growing that it, essentially, would be rendered moot.

Such knowledge could save the Duke, of course, Lord Milton was not going to let him know of this—let him find out on his own, the hard way—the painful way.

But, confound it!!—that Ruthven sole-slapper, Sage, had apparently read the same books. Under his guidance, the Duke stripped the Black Hat naked in his dungeon, and hauled in a steady stream of nostril-wrenching herbs and other noxious materials. The place stank. Milton could detect the smell all the way at his manor if the wind was right, causing him to require a perfume-laced hanky to clear his offended hooked nose.

The Black Hat's Shadow tech was, essentially, out-of-play.

But, Shadow tech wasn't the only tool available to her. No, no—she could shock the Duke to death with a Sten field. She could unleash the Mass, the infamous "Phantom Hand" and kill him from afar, or she could simply Point at him and watch the Duke explode. All of these illegal Black Hat gifts were based off of the Stare—a potent gift.

Of course, if they were to encase her in an arcane circle designed to counter-act the Stare, then all of those weapons would be denied to her. Only a heavy session at the library or on the holo-net would uncover that information. There was certainly no possible way the Duke and his noisome band of boot-knocking buzz-kills would figure that out.

A fie upon them! Sure enough, that annoying, nose-banging nerd, Sage of Ruthven, painted her into an arcane symbol-circle, effectively quashing her ability to use Gifts based off of the Stare. Miserable gods! More weapons to the bin!

So far, the Duke and his duster-wearing diaper-soilers had been quite capable at turning aside the first few aspects of this most perfect of assassination attempts. No matter, Milton would now take the situation into his hands personally. The simpleton's favor was off—now the hard gloves will be applied with vigor.

Lord Milton had at the Black Hat's manacles; he, using his little-known powers, snuck into the dungeon in the dead of night, through the window and crawling down the wall like a bug. Not even the Black Hat could detect him. First he electrified them. At the leisurely touch of a button, he could put an agonizing jolt into the Black Hat. And he jolted her often to make sure she was good and stoked at all times. Sometimes, in the middle of the night, he'd get up, trot over to his controller in his nightshirt, and give her a good jolting—just to make sure the Black Hat and the Duke were getting their beauty rest. Second, he tricked the lock. Again, at the touch of a button, he could unlock the manacles, freeing her at key moments so that the little maniac could escape and kill the Duke when he least suspected it. Again, that failed; the Duke able to fight her off and re-shackle her time and time again. The nearest thing was when one of the Ruthvens, the little one, got half-strangled to death: his head, caught in the locked vise-like legs of the Black Hat, ready to pop like a ripe grape.

Oh—but he wished he had a Vid-shot of that undignified scene to circulate.

Eventually, he shocked the Black Hat so much and so often that the current destroyed the unlocking mechanism, and he never had the opportunity to replace it as the Duke posted a guard around her to watch for further escape attempts.

Then there was the matter of her TK. TK was more often considered the venue of the Sisterhood of Light, and they could do wonders with it. However, Black Hat Painters also had a well-developed TK, and this specimen in the Duke's dungeon was clearly a Painter. Her TK also was not quashed by the symbol-circle as her Sten, Point and Mass had been. He, through wickedly subtle channels, made the Duke aware of a certain expensive amulet, one which, supposedly, diminished the power of the TK. In reality, it heightened and focused her power, her TK running rampant, even managing to throw the Duke out a window, too bad there was a reflecting pool waiting to break his fall. The main issue was that, in her sickened, diminished state with her Shadow tech kept at a low ebb, she couldn't focus her TK and rip him apart, she could only flail about with it, grasping at anything, making a mess but not able to finish the Duke.

Again, Sage of Ruthven, ever the library-lackey, ever the Billy Bookworm, discovered a real TK-suppressing charm and, getting it around her head, her TK was taken out of the game.

It occurred to Milton that, if success were to be achieved, he needed to separate the Duke from his trio of Ruthven touch-pots and pinch-pricks. John of Ruthven, the little one—"Little Johnnie"—though brash and youthful, was quick-witted and able to rapidly adapt to changing circumstances, Peter of Ruthven was a calm, collected, reasonable voice in the Duke's ear and his mechanical abilities could not be denied. And Sage, the eldest, the pseudo-intellect, the library-lounger, was learned enough to be a constant threat.

There was nothing for it—the Ruthvens had to go. This situation was to be a dance for two.

To get rid of the Ruthvens, Milton himself financed, through back channels, the "secret" transportation of a cargo of pure grain spirits to Hoban; an irresistible prize for an enterprising privateer like the Duke, as such a cargo would fetch a handsome sum in Xaphan space. Though ruinously costly to set-up, Milton knew he could recoup most of the cost in the end. He'd simply skim off a bit more than usual when he laundered the profits. The spirits weren't all that costly. It was the endless screens of secrecy and subterfuge: the paid-off merchants, the bought porters and bribed officials… all so that the "secret" shipment appeared to be sufficiently hidden.

All it took were a few well spoken words in the pubs, and news of the "secret" cargo spread like a bad smell. Sure enough, the Ruthvens took off to intercept the shipment, leaving the Duke all alone with his wailing, wretched Black Hat.

His quarry, alone and naked, Milton slithered in to begin "constricting" with a vengeance.

He gave ear to the Duke, listened to him lament that the turning of this Black Hat was not going well … that she failed to calm no mattered what he tried. He said that her health was beginning to fail, that she was injuring herself at an alarming rate. So, Lord Milton thought, the poisoned food he was able to slip her was finally taking effect—when the Duke was dead, he couldn't have a fully powered Black Hat running around, she could wreak havoc. The Sisters might arrive. He thought he'd seen a strange figure lurking about the Duke's manor. He thought, perhaps, the Black Hat had escaped, but, it wasn't her.

From his reading, Milton knew the old stories, that Black Hats were surrounded by a shell of darkness. This shell, though it could not be seen, kept them in a perpetual daze, in an evil trance from which they could do nothing but feel rage and hate. The old texts also said this darkness was eternal, that it could not be broken. Obviously, the texts were out-of-date, as, somehow, some way, Lord Blanchefort had done it several times. Must have used some sort of Vith magic on her. But, whatever, the Duke could not do what Lord Blanchefort did. The unseen darkness remaining stubbornly intact.

The Vith. If he was afraid of anything, it was the Vith. He had an ancient, inherited fear and loathing of them. Even the voices in his head were afraid of them:

The Vith are mighty, they drove us before them on the field …

Homma of the Vith, a great man …

We die! Eight arms, ten arms, a chest full of breasts—we die!

Enough of that. Now for it—the finale—the Master Stroke. Milton, whispering in his ear, told him of a magical Imp, a laughing silver creature that might be able to help him in this matter, to calm the Black Hat. Giving him a strange silver medallion, he bade him touch the Imp's image, and He will come. The Duke wasn't sure—surely Peter or Sage would advise against such a thing. But they weren't around. Milton lied and said he'd personally seen the Imp in action on the wharfs of Calvert, and it was a benign, wonderful creature. Nothing but good could come of this.

Smiling, hope in his eyes, the Duke took the medallion.

Of course, Milton had heard no such thing. Quite the opposite, the silver creature, he had heard, was an evil manifestation, one that will flay the flesh of any summoning it. That's what they said in Calvert. He'd stolen the magical medallion from some idiot Robber Lord from Planet Fall who smelled of catnip and wore a tabby cloak. Apparently, it had been a gift from a popular Lady of Standing whom he was courting at the time. The Robber Lord, drunk and capering about, was showing it off at a pub. Lord Milton, nursing a mug of warm ale, asked to see it. He accepted the medallion, palmed it, and gave him back a silver coin, which the foolish drunken lord did not discover. Certainly, this silver Imp, once summoned, will tear the Duke apart and feast on his bones. The Ruthvens will arrive home to find their Duke a torn, partially consumed carcass. Lord Milton's only regret: the he couldn't watch the flesh-eating spectacle in person. Perhaps he could get a vid network installed in the Duke's manor before the devouring.

Insufferable gods! Things could not have gone worse! Not only did the Imp *not* do him the courtesy of tearing the Duke apart and devouring his flesh, the foul creature apparently agreed to assist him, and was somehow *successful* in turning the Black Hat, calming her into compliance.

What the …

Whisked out of the dungeon into a soft bed, the Duke sat by her side, holding her little Black Hat hand as she recovered; her injuries healing, free of the poisoned food, her apatite returning.

So, the Duke survived and the Black Hat survived, the plot foiled, though unwittingly. In fact the plot had assisted in the happy outcome—the Imp connection being a complete, resounding failure. The only salvageable component of this whole, sad affair was the silver medallion itself. With the Duke pre-occupied with his "lady", Milton had no trouble re-acquiring it. Fascinating, it was apparently some sort of point-to-point portal powered by sorcery. He tried summoning the Imp himself, hoping to enslave it to his wishes. He "borrowed" a whole host of machines and equipment from some of his less-than-savory Science Ministry friends and made to way-lay the Imp when it appeared.

It did not come.

Later, as Lord Milton retired to his bedchamber, he was assailed with filth. As he pulled the door open he was hit by a cascade of feces and rotten fish held aloft in a rusty, now overturned, pail, hidden there by some miscreant.

There was a note at the bottom of the pail:

NICE TRY
--SIGNED: THE IMP

Miserable cretin. Milton sent the medallion off to a few of his Science Ministry friends for further study. What was done via sorcery could most certainly be reproduced mechanically. Lord Milton added the Imp's name to his revenge list along with the Duke's and the Black Hat—their name carved there in stone.

* * * * *

And now, here was the Duke, strolling in the sun with his Black Hat prize. Her hair was done, her face painted and her basket full of flowers. The Duke was doting on her like never before, as if her he actually cared for her.

Sighing, Lord Milton put his cup down and rang his bell.

A slight, wispy servant appeared.

"My Lord?" he said.

Lord Milton wiped his lips. He closed his eyes and took a deep breath. Something smelled good. "Ellington … what smells so tasty?"

"Lunch, my Lord, a lovely tureen of beef desjible. It will soon be ready."

Milton sat up a bit and rubbed his hands together. "Excellent, I am starved. Now, dear Ellington, please look down into the garden and tell me what you see."

Ellington, the servant, looked. "I see the Duke and a lovely lady enjoying the afternoon, my Lord," he said with a wheezy voice.

"Really?" Milton said grabbing his spoon. "That's not what I see. I see a dead man and a dead woman taking their last few breaths." Milton gawked at Ellington with his beady eyes Cloaked to look old. "I also see a man who is about to greatly improve his situation by making sure that those two end up dead."

Ellington grinned. "Yes, most certainly, my Lord."

"Do it soon … I have a plan."

Captain Davage, Lord of Blanchefort (From Carahil's Diary)

6—Captain Davage

Captain Davage, the Lord of Blanchefort, strode up onto the sunny platform. Down below, in the huge, trench-like pit, was a confusion of sounds—banging, clattering, shouting, welding, and whining machinery. Lt. Kilos of the 12th Stellar Marines, his first officer, joined him on the platform, her Marine boots clicking on the bare metal grating. She gazed down into the noisy pit: the partially-constructed skeletons of four gigantic *Triumph*-class starships were arranged one after another, stretching off into the hazy distance like a quartet of elephants being assembled from the bones up. The distinctive Double-

Teardrop shape of the *Triumph* design was unmistakable—how so very different from the beloved, swan-like *Straylight* ships that had served them so well. The *Triumph*-class had a very workman-like, up and down design by comparison.

The future of the Fleet was taking shape down there in the long pit.

Davage was decked out in his usual: his tailed Fleet captain's coat of dark blue felt with a stiff embroidered collar covered with ivy and stars, his black pants tucked into slightly over-sized Falloon boots. His white shirt was frilly. The sash going over his shoulder was black, denoting command. He wore a triangle hat as was the style in the Fleet, however his hat was a Vith hat, not the pompous regulation Fleet topper with a plume he was supposed to wear. As with any Programmable gentlemen in Fleet, Davage followed the regulations that he wanted to follow, often ignoring or making them up when they were not to his liking. He tried not to do it often, but he was a product of his station, as proven with his non-regulation civilian hat. His hair under the hat was wavy and dark blue, almost black in the Vith fashion. He wore it tied back in a tail with a small bow. Syg had put it there.

Gleaming at his side in a coppery flash was his CARG, the familial weapon of his Blanchefort line. The CARG was shaped something like a sword, but was rounder and straighter, rather like a water pipe with an X-shaped hilt. His CARG was well-known for being monstrously heavy, though Davage had no trouble lifting it. Holstered on the other side of his belt was his sidearm, a blue MiMs pistol. It was a tiny, underpowered firearm he rarely used; a ceremonial gun at best.

He pulled out a handkerchief and wiped his sweating brow.

"Feeling a little warm, Dav?" Kilos asked over the din of noise from the pit, already knowing the answer. Davage always found the Provst shipyards in the south of Kana a little too warm for his northern Blanchefort taste. Lt. Kilos, hailing from the sunny, golden south of Onaris, loved it like this—she liked it warm. Even though she was dressed in a thick Marine uniform consisting of a scarlet tailed coat complete with an embroidered "12" on her collar, white woolen pants and tall black boots, she was perfectly comfortable. She'd lost count of the number of times she had to struggle and strain to keep her teeth from chattering when visiting his chilly castle, and she enjoyed watching Davage melt a little. Turn about was fair play. She stood next to him, her long brown hair jostling in the warm breeze. She was almost, but not quite, as tall as he was; the two of them over six feet. Unlike Davage with his tiny MiMs pistol, her gigantic Marine SK jutted from its holster like a black slab of prehistoric metal, ready to unleash death. Also, unlike Davage who was a Blue from the Kanan north, Kilos was a Brown: a commoner from the nearby world of Onaris, so named for their brown eyes and thick brown hair. A "peasant" some called her under their breath, though Davage shielded her from much of that society nonsense. Davage and Kilos, worlds apart in terms of status and station, were unlikely best friends.

"So, Captain, which one will it be?" Lord Milos of Probert asked, making his way up to the platform. Milos, the League's Chief Engineer, a small, roundish man, was dressed in his garish best and beloved buckle shoes. He, like Davage, seemed a little warm in the afternoon sun, but not quite so much. A typical fellow from the House of Probert, his body was configured more east to west than north and south, and he was significantly shorter than both Davage and Kilos. "Which one do you want, Dav?" he asked again, holding his massive plumed hat.

Davage wiped his brow again and surveyed the ships taking slow shape in the pit. "I've been thinking, Milos, I'm not so certain I wish this course of action. I'm not certain I wish to leave the *Seeker*."

"Ahh," Probert exclaimed, "I suspected as much. You Fleet captains … you get so attached to your vessels. You must understand, time continues, things change. The day of the *Straylight* is coming to an end. I hate to say it, but their obsolescence grows by the hour. I'll not see you, our finest Fleet captain, in anything less than our finest new class of ship."

"I seem to recall, Milos, that I did pretty well in my sad old *Seeker* against your new leviathan here," Davage said, recalling his desperate battle with the hijacked *Triumph* several months back.

"Indeed you did, and I am thankful for it. But, you must acknowledge that the *Triumph* was under the control of novices who had no business flying such a ship."

Kilos remembered it well. The *Triumph*, on its maiden voyage, had been taken by Princess Marilith and her vile henchmen, the Fanatics of Nalls. Weapons blazing, they had sought to sink the *Seeker*, but had been unable to do so. The *Triumph* eventually came to a sad, wretched ending buried in the mud on the backwards world of Gelt. No thought had ever been made to lift and repair it. Let it die and be forgotten. Time to move forward.

"Additionally, given field data I acquired from that sorry incident, I made some important design changes. I found the original lacked maneuverability in the lateral, as you exposed, Dav, and the Lady Branna's damn Sar-Beams took a little too long to charge and fire. She has since improved the fire rate of the Sar-Beams, and I've added Battleshot batteries and lots and lots of thrusters."

"I can imagine what the Lady Branna thought about that."

"We nearly ended up in a fight to the death over it, me and that blue-haired, Remnath strumpet. But, as I do not see her around anywhere, I will proceed anyway."

Davage laughed. "It's too bad the Lady Branna is married—I think she would have made you a formidable wife."

"You've not heard, Captain? Lord Fallz, Lady Branna's husband, passed away recently," Probert said.

"Really? No, I've not heard that. I must send my condolences to Crewman Saari, my helmsman. I had no idea her father had passed on."

"Just happened. That's why Branna's not here. But, as you know, Captain, there is only one woman for me."

"I put in a good word for you with Lady Poe whenever I can … and I know that Syg is pulling for you too."

"Me too," Kilos said.

Probert kicked at the platform with his buckle shoes. "I am a fortunate man to have such true friends."

Davage again looked out at the unfinished ships. "I have an additional concern, Milos. I am afraid my countess will not wish to set foot aboard a *Triumph*-class ship ever again. You must understand … the scars of that day are still present and I will not subject her to them again."

"I fully understand, Dav, and I am not unmindful of her feelings—both myself and the Lady Branna are in her debt for getting us off the ship in one piece, and I have not forgotten that. I have completely re-designed the interior to give it a more *Straylight* appearance. I even empowered the Lady Branna a bit and allowed her to have a hand in the re-design—makes her feel important, you see. I also partially redesigned the outer hull a bit, to help incorporate the thruster changes

I made, completely enclosed the tach drives, and the added Battleshot batteries."

Davage and Kilos looked hard at the ships, searching for the changes.

"I assure you, the changes should be more than enough to quiet any fears that Countess Blanchefort might have."

An orderly appeared on the platform with a tray of iced drinks. Davage accepted his with much thanks. "Those sound like expensive changes to make, Milos."

"They are, they are, but I felt them necessary. So, Dav, what do you say? Will you delight me and please pick one out?"

Davage took a drink and thought a moment. "I tell you what, Milos, I will select one today and finance its completion … as I am certain you were about to ask for money. However—upon its sounding, I will bring my countess here to Provst so that she may inspect it fully. If, at that time, she determines that she will not be injured in any way—that no bad memories are brought to the surface—then I will face Appointment as its captain."

Probert smiled. "Fine, fine, fair enough. So, which one will it be? You've four to select from. The one at the far end is nearest to completion. And, as always, we have provisionally named these fine dreadnaughts, though, if you are graciously providing funding, then you may christen yours as you choose. The first here is the *Marionette*."

"The *Marionette*?" Ki cried in disgust.

Probert continued. "The next is the *Axelrood*, in memory of the House of Axelrood, then there's the *Bombastic* …"

"*Bombastic*?" Ki cried.

"… And, finally, there is the *Spaceworthy*. I picked those names out myself." Probert seemed proud.

Ki mumbled under her breath: "*Stick to designing stuff*."

Davage finished his drink and gave the empty glass back to the orderly. He noticed a small note attached to the bottom of his glass. He pulled it off and read.

It said:

STAY HOME, OR YOU'LL BE SORRY. –M

He turned to Probert. "Milos, what is this?" he asked holding out the note.

Probert took the note, glanced at it and laughed. "That capering hellion! Oh, no doubt this is from the Lady Branna. You must have received my glass, Dav. Certainly she doesn't wish me here in the yards making changes and good progress without her present to protest, badger and delay—the clucking hen!"

"It's signed with an 'M', Milos."

He threw the note away. "No doubt trying to pin the blame on me, when, clearly, she did it. Apologies, Dav, that you had to become involved in our ongoing confrontations. I'm going to tap her on the shoulder with an armored glove when next I see her. Now, sir, the question remains at hand. Will you pick one out?"

Davage put his hands behind his back and sighed. "Ki, you make the selection."

Kilos stood there holding her drink. "Me? You want me to pick, Dav?"

"I do, pick us a winner."

She set her glass down and stared at the ships in the pit, crawling with craftsmen and dripping with welded sparks. "That one," she said finally, pointing out toward the far end. "The second from the end there."

"Ah, the *Bombastic,* an excellent choice. Why that one, if I may ask as a matter of interest," Probert said.

Kilos shrugged. "It feels right."

Probert smiled. "Agreed then, and … what shall we call her? Shall we leave her be as *Bombastic*?"

Davage again turned to Kilos. "Ki?"

She thought a moment more. "We're changing the name. Your first ship was called the *Faith*, right, Dav?"

"Yes. She was an old *Webber*-class ship. Been scrapped I think."

Probert put his arms behind his back. "Yes, yes … a few years ago," he said. "Got re-cast as a *Tekel*."

"Then, we'll call her the *New Faith*," Ki said. "How about that?"

"Very well. A fine name. *New Faith* it is," Probert said.

7—The House of Xandarr

After their meeting with Probert on the warm, sunny platform, Davage and Kilos went into the massive Fleet complex and were stuck in meetings for several more hours—dry ones at that: Fleet concerns, logistical and supply distribution matters, and so forth. It was material to bore the life out of a person.

Every so often, Davage glanced out the window. Outside, his ripcar sat in the vast yard gleaming with afternoon sun along with various other Fleet craft: other ripcars, larger transports, small fighter craft, Sub-Orbitals and so forth. Soon, he and Ki will mount it and head north, home to the mountains and black rivers—to his village and castle … to Syg. He couldn't wait to see her. He wished he could bring her to these functions. She couldn't attend the meetings of course, but she could go and do her own thing and then meet up with him later. But, his castle needed its countess, even a part-time resident was better than none at all, there were guests and arrivals to attend, and Syg did a great job. She was still getting the hang of League society and was trying her best, rolling with the punches. Seeing her little green eyes flaming like two pinwheels on a creamy landscape after Carahil hit her with that pie was probably the funniest thing he'd ever seen. Any other countess would have been mortified into seclusion over such a thing, but not Syg. She went the rest of the evening with pie on her face like it wasn't even there, making all the guests look her in the eye and deal with it.

Ah, Syg … She will, no doubt, have discovered some new obscure part of the castle, take him there and, filthy, crouching in the dark, they will make love. Syg was enraptured with his old castle and loved to explore it, finding things that even he didn't know were there.

How he adored his countess.

A little while later, as the afternoon dragged on, an orderly entered the room and approached Davage. Leaning down, the orderly said he had a message from the League Office, marked Red for urgent. Excusing himself, and thankful for a moment to stretch his legs, Davage left the room and walked down the busy, marble-cased hallway. Eventually, he found a quiet, discrete terminal near the central cupola and sat down to take the message. He was certainly in no hurry to return to the meeting. As he waited for his terminal to connect, he noticed a slip of paper sitting next to the screen. "Lord Blanchefort" was written in a fine, flowing hand across the center.

Odd.

He reached out and unfolded the paper. It read in a stilted script:

YOUR COUNTESS IS IN DANGER. –M

As he pondered the meaning of that statement, the screen came on. His message was not from the League Office. It was the House of Xandarr.

* * * * *

He was used to getting messages from Princess Marilith of Xandarr, his old enemy and former fiancée. He was to marry her long ago, their proposed wedding a very public and celebrated event that promised to unite the League and their old enemies, the Xaphans, once and for all. Due to a complicated series of events, the wedding never happened, and fleeing from her side, Davage never saw her in person again. Her mind Zen-La'ed with his, Marilith became angry and spiteful, and they became frequent combatants, tangling in wild, cursing battles in space—Davage the usual victor, Marilith always escaping to try again another day.

Still, they had loved each other and Marilith often contacted him in private, and they sullenly stared at each other over the viewing screens. Davage loved her for eighty long years, until Syg came from out of nowhere and stole his wounded heart. His Zen-La passed from Marilith to Syg, and Marilith didn't take it well. She didn't take it well at all and she savagely attacked, recruiting a sect of rebels and malcontents to assist her called the Fanatics of Nalls. Syg, taking matters into her own hands, apparently killed Marilith and the Fanatics in the rain and mud of distant Gelt, nearly losing her mind in the process.

He'd not heard from Marilith since the terrible battle aboard *Triumph*, where Syg, initially subdued and tortured by the Fanatics of

Nalls, rebounded and killed them all. Princess Marilith was apparently lost—killed right along with the Fanatics, impaled on a Shadow tech stake. His cagey foe finally silenced it seemed.

* * * * *

There on the screen was House Xandarr. The whole Xandarr clan, as far as Davage could determine, was sitting at a vast feasting table in a grand Xaphan hall. There were no walls, just arched pillars opening up to an arid outdoor expanse. The sky on the distant mountainous horizon was a soft purple—a tell-tale feature of the planet Xandarr, their fief and great holding. At the front of the table was King Hezru of Xandarr, the family patriarch. Across from him sat Xanthipe his queen, and behind them were nine of their children. They sat at the grand table, as if ready for a sumptuous feast. A small house cat lazily wandered around the legs of the table, waiting for crumbs to fall.

Hezru and Xanthipe smiled broadly. They wore exotic, light veils of reds, pinks and purples in the Xandarr style, rather as Marilith once was prone to wear. Like Marilith, their airy veils did not fully account for modesty, with the king and queen's nude bodies quite exposed beneath them. The Xandarr children appeared to be a bit more covered up than their parents as they wore vests of slightly heavier cloth. The Xandarr children all sat there, princes and princesses, expressions blank, their necks craned to their right to look into the monitor. Each had a head of blue hair that was more garish in shade than the next—like eleven cones of cotton candy sitting on veiled sticks. Davage's hair was blue as well, but it was a much darker, more provincial blue, almost a black. The Xandarr's hair was a very icy blue in comparison.

"Captain Davage," Hezru said in a booming, joyous voice. "Felicitations!"

Hezru paused and seemed puzzled. "Hello, hello, Captain … are you there?? Xaphan's beard!!—have I properly operated this contraption?"

Hezru got up and approached the screen, his large, soft girth utterly filling it, open mouthed and many-chinned. He seemed puzzled. "Yes, yes, I know," he said to someone off the screen. "… but I see three of him. Three captains …"

Hezru backed up a step, and a technician's small, quizzical face slid into the screen from the left. He reached and fiddled with some unseen controls. "The channel is open and secure, my King," the tech said, sliding back out of the picture.

Davage had not seen Hezru in eighty years, since the wedding. He thought, given his famously contentious relationship with his daughter, that the rich Xaphan king should be a bit … angrier. But no, he smiled a jolly smile, as did his pretty, veiled wife. The Xandarr children beyond continued to stare at the screen, eyes blank and unblinking.

"King Hezru, well met," Davage said after a moment. "I must say, this is a … surprise."

Queen Xanthipe stood and bowed—again, nothing left for Davage to wonder about under her thin purple veils. Marilith clearly inherited her mother's great beauty and ample physique.

"Ah, Captain, there you are. My, sir, you are as handsome as ever. A great pity our two Great Houses could not have been wed in years past."

"Yes, a pity."

"Ohhhh," Hezru said again, "let's not wallow in trivialities that are forgotten shall we? Let us be frank and to the point. We both have profited greatly from your … animosity … with my daughter."

"Profited? King Hezru, I profited in no way that I can think of. I suffered … and my heart bled. Until the coming of my countess, I loved your daughter."

"She was greatly wounded by that, Captain," Xanthipe said. "She truly loved you sir … the Black Hat who stole your heart, broke hers—drove her into a final madness at last."

"Ohhhh, let us please discontinue this 'sadness fest'," Hezru said. "And, to your previous point, I shall argue that you, Captain, greatly profited from your dealings with my daughter. What about your notoriety, your fame? Yours is a common name in Xaphan Society. You, sir, are the subject of many Xaphan poems and stories right along with my daughter; the doomed lovers, they fought, yet they loved. Ah, very romantic, and again, very profitable."

Davage shook his head, not quite sure what to make of this. "So, King Hezru, what can I do for you today? Marilith is dead, and I am sorry for your loss."

"Captain, Marilith did our name proud. She fought you—House Xandarr fought you—and we have become rich. The Black Hats took everything we had after the damn *Triumph* Affair several years ago, and your lore has made us rich again."

"You grieve not for the loss of your daughter?"

"She lived long, she made a great name for herself, and she made her House a vast sum of money."

Davage had had enough. "Good King, I must away—I've duties to attend."

"Care you not to hear our request?" Hezru asked. "Care you not to conduct a matter of business, hmmm?"

Davage shrugged. "Fine then, I will give ear, but please ... be swift."

Hezru slapped his ample belly. "We wish the hostilities to continue, Captain. We wish to continue meeting you in combat. There are further riches to be made. Isn't that delightful?"

"And how so? Marilith is dead."

Queen Xanthipe stood, excited. "Let us show you, Captain, let us show you." She bounced away from the table, her veils streaming and light, and disappeared from the screen. Soon she reappeared with a small, blue-haired girl.

"Allow me to introduce my youngest daughter, Princess Vroc."

The girl stared at the floor, apparently painfully shy. Like Marilith, she had bright blue hair, though her hair was cut quite short in the back, with long straight bangs that hung down over her face in the front. Unlike Marilith, who was almost as tall as Davage and was as fit as a championship athlete, the girl standing in the screen was smallish and skinny. Unlike the rest of her family, she was quite heavily garbed. She wore a violet flight suit, boots, and a black jacket emblazoned with the Xandarr motif—a rampant Griffon. A gun belt was strapped at her waist. A large Mazan-style energy pistol was holstered to her right, and a finely wrought silver hilt hung in place at her left in a Xandarr saddle. It looked to Davage to be the BEREN, the LosCapricos weapon of House Xandarr.

Davage had to take a moment. It was odd to see a daughter of Xandarr so covered up: jacketed, shoed and armed. She wore a pair of boots! Not in eighty years did he recall ever seeing Marilith wearing a pair of boots. And a gun? Marilith never carried a gun. All she ever had was her knife, Moonglow, though she was never without it. This girl didn't seem at all like a Xandarr.

Hezru beamed with happiness. "We wish you to continue your battles with Vroc."

Davage was shocked. "I will do no such thing."

"Why not?"

"I will not fight a person with whom I have no quarrel, especially an innocent girl."

The girl, Princess Vroc, stood there gazing at the floor, blue bangs over her face.

"You will find, Captain, that our little Vroc, though she might appear shy and innocent, is in fact a mighty fighter. She is our eleventh daughter—a worthless addition to our household."

"The eleventh daughter is very unlucky, Captain," Queen Xanthipe added happily. "We had planned to sell her into prostitution for wont of anything better to do with her." She spoke as if the notion of selling her own daughter into prostitution wasn't any big deal.

"She was a poor, coinless prostitute—too homely, too bone skinny," Hezru said. "So, as a last resort, I was going to sell her flesh to the Burgon meat market so that we could at least make a bit of money off of her. But then, I had a stroke of genius, Captain. Pure genius! It occurred to me that, should anything happen to Marilith, should she be captured or killed, House Xandarr would require a suitable replacement for her; someone who could step right in and fill her shoes. And so, here she is … what say you?" Hezru blinked with pride.

Vroc lifted a hand and absently rubbed her nose.

Davage was shocked and disgusted. "I say be off. I am truly at a loss, King. You speak of your daughter as worthless—a prostitute, a carcass swinging from a Burgon hook?"

"Again—the eleventh daughter. Very unlucky."

"There are many eleventh daughters out there, King, and none of them, including yours, are worthless or unlucky. And now, merely to line your pockets, you wish to send her to her possible death in space?"

"You will find that she is a worthy opponent—possibly a better one than even Marilith. She has trained since her early youth to engage you in battle. She has studied you, absorbed you … learned your every move. She is a superior ship's captain and, like you, is a fine pilot in her own right. Also, she has mastered the BEREN lore—the LosCapricos weapon of our line, making her a deadly swordsman. Marilith never bothered with the BEREN. You will not be disappointed. Your CARG against our BEREN, which will triumph, I wonder?"

"As I said, I will not fight this girl."

Slowly, in the screen, Vroc lifted her eyes and stared at Davage for the first time through the curtain of her blue bangs. She was plain and forgettable in face, unlike her sister who had been a true beauty. She did, however, share Marilith's eyes—Vroc's eyes were long, thin and a little sleepy in appearance. They were also deep, deep blue.

"I wish to fight you ..." she said in a soft voice. "I wish to make a name for myself, to prove my worth. I'll make you look at me ... acknowledge me."

"You've nothing to prove, not to me or anyone else for that matter. We will not fight, child. I will not fight you."

"Then ... you will die."

Hezru stood up and joined Vroc near the screen. "You will meet, her, Captain, whether you wish it or not. There is too much money at stake, and too many poems yet to be sung. I will ask again—will you continue the game, Captain? Will you fight little Vroc here?"

"I will not."

Hezru rubbed his chubby chin for a moment. "Hmmm, are you struggling with this because you consider Vroc an innocent? Is that it?"

"I am a Fleet captain, King—I do not fight for personal reasons, for wealth or vanity. I fight as my duty calls. I fight to defend life, to defend it from Xaphans, like you, who seek to take it!"

"Ohhh," Hezru said, a little insulted. "I see, always that damned League righteousness. Always the Promise. Can you say, truly say, that you didn't enjoy fighting Marilith all those years? Was she really so skilled that she could have escaped your grasp time and time again—or, did you let her go? Did you 'take it easy on her' so that you could meet her at odds yet another day? One canister is all it should have taken ... and that fatal shot never came, not in eighty years. Your wife, it seems, had to do the dirty work for you."

Davage thought a moment—possibly... maybe. He had loved Marilith, and yes ... he did enjoy the game, the joust. Seeing that beautiful face on the 3D cone, covered in war paint, knife in hand and *Bloodsimple* carved on the wall behind her. Fighting Marilith was exhilarating.

He felt ashamed.

" … And, Captain, if our little Vroc suddenly became … a pressing 'threat'? What say you then?"

"You would dangle the soul of your daughter over the abyss? Princess Vroc, I implore you, find your own path. If you are skilled and you are mighty, then I congratulate you on what you have made of yourself. Make your own way. Be your own person."

Vroc shuffled a bit and looked down at the floor again. "You will die by my hand, or I by yours. And if I must shake a few trees to get you to face me like a Man, then I will do that. Such blood shall be on your hands if you choose to go the coward's route."

Hezru came forward and clapped Vroc on the shoulder, her gun belt jangling. "You do us proud, Princess. Be advised, Captain, do not underestimate her, for she is deadly. And, unlike Marilith, Vroc has nothing but hatred for you."

Vroc looked up and approached the screen. She looked intently, studying Davage, taking in all of his features. With Vroc's long, sleepy eyes filling the screen, it went black.

* * * * *

"Can you imagine?" Ki yelled as the ripcar tore across the sky, the mountains looming in the far distance. Her wind-blown brown hair sailed in the slipstream. "Being some poor Xaphan slob and having to trot home and tell your mates that you got handled in space … by the *Marionette?* Ha! Those were the worst ship names I've ever heard!"

Davage stood at the throttle, the blue tail of his long hair whipping this way and that. "I don't know, they had a bit of style to them, possibly."

Kilos sat there, shaking her head. "So, tell me about this message you received. You're saying that House Xandarr wants to continue fighting you?"

"That appears to be the case, yes. Apparently, they made great profits during all the years Marilith and I fought, and they do not wish the well to run dry, with Marilith apparently dead and all."

"They weren't upset that she's gone?"

"Only for their loss of capital, it seems."

"Well, what do you think? You think this sister of Marilith will make any noise?"

"Hard to tell. They claimed she is a fine captain. She certainly appears… motivated. She appears not to like me much."

"Does she wear clothes?"

"Actually, she does: jacket, gun, boots and all."

Ki was a little shocked. "Boots? Well, if she wants to come, then let her. I must admit I miss fighting with Marilith, those were some good, straight up battles. And, you won't have to worry about her attacking Syg out of jealously this time, since she appears to want nothing more of you than your bloody head on a stick."

"Thanks, Ki."

In the distance was a fast approaching line of steep mountains. Written in a series of small but bright dots on the face of several of the outlying peaks was:

REMEMBER: THINGS TEND TO
WORK THEMSELVES OUT

Ki leaned down to look at the message further as they passed over it. Davage pitched the ripcar down a little as the updraft from the approaching mountains jostled the ship.

"Dav, did you see that?"

"See what?"

"That message we just passed over."

"No. I saw several Com relay stations several miles away. I saw several hikers climbing the mountains due east and, I'm afraid to say, Carahil has run one of Syg's gowns up the Josephina Tower flag pole again."

"You saw all that but you didn't see the message in lights right in front of us?"

"No. You drink a little too much of that horrid Fleet ale?"

"Yeah, but, I usually don't hallucinate when I'm drunk."

Davage reduced the throttle a little. "Back to our previous topic, I feel a little 'unclean' about the whole notion of fighting with a girl for no other reason than her family wants to make money off of the spectacle. Perhaps she'll grow bored of such intrigues, find a good husband and pass the baton."

"You said she wasn't all that great looking."

"What difference does that make? There are other things to consider, Ki, beyond the merits of a pretty face. Perhaps she has great wit."

"Great wit—ha! Great wit gets you nowhere ... look at Lord Probert."

"What about him?"

"There's no wit greater than his in the League ... and look, in love with Lady Poe and can't get a second glance from her. So much for great wit. Apparently she places a lot of stock in a Great Face."

"Yes, and I am going to have a long talk with her about that. In any event, I've no great desire to see this Princess Vroc ever again."

Davage looked at Ki and gave her a nudge. "I believe I might owe you an apology."

"Why, Dav?"

"Today, when Lord Probert asked me to pick out a ship ... I automatically assumed you will be coming with me. I should be more mindful. Do you feel you are ready to strike off on your own? Shall we to the Admiralty where you may argue your case to become a ship's captain?"

"You need money to do that."

"Indeed—you've the Blanchefort fortune at your service."

Kilos beamed. "Trying to get rid of me, Dav? No, I'm not ready yet. I've still a lot to learn from you. Maybe one day, but not today. Thanks for asking, though."

The mountains loomed ahead. Davage kicked the thrusters and the ripcar surged forward. "Through the mountains, Ki, or over them?"

"Over them, please. My stomach ..."

Davage smiled. "Through them it is!" and he plunged the ripcar into the mountain passes, hauling the craft this way and that, Ki hanging on for dear life.

8—The Naked Countess

Davage dropped Kilos off at the village docks by the bay near the *Seeker*. The frontal section of the ship towered over the huddled buildings lining the dock. Kilos bounced out of the ripcar and, always thirsty, begged Dav to come have a drink with her at one of the pubs. She said it was honey ale night at the Drunken Eel, something not to be missed. Smiling, he gave in and had a glass or two, clapping shoulders with the locals and some of his crew who were there. He was enjoying the fellowship and had a mind to call up to the castle and have Syg come down and join him, he missed her so. She'll, no doubt, climb into her sedate little green ripcar and come blundering down the mountain road. Syg was a terrible pilot, but usually didn't trouble the staff to fly her down. She liked to do things herself, even when she was terrible at a thing. Her green ripcar was battered with dozens of little dents. Davage certainly hoped that their son, growing within her, didn't inherit her piloting skills.

He went outside to call Syg when he saw the ship parked at the far end of the bay. The small Vith ship was a Sister ship, no doubt about it. A few Marines were posted in front of it, standing guard. The Sisters were here? No announcement, no contingent? Without question, they were up at the castle. There was nothing in his village that otherwise interested them.

He could guess what they wanted—and he knew his countess wasn't going to take it well in the least.

He put his glass down, said `bye to Kilos and his crew, and blasted the ripcar up toward the castle, hauling it skyward in a steep climb to clear the mountain shelf. He maneuvered through the myriad of spires and towers of the castle, clearing its colossal width and lowering toward the vast green maze of the Telmus Grove.

Ahead, the old Vith chapel rose out of the tangle of trees. He knew the Sisters were there, waiting.

He knew they will not see Syg.

He knew that fact will enrage her.

Oh, Creation …

Lowering the skids and chopping the power, he dropped the ripcar like a rock and tore into the waiting chapel.

He knew exactly what the Sisters wanted … but he had no idea what he was going to say, not this time, now that he was married.

* * * * *

Lt. Kilos entered her quarters aboard the *Seeker,* and took off her red Marine coat and her gun belt. Outside, through her windows, were the carnival lights of the village, the black bulk of the mountains, and the massive spired castle high above. The bright northern stars twinkled beyond.

In a few days they will blast off on a new tour, the *Seeker* howling out of the bay and into the clear air, heading off to who knows where. A new tour—she loved setting out fresh. She enjoyed hanging out in the village, visiting Dav's castle and whatnot during these down times, but soaring the stars was her favorite. To set sail toward parts unknown, it gave her chills of anticipation.

She sat down at her desk and sorted through the bursar's notes. As first officer it was her responsibility to keep up on ship happenings, deal with any crew situations that might crop up, and otherwise command the docked vessel. As usual, Dav's crew was well behaved; the only incident of note was a crewman had failed to compensate a courtesan for a night's work, and she was handing the bill to the Fleet. A matter easily taken care of. She then thought she'd catch up on her Marine mail, freshen up, and see if Dav and Syg were up for some breakfast The sun will be rising soon—Ki being the consummate night owl, sleep was for the weak, the timid. Sleep was for nobodies. And Ki loved the pancakes they served up at the castle with that awesome Nadine syrup they made. Oh Feature; that was some eating.

She was a Marine of course; she wore a Marine uniform and carried a Marine SK. She went to all of the various 12th Marine Division functions, but, as Dav's first officer, she had little contact with Stellar Marine Command itself. She was fortunate that her high position on a Main Fleet Vessel of the line was greatly prized by the Marines. It gave them a great deal of prestige, and they allowed her all the leash she wanted. They hoped she would groom other Marines to become first officers in the Fleet as well. They'd sent a few officers her way, whom they hoped she'd train up, but, with her gruff nature and dour demeanor, they went away generally unassisted. There was talk about a disciplinary action against her, that a high-ranking Marine Commandant wanted her head for her attitude. But, again, her standing aboard the *Seeker* was a bullet-proof shield protecting her from attack.

Still, there was paperwork that needed done, her debriefs for her "commander" back at Marine station 0-Foxtrot on Olgolvy, and she, as usual, let it back up. She hadn't seen her Marine Commander face to face in years. Dav was all the commander she wanted.

Relaxing at her terminal, she logged in and began sorting through her Marine To-Do Box—200 plus items, Good Creation!

She'd finished a few items. One must have been a bit of whamic—junk mail. It was just a red pair of animated cat's eyes on a black screen that seemed to follow her around when she stood up from her terminal to get her mug. She was a little too tipsy from the pub binge to be startled or overly interested. She closed it and had more whamic in her list: a message, supposedly from her commander, said:

STAY AT YOUR POST! DON'T MAKE
ME COME FOR YOU! –M

Actually, it might have from her commander after all; she heard the man hated her for her insubordinate attitude and her immunity from persecution under Dav's wing. He was a Major, too: 'M' for Major.

"Sour Jo-boy," she said.

She finished a few more messages when a League Com screen popped up. She had an incoming message.

From: the University of Tusck.

Her husband!

Smiling, she ran a hand through her hair and opened the Com. There, on the screen, was her husband in his office at the old university; mid-day back on Onaris. He wore his usual academician's robes and scholar's hat. He was a handsome fellow, but small—a good foot shorter than she was. He was Syg-sized. His office was the usual clutter of stonework, artifacts and documents scattered about. In the background was an angelic, brown-eyed painting of Kilos; he'd done it himself. He was a good painter. He was good at everything he did. His skills as a researcher were demonic—legendary. There was nothing that was beyond his reach, no secret whose mysteries he could not fathom.

His whole office was lit up in whitish, silvery light.

"Hi, darlin'!" she said happily.

Before she could get two more words out, he interrupted, and said with a solemn, serious voice:

"Come home, Ki …"

* * * * *

Syg had been struggling for what seemed like hours, and getting nowhere. Time was wrapped around her, in a blanket, in a vortex, moving at a sprint. She might, with considerable effort, make it to the chapel eventually, but it will take days—by then the Sisters will be gone and Dav will probably be in a lather wondering where she was.

She was frothing mad. By the Elders, she was going to see the Sisters whether they liked it or not.

And she was not helpless, not at all.

She allowed her Silver tech to flow out of her hands, hitting the stony ground, bouncing up and coating her in a film of silver. The grip of time, accelerated around her tiny body, began to slip, to lose its hold. She let it grab onto the silver, like a banana being squirted out of its peel.

She could feel herself moving.

"You won't want to do that, Countess," Carahil said, floating on the air, his Silver tech body immune to the time wrap.

She ignored him. A little more … a little more. With a RIP!, she was free, and hurtled toward the waiting chapel, toppling to the ground with a thud.

She was there. She had made it.

She was also naked, her gown ripped away along with her Silver tech, locked in time, hanging there in effigy.

"Carahil, bring me my gown, please," she said, picking herself up.

"I got it! I got it!" Carahil cried as he seized the gown in his mouth like a life-sized anthropomorphic kite, and flew off with it, disappearing behind a stand of trees.

Syg fumed. Obviously, Carahil wanted her to follow him. Obviously Carahil, like Poe, like the Sisters, didn't want her going in there.

Too bad. She didn't care. She will settle with him over her gown and the pie thing later. By Creation, he better not lose or damage it.

She was going to see the Sisters, stark naked if need be—who cares! She wiped the dirt from her face, hauled back, and kicked the door open with her dirty bare foot.

BOOM! The door flew open with a heavy wooden thud.

She charged in.

Inside, as she recalled from her wedding, was a large ornate vestibule. Sitting properly on three little couches were the Sisters, each flanked by a Marine. Syg recalled their faces from dinner yesterday. Standing in front of them, was Dav, her husband, his hat off. His coppery CARG glinted at his side.

Dav!! Her heart fluttered.

Three Sisters? Weren't there four? She had seen four at the docks.

All faces turned to her immediately. Syg, standing there naked and dirty, bowed with all the courtesy she'd been taught.

Syg in the Chapel *(Carol Phillips)*

9—The Sisters Program

"I beg your forgiveness for my tardy arrival, esteemed Sisters, however, it appears I became engulfed in some sort of time vortex in the Grove. Most inconvenient. Strange, I'd not encountered one of those there previously."

Davage regarded her with a broad smile. "Syg! … I mean, Countess Blanchefort, well met and good evening."

Syg looked at Dav and burst into a smile as well. "Dav!! … err, Captain Davage, my lord. I am pleased that you are returned safely to your castle, at last. It appears that I have misplaced my gown in my haste to arrive here and attend honored guests in our home."

The love that passed between them warmed the room. Quickly, Davage took off his coat and draped it over her shoulders. She touched his hand as he put it around her, savoring his feel, wishing they were alone.

The Marines appeared both amused and touched by this display.

The Sisters were nonplussed and inscrutable as ever. They began speaking through the Marines.

"Lord Blanchefort, we will allow you to escort your countess back to the castle, spend a moment with her in reunion as you will, and then return when you can. We will await your arrival."

"Esteemed Sister," Syg said, "I have come all this way to humbly serve you and attend to your every need. I have even lost my clothing in my zeal. My Lord is no doubt tired and hungry from his important League meetings to the south, and shan't be further disturbed tonight. Please, to the castle, Lord Blanchefort, I will happily serve the Sisters here as best I can."

"Countess Blanchefort, you misunderstand—our business here is with Lord Blanchefort and Lord Blanchefort alone. You cannot assist us in this manner. He will escort you in safety back to the castle, and he will return here at his convenience. We assure you, there will be no further 'time entanglements' along the way."

Syg wiped the dirt from her nose. "Great Sister, Lord Blanchefort will return to the castle at once and be refreshed, and I will attend you here! We can bandy this topic about all night if need be, yet the outcome will be the same!" Syg said, the long tails of Dav's coat dragging on the floor.

There was a fierce standoff for a moment; the Sisters stiff, immovable, sitting on their couches and Syg, proud, naked, draped in a Fleet coat that was far too big for her. Davage and the Marines were forgotten for the time being. They looked around at each other… incredulous.

Finally, one of the Sisters smiled a bit. "Great Countess," a Marine said, "it is obvious that you love your lord very much, and such a display truly warms our hearts. We forget that Lord Blanchefort is no longer an esteemed bachelor, and has the love of his wife, his Great Countess, to consider."

"Thank you, Great Sister. And, should you wish to speak to me in private, recall that I can hear your thoughts without the need of a Marine interpreter."

The Sister went on, the Marine speaking for her. "That is true and thank you, yet not all in attendance can communicate in such a fashion. For Lord Blanchefort's sake, we will continue to speak through our Marines, with their kind permission, of course. Countess, you are still new to League Society, so we will understand your lack of knowledge in this area. Be it known, we wish to pay the Lord of Blanchefort one of the highest compliments we of the Sisterhood can offer. Be it known that he … and by proximity, you as well, are well favored and beloved by us."

"Thank you, Great Sister, I appreciate your compliments, and am flattered that you find my husband worthy. He is, of course, a great Elder, and I am not afraid to say it. No one is as proud of him as I."

"Indeed, and we wish to suitably honor him by having him participate in our Program."

"I see. And what is your Program? Can you be a bit more specific?"

The Sisters looked at each other for a moment. "We can say no further. That is for Lord Blanchefort alone."

Syg, allowing Dav's coat to come open, strode forward. The Sisters watched her with muted interest. "I am most concerned by the secrecy concerning this 'honor' you wish to perform upon my husband. We took an oath together, he and I, on the day of our wedding. Our hands held the wedding baton, and we became as one. We have, and maintain, no secrets … I have shared all the sordid details of my horrendous past as a Black Hat Hammer with him, and he loves me still. He has forgiven me the things I did in a past life. Certainly I can hear and stomach any honor the Sisterhood might wish to affect upon him. Certainly, such an honor will warm my heart."

Davage came forward. "Sisters, please allow me a moment alone with my countess."

A Sister stirred. "No, no, Lord Blanchefort. Your countess raises an excellent point, and we should not hesitate in sharing with her the honor of our Program. Certainly, none of our exploits should give a Black Hat pause."

"I am no longer a Black Hat," she replied.

"Indeed."

"Sisters, please," Davage said.

Syg looked up at him and winked. "It's ok, Dav," she whispered. "How bad can it be? How much money can they possibly want?"

"Lord Blanchefort, we insist. Countess, no doubt you have heard the term 'Programmability' used in various social circles. Programmability is a measure of a gentleman's worth and status in the League. Programmability itself is derived from a gentleman's participation in our time-honored Program. We wish your husband to participate in our Program today, and further enhance his already impressive Programmability."

"Yes, thank you, you have said that."

"Our … *mating* … Program."

Syg's eyes flared, her mouth dropped open.

"We have been blessed with a miracle, hence our haste. A Sister of great esteem, who was not due her time for several more years, has come into sudden fruit and requires proper seeding. Such things happen. We do not question the Elder's plan. It is a gift that we cherish. We have determined that Lord Blanchefort's Programmability is high in this case—which is a great honor. He is an ideal candidate to seed our Sister and create a fine, strong girl-child offspring. We apologize for the alacrity of these proceedings, however, speed is of the essence lest our Sister's unexpected time be missed. Fear not, you will not miss your husband… he will simply be gone one night and returned to you in the morning, harmed not in the least. Nothing more will be said or need done, and a grand dowry we shall pay in thanks."

Syg stood there, speechless.

"You see, countess, perhaps it was best not you inform you of the details regarding this matter. Rest assured it is a common practice throughout the League and is greatly appreciated by the—"

"I FORBID IT!" Syg shrieked at last.

Davage gently touched Syg by the shoulder. She was trembling with rage. "Syg, come outside with me for a moment."

"MY HUSBAND WILL REST IN THE ARMS OF NO OTHER!! I FORBID IT … NOT WHILST I LIVE AND DRAW BREATH!!"

"Clearly, you were unprepared for this information. Our Program is purely voluntary."

"AND HAS HE YET AGREED TO THIS … THIS ACT OF ADULTRY?"

"He had not, as of yet, agreed. We await his answer still. And, allow us to correct you. To seed a Sister, to engage in the time-honored practice of Programmability, is not adultery. The Sisterhood does not recognize the bonds of marriage."

"FORGIVE ME … FORGIVE ME!!—BUT I DO NOT RECALL OUR MARRIAGE VOWS TO ONE ANOTHER BEING WAVED, CIRCUMVENTED, COUNTERMANDED OR OTHERWISE POSTPONED SIMPLY BECAUSE THE SISTERHOOD OF LIGHT HAS A BITCH IN HEAT REQUIRING A STUD!!"

The Sisters appeared stunned, so did the Marines and so did Davage. Syg composed herself a bit. "I … am sorry, Sisters … that was most uncalled for of me," she said in a quiet, hurried voice. "However, you must understand, I will not see my husband in the arms of another … not even a Sister. Certainly you will understand that—certainly that fact is most plain!"

Another Sister spoke via a Marine. "It is most obvious to us how the Countess Blanchefort feels regarding this matter. Her thoughts are … most clear and we thank her for her candor. And so … how does *Lord Blanchefort* feel?"

All eyes turned to Davage.

Syg's eyes burned green in their wide, disbelieving sockets as she gazed at him.

He stood there for a moment and rubbed his forehead.

"Sisters," he said finally, "clearly I am in a most distressing position. I am certain, as my past actions have shown, I have been a willing and honored participant of your Program many times. Seven times you have come to me, and seven times I have gladly accepted. You have bestowed the Programmable ranking of *Magni* upon me, which has opened many doors for me in the Fleet and League at large. I can think of no other Lord who has participated so much in my generation."

"That is true," a Marine said, "your fine Blanchefort blood has done us proud many times in the past and you have earned your *Magni* ranking. Yes, that is true."

"And I am deeply honored, and flattered, that you have come again on this urgent occasion seeking my help. However, as my countess has put it, I am no longer single and have her feelings to consider in the matter as well. She is my Zen-La, and I shall not harm or diminish her so."

"And so, what do you suggest?"

"Yes, Lord Blanchefort," Syg said in a tart voice, "what do you suggest?"

"I recall the time-honored custom of *Perlance*, one that the Sisterhood has afforded to married Lords often in the past. Per the *Perlance*, I will gladly open my home to you as you need it, and offer a compensatory dowry for your inconvenience here today. I offer it willingly, as I heartily wish to maintain and perpetuate the open friendship with the Sisterhood my family has enjoyed over the centuries."

Syg looked at Dav and beamed with happiness. As usual, Dav appeared to have a knack for talking himself out of a tight situation.

The Sisters silently chattered amongst themselves for a moment. A third Sister began speaking. The Marine: "*Perlance* is your right to claim, Lord Blanchefort, however, this situation is a bit … different than most. Our Sister has specifically requested you for her Program, she was most adamant about your particular participation, and will accept no other. Our Sister's fertile period must not be missed, and no other candidates have been matched. We are afraid that *Perlance* is, regrettably, denied, though you are certainly within your rights to request it."

Syg instantly regained her previous fury. "Denied … DENIED? Sisters, you come here claiming to offer my husband a great honor. You claim it is purely voluntary. It, however, does not appear voluntary to me … RATHER IT SEEMS MOST COMPULSORY TO ME!!"

"Consider it as you will."

"Sisters, you claim to be so good … so pure and without sin. You come, polite, smiling, offering endless choice. Yet, you do not offer choice—there is no choice other than the one you have pre-selected!! You have run roughshod over the League, over fine men like my husband, since time immemorial, and that is over in this particular household! You claim to allow freedom, yet you take it away when you hear the word 'no'. I say NO! Let your … BITCH … find a stud in some other pasture!"

"Unacceptable."

There was silence for a moment. Syg and the Sisters faced each other relentlessly.

A Marine: "This exchange is unproductive and pointless. Countess, if you choose to impede us, if you choose to so inconvenience Lord Blanchefort and trouble his thoughts, then we will be forced to simply take what we want. Have you any illusions that we could not pass your time, the seeding done and gone at the blink of an eye?"

Davage faced the Sisters. "Should you do that, Sister, then, of course, we are powerless to prevent it, however, you may be certain that the friendship of House Blanchefort and the Sisterhood will be, henceforth, at an end. You will no longer be welcome here. I will give you no further ear, I will entertain you not, and nor shall any future Lords of Blanchefort. Finally, I will make it generally known what was taken here by force before the League Ex-Commons, and how we are all slaves before the Sisterhood."

The Sisters looked amongst themselves and appeared pained. "Forgive us, Lord Blanchefort, forgive us Countess, we sincerely apologize for suggesting such a thing. We are your friends, and are grateful for your council. We do not wish to … endanger … our standing with you. That is not our desire."

"Then why not display your good intentions … and leave—at once!" Syg said.

The Sisters sat silent for a moment. Finally, a Marine said: "Countess, our Sister has informed us that she knows you well, that she anticipated a scene such as this. She anticipated your pride, and your haunting of Lord Blanchefort's thoughts, forcing him into a very awkward situation. Lord Blanchefort, our Sister offers her apologies for the contretemps that have been made here today, both by our presence … and by the actions of your countess. Additionally, countess, our Sister wishes to distress him no further, and offers you sport."

It was Davage's turn to be enraged. "No sport will be accepted! Not whilst I am lord here!"

Syg turned to him and put her hand on his shoulder. "It's all right, Dav." She turned to the Sisters. "I will hear this … sport."

"Our Sister offers a contest with you to settle this matter, any contest you so choose, just you and she."

"You are saying that the Sister wants to fight, is that it?"

"If that is the contest you wish, she will meet you. She will meet you naked if you so choose. You may select terms."

"Is no one listening? There will be no terms. I will not allow it!" Davage said

"My Lord," Syg said calming him down, "My Lord, I do not see any other way around this issue. Clearly, the Sisters will not accept 'no' as an answer, and clearly I will not accept 'yes' as an answer either. I will meet this Sister, I will fight her, and I will defeat her clean."

"Then, state your terms," a Sister said.

"I will fight the Sister with the strength of my arm against the strength of hers. No weapons, no Gifts, no Silver tech, no TK, no illegal Black Hat Gifts or hyper Gifts. Just the two of us, woman to woman."

"Our Sister will agree."

Davage spun Syg around—his coat hopelessly big on her. "Countess Blanchefort, may I remind you that you are carrying our child."

"Our child is as a seed at the moment and will not be harmed." She turned to the Sisters. "I will further ask that the Sister refrain from intentionally striking my belly … or does the unborn life of our child also mean nothing to the Sisterhood?"

"Our Sister cherishes your unborn child and will gladly avoid harming him, however, your face and limbs will be fair targets."

"Fine, as will hers."

"Then it is done and bound. And, when you are soundly defeated you will trouble Lord Blanchefort no further regarding this matter."

Syg was defiant. "I will expect no further dalliances when I have won, and you will not come to our home with your 'Program' ever again. Not until our son is born and comes of age, then he may deal with you as he chooses."

"Agreed. And, where shall this humiliating, short-lived battle take place?"

"Carahil's Walk, in the Telmus Grove. Sunset. Two days hence, on the full moons."

"Done and bound."

* * * * *

Davage and Syg lay in bed, their arms tightly wrapped around each other. Outside, the stars hung bright in the northern horizon.

"Syg, I will not allow this."

"It's already done. My marriage vows to you are the most important words I have ever spoken, and yours to me are the sweetest I have ever heard. You will rest in the arms of no other."

"You will not fight a Sister."

"I will fight the Sister, and I will win."

"Syg, you cannot face a Sister … she is strong."

"I'm strong."

"You are, but you're not as strong as I am … even without the Gift of Strength. However, I am in no way as strong as a Sister even at full strength."

"Strength is strength. I know how to fight. I've been in lots of fights, Dav—with people a lot bigger than I am… and I won. You've also taught me how to fight up close. I will win tomorrow. I am fighting for my beloved husband."

"You're doing no such thing. You're fighting out of jealousy."

"And so … all the more motivation for me to win. I'll not share you with any woman, even for one night. If that's jealousy, then yes … I am jealous."

Syg looked at him in the dark and kissed his chest. "I'm sorry I made a scene. I … wouldn't have done that if I didn't love you so. You know that, right?"

"I know, Syg."

"And, on the moons I will fight this woman, beat her, and send her on her way. Then it'll be done. The Sisterhood will get over it. They will still be friends with House Blanchefort."

"And our son?"

"There is no situation in which I will ever endanger our son. Right now he is a seed, he will not start sprouting for another month or two. And, the Sister agreed to not strike my belly in any case. He will be fine."

"I've been thinking of a name for the little fellow."

"Oh," Syg said, glad to change the subject. "Tell me?"

"Kabyl, after Lord Kabyl, a Blanchefort of old."

"Hmmm, not bad, but we've a whole year and a half to plan a name, don't we? I have a few planned myself."

10—"Come Home ..."

Kilos and Syg were in the *Seeker's* gym working out: Kilos alternating between lifting weights and hitting the bag, Syg, body-suited up, nimbly climbing the bars. They always tried to set aside time to work out together.

"I've got to hand it to you, Syg—you certainly know how to make an impression."

Syg twirled around in the bars, her tiny body moving with the skill of a champion gymnast. "You think so? I'll bet that in-heat Sister never thought in a million years that she'd be getting into a fist fight with the Countess of Blanchefort when all of this started."

"I should say you're probably right. You sure you want to do this?"

"Positive."

"You're fighting tomorrow night, right? On the full moons?"

"That's right."

"I know it sounds a little strange, but the Sisters do this all the time. I believe I recall Lord Smithson had to service a Sister whilst on his wedding night to his countess."

"What? How could they?"

"When a Sister comes into fertility they don't dally around. Time is of the essence and, as they carefully scout out who they want to 'do the deed', they aren't going to take no for an answer—though nobody ever says no."

"How could Lord Smithson's countess allow this seeding to take place ... on her wedding night of all things?"

"I'm certain she wasn't too happy, but what was she supposed to do about the matter? I suppose she probably didn't have your guts, and, let's face it ... there aren't too many ex-Black Hat countesses out there. A standard countess or lady can't fight back like you can."

"The Sisters appeared rather nonchalant about the whole thing."

"They do it all the time."

"Call it what you will—but I'll not share Dav with anybody. He took a vow to be with me and me alone, and I'll be dead before I merrily send him off to bed someone else."

Ki pounded the bag. "Listen ... I want you to be careful, yes? You've never fought anybody like a Sister before."

"I know how to fight, Ki. Also, it's just going to be me and her: no Gifts, no powers, just the two of us."

"Do you realize how strong the Sisters are?"

"Yes ... and, let's be frank, this won't be the first time I've fought a Sister."

"This won't be on a battlefield, all laid out and lines drawn. This is going to be you and her, arm-in-arm. Sisters are as strong as earthmovers."

"Then I suppose I'll just have to make sure I don't get hit."

Syg came down from the bars and sat down next to Ki. "You remember the first time we were in the gym together ... rolling around, screaming, hitting?"

Ki laughed. "Yes ... you gave me a pretty hard time."

"I gave you more than a hard time, if I recall correctly. Didn't think I could fight, did you?"

"Nope."

"Proved you wrong, didn't I?"

"Yep."

Ki sat down and looked at the mat. She sighed. "Syg, I know you've got a lot on your mind ... but, I was wondering ..."

"Something the matter, Ki?"

Ki shrugged for a moment, then: "It's my husband."

"What about him?"

"... he wants me to come home."

"Again?"

"Yes, but this time I think he really means it."

"Did he say why?"

"Oh ... something about wanting his wife. Something about starting our family."

Syg smiled. "What a horrible man—to want his wife, to want to become a father. How could he?"

She stood up and hit the bag. "It's not fair!"

"Well, you can't blame him for missing you, can you? Don't you miss him?"

"`Course I do. It's just … I'm not ready to come home. I was a failure as a peasant, and then I was a failure as a Marine. I couldn't stay out of trouble … I was always fighting. I was in Hack more than I was out of it. It wasn't until I got here that things changed. Dav gave me a chance. He believed in me."

"You've been a good friend and a great asset."

"It's him—it's all him. He helped me find myself. And, Elders help me—I love this! I love being here!" She slammed the bag. "It's not fair! I'm not ready to go!"

"I know how'd I feel if Dav was gone for a long, long time—I'd be a basket case. I couldn't be without him."

"I can't think. I can't sleep. Nothing tastes good in my mouth. I've even been seeing things! Can you believe that?"

"Seeing things?" Syg asked.

"Yeah, strange things. I've been getting these vaguely threatening messages in my Marine Mail—they're probably from my rot-gutted commander. I don't know. And then I've also been seeing these weird, peppy little messages written out all over the place. I saw one in the clouds, another in the mountains, and one in the toilet of all things—which was gross!"

"What do the messages say?"

"Tuesday morning poetry. Stupid stuff like you'd see hanging on the wall in a locker room. One said: 'The Darkest Night begets the Brightest Dawn'. What a bunch of crap."

Syg thought a moment. "The threatening messages, Ki, were they signed: 'M'?"

"Yeah. How'd you know?"

"I've also gotten a few odd messages signed 'M'. Maybe they're connected?"

Ki ran her hand through her sweaty hair. "I don't know. I'm pretty sure mine are from my commander. His key is encoded in the notes, and the guy hates me, so they must be from him. And they're not really bad, I guess, they're just worded in a way that feels a little creepy. Maybe I just need some sleep. Me—needing sleep? Imagine."

Syg stood and held the bag—Ki pounded it. "You need to relax, Ki. I know—why don't you and me hit the bowling alley and throw it around a little?"

Ki managed a laugh. "You know, I'm really not much into bowling, Syg, and the last time we went to the alley you tried to get everybody to bowl naked. I got to tell you that really freaked me out."

"You try bowling in a gown."

"You know what I would like? Coming here as often as I do, I've become a big supporter of the Sarfortnim College brandtball team; the Magenta `40's. There's a match tonight, with the St. Edmunds Tarpons and the Feren Industrial Precision teams visiting. We could all go and sit in the Blanchefort box right down the center line and watch. I'd really like that."

Syg gave Ki a rap on the shoulder. "Sure, Ki, sure. We can do that. I'll have my staff tell the school to expect us this evening and have the box stocked with plenty of sweet meats and good ale."

"Make sure the ale's from the Drunken Eel, and don't forget those crunchy chips that I like from Sandy's."

"Fine, fine. Whatever you want, Ki. You know, I just had a thought about your situation. Why doesn't your husband come here?"

"Not a chance."

"As you touched on we have the college in the village—he could teach there. It's not a bad little school. I'm taking a few courses there myself. Dav sits on the Board of Governors and …"

"He won't come. He loves that university in Tusck."

"And you love this ship, so something's got to give, right? Why doesn't Dav just give you a little more time off, so you could go home more often?"

"Won't work."

"So … what's going to happen?"

Ki stopped and thought. "I don't know. I don't want to lose my husband, and I don't want to leave the ship either. I love this … all of this. I love soaring the stars, I love the exploration, the danger. I love getting into fights. I love wearing my uniform—can you picture me wearing anything but? Can you picture me in a dress and sandals?"

"Not really, no. I don't think I've ever seen your feet."

Ki smiled. "That's a good thing … they're ugly."

Syg put her arm around Kilos. "I'm sorry your husband is putting you through this. But, just think how he feels … his beautiful wife so far away. I know how I'd feel. You know you'd be greatly missed here, but, if it's any consideration, you and your husband will be expected as guests in our home often. If you were to leave, it won't be goodbye … just so long. Come on, let's get the ball rolling for the box and tell Dav we're all attending the match tonight. You're all going to have to help me out a little. I still don't understand all the rules of brandtball yet."

Ki walked at Syg's side and wiped her nose as they left the gym. She was eager for the match. It might put her mind off things.

Another one of those stupid messages she'd seen popped into her head; this one had appeared on the steamed up mirror behind the bar at the Drunken Eel. It said:

Somebody you love out there loves you too…

11—Carahil's Walk

The following evening Davage and Syg entered the courtyard deep within the Telmus Grove. It was twilight, and soon the Grove would be plunged into tangled, leafy darkness, the two full moons, Elyria and Solon, soon to rise. The courtyard, so far, was empty beyond the two of them.

This particular courtyard had lights surrounding the perimeter, but, in the fading dark blue of dusk, the lights weren't doing much good.

Syg was wearing her black body suit and light sandals. She had a thick shawl on to keep off the evening chill and keep her muscles limber, though she didn't really need it. Cold didn't bother her.

Carahil bounded around the corner, as if from nowhere. "My Lord and Countess, what a surprise!" he said happily. He had something in his mouth, which he promptly tossed into the bushes.

"Where's my gown, Carahil!" Syg cried, his whiskers drooping a little. "—don't think I didn't see you take it!"

"I was hoping you'd follow me, and avoid the Sisters."

"No chance of that! So where's my gown?"

"When you didn't follow, I chested it up and set it toward the far end of the Grove. I was hoping to prank my Mother into thinking that Countess Pardock had returned."

"Well, unchest it and return it at once, and my damn knickers too!"

"Aye, my countess … umm, before or after I've pranked my Mother?"

"Before! In fact, go get it right now, and you better not have made any teeth marks in the fabric, or I'll have you over my knee."

"Don't be in any hurry to return, Carahil," Dav said.

"Why?"

"There's going to be a fight."

"A fight? Who's fighting?"

"I am … and a Sister," she said removing her shawl and giving it to Davage. "We're fighting over Dav."

"You're fighting over Lord Blanchefort? Are you planning on running off with the Sister, my lord?"

"No, he is not. And, he is not going to be sleeping with one, either."

"A Sister will not be an easy opponent," Carahil said.

"Nor will the Countess of Blanchefort."

His silver book appeared. He opened it and scratched in a few notes. "I should stay, to ensure it doesn't get out of hand. This is not a duel, correct?"

"Correct, Carahil," he said. "Nobody is to be hurt. I am here to monitor the situation. You may take your leave."

He reached behind the wall and pulled out his box of sleeping kittens. He held it in his jaws. "I better get them out of here. Things could get a little chaotic."

"Yes, you better," Syg said. She looked at the tiny forms huddled in the blanket inside the box and smiled. "You know, Carahil, you do have a good heart. Perhaps that's why I haven't utterly destroyed you over the pie incident. Go on, take them someplace safe."

He bowed. "As you wish, my countess. Please fight well, and remember, keep her close and do not let her hit you." He took flight and was gone.

Syg looked up at Davage. He rubbed her shoulders. "Can I please have a kiss, love … for luck?"

Davage knelt down and kissed her, wondering what was about to happen here. He knew, if she lost this fight, and he had to seed the Sister, that Syg will never forgive him. And he knew if she somehow won, the Sisters will never forgive him either. Any way, he was in a bad spot.

* * * * *

A few minutes later, several Marines entered the courtyard from the far end. A moment later, there was the Sister, emerging from the dark. She appeared uncharacteristically angry, enraged even; Sisters were always so calm and collected. She strode forward across the courtyard, almost at a run, heading straight for Syg. She ripped her headdress off and threw it down—her platinum blonde hair all over the place. She pulled off her cloak and dropped it.

She was nearly to Syg. Davage backed away. The countess stepped out of her sandals and jumped aside as the Sister sent a hammer blow whistling her way. Moving easily in her black body suit, Syg nimbly avoided the blow. The Sister swung again and again, grunting with the effort. Moving surely and smoothly, Syg evaded one blow, then another, then another. She got behind the Sister after another missed swing, and punched her square in the side of the face.

The Sister tried to retaliate with a whooshing left.

Syg ducked and punched her in the face again, snapping her head back. Her blows were small, stinging, annoying … draining.

The Sister paused a moment. It appeared she had expected to have ended the fight with the first devastating blow. She appeared confused. She didn't expect the countess to still be standing. Syg, taking advantage of the moment, punched her in the nose. The Sister, stung and frustrated, tried to grab Syg, who easily side-stepped and put an elbow into the Sister's mouth, drawing blood.

The Sister realized she couldn't move properly with all her robes on; the countess was much better attired. She began pulling her robes off.

Syg didn't wait. She popped her in the face again and tackled her. Struggling in a heap, she hiked the Sister's robes up over her face and wrapped them around her head. She could feel her massive strength. Syg located her head in the pile of cloth and locked it with her arms. She kept her body close, refusing to give the Sister any leverage, any room to move. She tried locking the Sister's legs with her feet, and that was a big mistake. The strength in the Sister's legs was nearly enough to break her ankles. Freeing her arms, the Sister swung with a right. Syg rolled away, but the Sister caught her in the face. Though it was a glancing blow, Syg reacted like she'd been struck with an iron bar. She flew a short distance away and landed with a fleshy "plop!"

With a rip of cloth, the Sister emerged from the tattered remains of her robes. She was small, about Syg's size, her skin a fertile bronze color, and she was fit. Down to what looked like a white nightshirt, she threw herself at Syg. Syg was able to climb over her and latch onto her back, there she pounded the Sister in the base of the skull and kneed her in the kidney. They fell to the old stone cobbles and rolled about in a tangle of white cloth and black. The Sister just couldn't get hold of the squirming, moving Syg no matter how hard she tried. She kept trying for the big blow, the haymaker, while Syg kept moving for leverage and peppering her with small shots that were starting to add up.

It was obvious that the Sister was no good at fighting like this—up close. Apparently, the Sisters, like the Black Hats, expected to fight at a distance using their awesome array of Gifts, and to fight hand-to-hand was an unheard of indignity. Davage had taught Syg how to fight in close; that, coupled with her knowledge of fighting in the Black Abbess' Church, and her slithering expeditions through the castle tunnels had the added effect of making her very agile and able to move easily in confined areas. She now knew she was more than capable of chopping down this mighty Sister. All she needed was time.

Grasping, reaching, the Sister finally managed to grab Syg's left foot. She latched on and began twisting, trying to get Syg to cry out and submit. Twisting with the movement, Syg spun, trying to keep the Sister from being able to apply pressure to her ankle. The Sister became tired of this game, and she lifted Syg into the air and slammed her down head first.

The courtyard spun. Roughly, the Sister dug her knee into the small of Syg's back and reared back to hit her—all it would take is one good blow, and Syg will be done.

And the Sister will take her husband, her Dav, and have him for a night.

Take him into her arms … and love him.

Just one night.

A thousand nights too many!!

Syg, drawing strength from within, slithered out from under the Sister's knee, where it went roughly into the courtyard stones. As the Sister winced in pain, Syg reared back and slammed her in the mouth, snapping her head back and drawing more blood. Knocked off balance, the Sister staggered.

Syg was all over her. She hit her again and again, and then climbed up onto her shoulders. She clamped onto her throat, choking, clinging, ankles locked. The Sister tried to grab her, to pull her off, but couldn't reach. Soon, the Sister fell. She gasped for air.

"Submit, Sister!" Syg yelled. "Submit!! Or, I swear I'll choke you to death!!"

The Sister struggled feebly for another moment or two.

Then: "… I … sub—mit."

Syg released her, and the Sister wheezed for breath. Sweating, filthy, Syg allowed herself to relax. She could expect to be badly sore in the morning.

The fight was over … she had won.

Davage ran to Syg and embraced her. "You all right, Syg?"

"I am, love."

Davage looked over to the Sister. "Sister, are you all right?"

The Sister sat there and didn't respond.

"Do you require assistance?"

Again, nothing.

Davage picked Syg up, threw her shawl on, and began walking her out of the courtyard. The Marines approached the Sister, but she waved them away.

The Sister sat there on the stone: dirty, knee skinned, lip bleeding. She stared at the ground, and then began weeping, slowly at first, then growing to a sad, halting ululation. She put her face into her hands, her blonde hair in a tangle.

Davage stopped and looked at her. After a moment, he went to her and knelt down.

"Come on, Dav," Syg said from a distance, a painful knot growing on her cheek. "Let's go."

The Sister continued to moan. Davage, sitting next to her, tried to stop her crying. She looked at him as he dried her tears with a cloth. He wiped the drying blood from her mouth.

"Dav!" Syg called.

"Syg, have a heart for a moment!"

"Why should I? This is the Sister that wanted my husband! I won and she lost!!"

"Syg, let me tell you who this Sister is. Don't you recognize her? This Sister is the one who listened to me, way back when, when I wanted to see you for the first time. This is the Sister who had faith in me, even when all others wanted you dead. This is the Sister who allowed you to live the night you were mad with Shadow tech; again, protecting you from the others. This is the Sister who saved my life in Metatron …"

Syg slowly approached. The Marines parted for her. The Sister looked up at her with a tear-streaked face, her skin bronze—a sure sign that she was fertile and ready for seeding.

Syg sat down next to Davage and looked at the Sister. Her expression softened. "If that's the case, then I am in your debt, Sister. Look around you—look where I am today. Look where I came from; look at what I was, and all is partly thanks to you. I am in your debt, and to pay this debt, I will gladly give you anything you wanted in return, anything I had. Anything, except the love of my husband."

The Sister began weeping again.

Syg's heart softened. "Here we are Sister, locked at an impasse, but maybe, maybe we can reach a compromise. If I have learned anything being the Countess of Blanchefort, it's that compromise is always possible."

The Sister looked at her.

"You wanted one night with my husband … and I will not allow that. You have experienced the lengths that I am willing to go to prevent that from happening. We fought fairly over the matter, and I beat you fairly. You wanted a night, instead I offer you a day. One day, from sun up to sun down, with my husband. And, not as a Sister—no headdress, no robes, no Vith ships, no Marines… just Dav and you, as a woman. You may walk with him, laugh with him, and hold his hand. You may even kiss him on the cheek if you wish. Let him show you what it is like to be a woman—no sex, no seeding, just the simple joy of his companionship. Will you agree to that, Sister?"

The Sister thought for a moment and spoke to Syg. *<You will trust me … that I will not take what I want?>*

<I trust you, and I trust my husband … that's what it means to love someone—to trust them implicitly. My husband appears to be fond of you, for what you did for us, so I feel you are owed. So, what say you … will you accept my offer?>

<I will accept. But, just the two of us. You will not be present.>

<Agreed.>

Davage was puzzled by the furtive silence. "Syg, what's going on?"

Syg smiled and a tear rolled down her cheek. "Feel like going out on a date?"

12—A Day with Dav

The next morning, just after sun-up, Davage went down to the chapel, and picked the Sister up. She was wearing some of Syg's old cloths, and it took him a moment to adjust to seeing her—a Sister—so attired. She was very attractive with her platinum hair and bronzed skin. He walked her to the ripcar and they were off. He had so many things he wanted to show her.

He took her south, to the great caverns of Ienn. He showed her the quiet underground streams and glittering falls. He took her to the babbling black creeks hidden in the mountains, and they swam through the water. Drying, they sat under a tree, and she held his hand and laid her head on his shoulder. He began calling her Blondie, after her blonde hair. Not overly imaginative, but it would do.

They lunched in the high towers of Lyra, amid the lights and artificial dark. They saw the great works of art, and the massive statues.

They went all over the world as fast as the ripcar could carry them, seeing as much as they could. Blondie held his hand, and reveled in his touch.

Reveled in just being a woman for a day.

And before long, the sun grew tired, and the twin moons of Solon and Elyria rose. He brought Blondie home, to the chapel.

As he walked her to the door, Blondie looked at him, placed her hands on the back on his neck and slowly brought his head down to meet hers.

There, foreheads touching, he began to hear a voice, tiny, far away, but clear and plain.

<Can you hear my thoughts? I offer them as plainly as I can. You once asked me if I am happy—if being a Sister makes me happy. Indeed it does … I am proud to be a Sister. But, every so often I am reminded that being a Sister has limitations. Being what I am allows me to be strong, wise, powerful … everything except a woman. I am old… ancient. I recall

the Elders, and I walked among them and shared their thoughts. Shortly I will return to the stars and walk to Camalopardus, and be a Sister there ever more. You will never see me again. But know that I have never had what you gave me today. I have never, in my long life, had the occasion to be just a woman in the company of a fine man. Sharing your company was wondrous, truly wondrous. If I could be a mere woman, not a Sister … perhaps you might stretch out your hand and claim me yours. I will never forget you and this day.> A tear came to her face. <*I was so happy when I became fertile. It was so unexpected. I thought it was a sign, a miracle. I so wanted to bear your child …*>

Davage reached into his pocket. "Blondie, if bearing my child means so much to you, then I offer you this …" Davage pulled out a small decorated cryo-vial and gave it to her. "I have not violated my countess's bond by giving you this. For all that you have given to me, and to her … I want you to have it and do with it what you will."

She took the vial in her hands, and stared at Davage. She opened her mouth and struggled to speak:

"I … l-love … you."

And she kissed him, not on the cheek, but on the lips and for a long time, the single kiss that had to last her forever.

* * * * *

Syg spent the day in the village bars with Kilos. She hadn't bothered with a gown, instead, she wore one of her older flower-print dresses that Dav had bought for her. She was a nervous wreck, a bundle of angst. It was like Dav had been gone for years. After a while, she couldn't stand it anymore, and got drunk … roaring drunk. Kilos found it amusing that Syg, the Countess of Blanchefort and a fearsome ex-Black Hat, couldn't hold her booze. Ki wasn't kind either, prodding and harassing the drunk Syg without mercy. "Look, there's Dav!" she cried, or "Is that Dav I see kissing someone in the corner?" And Syg, drunk, fell for it every time. Then, nearly passed out, Syg resorted to mindless blubbering. "Why, why … why did I let him go?"

"Because you owed the Sister a debt."

"When's he coming back? I want him …"

"You gave him until sundown," Ki said smiling.

"The sun's down."

"No it's not, Syg."

"Then why's it dark out?"

"We're in a pub, Syg, it's dark in here. Look to the window."

Ki couldn't resist. "Hey, Syg—can I go out with Dav next?"

"… no …"

"I've also several sisters who would love to go out with Dav. Got about ten of them!"

"… I'll do to your sisters what I did to the Sister …"

Syg blubbered relentlessly. "Where's my Dav? I want my Dav…"

"Should my ears be burning?" Davage walked up to the table. "I thought I'd find you two here."

"DAV!!" Syg cried, falling out of her chair.

"Syg, are you drunk?"

"She's hammered, Dav. She's blubbered over you all day. I was thinking about shooting her just to shut her up," Kilos said.

Dav picked her up, and she was a drunken, clinging, kissing mess. It was good that the pub was mostly empty. The people didn't need to see their countess like this.

"Love you … Dav … love you …"

"I love you too, Syg. That was a very fine thing you did for the Sister. You helped make her very happy."

"The debt's paid … we owe her nothing … nothing from here on out."

Dav picked Syg up and walked her out of the pub. "Night, Ki, I'm going to take my drunken lady here home."

Ki lifted a glass. "See you tomorrow."

Walking out into the dark, Dav led Syg, arm-in-arm, to the ripcar. She leaned on him unsteadily.

"Very impressive with the Sister, Syg, I must say. You can fight."

"Yeah… well, you better watch it, see … or else … you'll get what she got …"

They climbed into the ripcar, and Dav took Syg home.

* * * * *

The next morning Captain Davage and Countess Sygillis went to the chapel to escort the Sisters back to their ship. As usual, they rode in enclosed litters surrounded by Marines in their long, open-air floats. Dav and Syg rode on Karb and Beryl, two large Silver tech horses created by Lady Poe. The huge silver creatures had no trouble keeping up with the litters and floats as they wound down the mountainside through the clouds. Syg, riding high in the saddle, was once again very stately in her fine blue Blanchefort gown. She didn't bother to disguise the ugly black knot on her face from where the Sister had tagged her. They enjoyed small talk with the Marines as they made their way to the village.

When they approached the dock, the litters set down, and the Sisters came out; three of them. Blondie was not present.

The Sisters approached Davage. A Marine spoke: "Lord Blanchefort, Great Countess, once again, the Sisterhood has benefitted greatly from its long-standing friendship with House Blanchefort, though, this has been a 'unique' visit."

"Great Sister," Syg spoke softly. "I wish to offer my apologies for …"

"Nonsense, Countess. You love your fine lord very much, rightly so, and you had the courage to not only speak your mind, but to back your thoughts up with deeds. It is most refreshing to treat with one such as yourself. And, as it turns out, our Sister is very happy with the gift you gave to her. She was profoundly touched." The Sister regarded her with a smile. "You do the name of Blanchefort a fine service, and we shall await the coming of your son with great interest. We are certain his Programmability will be high."

The Sister turned to Davage. "She asked us to tell you that she will not forget either of you, and that you have her love and her protection until the end of your days."

"Will we never see her again, Sister?"

"We do not think so. She is very far away."

"Then, if you've the occasion to relay a message, please tell her … that she will be very greatly missed," Davage said.

The Sister smiled. "We will do so, Lord Blanchefort."

The Sisters and the Marines piled back into their ship and, were gone within moments. The Vith ship floated away at speed to the east. The *Seeker* was once again alone in the bay.

Part 2— The Eleventh Daughter

One is for Love ...
Eleven is for Hate ...
Two is for Happiness ...
Eleven feels the Gate ...
Three is for Nostalgia, and Four is for Dreams ...
Eleven takes the blame and ruins everything ...
Five, Six and Seven are a repeat of the first ...
Eight, Nine, Ten, the womb is ready to Burst ...
And then there's the Eleventh Daughter, sitting in the dark,
The scorn of the world upon her,
And sadness leaves its mark.

--A Xandarrian rhyme

Lady Poe of Blanchefort and her Fabulous Familiars (cerca 003215ax)
From Left to right: Fins, Tweeter, a Tuleefly, Whisper, Snugs (flying), Shadow (in lap), King, Bark and ... Carahil.

c2010 Justine Marie Hedman
— And here is the 11th Daughter of Xandarr! Princess Vroc.
They said she's the bringer of disaster!
— SHE IS THE BRINGER OF DISASTER!
SHE HAS BROUGHT DISASTER!
— They say she was a destroyer.
SHE HAS DESTROYED!
- She is under the influence of many
- She fights with the strength of a dozen men.
- I CANNOT ALLOW HER A FREE HAND.
- I will not kill her in cold blood.
- I SHOULD KILL HER NOW AND BE DONE WITH HER!
- I must have faith in my friends.
- SHE MUST BE STOPPED!
- SHE MUST BE STOPPED!!
- I allow her to live at the PERIL of my Mother, the Countess AND my Lord!!
- Yet there is REDEMPTION to be had by ALL! Even the 11th daughter of Xandarr!
She's a Lynch Pin and will be Xandarr's down fall if allowed to live.
- mabs has had at her.
- The black hats have had at her.
- She has a Part to play.
- SHOULD THEY COME TO HARM IT WILL BE MY FAULT! ALL MY FAULT!
MY FAULT!!

Princess Vroc of Xandarr (From: Carahil's Diary)

1—The Shade Church

The surface of the island was bare, rocky, and covered with fitful patches of thin, sharp-bladed grass. The sky overhead was angry and turbid. Her thoughts in a jumble, she shut down the engines of her small craft and sealed the hatch.

You'll be back for dinner? We're having a feast, just for you …

Yes, Father, I promise. I'd not miss it for anything.

The wind whipped across the barren face of the island. It beat her short hair into an uncombed mass and made the lifting-body shape of her ship jump up a little.

She thought about the feast that was waiting for her back home; the grand table full of culinary delights. She had to hurry.

She made her way inland across the rough, uneven landscape, careful not to twist or possibly break an ankle. Her boots felt the way with every step and her gun belt jangling at her waist. She looked back. Her little ship sat lonely in the distance, framed by the angry line of the sea.

She wished she was in it, on her way home to her family.

She wished she was away from here. She hated coming to this forgotten, stormy place. Cloudy sky and frothing sea, she had to tell herself that her friends were here, and that she needed her medicine.

She needed it badly.

An animal cried out in the far distance, a big one—sounded hungry too. She thought she saw some sort of cat-like predatory animal with faint red eyes padding around in the distance, stalking her. She drew her Mazan gun and took the safety off. The butt throbbed with energy. She aimed and pulled the trigger. There was the micro-second delay as the gun charged, and then a messy lance of shapeless green energy surged out of the solid-faced head. She watched the lance spread out and dissipate after about three hundred yards, and let go of the trigger. The Mazan refreshed, and then gave the reassuring double thump in the grip, indicating, covertly, that it was trigger-ready. She looked around, didn't see the animal anymore, and warily continued, her gun held tightly in her hand.

Ahead lay the ruins of a temple—stony, fallen down. The remains of once tall pillars were scattered about like forgotten, doughnut-shaped toy blocks left out in the rain and covered with moss. The ruins seemed only just a few healthy strides ahead, but, no matter how far she walked, it got closer at nothing but the most painful and sluggish of rates. The going was rough; the flat ground was deceptively pocked with ruts, depressions and hidden drops. She frequently looked down to check her footing. Out of the corner of her eye, she was certain she kept seeing hints of a figure clad in scarlet standing amid the ruins. When she looked straight on, however, she saw nothing.

This was a hideous, haunted place and she wanted to be gone.

There was a strange smell in the air, an alkaline, salty, metallic smell, like blood or rust. It was strong, filling her nose, making her gag.

All the death this place had seen entered her thoughts.

Murdered! Hands at their throats.

Angry hands tearing! Hanging from a hook.

Burgon … Cat's eyes staring.

Shadow tech oozing from their mangled bodies.

She thought to turn and flee, to go back to her ship, hit the jets and never come back, but she was a courageous girl and she wouldn't back out … no matter what.

Her friends were here, with her medicine. She kept telling herself that.

The weather turned bad. It was bad to begin with, but now it was worse. In the far distance a black cyclone formed over the sea, dancing slowly, roaring, coiling. It approached, horrible to look at. It was Shadow tech. There was Shadow tech everywhere here.

She turned and continued.

Finally, the ruins. She stepped up onto the old, cracked platform. She could make out the weather-blunted indentation of an ancient basin—here's where they were brought in the old days, the Shadow tech girls, kidnapped from wherever. And here they were bled. Here, their eyes were shut.

Hanging from a hook … waiting to be bought.

This place was carved from cruelty and hidden pain. This sorrowful place and horrid sky was the last thing many a dying girl ever saw.

Looking back one last time, the cyclone was closer; a black thread hanging from the laughing sky. Her ship was nowhere to be seen—too far away. Her heart sank a little.

She spied a doorway in the distance, one that belched darkness. Spinning her Mazan with a showman's touch, she re-holstered it and went toward the door.

She reached the threshold and stood there a moment. Seeing nothing within, rubbing her nose, she entered, plunging into immediate, unyielding darkness. She fumbled about, trying to make her way down, reaching out with her hands.

Strangled them to death!

Feebly trying to lift her body up off the hook buried in her back. Cat's eyes.

She prayed to her father for guidance. She prayed for courage. "It is I, Princess Vroc!" she blurted out with a touch of panic.

After a moment she heard a distinct "… ssssssssssssss …" sound in her ear.

Something gently took her by the hand, and led her in some unknown, terror-filled direction. She tried to pull back, to flee, but whatever had her could not be escaped.

Composing herself, relaxing, she allowed herself to be led. Her uncertain boots slapped against the damp, gritty steps, going down to a cool, deep dark.

She had to remind herself she was a guest here—she was invited. She was the chosen.

This was a place made out of Shadow tech. A place built on the screams of the dying where the only thing more common than cruelty was the scarcity of mercy.

… The bodies hanging on hooks. Cat's eyes looking up at her.

Eventually, the guiding hand, or whatever it was, pulled away and she stopped, standing in total darkness, struggling to keep her balance. She knelt down; her searching fingers found the flat, damp stone floor all around her that seemed to go on for a good distance. She felt a bit claustrophobic. She was deep underground.

Something spoke; no, didn't speak—growled: "*… You have come again. The House of Xandarr still owes us much …*"

She spoke into the air. "I have been invited. Nothing is owed. I have done what you asked. I have listened to you."

"*Your debt continues … your debt is unending … for all we have done for you.*"

She reached down and felt for the gilded silver hilt at her waist. She unsaddled it and fumbled with it in her hand. Having the BEREN in hand made her feel a bit better. "I am grateful for those things, and I am here at your invitation," she said again. "I need my medicine."

"*… Indeed …*"

In the distance, she could make out several figures emerging in the dark. The figures were robed in scarlet. Their faces were hidden behind black sashes. They were lit straight down, as if from a spotlight high above, though no obvious light source could be seen. Their figures were distorted, as if she was seeing them through a dense, particle-laced black mist. They swayed in a deep trance.

Princess Vroc of Xandarr was surrounded by Black Hats in the heart of the Shade Church where the Black Abbess walked.

"I need my medicine. May I please have some?"

The Black Hats swayed and considered her request.

"*We have tasks for you.*"

"I've done everything you have asked! What more do you want?"

Suddenly, a creature emerged from the darkness next to her. It was illuminated in pale light. It was some kind of half-cat/half bone-thin monster standing on two legs with a sucked-in chest laden with teats. "... zaaaal ..." it hissed, red-eyed. Its arms were over its head, hands clenched into claws.

Princess Vroc jumped a bit and raised her BEREN.

"*Revenge ... that is what we want ... We want screaming ... We want blood ... We want locked doors and wary eyes peering out of darkened windows.*"

"G-Get away from me."

The thing faded into the dark. "*Misery and bestial screams ... heeheeeheeeeeee ...*"

"*We have allowed the League, and indeed the Xaphans, to go too long without a suitable display of our power. We shall make a bold statement. We've a grand venue set ... we intend to kill billions ... There will be fear sown in abundance ... and we shall have our revenge ...*"

"My medicine, please?"

A Black Hat appeared next to Vroc. The Black Hat danced with a light, airy grace.

"*Of course, child, I have your medicine here. Am I not your friend?*"

Vroc swayed. "Yes ..."

Cat's eyes. The clawed hands reaching up and pulling her off the hook.

"*Did I not free you from that terrible, terrible hook in Burgon?*"

Vroc wept at the memory. "Y-yes ..."

The Black Hat danced up to Vroc and raised a hand. She held a small vial with a mister. The Black Hat squirted Vroc in the face. Instantly, she straightened and regained her bearing.

"What do you want?" Vroc said in a firm, newly strong voice.

"*The Lord of Blanchefort,*" the voice spat with contempt. "*We want his bitch ... our bitch that he has stolen from our midst. We want her right here on her knees. And, we want his sister too ... By rights, she belongs to us ...*"

Another Black Hat spoke. "*We want them alive or dying, we care not ... but they must not be dead.*"

"The Countess Sygillis and Lady Poe, you want them here? And what of Lord Blanchefort?"

"*Leave Lord Blanchefort to us, he will die in a place of our choosing. We want the bitch and his sister. We want them alive or in the process of dying, but not dead.*"

"*THE BITCH AND HIS SISTER, THE BITCH AND HIS SISTER!!!*" something screamed.

Vroc, her medication in full effect, stood tall. "I want Lord Blanchefort for myself. I will give the Lord of Blanchefort to my father ... as a gift."

"*Lord Blanchefort is ours.*"

"It sounds like you're rather frightened of him, are you not? Afraid of what he can do? Afraid of his Light?"

Clenched hands came around her shoulders from behind and settled at her throat. Vroc, however, was unafraid.

"Yes … you are aren't you? Not quite sure what to do with him, yes? You've no defense against his Sight … his Light. He took one of the most mindless, most wretched of your ranks and turned her into a gown-wearing lady of standing. Think of what else he could do with his Sight."

The hands slid back into the dark.

"*THE SIGHT DOES NOT EXIST!*"

Vroc laughed. "Ha! Ask 'the Bitch,' about his Sight. Yes, Sygillis of Metatron … an evil, repugnant woman made comely and whole, full of love."

"*A trance she is in. We will … medicate it out of her, just like we medicate you. Purge it with pain and suffering. She will be evil again … or she will die as we watch, knowing there is no escape from our midst …*"

"I will give Lord Blanchefort to my father, then I will bring you what you want. I will have them before you; crying, on their knees, dying ... You will help me with Lord Blanchefort."

"*You are in no position to make demands, princess of Xandarr … Think of what we have done for you … Think of where you were …*"

The Princess suddenly shuddered and fitfully pawed at her blueberry hair. "I—I remember where I was … and what you did for me, and what you made of me. And I am grateful, still, you need me. You want dying, then you need me … and all I want is Lord Blanchefort. For what he did to my sister, and to my family, I want his head to give to my father."

The Black Hat sprayed her in the face again with the mister. Again, Vroc's bearing changed once sprayed.

"So, what about it!" she yelled. "Do I get what I want, or do I walk away with all the gifts you gave me! You need me!"

The gallery of Black Hats considered her words.

"*You require a strong vessel. We will give you one. Your tutor will come with you, guide you, and give you your medicine in timely doses.*"

"I have a vessel."

"*You have a weak, flawed Xaphan cruiser that Lord Blanchefort shall cut to pieces. We will give you a vessel. With it, you will face Lord Blanchefort if that is what you wish. You will then bring us his bitch and his sister. Listen to your tutor. She will counsel you.*"

Princess Vroc stood tall. "I was not aware that the Black Hats had a force of ships."

"*We have been at work. We have re-invented Shadow tech. It is a vessel of our creation. It is a Shadow tech ship. It is time for the League and the Xaphans to tremble at it. We are the new power. Under our reign, all shall die, none shall live … an empire of the dead we shall command.*"

Vroc wanted nothing to do with Shadow tech. "I will use my cruiser. With it I will defeat Lord Blanchefort."

"*You will die in your cruiser.*"

"Shadow tech is poisonous."

Something clattered to the Princess's right. There, gleaming in the dim light, was a black medallion.

"*You will not feel the Shadow tech around you. Now go and bring us the bitch and his sister. Not dead … alive, or dying, but not dead. If they are to die, it will be here, in the dreaded darkness, with us, and we will bleed them of what is ours.*"

She slowly picked up the medallion and placed it about her neck.

The Black Hats began a droning, melodic cackle that rose to a shriek.

Vroc, fully medicated, listened with mild interest.

Behind, in the dark, a cat meowed.

2—A Tearful Resignation

Captain Davage had never seen Lt. Kilos like this before. She was a hard-case, a lady who prided herself on being tough, being in control. When she came to him ten years prior as a Marine sergeant, she was hopeless: an uncontrollable, uncommandable, unruly wreck who had been selected by Lord Grenville to disrupt his command. She had been a test to see what Lord Blanchefort was made out of. Any lord, captain or otherwise, should have thrown her out immediately. But, Davage being Davage, saw untapped potential in this tall, sad Marine from Tusck. Under his positive influence, she thrived, excelled, became skilled, and became a friend— his best friend. She had mellowed to some extent, softened in these ten years. She allowed Davage to see her most guarded of thoughts and feelings. Still, she prided herself on keeping most things bottled up and hidden. If she had a problem, she spoke about it with him empirically, in a bland, sterile sort of way—as if it was someone else's problem, not hers.

But now, Ki was truly in pain, truly panicked and unsure of herself. He'd seen her red-faced with rage, belly-laughing, drunk, quizzical and stressed, but never trembling with uncertainly: tears flowing freely, her hands shaking.

"Dav … I need to resign my post … effective immediately …" she said wiping a tear away.

He was thunderstruck.

They sat in his office, the ship vibrating with near-launch activity: the last bits of supplies coming on-board, the last-minute touch-ups of hull plating and internal tubing, and so forth. Ki sat in her chair, slumped, weeping.

"May I ask what has brought this on, Ki?"

"My husband, Dav … he wants me to come home."

"I see. He's asked you to come home before, has he not?"

Ki put her face into her hands. "He said … he said he'd leave me if I didn't come home. I know it sounds strange, me being gone from home so much … but I love my husband, I don't want to lose him."

Davage got up from behind his desk and sat down next to her, taking her hand.

It was damp and trembling.

"I'm sorry for this, Ki. I understand what you must be feeling."

"No, Dav—you don't. I love this ship, I love my job. I love being here with you … you're my best friend! You're one of the few people who understands me; can see through all my crap. But I love my husband too … and he wants me home!"

She pushed Dav's hand away. He expected her, knowing Ki as he did, to stand and walk away, to work it out on her own. Instead she embraced him, putting her wet, teary face on his shoulder. "Order me to stay, Dav. Tell me I can't go!" she sobbed.

"I can't do that, Ki. You've served your time, whether you stay or go is up to you. You know you will be missed, terribly. You know you are my best friend as well."

"Tell me what to do, Dav—tell me please. Order me to stay."

She pounded his chest.

"Hey, hey. Ki—I order you … to be happy."

Ki bitterly wept into his shoulder. "I'm sorry this had to come up … I'm sorry, right before a launch and all."

"It's all right."

"No, no it's not … this ship needs its first officer. You're too nice sometimes, Dav. You should be chewing me out right now. You should be beating the hell out of me in the gym!"

"How about if I gave you an extended leave? I could deactivate you, then you could go home, take a year or so and see what shakes loose. If you get things sorted out, then you could re-activate."

"But I'd be-reactivating as a Marine … I'd not be here, I'd not be your first officer."

"No, you wouldn't. I wish I could say your job will be here waiting for you, but you know I can't. I need a First—though anybody other than you shall be a settle-for, you know that, correct?"

Ki pulled back a little, composed herself, drew her huge SK pistol, removed the magazine, checked the chamber, and handed it to Dav.

"Here's my gun, Dav … since I'm not your First anymore." She looked at it hard. "I never … ever thought I'd be saying goodbye to you."

Davage took the SK and set it on his desk. She looked at it sitting there and cringed. He lifted her chin. "What's this goodbye nonsense? Hmmm? This had better not be goodbye, Lt. Kilos. You and your husband are always welcome in my home. Syg and I will miss you, Ki, and I must have your word that you'll not disengage … vanish into the night and be gone forever. You'll promise me I will see you at home?"

Ki tried to smile. "I promise … my friend. I promise."

They embraced.

* * * * *

The following morning, Captain Davage and his Countess Sygillis, wearing a fine red gown, came aboard the *Seeker*. Usually, Davage, Syg and Kilos made an inspection of the ship, going over everything before the ship launched. But, today, it was very different. Syg knew he was sad … no Kilos. She pulled him aside when she could and hugged him; she kissed him when nobody was looking, trying to cheer him up. He was grateful for her love, but, things just wouldn't be the same.

They entered the engineering bay. The coils thrummed and sparked with life. Commander Mapes, Lord of Grenville, came forward. Davage shook his hand and kissed Syg's hand. Lord Mapes and his wife, Lady Suzaraine, were good friends.

"Commander, I wanted to let you know that Lt. Kilos has resigned her post."

"What? Why?"

"Personal reasons. I must say this is very sudden, and I'm quite at a loss to appoint anyone else. I also wanted you to know that, if you weren't an appointed officer, I'd ask you to take her place without question."

"Thank you, Dav. I appreciate that."

"Do you have any thoughts on the matter? Any possible candidates?"

Commander Mapes rubbed his chin a moment. "I'll check my roster. I can't, at this point, think of anybody free to assume the role, however."

Davage suspected as much. He smiled. "Well, keep a weather eye, and let me know should you have any thoughts."

"I will, thank you, Dav."

With that, they completed their tour of the engineering bay.

When they finished inspecting the ship, they made their way back to his office and closed the door. Syg, carefully arranging her gown, sat down on Dav's lap. Gently, she kissed his cheek and neck.

"Well, I'm at a loss, Syg. I've no idea who I'm going to get to replace Ki."

"Will someone on the bridge crew do?" Syg purred.

"Probably. I was thinking about crewman Sasai from Sensing. She's very solid."

"You think she will do as well as Ki?"

"No, but each to their own, I'm certain she might excel in other areas. Ki was lousy at paperwork."

"What about Crewman Saari, the helmsman?"

"Lady Saari is just now becoming a fine helmsman. I don't want to take her from it. She appears to love it so. Do you know her father, Lord Timmon of Fallz, recently passed away? Milos told me."

Syg was shocked. "No—I didn't. Oh, the poor thing, her father dead."

"Yes. I took the liberty to send her mother a basket of flowers and a note. I hope Lady Branna is all right."

"You should have let me have a look at those first, Dav. That's my area."

He stood and put Syg down. "Yes, sorry. Well, let's to the bridge and get under way."

Syg looked out the window, at their castle in the distance. "I always hate this part."

"I know, Syg."

They exited the office and walked a few steps to the bridge. As usual, the crew snapped to attention. Davage put them at ease and Syg took a seat in his chair as she always did. He signed a few reports and went to the Com station; Lt. Gervin manned it as usual for a day shift.

"Com," Dav said. "Please make a note—as of this entry, Lt. Kilos, lieutenant of the 12th Stellar Marines, and first officer of the *Seeker,* has resigned her commission and her esteemed post."

There was a gasp as the crew listened.

"Additionally, please note that her years of service have been exemplary, and this vessel will sorely miss her presence. We will make do as best we can and will want for her wisdom and bravery. Please send to Fleet Command, that Davage, captain of the *Seeker,* requests suitable candidate for the post: vacancy—immediate. Also, Com, send to Crewman Heartford to assume the Ops position on the day shift until further notice, and make a note in the duty roster."

"Aye, sir."

Davage looked around. "Well, there you have it, I am certain that you are all as saddened by Lt. Kilos' departure as am I, and I am also certain you will join me in wishing her nothing but the best. She is … what is best in all of us. In the meantime, the ship sails and life goes on. I am, of course, unwillingly in the market for a new first officer. It's a tough job, a serious job and … the hours can be terrible. The responsibility is immense, and the boss is, so I'm told, a real axe-wielding closet-case ..."

The crew laughed.

"… but, as with anything, the rewards can be without limit. I have put a call out to the Fleet for a replacement as is standard procedure, however, as I hope you are all aware, I value my crew above all. If any of you here wish to accept the challenge and throw your name into the hat for consideration, then I'd be happy to take a moment, sit with you, and hear what you have to say. As usual, my door is always open."

After a moment, Davage strode to Syg's side. She was always careful not to touch him too much when on the bridge. He put his hand on her shoulder and, looking up, she lightly touched his hand.

The lift door opened, and Crewman Heartford entered, scurrying to the Ops position.

"Crewman," Davage said in a cheerful voice. "I hate to put you on the spot, but, when you are ready, could you give me ship's compliment? Take your time, get settled."

Heartford logged into the station and tapped a few buttons. He looked nervous and flustered.

"Take your time, crewman, this isn't a race. The only danger we face is that some of the hanky-wavers on the dock might have sore arms in the morning."

Heartford chuckled and continued what he was doing. After a minute or two, he spoke up. "Sir, ship's compliment is all present and accounted for."

"Did we have any late arrivals this time?"

More key tapping. "No sir. Additionally, all provisions stowed and manifested."

"Excellent. Do we owe anybody any money?"

"No sir. Paymaster Milke reports all ledgers clear."

Davage smiled. "Fine, fine, and well done, crewman." He turned to Crewman Jonas at the navigation post. "Navigator, status?"

"Sir, navigation is caged and pegged."

He turned to the Missive. "Missive, report."

"All ship's systems reading as nominal."

"Thank you. Please release the viewing cone and enable ship's sensing."

The Missive worked his large, but rather obsolete panel. The Holographic main viewing cone came on in glorious 3D, and the various sensing stations shot to life. The Missive was an endangered posting—Davage had heard the Missive's station was to be deleted in the next generation of ships altogether. Time moves on.

He turned to blue-haired Crewman Saari standing at the helm. "Helm, status?"

"Sir, the Helm is available and fit for travel."

Davage straightened his hat. "Very well, Com, please send to Fleet Command, it is time for our Pledge."

"Aye, sir."

A moment later, a Fleet adjutant popped up on the cone. Resplendent in his fine blue uniform, the adjutant looked at the crew with a haughty, somber brow—the usual look from the Admiralty.

Davage spoke up. "Adjutant, well met. Captain Davage reports that, as of this moment, the Main Fleet Vessel *Seeker* is ready and able to travel. We await our Pledge."

"Captain Davage, Lord of Blanchefort, well met," the adjutant said in a somewhat unpleasant Remnath drawl. "So be it, as of this moment, the Admiralty acknowledges your ready status, and fully expects you to perform your duty, in and out of the face of the enemy. Will you submit to the Pledge, sir?"

"We will."

"Very well, a moment please."

The cone went black, then came back on. A Fleet Admiral appeared: wigged, powdered in his elegant blue uniform and knee britches. It was Admiral Scy, of the 10th Fleet.

An Admiral's uniform was very garish and civilian-like. It was a composition of a long blue coat that went to the floor, huge buttons and end-sleeves, white hose, buckle shoes, and a massive plumed hat. He carried an Admiral's command scepter. The whole ensemble was one reason why Davage never wanted to be an Admiral.

Davage was elated that it was Admiral Scy who was Pledging them today. Scy, unlike many of the Admiralty, didn't make an overly big to-do of the Pledge ceremony. He normally gave the Pledge, and sent them on their way with a minimum of fanfare. Some Admirals, like the infamous Admiral Pax, liked to make a huge fiasco of it, taking hours.

"Bridge!" Davage barked. "Be at your guard!" The bridge came to attention. Syg stood with head bowed, in the traditional manner for a civilian.

The Admiral looked the scene over, and, when satisfied, spoke. "Great Countess Sygillis, well met. You are as radiant as always."

Syg responded. "Thank you, and well met, great sir."

"My wife informed me that an unthinkable event having to do with a thrown pie occurred at a recent ball you were graciously hosting. If true, has the throwing party been caught and appropriately penalized?" Scy was a remarkably conversational man for an Admiral.

Syg turned a little red. "No, great sir. However I have a prime suspect in mind and will deal with him when the time is right."

Scy laughed. "I see. Captain Davage, well met as usual. You sir, are entrusted with a heavy burden, one passed down from the time of the Elders to the present. I put you to the Pledge, are you ready, sir?"

"I am."

"Will you Pledge to defend life, in all its forms, wherever it is threatened?"

"I Pledge to do so."

"Will you Pledge to protect and defend League citizens, wherever they may be found and whoever they may be?"

"I will Pledge to do so."

"Will you Pledge to fight the Xaphans wherever they may be found?"

"I Pledge to do so."

"And, will you Pledge to harm not the Xaphans themselves … but to endure their evil as a good servant of the Elder's memory?"

"I Pledge to do so."

The Admiral looked the scene over again. He seemed about ready to bow and conclude the matter when he suddenly spoke again—his image lit-up with silvery light.

"Captain, you are hereby Pledged and Bound. I entreat you to go forth and do your duty as the Elders see fit. In this, Captain, you must always remember you are Pledged to defend life … wherever it is threatened, regardless of position, standing and group affiliation."

"I have so Pledged to do so, Admiral," Davage said.

"Always remember, Captain, life knows no political boundaries. Please remember that, I beg you."

"I will remember that, Admiral," Davage said, puzzled.

The silvery light faded, and the Admiral stood there, perplexed for a moment. He then made a sweeping gesture with his scepter. "Then, so Pledged and Bound, may you Speed Well, protect the children under your command, and forget not your duty." With that, the Admiral bowed and the cone went black, reverting after a moment to the Blanchefort dock and the crowds gathered there to see the ship depart.

The cone briefly warbled. Syg seemed shocked and pointed.

Davage sighed. "Always seems like that takes forever, doesn't it? At least it wasn't Admiral Pax this time."

<*Dav,*> Syg sent via telepathy, <*Dav, did you see that?*>

The crew, still "At Guard" concurred.

<*See what, darling?*> Davage smiled. "Shall I contact the Admiralty again and get him … get Admiral Pax? I'm certain he'll …"

"No sir!" the crew said in unison.

Davage laughed. "Well then, bridge crew, be at ease." They relaxed and Syg stood there slightly bouncing up and down. She seemed in quite a state.

<Admiral Scy! The cone switched back to his office for a brief moment, and I saw him standing there, spread-armed and bent kneed, covered in pie! I know I saw it!>

<Syg, you will not let that pie incident drop, will you? If it bothers you so much why don't you hit Carahil in the face with a pie of your own?>

Davage walked over to crewman Saari, his helmsman. "My Lady," he said under his breath, "are you certain you are up to this, with the recent passing of your father? I could arrange you some additional time off."

Saari's face saddened a bit. "Yes sir, thank you, sir. I am fine. Please, I want to fly."

Davage smiled and patted her on the shoulder. "Then, take us up, fifteen thousand feet and hold, and mind the crowd, there's a lot of them out there this morning. I'd certainly love, for once, to give them a good, friendly soaking, how about you, crewman?"

"I would sir."

<*You didn't see it, Dav?*>She was hopping up and down.

<I did not!>

Davage thought for a moment. "Well … we'll let them go home dry today. Take us up."

"Aye, Captain," Saari said and the *Seeker,* rumbling, quickly screamed up out of the water and into the cold air above the cheering masses on the dock.

"Cone to ventral," Davage said, knowing that Syg liked to see the castle fade into the distance. The cone popped to the ventral view, and his old Vith castle came into view as a huge, sprawling red edifice, the tumbled green of the Telmus Grove stretching off beyond the edge of the field. Syg looked at the castle fading below and gripped his hand tightly.

<I'm certain I saw him standing there face-hit with pie!>

<Again, I saw nothing, now please …>

"Sir," Saari said, "Fifteen thousand feet, standing at station."

"Sir, the screens are clear and we are free to navigate," Sasai said from her sensing position.

"Very well. Set to standard orbital tachs and ease us up."

"Heading, sir?" Jonas asked at the navigation station.

Davage stepped away from Syg. "That's a good question, crewman. Point us at Planet Fall and wind for 1/16 Stellar Mach. I'm to the books to see if anything's hot."

Davage made his way toward his office door and waited.

"Crewman Heartford, I require your presence in my office please, sir."

Heartford adjusted his uniform and bustled into Dav's office, the captain following. As he entered his office he caught a glimpse of Syg looking at him from her seat. Her eyes were big, shuffling, red hair quizzical around her head, mouth set in a long straight line. She always wanted to come into his office with him when the ship's destination was being decided upon, but, she was not allowed. Just the captain and the first officer, or, in this case, the Ops crewman, nobody else—not even wives, not even Great Countesses.

With Davage getting "The Look" from Syg, the door closed unceremoniously.

Davage and Heartford sat down to discuss the ship's destination. As Heartford began reading off the hot listings on the wire, he looked over his shoulder, to the little hidden panel on the wall, where he kept a tall tankard of buncked narva.

Ki. How Ki loved her narva.

c2010 Justine Marie Hedman
To Do List:
1. Feed Kittens.
2. Get mother's favori hat and hide it!
3. Save Planet X!
4. Hide Lord Blanchefor hat. (Some-where different today. He found it t easily las time.
Thought of the DAY! When in doubt, do what mother would do.
5. Enlist Lt K to hel you aquire a Brightstone.
8. Decide what kind of miracle to preform on Planet X!
6. Perform miracle on Planet X.
7. Throw pie at Lady Blanchefort.
(you can do it tonight! You will!)

Lady Poe of Blanchefort (From Carahil's Diary)

3—Lady Poe of Blanchefort

"Can you see it, Lady Poe, a solemn union between Houses Merryweather and Blanchefort? It could be a match that shall have the whole of the League talking."

Lady Poe and Lord Haverell of Merryweather stood on the roof of his sprawling ancestral home in the sea-side city of Bern. It was a Vith structure, but not a castle like Castle Blanchefort, instead in was an estate, spread out on lovely, manicured lawns of only the most perfect green. From here, the skyline of Bern rose in the distance—green-flagged, the seat of League money and finances. The Merryweathers were noted bankers and owned several influential banks in Bern. Certainly, it was a pretty place, an exquisite place. It was a beautiful day, but, Poe, coming from the cold north, felt it a bit hotter than she liked. From the patina-capped green roof, Poe saw the Merryweather ladies strolling about the grounds; their brightly colored pastel gowns making them look like tulips in the bright afternoon sun.

They had spent the day touring Bern, visiting the banks, the vast marketplaces of bustling commerce, and ancient buildings. It was all beautiful and interesting surely, but, Poe had seen so much the same in recent weeks, as the various League Lords vied for her attention. She found she was getting a bit bored with it all, actually; the trips, the villas, one beautiful site blending into another. One handsome League Lord after the next. Perhaps she might take a break, catch her breath, and take a moment to reflect.

Strange, how most of her life she'd been social poison—no self-respecting Lord worth his shirt daring come near her and court the "crazy woman" from the north, as Poe had been thought to be.

Now, she was no longer crazy. Now she was a Shadow tech female.

Now, she was almost a Black Hat. Poe had heard that Dav's turning of Syg and Bethrael of Moane, and Commander Mapes saving of Suzaraine of Gulle had ushered in a new craze called "Black Hat Fighting". Various fool hearty Lords of the League were actively setting out hoping to encounter a Black Hat, capture her and turn her, as Dav had done with Syg. She had heard that, of all people, the Duke of Oyln from the region of Esther had fought a Black Hat Painter on Xandarr, and had her in chains in his dungeon. He was trying to turn her—only he was having great trouble getting her to quiet and cooperate. She had also heard that Lord Finster of Rustam had tried something similar, and had been horribly killed in the process. The parts of his body were sundered and fed to a pack of wild attack birds. It was a grim warning that Black Hats were not to be trifled with. Lady Poe, a Shadow tech female and civilized northern lady, was a much safer, much more docile choice, and that made her a valuable commodity. Lords from everywhere sought her attention. They lined up to spend a bit of time with her, to make their respective pitch to have not only a Lady of Blanchefort at their side, but an "Almost Black Hat" as well.

She'd been delighted with the attention; she'd been swept off her feet certainly. She'd always dreamed of a gentleman, any gentleman, coming to take her away. For two hundred years, that's what she longed for in between bouts of agony and Shadow tech poisoning.

Funny ...

Now that she was getting her lifelong wish, she found herself remarkably indifferent with the whole process. The gentlemen were all handsome and proper. They lived in grand castles and estates, and they said all the right things, but she just didn't feel much of anything toward them in return.

She wanted something like what Dav and Syg had: a full, devoted, body and soul love. She watched Syg as she gazed at Dav … seeing the love pour out of her.

That's what she wanted. That's what she wanted to give, and she knew she had it in her somewhere. All she needed was the right man to set her soul ablaze, but, so far, none had done it. She remained as cold as her northern home.

She had tried to love Milos of Probert, that wonderful, witty man. Dav and Syg were always pushing her to court him. They were afraid that she didn't because of his plain, dumpy appearance. Such wasn't the case—she didn't care what he looked like. She just didn't love him, that's all. She had tried … desperately she'd tried. She cherished him as a friend, as a brother, for both his sharp mind and the tenderness he'd shown her the years she'd been sick.

She hated herself for not being able to love him—she felt ungrateful and low.

But, it just wasn't there.

She wondered if she'd ever love anybody.

As she pondered these thoughts on Lord Merryweather's patina-covered roof, she barely noticed the odd, black vessel that came down through the clouds and landed on the green. Winged, pinnacled, somewhat on the smallish side, black as charcoal, it wasn't any sort of ship she had ever seen before.

The house staff approached the ship. Merryweather ladies, those colorful tulips, curiously walked toward it to get a better look.

"Are you expecting visitors, Lord Haverell?"

"Oh, vessels are always coming and going. My brother, Lord Kesvan, is always picking up odd starcraft from exotic locales—it's a hobby of his. An expensive one too—the taxes are truly astounding." He looked at the black ship. "Ah … that's a novel one down there, isn't it?"

Poe didn't like the look of it.

And it smelled, on the wind, it smelled plain as day.

Shadow tech! She'd know it anywhere.

"Call your guards! It's Shadow tech!" she said.

Lord Merryweather pulled a small communicator out of his coat and began speaking into it.

As Poe watched, the black ship pulsed. A wave of black in a filmy, slimy sphere came out of it, and, expanding, it enveloped the green and the house grounds. Where the wave passed, the grass turned brown, the stone cracked, and birds fell lifeless out of the trees. And, ladies in their colorful gowns wilted to the ground, scattered about like fallen flowers.

The wave passed Poe and Lord Merryweather. Instantly, she felt dazed, stunned … the Silver tech within her reacting badly to its passing. Merryweather dropped his communicator and slumped to the rooftop.

Poe felt sick to her stomach, her insides blanching. The roof spun. She collapsed to the flagstones, her limbs growing heavy.

"Haverell?" she cried weakly.

She couldn't move, her limbs were so heavy. With supreme effort, she lifted a finger and sent a thin stream of Silver tech toward him. It contacted his hand and wrapped around it.

No heartbeat, no breath.

No Life ... Haverell, Lord of Merryweather, was dead.

Time passed, all was deathly quiet. Poe, unable to move, lay there in the sun.

She dimly saw a door at the end of the run open. A small figure stood there.

The figure looked at her a few moments, and then began walking casually toward her. It was a girl, a blue-haired girl wearing a black jacket. Poe could hear the soles of her boots treading on the flagstones. She could see a large energy gun swinging holstered at her side.

"Lady Poe?" the girl said nearing her. "You're a surprisingly difficult person to track down. Here one day, across the planet the next. Must be nice having so many gentlemen lining up to see you. My associates also wish to see you. They wish it very much, and are greatly looking forward to meeting you. They insist, in fact …"

With a smile, she continued nearer. Poe was certain she didn't want anything to do with these "associates" of hers.

As the girl approached, Poe struck. She roped her around the neck with Silver tech, and lifted her off the ground. A fast series of wind blasts came from the girl. She was trying to Waft out of the noose Poe had her in, but couldn't; Poe's Silver tech bound her in place. She then threw her, arms flailing, legs akimbo, over the side of the roof where it was a good two hundred feet to the ground below. She threw her like she was casting a fishing line from a rod. She could dimly hear the surprised gurgling sounds the girl made as she fell with Poe's Silver tech cord around her throat.

Still suffering the effects from the Shadow tech blast, Poe felt dizzy. Her Silver tech lost its cohesion and faded into silvery mist. Poe got sick.

There was a blast of cold air.

The blue haired girl emerged from the Waft cloud. Her Mazan gun was drawn.

She was enraged. She fell on the near helpless Poe.

"… Blanchefort bitch …" she muttered, and she reared back and pistol-whipped Poe mercilessly about the shoulders and face. Over and over again, the cruel butt of the gun making a sickening "smack" with every raw hit.

Soon, her gun butt covered with blood, she holstered it, and easily picked Poe up. She was oddly strong for such a small, skinny girl. Must have the Gift of Strength.

Poe hung there, an unwilling, unable passenger. Through swelling eyelids she saw the pebbled surface, the fine patina covering of the roof and the back and forth movements of the girl's legs and booted feet. With all the strength she had left, she slowly moved her hand up to her throat, to the silver medallion that hung there. With shaking fingers she flipped it over and frantically touched the embossed image: the whiskered, bright-eyed, happy image of a seal.

"Carahil …" she said. "Help me …"

"Shut up!" the girl said.

"Carahil …"

And Lady Poe of Blanchefort fell into blackness.

Tweeter (*Carol Phillips*)

4—The Cavern

Kilos had never been so miserable in her life.

She stood there on the dock, amid the crowd of cheering people, watching the *Seeker* take off. The ship created an artificial rainstorm as it rose, water pouring off of its belly.

She felt a whole bunch of things as she stood there on Blanchefort dock—she felt left out, unimportant, insignificant, sad, anxious … angry. Standing there amid the waving, cheering crowd, the husbands and wives, the boy and girlfriends, she felt like she used to long ago in Tusck as she trawled the marketplaces with her brothers and sisters looking for food: she felt like a peasant.

It was a feeling she didn't like one little bit.

Kilos was wearing a long, tan dress, and a pair of soft leather boots that she'd bought in one of the shops near the dock earlier that day. She just stomped into the shop and pulled the dress off the racks without bothering to look at it much. It didn't have any obvious patterns or prints, which was how she wanted it, so she bought the thing, the boots too. The dress didn't fit. It was too big, draped over her lean body like a billowy flag tangled around a flagpole, but she didn't really care. It was something to put on—better than going naked. Her new, soft boots, without a heel and a hard sole, hurt her feet. They felt like she wasn't wearing shoes, and unlike Syg who could walk shoeless over broken glass, Ki, tough as she was, was a real tender-foot. Top to bottom, without her beloved Marine uniform for the first time in a long while, she felt very naked. She carried a large bag—a purse, also new—that she stuffed her things from the ship into. She hated dresses, she hated purses—Gwwahh! She felt like a girl. She wanted her uniform back!

* * * * *

Ki had been amazed, but not necessarily surprised, how quickly she'd been debriefed and shuffled out of the Marines. They'd arrived that morning in a Marine cutter ship and, in a matter of an hour or two, she was out-processed, removed of all her uniforms and rank insignia, and loudly de-oathed. As a final bit of good-measure, she was thrown into the brig for forty minutes. When they let her out, she was busted down to private—for not following her chain of command, they said in angry tones.

When it was finally over, they escorted her from the cutter ship to the dock at gun-point no less. The Marine Command at 0-Foxtrot was not happy about her sudden and un-discussed departure from the *Seeker,* they were not happy at all. They were incensed that she hadn't consulted with, or suitably warned them ahead of time regarding her desire to leave. They wanted a Marine in as a first officer on the *Seeker,* and they wanted her replacement to be a Marine as well. The posting gave the service a fair amount of prestige. Now, no doubt, some Fleet character will be trotted out to fill the role, and they needed to scramble if they wanted to salvage the situation. She heard one of the big shots down at 0-F wanted to launch a full-scale investigation into the matter and uncover the scope of her misconduct. Apparently, nothing came of it.

When they were done with her, they put her off on the dock in a disposable prisoner's jumpsuit (complete with the word INMATE printed across the back) as she had nothing else to wear. They handed Ki her final back pay, and threw her personal possessions at her in a small heap. Then they took off ... not even asking if she needed a lift to wherever.

* * * * *

She stood there in her brand new dress and peasant boots—feeling sad, feeling the wind creep up in places she wasn't accustomed to.

Her world spun around her. Her replacement? A dishonored private? How had all of this happened?

It still didn't feel real to her.

She watched the *Seeker* rise as long as she could stand it, stoic, arms crossed at her chest. Then, grimacing, she plugged her ears and gritted her teeth—the *Seeker* was, even at a distance, deafening. These people, grinning, waving, must all be half-deaf or something.

When the ship was no longer in sight and the people on the dock went their separate ways, she stood there alone, not quite knowing what to do. Like a ghost in a sheet, she numbly whirled around after a time and wandered into a pub—one that she normally didn't familiar. She didn't want anybody she knew to see her like this; a nobody. She saddled up to the bar and drank—she wanted to get good and drunk. If things went well, maybe she'd end up in a nice, soothing fight with some urchin or dirty courtesan. She hoped so ... she felt mad. She felt like hitting. But, getting into a big brawl dressed like this just won't do—she'd probably get beaten up, her dress hiked up over her head, her exposed knickers laughed at by all.

She wanted to be on that ship. Creation—what was she doing here?

Finally, drunk, feeling sorry for herself—feeling abandoned—she stumbled out of the pub, and began slowly walking toward Dav's castle. The castle loomed over the village in the mountains high above.

Nobody had the decency to pick a fight with her all afternoon. Nobody even messed up her name like they always did ("No, no, you piece of bat-shit. It's not *kilos*, as in your head weighs ten-thousand kilos. It's *Ki-los*, 'ki', as in *kite,* then 'los' ... *Kilos*, you get me?") Nobody even asked her name, come to think of it. They left her alone and let her drink, let her wallow in self-pity. Nobody even propositioned her. She was always getting propositioned in the pubs, at least a couple times a night by sailors and frat boys from the college, and she'd show them her wedding ring or pop them in the nose if they got too forceful. But, that was when she was a somebody, a Marine lieutenant. Now she was a nobody in a sheet-like dress and a pair of ugly boots, not worth approaching for a one-night stand.

She initially had thought to check herself into an inn until she could book passage back to Tusck, but Dav had talked her into staying at his castle—he pleaded with her in fact. Handing Kilos a key to one hundred-ten story tall Pendar Tower, a medium-sized tower in the north-west section of the castle, he begged her to stay there, for as long as she wanted. He said the tower was hers.

He needn't have begged—she wanted to stay there. She wanted to hold on to as much of him as she could.

Lady Poe, always kind and matronly, had conjured up a Tweeter for her to use while she was a guest in the castle. Ki's sense of direction was every bit as bad as Poe's, and her tiny, chirping, Silver tech familiar was dynamite for finding one's way in uncertain situations. The first time Poe had created Tweeter—specifically for the purpose of helping her find her way through all the unfamiliar cities and castles she was now getting to see as a rising star in League Society, it had taken days of careful thought and planning, with a great number of frustrating missteps in between, to get him right. With practice, she could now pop one up as needed in just a few minutes. All you had to do was tell Tweeter where you wanted to go, and he got you there without fail. Infallibly accurate, able to operate indoors and deep underground, he was much better than a hand held ranger device.

And, Ki had to admit, he was cute—a cute little guy. He appeared as a mechanical silver bird with a slightly over-sized belly area, like a golf ball with wings and a beak. Lady Poe loved happy faces, she made all her Silver tech creations that way, and Tweeter was no exception. He had bright, winsome eyes and beak that was curved into a permanent smile. His delicate legs and bird feet were articulated in a mechanical fashion. Under his right wing was Lady Poe's stamp, her Blanchefort Coat of Arms, another common feature of all her Silver Tech creations. Poe's stamp was her seal of approval, an assurance that he would work as he was supposed to.

For stays alone in Dav's massive castle, Ki needed Tweeter—badly, the place was a confusing maze of passages, corridors, halls and stairs where she got hopelessly lost at the drop of a hat. Syg loved the castle like that, a tempting black forest of undiscovered places to explore. She always wanted Ki to follow her into some tiny, dirty crawlspace she'd discovered. But Syg could get around with ease—some sort of arcane, internal Black Hat sense-of-direction deal that she had.

Ki, though, had no patience for not knowing where she was going, and Dav's castle was impossible. She recalled staying there once with her husband for a celebration and, leaving their guest tower in the middle of the night to get a little something to eat, she lost her way. She wandered around the endless corridors in her pajamas like a ghost. She was lost until daybreak, when she encountered a staff member.

With one of Poe's Tweeters though, Ki had no worries. The Marines had wanted to confiscate Tweeter and the Pendar Tower key as they roughly out-drummed her. They went over Tweeter's little chirping silver body with a microscope, looking for any serial number, laser sprand or other mark identifying him as Stellar Marine property. They found no marks other than Lady Poe's Coat-of-Arms, and, grudgingly, gave him back to her, along with the key, tossed in the pile with all her other worthless stuff.

* * * * *

Walking out of the pub, in the amber light of dusk, Ki fished around, digging Tweeter out of her bag and let him go. With silver wings, he fluttered up to a nearby window sill and looked down at her, happy-faced, eager to get started. His little head twitched about in a bird-like fashion.

"Get me to my room in Pendar Tower, Tweeter, as quickly as possible," she muttered.

He chirped and fluttered a bit down the lane. There, he stopped and waited for her on an eve amid the glowing lanterns, banners, and colorful lights that were softly lighting up the dusk. It was a party atmosphere tonight in the village near the dock, and locals were gathering in the streets to celebrate. Slowly, she staggered down the lane, past all the people and street vendors. When she got near, Tweeter took flight and went a little farther. The process repeated until she had gone several blocks down Bloodstein Road. The crowd thinned accordingly as she passed into the quiet outer reaches of Cyan-Towne, where many of the villagers lived. She expected Tweeter to take her east to Hannover Road, through the old brickyards then up the long switchback road to the castle. How else could one get up there? It was going to be a long walk up the steep road. She didn't mind, she felt like a long, lonely slog.

Maybe she'd get sick somewhere along the way. Maybe she'd pass out.

Instead of all that, Tweeter flew into a shop, a small quaint grocery lit up in soft white light.

Kilos, curious, walked in after him. "Evening, Miss," the grocer said with a smile as he restocked his shelves after a busy day. The store was empty of customers. The grocer had a small Aire-net terminal powered up at the counter: some sporting event droned on the floating screen.

"Miss," he called her *"Miss"*—she fumed. Peasants were called "Miss." She'd rather be called "lieutenant". Of course, she wasn't a lieutenant anymore. She'd even settle for "Hey, you!" Anything but *Miss.*

She made her way into the brightly lit interior of the store, Tweeter was sitting on a basket of apples, casting the fruit in a pleasing silver glow. As she approached, he fluttered even farther into the back.

"What are you doing, Tweeter?" she whispered, annoyed.

He landed on an odd pillar in the very back of the grocery butted up against the wall, where strings of garlic hung. As Ki approached, he hopped down and flew into a small hole at the bottom of the pillar, partially blocked by a basket full of turnips. She would never have noticed the hole if he hadn't gone into it. "Tweeter!" she hissed in a loud whisper.

The Aire-net terminal up front suddenly gave a roar—somebody must have scored.

She moved the basket aside and looked to see where Tweeter went: the hole traveled down at an odd angle and disappeared. To her eye the hole looked nothing more than a shallow air vent. She could see Tweeter's silvery light inside bouncing around. Ki knew that Lady Poe, after a few embarrassing misadventures, had redesigned Tweeter so that he won't try to take you any way you couldn't possibly follow. So obviously, though the hole seemed impossibly small, she should be able to fit. And, she did tell him to get her back as "quickly as possible." This must be a shortcut, one of those odd tunnels Syg was always raving about.

"Miss?" the owner asked from the front of the store.

Again with the "Miss" thing, she thought. She considered waiting for the grocer, and telling him that she'd lost her bird, then walk out into the new night and take the dark switchback up to the castle.

But then she pictured Syg, fearlessly crawling through the tunnels scattered throughout the castle and the village in her Hospitaler bodysuit and bare feet. She recalled the villagers speaking about their countess, how she could suddenly appear from nowhere, but without the wind and noise of a Waft. Obviously, this was the entrance to a tunnel. She wondered if Syg, filthy and exhausted, had popped out of this hole at some point in the past.

Syg. How Ki loved her … and disliked her a little bit too. How Syg had taken Dav—her best friend—and married him, dominated his time, kept him for herself; her love endless and smothering. Ki felt ashamed for those thoughts—Dav was happy, Syg made him so happy, and that should be enough for her. She should feel glad that her friend's wounded heart was finally healed.

Still, she longed for the old days, when it was just the two of them, best friends, inseparable.

She made up her mind at that point. She was determined to not be outdone. If Syg could do it, so too could she. She knelt down, stuffed her bag in and crawled into the hole.

The hole was small, only about fourteen inches high, and went down at about a nineteen degree angle. The dirty stone pressed on both her back and her stomach at once—like an unmovable straightjacket. She could feel her dress catching on the rough surface.

Ki struggled … she didn't really like tight spaces.

After a few more thrashes she was wedged in like a sausage, and quite stuck.

If she hadn't been so drunk, she felt she might really start panicking. She supposed she could start screaming, and hope that the grocer heard her, but that was a scenario that she really didn't want to be any part of.

Here's how she foresaw it happening: she'd scream until the grocer heard her. Then, unable to free her himself, he will go and get help, probably from the town Magistrate. The Magistrate of Blanchefort, like any officer with very little to do, will no doubt make a big spectacle over this, and, sounding the alarm, he'd bring half the village to witness him presiding over this event, this noble rescue. Then, standing over the hole she'd got stuck in, he will piously lecture the bottoms of her boots as he pulled her out.

No thanks ... she'd rather not.

So, here she was, stuck in a tiny hole. Tweeter ahead, patiently blinked, waiting for her to continue.

Being a Brown, nothing overly impressed her—not even her fears, and she had a lot of those if she thought about it. Fear, though initially "scary", wasn't really a big deal—just a lot of nonsense once you faced up to it and let it pass by. She'd been in a lot of gunfights, especially in her early days in the Marines, where she'd been paralyzed with fear at the outset. Once the bullets started flying and she got a good look at the Jo-boy shooting at her, her fear quickly dried up, replaced with smug indifference. "Hey, look at that loser over there, must have lost his razor or possibly his mother dressed him blindfolded that morning." TACK! TACK! as she leveled her SK and blasted away, belatedly joining the party.

She couldn't go back, so she might as well go forward. She took a moment, composed herself, let all the air out of her lungs, and began crawling. The space was too small for her to get up on her elbows and crawl, so, arms out in front of her like a diver, she used her long, strong fingers, moving one finger-length at a time. The tight hole was illuminated in silver light by Tweeter standing there in the distance. As before, he hopped away as she neared him. Slowly, pushing her bag ahead of her, she moved deeper and deeper into the tiny hole dragging herself with her fingers, embracing the stone, not fearing it any longer.

"You're going to get it over this, Tweeter—as soon as you get me out of here," she grunted, her voice in a tin can as she pulled herself along.

After about a hundred feet, the hole opened up a bit. She emerged in a lemon-shaped chamber of rock about three feet high—a luxurious amount of space after the tight confines of the squeeze she just came through. Tweeter waited for her there. It was a sort of crossroads—many dark holes lined the walls leading off in various directions. Kilos, on her stomach, looked at the quiet, imposing holes, and then looked at Tweeter; bright, chirping, her only way out of here. Her head had cleared quite a bit—the bulk of her intoxication had been sweated out in the crawlspace. She peeked into one of the holes—it trailed off into the dark, going somewhere. The quiet in the chamber was profound, was enveloping. All the chattering and evening noises of the village above were gone, silenced. As she sat there in the chamber, other normally imperceptible noises became deafening: her heartbeat, the stretching of her joints, the wheeze of her breath, and the padding of Tweeter's silver feet on the cool stone. She entertained the fleeting thought of leaving Tweeter's side and crawling into a random hole, just to see how brave she was, but then gave up on the thought. She wasn't that brave.

"Lead the way, buddy," she said, her voice bouncing around in the chamber.

He hopped off toward a hole—the smallest one, of course, and went into it. Now that her eyes were accustomed to the dark, and her head was sobered up a bit, she was amazed how much light Tweeter put off. She could clearly see his effervescent silver glow, bubbling around on the other side of the hole ahead. She felt like she was in a darkened theater looking at a brightly lit stage. Kilos hauled herself into the hole and squeezed through, again having to force all the air out of her lungs to fit. She found that, though small, the hole opened up into a large, silent underground cavern easily large enough for her to stand. Tweeter flapped his way up onto her shoulder and fluttered there, his light clearly illuminating the rocky features of the darkness-soaked cavern. The way ahead at this point was clear, and she started walking, following a long gentle slope upward. As she made her way up the rocks of the slope, grunting and sweating, she could see why Syg liked doing this so much. It was actually pretty fun to move about in the dark, unseen, discovering what was there to discover—just like exploring space—it required the same energy, the same spirit. She admired Syg's guts to do this in the dark all by herself. She felt ashamed for being jealous of her. And, as long as she had Tweeter to keep her from getting lost and providing plenty of light to see, she found she was enjoying herself. It took her mind off of the ship that was now far away.

The ship that she wanted to be on.

She wished Dav and Syg were here. She wished they could explore the passages together, get filthy, get tired and then wash out all the dirt and grime in a pub somewhere in the village. The Drunken Eel, that one was her favorite.

She badly missed her friends. Why did she ever hand Dav her SK?

Moving through the cavern was a complete sensory experience. It was cold in there, near fifty degrees, but as long as she kept moving the temperature felt just right. The air was thick with humidity—near 100%, and with every wheezing breath she tasted the salts and silicates hanging in the air and felt the grit of minute eroded particles of rock in her teeth. She felt it condensing on her skin in dirty droplets. She could smell the minerals and hard water, mixed with the slight perfume of her own sweat marinated with the traces of hard booze consumed hours ago. The rocks she treaded on were smooth, slippery with moisture, and stained with streaks of rust from the iron substrates above. Water dripped onto the rocks in a quiet hammering, made loud in the unearthly silence of the cavern. There were twisted formations overhead dripping water that reminded her of bacon. She'd had nothing all day and a torrid liquid lunch, so she was feeling pretty hungry. She'd have to grab a snack when she got to the castle—the kitchens were always going. It was a rule Dav had that food always be available to those who were hungry. She imagined bacon, and her favorite, pancakes. Oh!—with that rich, dripping, lip-smacking Nadine syrup they boiled down every morning. Ki remembered literally fighting with her sister, Maia, over the jugs of Nadine syrup she brought home from Blanchefort castle. Her mouth watered with the thought.

The cavern appeared to come to an end in a sloping wall of rock, Ki scanning the rock face, seeing nothing and certain Tweeter had led her to a dead end. But invariably, he'd hop into an imperceptible fold in the rock and push in with gusto, revealing a squeeze. Ki knelt down and was appalled, the rising and falling squeezes, at first glance, looked impassibly small, and, without Tweeter's light, were nearly impossible to find. Taking a breath of gritty air, Ki plunged in after Tweeter, feeling the wet rock closing in on her in a uterine embrace, locking her into a twisted position. Her arms and legs felt far away from her, separated by an ocean of stone. Hard water dripped into her eyes and the rubbing rock began irritating her skin, making it itch, but she couldn't reach her face to rub away the water or scratch with her stone-locked hands. She had to concentrate, forget about minor distractions like watery eyes and itching skin, and keep moving.

Going forward, following Tweeter's light and accepting what the squeeze dished out, she was fine. Going back, plunged in darkness, was impossible.

She emerged and basked in the open, humid air of the cavern, the luxury of freedom of movement a precious gift given back to her.

Moving on she eventually reached the top of the cavern and Tweeter flapped into another crawl space—a more manageable one this time. As she readied to get in and follow him, she looked back once … and did a double take.

With Tweeter ahead in the tube, the cavern behind her was again plunged into thick darkness. Down far below, where she had been just minutes earlier, was a pair of eyes: glowing, animal-like, looking at her in the dark. Frozen in place, she instinctively reached for her SK, but, of course, it wasn't there. Swallowing, she entered the crawl space as fast as she could. Whatever was down there, she wanted no part of it.

Soon she caught up to Tweeter. He was perched on the rungs of what appeared to be an ancient stone ladder, going up into the dark reaches. He fluttered upward, his light making a bright silver circle illuminating the interior of a small tube going up. Ki looked back toward the tube opening she'd just crawled through, remembering the eyes in the dark. Quickly, she began climbing.

After a long climb of about three hundred feet, she emerged under a beech hanger in the vast Telmus Grove. The bright northern stars were out of the bag and glittering, Dav's looming castle back-lit in mute light. Here she was, she'd arrived—she couldn't believe it. She smiled and felt proud, like she'd just accomplished something. She sat for a moment on a low stone wall and enjoyed the night air. Normally, the air this time of night was too chilly for her liking, but, after all that activity in the caverns below, the air felt good on her dirty, sweaty body. She wanted to come back soon and do this with Dav and Syg—to crawl in the unseen places, it was a lot of fun—except for the creature in the dark bit.

She got up after a time and began toward the castle, walking easily. She followed Tweeter through the twisting passes, where she let herself in with her key. She directed Tweeter to take her to the kitchens and had the staff whip her up a quick plate of bacon and pancakes dripping in dark brown Nadine syrup, just boiled. The staff eyeballed her filthy clothes and wanted her dress to wash, but she waved them off. Still flush with her adventure through the cavern, she sat down and ate with gusto and reviewed in her thoughts everything she'd experienced that evening. Creation, the food was good. She finished up and began to feel tired and dirty, Tweeter leading her to her tower. Pendar Tower, like most in Dav's castle, wasn't just a room—it was an entire, self-contained multi-leveled structure, one hundred stories tall complete with bedrooms, sitting rooms, game rooms, bathrooms, terraces and small libraries, the only thing it lacked was a fully functioning kitchen. If Ki had been more of a reader, she could spend days and days going through all of the inviting books in the tower's many libraries. As Pendar Tower was usually reserved for guests, it had a lift that could speedily reach all hundred floors. Dav and Syg's Grandia Tower had no lifts—they simply Wafted up. Blues… Got to love them.

She was tired. She unlatched the tower door and went in, eager for a wash and her bed. She went up the lift and approached the room that she had selected to sleep in. It was on the sixty-third floor, adjacent to a large open-air terrace overlooking the village. There were plenty of rooms to choose from, but she'd liked this one for some reason. It had a nice bed that she found quite comfortable. The staff knew she liked her room warm, so they probably had already turned up the heat. It should be nice and warm. She opened the door.

The shining eyes in the dark of her room startled her—brought her heart into her mouth. She dropped her key.

The eyes, fixed on her, approached in a lope.

* * * * *

The Com Officer entered Davage's office, handed Crewman Heartford a report pad detailing all current League activity and a stack of printed paper tags from the Marines, and left. As per usual tradition, the captain and first officer, or, in this case, acting first officer, sorted through all of the current League dispatches and tags, and determined which were likely to be served. Usually, any imminent Xaphan movements received priority attention, followed by League matters, local situations, and so forth. It was up to the captain, the Admiralty traditionally having very little say in the matter unless in times of war or the declaration of a General Battle.

Heartford read through the papers and the pad, his hands shaking a bit.

"Take your time, crewman. Nothing to be nervous about. Care for something to drink?"

"No sir, thank you." He re-adjusted his papers, wiped off his pad, and read through them again.

"So, crewman, anything hot out there?" Davage asked after a time.

"Sir," Heartford said, "we have currently no tags marked Red. There are also … no general call outs or Xaphan issues."

"All quiet out there, eh? Good, good."

"There are a number of call outs from Fleet Admirals requiring ferrying."

"Oh dear …" Davage shrugged. "Skip those."

Heartford appeared shocked. "Sir, I …"

Davage saw his discomfort. Clearly, to a crewman, a grand personage such as an Admiral sounded impressive enough, however, most Fleet captains at sea generally gave land-locked admirals the brush off. He sighed. "All right, crewman, go ahead and read them."

"From: Pax, Admiral of the Fleet, 9th wing—require immediate transport in show to Tantan for summit meeting and League junket. Require warship of *Straylight* configuration, and two more in tail. Request, per command: *Seeker*. The Admiral hopes we will ferry him, sir. The tag also notes the Admiral has Programmability *Profundni,* and that there could be profound consequences should his request go unheeded."

Davage rolled his eyes. "Oh, *profound consequences,* eh? As you can see, I am shaking at the thought of what those consequences might be. Crewman, I … *hate* … ferrying Admirals around; all that strutting and clucking … the entourage, every meal a full blown formal affair, the gossip and the Blue League nonsense. Can you imagine? And, please, refresh my memory as I wasn't really listening the first time—how many warbirds does he wish to inconvenience on his little joyride to Tantan?"

"Three, sir."

"Three warbirds impressed into vagabondage! Why not ten, or a hundred—how about the whole 3rd Fleet to go to Tantan with the Admiral? What a criminal waste of resources. Let him take a scout ship or a transport like everybody else, for Creation's sake. *Tekel*-class scout ships are indeed marvels of engineering. And, do you care for a brief lesson in League society? Shall I tell you why he wants three warbirds to go to Tantan?"

"Yes, please."

"If there's anything the lords and ladies of the League are impressed by, it's *Frundage,* an excess of things. A great amount of money, a great collection of clothing, beasts or spices, a massive Programmability—that's *Frundage.* All those things open doors and turn heads. So, picture this, if you will: the Admiral arrives at his summit meeting with his little armada of warbirds in tow, hoping to sway the proceedings to his liking merely because of all the metal he has floating around in orbit. If he wants to dominate the day, I say let him do it with scalpel wit and speed of tongue, with naught but a scout ship to take him home when it's over."

Heartford looked uncomfortable. "But, sir, the Admiral has Programmability *Profundni.*"

"Really? If we are going to go in that direction, crewman, be aware that I have more Programmability with the Sisters than he does. I hold the *Magni* status, therefore his *Profundni* is nullified. What is the Admiral's current location?"

Heartford was astounded—clearly Davage's *Magni* impressed him. He looked at the pad. "The Admiral is currently on Hoban."

"Ah—Hoban. Let's assume for a moment that my Programmability did not out-strip his. Admirals such as he, may usurp command of a Fleet warbird if said vessel is within 100,000 stellar miles of his location. Fortunately, Hoban is much farther out than that, so, therefore the Admiral is out of luck on multiple points."

Heartford still looked dubious.

Davage relented. "You're making me feel guilty, crewman. Has anyone already answered the charge?"

"Yes sir, several scout ships."

"Good, good … they can take him. You see, the Admiral will be well served, and thank Creation for it—next!"

There was a soft knock at the door. "Captain …" Syg said from the other side. "May I come in?"

Heartford looked at the door and stood up.

"Not now, Countess," Davage said. "Ship's business. I'll be out soon." Syg did that often, just to let him know she was still out there—

she hated to be left out. If she really wanted in, she'd be pummeling him with telepathy.

Davage turned back to the crewman. "What else?"

"From Captain Bertus, MFV *Gauge*: require a flight of vessels to go in force to Tubruk to exact delinquent tribute from the local sovereign."

"What!" Davage cried, outraged. "We're collecting taxes now, are we? Oh, what have we become? Crewman, delete that tag from the pad at once, for Creation's sake!"

Heartford deleted it.

"What's left?" Davage asked.

He looked over his pad. "Sir, there is a call from Captain Mennader of the *St. Cloud* for a four ship combat box to quest to the Liteal System for palladium."

"Interesting … interesting, we'll keep that one in mind. Next."

"That concludes the current tags. Except for standard Marine traffic and …"

"Marines? What do they have going on?"

Heartford looked through the notes. "Troop transports, base re-supplies, and the standard raider and pirate patrols."

"Hmmm, read me a few."

He read through the stack. "From Commander, Marine vessel *Wardiner*: Lt. Westrich of the 44th Marines reports he is in trail of a vessel of unknown configuration, and requests a Marine detachment at Bazz to assist in intercepting."

Davage thought for a moment. "What is the heading of this unknown spacecraft?"

"From Heron 7, it is bearing 3:30am of 10pm."

Davage brought up a 3-D map and punched in the coordinates. A star map of Heron 7 popped up. "Here's Heron 7… and just over here is … Xaphan space," he said tracing the route out with his finger.

Heartford spoke up. "Sir, the notice is marked 'X' for suspected raider/pirate activity, the usual purview of the Marines."

"Nonsense, crewman, we're all one big happy League after all." Davage gazed at the map. "Let's plot solution and have a look. Besides, the Marine vessel in tail is a *brigantine*, that's barely bigger than a mail tender, and I imagine they shall appreciate the attention."

Heartford stood back up. "Aye, sir. I'll inform navigation at once."

"Excellent, and thank you, crewman, well done."

Heartford opened the door and exited.

Syg was standing there, leaning against the wall with her hands behind her back. Heartford greeted her, and she acknowledged, allowing him to pass by and then walked in, closing the door behind her. "Well now, all the 'Official Stuff' concluded, is it, Captain Davage? May I have my husband back?"

Davage stood and poured her a cup of coffee. He sat back down, and Syg got into his lap and toyed with his blue-haired bangs.

"So, where are we headed?" she asked taking a drink from her cup.

"Heron 7, to assist the Marines in tailing an unknown vessel."

"An unknown vessel? We don't normally do things like that, do we?"

"No, not normally. But … I've a feeling about this one."

He gazed at the 3-D map. At Heron, at Xaphan Space nearby …

At the planet Xandarr … and the princess who wanted to kill him.

5—Carahil

"I am sorry if I startled you, Madame Kilos," Carahil said emerging from the darkness at the far end of her room.

Ki, heart pounding, took a moment to compose herself. She fumbled with her bag and picked up her key. Her hands were shaking.

"Was that you I saw in the cavern?"

"Yes, Madame, it was."

"You scared me to death, and if I'd had my SK with me I probably would have shot you. Don't skulk about next time! Come and see me if you want to see me, understood!"

"Yes, Madame, I will."

"And don't call me `Madame'! Makes me feel like I'm two hundred years old or something! Either call me Kilos, or don't call me anything at all, got it?"

"May I call you Ki?"

"No! No, at least, not yet. I don't know you well enough for that at this point."

Carahil's smooth silver body glinted in the dim light. "Yes, Kilos, of course."

Kilos walked to her desk and sat down . Uncharacteristically, she was incredibly tired, right down to her bones. Where was the night owl? Where was the energy? All she wanted to do was close her eyes and sleep.

"By the by," she said in a sleepy voice, "have you been leaving me little nuggets of inspiration all over the place lately?"

"Yes I have. I felt you could use some cheer."

"I don't mean to sound ungrateful, but leaving me thoughts of encouragement in a toilet is just plain gross, ok?"

A large book appeared, along with a marker. Carahil took the marker with his teeth and jotted in a few notes. The book and marker then vanished. "I'll remember that for next time," he said. "So, Kilos, do you have a moment?"

She threw her bag into a corner and Tweeter, ever glowing, settled on a high bookshelf, awaiting his next task. Outside, through the window, the stars gleamed. Far below in the village, the celebration was winding down; the lights shutting off.

She was filthy. "I need to get a wash, Carahil. Can this wait?"

Patiently, Carahil lowered his head and retreated. Kilos pulled her boots off, threw them in a corner, and walked into the large bathroom, stripping off her brand new but hopelessly stained dress. She hopped into the huge shower stall, tiled and inlaid with mosaics of fish, and hit the jets. Hot water and steam drifted up around her from several nozzles. It felt good. Through the misted, pebbled glass, she saw Carahil peek into the bathroom. "Don't worry," he said, "I can't see anything."

Ki closed her eyes and let the hot water soak her. "So what is it?" she said yelling over the hiss of water. "What can I do for you? I'm certain you didn't come up here for nothing."

Carahil loped up to the glass. "I need your help."

Kilos was sore all over. She selected a variety of colored soaps from the many ornate dispensers built into the wall and began washing her long hair. "My help?" she said, scrubbing the soap in, stepping around the grit that poured off of her, "haven't you heard … I'm not a Marine anymore ... I'm just Kilos of Tusck." She could see Tweeter sitting on top of the steamed-up mirror, a little ball of light. "I'm Kilos of the Silver Bird."

Carahil replied. "Yes, I know, and that makes you a perfect choice to come and help me. I know quite a lot regarding your situation. I know you've quit the Marines, and I know why you did it too."

Kilos, skeptical as always, was unimpressed. "Really … enlighten me then. Why'd I do it?" she said as she rinsed.

Tweeter chirped from the mirror, his little body starting to sweat.

"Pride, Kilos—isn't that obvious? I wonder, how does leaving the Marines make you feel at this moment?"

"Why don't you go ahead and tell me. How do I feel, Carahil?" She shut off the water and walked to the far end of the shower stall several paces away. It had a selection of folded towels, and a tiled vaculator seat that would dry her in a few moments in a rush of air. Ki opted for a towel. She grabbed one and began drying off.

Carahil nudged the shower door with his nose. "You feel a number of things, none of which are good. You've clouded the issue this evening with drink, denial and exhaustion. You are sad—that's clear. You are angry, that is also clear. Tell me, how do you feel about your husband right now?"

Kilos closed her eyes and felt tears welling up. She buried her face in her towel. "I … hate him right now. I hate the fact that I'm stuck here wearing a dress. Yesterday I was somebody … today I'm a Brown peasant."

"A Brown peasant? A peasant with the free run of Blanchefort Castle? How many peasants can say that? And, your husband—you hate him for doing this to you, for turning you into a peasant?"

"Right now I do."

"Please, Kilos, let us not indulge in games here—he did nothing of the sort. He was lonely; he asked you to come home, as he often has in the past. It was you who forced the matter, inflated it. It was you who handed your weapon to Lord Blanchefort. It was you who quit the Marines. So, just who was it who put the dress on your back, Kilos? It was you, and you know it."

"Why would I do that?"

"Pride … as I said. You've been feeling left out, indeed, you've been feeling a bit jealous—since Lord Blanchefort married his countess. You long for the old days—when it was just you and he, as best friends tossing them back in the bars by the docks. Now, time he once spent with you, he spends walking the Grove in the countess's arm, or in the bowling alley watching her throw gutterballs, or in bed conceiving young little Blancheforts. Your husband Com'ed, asked you to come home again, and you, feeling jealous and left out, embarked on an emotional tirade that quickly spiraled out of control, culminating in you leaving the Marines. You wanted Captain Davage to beg you to stay, didn't you? You wanted him to plead. You wanted him on his knees, didn't you? Your husband had nothing to do with that—that was all you, that's what you wanted."

Ki thought a moment. Carahil had her knocked—she didn't bother to deny it. She grabbed a fresh towel, wrapped herself up in it, and emerged from the shower. She walked past Carahil, re-entered her room and flopped onto her bed. The sheets felt warm and inviting against her washed body. "And what's wrong with that," she said. "To want to be needed, to be indispensible?"

Carahil followed her out of the bathroom. Tweeter flapped out and settled on the bookcase, lightly pecking its surface.

"Nothing, perfectly natural," he said. "And, I can tell you that Lord Blanchefort is very sad right now. He is sitting in his office, looking at the wall where your tankard of unauthorized buncked narva is kept."

Ki got annoyed. "How do you know there's buncked narva in a hidden panel in his office?"

"I know lots of things, Kilos. I also know Lord Blanchefort misses his first officer. He misses his friend. So too does Countess Blanchefort. She loves you as well, though, as you recall, you two got off to a rough start. She hits pretty hard, doesn't she, the countess?"

Kilos thought back. "Yes, yes she does." Syg had knocked out a few of her teeth.

"So, Kilos, there it is, you have your wish … you are missed and pined for. And, I can tell you that lots and lots of people are in the process of clamoring for your job. How does that make you feel?"

Kilos felt a sting deep down. All this—this "Going Home" thing was suddenly very real. She felt trapped and alone, locked in a tiny little box of her own making. "Great—feels great," she said running her hands through her damp hair. "So, Carahil—what do you want?"

"To repeat myself, I need your help."

"My help?"

"Yes. I am Lady Poe's guardian. I protect her—I protect all those whom Lady Poe loves. I guard you as well."

Kilos gave a chuckle. "Lady Poe loves me, does she?"

"She does, after a fashion, yes. You are a good friend and she acknowledges that."

"I'm honored."

Carahil smiled at her. "As you should be." He regarded her for a moment. "Do you realize what I am? I feel I can be frank with you."

Kilos rolled over and looked at him. He stood there in the dark propped up on his silver flippers, big eyes blinking, whiskers twitching, the smooth dome of his silver head shining in the dark. She didn't think she liked the tone of his question—he seemed oddly sinister to her. She wished he'd go away and let her be. "Ummm, you're a seal that likes to take care of kittens and throw pies. You know Syg is still fuming over that, right?"

"I know, but I made up for it by running her green gown up the flagpole. But those are easy—what else am I?"

Ki laughed. "I suppose you're like him up there." She pointed at Tweeter. "Instead of a bird, you're a seal. You're a Silver tech gadget made by Lady Poe."

Carahil glanced up at Tweeter on the high shelf. "Gadget? Ohhh, you wound me. Me, like Tweeter? It's a scandal!"

He lifted his nose Tweeter fluttered down and settled on it. "Allow me to inform you—I am not a gadget, and I am nothing like Tweeter here. Tweeter is a Silver tech Familiar. He is nothing more than a bit of Silver tech with a small soul. He accepts commands, he carries them out, he does his job, but nothing more—there is no intelligence, no heart, just like those fish my mother makes. He's the gadget, not me. Shall I pop him into my mouth and swallow? He'll not care in the slightest."

"But, I'll care—I need him. Put him back, please."

Carahil flipped his nose and Tweeter went back up to his shelf. "Indeed …"

"So then, Carahil, what are you then? You seem to be dying to tell me."

"I, Kilos, am an Elemental Spirit. I seek to expand my knowledge, serve and protect. I must say, my Mother, Lady Poe, had no idea the … force … she was unleashing in that Vith fountain when she made me."

Kilos relaxed a bit. "Feeling a little happy about yourself, Carahil, are you? And so, 'Mighty Elemental Spirit', you said you need my help? What do you need, and why?"

"I need you to come with me. There is a place that we need to go together."

Kilos was intrigued. "Yeah? Where are we going?"

"What's your answer?"

"Don't you know?"

"I do, but you have to say yes. I have to give you a choice. I am … good … after all."

Ki sat up. "I have to go, Carahil. I have to go home, to Tusck, to my husband. I just gave up my career, my rank—my friends. I might as well finish the trip. Besides, what good would I be?"

Carahil eyed Tweeter sitting on the shelf. "Going home right now is not a good idea. As we previously established, your pride created this mess, and if you go home now, your pride and anger will bubble up in full force and plague your husband. It won't be long before he hates you and you he—for real this time. Really, you and your husband do much better at a distance, so that you two can revel in each other on those select occasions when you are together. Your personalities are such that too much close proximity is a bad thing. Certainly, you don't need me to tell you that."

"I suppose not."

Kilos rolled over in bed. Carahil came forward and nudged her in the back. "So, what do you say, Kilos? Are you going to help me or not?"

"What if I say no? What if I just go home?"

"And fade into the crowd of Browns in Tusck, never to be seen again? That will be a death sentence for you."

"You're serious about this?"

"I am."

"Then answer me two questions, truthfully, and maybe I'll help you. First question: who's been leaving Syg all those messages?"

Carahil thought a moment. "I don't know." Out came the book and marker again. A few scribbles and it vanished. "And, that should tell you something, Kilos. If I don't know, then that's possibly a good reason to be concerned. Tell you what, when I know, you'll know."

Ki lay there, half asleep. "Now, for my second question. Where are we going?"

"South, where it's warmer. You'll love it. So, what do you say?"

"Sure. Sure, I'll go."

"Well, that's great news. I will be calling on you. Get some sleep and eat hearty in the morning. You shall need it."

He turned to leave. "Oh, are you sure I can't devour Tweeter right now … we've a long way to go, and I'll need a snack."

Kilos threw a pillow at him.

6—Lt. Carbomier

"Dav, I'm sick of you going into your office and not letting me in," Syg said in their quarters after day bell. She poured herself a cup of coffee, and sat down next to him on the couch. She had removed her gown and was down to her petticoat and undergarments. She jammed her feet into his ribs.

"You know you can't be in there when I am discussing ship's destination. Those are the regulations."

"I thought you made up the regulations."

"In some cases I do, but not this one. The Fleet regs are plain—it's supposed to prevent tampering and corruption."

Syg jabbed him with her feet again then snuggled up next to him. This was his favorite part of the day, to just sit and relax with his wife.

"I don't care," she said, "it's not like I'm going to know what you're talking about anyway."

Syg wrapped herself around him. As she often did, she slid her soft feet into the interior of his boots and rubbed them down to his ankles. Dav's boots, big, and rather over-sized in the Fleet tradition, were large enough to accommodate his leg and both of Syg's to some extent. The big Fleet boots were based off of the old Falloon-style boots of long ago. "Rain-catchers" the Marines called them; they wore smaller, leg-fitting Brusards.

"You could be an enemy spy," he said laughing.

"Yes, Dav … I'm a Xaphan spy. I'm in so deep, I even married my mark, got pregnant with his child, have wonderful sex with him several times a day, and have to wear his clothes to boot."

"Is that all?"

"No, that's not all, the spy fell madly in love …"

"It's only for a few minutes, and only every so often. Why's it bother you so much?"

"Because, it does." She put her cup down and sighed. "I suppose I'll need to apologize to you now, Dav."

"Why is that, Syg?"

"Because I feel it coming on."

Davage became a bit apprehensive. "Feel what coming on?"

Syg smiled. "'The Rush'. It's just my body adapting to being pregnant. A year and a half is a long time, and my body has to ready itself for nurturing our son. The down side of that is my emotions might be a little out-of-whack for a while. I was reading about it a few days ago in some literature Ennez gave to me."

"I must admit," Davage said, "I've not spent a lot of time around pregnant women previously—other than my sister, Pardock, when she was pregnant with her children, though her emotions seemed no more out of sorts than normal. You mean you might be feeling a little moody from time to time? I'd think that's only natural."

"Moody's part of it," Syg said. "I'd say it's more like hyper-sensitive and needy, and a bit erratic as well. I might do strange things, and my temper might be a tad short. I might be pretty clingy as well. Just remember that I love you."

Davage embraced her. "That's fine, darling. Maybe that's why you think you saw Admiral Scy getting hit with a pie."

"I didn't think that, Dav, I saw that."

"I didn't see a thing, and you know me, I see everything."

Syg smiled and ran her hands up his chest. "Well, maybe you're getting soft …" She then hauled back and slugged him in the stomach. "Oops," she said, "did somebody just slug you?"

"How long will this erratic behavior last do you think?" he asked, astonished.

"The whole time, from here on out," Syg said happily. "The whole year and a half."

Dav reached down and felt Syg's belly. She put her hand over his. "How's he doing?"

"He's fine, Dav. He's going to be a lovely, handsome boy."

She put her coffee cup down and began kissing his neck. "Mmmm, let's start practicing for our next child. You want another boy or a girl?"

"How about a girl. Kilos … we'll name her Kilos."

Syg continued working his neck. "Lady Kilos of Blanchefort, sounds good to me. I miss her. I wish she hadn't left."

"Me too, but, I think she needed to work something out, Syg. Her husband, he didn't pressurize her any more than normal—I could tell it in her face. I think she was conflicted with something, something she'll need to work out on her own."

"Your Sight tell you that?"

"Yes, it did. I only hope she's not regretting her decision right now. To take such a drastic step, to lose her situation. I hope it's worth it to her."

"Just remember, it's not goodbye, we'll be seeing her often."

The Com rang in. "Sir, I have a message for you from Stellar Marine Command, Lt. Carbomier standing by."

Davage shrugged. "Aye, Com, I'll take it here." He stood up and kissed Syg. "Looks like the Marines are wasting no time casting their bones for a replacement for Ki—they seem to be rather keen on it."

Syg trotted over to the far side of the room. "I am I off screen, love?"

Davage walked over to his terminal and punched up the Com header. "Yes, yes, darling, you're fine where you are."

Syg winked at him and sat down. She created a rack of Silver tech ten pins at the far end of the room and a shimmering silver bowling ball in her hand. She took position and readied to line up for a shot.

<*Syg, don't you dare bowl that ball!*> This is going to be a long year and a half, Davage mused. He hit the switch, and Lt. Carbomier popped up. A smiling, handsome fellow, his red Marine uniform was as neatly trimmed and pressed as Kilos' used to be.

"Captain Davage, well met, sir! I am sorry for the hour."

"It's quite all right, Lt., greetings. What can I do for you?"

"Sir, we—here in Marine Command—"

The Silver tech bowling ball sped across the floor behind Davage, skittering a little on the rises in the carpeting, and crashed into the tenpins with a massive tumult. Lt Carbomier heard the noise and was distracted.

Davage glanced over. Strike—not bad.

The Lt. continued. "...wish to offer our most sincere apologies regarding the untimely and sudden departure of Lt. Kilos as your standing first officer. We certainly hope that you are not overly offended or inconvenienced, and we assure you the matter has been promptly dealt with."

"Promptly dealt with, Lt.? Lt. Kilos was, without question, one of the finest officers I have ever had the pleasure of serving with, and I fully understand her pressing personal need to return to her home. I am curious, just how has this matter been … 'dealt with' as you put it?"

Davage didn't need to ask, he could guess—Ki was probably dressed down, stripped of her uniforms, de-drummed and kicked out in short order. And, if she managed to be out-processed as anything more than a private, he'd be surprised.

The Lt. shuffled uncomfortably. "Sir, I … I only meant that her immediate wishes were attended to in short order, to speed her transition to …"

"Lt., I will be speaking to Madame Kilos shortly and, if I hear that she was treated with anything but the utmost courtesy and respect due to any long-serving officer in good standing, if I hear that she was out-processed as anything but a lieutenant, and if I hear she was abandoned at dock in Blanchefort village … I will find that situation most unfavorable. Indeed, I will be quite annoyed."

Again, the Marine looked like he'd been run-over. "Sir, I assure you, we will attend to her every need. She will lack for nothing as she makes her way to wherever she is going. She will always be a Stellar Marine in our eyes."

Davage eyed him skeptically.

Syg, forming a fresh Silver tech bowling ball, smiled. <*Well said, Dav—stick it to him.*>

"Glad to hear it … Lt."

Carbomier cleared his throat and continued. "Sir, I have been asked by my Command to relay you a message."

"Indeed. Please proceed."

"Sir, our Command has been pleased that a Marine was selected as first officer of such an esteemed Vessel of the Line. Our Command wishes to humbly submit to you a potential replacement; an officer whom we feel will serve with all the skill and professionalism you have come to expect."

"I see. I was hoping to promote from within, as I did with Kilos years ago. Though she was Marine and I Fleet, I considered her as one of my own."

"We … were hoping …"

Behind Davage, the Silver tech bowling ball again raced across the carpeting and crashed into the pins.

"God's Bodkins, Captain," Carbomier said, "was that a bowling ball just now?"

"Yes it was, Lt., please continue."

He composed himself. "We were hoping not to sway your decision, sir, but to simply make you aware of all options available—so that you can make the best choice possible. We are sending a Marine cutter to high noon of Bazz. We are hoping, at that time, to have permission to come a-beam, hail and board. Will you grant a boarding?"

Davage thought a moment. "I will tell you … after I have spoken with Madame Kilos regarding her treatment. Not before. Davage out."

With that, he cut the connection.

Syg bounced up from her seat. "Not nice, love …" she said throwing her arms around him.

"I suppose not, but, I'll not reward them for ill-handling Ki."

"You really think they gave her a rough time of it?"

"Without question."

Syg smiled. "Speaking of Kilos, shouldn't we be practicing for creating the next Kilos … Lady Kilos of Blanchefort?"

And they made love on the floor.

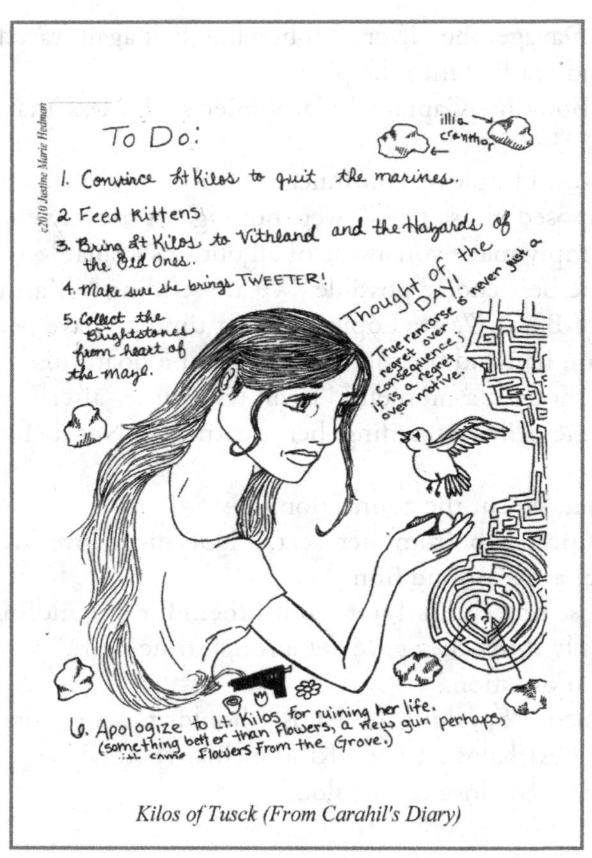

©2010 Justine Marie Hedman
To Do:
illia
cranthor
1. Convince Lt Kilos to quit the marines.
2. Feed Kittens
3. Bring Lt Kilos to Vithland and the Hazards of the Old Ones.
4. Make sure she brings TWEETER!
5. Collect the Brightstones from heart of the maze.
Thought of the DAY!
True remorse is never just a regret over consequence; it is a regret over motive.
6. Apologize to Lt. Kilos for ruining her life.
(something better than Flowers, a new gun perhaps,
Flowers from the Grove.)

Kilos of Tusck (From Carahil's Diary)

7—The Eleventh Daughter

When Ki awoke in her bed, she felt as if the last day had been nothing more than a strange, uncomfortable dream. She was certain she'd awake in her familiar quarters on the *Seeker*, still a first officer, still a Marine.

She looked around and her heart pinched. She was in Pendar Tower certain enough. She was in her vast, comfortable guest bed, nude, her towel thrown aside. Her dirty dress was sitting on the chair in a corner. Tweeter, silver and glowing, was fluttering about on the window sill.

She was slightly hung over.

Carahil was nowhere around—back to the green of the Grove, she guessed. He had seemed strange last night; intense, frightening in a way. She wondered if she had dreamt the whole thing.

There was a scratch at the window and Tweeter fluttered up. At the window a small cat gazed in, apparently wanting to eat him. She gave the pane a stiff rap with her knuckles. "Go on, get out of here!" she said and the cat moved away.

She grabbed her towel and wandered out onto the terrace. Far below, down the precipice of the mountains, was Blanchefort village huddled by the bay. She could clearly see the long, straight run of Bloodstein Road. To the south of it were the orderly residential nooks of Cyan-Towne; to the north the craggy confusion of shops, chapels, inns and pubs. The grocery where she began her subterranean adventure was along that road somewhere.

Wearily, she put her rock-stained dress and boots back on. She had nothing else to wear. She asked Tweeter to show her where the kitchen was, and she followed him down. There she met the staff. Once again they eyed her filthy dress and bade her allow them to wash it. They gave her a thick robe to wear and, putting it on in a bathroom, she handed over her dress. The staff then made her breakfast. Thanking them, she ate alone in brightly lit, colorful Capricos Hall at the huge feasting table there.

Dav and Syg … gone.

Lady Poe, out on yet another date.

Eating alone at the huge, two-hundred foot long table was horrible. The last time she'd been in Capricos Hall she was with Dav and Syg, Ennez and Bethrael of Moane; the five of them one big happy family. She stared at her plate of pancakes and ate her food mechanically. The staff came out every so often to see if she needed anything. The table in the hall could probably seat three hundred people, and there she was alone, sitting meekly at one end.

"Looks like it's just you and me, Tweeter," she said as he bounced around on the tabletop. She recalled Carahil saying Tweeter was just a Silver tech automaton, a gadget—no heart, no soul. But, to Ki, especially after his performance yesterday, he was her chirping little friend. She broke him off a little bit of pancake and he pecked at it with gusto. She had no idea if he was actually eating it or simply simulating the act; still, watching him work on it was comforting.

Tweeter, her only friend in this huge, mostly empty castle. Kilos of the Silver Bird she had thought of in the shower—she sort of liked the way that sounded.

She finished her lonely breakfast and decided to go out into the Grove. "Take me to Carahil's Walk, Tweeter," she said and he guided her out into the sunny morning. It was a typical bright, yet chilly northern set up. She closed the folds of the robe and held it shut.

She wound her way through the huge Grove with Tweeter leading the way. The complex twisting layout of the Grove with avenues of trees, dead-ending in old Vith courtyards laid out in no particular order, was boggling. Without Tweeter, she'd be lost once again.

He took her through a clearing in the trees crisscrossed with walkways leading in various directions. This was the Inner Plaisance of the Grove. In the center of the clearing was the statue of a large fox in a vaulted gazebo of stone, surrounded by well-tended flowers. Foxes were sacred animals for Vith families like the Blancheforts. Foxes were said to commune with the Elders in days of old, and every Vith estate had a fox shrine somewhere on the grounds. The fox was carved in a sitting position, its dog-like face looking up to the heavens. Dav once told her there were over a hundred fox shrines located on the grounds, scattered about.

Continuing on, Tweeter led her toward a dense growth of beech trees.

Wait!

She stopped. She was certain the saw the fox statue move. She looked at it; just a large statue of gray stone, marbled and blended somewhat with bits of garnet and olivine. The statue just sat there in its little gazebo looking at the sky.

Following Tweeter, she plunged into the line of beech trees and left the statue behind, though she was certain she saw it move again, poking its head out of the gazebo.

She arrived after some time at Carahil's Walk, and sat down on the low stone wall surrounding the courtyard, waiting for him. He usually came blundering around a corner, full of charm and wit. The beech trees here were huge and twisted; a black framework holding up a green canopy. Nearby a fast moving creek flowed with dark, cold water. Tweeter flew off to a tree, and hopped around on a branch. He argued with other birds in a fuss.

Carahil was nowhere to be found. She waited and waited.

Nothing.

Through the breaks in the canopy she watched the sky get progressively darker blue as noon approached—a sure way of telling you were far to the north. Every so often she caught a glimpse of silver moving through the green. She saw glimpses of silver horses, birds—much bigger ones than Tweeter—rabbits, frogs and, something that looked like a bear gazing at her through the branches. Lady Poe sure loved creating Silver tech animals.

But, no seal. No Carahil. Maybe he didn't need her help after all. Knowing his love of pranks, maybe he was jesting. Maybe it was all a big joke.

Ki felt a bit of disappointment pass through her.

She saw something sitting on the courtyard wall near the trees. Curious, she got up to see what it was. It was a book entitled *Carahil's Magic Book of Things To-Do and Memorable Quotes.*

His diary, the one he brought everywhere with him, conjuring it up whenever he wanted to write something down. Her husband also did things like that. He was a note-taker too.

She picked the book up (it was way heavy) and opened it. The silvery pages were lineless (Ki hated paper with no lines), with little illegible scratchings here and there. Carahil needed to work on his penmanship. Of course he didn't have hands, so perhaps he should be forgiven.

Leafing through, she turned to a series of simple sketches. The sketches were three-quarter bust shots: scratchy, child-like, and they were vandalized with Carahil's beloved TO DO lists and little random doodles. Yet, they had definite sense of style and she could recognize each one. There was Dav and Syg, drawn full of life and bounce, several of Lady Poe, and one of Ennez the Hospitaler with his winged helmet. Another drawing was of a stocky fellow wearing a triangle hat and trench coat. He smoked a pipe. She didn't recognize the man. Standing next to him was a tiny, black-haired woman with round eyes and a ridiculous smile. She seemed to have a Shadowmark, just like Syg and Lady Poe—odd. On the next page was a drawing of herself, holding a mug. It was just an abstract sketch, but she liked it, was flattered by it. Her husband had painted several portraits of her back home in Tusck, but they were all very ideal and angelic, painted in a fashion that her husband wished her to be, as opposed to what she actually was. This sketch here was grittier, slightly annoyed. It was more true to her.

She'd have to ask him if she could have it, or, maybe he could do another one. On the next page was an abstract sketch of a weird tree with branches like tentacles. She got the hint of planets and galaxies nurtured in the twisting branches of the tree. At the top of the drawing Carahil looked down on a basketful of kittens nestled in the branches. Carahil and his kittens.

Looking at it further, the sketch was odd. The basket the kittens were in was round instead of rectangular. The kittens were drawn all around the basket, some were even upside down. Carahil had drawn himself holding something in his flippers; several oblong objects that looked like dolls. And, he drew himself with a tear rolling down his face. It was actually kind of a sad sketch.

On the facing page was a series of quick jots. These Ki was able to make out, but just barely.

They said:

COMPLICATIONS

1)—Sisters

a)—Why did the Sisters come to Blanchefort?

b)—Sister, dubbed "Blondie" by LB, was not due her fertile period for years hence. What happened? Why that particular Sister, who had a long-standing affection for LB?

c)—Did someone tamper? Somebody must have tampered with Blondie to create chaos. Need to investigate.

2)—Messages and other Ill portents

a)—Have become aware of a troubling series of messages that have been showing up with fair regularity. Didn't see anyone leaving messages. I should have seen.

a)—CB has received messages and heard voices.

b)—LB has received messages. I think he has seen things too.

c)—DO has received messages. DO is a project. Need to properly motivate DO. His help will make this easier.

d)—MK has received messages, heard things and seen things. Something pursuing MK. Need to keep a sharp eye. Provide encouragement.

e)—Messages all signed: "M"

3)—Wildcards

a)—Several characters have made their way into this scenario that could be problematic.

b)—PV, a sad case. Very powerful—someone has had at her and made her greater than what she was. Must let her play her part, if this is to be a success, no matter how much it hurts. Her role is key.

c)—LM: ????????? What is LM? Who is LM? Got a mind like a jar of peanut butter—can't sift through it. Don't understand. Mutation? And what are those things under his clothes?

TO DO: Research LM.

4)—Assessment

a)—Somebody's cheating. M is cheating, and annoying me too.

b)—Checked with CA—claim innocence.

c)—Allow PV to continue. Though, if she harms anyone it'll be MY FAULT!!

d)—Watch LM and assess his situation.

e)—Messages: a demon's hand is at work. One Demon or several Demons might be doing it.

f)—4 Demon's missing from Windage—checked roster.

g)—Identity of Missing D's (as posted in the weekly Windage rostrum): Barr-Igura, Ibilex, Mabsornath, Maiax

h)—Probable candidate of message-sender: Maiax. Need to keep a sharp eye.

i)—Maiax's presence will prove problematic. Must protect MK.

Maiax? Who's Maiax?

She put the book away. On the other side of the wall was a small box full of sleeping kittens. She knew Carahil liked to adopt lost kittens, and here was the proof. She thought to bring them in out of the chilly air, but they seemed perfectly happy where they were. Several smooth rocks bunched around the box were warm. He must have heated them up somehow. Sitting on the rocks was a kettle with "MILK" printed on the side. A saucer sat nearby. Carahil was doing a good job taking care of them.

She looked around again. Still no Carahil, just his book and his kittens. The kittens were fine, saved by their silvery protector. When was he going to come charging to her rescue? She left the courtyard, and, with Tweeter's help, made her way back to her tower. She found her dress, cleaned and folded, sitting on her desk chair when she arrived.

There was also a note sitting on her desk. She thought about putting it aside unread, but her curiosity quickly got the better of her. Opening the note, it said:

DO NOT GO TO *HIM*!! YOU
HAVE BEEN WARNED!! –M

Another creepy note. "M" again. Who was "M"? What was "M"? This one couldn't be from her commander. Carahil seemed to think "M" stood for Maiax.

"Who's Maiax?" The chicken-scratch in Carahil's diary mentioned something about Maiax and demons. Demons? She didn't quite like the sound of that. She sat down at the Holo-net terminal and fired it up. She tried looking the name up, but, being a novice at using the Holo-net, she came up with nothing but several entries for businesses and places named Maiax. There were quite a few. She hated the Kanan Holo-net—too hard to use. The Blues had it all yucked up. The Archen-net back home on Onaris was much more to her liking.

She supposed she could check with her husband. He'd probably be able to tell her who Maiax is right off the top of his head. But, checking the time, he was conducting class now, and she was mad at him to boot. She'd figure it out herself.

She looked at Tweeter sitting there on the shelf. She had a thought.

"Tweeter," she said, "I'm looking for information on a creature named Maiax. Can you lead me to anything pertaining to this entity?"

He chirped and flew to the door. She got up and followed him out into the corridor and down the lift. She wondered just how abstract a command she could give to Tweeter and expect him to successfully execute it. If Tweeter could lead her to pay dirt on Maiax, then who knows what his full capabilities might be. Did Lady Poe realize he could do things like this? Probably not.

He led her out into the main hall of the castle and into the quiet southern wing. This was a part of the castle she had never seen. Things looked even less familiar to her than usual. She saw no staff along the way; the southern wing appeared quite deserted. Tweeter wound through several long corridors into a central nave where four large cathedrals loomed side by side. The cathedrals were empty and silent; murky with the solemn light of stained glass. The tart smell of age-old incense hung in the air. Tweeter veered to the right and flew into a medium-sized library tucked snuggly off the main drag. She followed him in.

He settled on a cozy confusion of bookcases in the rear of the library and came to rest in front of a thick, hide-bound tome.

Ki grabbed it by the spine and slid it out. "This the one?" she asked.

It was a thick book of mythology and lore. Surprised by its weight, she lugged it with two arms to a reading table. There was a book already sitting on the table on a wooden stand. It was opened to a colorful illustration of several spherical gems that caught her eye. The gems were colored with reds, purples and greens, like fruits. Pretty to look at. There was a short notation.

BRIGHTSTONES

Vith Name: *Illia-Cranthor*. Ancient beryl stones once used by the Elders for the purposes of operating a number of wondrous technological devices, most of which have fallen into obscurity. The Brightstones have been attributed with a number of various useful properties over the centuries, including:

1) Unlimited power source.
2) Ability to affect climate over a large area.
3) Self-Replication.
4) Ability to teleport from place to place over vast distances

In 004562ex, the Sisterhood of Light undertook a series of quests over the course of one hundred years to gather all known Brightstones (referred to collectively as the Tasks of Va and Falquil). The origins of the Stellar Fleet can, in part, be traced to these quests. The Sisters recovered, as a result of these quests, 10, 500 Brightstones (all documented). The recovery of the Brightstones coincides with the ascendency of the Sisters as a major League sect in 004663ex. No further Brightstones have been uncovered through the centuries, though four are thought to reside somewhere in Xaphan space. It is also suspected that the House of Want discovered the methods used to create Brightstones, and incorporated them as functional parts of the various advanced machines they invented before departing the League in 000011ax. The current whereabouts of the stones recovered by the Sisters is unknown outside of the Sisterhood.

Cool stuff; she'd have to look at it further later. Ki pushed the book aside and threw the one she'd been carrying to the tabletop. Smelling of old leather and vellum, she leafed through the thick pages. Lots of stories written longhand in both Vith and in the common League tongue; lots of pictures too. She found a detailed picture of a space station being destroyed. Zall 88; she remembered that one from when she was a kid. Zall 88 was a Xaphan space station over Gothan; a place of great learning and enlightenment, which was odd for them as such things usually weren't high on the Xaphan's list. It was looted and destroyed by the House of Xandarr centuries ago, who was jealous of their secrets. All dead. Xaphans loved to beat each other up.

Moving on, she eventually found what she was looking for in an illustrated story called: *The Death of the Bodice*.

The story was long and sad recounting the history of the House of Bodice, and their eventual extinction three thousand years ago. There it was, Tweeter was right on the money:

Maiax was a creature whom the Bodice turned to for help.

Maiax lied to the Bodice.

Maiax tricked them and offered up their bodies as a burnt offering to a horned god.

Maiax was a demon ...

Maiax deceives the Bodice

Demon? The Bodice were gone, and it was Maiax who did it.

There was an illustration of the Bodice being sent to their fiery death. Looming over them, wringing his hands, was a lurid, monstrous thing with lust-filled eyes and a huge head watching as they died. Maiax. It was a creepy picture.

So, was this Maiax fellow at work here? Was he leaving she and Syg little notes? Why? What for? Did he want to sacrifice her to a horned god too? Where would that get him?

She heard a bumping in the shelves and a rustle of paper. She looked up from her reading and whirled around. She no longer felt alone. Ki closed the book and made to put it back. She heard something: "… zaaaaaaaaaaaaal…"

She listened a moment. Another bump, shuffling and a hint of movement. Something was moving through the stacks. "Tweeter?" she said. "Let's get out of here!" She left the book where it was and tore out of the library into the hallway, moving fast on her long legs. Abandoning any pretense of noble decorum, she fell into a full sprint in her robe. Tweeter flapped slightly in front of her. She thought she saw something come to the library threshold in her side vision, but she didn't look back. She didn't want to see.

Tweeter led her back into the familiar areas of the castle and she began encountering the staff going about their work. They wanted to know why she was running. She told them she thought she saw an intruder in the southern wing. Several staff went back there, and returned several minutes later.

They saw nothing.

Ki calmed herself and caught her breath. She felt a little silly for panicking, and for informing the staff. Dav always told her his old castle was haunted, and now she'd probably experienced her first ghost and freaked out over it. The staff didn't seem to think anything; they were probably used to ghosts. She followed Tweeter back up to her room; her thoughts full of Zall 88, the Bodice, and Maiax, a demon. Her imagination was certainly working overtime.

She was determined to sulk when she got back to her room, to sit there in her robe and feel sorry for herself some more—to be mad at the whole world: to be mad at her husband for kicking this whole sorry mess off, to be mad at Dav for not having the decency to beg and plead her on his knees to stay, and, to be mad at Syg, the interloper, for breaking up the fellowship in the first place.

And, lastly, to be mad at herself, for allowing her pride to ruin her life.

She sat on her bed and stewed for a bit, then, bored, she went back out on the terrace. In the clear air she could see all the way down into the brandtball pitch at Sarfortnim College; Pendar Tower had a great view of it. A game was in progress, and she watched the tiny movement back and forth across the pitch as the three teams, mounted on wheeled cars, jostled the ball around. The yellow team from Saga Convent appeared to be cleaning up the magenta and sky blue teams: the `40's appeared to be in trouble in this set. She loved brandtball, it was much more suited to her personal taste, unlike bowling which she disliked, especially the prospect of having to do it naked, which Syg was pushing hard for. Tweeter sat with her on the terrace the whole time, bopping around in her lap, occasionally flying off and disappearing to chase other birds, though all she had to do was say "Tweeter" and he'd reappear, ready to go. She looked around for that cat she'd seen earlier, in case he was still hungry for Tweeter. She didn't see him. She got up and looked over the side of the terrace.

Just a sheer drop down to the rocks far below. It made her a little dizzy. Brave cat.

She returned to her seat and sat out there until the game ended; the yellows from the convent appeared to win in straight sets despite being double-teamed by the blues and magenta clad `40's. Ah, you can't win them all. She went back into her room.

She was restless. She sat down at her desk. The creepy note was still there, possibly written by a demon's hand. She pushed it aside and fired up her terminal.

A message appeared as the cone began to form:

Lost kittens are where you find them. Think happy thoughts!

Ki chuckled a little. She must be losing her peasant mind.

The cone was ready and she checked her Marine login for messages—more out of habit than anything else. She figured, given her hasty gate the other day, her account would be dead. To her surprise, it was still open. To her further surprise, she had several new messages from her Commander's office. The messages were long and rambling, apologizing to no end for her treatment, for her drumming out, and for the seizing of her uniforms. They stated she was retroactively promoted from private to X-Lt, a de-facto major, a jump of two grades. They also stated she was to receive a commensurate back pay of two months reflecting the grade change. Another message said that a Marine cutter ship will be arriving at noon on the morrow to take her anywhere she wanted to go. Lastly, they asked for her to contact Captain Davage at once and perform a final de-brief. They enclosed an active authorization code for her to use when contacting him.

Dav.

No doubt the Marines had already contacted him regarding getting another Marine installed as her replacement, and he, suspecting her treatment, made his displeasure known. Scrambling, they sought to make amends for they sorely wanted a Marine as his first officer, and they were willing and eager to thoroughly grease her to help pave the way for it.

It was good to have friends.

Smiling, her previous bitterness falling away, and, wanting to see him and hear his voice, she responded to the commander's message, stating she shall accomplish the debrief as requested. She then contacted Fleet Com, gave them the code and, after a few minutes, Dav appeared on the cone. Her heart jumped. She was grateful they were still in Com range.

He was in his quarters, his coat and gun belt off—it must be night bell. Behind him, the stars moved across the window.

"Dav!" she said with glee. "It's good to see you!"

He moved the screen to face the couch and sat down. Syg, wearing her nightgown, appeared and snuggled in next to him on the couch. They were both all smiles.

"Hi, Ki!" she said.

"Ki, I've been so worried about you," Dav said, the relief at seeing her clear in his voice. "I inferred from my previous conversation with Lt. Carbomier, of the Stellar Marines, that your out-processing session didn't go well."

"Well, Dav, I can't really blame them. I gave them no notice, I didn't even let my commander know what was going on. I didn't show them the proper courtesy either—it goes both ways I guess."

Her arms around Dav's neck, Syg chimed in. "They are sending a ship or something to meet us in space. They want to board. Dav hung up on them, you should have seen it," she said happily.

"Dav, they really want my replacement to be a Marine—it's important to them. Please, as a favor to me, at least let them come aboard and hear what they have to say. This whole deal ... it isn't their fault."

"Have they made amends? Are you a Lt. still?"

"I am Dav. Actually, they made me an X-Lt."

"Really? And passage? Are you stranded there in Blanchefort?"

"They are sending a cutter ship tomorrow."

"Good, good. Take it if you wish, or stay and be our guest for as long as you need."

"Hey, Dav, is the southern wing of the castle haunted?"

"Yes," he said.

"The whole thing is haunted, Ki," Syg said. "Isn't it neat?"

Ki shook her head and got her Pendar Tower key out. "Wonderful. Where should I leave this when I depart?"

"Keep it, Ki, and use it whenever you want. Pendar Tower shall be your home away from home."

"How's the castle, Ki—do you need anything?" Syg asked.

"Castle's great, a little empty and frickin' haunted, but great. And no, I'm fine. I don't need anything."

"If you change your mind, be sure to see Madastrella, our Head-of-Staff. She'll get whatever you want. Also, I'm certain that Poe's gone on another outing, yes?"

"She is."

"Did she leave you a Tweeter?"

"Yes, she did." Kilos reached up. "Come here, Tweeter." Tweeter came down and settled on her finger. "Handiest thing. How long will he last do you think?"

Syg thought. "How long? Well, if Poe made him for you, then, I suppose he'll last as long as he's in fairly close proximity to you. There's no expiration date on Silver tech, he'll last as long as he was made to last."

"Good, good. Hey, Syg, I wanted to ask you. You like crawling around in the tunnels under the castle, right? Have you ever ended up in that little grocery in the middle of the village on Bloodstein Road?"

Syg rolled her eyes up and thought for a moment. "The little grocery on Bloodstein Road? Oh!! Oh, yes!! I believe so. There's that strange pillar with the garlic in the back, right, with the hole at the bottom? I think I scared the grocer half to death when I popped out. The poor fellow was all 'My Countess' this and 'My Countess' that."

"He was coming back to see if I needed anything and then I was gone—stuck in the hole. He probably thought I was a ghost or something," Ki said.

"Did you make it all the way to the castle going that route? That's a pretty tight squeeze."

"What are you saying, Syg?" Ki asked laughing.

"Nothing, nothing … it's just that's pretty small going. Even I got a little stuck. Also, you shouldn't do any tunneling alone—that can be very dangerous. I don't want to have to worry about you."

"You do it alone."

"Well yes, but I can always Waft out of a tight spot—I'm not a good example to follow. If you want to do some exploring, there are a lot of fun, beginner-level tunnels near the Holt courtyard in the Grove. You can't get in trouble in those. Just make sure to let the staff know where you're going and when you're planning to finish up, so they will know to look for you. That's the main thing about tunneling and caving—someone always needs to know where you are—just for in case."

"No sissy beginner's tunnels, Syg. And, I'm not alone—I've got Tweeter with me. I asked Tweeter to get me up to the castle as fast as possible and up we went. It was fun … I can see why so like exploring those tunnels so much."

"Wait a minute!! You used Tweeter to get through—that's cheating!"

"Well, scrabbling around in the dark, hopelessly lost, doesn't sound like fun to me. Besides, Syg, not all of us have an arcane Black Hat compass buried inside us like you do."

"Alright, touché," she said laughing.

"Hey, maybe when you get back, we can all hit the tunnels together, and crawl around a little. You haven't explored it all yet, Syg, have you?"

"No, not by a mile."

"Good, then we'll make it a date. We'll crawl around awhile, and then wash the dirt out at the pubs. Maybe catch a match. Just the three of us."

Davage laughed. "You two … love mucking around in the dark, don't you?"

"What do you say? Is it a date?"

"Fine with me."

"Me too."

They talked for a bit more, then the cone went blank as they Com'ed out, and Ki was all alone again in Pendar Tower. Still wearing her robe, she fell asleep in front of her terminal, the holos swirling in a dance around her sleeping head. She dreamed of her friends.

* * * * *

Ki awoke the next day. As before, she took Tweeter and went down to the kitchen.

Again she ate alone in the huge, empty, Capricos Hall. When she finished, she went back to her room to dress, and then stepped out onto the huge terrace overlooking the village and the bay. Down below, she saw the red and black rocket-shape of a Marine cutter ship at rest at the dock. All she had to do was go down there, get on and go home, to Tusck.

Home. Where she could be a peasant along with everybody else.

She grabbed her bag and followed Tweeter back out to the Grove. She was going to walk to the beech hanger and go back in the hole. She was going to go down the ladder, through the cavern, into the crawl and out the hole in the grocery—probably giving the grocer the fright of his life again. Then, she was going to go to the cutter, go home, have kids and become an old woman.

She locked up Pendar Tower, and followed Tweeter out into the green.

Ahead, to her right was the huge mushroom-shaped mound of Dead Hill, a massive Blanchefort necropolis. She remembered Dav telling her that he often could see the ghosts of his ancestors looking down from up there. Their withered faces, their reaching hands …

A disembodied spectral gown jumped out at Ki from a stand of trees. Headless, its arms waved.

With a cry, Ki jumped back, again reaching for her SK that wasn't there.

The gown slumped, shiny strings caught the sunlight, and a laughing Carahil came from around the corner. "Hohohoh! Oh, Kilos … forgive me … I couldn't help it!! Thought you could use a little good humor. You screamed almost as loud as my mother, Lady Poe, did the other day!! Hohohoho!"

Ki glared at him. "V-Very funny, Carahil."

"Oh, please don't be sore, just a bit of good humor. I've got to get this gown back into the Countess's closet soon or I'm a goner … but it's just so much fun!"

"Goner, huh," Ki said with thoughts of stealing the gown dancing through her head.

Carahil cut down the gown and, holding it in his mouth, shook it to clear the leaves and dirt. "So," he said, "are you going somewhere?"

"I'm leaving on the cutter ship that's waiting for me in the village."

"Really, heading home, are you? And … our agreement?"

"What about it? Where were you yesterday? I waited for you. Didn't see anything but your book and your cats."

"The kittens you mean? Did you feed them?"

"What?"

"Feed them. Did you feed the kittens? I left some milk."

She was a little taken aback. "No, that's your job. They're your cats."

He smiled. "Sure it's my job; doesn't mean I don't need a little help sometimes. I was hoping you'd feed them for me; now look, they missed their lunch yesterday. And, by the way, they're not my kittens. I have simply been entrusted with their well-being." He looked up at her. "Can you take this, please? The countess's gown I mean."

Ki took Syg's gown and Carahil reached behind the wall, taking the kitten's box in his teeth. "Well, no harm done. I gave them an extra-big breakfast this morning. Come on, let's get them inside." They began walking back toward the castle.

"Sorry," Ki said. "Sorry about the kittens. I should have given them a little milk. So, where were you yesterday?"

"I was indisposed yesterday—there is a great deal to prepare. I left a note here somewhere," he said looking around. "I am ready to begin now, however." His voice was a tad muffled from carrying the box.

Kilos held Syg's gown aloft as she walked, trying to keep it from dragging. "Well, I'm not. I'm sorry, Carahil, but I have to go. My ship's waiting for me in the village. My husband is waiting for me."

"You're going to play this out to the bitter end, aren't you?" he said.

"What do you mean?"

They walked into the clearing. To their left was the fox statue in its stone gazebo. "Kilos, as time is short, I'll bite—I'll say it."

"Say what? By the way—that fox statue was moving by itself yesterday."

"Of course it was moving. It was possessed yesterday, but it's fine today. I really need you. I need you to help me. That's what you wanted to hear, isn't it?"

Kilos looked dubiously at the statue. "Possessed? By what? And, what do you need me for, oh 'All-Powerful Elemental Spirit? I'm a Brown, I can't do anything. I have no Gifts. I can't see through walls, I don't have super strength, I can't teleport or disguise myself, I can't Dirge, and I can't look into people's souls."

"It was possessed by a demon. Don't worry about it. It's gone. That is precisely why I need you. You, Kilos, as a Brown, can go places and do things that no Blue could ever hope to—did you know that? You've no Gifts of the Mind, and that is true, yet you've still your heart and your courage and your devotion. How many times did you stand Giftless, back-to-back with Lord Blanchefort, you saving his life and he saving yours? I am asking you to show that same courage now … to stand with me and help me save them."

"I don't even have a gun."

They approached the castle. "No gun? Oh, oh … what's this? What's this I wonder?"

Kilos felt something heavy and solid suddenly fill up the limp structure of Syg's gown. She reached down through the neck and found a large gun hidden within. It was a Marine SK pistol, full magazine, in excellent condition.

She felt the weapon with her hands. "This … is my SK, the one I turned in, I'd know it anywhere. How'd you …"

"Yeah, I wasn't sure if you wanted a brand new SK or your old one back. So, I gambled and got you your old one. You want a different kind of gun? You want a Grenville 40, or a Hertamer? How about an Inseroth D series?"

Ki was disgusted. "How about no! An Inseroth? Give me a damn break. I'll take an Inseroth if I want to die." Expertly, she worked the finely crafted controls, cocked the primers and set it to safety.

"The SK's the best gun ever made. Inseroth my butt! I could use a holster, though," she said.

"Oh, oh … what's this …" A holster and belt came out of the gown next.

"It's great to be me," he said.

"Certainly don't mind doting on yourself, do you?" Kilos smiled, put the belt on and holstered the SK. A wave of relief spread over her, its familiar weight at her hip a huge comfort.

They arrived at the rear of the castle. Tweeter popped up and flew into the trees, again feisty with the other birds. "One moment," Carahil said, loping into the castle with his box of kittens. Ki pulled her SK and checked the magazine: fully loaded, twenty-five shots, .50 caliber short jacket. The good stuff.

After a minute or two, Carahil returned, minus the box. "The kitchen staff promised to feed them three times a day. They'll be fine." His diary appeared. He scribbled in a few things with a marker in his teeth. It then vanished, along with the marker.

Ki popped the chamber and re-holstered her gun. "What about my ship, how am I going to get home?"

"If, after all this is over, you still want to go home, I will take you there. Now, shall we? We've far to travel."

Ki was still holding Syg's gown. "What about this? This needs back in Syg's wardrobe."

"Here," Carahil said, "let me." He took the gown in his teeth and bounded into the castle. He returned a few minutes later. "Done. Are you ready?"

Ki looked up and saw Tweeter sitting in the dark branches of the tangled ash trees, still fussing with other birds. Smiling, she opened her bag. "Hop in, Tweeter, we're going." Tweeter winged down from the branches and disappeared into the depths of the bag.

Carahil shook his head. "Tweeter … he sure does look delicious."

Ki glared at Carahil. "If you're hungry, I'd go a get a sandwich before we start, if I were you, and leave Tweeter alone. By the way, where are we headed?"

"South, about fifteen hundred miles."

"Where's the ripcar? I guess I'm driving since you don't have hands. I'm not a very good driver, I'm warning you."

"No foolish ripcar, Kilos. You'll be taking Air-Carahil. Much more stylish than a ripcar any day."

Kilos looked at Carahil and laughed. "Little small, aren't you?"

Before Ki could blink, Carahil was suddenly huge. Dav had said the original Carahil was fifteen feet tall. This Carahil was now easily that big.

"You were saying? Hahaha! Now, time is of the essence, let us be off," he said, his voice echoing a bit with his size.

Dubious, Kilos, holding her bag, climbed up his back—his skin was smooth and strong. She found a comfortable spot on his back and sat down. After another moment, Carahil took flight. Not the quick, jerking movements she was used to with Dav in the ripcar, but, smooth measured strokes. Soon, they were high in the air, level with the tallest castle spires. Ki felt safe and snug on his back. She didn't even feel cold.

Hey, wait a second! Ki saw that one of the noble bronze statues lining the battlements of the northern wing was wearing Syg's gown. Others had several of Syg's knickers pulled over their heads like little caps. Ki was open-mouthed in shock, but then she started laughing; Carahil's sense of humor starting to agree with her.

He veered easily to the south, the vast mountains stretching as far as the eye could see. There was huge Mt. Vith, big and cone-shaped, and to the west was the slightly smaller Mt. Durst, also cone-shaped. Far away, past Mt. Durst, like a white and green toy, was Castle Durst.

"Through the mountains, or over them?" Carahil asked as he settled into smooth level flight.

"Over them, please."

He smiled. "Over the mountains it is."

8—Larsen of Zenon, Verlin of Hobby

The Marine cutter *Quincy* appeared through the murk. A tiny ship, not a sixteenth the size of the *Seeker,* it Com'ed in the traditional manner, sought permission to come a-beam, or directly in front of the ship, and dock. The cutter, though small, was a bit too large to fit into the *Seeker's* internal docking bays. Deftly, the little red and black rocket-shaped vessel maneuvered into position and docked with a clank. The colorful Marine cutter stood in contrast to the white Fleet *Seeker*—all Fleet vessels were painted white.

It wasn't long before another small vessel emerged from the darkness. This time it was a Fleet *Tekel*-class scout ship, the *Dorset. Tekels* looked like three bananas evenly spaced around an ovular-shaped saucer, hence their apt nick-name: the Banana-Boat. It, like the Marine vessel, wanted to send a party aboard. After the usual courtesies were exchanged, a ripcar from the *Dorset* made berth in Bay 2.

* * * * *

<You're going to get it later, Dav! What have I told you about this?> Syg, hands on hips, telepathied as the door to his office closed. She looked good and furious standing in the corridor in her gray gown, her big green eyes on fire.

Davage sat down behind his desk, the white painted *Dorset,* the Banana-Boat, standing at nine, appeared motionless several miles away through his windows.

<Dav … open this damn door right now, or, I swear I'll blast it down! Dav!>

Syg wasn't kidding when she said her emotions were going to be out of sorts—she was frothing mad. The chairs in Davage's office were in short supply. Two Marines, a male and a female, glorious in their red uniforms, sat to one side, and two Fleet officers, a Commander and a Lieutenant, both men, sat on the other.

<Dav!! Answer me!! I want in!!>

<There's no room, Syg, and, again, this is Fleet business!>

<Then move to the conference room if there's no space!! I'll be waiting for you there—and you better show, or you and I are going to have a fight like never before!!>

He thought he heard something hit the door. She appeared to be very put off.

"Sir," the male Marine said, "this is a great honor. I am Major Westwind, 53rd Marines, and I wish to proudly introduce Lt. Verlin, also of the 53rd Marines."

Lt. Verlin spoke up. "Sir, it is a great pleasure for me to be here. I have long followed your exploits," she said in a cultured, South Kana accent. Distinctly Remnath if he wasn't mistaken.

Davage looked at Lt. Verlin; she was tall, blonde-headed, very similar to Kilos. The Marines, apparently, were hedging their bet by trotting out a virtual Kilos look a-like. But, in this case, Lt. Verlin wasn't a Brown, clearly she was a lady of standing, and a Remnath at that. She sat properly, with lady-like grace. Her face was made up, within Marine regulations, and her golden hair was set in a Remnath style. Her eyes, her cheek-bones, her accent, her hair; she had the Hobby look, an old Remnath Great House from Howell.

"Lt.," Davage said, "are you by chance a lady of House Hobby?"

"I am, sir, yes."

"You father is Lord Merivel?"

"He is, sir."

"Good man, honest merchant," Davage said.

Verlin blushed and rustled a bit in her chair. "Sir, I had the pleasure of briefly meeting you some years ago, before I joined the Marines."

Davage was interested. "Really?" he said looking hard at her. "I must apologize, Lt., you have me at a disadvantage. I take great pride in being able to recall faces and … I cannot place yours."

"Oh, I was wearing a muffler. My face was obscured."

Davage smiled. "All bundled up, eh? I suppose that Blanchefort is uncomfortably cold for someone from Howell. I am assuming we met in Blanchefort village, yes?"

"Yes sir. It certainly was cold, however, I assume that Howell might be a bit too warm for you as well."

"Indeed, I just about melted in Provst not long ago."

Major Westwind spoke up. "Sir, we feel Lt. Verlin will be an ideal candidate for you to consider in your selection process for first officer. She graduated top in her class at Marine Academy 4 on Bonham. She is expert on Marine sensing stations, and in Xaphan history and tactics. She is also fully briefed on *Straylight* operations, including Ops, Missive and Navigation, and should hit the ground running for you."

Lt. Verlin smiled, sitting straight and tall—again, sort of like Kilos, but more regal; clearly a Blue Lady, not a Brown.

"Lt., it is your wish to serve as first officer aboard the *Seeker*?"

"It is, sir. I have followed your exploits through the years with great interest, and very much wish to serve, yes sir."

Davage was impressed—certainly seemed eager enough, this lady of Hobby. But, what about her soul, her spirit? Davage could teach any person to be the first officer, he couldn't however, give her a heart. That she had to bring with her.

House Hobby—Davage couldn't think of any other Hobbies in the Fleet. Merchants, a long line of them.

"Lt.," he asked, interested, "if I may? House Hobby is a fine and honorable southern House, merchants plying an honest and true trade. I have transacted business with them many times myself, and have always come away satisfied. I cannot recall any other member of House Hobby currently in the service, be it Fleet, Marine or otherwise. May I ask, why you have chosen to serve, and not batoned to some fortunate gentleman at this point?"

Verlin looked down a moment, then smiled. "Sir, it's true, my House has not done its fair duty in the past."

"I did not mean to imply that your House has not done its duty for the League."

"No, I know, sir, thank you. I … I always wanted to see the stars … to leave Howell and find my own way for a bit. I looked up into the night sky, and watched the Fleet ships coming and going through my brother's telescope; the stories that each of those ships could tell. And, I remember Mirendra … watching all those ships coming home blackened, ruined, and I wanted to do my part. I wanted to make something of myself, so that, someday, when I have children, I will have stories of my own to tell. I want to be able to teach them something too."

Davage bowed. "I see, and yours is a sentiment that I share with you. I understand fully. Thank you for sharing that with me, Lt."

He sat and thought a moment. "Major Westwind, may I borrow your SK please?"

The Major looked a bit confused. Tentatively, he unclasped his holster. "My weapon is not palm spranded, sir," he said, and carefully handed Davage his SK, butt first.

Davage accepted the weapon, pulled the mag out, cleared the chamber, and set it down on his desktop.

"Lt., I'm afraid I hear the stun bottle leaking."

"Sir?" she said confused.

"Yes, most definitely. It's making a dreadful noise. Will you be good enough to clear it for me, please?"

The Major smiled, sat back and watched.

She slowly picked the gun up. With her graceful Hobby hands she then began taking the huge pistol apart.

"With your eyes closed, please, Lt.," Davage added. "*Straylights* ... one never knows when the lights will go out."

Verlin looked at him, then closed her eyes and began working. She started slowly, hesitantly, feeling the gun with her long, slim fingers, removing the pins. After a few seconds she picked up the pace. Soon she was expertly departing the weapon, turning it this way and that, removing small piece after small piece and setting them in an orderly fashion on the desktop. After several more seconds, she had the gun in seven pieces and held the stun bottle aloft.

Davage sat there a moment. He could smell her perfume, a fine southern Remnath scent. Kilos wore perfume about as often as Syg wore shoes.

"My mistake, the bottle seems fine," Davage said. "Please reassemble, and, again, you needn't open your eyes."

Eyes closed, she deftly reassembled the gun, and soon, it was back together. As a final test, she dry cocked the chamber with the usual, satisfying "Chu-Chuck!" sound.

"The SK is the standard weapon of the Stellar Marines, it is our lifeblood and heritage, Captain. Every Marine should know its workings in and out," she said handing it back to the Major.

"I agree fully, Lt., and well done. Really, an expert showing."

Davage offered her a cloth, and smiling, she wiped her hands, removing the light oil and grease from the SK's innards.

<Dav!! I'm sitting here in the conference room awaiting your arrival. I'll not wait much longer! If I have to come marching back over there, you can rest assured that I will be blasting down the door, and a scene will commence to be made!!>

The Fleet contingent began stirring. "Captain if I may interrupt for a moment. I am Commander Forsburg, Lord of Wiln, adjutant chief to Admiral Garth of the 10th Fleet. Sir, we are shocked at the sudden departure of your Lt. Kilos, however, we at the Admiralty see this occasion as a grand opportunity. Sir, the Admiralty feels the fine vessel *Seeker,* once our proudest war bird, is falling by the wayside to other ships."

"I see," Davage said. "And how so?"

"It is obvious sir, the *Seeker* is always off in some far-flung reach. Never in the League, never accommodating an Admiral, or other distinguished passengers of note."

The Marines looked at each other.

"Sir," Davage said, "the *Seeker* is, first and foremost, a war vessel. The sworn mission of this ship is to uphold the ancient Elder Promise, to fight the Xaphans and defend life, and the *Seeker* has done that. Ferrying passengers, grand and noteworthy as they may be, is a secondary concern."

"Sir, the day of the Xaphan is past. The League is victorious and there are none with strength to stand before us. There is no more evil to fight, sir."

"Commander—there is always more evil for good to fight."

The Commander gave a curt smile. "And so, well said. I have in attendance with me Lt. Larsen, formerly of the 10th Fleet office in Bern. We strongly suggest that you consider him for the position of first officer. We feel, with his assistance, the *Seeker* will once again be the talk of the Fleet, as it rightly should be. And, please note, Captain, Lt. Larson's Programmability is rated at: *Ellendni.*"

Lt. Larsen sat there, be-decked in his Fleet uniform, and blushed a little. Oh, the Fleet and its love of the Sisters. Programmability was *everything* in the Fleet, Davage thought. He looked him over: tall, black-haired—clearly a Lord of Zenon, a centrally located House at Blue Pierce.

Davage had to take a moment—for someone who prided himself on not being overly enamored with League Society and posh inner-circles, he was certainly up on most if not all of the Great Houses, despite himself. As a boy, his father, Sadric, had beat it into his head. Hours and hours of Society this and Society that. As his grandfather Maserfeld had drummed CARG lore into Sadric's head, he, in turn, forced League Society down his. Hours and hours learning to recognize minute detail: a distinctive turn of the brow, the tint of the hair, a certain fabric or scent. Sitting there as a boy, stewing, wanting nothing more than to run off, hide or get into another knuckle busting fight with his sister, Pardock. But, as a Fleet captain, Davage had to admit, the ability to recognize familial traits, their likes and dislikes, their history and family tree; to know a bit about the person before a word had been spoken without having The Stare was very handy indeed. His son, Lord Kabyl, once born, shall have both CARG and Society lore applied to him. Both, it seemed, were handy in a pinch.

"Lt. Larsen," Davage said. "You are, no doubt a lord of House Zenon?"

"Yes, sir, well determined."

Commander Forsburg chimed in. "Yes, Captain, Lt. Larsen has a very high Programmability with the Sisterhood, I thought I might mention that once again."

Davage had to keep himself from rolling his eyes. "Yes, very commendable. Bear you the LosCapricos weapon of House Zenon—the GREAT DORE?"

Larson gave a respectful smile. "I do, sir."

"May I see it, please?"

"Yes, sir."

Davage and Larsen stood. Davage unsaddled his CARG and offered it to Larsen—common courtesy dictated a mutual exchange of LosCapricos weapons. Larsen opened his coat and pulled out a silver rod about eight inches long. The rod was handsomely filigreed with a bluish inlay. The Lt. gasped as he took his CARG.

"Elders!!" he said. "It's heavy. I'd heard, but was not fully prepared for its weight."

Davage looked over the GREAT DORE, and admired the craftsmanship. "Sir," he asked. "If I may?"

"You may, sir."

Davage found the hidden stud, and, with a snap, the rod expanded into a man-sized javelin. It vibrated with energy.

"Yes, very finely made. I must say I've never been much to dwell on tradition, but the LosCapricos weapons of old is one tradition I find very much to my liking." Davage retracted the weapon and handed it back, taking his CARG in return.

"Lt., have you ever served aboard a Main Fleet starship?"

"Yes sir. I was the Com officer aboard the *Exody* for three years." Davage's ears pricked up—the *Exody*, a sister vessel.

"Ah, the *Exody*, obviously a ship that is very near to my heart. The Com is a very busy position, full of responsibility."

"Yes sir, it was my honor to serve in that role."

Davage reseated himself and thought a moment. "I appreciate your coming here today, the pair of you," he said addressing both of them. "If I am to be perfectly frank, I tend to promote from within, to suitably reward one of my own for their hard work and dedication."

"Sir," Lt. Larsen said, "that is a wise policy and your crew no doubt appreciate the devotion you show them. However, I am certain that I am not speaking out-of-turn when I say that, given the short notice of this situation, your crew are urgently needed where they are, and shan't be spared."

Davage thought a moment. "Yes, that is true, well said."

Larsen continued. "We strongly feel that, given your dangerous charge, a purpose-assigned officer will not only allow you to keep your valuable crew where they are, but provide you with instant experience and skill at the position."

"So, you both wish to serve aboard the *Seeker*. This is your wish, and not hopes and designs imposed upon you?"

"I wish to serve, sir," Verlin said.

"As do I," Larsen said.

"This vessel shall be in harm's way. Make no mistake, the Xaphans are still out there and they thirst for revenge. Their sects are on the rise, and they are potent with the Gifts. They are spoiling to engage the League afresh, and are simply waiting for the moment to do so. Does such a prospect give either of you pause?"

"No sir," Lt. Verlin said,

"I am eager for the challenge, sir."

Syg barged into his head. *<All right, Lord Blanchefort, you had your chance! Sygillis of Metatron is coming for you, sir, and she is good and angry! I wouldn't want to be you right about now!>*

Whenever Syg referred to herself with her old Black Hat name, Davage knew she was peeved. Quickly, he Sighted in the direction of the conference room, and sure enough, there was a rather rank Syg, rolling up the sleeves of her Blanchefort gown, stomping in his direction. She looked very dissatisfied to say the least. Several crewmen scrambled to get out of her way.

Quickly, Davage continued. "I must say that I am at a loss here. I can see no fault in either of you, at least from this brief initial encounter. There are certain advantages of having a Marine first officer, but I suppose I could use a Fleet voice in my ear as well, least I forget myself."

He stood up. "I will request that both of you remain aboard for the time being, assume the joint role of acting first officer, join me in council and test the waters. There, under trial, we will see who has merit over the other. Also, during this interim period, I will continue to give ear to my crew, should any choose to present themselves as a possible candidate. I suppose when we return to Kana in a few weeks a clear choice will be apparent. Does that meet with your approval, gentlemen and lady?"

Major Westwind stood, and bowed. "It does with us."

Commander Forsburg stood. "Indeed. I am confident you will be delighted to select Lt. Larsen at the conclusion of this trail period."

"It's agreed then. On the morrow we shall begin, that will give the pair of you time to settle into your quarters, and be refreshed."

Davage walked to the door. "Oh, if you will please to allow me to introduce Countess Sygillis of Blanchefort, my beloved wife."

Davage opened it and there was Syg, arriving in a thunder. She looked about, saw all the people staring at her, and bowed in a courtly fashion.

<Oh, that's dirty pool, Dav! Not fair! How am I supposed to yell and scream at you for locking me out when I've been properly introduced?>

<My very thought.>

9—The Hazards of the Old Ones.

After an hour or so, Carahil descended through the layers of light clouds. Though it hadn't felt like it, they must have traveled far. The ubiquitous northern chill was gone, replaced with a comfortable, temperate climate that was much more to Kilos' liking. The mountains rising up all around were also different. Not the bare, jagged, cornice-laced peaks of the Kanan north, these were gentler, covered with purplish growth, overlooking vast conifer forests and quiet lakes. A very lovely area all in all. Carahil landed in a grassy clearing, and Ki jumped off and stretched her legs.

He shook his silver head and scratched. He looked around, made his book appear, consulted it, and then made it vanish just as quickly. "Any thoughts as to where we are, Kilos?" he asked shrinking back down to his usual smallish size.

She looked around. The surroundings looked familiar to her, but she couldn't quite place it. It sort of reminded her of home: of Tusck, of wild Onaris. "No," she finally said. "Nice area, pretty."

Carahil patently lifted a flipper. "Yes, very pretty. That way, about ten miles yonder, are the Tartan Plains, several old Vith chapels lying in ruin. A very lovely setting for young lovers: the solitude, the mountains, the flowers, the picturesque ruins ..."

Ki squinted her eyes. Way off, to the south, she thought she could see the low, spread-out remains and stony ruins of a Vith chapel, scattered before the edge of a dark green forest. She could make out the remnant of a dry riverbed running from the ruins to pretty much right where she was standing. The edges of the ancient riverbed were marked, at regular lengths, by flat objects overgrown with weeds. "Oh, the Tartan Plains! I remember Dav taking Demona of Ryel there once on an outing. Is that where we are headed? I've never been there myself."

"No, Kilos." He pointed with a flipper in the opposite direction. "That's where we're headed. Right there."

Through a stand of trees to the north, were the bases of several tall, purple mountains, about half a mile distant. Dug into the bases of the mountains were six black holes. Even at this distance the holes were the murkiest patches of midnight she'd ever seen. Carahil began loping toward the mountains, with Kilos reluctantly following.

"Those holes? What are those?" she asked.

"They are called the Hazards of the Old Ones."

Ki stopped dead in her tracks. She swallowed. "I've heard of those. Dav's told me about them—warned me about them." Movement in the trees caught her eye. She thought she saw a small, long-armed creature hanging in the branches.

"I see," Carahil said, also stopping. "And, what did Lord Blanchefort tell you?"

The wind picked up a little; a gentle comfortable breeze. The trees swayed a bit. A strange pink bird with a long neck and stilt-like legs took flight and winged its way north. Ahead was another flat overgrown object dotting the edge of the old riverbed that she'd seen running along its length. Ki approached it and knelt down, pretending to examine it.

Something jumped out of the growth and nearly stopped her heart. It was a cat that spat at her and darted away into the trees. Ki put her hands into the tangle of weeds the cat had been hiding in. The old growth was convenient; it hid her fingers … her shaking fingers.

The Hazards of the Old Ones …

"Kilos?" Carahil asked.

She couldn't make her hands stop shaking, and she was determined to hide it. "They're tunnels of some sort, right?" she said digging her hands deep into the growth. "I also remember Dav saying something about strange animals coming from the Hazards of the Old Ones."

She looked around. "That must be it, I saw a weird pink bird and a cat, and something hanging in the branches. Right?"

Carahil laughed. "That was a monkey in the trees, and you missed the elephant."

"Elephant?" she said looking around.

"Yes. I believe you're referring to the Grand Animaliums, that one of them is said to reside hidden in this area; and you and Lord Blanchefort are correct, there is one hidden around here somewhere.

All sorts of novel animals come wandering out of it. But that isn't really related to the Hazards per se—what else?"

"They're … evil. That's what we say back home."

Carahil watched her examine the growth. "Evil?"

"We've got all sorts of stories about them in Tusck. There's something inside, something hidden in the dark, so the stories go. My parents used to say the Devil lived in them. Dav's told me that the Great Lords used to come here to test their bravery, to see how far they could get before turning back. He said nobody ever gets more than a few paces in. Even Dav couldn't get far—he said he saw something in the dark with his Sight."

"Indeed he did. And, to bring you up to date, the Great Lords no longer make a show of attempting to enter the Hazards—that was too disturbing and the fad fell out of favor. They now have refined the practice to simply having lunch in this area. A 'Hazards Lunch' it's aptly called. Very quaint."

She heard a shrill cry off in the distance. "Zaaaaaaaaallll! Zaaaaallll!!" An animal making noise; it stabbed Ki in the soul. Suddenly, the simple act of merely eating lunch in this area seemed a real test of bravery. She had to take her hat off to the Great Lords after all. She wished she could get on Carahil's back and take off; forget this place. Forget lunch.

"Zaaaaaaaaaaaaaall!" came another shriek.

Tasting bile in her mouth, she turned back to the growth, pretending to be interested in it. She cleared the growth and twisted vines away. A plain stone platform was revealed: cracked, overturned, obviously very old. It was decorated with some sort of strange, twisting writing. She thought she could make out the stained image of footprints on the platform's face.

"Kilos?" Carahil said over her shoulder. "Would you care to come with me, please?"

She didn't move. She sat rooted at the platform.

"I think I should tell you," he said. "The 'Message Sender', who's been leaving you and the countess little notes all over the place, is here with us."

Ki reacted, whipping her head around. "Maiax?"

"Yes, he's here too …" Carahil turned and began loping away toward the distant holes in the mountains.

The picture she saw in the book, the scary one, flashed through her mind. She got up and quickly followed him. "Are we in danger?"

"Depends," he replied.

They reached a break in the trees, their branches bobbing in the wind. Ahead, looming, sixty feet high, were the six rough-hewn black holes bored into the base of three mountains. They were spaced out about five hundred feet apart.

Ki could feel the darkness pouring out of them. "What are we doing here?" she asked. "Are we going to have lunch or something?"

"We, Kilos, are going into one of these tunnels."

"We are?"

"Yep."

"And I'm supposed to assist you in some way once we're inside?"

"Yes."

I think you've got the wrong girl. I'm pretty sure you got the wrong girl!! she thought frantically, trying to appear poised and nonchalant. "Not really sure how I can help you, here, Carahil," she said.

"No, I've got the right girl, no doubt about it," he replied, as if responding to her thoughts instead of her words.

Ki felt the hairs standing up on the back of her head. She felt her legs locking. She kept her feet moving, and rocked from side to side. A Hazards Lunch—she doubted she could finish a lunch here, or even gen up an appetite. She wanted to be miles away. She wanted to be back on the *Seeker*, or in her bed, safe and hidden away in Pendar Tower.

"Zaaaaaaaalll!!" came the animal cry again.

* * * * *

Coming from Onaris, Kilos grew up with all sorts of stories of their rich celestial neighbor, Kana. Dirt poor, dressed in rags, she and her huge family didn't have much in terms of material and technological items. Sitting in the dark, for they couldn't afford lighting either, they told stories. The stories often spoke of Kana, and they usually weren't flattering.

Kana, where the Blues lived: those demented, blue-haired souls armed with the Gifts of the Mind, playing at being gods, usurping the Elders themselves. Kana, where the Browns from Onaris worked as lowly servants; toiled for the Blues, cooked for them, fought and died for them.

Being a Marine, being the best friend of a famous Blue Lord, and having seen much of Kana herself, she now thought of the place as a second home. The home of her best friend, and all those old, unflattering stories she remembered seemed silly and quaint.

As a girl, she recalled being terrified of Kana—the Monsters that were there on Kana. The Giants on Kana.

The Devil came from Kana.

She realized that you never really stop being afraid of things that scared you as a child. The fear is trussed up, pushed to the side and rationalized away; but it's still there, just waiting to come out.

The gates to Hell are on Kana. Those stories used to keep her up at night.

And here they are: the Hazards of the Old Ones.

Impossible!

But look!

* * * * *

"Carahil, I don't see any productive reason to go into these holes."

He put his nose down and gently began nudging her toward the openings again.

"Oh, but I do. Come now, where's that Brown skepticism you're so famous for? What could possibly be so bad down there, in the dark?"

"It's pitch black. We could walk off a ledge, or get brained on a low hang. For safety's sake, we ought not to go in there."

Safety—yes, that sounded good.

Carahil looked at her and smiled with his seal face. "Please ... I can see just fine. I'll guide us. And, I'll make sure to say 'duck' if we come across a low hang."

Ki felt like running, but managed to control herself. They passed through the trees and soon they were standing right in front of the middle tunnels. The orange, circular walls of the tunnels were tiled from top to bottom. The tiles were covered with some sort of strange writing; she didn't recognize it. It wasn't Vith, which, though she couldn't read or write, she could recognize easily enough. This writing was elongated, twisting, and rather unpleasant to look at. "What's this writing?" she asked.

"It's Magravine."

"Never heard of it."

"It's an old language … an extinct one. The Sisters once spoke it way back, ages ago when they still used their mouths to speak. They used it to guard their knowledge from the troublesome Vith—always secretive, the Sisters, even back then. The Grand Abbess of Magravine developed the language, you know who she is, correct?"

Ki thought a moment. "She … was the founder of the Black Hats, right?" Ki said in a questioning fashion, even though she knew perfectly well who the Black Abbess was.

The Black Abbess was a big celebrity on Onaris, a fixture of their fears and folklore; a demon in female form. She was an embodiment of evil that you could blame virtually anything on.

Something bad has happened to you? The Black Abbess did it.

"Not *was*," Carahil said, correcting. "She *is* the leader of the Black Hats. I believe Lord Blanchefort had the pleasure of meeting her some time back."

"She's still alive? That would make her thousands of years old, right?"

"Correct—your math is impeccable. So, here we are, in this lonely place of strange, wandering animals and whispering winds, where the Black Abbess once walked. Shall I tell what happened here, long ago?"

Ki was about to say "No thank you," when Carahil cleared his throat and began telling the story anyway.

"It was here," he said, "ages ago, that Magravine and a few of her demented followers began experimenting with Shadow tech."

Something stirred in the trees. Ki whirled to look, but didn't see anything. Carahil, apparently unconcerned, continued.

"This region has always carried an odd air about it. It was once thought that a precursor city stood here in the mountain passes, populated by strange folk who fled the coming of the Elders. And then, of course, there's the Grand Animalium connection, whose defenses are said to affect the mind and alter perception in various ways."

Carahil pointed with his flipper to the temple ruins through the trees, far to the south. Ki looked; the wonderful afternoon setting began to take on an ominous light.

"That ruined temple yonder to the south, where young lovers today enjoy the sights, is where it all happened—where *they* were taken, those poor Vith girls. That's where the Vith eventually came in force, and knocked it to the ground—trying to rub out the memory of what had been done there. In those days, as the Elders orbited the skies, Shadow tech was nothing more than a crude brown substance that issued from the orifices of various Vith females of the line of Subra of the Mark. It came out of their eyes mostly—they wept a brown mild form of Shadow tech. The Sisterhood noticed that, sometimes, these dark tears floated and darted about, that the girls could make the tears 'dance' if they tried very hard. The Vith also found these odd tears could be extruded and worked into simple things. It was a 'disgusting' Gift, a minor inconvenience, a novelty … nothing more. The Grand Abbess of Magravine, though, became obsessed with it; she was always so jealous of her elder Sister Subra—and was convinced that this odd, messy substance was the ultimate Gift, the ultimate power, it just needed proper cultivating. She began seizing the Vith females who could create it, and experimented on them, torturing them, dissecting them out in the sunshine, flowers and mild breezes of the Tartan temple.

"She found that the more pain and suffering she created in them, the more focused and potent Shadow tech became—it turned black, it flew, it became poisonous. It seethed with life. And, as a side benefit, Magravine also discovered that she enjoyed hurting those girls … that she enjoyed inflicting pain.

"The Vith, once they discovered what was happening, were dumbfounded. They were innocents at that point in time—before the Giants came. They'd never seen such a thing; such brazen, unwashed cruelty—even the main body of the Sisterhood didn't quite know what to do. They went to the Elders orbiting high overhead, and asked for help. And the Elders, in typical fashion, told them to remedy the problem themselves. So, they went to Magravine, asked her to stop, pleaded with her to stop. She simply laughed, and continued, daring them to challenge her. Magravine's power among the twenty five Grand Abbesses was unmatched.

"Her work continued. She discovered the Shadowmark and the genetic markers that governed its use. The Sisterhood, afraid to face Magravine in a direct conflict, tried to save the Vith by breeding Shadow tech out of existence. Once it was extinct, they reasoned, Magravine would forget all about it and turn her interests elsewhere. But, Magravine was undeterred. Even as the Sisterhood tried to breed

Shadow tech out of existence, Magravine undertook steps to breed it right back in again—the two sides working against each other and getting nowhere. Discovering the existence of the Invernans, the Shadow tech males who pass the trait down to their female progeny, she enslaved those that she could get her hands on, and murdered the ones that she couldn't. As her slaves, she set them to her bidding, to create, by force, as many Shadow tech females as was possible.

"In time, she also discovered that these poor Shadow tech females continued to create the substance even after death, if their bodies were properly treated. She created a whole, dark forest, the Landscape of Tithmus: dead female bodies, posed to resemble trees and oozing Shadow tech sap."

Tithmus—Ki shuddered at the name. The forest of the dead by the black lake. All the old stories were ramming their way out of the furnace of her inner-mind and burning bright right in front of her.

The pink bird was back, rutting around just within the line of trees.

Carahil continued. "In time, the forest of Tithmus created so much Shadow tech that a lake of it began to form. Magravine bored six holes in the mountains before us and dug out the riverbed we now stand in. The Shadow tech lake flowed from Tithmus and poured into the holes in the mountains where she could store it indefinitely. The river she created was once lined with dead Vith girls, posed on stone platforms—recall the one you were looking at not long ago? The river of Shadow tech was called Tarbor. Ever heard of it?"

Ki winced, she knew the name: Tarbor, the road to hell ... The dry riverbed she saw ... the one she was standing in. The platforms lining its sides ... the one she just touched, once supported the feet of a dead Vith girl, spewing Shadow tech.

She cringed. All the things she was told as a child, but thought were just frightening stories—all true. All true ...

Something big moved through the trees. Ki couldn't see what it was. A huge squared-off machine, or something.

Carahil, unmindful, relentlessly continued. "Eventually, the Sisters and the Vith had enough. The Vith, under the leadership of Holt of the Mountain and the remaining twenty four Grand Abbesses, rallied and attacked. Weeping, they burnt the forest of Tithmus to the ground, and, with their combined strength, destroyed the Tartan temple and drove Magravine and her followers into the holes in the mountains. There, in the darkness, she became the Black Abbess, a demon of pain and delights. The Vith, in rage and fear, also destroyed her temple at Magravine for good measure. They thought they had beaten her, that she was done—withering away and passing out of memory in the dark under the mountains. Obviously, that was a bad bit of wishful thinking."

Ki stood there and looked at the trees. The monkey she'd seen earlier was swinging about in the high branches. This strange assortment of animals had to have come from the Grand Animalium that Carahil said was around here somewhere.

Carahil continued on. "The Black Abbess was far from done. Safe in the darkness, she snared the tunnels to keep out the Sisters and the Vith—the Blues— and there she remained for centuries, continuing her studies, luring in and enslaving the weak Sisters and Vith who dared come too close. To those followers, she imparted her love of pain and suffering, and they kept her fresh in new Shadow tech meat. Eventually, after the Great Betrayal, she took her followers and fled to the Xaphans. And then, eventually, the Black Hats …"

Ki swallowed hard and watched the monkey climb up a tall, curved tree with a white trunk. She could see the ruins of the Tartan temple far off to the south. "I thought all that was just folklore."

"I'm afraid not. All that and more happened right here. These holes, the Hazards of the Old Ones, is where the black river once flowed. Here countless unhappy females were dragged into the interior, never to be seen again. Only their screams were heard, drifting pitifully out of the holes, carrying on the wind, and all the old blue-haired Vith heroes, and even the Sisters, were powerless to enter and save them. On her victim's pain, the Black Abbess invented the Sten, the Point and the Mass, the Phantom Hand first issuing out of these holes to kill and cause fear. Then, when Magravine and her followers fled to the Xaphans, they abandoned these tunnels, leaving behind only ghosts, despair and bad dreams. Do enough evil and a place can become evil as well. So, yes … as you mentioned before, this place is evil."

Ki took a few steps back, her imagination began to run away with her. She noticed that the white tree the monkey was climbing wasn't actually a tree—it was smooth and shiny, like a whale-bone … or a tusk! There was another white tree nearby in a similar shape to the first one—a pair of tusks, but they were impossibly huge! There was a dark shape behind the tusks, so square and massive Ki hadn't acknowledged it as a shape at all, something that spanned the tree-tops. She thought she could see it moving slightly. "Carahil! Is that the elephant you were talking about?"

Carahil turned his head. "Yes."

"What is it? Where did it come from? Should we get away or something?"

A cat wandered out from the trees and licked its paws. It stared at them, and Ki thought she could see red eyes.

"*Don't go in there …* " came a soft voice.

Ki held her bag and stared. How could this be? Did the cat just talk? Carahil seemed nonplussed.

"Do go away," he said. The pink bird took flight and the monkey bounded into the trees. The great bulk of the elephant slowly turned away.

The cat sat there a moment. It sat with purpose and grim intent. "*You'll be sorry …* " it said as it padded into the trees and vanished.

Carahil twitched his whiskers. "Now then, where were we?"

"What was that?" Ki cried. "Did that cat just talk?"

"Yes."

"Cats can't talk!" she cried.

"Neither can seals normally, but here we are, chatting away. Let's suffice to say that that isn't really a cat."

"What is it then?" She considered recent events. "Is that what's been leaving the messages? Is that Maiax?"

"That's not Maiax. Let's not lose focus, shall we? They are gone and let us return to the task at hand."

Somewhat dubiously, Ki turned back to the tunnels. Wind circled around the mouths of the holes. Noise came out of the tunnels.

The tunnels began moaning. "*Don't go in there …* " she heard again.

"You hear that?" Ki said as casually as she could.

"I don't hear anything."

She could see a few feet into the tunnels, but no further. A wall of cloudy dark was hopelessly entrenched within. The dark was oily and swirling. Ki imagined she could see hints of the Black Abbess dancing in the folds; a wagging finger, a bit of red cloth … a demon in female form, reveling in the torment, beckoning her to enter. She looked back at the ruins far in the distance to the south. The odd animals were gone and she could follow with her eyes the path the black river took. The Shadow tech flowing from all those dead girls …

The wind picked up a little, making a whiny sort of drone against the mouths of the tunnels, other than that, then was no other sound. No birds chirping, no insects buzzing … nothing. Even the purplish groundcover that gave these mountains their distinctive lavender color didn't grow near the holes—they were bare orange stone.

Life seemed to want to avoid these tunnels.

"I've no hankering to go in there myself, Kilos, you must believe me … but I do what I must. I protect and serve, and to do that, I must go in. I must prevent what is to come. And you also must go in. You also must prevent what is to come."

"Carahil, I …"

"We've a job to perform, Kilos. The sooner we begin, the sooner we finish." Carahil said moving toward the third tunnel from the left.

Kilos, her wide eyes fixed on the hole, gripped her bag. Her hands were shaking again.

"Listen, before we start, I need to know what we're doing here. I need a mission breakdown, and I need to know what my role here is going to be. You promised to tell me." She could hear the fear in her own voice, the panic.

"I certainly did. We are going into the third tunnel here. We are going to feel around in the dark for a few miles until we come to the Heart. There, you will search for a Brightstone and secure it."

"Brightstone? What's that? Sounds familiar."

"A bit of the arcane I've had my eye on for some time now. It's a beryl, a roughly spherical blue, green, pink or clear jewel. Very pretty, actually."

"How big?"

"About as large as your fist. There's actually quite a few in there … we only need one. You may take your pick. The color will matter not, but please, pick a pretty one by all means."

"And I'm getting this Brightstone for you? You're not getting it?"

"Correct—if I could retrieve a Brightstone on my own, I would do so. I cannot, therefore I need you to fetch one for me."

"And what do you need me to do with it?"

"I need you, once you've secured one, to put it into my mouth."

"Put it in your mouth?"

"Yes."

"Is that all? Do you need to chew it or swallow it?"

"I will need to swallow it, yes. Excellent question, Kilos."

"All right, then what?"

"Then we leave, exit the tunnels. Easy enough, yes?"

"That's all?"

"That's all."

"Why's this Brightstone so important? Why do you want it?"

"Because, I currently cannot be in more than one place at a time. I will have a need to be in many places at once, if we are to save those we love. The Brightstone will allow me to do that."

Kilos stood. "Who are we saving everybody from?"

"The Black Hats … they've gone mad. They want blood and they don't care where it comes from. They also wish to make a point for all to see, and that point will be bought by the deaths of billions."

Kilos gripped her bag, and looked at the tunnels again.

"And, if we do not do this here, they will have the blood of everyone we love and more … much more."

She swallowed. "All right, for my friends, for Dav, for Syg … I will do this. You're not going to disappear on me in there, are you?"

"I shall do my best to survive the whole way."

10—Heron

Before morning bell, the *Seeker* blasted out of Stellar Mach outside of the Heron system. Heron was on the edge of a massive, energetic nebula—the charged gases and dusts made for a sparkling, colorful display. Beyond the nebula was Xaphan space, the enemy's territory. Trimming the helm, the huge ship bared down on the system, moving in a gale.

Davage and Sygillis ate breakfast together in their quarters, Syg sitting there with a huge bib, so as not to spot her gown. As much as she complained about her gowns, Syg treated them tenderly, always careful not to stain or damage them, and whenever one got destroyed, she took it personally. The gown Carahil had stolen in the Grove was still a sore point. She had four wardrobes full, even surpassing Poe in the sheer volume of gowns that she possessed. While Poe tended to keep her gowns in the soft blue, red and green range, and Countess Pardock's old Blanchefort gowns tended to always be in the white or cream tones, Syg's spanned the color spectrum. She had a good number that were completely black, while others were pleasing in soft pastels of varying shades. She also had a few that were garishly hued—shockingly bold and skirting the boundaries of good taste. During their travels, if she came across a bolt of interesting fabric, she usually bought the bolt and took it home, and soon she'd have a new gown. She'd come up with a new design for a gown that was designed to help her bowl better, and the idea of designing clothes took flight in her head. She began sketching gown designs, and even was toying with the idea of designing her own fabrics and patterns. She often went down to the factories in the village with an armful of sketches and swatches and assailed her thoughts upon the designers, who patiently listened—though they probably wished she'd stayed in the castle.

She also did her hair in the elaborate Blanchefort style when she wore a gown, though she didn't have to. Her Silver tech allowed her to set it place in a matter of seconds. Dav suspected she liked wearing her gowns because she could go around and not wear sandals, her large petticoat covered her bare feet completely. The only shoes she ever wore were her little bowling shoes that she looked so cute in.

Once they finished their breakfast, they went to the bridge, where Lt's Larsen and Verlin were both waiting by the Ops station. Though they were competing for the same job, they seemed to be pleasant enough with each other, making small talk and getting acquainted. Davage called them into the conference room. Syg, nearly at a run in her lovely brown Blanchefort gown, glided into the conference room ahead of them all, not waiting to give him the chance to shut her out.

<*Syg, where are you headed?*>

Seating themselves, Davage came in last. "Good morning," he said

<*You're not shutting me out again, Dav!*> she telepathied as she allowed him to seat her.

"Good morning, sir," Larsen and Verlin both said.

"Morning, morning. I trust you remember my countess, Sygillis of Blanchefort?"

<*I wasn't planning on doing that. I was going to invite you in, honestly.*>

"I do," Larsen said. "Good morning, Great Countess."

Syg nodded in a courtly fashion.

<*So you say. Let's see you throw me out now, HAHA!*>

"My countess is an invaluable asset here on the ship, and, if you are to be first officer aboard the *Seeker*, you must accept and value her presence as I do. Her knowledge of Xaphan Society and her war craft is without peer. She's also not too bad in a fight. Now, anyone for a cup of coffee?"

They all nodded.

Davage made a cup for everyone, and, after they had drunk a bit, Davage spoke up.

"Doubtless, you have perused our destination."

<*I think you're cute, Dav ...*>

"I have, sir. The Marines will be very appreciative of our presence here," Verlin said.

"Yes sir, however, I am wondering, is it usually the duty of a Main Fleet Vessel to intercede in a minor Marine interdiction mission?" Larsen asked.

<MMMMM … I am going to tear you apart as soon as this silly meeting concludes …>

<Syg, not now, please …>

Davage smiled. "Normally it is not. The Marines are fully capable of handling such things on their own, and, should they require assistance, the Fleet will always be on station to assist at once. However … there are certain matters that you must be made aware of."

Davage worked a few controls at the table and a large 3-D map of the Heron system popped up and slowly spun. "Can anyone tell me where we are?"

They looked at the map. "We are approaching the Heron System, sir," Larsen said. "There is the Tammarak Cluster at 12am, and, at 6am, are The Kills."

"Indeed, well done. What else strikes you about the Heron System?"

<Daaav … ??>

They studied the map. "Heron is an energetic T-Tauri star in the F spectral range. No life capable planets due to the youth of the star and because of the Great Heron Nebula hanging at 7am," Verlin said.

"And?" Davage said.

Larsen rubbed his chin. "We are very near to Xaphan space."

<Daaaav … ??>

<Syg, stop this. I am trying to conduct a serious briefing.>

"Correct," he said. He pressed a few buttons and the map spun. "More specifically, Heron is rather close to the planet Xandarr."

Davage hit a button and a planet just within Xaphan space began blinking: Xandarr. "Yes, at 1am, barely four light years from Heron. You two, of course, are aware of my ongoing issues with House Xandarr?"

<I love you!>

"Yes, sir," Verlin said. "However, I thought the Princess Marilith was dead."

"As did I," Larsen said.

<I love you too, Syg.>

"She appears to be dead, true enough. However, before we sortied, I received a rather disturbing message from Hezru, King of Xandarr. To sum up the conversation, the King was wanting to 'keep the hostilities going' to use his words, and introduced me to his eleventh daughter,

Princess Vroc. Apparently, our battles over the years made House Xandarr a great deal of money."

Syg chimed in. "You see, House Xandarr had fallen out of favor with the Black Hats. A promising snare operation aboard the foreign vessel *Triumph*, authored by Princess Marilith several years ago, went badly and many Black Hats were killed. In revenge, the Black Hats fell upon House Xandarr, seized their assets, condemned Marilith to death, and swore eternal revenge. They have hated House Xandarr ever since."

"To expand, you have both probably heard of the '*Triumph* Affair' that the countess refers to, yes? Princess Marilith enlisted the aid of the Black Hats to perform an extensive Shadow tech snaring operation on the *Triumph*. Marilith did not like Demona of Ryel, the captain of that vessel, and …"

"She was the captain's girlfriend," Sygillis said dryly.

<She was not, Syg, will you please drop that?>

<She was too—don't try to deny it!>

"Yes, well, the plot was uncovered a bit prematurely. Princess Marilith, apparently eager to brag, began boasting before the Black Hats were fully ready. The Fleet and Sisters interceded, boarded the *Triumph,* and over twenty Black Hats were killed in the ensuing battle. That was the first battle in recent memory where a force, other than that of the Sisterhood of Light, had met and defeated the Black Hats. For that loss of face and station, they were exceeding angry with House Xandarr and have been so ever since …"

<Davage and Demona sitting in a tree …>

Davage gave Syg a dirty look and continued. "Impoverished after the Black Hats took all their assets, House Xandarr was able to enrich itself afresh by banking on their daughter's ongoing battles with me. And so, this eleventh daughter of theirs, Princess Vroc."

"I understand that the eleventh daughter is considered very unlucky in Xaphan Society," Verlin said.

"The king did mention that, yes," Davage said. "Can you expand upon that further, Lt.?"

"Aye sir. Xandarr lore teaches that the eleventh daughter is the accursed daughter, the worthless daughter, bringer of unluck and ill tidings."

"Lt.," Syg said, interrupting.

She continued on. "In the Xandarr pantheon of gods and goddesses …"

"*Lieutenant!*" Syg said again, louder.

Verlin stopped her oratory and turned to her. "Great Countess?"

Syg smiled. "Lt., what is your bowling average?"

Verlin was open-mouth shocked and blushed. "My bowling average? Great Countess, we do not partake of bowling in Remnath."

Syg narrowed her eyes and ground her teeth. "*Liar* …" she said.

<Syg! Holy gods! We do not speak openly of bowling! You have just embarrassed her!>

<So? She's been bowling since she could crawl, I'll bet, and I wish she'd admit it.>

"Countess," Davage said, "we will discuss this further later. Lt., please continue."

She straightened her Marine coat and went on. "As I was saying, the eleventh goddess of the Xandarr pantheon is Mabsornath, goddess of pestilence, infidelity, infertility and bad luck."

"Goodness."

"The eleventh daughter is something they take seriously on Xandarr."

"Sounds like nonsense to me," Davage said. "Regardless, I told the king that I had no interest in fighting an innocent girl; that I fight as my duty calls. He, however, was quite determined and said, in no uncertain terms, that Princess Vroc will not stay innocent for long, that they will seek a fight in League space … shake a tree or two."

"So, sir, you are thinking that this unknown vessel might be your Princess Vroc?" Verlin asked.

"That is my belief, and hence our presence here. We shall ask the Marines to withdraw, and we shall investigate this ship further. I'll not have any needlessly endangered over this Xandarr entanglement."

Davage turned the map off. "We are set to make contact with the unknown vessel in one hour. I will await your thoughts and opinions on the matter as we engage. And remember, I want nothing taken for granted."

"Aye, sir," Verlin said.

Larsen nodded.

"Dismissed."

The two officers stood and exited the room.

Syg, now that they were alone, allowed her courtly demeanor to fall away. She sat there sheepishly and smiled. "Hi, Dav ..."

"Sygillis ..." Davage said in an angry tone.

"Ut-oh ... I'm in trouble, aren't I?"

"Yes indeed. What were you doing just now?"

"Nothing, Dav ... just telling you that I love you."

"I know you love me, now please allow me to do my job unmolested."

"Your 'job', sir, is to be my lord." She stood and put her arms around him. "Can't a countess dote upon her husband?"

"Certainly, but there are serious matters afoot. Now, I am certain that Lt. Verlin enjoys bowling, all Ladies do—however, it is not spoken of. You know that."

"That is stupid, Dav."

"Regardless, that is the custom, and especially in stodgy Remnath of all places. I'll expect you to apologize to her in private later. And, additionally, I am tired of you harping on me regarding Demona of Ryel—a woman who came and went years before you happened along."

"Yes, well, you should pick your girlfriends more carefully. You should have anticipated my coming, either by vision or dream quest, and dismissed her, knowing that I, one day, would be your wife."

Davage shrugged—the Rush was manifesting itself full force. Syg's emotions and her logic certainly were teetering a bit.

"You really think this vagrant ship has a Xandarr connection?" she asked.

"I do. Just a feeling."

Syg kissed him. "I trust your feelings. Should I change into a body suit and be ready for action? I'll not have another gown destroyed."

"If there's any 'action' as you put it, you will be safe in our quarters, riding it out."

Syg smiled and grabbed him by the collar. "Incorrect, sir. I will be right at your side, as always. You always bring this up and you always lose this fight."

Davage smiled and lifted her off the floor. "That's fine, I suppose. Better to keep an eye you."

11—The Heart

The dark was like nothing Ki had ever experienced before. Certainly, the cavern beneath Castle Blanchefort was murky and pitch black, but it could be comfortably illuminated witht the smallest of lights. Here, the darkness moved and thrived. Here, there was no casting it aside. She even thought she tasted it crawling into her mouth. She looked into her bag where Tweeter was. She could not see him—his silver light swallowed up, but she knew he was there. She heard him stumping about at the bottom of her bag. The dark air was heavy in her lungs; she gulped for breath, on the verge of hyper-ventilating. She imagined she could see colors floating about in front of her, she even thought she could see her hand in front of her face, but no—she saw nothing but black in this place where light and color had no meaning.

Carahil was next to her, loping along, leading the way. She kept one hand on his smooth back, the other on the side of the tunnel. She could not see him either. Every so often, the wall to her right opened up into a drafty, soul-shattering empty space, obviously an intersection. When that happened, she would tarry there a moment and listen. In the quiet, she could hear the breeze flowing past her, and something else: a faint, monotonous, slightly industrial sound far away. After a moment or two, Carahil would return to her and nose her forward, the empty chasm soon filled in by the continuation of the wall.

She kept thinking she was going to step off the edge into a long drop. She couldn't orient herself. Though she could feel the ground under her boots, she felt like she was falling. She stumbled often, having trouble determining which way was up. Always, Carahil, stopped and helped her to her feet.

She thought of the screaming these passes had once heard, the sadness. The Black Abbess's servants cooing in the ears of those poor, innocent girls:

"*Come, child … we've a gift for you …*"

And with them they went, unknowing of the agony they were soon to feel.

"*Take a last look at the sky, my dear … FOR YOU SHALL NEVER SEE IT AGAIN! AHAHAHAHAHAHAHA!!!*"

The pain that had been inflicted here. All the old, sad ghosts lost in the dark. The Black Abbess once walked these dark tunnels, spewing her darkness, reveling in the misery around her. She still got goose bumps when she recalled Dav speaking about his encounter with her, how she was tiny, like Syg, but huge in power and utterly evil. How she had a Phantom Hand waiting for Dav, and, without the Sisters protection, he'd be dead.

Her heart was pounding, she couldn't catch her breath. She was near to the Black Abbess … near to the evil she had done. She could feel it.

She could hear the Black Abbess's heart beating!

I can't! I can't do this! She reached out for Carahil.

Where was he?

"Carahil?" she said waving her hand, looking for his reassuring smooth bulk in the dark.

She heard something approach her from behind.

"I told you … not to leave your post …"

Hands at her throat! She couldn't breathe. She reached out to grapple with whatever had attacked her, but there was nothing there, and she fell, lost in space. Lost in the dark.

"Carahil?" she whimpered … all her Marine toughness was completely overwhelmed and cast aside. All she could feel was fear … raw fear. "CARAHIL!!" she shrieked.

Something nuzzled her back. "I'm here, Kilos, I'm here. I'm sorry."

Kilos rose and, reaching, found his neck and put her arms around it. "I—I can't do this. I can't go any further!"

He came to her side and nudged her, his whiskers tickling her face. "Here, Kilos … I will carry you."

Shaking, ashamed, but grateful, she felt around, picked up her bag, and slowly climbed up onto his strong smooth back and held on as tight as she could.

"Are you all right?" he asked.

"No … I hear laughing … I hear screaming. I hear all those Vith girls …"

"There is no laughing, Kilos. There is no screaming …"

"I want out … I feel the Black Abbess's hands at my throat!" She buried her face into his back.

"You know the Gifts, yes?" he said loping along, trying to occupy her thoughts.

"I—I do."

"Name them for me."

"T-There's the Sight, Strength, W-Waft, Cloak, Dirge and S-S-Stare."

"That's only six," he said loping ahead and turning to the right.

"What do you mean? There are only six."

"You're wrong. There are seven."

"There is not a seventh."

"There is, not counting youth and health—those are for granteds. And that's the whole reason why we're here today, because … of the seventh. The Seventh Gift, or, more precisely, the First Gift."

"What is it?"

Carahil paused a moment. "Immortality."

"What?"

"Immortality. You, Kilos, are immortal just like I am."

Carahil stopped, seemed puzzled a moment, then turned to his left and continued.

His efforts to put her mind to work on something other than her fear appeared to be working. Ki's Brown skepticism was beginning to win out; the smothering fear she'd felt was falling to the rear. "I've got a whole graveyard full of relatives who might disagree with you on that immortality bit," Ki said hanging onto his neck, slowly forgetting about her fear. Colors, previously lost in the dark, began to fill her mind again; the graveyard outside of Tusck where all her family was buried, awash in the golden color of the fields. It was near the sea, the lapis waves breaking nearby.

"Oh yes, and you being a Brown, I'll wager that's one huge graveyard," Carahil replied. "Here is what it is: long ago, during the CX time epoch when your people lived with the Elders on Cammara, you were made immortal. Through genetic engineering the Elders had already purged your people of the ravages of disease and old age, as thanks for your good service. They then determined to take the next step and make you immortal as well. This was hundreds of thousands of years ago, before there were any Blues or Browns, before the advent of the seven tribes. It is often thought that the Sisterhood was originally created to investigate the Gifts of the Mind. That is not quite true. The Gifts of the Mind didn't come until much later during the EX epoch here on Kana. The Sisters original mission was to investigate Immortality and determine what was to be done with it."

"Done with it?"

"Yes. The Elder-kind were not originally immortal beings. You do not have immortal psyches—you couldn't accept it. You went mad with it. Endlessness was too much to bear, and the Elders did not count on that. The immortality they built into you was complete. Imagine, being cleaved in two on the battlefield and not dying. Imagine having nothing left of you but a bit of brain matter in a pan—and that brain, festering and insensate, is alive and everlasting. Horrible isn't it? It was therefore decided that, though you be immortal, you needed to be put to the grave, you needed peace—the standard agreed upon time limit being two hundred, twenty years."

"Who decided that?"

"The Sisters, who else?"

"Are you saying that the Sisters decide arbitrarily who lives and who dies?"

"I am. The Sisters spent centuries figuring out how to get past the Elder's engineered immortality, and, the splinter sect of the Sisterhood that does the killing is what is at the heart of these dark tunnels ahead."

Ki suddenly felt like jumping off of his back and running. "You said the tunnels were abandoned!"

"I said the Black Abbess and her dark followers abandoned the Hazards ages ago. They didn't stay abandoned for long. The Sisters, following her departure, devised methods to defeat her snares and traps. They entered the Hazards and found them to be a perfect place to perform their "service" for the Elder-Kind, safe behind walls of darkness, a ready-made venue, and a veil of fear and superstition already keeping the locals away. The bad thing is that little bits of the Black Abbess are still here, and not even the Sisters, with all of their might, can fully be rid of them. And here they have been ever since, living in the Black Abbess's Heart, guarding their secret well."

"They are murdering people …"

"Let's not be overly-dramatic, shall we? Yes, they are killing people, but they do it because they care—because they truly feel that immortality is a terrible thing, and they are correct. It is not remembered today how horrific the last ages on Cammara were—the madness, the insane tyrants living forever. The roaming body parts that never die; dreaming of what they once were. A beginning and an end is a natural course, Kilos—remove the end and the beginning no longer has meaning. The Sisters saw it and begged the Elders to rid them of the Gift, for it was causing harm. But they would not, and so the Sisters took matters into their own hands. Through research, they discovered methods to suppress the Elder's immortal engineering to the point that sustained wounds would kill—no more bits and pieces of bodies that will never die. Now, they have it diluted such that you'll live as long as you're not killed by something. As for the rest of it, they watch over and attend to everyone in due time. They try to give the people their fair share of life, and when they feel it is over, when they feel the person cannot grow any further, they end their life, quietly, peacefully. And, if they feel you've suffered a bad draw, they take that into account and award more life to compensate. Ever had a relative who lived for a very long time, much longer than normal?"

"My aunt, Old Wisathelia, she lived to be almost three hundred."

"I see, and was your aunt somehow sick or otherwise unfortunate at any time during her life?"

"She was never sick that I recall … oh, she was enslaved in Xaphan space for a good portion of her youth on Midas."

"Ah, you see … so, the Sisters, seeing your aunt inconvenienced, gave her more life accordingly. They do that a lot, they try to be fair. This is a task they do not take lightly. The Elder's engineering is persistent—it keeps coming back. That was the beginning of the Sister's Program, to introduce agents into the bodies of the elder males that help suppress Immortality, so that severe wounds, such as a bullet to the head, would be fatal."

"The Sisters use sex to kill people?"

"In a manner of speaking. The agents they introduce during intercourse with League males make it possible to end your lives, though you would, in fact, still live forever should you not be killed by external forces. It's not perfect, and things like Shadow tech complicate matters, making the person much more difficult to kill."

"What about the Xaphans? They're basically nothing but runaway Vith, so that would make them Immortal too, right? What about them? I've killed lots of Xaphans."

"The Sisters are a little less demure with them than they are with League gentlemen. Ever hear the old Xaphan stories of the Succubi, the creatures who come to Xaphan men in the night and take them in their sleep. Yep, you guessed it—that's the Sisters again, doing what they do. The Sisters certainly get around. They use the Brightstone, which again is why we're here."

"Why are you telling me this?"

"Because you'll not remember it when this is over. Knowing too much about this place is a death sentence. Though the Sisters do this for the good of the people, they do not wish this activity known—obviously few would understand, might even go to war against the Sisters over it. Such knowledge, generally known, could be the end of the League. The Sisters within, living with the pall of Black Abbess's crimes, are savage and ancient; they have changed, evolved, become monstrous, and they will kill to keep this secret without mercy, and any entering their dark realm is, by consequence, their mortal enemy. This place is snared for death. For those select individuals who overcome the snares, they've machines roaming these dark holes, waiting to fall upon any who might enter. And then, there's the Sisters themselves. All they need is to catch a slight whiff of you, and they can hunt you down, fall upon you in the night and bear you away, never to be seen again. Once they have your scent, they will never stop looking."

Ki closed her eyes and shuddered.

They reached some sort of precipice or drop. Carahil stopped and Ki climbed off. Righting herself in the dark, she knelt down and felt the cool, earthy rim of the drop. Down below, in the far distance, she thought she could see a cool, grayish-green light, shaped like a tall doorway or threshold. She thought at first that it might be her imagination again, but no, it was there.

Ki felt one of Carahil's flippers touch her face and she could see it glinting in the greenish light. "Now, we'll wait here a moment," he said in a quiet voice. "Be proud, Kilos, you have gone several miles into the Hazards of the Old Ones. You have done something no Blue Lord could ever have done, not even Lord Blanchefort."

"I'm in no way braver than Dav," Ki said defiantly.

"Bravery has nothing to do with it. These caves are snared to react with the Gifts of the Mind. It's impossible for a Gifted Blue, other than a properly trained Sister, to enter here. Their brain will short-circuit before they got twenty paces in—the Black Abbess snared it herself. It's a safeguard to keep the curious out."

"What about Browns?"

"The old snares don't work on the Browns. There are those nasty machines roaming around that I mentioned to you earlier; they're there to clean up anyone who somehow gets past the snares. But, all in all, nether the Black Abbess, or the Sisters for that matter, properly consider Browns, to their detriment. They think of Browns very much the same as you think of Browns—without concern or proper respect. Certainly no Brown—no Giftless peasant—would ever dare enter here in the first place. Peasants are moldable creatures, swayed by folklore and myth, too busy wallowing in their superstitions to be a threat—that's what they think. The Sisters cannot conceive of a Brown ever daring to set foot in the Hazards. Yet, even peasants can have a heart. Even peasants can be brave, as you have been. Now, let's to it. Can you see that light in the distance?"

"Yes, barely."

"That is the Heart—that's where you need to go. Inside are the Brightstones. Remember, you must get one and put it in my mouth. Ignore what you see around you, ignore what you hear. Concentrate on the Brightstone. You, as a Brown, will not be noticed as long as you stay quiet. They will not be able to detect you. Now go, my time is running short."

"Running short?"

Carahil nuzzled up next to her. "I am … under attack, Kilos. I am struggling to maintain my sanity—even now. The snares are … taking effect. I can go no further. You must, on your own, go and get the Brightstone, and put it in my mouth and make me swallow it, even if you have to stuff it down my throat, understand?"

"You'll choke."

"I will not. As long as there is a spark of life in me, then everything will be all right."

"Carahil, you're scaring me. I don't think I can do this."

"Yes you can, look how far you've come."

"You got me here. You carried me."

"You walked at my side, willingly, for as far as you could, and then you had the courage to ask me for help when you needed it. That is a leap a surprising number of people are unable to make. You have shown great strength. Now, you must show a bit more … finish the journey … for me."

His voice choked. "Kilos, you must hurry. My time is almost up. Remember … do not worry about me, just get that jewel into my mouth at all costs."

Ki started for the drop, then stopped. "Hey, Carahil …"

"Yes …"

"Just call me Ki, ok?"

He nuzzled her cheek.

She drew her SK and cocked it. Stumbling forward on all fours, her bag slung over her back, she groped her way toward the light and slid down the shallow drop.

Ahead the light got slowly closer. Looming in the distance, its size exaggerated in the dark, was a massive stone doorway. It was covered in Magravine script, which, in the backlight, gave it an intestinal sort of look. Beyond it was some large open space filled with bright greenish light. The light was blinding as she got closer.

Ki slid forward, her shaking hand tightly gripping her SK.

The Sisters, he said, killing people out of kindness.

Immortality ...

If she thought about it, the idea was frightening: to live forever, to always be. One day dripping into the next and so on, without end. She imagined being an arm or a leg flopping around alive … forever. No thanks. Small wonder the ancients went crazy with it. No wonder the Sisters did what they did. Ki was a sensible person, she understood, though she wondered how such a thing might go over in the League, should it ever come out. Probably not very well. The knee-jerk reaction against the Sisters would be strong. The old graveyard back in Tusck, under the sun, awash in color, felt awful friendly at the moment.

She continued, sliding on her rear-end; just she alone in the dark with the Killers. The Sisters killing their "customers" with thought and kindness, and killing intruders at their gates with wrath and malice.

When she was about a hundred feet from the doorway, a black shape appeared in it. It was hard for Ki to make out detail; her eyes so starved for light, the sudden abundance of it from the door was blinding.

The figure in the doorway looked like a person, only incredibly tall and thin. It must have been at least twenty feet tall, naked apparently, for no garments or hanging cloth could be seen, its arms legs and neck were three or four times longer than normal. It was bone skinny.

It appeared greenish or black in the light. Its stomach cavity was exposed, she could see its innards pumping and pulsating.

Its head, atop its stalk-like neck, was strange: small-eyed, hairless. Its head was high-domed and egg-shaped, with the top of the skull dotted with upward-pointing knobby protrusions, like a bony crown.

Kilos looked at it in horror. This thing was once a Sister. She was old, ancient, evolved. She might not have seen the sun in literally thousands of years.

<*Sister,*> she thought. <*... someone ... is out there... in the Dark ... hiding ...*>

Kilos, a trained Marine, was fully able to hear her thoughts, though, they were strange and jumbled. She couldn't understand it all.

Another "Sister" came to the doorway, a monstrous giant like the first. They looked around.

This couldn't be real ... these monsters couldn't be Sisters.

<*There, there ... on the parapet! I feel it!! Elders!! It's a Wumalaar!!*>

<*Yes, yes ... Wumalaar!*>

Moving with the speed of demons the "Sisters" tore out of the doorway, flew past where Kilos was crouching, and shambled up the side of the hill, toward where Carahil waited.

Looking back into the dark, Kilos heard the sudden sounds of a scuffle.

She heard a pained cry.

She heard flesh tearing.

<*Wumalaar!! Your life ... forfeit!!*>

She heard agonized screaming.

* * * * *

The *Seeker,* upon entering the Heron system, flew side-by-side with the spry Marine *Brigantine* for a time.

Lt. Westrich, aboard the tiny red and black Marine ship, was elated to see the massive *Seeker* park along side of it. He gave the *Seeker's* Com officer all the information he had on the unknown ship: how it was a strange vessel, huge and black, seemingly dead and unpowered yet moving with purpose.

He said it was several thousand stellar miles right ahead ... high noon.

Again, the Com thanked the Lt. and bade him fall back with his vessel to Bazz. Banking his *Brigantine,* he retired the area and gave it to the *Seeker*.

* * * * *

Kilos covered her ears, scooting along in the dirt.

She could hear the horrible sounds coming from the parapet, the struggling, the distressed screaming.

There was a ripping sound. Something landed in the dirt nearby. Though she couldn't see it clearly, Ki thought it might be one of Carahil's flippers.

They're hurting him! They're killing him!!

Unable to stand it anymore, she leveled her SK and fired in the direction of the sound.

TACK!! TACK!! TACK!!

The flash from her shots lit up the chamber in a series of flash-bulb moments. She was in a massive, half-moon shaped dome, the walls covered to the top in Magravine. The inky un-natural darkness flooding the tunnels ended just beyond the parapet. This whole area appeared to be a dry basin—a basin where Shadow tech once was collected, where the Black Abbess took it and created all sorts of terrible things. The blood of those innocent girls pooled here. Here was the end of the Tarbor—Hell itself. There was an overturned statue at the far end of the chamber. It was a proud, robed, masked female—possibly the Black Abbess herself.

<*Who is there??*> the Sisters thought.

<*How, how can … this be?*>

<*Is it another Wumalaar?*>

The giant Sisters stormed down from the parapet on their long, thin legs, the ground shaking slightly as they walked.

In a panic, Ki kicked at the ground, scooting away toward the door. In the greenish light she could see the two huge creatures who once were Sisters come striding toward where she previous was. They pawed at the ground, throwing dirt and bits of stone high into the cool air.

Ki sat there, only a few feet away and watched in disbelief.

"*We will find you,*" they hissed, speaking with a distorted accent. "… *and you will die!!*"

They came forward and, after another step or two, were standing right over her, Ki looking up into their naked, lofty crotches. They bent down and began pawing the ground again. They did not seem to be able to see her.

<*Harken!! I believe I smell something …*> one thought.

There was a pitiful, anguish-filled groan from the top of the parapet. They turned.

<*The Wumalaar … it lives …*>

Quickly, they strode back to finish Carahil once and for all, the kicked up dirt from their huge feet landing on Ki in a gritty shower.

The screaming resumed.

Carahil!! Her heart ached for him. They were killing him right at this moment. She had to do something!!

The Brightstone!! She remembered the Brightstone.

Scrabbling in the dirt she made her way to the doorway and went in.

Inside was a vast underground vault. She covered her eyes. Being in total darkness for so long, the bright green light within was enough to put her eyes out. She covered her face with her hands.

When her eyes cleared she looked around.

Her heart froze.

She was in a huge, vaguely circular open space at least a mile in circumference with a vaulted ceiling looming thousands of feet overhead. The size of the room made the huge dome on the other side of the doorway look like a tiny antechamber in comparison. Light poured down from an unseen source. In the center of the room, directly under the dome overhead, was a circular, aqua-marine pool that was large enough to be a decent-sized lake. The water was a sparkling sort of blue, like what you might see in a tropical resort, like in Fazo on Onaris where the Blues liked to come for vacation and get sunburned. There were yellowish masses moving about in the water just beneath the surface. They moved in a rhythmic sort of way.

Looking around, there were at least a thousand Sisters in the room: each tall, skinny, green-skinned, open-gutted and monstrous. They stood tall at large, arcane control panels that lined the circumference of the room for as far as the eye could see. The panels were made of ochre stone. A polished marble slab hung on the wall above each control panel, like a terminal screen. The control panels thrummed with energy.

With a wave of their over-sized, black hands, the marble screens came to life. In the screens were images of people: sleeping people.

The Sisters, standing there, tall and green, gazed at the people on the screens, squinting with their tiny, near-useless, reptilian-like eyes. A nearby Sister looked at a sleeping woman, resting in her bed through her screen. The Sister's strange, ancient face appeared sad, lips trembling.

<*To save you … I must kill you. Long time I have watched you … you have lived long and well, a fine family you have nurtured, and proud you have good cause to be. Many good works you have done, you can do no more. Well done on a full life well-lived. Sleep, dear friend …*> the Sister thought.

The Sister reached through the screen, as if it was an open portal, and gently touched the sleeping woman on the head. The woman shuddered and died. Ki got a good look at the Sister's hands as she reached in. Her palms and the pads of her fingers were covered with some sort of intricate black tattoo or complicated circuitry. Her touch was utterly deadly.

The Sister reached back through, and the screen went black, back to marble as before.

Ki stood there and watched for a moment … horrified, yet, understanding. Ki certainly didn't want to be immortal—what kind of life was that? You live, then you die—that's how it should work.

These ancient, deformed Sisters did what must be done. Their work was unknown, unthanked. They were entombed in the middle of this cursed maze; their existence a carefully guarded secret.

A Sister turned from her console and came striding toward Ki's position. She didn't know what to do for a moment, and then dove aside. The Sister passed without notice and stopped at the lapping rim of the pool.

<*We have a schedule to maintain! You are late as usual!*> she thought.

<*Sc..ewl.. Y..r Pa..s..ion…s*> came a reply that Ki couldn't understand.

A shape rose out of the blue water. It was a Sister, but in a very different form than the monstrous green ones. She was golden in color. Her skin was smooth and slightly scaled. She had lacy fins sprouting out of her back that moved around her in an airy fashion.

She floated past the giant Sister, who looked at her in an envious sort of manner. Ki stared at the golden Sister; she was alluring, seductive. Ki had to shake her head and snap out of it.

The giant returned to her console, waved her hands over its face, and the marble screen came to life. A sleeping man appeared. He was scruffy and obviously passed out. He was dressed like a Xaphan sailor; Ki had seen enough of those in her day to be able to recognize them at a glance.

<*Here is your party. Now, be quick about it!*> she thought.

The golden Sister floated past the giant and through the screen. She hovered over the man and then set to work on him. He began laughing in his sleep.

That was one lucky Xaphan, she thought. Ki looked on, captivated. The Xaphan guy in the screen was having the immortality screwed out of him as she watched.

Two Sisters came striding long-armed through the doorway at that moment. Ki's blood froze.

They were looking right at her. She had been entranced.

They turned to their right and continued farther into the room—as Carahil had said, they couldn't see her.

Their strange thoughts fluttered about the room.

<*What was it, Sister …?*>

<A *Wumalaar of some sort … a sorcerous creature…*>

Carahil!! Oh, Carahil…

<Is it dead?>

<It is dead.>

Dead!! Ki's fear and allure turned to fury. Her hands trembled with rage. She was ready to raise her SK and start shooting, to kill as many as she could. She barely knew Carahil, was annoyed by him most of the time—but he was good, he was true and brave.

Dead! She thought of him, caring for his kittens. She thought of the sketch he'd drawn of her. He had comforted her in the dark when she thought she might die. And whatever he had seen, whatever evil was coming to kill her friends, its secret was now dead with him.

And she was buried alive in this terrible place, with no possible way out through that pitch maze without him to guide her.

She approached a nearby Sister and palmed her SK. The Sister, unaware, waved her hand at the control panel. Again, the screen lit up. A sleeping man appeared.

Another Sister approached. *<No, Sister … we have discussed this. He is to have more time … he wishes to go on a pilgrimage, it is important to him. He ought to have that experience.>*

<I cannot not tarry much longer. He is well past his time.>

<Allow him his pilgrimage. Then, grant him peace.>

<As you wish …> The Sister waved her arm and the screen went blank.

The stony control panel the Sister manipulated was a flashing gallery of colored lights. Ki took a good hard look at it from a distance: polished stone, studded with colorful jewels that she could see blinking in a rhythmic pattern.

Colorful jewels!! Brightstones!!

Remembering her promise, she holstered her SK and controlled her anger. She had made a promise, and she was going to keep it. She made her way to an unoccupied control panel. She was going to get a Brightstone and take it to Carahil, and put it into his mouth as he had asked. After that, she didn't know. She might just sit there forever.

She stood at the panel and looked up. The smooth stone surface rose up to about ten feet and then slanted inward toward the marble screen high above—in the slanted portion, that's where the stones were embedded. She couldn't reach … no way. The stones, within easy reach of these long-armed, giant-sized Sisters, were hopelessly out of Ki's grasp. She stood there and stretched. She jumped up and down as high as she could.

Too short. She leaned up against the stone panel in frustration, having no idea what to do.

She noticed activity at the far end of the room. A group of smaller Sisters moved from giant to giant. They stopped at each one and fed the Sisters from buckets they carried using TK to lift and maneuver spoonfuls of food into their giant mouths. They also washed the giants with loving care, using damp cloths wetted in the nearby blue pool; the cloths floated through the air on precise TK. The big ones were careful not to let their lethal hands touch the smaller Sisters. When the smaller ones had finished, they wiped the giant's lips, and moved on to the next one to begin the process again.

Wait…

Mixed into the group of smaller Sisters was an even smaller one. Hunched, bent over, she seemed infirm, which was rather shocking; a Sister, sick? She carried a ladder with her, transferring it from panel to panel. As the others fed and washed the giants, this one climbed up her ladder and cleaned and straightened the giant's control panel. The giants treated her with reverence, bowing in her presence. Must be important. Probably thousands of years old.

As they neared, Ki saw the smaller ones were also in a sort of evolution. They appeared to be in the early stages of becoming monstrous. The one using the ladder was covered in rock-like bulges.

Ki watched as the procession moved closer and closer. She carefully studied them, getting the feel for their routine as they moved from one Sister to the next.

The TK, the buckets of slop floating, the preening, and then the moving on. The ladder propped up against the control panel …

When they got to the Sister nearest her, Ki didn't wait. She charged, knocking the smaller Sister aside, where she toppled over with a cry. Ki clambered to the top of the ladder and sprang as high as she could.

For just a moment she could see over the top of the control panel. Arraigned in neat rows, were colored jewels, slightly glowing, bulging out of their sockets. Ki reached out and clawed for one, knocking a pink stone from its place. As she reached for the stone she knocked a small vase off the panel. The vase fell to the floor and smashed.

It was full of fresh lilies. Flowers picked from the surface to provide the entombed Sisters with a bit of sunshine. Ki landed in the mess of flowers and broken vase.

<*Villains!! Someone is here!*>

<*It has taken P3847!*>

<*The Superior has been touched! To her side at once!*>

The room roared with shock and horror.

Ki picked up the pink stone and tore toward the door, running as fast as she could. She moved at what seemed like a nightmare crawl.

Behind her death pursued. <*What is it? Where is it?*>

She felt pillars of TK whizzing about the room, groping for her. There was a splashing: about a hundred golden Sisters from the pool rose into the air and glided about, fruitlessly searching for her.

Ki glanced back once. A hoard of Sisters, big, small, and golden, moved about in confusion, but quickly covering the ground, gaining on her.

There was the threshold, only a few more steps.

Something was sitting in the dark just beyond doorway. It was a cat.

As Ki neared, the cat puffed up somehow. No, it didn't puff up—it stood up, like a half cat, half human monster. It shrieked: "ZAAAAAAAAAAALLLL!!"

Ki was blasted backward. Suddenly, she was laying there surrounded by hundreds of Sisters. They stomped about, reaching with black hands and pointed TKs.

There was no place for Ki to go. They were seconds away from lucking into her; and then that would be it.

Something hurtled through the air and hit the ground with a heavy crash.

The Sisters, startled, turned to it, forgetting about her for the moment.

Laying there was a silvery book: Carahil's diary, much bigger than she was used to seeing it.

<*Harken … what is it?*>

<*'Tis an arcane book. It's the Wumalaar's Book. Behold, it courses with power.*>

<*Destroy it!*>

<*No, no, we must study it …*>

One of the giant Sisters came forward and TK'ed the book off the ground. Several others gathered around. They poked and prodded it.

<*Some strange, ancient writing on the cover. What secrets are held within?*>

One of them, using TK, opened the book.

A giant-sized cream pie shot out and hit the Sister square in the face. She dropped the book and stood there, open-mouthed. "Euuhh!" she said. Probably never in her ancient life had she been hit in the face with a pie, and she reacted just like Syg did, with complete disarmed shock. A blast of Shadow tech would have troubled her less. The others reacted the same way. They began attending to her, trying to clean her astonished face.

The way was clear. Ki crawled on all fours through the Sister's legs and then made a break for it.

She saw red cat's eyes in the dark on the other side. She drew her SK and fired. TACK!

The eyes vanished.

She emerged through the doorway and continued up the parapet into the dark. A gaggle of Sisters, small, large and golden emptied out into the chamber hot on her heels, they blundered about, still not able to properly see her.

Their thoughts were a panicked, enraged racket.

<*What is it?*>

<*What is it?*>

<*What was our Sister attacked with?*>

<*It seems to be a pie …*>

<*No, no, it cannot be a pie! Who would dare strike a Sister of the Deathhand with pie? She must receive medical assistance at once!*>

<*We will peel the flesh from its bones!!*>

<*What if it escapes? What are we to do?*>

<*It shan't escape … for our wounded Sister, it shan't escape!*>

<*It was pie, Sister. She is fine!*>

<*Where did it go?*>

She reached the top of the parapet as the area below filled with ant-like activity. "Carahil …" she whispered. "Carahil!" She hoped beyond hope that he responded.

<*Harken, did you hear? Is it the Wumalaar again?*>

<*The Wumalaar is dead.*>

Looking around a moment, she found his body, mangled, torn half apart, mashed into the dirt. His silver, seal body was ripped open.

"Carahil?" she said, choked with tears. "I got it … I got a Brightstone."

She shook him. "… Carahil?"

She felt him tremor a little bit.

Still alive!!

Quickly, she opened his mouth, and stuck the Brightstone in. "You and your pies, Carahil …" she said, trying to generate a laugh.

It rolled out, his silver tongue lolled.

"Carahil, please …"

His tongue moved slightly. Recalling what he said, she picked the Brightstone up, opened his mouth, and literally stuffed it down his throat, lodging it as far down as she could reach.

<*What could penetrate this far into the Hazards?*>

<*I do not know … but it will die!*>

<*To the gates … guard all of the gates … it will not get past us!*>

Kilos sat there a moment, waiting for something to happen. Nothing did. Carahil, his silver body in ruins, did nothing. He lay there, unmoving. She could see the bulge of the Brightstone where it lay in his throat.

A sinister, hissing alien voice spoke in the dark. "*We will find you, intruder … we will get you. We will not rest until you are dead. Your life is forfeit. There is no escape!*"

Ki was angry … angry at what they had done to Carahil. "Murderers!" she shouted in return. "I'm going to leave, I'm returning to the sunshine, and I am going to tell what passes here!! All will know what is done in this place! You and the Black Abbess—one in the same!!" she shouted.

There was a chamber-filling shriek—a din of angry screaming, mixed with a bit of fearful moaning. Thundering about, the Sisters desperately searched the area.

<*Where is it?*>

<*Where!!*>

<*It has stolen P3847! Its soul is forfeit!*>

<*I heard it over here!*>

<*No, it was from this direction.*>

<*Ages!! This is the end of us!*>

<*The people … the people … they will never understand!! They will never forgive us!!*>

<*This is the end!! This is the end!!*>

<*The people will know nothing!! The intruder will die here and we will recover P3847!*>

<*Perhaps it went this way …*>

<*It must not escape … It cannot!!*>

Kneeling next to Carahil's body, Ki sat there miserable. A moment later, a frantic giant-sized Sister approached, thundering on her long legs. She shook his carcass, then, satisfied he was dead, moved on. Kilos could feel the hair-raising power of her killing hands as she passed so close, yet completely unable to see her.

Alone in dark Kilos sat there for a bit, and, having nothing better to do, cried.

Carahil had brought her here—*put the stone in his mouth and everything will be fine.*

Ki's thoughts were in a tempest: Carahil's dead. He had seen something terrible. He was trying to help. He had tried his best. Many will die. He was trying to save *them*, whoever *they* were.

Dav, Syg in danger. She had to warn them!

Lady Poe … in danger.

Slowly, pitifully, she began crawling away from Carahil's ruined body. Sliding further and further into the thick darkness, she followed the walls for a bit, then came to a crossroad. The darkness was comforting as she sat against the wall, the Sisters pounding about, wailing. Again, she could slightly hear the faint, monotonous sounds of machinery far away—it was a sound she thought she could fall asleep to.

The Sisters wanted to touch her with killing hands, her body never to be found. No sun-strewn grave in Tusck with the family for her—instead, to be entombed with the monsters in the most evil place on Kana.

<*We are going to get you!*> the Sisters thought.

Everybody wanted a piece of her.

Leaning against the wall, she curled up into the fetal position, and decided to wait for the end; surely one of the wailing Sisters will be by soon to collect her. To pick her up like a piece of mail and take her someplace.

She heard a faint chirping.

Tweeter came hopping out of her bag. She'd forgotten all about him. Given all the nasty things in here, the ancient snares and traps, the fences and safeguards meant to disrupt and shutdown Gifts, she figured Tweeter was a goner, or soon to be dead or insensate, take your pick.

But no, there he was, rooting around in the dark, his silver light swallowed up, but not his life, not his spirit. She reached out to Tweeter and held him to her; his tiny silver head nuzzling against her face. "Hey, Tweeter, hey ..." she said to him softly through tears. "It's good to see you."

She held him for a bit. He made her think of Poe, the lady who had made him, and Dav and Syg ... her friends. She recalled watching Lady Poe sit down and begin creating him for her. Lady Poe of Blanchefort, ever thoughtful and concerned, wanted to make sure Ki didn't get lost while she was a guest in the castle. She had been in a hurry. A coach had come to take her to the windy, western city of Saga for yet another outing with yet another expectant League Lord—and she was late, but she took the time to make one for her anyway. She remembered the little ball of silver that formed in her lap, and, watching, saw it condense into the shape of a small bird. She remembered the first thing Tweeter did was flap up and land on her nose. "He's all yours," Poe had said. "I made him just for you."

"Will this really work?" Ki had asked, looking cross-eyed at Tweeter sitting on her nose.

"He sure will," Poe said happily. "With Tweeter at your side, you need never be lost again."

You need never be lost again ...

The memory was a happy one, filled with light and good friends. She began to take heart.

Certainly, Tweeter couldn't work properly in here ... in the center of hell? All the old snares lining the passages, he'd probably fall to the ground and hop in circles.

The two of them were to be buried here together; buried alive.

At least she had him—a reminder of the light beyond the tunnels.

"Can you get me out of here, Tweeter? Can you do that for me?" she asked, expecting nothing.

He chirped and flew off into the dark.

Seemed eager enough.

Slowly, crawling on all fours, she followed, tears dripping off her nose. She couldn't see Tweeter in the smothering dark, but she could hear him just fine. He was hopping around just ahead, waiting for her to follow.

Stopping, she took one last look back.

She couldn't see Carahil's body. In the dark, she couldn't see it.

12—Pieces in Play

Torrijayne of Waam walked through the manor on her way to the study. She was freshly washed, ready for the evening; her pale skin silky and smooth. She wore only a small flower-print silk robe. Her hair and slender feet were still slightly damp from her wash. She had bathed at her leisure in a huge tub filled with rose petals that she had gathered, and washed her long black hair, scenting it with blossoms. Her Duke liked her scented and pretty. She wanted to please her Duke.

She remembered, not long ago, being a Black Hat Painter. She remembered doing terrible things. She recalled her X-shaped temple in the Xaphan city of Waam, how her temple was an accursed, feared place. She remembered the pain she'd inflicted there, and the terror she had inspired. It all seemed like a blurry, strange dream to her. Just like the illusions she was so good at creating—her whole life a long, dark illusion filled with the nightmare images of dying faces and tortured bodies. If her Duke hadn't told her it was all right, if he hadn't told her the things she'd done weren't her fault … then the guilt should have consumed her.

Only the last week seemed real. Only her Duke, sitting at her bedside, seemed real. She was eager to put her past life behind her and be forgotten. She had so much to look ahead to, she and her Duke. Perhaps soon he'll ask her to marry him.

Her life began when she opened her eyes in the dungeon below. She was naked, shackled, surrounded by herbs and plants that made her feel slightly sick and weak. She remembered hating the man, wanting to kill him; desperate to kill him and escape, back to Waam and her dark temple. She remembered something bright and silvery with glowing eyes … eyes that reached out and warmed her.

She recalled suddenly feeling many things. She wondered where she was. Her arms hurt. She was terribly hungry. What is that smell? Who is that man?

She slumped in her manacles and he freed her, cleaned her, dressed her, and he told her his name: Lord Fallsworth, the Duke of Oyln. As she lay there, all the hate draining out of her, she told him hers, she wanted to tell him: Torrijayne of Waam. Telling him her name was like lifting a weight off of her soul. After that, everything else flowed together. After that, her life began.

She was carrying a tray of spirits and mixers. She loved it when her Duke made her a cool drink, and they curled up together in the study or the bedroom, or out on the lawn and he told her stories. Stories of romance and adventures. She loved them, couldn't wait to share in his adventures herself. She sometimes sat in the Duke's library and marveled at all the books neatly lined up in towering shelves. She longed for the day that she could read them herself; her Duke was teaching her, he was such a patient man. The Duke told her that this was her library too, that everything he had was hers also, if she wanted it.

Oh, how she wanted it: to pick up a book and read it, to train her attention to things other than illusions and killing.

And the flowers that they picked together in the garden; wondrous, simply wondrous. She loved to smell and arrange them. His study, once a drab, airless, lightless place of olive upholstery and cream-painted woods, was now filled with huge Moorland vases full of colorful flowering plants that she cut and potted. The curtains were thrown open admitting life-giving sunshine.

She and her Duke.

Her tray was full of colored bottles that clanked together as she walked. She didn't know what was what yet; she couldn't read the labels. She always carefully watched what he was doing when he made the drinks and tried to remember what bottle did what, so she had loaded as much onto the tray as she could from the bar.

Let's see: a few splashes from the pink bottle, a long pour from the green bottle shaped like a pear, and a healthy shake should create what her Duke called a martini. What a yummy drink. Oh! The olives—she cannot forget the olives.

She wanted to surprise him with the drinks. She will go into the study, and she will take the bottles and make him a martini. They will drink their drinks, he'll hold her and tell her a story, then they'll make love.

As Torri approached the door, she thought she could see something crouching in the shadows at the end of the hall. Stopping, she stared, trying to get a better look.

"Who is there?" she asked holding the tray. She wasn't scared—she didn't feel fear, per se.

Something moved. Something spoke: "Good evening, ma'am, I hope I did not startle you."

"You didn't. Who are you? Why are you hiding?"

It came out of the shadows and bowed.

"My, but you are a vision, ma'am. May I ask your name, please?"

"Torrijayne. Torrijayne of Waam."

"That is a beautiful name. Will you please tell your Duke that I have come calling on him. It is time. He'll know what you mean."

As Torri reached for the door handle, it spoke again. "I'm sorry," it said.

"Why?" she asked.

"Because you appear to have washed for the evening. I am afraid that you'll be heading out soon."

* * * * *

The bridge crew gave each other knowing glances—they'd heard that something was up, something interesting.

They knew their destination was an unknown derelict ship bearing out of Heron.

What was a Main Fleet Vessel like the *Seeker* doing on a paltry mission like that? That's what the Marines were for.

They suspected House Xandarr and Princess Marilith. Tense, eager, ready for action they waited to intercept the ship, wondering if at any moment that fierce painted face would appear on the cone as it had so many times in the past: dressed in veils, nearly nude, holding her legendary knife.

Davage saw it. "Now, everyone, this exercise here today is merely to spare us the drudgery of having to play taxi cab for a stodgy, pedantic Admiral. I expect no unusual happenings here and merely wish to assist our Marine friends as best we can. We will, no doubt, locate some marginally functional tramp vessel ferrying unfortunate Xaphan refugees. Stay sharp, fly true, and I am certain this will pass without notice."

Syg looked at Dav from her chair. <*You really believe that, love?*>

<*Certainly.*>

Syg smiled. <*Oh, I see—too bad nobody else does.*>

As Syg touched upon, none of the crew listened to Dav's speech. They'd heard whispers in the pubs and in the mess … of a new enemy. A new Xandarr princess who wanted to kill the great Captain Davage. They'd heard this princess was some sort of trained weapon—that she'd prepared her whole life to meet Lord Blanchefort and kill him.

Now, that's adventure. That's excitement.

None believed such a thing could happen. They had Captain Davage, he of the Sight, he of the Helm. Captain Davage could not be beat. All they had to do was hold on, do their jobs, and enjoy the show.

Full of confidence and hoping for some action, they sailed into the Heron system … ready for whatever.

A familiar hush fell on the bridge as the strange, black ship appeared on the holo-cone, right where the Marines said it should be.

The crew was excited. They remembered Princess Marilith, the battles, the victories. The twisted metal, and captured prisoners. The crew thought of the old fights with Princess Marilith with a gleam of nostalgia.

Manning their posts, they waited for the usual screen on, the war-paint, the bare chest in 3-D on the holo-cone and the brandished knife that she longed to stick into Captain Davage's chest. The insults and threats.

But, there was nothing … a long, shadowy silence from the vessel ahead.

* * * * *

Davage stared at the ship—he'd not seen anything like it before. It was large—huge actually—possibly twice as long as the *Seeker*. It was situated around a central cylinder, like a toppled-over column. The cylinder appeared to be segmented at regular intervals. In the center of every tenth segment was a large set of antenna dishes or wings, articulated in a curve and swooping like a bat's-wing. There were ten of these winged-arrays spaced evenly along the length of the cylinder.

The ship was dead black, with a slight burnish of brass, lit up by the yellowish light of the Heron Nebula.

"Fore Sensing, are you reading anything?" Davage asked.

Sasai stared into her view screen. "No, sir. Not reading any life signs, any obvious source of power or propulsion, or any known metals."

Davage, as usual, Sighted the ship, his glowing eyes lighting up the bridge. None paid any attention except for Syg, who still couldn't resist looking at them. In his Sight, he could see the finely detailed exterior of the central cylinder, the delicate structure of the wings, the absolute lack of usual starship activity, power, moving parts … and people.

"It looks like Shadow tech," he said finally. "A lot of it. Countess," he said addressing Syg formally, which she hated, "do you sense anything?"

She stood up and walked toward image on the holo-cone. "I don't feel anything here. I need a window."

"This way, please." Davage motioned for her to step into his office. She did with a proud gait—finally, she got to go into his office for something "official".

They walked in and closed the door. Syg huffed. "I wish you stopped calling me 'Countess'. I am your wife after all."

"Just protocol, darling," he said.

She kissed him, then looked out the window. The black ship was huge, its size much more apparent through the windows than it had appeared on the cone. The large shaft of circular light from the Main Sensor traveled up and down the ship's length. The illuminated area was just as dark and lifeless as the rest. Syg gazed at it. "I'm not sensing any Shadow tech. I should be feeling it heavy."

Davage Sighted it again. "It has the look of a lot of Shadow tech, Syg, but it's rooted … not bubbling like Shadow tech usually does. If it is Shadow tech, it's not like any I've ever seen before."

He glanced at the ceiling. "Com," he said.

"Com here, sir,"

"Send transmission to the unknown ship."

"Aye, sir. No reply."

Davage thought for a moment. "Syg …"

"Oh, now it's 'Syg', is it?"

"Your Silver tech, I wonder, if you touched the ship with a stream, and it is Shadow tech, then there will be a reaction, correct?"

"Yes, I suppose."

"Then let's to a hatch and …"

Syg smiled. "No need." She lifted a finger and sent a small stream of silver to the window. It splattered and collected there for a moment, then a gossamer strand emerged on the other side of the window. She then sent it streaking toward the ship.

"See, love, Silver tech can find the tiniest of imperfections, even at the atomic level, and move through."

She put her free arm around Davage and closed her eyes. "It's cold out there."

"No doubt."

The stream reached the ship and touched the surface.

Startled, she lurched away from his side.

"Dav!!" Syg screamed. "It is! It's Shadow tech, of a type I've never seen before either!"

A dark wave passed across the ship and a surge sizzled through the stream into Syg's arm.

There was a flash.

She clenched her teeth and fell to the floor.

* * * * *

Kilos had been crawling for hours it seemed, though she couldn't be sure. Time here in the dark had no meaning.

She was following Tweeter, following the sound of his chirps. She had no idea if he actually could get her out of here or not—certainly this place will foul his inner workings sooner or later. He was just a toy, a clever bit of Silver tech created by her best friend's sister to keep her from embarrassing herself in unfamiliar places. A "gadget" she had said. Surely he was no match for the ancient evil lurking in the damned dark; the same evil that had kept out all the old Vith heroes, and even the Sisters for centuries. Surely Tweeter was on borrowed time, and so was she. She expected him at any moment to simply keel-over and die.

But on he went, just as bouncy and cheerful and ever.

The dark was shocking; devastating. Every so often, she thought she could see light in the distance and she tried to quicken her pace, but, like a shimmering mirage, the light never got any closer. It was just a bit of hopeful thinking courtesy of her color-starved imagination.

Tweeter was hopping along confidently. When he wanted to go left or right, he pecked the walls, and Ki, dirty, exhausted, knees skinned, followed. She didn't bother to try and walk any more. Whenever she tried to stand and walk, the unseen ground invariably rose or fell sharply, sending her toppling.

It was better just to crawl.

She became aware of being exhausted—bone tired. How far had she crawled? How long ago it had been since she'd eaten her lonely breakfast at Castle Blanchefort? She stopped and leaned against a wall. "Tweeter!" she gasped. "Give me a moment, please."

Kilos' hearing, made acute in the pitch black, picked up the minute sounds of Tweeter hopping toward her. He chirped. Though she couldn't see, she could imagine him looking up at her, patiently waiting for her to follow.

She closed her eyes, letting sleep take her away toward lighted passes and friend-filled vistas. Dav and Syg, dear Lady Poe, and … Carahil. He was a friend too.

She heard sounds in the distance. A mechanical droning, accented by industrial hammering and other metallic sounds. It was the same clatter of sounds she had heard before, far off in the distance. It was a vaguely soothing collection of noises; though loud, she could easily sleep to it.

The sound was getting closer.

Tweeter suddenly flew up into her face. She could feel his wings beating in a flurry, feel the breeze.

"What, Tweeter?" she said, wanting to sleep.

He jumped onto the bridge of her nose and began pecking her cheek.

She had a mind to give him a good cuff across the beak.

Let me sleep! All I want to do is sleep.

The ground began to vibrate. Something was approaching.

What had Carahil said—there were not only snares for the Gifted here in the Hazards, there were machines too, waiting to fall upon any who might have gotten through.

A machine approached.

Kilos pulled herself from her delirium. The sound was loud—the machine could be upon her at any moment.

"Tweeter! Get me away from this thing!"

He hopped onto her right shoulder and began pecking her right ear.

"Right, you want me to go right?" She started moving to her right, down unseen passageways toward the nearing machine."

When she had gone right enough, Tweeter hopped off her shoulder and got in her hair. Straight, she guessed he wanted her to go straight.

She crawled straight.

The sound got loud to the point of being deafening. It had to be right in front of her.

Tweeter hopped onto her left shoulder and she dove to her left and kept moving.

The sound reached an apex; the squeaking of wheels, the rolling of treads, and then began slowly fading into the distance. Soon, it was nothing more than a pleasing, industrial drone again.

Kilos, crawling, smiled. "Thanks, Tweets."

He chirped in response.

"Get me out of here, okay, and go ahead and peck my eye out if I start to fall asleep again."

Following his lead, Ki crawled on, still forever deep under the Hazards of the Old Ones.

* * * * *

Sometime later, Tweeter's little silver wings stopped flapping and his chipping was silenced. He stayed quiet for what seemed like a long time. Was this it … was he dead? She was about to call out to him, when her blood froze.

Something was nearby, in the dark. It wasn't her imagination. Something was there … stirring, huge and rustling. She could feel it.

There was a hideous voice: "*COME HERE!! COME TO ME!!*"

It was the ugliest voice she had ever heard; the voice of the devil. It blasted her ears, filling the tunnel.

The Dirge—the giant Sisters, unable to root her out of the dark, unable to trust their machines, were trying the Dirge to command her to come to them.

She could feel her muscles begin to clench. She began moving.

But wait … what had Dav told her once, about the Gifts and Browns? Something about the Dirge. She knew the Dirge was considered a bad Gift; a rotten, rude, dirty Gift. Using the Dirge to force someone to do something they didn't want to do, it tended to create bad feelings. Those Dirgeists who plied their trade too often found themselves with few friends, lots of enemies, and were generally given a bad time of it. They often ended up in prison. The Dirge was best left as a parlor trick, an amusement for children on lazy afternoons.

"*COME TO ME! WE WILL MAKE IT QUICK AND EASY!! WE COMMAND IT!!*"

Again, her muscles clenched. Again, she started moving against her will.

Wait …

That's what Dav had said. The Dirge didn't work on Browns, only Blues.

She closed her eyes and relaxed, allowing the massive Dirge to paw fitfully at her soul; formidable, impressive, but doing nothing.

"*COME HERE!*"

Ki rode it out.

There was silence for a minute or two. Then:

<*Can you hear our thoughts? Yes … you can, can you not?*>

The Sisters, they were here and they were close. They hadn't given up searching for her. Their eyes had failed them, their machines roving the tunnels had failed, their hyper-powered Dirge had failed, now was the time for intimidation and threats.

She cleared her mind … kept it quiet.

<*We do not know what you are … or how you have stood where none could stand, or how you resist our Dirge, or avoid our mechanical cats, but no matter. Have no illusions, we will find you … and we will determine all your secrets … wrung from your living flesh.*>

Ki, leaning against the wall, heard a rhythmic pounding—the huge dirty footfalls of a giant-sized Sister. She was near; she was very, very near, just a few paces ahead.

<*Come to us … wait for us … All of the exits are being watched … all the passages are being sifted. You cannot get out … Be reasonable. Wait for us …*>

Her ears, sharpened by hours of pitch black, picked up a faint rasping.

<*We will make it quick and easy, you have our word. Come to us … we command it!!*>

They couldn't detect her. They were desperate to stop her; to silence her.

<Heed not our command, continue running, and, when we find you, we will first kill everyone you have ever known as you watch: your friends … your family … your loves. All will die and you will be the last. Come to us … end this now. For the sake of the League, end this now …>

More pounding, the Sister couldn't be more than a few feet away. Ki could hear her ragged breaths, could smell her exposed innards. She heard a claw scraping the ground. She heard a sniffing.

<You were here … at one point. Yes, you were, I can smell you. Could it be that you are a … Brown? Yes … a Brown … we hadn't considered … we hadn't considered … We will have to remedy …>

More sniffing.

<You … are from Onaris, yes? I see golden fields, I see serfs working in the sun. You are a serf, too. Know, this, Brown … Serf, we will eventually determine your identity … we will … we've all the time in the world … You could be safe in your bed, a million miles away and it matters not … And when we find you … woe to you and those you love …>

Ki quietly drew her SK, scooted forward a bit and was ready to fire, ready to shoot the Sister nearby. Whether the giant Sister, a master of life and death, could be gunned down, she didn't know.

She cocked her SK, and the sound was huge in the dark. CHU-CHUCK!!

"Erraah!" she heard the Sister grunt audibly.

The poundings approached at a run.

Ki rolled to the other side of the passage and, a moment later the Sister was standing right where she had been, clawing at the ground. Little bits of dust and crushed stone rained down on her.

<BROWN!! We will trample in your flesh!>

Ki aimed where she thought the Sister's torso might be. She put pressure on the trigger. She could feel the Sister's rage. She could feel the pure malice streaming out of her.

These Sisters, hidden in the cursed dark, stained by the Black Abbess, doing work they felt necessary and just, had become sour; become paranoid. And to keep their secret, the things they would do to her flesh. The agony they would inflict. They had become monstrous, body and soul, just like the Black Abbess before them.

Just a little more pressure and the SK will go off, and then Kilos of Tusck will come face to face with her eternity, swallowed up in the Hazards of the Old Ones …never to see the light of day again.

<*Wumalaar!*> came a frenzied thought from far off.

<*How can this be?*>

<*There is a Wumalaar at the gates!! And it has P3847!!*>

<*P3847!*>

<*North passage!!*>

<*Hurry Sisters … hurry!! The Wumalaar is powerful!!*>

The Sister pounded the wall of the passage in frustration.

<*We know you are here, little intruder, cowering in the dark. Worry not, we shan't be long … we will be back for you … and when we get hold of your blessed form at last … your torment will be the basis for a whole new branch of suffering. The Gates are watched, and you cannot exit them. Upon your flesh we will know how our fences were cut!*>

There was a clatter of ceramic tiles smashing and breaking under the Sister's fist. Then, a second later, she was gone, striding down the passage to go get the "Wumalaar".

Ki sat there for a moment and caught her breath. The Sisters, just by smell could somehow piece together who she was—after just a few moments they had already determined she was a Brown from Onaris. How long after that will they know she was from Tusck? How long after that will they learn her identity, and kill everybody: her family, her husband … Dav, Syg …

Perhaps, there was no escape from the Hazards. Perhaps this was a one-way trip. Maybe Carahil knew that all along.

Something nuzzled up against her face. It chirped.

"Hey Tweeter …"

Tweeter!! She'd forgotten about him yet again. She thought he was gone, dead, swallowed up at last in the presence of the enraged Sister.

But no, here he was. Unseen in the dark but felt none-the-less. She petted him for a moment, then he fluttered off and chirped. Slowly, she holstered her SK and crawled after him. He came back, fluttered in her face a moment and then flew away. Apparently, he wanted her to hurry.

She stood and stumbled ahead, careful of the rises and falls, her unseen legs unsteady.

Tweeter, chirping, turned to the left. Feeling for the walls, she followed.

Light far ahead … another mirage.

No, no, there was light, in the distance, a distant dark blue smudge! She looked down and could see her legs and the ground in a brackish light. Ahead she could see Tweeter's silver light, the relief of the Magravine tiles standing out sharply in a ring as he flew. She looked back, the thick unnatural darkness ended several paces to the rear.

She quickened her gait—she ran. She will get back to civilization, contact Dav, warn him of danger … then, she will probably kill herself to protect him, to keep the Sisters from discovering her.

She ran out of the mouth of the tunnel. It was night, the stars were out, the distant mountains lined up like lavender shells under the dusty sandbag of starlight.

Stars!! Fresh air!! Tweeter ahead, glowing as a candle.

She ran, though her heart and legs demanded respite. Where was she? Where could she go? Where was the nearest town or estate?

It didn't matter. Anywhere but here was better.

Suddenly, a vise came down on her.

She'd gone about three hundred yards from the tunnel when she was stopped cold. She was held fast in place, defying gravity. She dropped her SK and it hung in the air, held fast just like she was.

TK'ed.

She couldn't move a muscle. She squirmed and struggled. She couldn't breathe. She was caught in an invisible death grip from top to bottom.

Panic took her.

The Sisters … they had her at last.

* * * * *

"Syg!! Syg, are you all right?" Davage cried picking her up off the floor. He glanced at the wall and Sighted through it.

The ship. He Sighted the Black ship moving, firing black weapons. He Sighted the *Seeker* being latched onto and squeezed.

"Lt. Verlin, he yelled toward the ceiling. "Get us out of here, maximum speed!! Lt. Larsen, mark bearings and fire!"

He loosened Syg's gown. Her heart—it wasn't beating. Her eyes rolled back in her head. "Hospitalers to the Captain's office!!"

He could feel the ship hauling around. Several thuds: canister missiles exiting the ship.

Something was hitting the ship—not cassagrains, rather something big and jarring.

"Captain!" Verlin cried over the Com. "The ship has been grappled! We are held in place!!"

The ship shuddered again.

"Captain," came Larsen's voice. "Canisters have impacted the enemy vessel but damage cannot be assessed!"

"Keep firing! Evasive maneuvers!"

He couldn't leave Syg's side. His wife, his beloved Syg, was dying in his arms. He couldn't open her mouth to breathe for her—her mouth was clenched shut.

The door flew open, and Ennez, his Hospitaler Samaritan, entered with two Chancellors.

"Ennez, it's Syg! Her heart's not beating!"

Ennez knelt down and pulled out a scanner. "What happened?"

"She was scanning the unknown vessel, screamed and fell!"

Ennez moved his scanner about. "Elder's Balls, Dav—her body is flooded with energy! That's what's keeping her heart from beating!"

The *Seeker* rocked again, and was listing to port.

The Chancellors opened her gown, and quickly affixed several electrodes from a small device to her chest. "Armed!" one said.

"Fire!" the other said. They jolted Syg, trying to shock her heart into beating.

Nothing.

Ennez scanned. "She's still getting shocked—energy's flooding her nervous system!"

The Chancellors tried to lift her chin and breathe for her, but she was rigid, like a statue.

"Shocked? From where?" Davage asked. "How!"

"I don't know! You tell me!"

The ship's list grew more pronounced. More thuds.

"Captain!" Verlin cried over the Com. "We cannot break free!"

Davage thought a moment. "Wait, Ennez … here! Look here!" He looked to her small, elegant hand, and there was a tiny strand of Silver tech. She was still connected to the monster ship outside.

He took the strand, and tried to break it with his hands. He pulled and pulled, it didn't budge. He could feel the shocking power coursing through the strand. He tried again—still nothing.

Ennez scanned it. "Dav—this strand has to go. I'm reading massive energy surging through it!"

Another thud from outside.

Ennez pulled a pair of cutters out of one of his pockets. He tried to cut the strand, and got the shock of his life, the cutters flying out of his hand and sticking into the door.

Davage stood and unsaddled his CARG. "Stand back, Ennez! Everybody stand clear!"

Ennez, and the Chancellors backed away, and Davage cleaved down with his heavy, coppery CARG. The Silver tech strand, no thicker than a hair and as delicate as spider's silk, met the cutting blow and resisted. It didn't break. He gritted his teeth as the shocking power of the strand flowed up the CARG into his body, blowing his hat off.

He staggered.

Recovering, wheeling back, Davage raised and lowered his CARG again, this time with Full Strength. It cleaved the silver strand and made a deep furrow in the floor.

The silver snapped with a high-pitched "TINK!"

Syg, free of the shock, went limp.

The Chancellors set their equipment back up, and hit her again.

"Armed … fire!"

"Beat! Good beat!"

Ennez removed the electrodes, and began massaging her chest, and, after a moment, Syg exhaled roughly. He got his scanner out and waved it around. "Looks good, Dav, her heart-rate is returning to normal."

"Get her to the dispensary, Ennez, and don't let her leave!"

Syg took a few pained breaths. "Dav …" she said weakly. "What's going on?"

"You're going with Ennez to the dispensary."

"What? I'm … I'm all right, Dav. I don't want to go with Ennez, I want to stay with you!"

Davage picked her up and handed her to Ennez. "Get her to the dispensary and that's an order!"

Ennez began walking out. "Dav!" Syg cried. "DAV!!" She weakly kicked in his arms.

Davage steeled himself, and headed for the bridge.

13—The Goshawks

Ki couldn't move an inch. She couldn't blink; she couldn't breathe. Her SK floated just out of her grasp, also stuck in the TK.

Away from here, she wanted away! To flee and never stop.

She expected the giant Sisters to come roaring out of the tunnel at any moment. Unable to breathe, she was on the verge of passing out. Her heart was pounding, palpitating; her lungs screaming for air.

Someone spoke from nowhere just then. "It's a lady! A tall one, Fall!" she heard a small female voice say.

"Does she have blonde hair?" she heard another voice say, a male voice this time, with a weird accent.

There was a tentative pause. "Hard to tell, really," came the female voice. "It's sort of brownish-blonde, I guess. She's got a big gun with her."

"Well that's her then. Let her go, Torri!"

Ki was suddenly released. She plopped roughly to the ground, her SK too. She sucked in air, trying to fill her lungs.

She looked up. In the abundant starlight, a woman appeared in front of her. The woman was small and slender with long, styled black hair. She wore a black flight suit with a black duster over top of it. She had on padded, Macco-style boots, (like what they wore in the Astro-Merchants), which made her appear a bit shorter than she actually was. Her long black hair was elaborately styled and held in place with a few barrettes enameled with flowers.

She also had the mark: the Black Hat's Shadowmark on her face. It stood out sharply in the dark on her pale skin. Ki thought she might have been Bethrael of Moane for a second, but she didn't have a mole on her cheek, and her hair was the wrong color. The woman had a friendly smile, just like Beth did.

"Hi!" the woman said cheerfully. "Sorry about that—the TK I mean. You can't be too careful, you know. Right, Fall?"

A tall, blonde-headed man appeared. He was dressed in a similar style to the woman, only he wore a black triangle hat and had on a long black scarf. A large pipe jutted out of his mouth. Ki's long stint quelling rowdies in the Marines told her this man was armed to capacity, she could tell by the fullness of his duster.

"Are you Madame Kilos, formerly of the Fleet Main Starship *Seeker*?" he asked with a mildly accented voice.

"I am," Kilos said picking up her SK. The woman, the Black Hat, though smiling, watched her closely. Tweeter landed on Ki's shoulder, throwing her face into silver relief.

She turned to the Hazards, fear welling up inside of her.

The exits are being watched!!

"Neat bird," the woman said looking at Tweeter. "What is it … it's sort of like Shadow tech, right?"

The man took his pipe out of his mouth and held it. "Please allow me to introduce myself. I am Lord Fallsworth—" he said.

"—The Duke of Oyln," the woman added with a touch of pride looking up at him.

Kilos thought she could hear something coming from the tunnels.

The Holes! The Sisters. Coming to kill her!

"Do you have a ship? Can you take us out of here quickly? I—I can pay you …"

Oyln laughed. "Yes, yes … But first, please allow me to introduce this lovely lady here …" He put his arm around the woman, and she leaned her head against his chest affectionately. "This is Torrijayne of Waam, my better half."

"Please, Duke we must away!" Ki said.

"What's the rush?" Torrijayne asked looking around at the darkened landscape. "It's pretty out here. Don't you think it's pretty, Fall? I'd love to come back here in the daytime."

Before the Ki could answer, there was a horrid cry from the depths of the tunnel. She looked back at it, the fear visible in her face. The Duke and Torrijayne turned to look at the tunnels in a nonchalant manner.

"Have you a vessel?" Ki quickly asked. "We need to be away from here at once! Please!"

"Right this way," The Duke said motioning toward a clearing.

"What was that noise?" Torri asked casually.

"Nothing—please we must go, quickly!" It was like a nightmare, everything happening at a snail's crawl. Everything needed explaining and mulling over.

They didn't have much time. Out of here—now!

Suddenly, a wheezy voice spoke up. "Drop your weapons if you please."

On a nearby ridge, a motley group of seven men and three women stood holding an equally motley assortment of weapons: hunting rifles, Hit-6 Frag-locks, old Marine surplus R4e breech-loaders, and a few aftermarket blundercannons—an old-fart Brown favorite that was unreliable, unaimable and ridiculously cheap. Another group, ten more men, and four women armed in a similar fashion, appeared behind them as well.

Ki, the Duke and Torrijayne were caught in a circle of fire … and the Devil coming from the holes.

<ARRRRRAAAHHHHH … We are coming for you, Brown! Soon, soon … Enjoy the night air while you can!>

They came forward a few steps, weapons leveled. They were a scabby group: scarecrow thin, dressed in knickers, knee-britches and waistcoats. They looked to Ki to be a group of butlers, servants, cooks and maids—a dirty, treacherous bunch of Browns if she had ever seen one.

The Duke squinted in the dark. "Ellington, is that you?"

"Correct, dear Duke," he said. "Lord Milton gives his regards. Now, if you'll be so kind, your weapons, please."

"Ellington, I am certain the night air will be bad for your fungal lung condition. Go on home, and take this lot with you, and tell Lord Milton that I'll be speaking to him regarding this matter in the morning."

Ellington stifled a cough and shook his gun. "Your weapons, Duke. I'll not ask again." He cocked his hammer.

"You've been more than patient, Fall," Torrijayne said. "Let's drop `em!"

The Duke smiled. "My weapons, Ellington, certainly." He pulled his finely-made Grenville 40 pistol from his duster.

POP! One of the maids holding a breechloader fired. The bullet bounced off of a Sten field surrounding the Duke. He lifted his

Grenville 40 and promptly returned fire, shooting one of the attackers dead with a roaring BANG!

"Gah! Treachery!" Ellington yelled, firing his blundercannon. His shot hit a rolling Sten floating in front of the Duke and sparkled as the pellets bounced off. Ellington did an inept, arms and legs, shoulder roll into the bushes. His cronies did the same, their assortment of weapons popping off in a variety of reports.

Ki hit the ground and drew her SK. She couldn't believe this. With a TACK!, TACK! she blew two away before they had a chance to dive for cover themselves. She just had enough time to roll away before shots from the group behind her sprayed the dirt between her legs.

A shootout! She had no time for this! An ancient evil was about to come screaming out of those holes and land right on top of them.

"Listen to me! We all have got to get out of here!! We are all about to die!" she shouted.

"You're about to die, certain enough, hot blood!" a bent servant with a blundercannon said, discharging it with an unhealthy "BARP" sound.

Gunplay was everywhere: BARP!!, TACK, TACK, TOMB, TOMB, BLAM, BLAM, BOUM! PHAM! BARP!! BOUM!!

Somebody flashed a blundercannon and a slug of pellets went off proudly in some random direction. It was often safest to be standing right in front of a blundercannon when it went off.

Someone leveled at Torrijayne of Waam and fired. The bullet hit her Sten field and bounced away. Smiling, she Pointed and the man exploded, instantly.

The Duke rolled to his left, and, drawing a small brass device from his duster, lobbed it into the Brown's midst. Before they had a chance to react, a series of wiry tentacles emerged from the device with an ugly, swishing whine, enveloping several attackers in a cutting and cruel embrace. In pieces and in a drone of dying screams, the men fell dead; their weapons cubed just as easily as their flesh had been. The surviving attackers, horrified, moved away from the terrifying weapon.

That was a LosCapricos weapon, that thing he just threw, Ki thought, though she couldn't recall which one.

Torrijayne of Waam was taking fire from all around. She was just standing there not making much of an effort to move or duck, and was an irresistible target. A steady stream of bullets and shot bounced non-stop off of her Sten field. It really wasn't fair—not much could penetrate her Sten, yet she could freely send things out through it as she would. She was holding a wiggling black snake, which she calmly tossed into a group of firing servants. The snake grew to a huge size, wrapping up and eating one of the screaming attackers whole, head first, in a horrid ophidian embrace.

Shadow tech; Ki'd know it anywhere. The snake slithered off to terrorize more of the attackers, bullets and blundercannon shot peppering its length.

The Duke drew something else out of his coat—some sort of black stick. Another LosCapricos weapon. Using the head of the stick he traced a blue design into the air where it glowed and then shot forward. Two men and a woman were severed by it as it passed.

Another man, trying to reload his smoking blundercannon, was suddenly wrapped up tight in Shadow tech. Torrijayne then, with a flick of her wrist, sent the man hurtling away like a screaming stone from a slingshot. His dark, spiraling form, arms and legs splayed helplessly, flew at speed and disappeared over the crest of the mountains. "Creation, I've always wanted to do that to somebody!" she piped.

The group from behind them moved into a better position, they scrabbled for footing and leveled their guns readying to fire a volley.

Three men, dressed in black flight suits and dusters appeared in their midst. With strange, thin swords and pistols they routed the attackers; some falling, some dropping their weapons and running,

"Oh, where're you going!" one of them taunted.

There was another cry from the tunnel … much nearer this time.

"Duke! We must be gone from here!"Ki screamed, nearly in tears. "For our souls, we must be gone from here!"

The remaining attackers stopped firing and stared at the tunnels; they heard the noise as well.

The Duke appeared completely unconcerned. He put his stick away, gathered his small brass capsules and puffed on his pipe. After a moment, he disappeared, so too did the newcomers. Torrijayne too. All gone.

Ki was now alone in the starlight with the remaining attackers: about five of them.

"Where'd they go?" yelled one of the attackers holding a smoking breecher, looking through his night scope.

"Did you hear that?" a frightened woman said holding her blundercannon. "It's the devil! You know the stories! It's the devil!"

"Maybe we should get out of here?" one of the other survivors said. "Use your thing, Ellington, and let's go!"

Just as Ki was about to stand and make a panic-filled, screaming run for it, three giant-sized Sisters came out of the tunnel entrance, striding in a rage. Ki felt her heart ready to seize.

<BROWWWWWWWWWWWWWN!!!!!>

The remaining attackers looked at the horrific scene, screamed, and began firing at the gigantic monsters charging toward them.

After a moment, guided by the gunfire, the Sisters waded into the mass of firing men and women, groped around a bit and seized several of them. The men died instantly in their grasp. They held the men close to their huge, strange faces—not able to see them, but able to smell. They sniffed the dead men.

"Brroownnns," they said in monstrous voices. They began tossing the dead men toward the tunnels.

A woman dropped her blundercannon and fell to her knees. "Mercy!" she cried. "Mercy!"

A Sister, reaching for the sound of her voice, seized her prostrate form, and threw her newly dead body onto the pile along with the others.

Another Sister grabbed Ellington by his waistcoat and regarded his bent, shrieking form. He unloaded his blundercannon right into her huge, demonic face. She recoiled and dropped him, holding her face with the backs of her hands.

Another Sister groped around and found Ellington again.

<You will live. We must experiment upon you, Brown … to prevent further incursions, to improve our machines. Upon your flesh we shall know the answers. Take a final look at the stars … it will be your last.> the Sister thought.

With that, arms swinging, the Sister took the terrified man by his coat back into the dark of the tunnel. The other Sisters, feeling about, collected the dead from the pile and were gone. The last remaining Sisters helped the one, still holding her face, who'd been shot by Ellington into the tunnel.

Ki could hear his terrified wailing through the dark hole—his screams now mingling with the old ones. She winced; she'd hear his pitiful, terror-laced screams for the rest of her life.

The Duke and the woman re-appeared. "What in the name of Creation were those?"

Ki didn't say anything … she felt her heart ... the pain in her chest.

"You ok?" Torrijayne asked.

"Can we … please go now?" Ki said choking back vomit.

Torrijayne smiled. "You needn't be so frightened—I Cloaked us," she said happily. "I was a Painter, you know. I can throw up a mean painted Cloak in a hurry. Those things have no clue we're here. I Cloaked you too, but I didn't have enough time to set it up so that you could see us at the same time. They couldn't detect you."

The three men appeared. One of them looked back at the holes with a great deal of concern. "By the Elders … what were those things? I'd read about the Hazards, but didn't believe the old stories. Creation—if those things find out we're here—"

"THAT'S WHY WE NEED TO LEAVE!!" Ki screamed.

One of the three men, the shortest of the three, strode up to Ki. "Is this Madame Kilos? Whoa, but isn't she sweet?"

"Not now, Johnnie," the Duke said. "To your vessels. Peter," he said to one of the men. "Scan for more intruders. Torri, if you please."

A large black ship and three slightly smaller ones appeared. From what she could make out in the dark they weren't like any ships Ki had ever seen before; not a Fleet vessel or standard merchant ship, they must be fancy yachts of some sort. They were fairly large for a private yachts, each being at least twice as big as a Marine cutter. They were black, winged and turreted, barrel-shaped and, as Ki noted, armed.

Peter waved a small hand-held scanner about. "We're clear, Duke. I suggest a rapid departure."

The three men scattered toward their various ships. "Hey, babe!" the shortest of the three said. "Want to come with me? Want to fly with Little Johnnie?"

Ki scowled and quickly made her way to the largest of the four ships. "Married," she said. "Not interested."

"Awww," the man said climbing into his ship.

The man named Peter opened the hatch to his ship. "Please don't mind him, ma'am. He's always fancied himself a lady's man, but he's harmless."

Ki shook her head and boarded.

The crew section was spacious and comfortable. The Duke flopped down into the pliot's seat and began hitting switches. Torrijayne sat next to him. Ki, with Tweeter sitting on her shoulder, buckled into her seat, and, a moment later, the ship blasted away into the night as fast as it could carry them.

Ki stared out the window, watching the Hazards of the Old Ones drift into the distance and get lost in the dark. Somewhere down there, under the mountains, Ellington the Brown servant was about to have the life wrung out of him. She felt for him … for what he was about to endure.

"I'm concerned about the noise of our departure," Kilos said thinking of the Sisters hearing them. She was certain they were to haunt her nightmares for some time to come.

She closed her eyes , and there they were: tall, green, reaching. Heads crowned with knobby protrusions; Ellington's severed head, still screaming, in their hands.

"Don't be," replied Torrijayne. "I've Cloaked us again." Torri looked at a few of the scanners mounted in the cockpit. "Hey, Ellington and his crew, where'd those guys come from I wonder? I don't see any ships down there in any of the screens."

"Don't know … but Lord Milton needs to stop. These assassination attempts are becoming tiresome."

"I can take care of him for you, if you want me to, Fall," Torri said.

"No, no, I'll deal with the matter."

"I thought the whole thing was kind of fun actually. Did you see me toss that guy? I wonder if he's hit the ground yet."

Ki sat back in the chair and took a deep breath. She was utterly exhausted. She closed her eyes, seeing the Sisters, seeing Carahil's dead body. Tweeter gave a chirp, and she rubbed his beak.

Tweeter, her savior. She hoped, after all of this, after how far he'd taken her, that he'd last forever.

Torri turned around and looked at Tweeter with interest. "So what is this little bird? It's sort of like Shadow tech, right?"

"It's Silver tech. I guess you could say it's 'happy' Shadow tech. You'll see, yours will do the same in time."

"It will? It'll turn silver?"

"Do you love anybody?"

She smiled and glanced back at the Duke. "I suppose that big scruff over there. I suppose I love him with all my heart."

"Then yes, it'll turn. Lady Poe made this little bird for me."

Torri leaned forward. "Can I see him?"

Kilos gently handed Tweeter to Torri. She cupped her hands and held him, examining his tiny silver body. "Hmmm. Wow, look at that," she said with admiration. "Who made this did you say?"

"Lady Poe of Blanchefort. She's the sister of my best friend."

"I've never heard that name before … I know all of the Black Hats by name."

"She's not a Black Hat," Kilos added.

Torri continued to admire Tweeter. "Well, in any event, this Lady Poe is a Shadow tech Master—a genius. How many months did it take for her to create this?"

Ki managed a laugh. She forgot about the Sisters for a moment. She loved the fact Torri was making a fuss over her little Tweeter. "Months? It took her about two minutes. I watched her do it."

Torri gasped. "This is a Familiar? Creation! There's a lot of … Silver tech did you call it … here, more than I've ever seen in a single Shadow tech familiar. It's very handy work. Lots of Black Hats I know would be drooling over something like this."

Torri handed Tweeter back to Ki. "He seems tired. I think his time's about up."

"What do you mean?"

"Well, Shadow tech familiars are usually timed. They only last for a few days, mine always do. Shadow tech needs energy to stay combined, even a big, complicated monster like this one," she said pointing at the tiny Tweeter.

"A monster, Tweeter?"

"Size doesn't mean much when you're talking about Shadow tech. You'd be surprised how little Shadow tech goes into a thirty foot tall beast. This one's got layer after layer of complex programming, so, even though he's tiny, he's packing a ton of … Silver tech I guess it is."

Ki felt a tear coming to her eye. "You think he's timed. You think he's going to die?"

"Looks to be."

"He's been to hell and back with me. I'll not say what I saw in the depths of those tunnels, but this little guy was equal to it; to all the ancient evil and traps they could muster … he got me out. You can't die, Tweets, you just can't," she said looking at him.

Tweeter sat there in her hand and, sure enough, didn't seem his usual energetic self.

Ki rubbed Tweeter's beak. She noticed Torri's big, padded Macco boots. "I didn't think Black Hats liked shoes," she said still worried about Tweeter.

Torri looked down at her boots. "Oh, I love shoes … got a whole closet full. Fall bought them for me. Know a lot of Black Hats, do you?"

"I know three, not including Lady Poe."

"Hmmmm … They must all be Hammers. I was a Painter—we don't wear Dora very often—too hard to concentrate with those damn things on."

Torri opened a small locker full of iced bottles. "I'm thirsty." She called up to the cockpit. "What do you want to drink, Hon?"

"D-Sprig!" he said through his pipe.

"Ohhhh … me too! That's two clear bottles, a little green and a splash of blue, right?"

"Right."

"See, I'm getting the hang of this," Torri cried, triumphant. "Kilos, you like something?"

Kilos, answered. "No thank you. So, if I may ask, what are you doing out here? Not that I'm not grateful. I am … I've never wanted to be farther away from someplace, ever."

Torri laughed. "We were asked to be here. We were supposed to pick you up," she said mixing various liquors together. "He said you'd be a tall, blonde-headed lady with a big gun." Torri looked hard at Ki. "I'm not sure about the blonde hair bit, though … looks more brown to me."

The Duke, sitting in the pilot's chair, pipe smoking, looked back. "Sorry about Ellington and his bunch. I suppose I'm going to have to speak with Lord Milton regarding these attempts to kill me, now that Torri's around."

"Don't become an old fud' on my account, Fall. I think they're fun. Bring `em on!"

She turned to Kilos. "You see, there's this scary-looking fellow over in the other manor who …"

A voice piped in over the Com. "Duke, we're eighty thousand and climbing, what's our heading?"

"South, Johnnie," the Duke replied.

"South it is. Hey … babe?" he said to Kilos through the Com. "You there?"

Kilos was annoyed. "The name's 'Kilos'. Call me 'babe' one more time, and I'm going to flatten you the next time I see you, got it?"

"Will you promise … babe?"

Ki, dead tired, let her eyes close. "Oh, I promise … 'tiny'. You are the little one I saw, right?"

Sisters … death hands reaching. *<BROWN!!>* she heard.

"Tiny?" Johnnie said. "Listen, not everything's tiny on me, babe."

She opened her eyes, forgot about Johnnie, and turned to Torri. "Oh, I almost forgot, who asked you to be here?"

Torri giggled as she finished up with the drinks. "He's in the back bay actually if you'd like to see him. You showed up pretty much exactly like he said—except for the hair part. I mean, what do you think, if I may ask—are you a brunette or a dirty blonde?"

<This pathetic creature we dragged into the Heart … he doesn't smell like you, Brown! No he doesn't … admirable effort! Our search for you continues!!>

Kilos was shocked. "He's here, now?"

"Yeah … he's really busy with something."

<We are going to get you … no matter where you hide!>

Shaking, assailed with voices in her head, Ki stood up and walked toward the back of the compartment where a hatch awaited her. "Through here?" she asked.

"Yep!" Torrijayne said taking a drink from her glass. "And tell him he needs to get his hair colors straight."

Kilos opened the hatch and looked through.

Her jaw hit the floor.

"Carahil!!" she exclaimed.

14—The Eleventh Daughter

When the Captain and the Countess left the bridge, the Black Ship suddenly came to life. It changed course and headed for the *Seeker* with remarkable agility for such a big, unwieldy-looking ship.

"Helm, hard to port and make rotations for full Sub-Stellar Mach!" Lt. Verlin yelled.

Saari spun the helm and the ship heeled around. The Black Ship turned to intercept. Several of the wing arrays at the forward part of the ship then "reached out" like a set of tentacles and slammed into the *Seeker's* aft. One of them hit the rear hull and poured into the coil vents, clogging them.

"Engineering reports Stellar Mach coils 3, 5 and 7 are down!" Sasai yelled.

The ship began a distinct list to port. "Canister control, fire a four-shot burst amidships, set to maximum safe distance!" Larsen said.

The canisters thudded away. Two of them got picked off in mid-flight by the flailing black arms of the enemy ship. Two detonated the enemy vessel right down the center. The black ship deformed for a moment, then righted itself, stretching back into shape; no apparent damage. More black arms shot out and caught hold of the *Seeker*, pulling and squeezing it roughly. Everyone on the bridge could hear the superstructure groaning and complaining.

"Are we in Battleshot range?" Larsen asked.

"No, sir!"

"Can we pull away?" Verlin shouted.

"The remaining coils are at max, and must wind down!"

Another arm … moving fast.

BOOM!!

"Ma'am, direct hit, frontal section, decks five and six. We are venting!" Sasai yelled.

More arms, more impacts, more list.

"Com," Verlin said hanging onto the rail, "send as General … prepare to abandon ship!"

"I agree," Larsen said.

The door opened.

"Belay that!" Captain Davage said as he strode back onto the bridge. "Situation!"

"Captain, we are in desperate shape!" Verlin said. "SM Coils 3, 5 and 7 are choked and down! We are venting in Frontal Section decks 5 and 6 and the enemy vessel has us gripped tight."

"Have those sections been evacuated?"

"Yes sir, they have," Sasai said.

"Can we wind the remaining coils and break away?"

"No sir, we are at max and must wind down!"

"Captain," Larsen said. "We have impacted the enemy vessel with no less than two direct canister hits with no apparent damage."

Davage thought a moment. "Stop the coils and power off all external lights. Additionally, counter flood to port."

"We should counter flood to starboard," Larsen said. "We'll be skirting Zero."

"Have faith."

The orders went out and a moment later the ship listed hard to port, the crew having to hold on to something as the *Seeker*'s gravity didn't function in the perpendicular to the standard AM orientation.

Davage took a moment to Sight the dispensary. There he could see Syg in her usual bed. Davage had been the *Seeker's* captain for sixteen years, yet Syg, in her relatively short time being on the vessel, had been confined to the dispensary many more times than he ever had.

She looked upset.

<How are you doing, darling? Is Ennez being good to you down there?>

She didn't answer. That wasn't like Syg, who was usually very chatty. Must be tired.

"Sir," the Com said, "we have an incoming message."

"Fine, fine. Let's give ear."

The holo-cone snapped on and they were seeing into the dark, forbidding interior of the ship. There, sitting in a crampt, mirthless control area, was the ghostly image of Princess Vroc of Xandarr. Her blue bangs still in her face. Her eyes glinting with triumph.

"Well, well …" she said. "So, here we have the mighty Captain Davage. Invincible, they say. Unbeaten, they say … unhittable. I cannot help but be somewhat disappointed."

Davage adjusted his hat. "I must say, that is a novel ship you have out there. Shadow tech, if I am not mistaken. I thought the Black Hats were angry at House Xandarr."

"Marilith's dead, Captain. We are once again … favored." She shifted in her seat. "So, how shall we do this, sir, hmmmm? Shall I pull your ship apart? Shall I crush it? Should I just kill everyone aboard, and take the *Seeker* as a prize? What do you suggest?"

Davage glanced at Verlin. <*Lt., can you hear my thoughts?*>

Verlin looked at him. <*Yes, sir!*>

<*Good. Send text to Engineering. Wind engines for full reverse.*>

<*Reverse?*>

<*Do it now!*>

"My dear, I believe that I told you that I have no wish to fight."

"Yes, and I replied that I, on the other hand, most certainly wish to fight you. And here we are … in our first and last battle. I had been expecting more. Do you wish to beg for terms?"

"Terms? No, no terms. If I am to die, I wish all here to die with me."

Vroc looked a bit confused. "Really, I'd expected a bit more nobility from you, Father. You are, no doubt, trying to confuse me,"

Father? Davage was puzzled. "Pardon?"

Vroc looked hard at him and blinked. "No … you're not my Father, are you? You're Captain Davage. Yes, yes, you're Captain Davage. You are on the *Seeker*. How's your Countess?"

"In poor shape, down in the dispensary. That was quite the jolt you put to her."

"Not acting a little … strange is she?"

"Let me look and see how she is doing." Davage lit his Sight and pretended to look down into the dispensary. Instead he looked the black ship over. His Sight penetrated the layers of concentrated Shadow tech, and he was amazed, there was so much that there was enough to make several Dark Man totems. Finally, deep within the forth-to-last segment, he saw Vroc sitting in her crampt control room—hidden. Scattered in other segments were a few Xaphan crew members, also sitting at black controls. He also thought he saw a prisoner confined in the forward part of the ship. Damn! That complicated things.

<Lt. Verlin, when we reverse, I want a 17 degree roll to starboard—text that to the helm. Also, send to Canister Control and all Battleshot batteries, I want the forward part of the enemy ship untouched—there are prisoners located there. Understand?>

<Aye, sir.>

Davage adjusted his hat. "She seems in weather shape. I'll sell her to you, if you like."

Vroc seemed shocked. "You'll what?"

"Sell her. I suppose if I sell her to you, that will at least keep her alive, though in bondage. In bondage is better than dead, I might argue."

Vroc blinked and looked lost for a moment. Her image floated in the holo-cone. "Sold … I was sold once …"

She seemed confused, unsure of herself.

<Sir—Engineering reports engines wound for full reverse.> came Lt. Verlin.

<Aye. Be ready for my command—and do not forget, spare the forward section.>

Princess Vroc shook her head and smiled. "I'm not purchasing the goods you're trying to sell me, Captain," she said. "Seems to me you're trying to bait for time … it won't work. You have moments to live."

"It seems to me, your father, the King of Xandarr, wants me alive. There's money to be made."

"My Father …" Her eyes went glassy, her face once again distant and confused.

Clearly, Vroc was struggling with her sanity. "May I sit at the table today, Father? May I eat with you today?" she asked.

Davage thought a moment. "Certainly. We have prepared your favorite."

Vroc's head dipped and she clawed at her blue hair. "Don't … LIE TO ME, FATHER!! ALL I WANTED WAS TO SIT AT THE TABLE AND EAT MY FILL … AND YOU … YOU NEVER LET ME!! YOU KEPT ME LOCKED IN MY ROOM LIKE A DOG!! I'M NOT A DOG!! I DIDN'T ASK TO BE YOUR DAMNED ELEVENTH DAUGHTER!!"

Vroc put her face into her hands and sobbed bitterly. Davage couldn't help but feel a bit sorry for her.

A crabby pair of gloved hands slithered into the cone and squirted her in the face with a thick-looking, pinkish spray. A moment later Vroc seemed to recover—her brief spin with raving insanity subverted.

"And now, Captain … where were we? Oh yes, since you have fallen well short, I shall simply find another League hero to fight. The Duke of Oyln, perhaps? I'd heard he captured himself a Black Hat. What was her name?" She leaned over her console to look something up.

Davage saw his moment. <*Now, Lt.—full reverse*!!>

The coils screamed and the *Seeker* rocketed back in the direction of the enemy vessel—the grasping tendrils holding the ship not expecting a sudden reverse movement. The Helm rolled, the thrusters ticked, whipping the head of the *Seeker* around.

Surprised, Vroc began rapidly working her controls.

"You wished to take this vessel, to kill its crew," Davage said. "No provocation, no parlay … to kill me … to kill my wife! This matter is at hand, Princess and this contest begins afresh—and I certainly hope you know what you've gotten yourself into, though I question your sanity."

The *Seeker*, heeling around, slammed into the side of the Black Ship with a "splash" of metal and Shadow tech.

The two ships, locked together, did a waltz over Heron 7 for a moment.

"Port Battleshot batteries open fire and hold!"

The Battleshot batteries opened up and the whole ship vibrated. The Black Ship, in a hail of explosive shot, puckered and deformed, the Shadow tech cringing and temporarily vaporizing. It screamed out a mental note that crashed into their brains. Some put their hands to their heads to attempt to drown out the noise.

Davage Sighted. He saw Vroc's control room under heavy fire, walls collapsing, opening to space.

Vroc, though, was not there. After another moment, the Black Ship broke in two near its aft quarter, with one piece being extremely long and the other rather short and stubby. The forward part of the ship where the prisoner was held appeared to be sound.

"Captain!" Larsen yelled. "Battleshot batteries overheating."

"We're free," Captain!" Verlin said.

"Cease fire! All ahead full!"

The *Seeker* blistered away from the bubbling, churning ship: the two blasted pieces nudging against each other randomly in the *Seeker's* expanding gas wash. Davage ran to the helm and grabbed the wheel, Saari giving it up as usual to the captain.

"Engineering," he said, "Counter flood to starboard and null the wheel! And, what is our coil status?"

Mapes voice came back from engineering. "Three coils down. Stellar Mach still available though not recommended."

"Standby," Davage said. He rolled the wheel, turned the nose of the *Seeker* back toward the Black Ship.

Sight—several reaching tendrils. He yanked the wheel and the ship rolled out of the way.

"Canister control, set pattern Gamma-Gamma-Tau and allow for maximum spread. Go now!"

Five canisters shot out of the *Seeker* toward the flailing pieces of the Black Ship. The tendrils reached out and tried to grab them when all five exploded. Not a usual simple detonation, the canisters instead burst outwards in a rapidly expanding arc, five growing circles of energized, charged gas and plasma. The circles surrounded the ship, not destroying, but deforming and flattening it, stretching it, mangling the Shadow tech like a thin piece of beaten copper.

Davage hauled the *Seeker* around.

"Starboard Battleshot batteries, open fire!"

With the usual "Buuuuurrrrrrrr!!!" the Battleshot raked the ship. Davage Sighted and saw the barrage had torn open a segment, spilling a portion of the sparse, struggling crew to cold space.

"Lt. Verlin, I need the Sisters here, immediately to mop this up."

Davage swung the ship back around.

To his horror he saw ten of the remaining winged segments on the larger piece separate into individual units and come swinging around with great agility. Like a squadron of fighter craft they attacked en masse.

"All ahead full!" Dav cried.

"Sir, coils at maximum!"

He cursed under his breath. Those missing coils were problematic. He turned to Saari who was standing behind him. "I want 72 degrees nose up!" She began flipping levers and Davage wrenched the ship upward, toward high noon.

The trailing ships followed.

Sight—a blast of black spheres. He yawed the wings as a huge, but fairly slow moving cluster of ugly black spheres bubbled out of the lead ship. The spheres came forward in a large group, bouncing into each other, expanding and changing. Davage could see that they seethed with deadly energy. Fortunately it wasn't difficult to avoid them with his fast maneuverable ship.

"Lt. Larsen," Davage said, "I want a full canister barrage, set to …"

The lift door to the bridge opened, Syg came marching out. "Dav …" she said.

"Countess I ordered you to dispensary!" he said spinning the wheel again.

"But you're not in the dispensary …"

He had no time for this. <*Come on, Syg, please! Go to the dispensary and rest, will you? For me?*>

Syg looked at him. <*AAAAAAAAAAAAAAAAAAAAAAAAAA!!!!!*> came back.

She took off her Blanchefort gown and let it fall to her ankles. She kicked it away.

"Countess?" Davage said looking at her naked body.

He Sighted something: claws, black claws.

"How can I … KILL YOU IF I'M IN THE DISPENSARY??" Syg shouted, lunging at him, black claws growing out of her fingers.

Part 3— The Shadow tech Conspiracy

We are Mighty…
We are Strong…
Give to us our Arms
… by being Mighty and Strong.

-- The gods Lament to Man.

1—Destination: Xandarr

Kilos threw her arms around Carahil, who was sitting in a large cargo bay, his silver light filling it. His whiskers twitched with happiness.

Kilos pulled back and framed his face with her hands. "What the hell happened? The Sisters ripped you apart, I saw it, I heard it! Good Creation—it was horrible!"

"Not totally, as you can see, I still had a spark of life in me when you put the jewel in my mouth. You did well, Ki. I am very proud of you."

"You scared me to death, you lug!"

"I am sorry, but, it all worked out as I had hoped. Even poor Ellington took the fall for you. At this moment, he's being whisked into the Heart where, I'm afraid, horrible things will soon be happening to him. Such is the price for being greedy."

Ki thought about the poor man's fate and shuddered. "I can still hear his cries, Carahil."

"I know, Ki … I know."

She wiped her nose. "You lost your book. Thanks for the help."

Carahil's book appeared in a flash. "You mean this one? I didn't lose it."

"You know, you could have had something a little more dangerous come out of that book to help me than a pie. A pie?"

"Seemed effective to me, and nobody got hurt which is good."

"They kept mentioning 'P3847'. What's that?"

"That's the Brightstone you took. They have them all numbered. They're not too happy down there and will probably never stop searching for it. S'ok. Let me worry about that. Everything worked out."

The Duke and Torrijayne, hand in hand, entered the bay. "Well, we are cruising high and fast, safe under Cloak. Now, where shall I take the lovely Madame Kilos, here?"

Kilos looked at him. "Just Kilos, sir, please. I'm not an old maid … not yet anyway."

The Duke tipped his hat.

Carahil shuffled his whiskers. "Xandarr, Duke. We would like to go to Xandarr, right away please."

"Xandarr?" the Duke and Kilos repeated in unison. "Xandarr? The Planet Xandarr … in Xaphan space?"

"The same, I am aware of no other."

The Duke pulled his pipe out of his mouth. "Creature …"

"His name is Carahil," Kilos said.

"All right, 'Carahil', I promised that I would pick up the lovely lady here, and then take her to a remote location."

"Indeed, and the remote location in this case happens to be the planet Xandarr."

"Why am I going to Xandarr, Carahil?" Kilos asked.

The Duke shook his head. "Out of the question … the Fleet is probably in the area. They rotate over in that direction about this time of the month to cover The Kills. We'd have to run them and possibly be boarded. It's simply too dangerous."

"And so? You're a League citizen. You're not running contraband this time, just passengers."

"True … ferrying passengers in a fleet of illegal, armed yachts which, additionally, have no taxes paid and fly no flag."

"Why did you not pay your taxes, Duke?"

"And what should I tell the tax collector, sir? 'And here we have a fleet of illegal vessels, armed, packing Xaphan tech and forbidden scanners right out of Ming Moorland, so, shall I pay my taxes before or after I return from prison?'"

Carahil shrugged. "Such is the risk you run being a pirate. So, back to the planet Xandarr …"

"Alleged pirate, sir, and we are not going to Xandarr."

"Are you going to renege on your promise, Duke? I thought you had turned a new leaf in the influence of your love here."

"I am grateful for what you did for me … for us. I can't now imagine being without my Torri—you were right about that too. But, as incarceration is not something I crave, I am not going to Xandarr, pick another place, preferably one that's not so crawling with Fleet activity."

"But, we've our hearts set on Xandarr, Duke. What's the matter? What are you not telling me?"

The Duke hesitated. "I have recently received a number of messages warning me not to go to Xandarr. They say the planet's cursed; that bad things are soon to happen there, and I want no part of it."

"Always do what you're told, Duke?"

The Duke laughed and put his pipe back in. "You know, that might have worked on me a few weeks ago, but not now. We're not going to Xandarr. Pick another place—I'll not endanger Torri. Besides, beyond the sinister messages, I have heard something big is going to happen on Xandarr soon. Best to leave it be for awhile."

"Something real big is going to happen," Torrijayne said. "The Black Hats have Painted half the planet, though I was never told why." Torri threw her arms around the Duke and gave him a big kiss.

Ki rolled her eyes. "Torri, I'm going to have to introduce you to a friend of mine—she acts all sappy just like you do. I've told Syg a thousand times—"

Torri was puzzled. "Pardon me—who?"

"Syg, the Countess of Blanchefort. She's also an ex-Black Hat. Hates shoes."

"Really," Torri said interested. "What's her name again, her full name?"

"Countess Sygillis of Blanchefort, formerly of Metatron."

Torrijayne's smile vanished. "Sygillis of Metatron ... really? You mean to say Sygillis of Metatron lives?"

"Yes, she's a good friend of mine."

Torri stood up. "Excuse me," she said walking away.

They watched her walk off.

Carahil continued. "Think of it as a reunion of sorts,"he said. "The site of your first date."

"Not funny," the Duke said.

Carahil smiled. "Not intended to be funny. I need you to take me and Kilos to Xandarr ... immediately."

Torrijayne, sitting at the cockpit, spoke up. "Aww, come on, Fall, it'll be fun. What's the big deal?" Besides, we'll be under Cloak the whole time. If the Fleet is out there they won't find us. Maybe we'll get to see Sygillis of Metatron. Maybe, I'll get to say hello." Torri sounded a bit ominous.

The Duke puffed his pipe and thought a moment. "Torri, you don't sound too happy."

"I'm fine. Think of Sygillis as my version of Lord Milton … we have a 'special' relationship."

"You mean you want to kill her, right?"

"Killing her is a good a start. Come on, let's go. I want to do this. Nobody will find us under Cloak."

The Duke thought a moment. "Very well, the Planet Xandarr. Torri, will you please send word to Peter?"

"Yep."

Carahil thought a moment. "Oh, Duke, on the way to Xandarr, we'll need to make a quick stop or two, nothing too out of the way, and nothing dangerous, I assure you."

The Duke sighed. "This keeps getting better and better, Carahil," he said. "Where are we going?"

"I'll tell you when we near."

The Duke stood and left, joining Torri in the cockpit.

Carahil nudged Kilos. "How are you feeling, Ki?"

"Terrible. I want to sleep, but, I can't close my eyes … I see them, in the dark."

"The Sisters, you see the Sisters?"

"Yes."

"Close your eyes, Kilos."

"I don't want to close my eyes … I'll see Them again." Ki looked down and fumbled with her hands. "I'm … scared. I guess I don't mind telling you that, since you probably already know."

"Don't be. I'm here."

Ki felt the inevitable hand of sleep reaching out for her. She tried to keep her mind going to stave sleep off. "'Wumalaar', they kept saying the word 'Wumalaar'. What's it mean?"

"The Wumalaar is a mythical beast that the Sisters believe in. Essentially, the Wumalaar is a creature that will break through the Sisters lines of defense and steal all their secrets. It is a creature they dread and fear. The day the Wumalaar comes, so say the Sisters, that is the day of apocalypse … the last day of the League."

Carahil leaned down and nuzzled her on the cheek. "But, in modern terms, 'Wumalaar' is anything that frightens a Sister, so, I suppose that you, Ki, are the Wumalaar in a manner of speaking. Enough bedtime stories, go to sleep … rest."

She closed her eyes.

Green-skinned, giant Sisters. Leering. Reaching out for her.

<*We will never cease looking for you … Brown!*>

Ki grimaced. "I see them, Carahil … I hear them. They're speaking to me, even now."

"Nobody is speaking to you. You are safe. It's just your imagination. Close your eyes, Kilos, and rest. You'll see no specters, you'll hear no voices … I promise, and when you wake, you'll remember little of what took place in the Hazards, I swear it. All the things you saw and discovered, will be gone."

"Immortality?"

"Shhhh, that too."

"I'm scared, Carahil."

"I know … but I am here, thanks to you. And I will protect you. I will guard over you as you sleep. I'm not going anywhere."

She settled back with Tweeter sitting on her shoulder. "You drew a picture of me, in your book, Carahil. I liked it."

His book appeared and he spun it around, opening to the sketch. "You mean this one?" he asked.

"Yes," she said, becoming drowsy.

"Well, once this is all over, I'll frame it and give it to you. Sleep now."

She closed her eyes, seeing Carahil's smiling silver form looking down at her.

She saw no monsters. She heard no voices—she slept.

2—"You have murdered your Countess ..."

Syg sprung at Dav, and swiped at him with a claw, tearing a bit of his coat. He darted away, not quite sure what to make of this.

"Countess?"

They played a momentary game of ring-around-the-rosie, Syg, naked, chasing Davage around the helm.

She laughed. "Come, Captain ... show me that CARG of yours. Kill me with it if you are able. Come over here!"

Saari backed away, watching this odd game with horror.

Davage Sighted, then cranked the wheel as another blast came in.

Syg, chasing him, pouting, head cocked. "What's wrong ... don't you want to embrace your countess?"

"Syg, you're out of your head, from your shock." He looked up to the ceiling. "Hospitalers to the bridge!"

"Oh, I'm fine, Captain ... never better. Come now ... get your CARG out and kill me with it!! You and I—let's fight! I have been waiting for this. Xaphan's beard, how I have waited!"

She lunged again, and Davage rolled aside. He turned and lit his Sight, hoping to calm her. Instead of gazing at his eyes with wonder as Syg always did, she crossed her arms in front of her face, her claws glinting. "Remove your light, Captain, or I'll kill everyone on this bridge! Off, I say, or they die!! Die!!"

The ship rocked with an impact. Saari, hands shaking, grabbed the wheel. The captain, otherwise occupied, Lt. Larsen spoke up. "Helm, aft quarter!"

"A-Aft quarter, aye!"

Davage looked Syg over. She appeared normal in his Sight; heart, lungs, kidneys, good strong bones, everything looked as it should.

It was Syg—no doubt about it.

Lt. Larsen again. "Helm, right full wheel and Mark for 2am!"

"Right full wheel, mark 2am, aye!"

Davage had no idea what to do; Syg, crazed, wanting his blood. With a pang, he realized he was going to have fight her, to incapacitate and get her back to the dispensary. And, if Ennez couldn't figure out what was wrong with her, then he didn't know after that.

Wait …

His Sight; he saw no child—no son in her womb. It wasn't Syg—it's not Syg, it couldn't be Syg!! He could breathe again.

She glanced at the helm, sprung, and clawed at Saari. She ducked, and the swipe took off the top half of the helm, Saari looking at it wide-eyed, in horror.

"Get your damned eyes off of me, Captain!" she said. "Get them off or … I'll start killing! I'll take this blue-haired bitch first!"

He enveloped her in his gaze again, hitting her hard, and she trembled in it. Her naked skin began to smoke.

"Port Battleshot batteries, open fire!" Larsen said.

BUUUUURRRRRRR!!

He looked around. There was no Silver tech that he could see in her body—not a bit of it. No Shadow tech either. That was not possible. He looked further, looked deeper—she cried out in pain as he did.

There, deep down, embedded in her tissues, in her bones, there it was. Shadow tech. It was everywhere. Every bit of her was Shadow tech. She was a Shadow tech totem, of a type he'd never seen before.

"It's Shadow tech!" Davage yelled unsaddling his CARG. "Everybody get away from it! Sisters to the bridge!"

With great agility, she sprang to the other side of the bridge, near the navigator, he scrambled out of his seat to get away from her.

"What have you done with the Countess of Blanchefort?"

"I killed her," she said smiling. She looked at the terrified navigator, and raised her arm. "Be happy, Captain … you're now a bachelor again."

There was a whistling.

His CARG buried itself in her chest, knocking her backwards and into the wall with the weight of it.

She rose. "Not nice … lover boy," she said unfazed. She pulled the heavy CARG out and threw it aside where it thudded thickly to the floor. She raised her arm again to kill the navigator.

TACK!

Lt. Verlin shot her in the chest. She recoiled, smiled, and attacked again.

Verlin switched to full auto and put a long burst into her, the bridge filling with gun smoke. Syg, shot enough times to kill a dozen men, leapt through the hail of lead and clawed at Verlin. Her SK fell to the floor cleaved in several pieces. Landing on top of her, gushing Shadow tech blood, Syg reared back to kill Lt. Verlin.

Davage shoulder-tackled Syg. They rolled on the floor for a moment, then Syg managed to get on top of him. She held her long, slick claws at his throat.

She cackled. "My … look who is under my claws. I suppose this means I wish a disillusionment to our marriage … Dav …"

"I am not married to you."

"Oh but you are. I am Sygillis of Metatron … come to her senses. The shock broke the trance you had me in. I am myself again, and now, I'm going to kill you."

Jonas, the navigator, tried to intercede.

"No, Jonas!" Davage shouted, but it was too late, Syg slashed him across the chest. He flew back, blood flowing.

Syg turned her attention back to Davage. She spoke softly, almost tenderly, her long claws dancing at his throat, micro-cutting the skin, turning it red. "Did you really think I could ever love a weak, pathetic Blue such as yourself. Look at you … soft and worthless. And now …"

Poof!!

Davage Wafted across the bridge. Syg snarled and made to leap at him.

Lt. Larsen drew his GREAT DORE from his coat and extended it. Moving with trained grace he threw it at Syg as she coiled to attack. As the GREAT DORE left his hand it became as energy, turning red, like a laser bolt. It hit Syg in the mid-riff, throwing her back against the wall yet again. Recovering she tried to pull it out, her claws sizzling on its radiant shaft. The moment she touched it, the red energy lance sprouted many more red arms, like a thistle seed, thoroughly impaling her.

She screamed and could move no more.

Larsen was enveloped. Syg's gown, which had been lying on the floor, came to life, flew through the air, and wrapped around him, covering his mouth. His muffled screams could be heard through the cloth.

Verlin and the Missive came to his side and tugged at the gown. It hugged his face tightly, it didn't budge.

Davage pushed them aside and blasted the gown with Sight. It cringed and mewled and began to smoke. After a moment it charred to ash, and Larsen could breathe again.

Verlin helped him, gasping, to his feet.

The lift door opened and Ennez and several Sisters entered the bridge. They stared at this situation in horror.

"Lord Blanchefort …" Verlin said for one of them. "What have you done? You have murdered your countess."

"Sisters," he said. "It's not the countess. It's Shadow tech. I am not certain how, but it's a Shadow tech totem."

The Sisters looked at the impaled Syg. "There is no Shadow tech here, Captain," Verlin said for the Sisters.

"Sisters," Syg cried. "He's gone mad. He's trying to kill me … his wife … My head was foggy, from the shock I took. Help me … please! Don't let him kill me!"

"It's not my countess … she's not pregnant. It's Shadow tech, Sisters," Davage said. "It's a strange type—her whole body is made of it. Could the Countess Blanchefort have been CARGed, shot, and DOREed and still live?"

The Sister's looked confused. "Lord Blanchefort …"

"Look to her gown. It came to life as a monster."

Davage, in, frustration, hit Syg with a powerful Sight. The Shadow tech Syg writhed in fresh agony.

The Sisters gazed at Syg. "Yes … yes … see, it is Shadow tech … strange, evolved, elegant. It does not flow. It is fixed in state. Remarkable, remarkable!" the Sisters said through Verlin.

Davage quelled his Sight.

"Captain," Verlin said again. "We must have this specimen. We must take it back and perform a series of tests on it immediately."

Syg cringed. "Dav …" she moaned, "don't let them take me … don't let them hurt me, please …"

Davage, even knowing that this was a Shadow tech image, felt his heart break a little.

"Where is my countess?" he asked.

"I'm your countess. I love you."

"Where is my countess!!" he shouted.

"I don't know!"

"How did you exchange places with her?"

"I don't know!" she cried. "Please, Dav!"

Davage rubbed his eyes for a moment. "Lt. Larsen, please withdraw your GREAT DORE. Sisters, you may have it."

Lt. Larsen, still a bit shaken, waved with his hand, and the GREAT DORE retracted and flew back into his grasp.

Instantly, Syg sprang at Davage, claws extended. "DIEEEEEEEEEE!"

The Sisters, calm and collected as ever, coiled her in a devastating TK. She hung in the air for a moment, held in place in mid-shriek. Then, in a bone-splintering, cracking confusion of noise, they crushed her down to a small cube-shaped block."

The whole process was rather horrific to watch.

"Thank you, Captain," Verlin said. "We will take this and examine it fully, and, if there is any information regarding your Countess's current location, we will extract it and update you immediately."

With that, they took the Syg-cube, the ashes of her gown, and left the bridge.

Davage took a deep breath.

"Are you all right, Captain?" Saari asked picking up the pieces of the helm wheel.

"Fine, crewman, fine. Thank you—please inform engineering we shall need a new helm wheel at once. Lt. Larsen, what is our situation?"

"Sir, we came about and broad-sided the Black ship in a long burst. It disengaged, apparently damaged, and withdrew toward Heron."

"I see, and well done, Lt. Quick work in an unusual circumstance."

"Thank you, sir," he said, still winded from his encounter with the gown.

"Are you all right?" Davage asked him. "Do you need a Hospitaler?"

"No, sir. I'm fine."

Davage went to the fallen navigator. Ennez was busy trying to stop his bleeding.

"How's Jonas?" he asked.

"Bad, Dav," Ennez replied. "He must to the dispensary. But, he should live. I think he'll live."

Davage nodded in a bit of relief.

A few Chancellors entered the bridge with a float litter, and carried Jonas away.

Davage looked around, his mind locked on Syg, his wife.

Where was she? What had happened?

He picked up his CARG and went to Verlin. "Lt., are you hurt?"

"No, no, sir. Just my SK. I'll need to requisition another from the Marine locker."

Davage smiled. "Good. Fore Sensing, what's the status of the enemy vessel?"

Sasai checked her scanner. "Sir, the sector is clear. The enemy vessel is gone."

Davage looked at the empty monitor screen.

"Com, send to Marines at Bazz. Inform them enemy ship headed in their direction. Inform them it is armed, hostile and extremely dangerous."

"Aye, sir."

Syg—she had to be on that ship. Where else could she be?

3—Sygillis

When Syg opened her eyes, she was in a dark place. Her hands and feet were shackled with black chains.

Shadow tech by the smell of it, though she couldn't sense it like she normally could.

What had happened? Where was Dav?

She recalled touching the Black Ship with her Silver tech. She remembered the ship reacting violently to her touch.

She remembered getting a jolt. And now, here she was.

She was lying on a bare metal floor in a dark room. The metal didn't feel like metal—it felt a little like Shadow tech, but she couldn't be sure.

The Black Ship—she must be on it. Somehow, she was now on the Black Ship. And, apparently, the whole thing was made from Shadow tech, as Dav had suggested.

Her hands were bound, she tested the chains. They were solid. Her feet were the same.

In the distance she could hear buttons clicking and people talking. She could hear the structure of the ship groaning.

She looked at the chains—again, they were black. Shadow tech, though they felt odd.

She flooded her wrists with Silver tech. As if acid had been poured on them, the chains melted away. In a moment, she freed her feet as well.

Standing, she snuck over to the end of the room. She made a tiny bit of Silver tech, and sent it around the corner, careful to not let it touch the walls or floor. She didn't want to risk another violent reaction.

Around the bend was a small bridge. Several people sat at their stations: they looked like Xaphan sailors from Midas. In her travels with Dav, she'd come to know well what those sorts looked like. In the center chair, a small, blue-haired girl sat with a Black Hat standing next to her.

"What is our status?" the girl said.

"Near full regenerated."

"Inform them that we have the Countess of Blanchefort, and are bringing her back at once, along with the other one as well."

The blue haired girl suddenly looked down and began chewing her fingernails. The Black Hat saw this and squirted her in the face with a strange, thick-looking liquid. Almost instantly, the blue-haired girl seemed to recover.

The girl stood. "I wish to know once we're fully functional again, then we drop off our cargo. Then we come about and finish the *Seeker*."

Dav … was he all right? She closed her eyes. Yes, yes … he was fine. She would know it if something had happened to him. Her soul would die along with him.

Whoever took her by force from her ship—from her lord—was in deep, deep trouble. That was a killing offense.

Syg pulled back her strand. She made to go back where she was and pretend to be tied up. There, she'd come up with a plan of some sort.

Someone passed by.

"Princess—the countess is free!!"

The crewman drew a gun, and Syg Pointed at her, sending her body hurtling back where she exploded in a terrible fuss a few seconds later. Syg readied herself. She heard a commotion of people scrambling in her direction.

Here goes another gown, she thought as the first person came around the corner.

Syg threw up a fast Sten. She stood there, rooted in place as the sailors peppered her with shots, both energy and projectile. There they all were, just standing there firing; sitting ducks. Well, she guessed if they were going to give it to her, she might as well take it.

She casually extended her Sten field and sent it diagonally across the floor to rest against the wall, pinning most of the sailors.

For a moment, the room was full of sparking and horrified screaming.

Then, silence, except for the clicking and groaning of the ship.

What a bunch of idiots. To stand there in a mass, and let a Sten spark them to death. They didn't even make it difficult for her. They deserved to be dead. She felt a small bit of freedom fighting here without Dav around. Here she could do whatever she wanted, fight anyway she pleased. With Dav, she had to control herself a little bit. She didn't want him seeing her as a terrifying murderess. She sometimes lay there next to him at night, troubled. She knew, deep down, that the Black Hat, the remorseless killer and inflictor of pain she had been, was still there just waiting to come out. As long as she had Dav, she knew she'd be all right. But, remove Dav, take him away from her for any length of time, and she wondered if she could keep the Black Hat from taking control of her soul again.

That tormenting thought terrified her.

She dropped her Sten and made to exit the room. "I'll make sure to pray for your souls when I get home," she said to the dead bodies.

A waft cloud appeared next to her.

Princess Vroc quickly stepped out of it and socked Syg square in the cheek, one of the hardest punches she had ever felt.

"You'll pay for that," the Princess said. "That's for the mess I'm going to have to get someone to clean up."

Recovering, Syg and Princess Vroc faced off

There was a large, smoky blast of air, and the Black Hat appeared.

The three faced each other for a moment in a triangle.

"... traitor ..." the Black Hat hissed. Twisting her hands, she created a large blob of Shadow tech that began throbbing into the shape of a strange, frog-like demon. A Shadow tech familiar if she'd ever seen one

Syg began forming her own blob of Silver tech which compressed into the shape of the *Seeker;* her Silver tech familiar of choice. It took flight. "Ignorant bitch," she said in return.

The Shadow tech creature charged, and the *Seeker* came down in front of it, blasting with tiny Silver tech Battleshot ports. Baaaaaaaaaaaaaaaaa!

The weight of the blasts sawed the demon in two, the Silver tech eating through its body, and it wailed in a death moan. The Princess drew her Mazan and fired at the *Seeker*, but the green seething blast had no effect. Syg swung the *Seeker* around to get the Princess. It loosed a tiny silver canister missile.

Vroc dove out of the way as it exploded in a pint-sized but very lethal explosion that created a huge hole in the floor

With a rope of Shadow tech, the Black Hat covered it in black, pinning it against the bulkhead wall, where the Shadow and Silver techs mixed and swirled for a moment, and then dissolved.

Syg sprang, and, before a moment had passed, had her hands around the Black Hat's neck. Surprised, mortified, that Syg actually wished to physically engage her, the Black Hat flailed about.

Then Syg broke her neck with a subdued pop. A small glass spray bottle fell out of her sleeve and broke on the floor, filling the compartment with a strange, cloying smell.

"Oh, that wasn't nice ..." the Princess said, standing.

Syg blasted her with Silver tech, but the Princess, her Waft maddeningly fast, got out of the way. Syg threw up a quick Sten and, a moment later the Princess appeared behind her and swung with her drawn BEREN. Its invisible blade sparked off her Sten. Dropping her field, Syg punched her in the face with a satisfying smack.

"That's for taking me off my ship, and away from my husband!!"

Vroc wiped a bit of blood from her lips. "Your husband ... the man I am going to kill. You're never going to see him again, are you?"

Enraged, Syg lifted her arm to Point at Vroc.

The Princess quickly Wafted away and appeared to her left, punching her in a blast of wind. She then followed up with a quick, damaging kick to the belly.

Her belly—their son!

Furious, Syg grabbed her in a full TK and lifted her into the air. She struggled for a moment then Wafted just as Syg readied to rope her up in Silver tech. Her Waft was blazing fast. Just as fast as Dav's, if not a hair faster. Such speed disarmed her of near three-quarters of her arsenal: the Sten, the Point, the Dirge, Silver tech blasts—all too slow. Syg's Waft was very slow in comparison.

She appeared beside Syg and hit her in the face yet again before she could lift a Sten. Vroc was so quick. The room began to spin, she felt a tooth come loose. This Princess was doing to her what she previously did to the Sister in Carahil's Walk—slowly knocking her down, draining her strength. Her speed and raw savagery disarmed most of Syg's weapons.

She swung to hit her back. Again the Princess Wafted. Again she hit Syg in the face. Grinning, the Princess reared back for another tormenting blow.

This time Syg Wafted, the blow missing. Syg appeared on the other side of her and smashed Vroc in the face, giving her a good taste of her own brew. Vroc appeared stunned. Syg seized her by the shoulder and hauled her down to the floor just as she feebly drew her Mazan. It fell from her grip and clattered across the room.

Countess and Princess, they thrashed about on the floor of the dark ship in a mortal contest, struggling for grip and leverage, Syg's gown becoming a torn, oily mess. They fell through the hole in the floor to darkened level below. Vroc, trying to get away, began to Waft.

Syg forced Silver tech claws through the ends of her fingers. They bit deep into Vroc's flesh and she screamed. Her Waft fizzled. Syg's skill at in-close fighting was winning out. She got her arms around Vroc's throat and began squeezing.

Gurgling in breathless pain, the Princess gagged and struggled for air, whooping for it. Blood spurted from her wounds. Her tongue hung limp, her eyes bulged.

Just another moment, and Syg would crush her throat and be done with her.

On the verge of death, the Princess showed remarkable poise. She managed to Waft away to the edge of the hole, one level up. She re-appeared, holding her throat, gasping for ragged breath. She bled from many deep punctures.

They stared at each other for a moment.

Syg fired a blast of Silver tech upward.

The Princess threw her BEREN down into the hole.

Syg's blast had partially found its mark—the meaty part of the Princess's left arm above the elbow was blown off, and she screamed in terrible agony.

Syg looked down.

The Princess's BEREN also found its mark—its silver hilt dancing in mid air on its invisible blade. Then, blood came gushing out. The invisible blade was buried deep in her chest, just under her ribcage.

Wide-eyed, holding the hilt, Syg fell back, blood pumping out of the wound.

"Dav … Dav …" she said weakly.

The Princess, holding her mangled arm, jumped down into the hole and stood over Syg. She grimaced in gut-wrenching pain.

The last thing Syg saw was her boot: the waffle pattern of her tread coming down on her face. And everything faded; only the sensation of her life draining out of her remained.

She had visions of her husband … and her son …

4—Fins

Lady Poe of Blanchefort awoke in the damp, smothering dark. She didn't know where she was, nor how long she had been out.

It must have been awhile, but she couldn't be sure.

She looked around. She was in a misty sort of dark; no light. The cool air was damp and heavy. She couldn't see. She had the impression that she was underground in a vast open space. She felt that there were unseen people all around her. She heard their shuffling movements in the dark.

She knew that she was in deep, deep trouble.

Her face hurt … ached. She touched it with her hands; it felt strange, lumpy.

She recalled standing on Lord Haveril's rooftop, the lovely day, the Merryweather girls in their pastel gowns.

She remembered the black ship that came down, the dark surge. She remembered Lord Haveril falling—dead, and the blue-haired girl. She remembered throwing her off of the roof on a Silver tech line.

She remembered the girl hitting her with the butt of her gun, over and over.

She felt her face again—it was swollen and painful. The shape of her face didn't feel like her face—it felt like an oblong melon.

"Hello?" she called out, her voice echoing back.

She heard a soft tittering of laughter in response.

A bit of dirty light appeared in front of her in a circular pool. Someone was there, prostrate on the ground, someone in a torn brown gown.

Weakly, with swollen eyes, Poe approached the figure.

"Syg … Syg!!" she cried. Poe dropped to her side and shook her, but Syg's tiny body was limp, boneless ... lifeless.

Blood! Blood was seeping out of her chest.

"Syg!" Poe whispered.

Syg moved a little after a moment. She opened her eyes to cloudy slits.

"… P-Poe … is that you? Dear Poe …"

"It is, it's me."

"… Poe …" she whispered. "Dying … I'm dying …"

Tears stung Poe's already painful eyes. "You're … you're not dying … Syg. You're going to be just fine. I promise you. I'm going to get us out of here."

Syg's eyes closed. "Tell … Dav … tell him, how happy … he made me … how I love him. How blessed …"

She grimaced. "Our … son … he dies with me … I'm sorry … Dav …"

Poe lifted Syg's tiny body up and cradled her. The heaviness of grief was building up within. "My nephew is fine, Syg. Your son is going to be a fine, handsome man. And, I'll tell Dav no such thing. You tell him. You tell him yourself when I get you out of here."

Poe kissed her clammy cheek. Syg didn't have long. She was watching the life drain clear of her.

She looked around … at the unseen people watching her. "Hello? Can someone please help us? Please … she's dying! We need a Hospitaler."

Shuffling, muted laughter was her response.

"Hello?"

Then, a grating, crawling voice came from somewhere: "*Repair her yourself … you have that odd infected Shadow tech flowing within you.*"

"I can't ..."

"*Repair her … your familiar ... the fish …*"

Poe shook her head. "Fins? You mean Fins? He's just for bumps and bruises … small cuts."

"*Repair her! We wish to observe the process.*"

"I can't!"

"*Then … watch her die …*"

Poe carefully laid Syg back down and opened her gown. Ripping off a large piece of cloth, she cleaned the blood from her chest as best she could. There, just below her ribcage on the left side was a large, jagged cut that rhythmically pulsed blood. The wound was deep, and very mortal.

Fins—the voice said to use Fins. Fins?

For this? She needs a Hospitaler. She needs blood.

* * * * *

Some time ago, she had designed a simple Silver tech familiar named Fins that looked like a big-eyed goldfish for Lord Duff's many nephews; Lord Duff being one of her many suitors at the time. Poe loved children, and his dozens of nephews and nieces were always jumping and falling off things, cutting themselves on this and that—they were simply being children. Poe remembered feeling so sorry for the children as they waited by the grand fountain crying, sometimes for hours, for Lord Duff's lone over-worked Hospitaler, Sancho, to attend to them. So, ever the tinkerer, she decided to try and do something about the problem.

Poe had already created a number of Silver tech familiars to assist her in doing various tasks. They were a challenge and a thrill to conceive and put together. Poe had created a small workshop out in the beech tree area of the Grove near the Greyson courtyard (soon after known as Carahil's Walk) where she undertook the task of forming them in silver. She'd perfected four familiars out in the courtyard: Tweeter, Shadow, Whisper, and Bark, and they functioned at a level of complexity that had Syg scratching her head half the time. Poe could do things with Silver tech that Syg had never seen.

So, here was the problem: Lord Duff's nephews and nieces needed something that could patch up small scrapes and bruises, something that would be fun and inviting—something they would want to use. As they often waited near a fountain for aid, she reasoned a silver fish, possibly a little goldfish, swimming in the water would be a nice touch. She hit Greyson's courtyard and threw herself into the task. Taking knowledge directly from the popcorn-haired head of Davage's Hospitaler, Samaritan Ennez at a dinner one evening, she began working on Fins: a little silver goldfish that could fix cuts and other small injuries in a snap. Once she had most of the bugs worked out—there were always lots of bugs—she filled the fountain basin at Lord Duff's home full of them where they swam about in a silver school. Whenever somebody hurt themselves, they could simply go to the fountain, pull one out, and heal their cuts and bruises in no time.

He seemed to work pretty well and was a big hit with the children, they gladly pulled the happy-faced Fins out of the fountain for even the most miniscule of scrapes and cuts. Sometimes they scuffed themselves up a little just to create an excuse to go get one. He was like a mesmerizing toy to them. A neat, handy novelty.

But Poe had stopped seeing Lord Duff sometime ago, and hadn't created Fins since. And Syg didn't have a scrape—she was dying of a terrible wound.

Repair her!

With Fins? With a toy?

She couldn't just sit here—this was Syg: her tutor, her brother's wife … her friend. She loved Syg as a sister. Syg was mighty, a Black Hat Hammer. And what was Poe, who was Poe? Just a foolish woman who could create cute little animals.

She had to try. For Syg …

* * * * *

Poe rolled up her sleeves, and began the delicate process for creating Fins; her fingers moving, spinning, fastening together. She imagined the movements. She imagined herself sitting in Greyson courtyard on a sunny afternoon, whipping him up.

Silver tech formed as a spiral in the air.

She could feel many eyes watching her as she worked. She thought she could hear gasps of astonishment and adulation as the various layers of Silver tech formed together into a solid mass and were stamped with the arcane coding required for him to function.

No, no … it was wrong, not coming together. She was nervous, out of her head with grief and worry, eyesight limited, and she hadn't tried making a Fins in some time. Silver tech familiars required practice, and she hadn't practiced with him. Why, why hadn't she practiced? Why did she let him fall by the wayside? All the movements had to be right, just right. She failed, and the Silver tech drifted away, unformed.

She started again, erred, and re-tried several times. Sniffling, wiping tears away, she finally had a ball of silver floating in the air, molding, forming, compressing into the shape of a tiny goldfish. This time, Poe felt him coming together. This time it felt right. After a few more moments, Fins was sitting in her hand, happily looking up at her; his big-eyes blinking. The finishing touch, the lozenge of Poe's Coat-of-Arms, appeared under his right fin. She knew he was right.

He looked happy. Poe always made her animals happy and bright-eyed. Even in this dire, hopeless situation, she still added that little touch.

"Save her, Fins," she said to him. "Save her …" She placed him on Syg's deep wound. He looked up at Poe for another moment as blood splattered onto him, then he disappeared into the depths of the bloody tear.

Poe sat there in the dim light, holding Syg's hand; watching her shallow breaths, wondering if each would be her last.

Fins was for small cuts … how could he repair a terrible wound like this?

He couldn't—he couldn't! He'll try his best, then he'll fail and Syg will die.

All the old helplessness began to fill her once more.

"… Poe …?" Syg whispered.

"I'm here … Syg … I'm right here …"

"I … f-found an abandoned hall … in the c-castle … Wanted to restore it … name it 'Davage Hall' … I wanted to dedicate … to Dav … with a big p-party …"

Poe brightened and stroked her sweaty face. "A party … that sounds wonderful."

"… Wanted to ask … your … h-help … planning it …"

"Oh yes, yes Syg, of course I'll help. It'll be … a grand affair, the talk of the League …"

Syg's eyes closed.

"… and we'll have a thousand guests, Syg … and those who don't make the list … will be so jealous …" Poe sniffled, and wiped tears away from her swollen eyes. "So jealous …"

Syg was still.

"Syg? Syg, please talk to me … SYG!!"

Something moved in the darkness.

Head on a swivel, Poe looked around. "Who's there?"

Something spoke. "*Come now, child, why so scared? We aren't going to hurt you … rather, we wish to help you.*"

"Keep away—I'll, I'll defend us!"

"*We are your friends … we've been waiting for you a long time. You are going to become what you were born to be at long last.*"

"SYG!!" Poe screamed, tears leaking down her face. Syg didn't move. The blood had stopped pulsing from her wound.

Something moved toward her and grabbed her by the ankle. "… *Welcome Home …*"

Poe blasted a gout of Silver tech in the direction of the thing that had grabbed her.

"*HAHAHAHAHAHAHAHAHAHAHA!*"

She was being dragged away.

Poe clawed at the damp, stony ground, trying to find something to hold onto.

"Syg!! Syg!!" she screamed. In the distance, still illuminated in the pool of light, Syg lay there, unmoving.

There was nothing—nothing! In the dark, she felt the walls closing in on her. She was being pulled down into a tiny space. She recalled Syg telling her about the Black Abbess' church—about the tiny spaces she was forced to inhabit for years. Not being able to stand up straight, and to be small was an advantage. Poe was not small.

"*You will not see light again for decades!*" someone said with glee.

Something turned her over, and she was forced into a kneeling position, face down. She felt a pair of hot, crabby hands reach into her gown and settle on her ribs.

Suddenly, she felt agony. Silver tech began pouring out of her mouth. It pooled on the ground in a bright stream for a moment, then trailed away and went down a dark grate. After a minute, it was over—she was totally drained of Silver tech. She felt as if she'd had the wind knocked out of her.

Terror filled her. All of the light drained out of memory. Desperate, out of her head with fear, she felt for the small silver medallion at her throat.

There it was—small, cool, solid. She touched it with her fingers.

"Carahil!" she cried. "Carahil … help me!!"

She was pulled into a tiny hole in the dark.

"CARAHIL!!"

* * * * *

Davage, Ennez and Lt's Larsen and Verlin walked into his office.

Davage was uncharacteristically unsettled and rank. "It must have been when she was shocked by the Black Ship. That's when she must have been taken somehow, and replaced with that thing out there."

Ennez got a scanner out of his pocket. "I see a bit of residual energy, Dav, and I'm detecting a trace bit of Shadow tech … but that's all." He adjusted his winged silver helmet and looked at his readings.

Verlin knelt down and examined at the floor. "Sir, I've recently reviewed several Science Ministry bulletins regarding the functionality of the matter/teleportation device being installed on the new *Triumph* class of ships. In theory, an instantaneous teleportation is possible, but requires a tremendous amount of power, and requires a direct connection to the endpoint."

"Yes," Larsen said. "However, such an operation discharges a great deal of energy."

Davage thought a moment. "As the countess was incapacitated, I recall seeing a bright flash, and, of course, she was directly in contact with the Black Ship via her Silver tech strand."

He lit his Sight and looked down at the floor. Verlin and Larsen watched in admiration.

"You have the Sight, sir? I too have the Sight," Larsen said.

"Then, if you would be so kind as to assist me."

Larsen lit his Sight, a very blue-tinted glow. "What are we looking for, sir?"

Davage scanned the floor, his golden gaze panning this way and that. "I'm looking into the past, Lt."

"The past? With the Sight?"

"Indeed."

"I hadn't thought that possible."

"It is, it is …."

Larsen extinguished his Sight and got out of the Captain's way. "It's one of the aspects of the Sight—to be able to see things that recently happened," Davage said gazing at the floor. Larsen shook his head.

He stopped and knelt down. "Here, here, Lt. … right here!"

"Do you see something, sir?" Larsen asked.

"Yes! I see my countess … lying on the floor. Here is the flash … and here!! Here!! I see two of her … occupying nearly the same bit of space for the briefest of times: one, my countess, the other, the Shadow tech fake."

Davage calmed his Sight, and looked out the window. "She's on that ship. Lt. Verlin, during the battle, do you recall scanning its propulsion source?"

"Yes, sir. No propulsion or motive form of locomotion was detected."

He put his hand to his chin. "They have to be using something. It was Shadow tech … how does Shadow tech move?"

Ennez put his scanner away. "Shadow tech moves as a result of thought and will. Destroy the source, the Black Hat, and Shadow tech moves no more. I don't think there is a way to detect raw thought."

Larsen popped up. "No, but, we badly damaged the Black Ship. It was trailing a great deal of material. I believe the Shadow tech facsimile of Countess Blanchefort was a diversion, to keep our full attention from the Black Ship, allowing it to escape. Perhaps its goal from the outset was to fetch her for purposes unknown."

Davage strode to the door. "The Black Hats have made no bones about their desire to re-acquire Countess Blanchefort to their ranks. That's an excellent point. Lt. Verlin, please ask the Sisters, using data derived from the Shadow tech countess, to help us follow the ship. Not only will we be able to save my countess, but we can possibly apprehend Princess Vroc as well."

"Sir," Verlin said. "Using the Sisters will work, but it will be extremely slow, taking us literally hundreds of years to follow and locate it. Sensory equipment was my specialty and, in the Marines, one often needs to improvise. I believe I can enhance the main sensor to be able to detect the Shadow tech trail at speed."

"What will you require?"

"I'll need an A7 logical unit, an A4 to serve as a co-processor and a power link," she said.

Larsen shook his head. "We don't have Marine stand-alones on a Fleet vessel, but I believe there is comparable equipment available in engineering."

Davage stared at the floor, where Syg had been stolen. "Take what you need, and if you encounter any resistance, have whomever come and see me at once. I'll expect a briefing at the top of the hour."

"Yes sir!" they said.

5—The Black Hat's Mercy

"*Is she dead?*" a crawling voice asked.

"*Nearly … soon enough. She is in her final moments …*"

In the dark, red figures danced around a fallen form.

"*'Tis a shame … evil such as hers does not emerge often.*"

"*She chose her path … to go with Him. It is his fault.*"

"*He will soon be dead … let no other attempt what He did. After another day or two, fear of the Black Hats will be universal.*"

One of the dancing forms stopped, was puzzled, and knelt down over the limp figure.

"*Harken!! She is pregnant!*"

"*We cannot harm the unborn … so is our pledge.*"

"*The Pledge is obsolete. This is a time of madness and fear.*"

"*True … many unborns are about to be killed, still, she was one of us … she shall have the benefit of the Pledge. Her unborn will not be harmed.*"

"*Then, what is to be done?*"

The remaining dancing red figures stopped. They regarded the fallen form on the wet stone.

"*She is dying. Expel the foal from her womb … before she dies. Let it struggle for life on its own.*"

Black hammers appeared in the Black Hat's hands. Shadow tech hammers.

"*See … we are merciful … allow her foal to struggle for life. We shall not kill it.*"

"*We are merciful, we are Black Hats. Sygillis of Metatron is also a Black Hat.*"

They raised their hammers and approached the fallen, unmoving form of Sygillis of Metatron … the Countess of Blanchefort, possibly in her last few moments of life.

"*Expel the foal from her womb … we raise not a sword. We are merciful.*"

They rolled her over and began pounding her belly—over and over again with their hammers.

There was silver light. They stopped.

6—A Friend in the Dark

Poe lay there in the dark, shackled. Her gown was shredded. Her Silver tech had been forcibly ripped from her. She had no idea how long she had been there.

Syg—where was Syg? She had been pulled from Syg's side. Was she still alive? Carahil—she had called to him, but he hadn't come. When she closed her eyes she sometimes thought that, for a fleeting second, she could see his silver, happy face.

She became aware of a roaring, smothering pain coming from her feet. She tried moving them and the pain that passed over her took her breath away, it was like a straightjacket, the agony inescapable. She moved her feet around trying to get comfortable. She was wearing an odd pair of shoes on her feet. They felt like they were made of metal.

Dora, Syg had called them. Shoes that were meant to create pain—and they did their job well. Confining, studded with blades and torturous ribs and pins, the pain they created was entirely overwhelming. The pain … the pain was mounting with every second. She tried to take them off, but they didn't budge.

The Pain! The Pain!

How could anyone wear these terrible things?

The agony was quickly driving her mad.

"S-Somebody help … me!" she managed to say. "Please!!"

Through the layers of mounting delirium, she dimly felt something nuzzle up against her.

She heard a clatter of metal, and shuffling in the dark.

Free, she was free of the Dora, they were gone. Though still in wrenching pain, it was bearable. It was just within her capacity to endure.

Slumping in her chains, arms shackled together, she managed a fitful bout of sleep, the hand of pain with her in her dreams.

She dreamed of her home, lit up in sunlight, all her family around her.

* * * * *

Sometime later, she was jerked from sleep.

A pair of unseen hands unshackled her, and began dragging her in some unknown direction.

"Stand up," a cruel female voice growled.

She tried to stand. She put her foot down and felt a bomb-blast of pain surge up through her leg.

Crying, Poe cringed in agony. "I-I can't …" she wept.

With a grunt of disgust, something grabbed her ankles, and felt around her feet. The wrenching, soul-bursting agony that hovered over her as they did so was nothing short of indescribable.

"You—how did you remove the Dora?"

Poe, craned her neck in pain. "I—I didn't."

A crabby female hand cuffed her across the mouth, drawing blood. "Liar! No matter, no matter. You … come with us!"

Slowly, painfully, Poe tried to stand on her shredded bare feet again, and quickly hit her head. She had to stoop, the room or passage or whatever she was in was no more than four and a half feet high.

Claustrophobia set in and Poe felt like panicking. Roughly she was pushed forward.

"Where … where am I going?"

"The Pit."

"What … why?"

"You are going to fight."

"Why?"

"To see if you're worth your bread. You will fight and either you will kill or you will die."

"I can't walk … I can't see … I don't want to fight …"

"You are a worthless coward."

"I don't want to fight!"

"Then sit there and die."

She was dragged stooping through a twisting series of passages, and then she was pushed into a yawning empty void. She fell for a few moments, twisting feebly and then hit the bottom of a greasy, cold pit.

"Stand up!" someone ordered from above. Poe tried to stand, but couldn't—her feet were two wretched stumps of pain. No wonder Syg hated shoes.

There was cheering in the distance, and she sensed that someone else had joined her in the pit—she could feel the presence. She heard the person's feet slapping against the floor of the pit.

Poe thought back. Syg rarely spoke about her days as a Black Hat and the training that she underwent in becoming one; the Black Hat Adepts, the trainees who were killed by the dozen every day. She remembered Syg saying that she often had to fight in pits—fights that were to the death. She never said how many Adepts she killed in such a fashion.

She found herself wondering if Syg had ever killed anyone in this very pit, the one she was in now.

There was ragged breathing. "*I'm going to kill you, I'm going to kill you …*" a small, but malicious female voice chanted at the other end of the pit.

"Fight!" someone above yelled.

The person on the other side of the pit charged toward her. No Silver tech, her feet in agony, all the color fading from her memory, she sat back, swallowed, and waited for the end to come.

There was the rapidly approaching slapping of feet on the damp stone. There was a lust-filled shriek that filled the dark.

There was a BONK! and a shocked, agonized cry.

Then, there was the sound of someone hitting the floor of the pit.

Poe, vaguely curious, strained to see in the dark and looked in the direction of the sound.

Something blossomed in front of her.

Light! She saw light, cool, growing to a soft white. She began to make out the outline of an earthen pit, the walls rising up about twelve feet. Lying on the floor of the pit about twenty feet away was the body of a ragged female. She wasn't moving. Next to her was a large glowing book—the light filling the pit was coming from the book. Quickly the book rose off the floor of the pit and spiraled into the air, its light intensifying.

A happy face looked down at her from the top of the pit. Blinking eyes and whiskers.

Carahil!!

"I'm sorry it took me so long, Mother, but I had preparations to make. I am here now!"

"Carahil, I can't stand up … my feet!"

He bounded down into the pit and came to her side. He expanded in size. "Climb onto my back," he said.

Painfully she got up onto his strong, silver back. Looking to the other side of the pit, which was about eighty feet wide, many forms were dropping down; ragged, tiny female forms. They charged forward.

"How many people are in this hovel?" a male voice said from above.

"Lots!" Carahil replied.

"Lots? Lots! I think you forgot to mention that!"

A loud din of shooting, mixed with enraged shouts, erupted above. There was the throaty report of a large gun of some sort, mixed in with the "FWWIEE!!" sound of an energy weapon. She saw the lances of red energy threading out.

There was a panicked cascade of screaming and shouting.

"Johnny, Johnny, look there, to your left!"

"Ha, ha! Roll `em up, Peter! And shoot to kill next time, will you!"

"Torri, what happened to our Cloak?"

"Cloak won't work in here—they've my key!"

"Wonderful, just wonderful! Sage—plan B, and hurry it up! Peter, set the charges!!" he shouted.

Shadow tech … Poe smelled it. Someone was throwing a lot of Shadow tech around up there.

A Shadow tech serpent, huge and grinning with anticipation, fell down into the pit. Instead of attacking them, it slithered away.

Poe winced. In a moment, the snake had a struggling form by the head and was quickly devouring it whole. She turned away, unable to watch any further.

Someone jumped down into the pit next to Carahil—someone with a huge, black gun. It was a lady—a tall one. A little silver bird sat on her shoulder, glowing like a candle flame. It looked like a Tweeter.

"Lt. Kilos?" Poe asked.

She looked up and smiled. "Lady Poe, good to see you!"

Ki leveled her gun and popped off several thundering shots. People in the distance fell.

"Lt., what are you doing here?"

"Long story!" she said hopping onto Carahil's rear end, and dropping a few more figures in the dark with her huge Marine gun.

"Lt., Carahil!' Poe cried. "—Syg! Syg's around here somewhere, and she's badly hurt. We've got to locate her!"

"Syg's here?" Ki asked, shocked.

There was a massive CRACK! from above, like the sound of a huge, flesh-tearing whip.

The Rescue of Lady Poe *(Chantal Boudreau)*

Carahil loped out of the pit. Poe looked around. In the dim light of his spinning book, and the frequent strobe of bright muzzle flashes, she could see that she was in a large, semi-circular cavern. The walls of the cavern were lined with small holes. Ragged, dirty women were pouring out of the holes. The floor of the cavern was pocked and rolling with hummocks and pits—people were climbing up out of the pits in force. Standing nearby in a mass were four people, three men and a woman, all dressed in long black coats. One of the men, wearing a triangle hat, had a massive whip and a small, but loud, pistol. Another man, a shorter one, was moving about firing energy weapons with both hands, and the third was on his knees, setting up some sort of device. There were black Shadow tech snake creatures moving about, attacking the ragged Adepts, killing them, eating them head first. The woman, apparently, was a Black Hat who was on their side—she was creating the snakes with slugs of Shadow tech from her hands.

"Peter!" the man with the whip yelled. "Are you ready?"

CRACK!! came the whip. Heads were loped off, bodies falling in the distance as the whip stretched out to an impossibly long length.

FWWWEEEEEE! came more blasts from the energy weapons.

"Nearly," Peter said.

"How long!" roared the tall, blond-headed man with the hat. With his huge whip he was taking off heads at a stroke, each with a life-ending crack.

More and more Adepts poured from the walls. The tall man put his whip away and got out a small black stick. Moving the stick around, the tip began to glow, tracing a blue shining pattern in the air. The pattern became solid and then shot forward like a laser beam, slicing and chopping everything it passed. It bisected a Shadow tech snake, which then grew back and began attacking in twain.

Several Black Hats Wafted into the far end of the cavern with a blast of brimstone. Hulgismen, the growling and naked personal guard of the Black Hats, began streaming out of the wall holes. They bounded down to the floor.

They were rallying. The Black Hat masters were unprepared to be attacked in their own backyard, but now they were rallying.

The Shadow tech snakes slammed into the mass of Hulgismen, attacking them, coiling them up, squeezing the life out of them. They devoured their flesh.

Some of the Black Hats began throwing out Shadow tech of their own: huge black spiders and black winged reptiles. Snakes, spiders and reptiles met and locked up in a terrifying dance; the snakes coiling and devouring some, the spiders putting their fangs into others, wrapping them up with their legs. The reptiles swooped and darted about, carrying some snakes away in their claws. A snake was in the process of eating one of the reptiles.

A raging group of Hulgismen approached, oblivious to the shots and energy blasts raking their ranks. Carahil's book landed heavily on the cavern floor before them, cracking the ground beneath it. It opened, grew huge, and the whole lot of Hulgismen were sucked off their feet. They tumbled across the floor and disappeared into the book's open face, as if eaten by it. The book closed, then quickly re-opened: kittens, rabbits and little birds all flew out and jumped around.

The snake-casting Black Hat got into a sparking, clashing Sten duel with one of the attacking Black Hats, their invisible fields banging into each other in mid air.

The man named Peter took a few steps forward and aimed some sort of small device toward the rock ceiling high overhead. A reptile from above swooped down, Peter standing helpless in its sights. The tall man took several shots at it with his pistol, but it didn't seem fazed.

"Peter!" the man yelled.

"I'm nearly finished!"

"Peter, forget it, and jump aside!!"

In a moment, the Shadow tech reptile would have Peter in its claws.

Carahil, open-jawed, head and neck stretching, plucked the Shadow tech reptile out of the air with a bone-splintering crunch, shook it, and sent it, spiraling and broken, back into the Black Hat ranks.

Peter loosed a shot of some sort toward the cavern ceiling.

The tall man with the stick traced out another blue line, sent it flying, killing many Hulgismen but being foiled by the Black Hats Sten. The surviving Hulgismen bounded in on them in a fury. Kilos, setting her SK to Full-Auto, mowed them down in a strobe-light of destruction.

"Peter!!" the tall man roared. "Light it off!"

"The charge is set, but we need to take cover first, Duke!"

"Peter—blow it! Blow it now!!"

Peter pressed a button and there was a huge explosion from above. A large hole opened admitting turbid, cloudy daylight into the chaotic cavern. Jagged bits of cracked stone came down. The Black Hat standing with the men created a Shadow tech shield, the chunks of rock bouncing off. Carahil arched his neck back and protected Lady Poe and Kilos from the falling rock. The attacking Black Hats followed suit. Many of the Hulgismen and Adepts filling the dome floor were crushed by falling stone.

A winged ship, black as coal, hovered there.

"Everybody on my back!" Carahil shouted, shrinking a little. The men and lady climbed on and Carahil took flight, the passengers still firing at the masses below.

"Wait!" Poe cried. "What about Syg?"

A blast of Shadow tech came up from below.

"Hold on!" Carahil roared, and twisted away from the blast in a gut-wrenching turn. In a moment, he was up and through the hole.

The cargo door on the winged ship opened and Carahil flew in.

* * * * *

The Duke jumped off of Carahil's back. "Sage!" he yelled. "Get moving!"

Sage of Ruthven, sitting in the cockpit, banked the ship and they headed east as gouts of Shadow tech began shooting upward.

The Duke took over the controls and hit the thrusters. The sky was blackening with Shadow tech. The Goshawk shook with turbulence.

"Syg!" Poe screamed on her knees. "What about Syg? We can't leave without Syg!!"

Torrijayne's normally cheerful face darkened: "Sure we can …" she said under her breath.

The ship lurched: the Duke just managing to bank away from a Shadow tech lance.

"All right, all right, I think we're clear. Torri, can you Cloak us?"

"No, Fall … they know who I am, they know my key!"

At altitude, the ship leveled. "Three minutes until we link up."

Poe was sick with worry. "Syg! We can't leave without Syg! Even if she's dead, she needs to be buried on Dead Hill where we can mourn her as a Blanchefort!"

Carahil moved to a larger area of the cargo hold. "Mother, Madame Torrijayne, Kilos … please look away or close your eyes for a moment."

"What for?" Kilos asked.

"If you will … humor me."

They looked away.

There was an odd "BLECH" sound.

There, lying in front of Carahil, was a slightly slimy Syg, her ruined brown Blanchefort gown a slick cocoon around her. Her red hair was a sticky paste stuck to her head.

"I would not allow us to leave without my countess either, Mother, though I had to improvise a place to put her."

Poe clambered to her side. "Syg!! Is she alive, Carahil? Can you help her? Please help her … she's terribly wounded!"

Carahil smiled. "You're mistaken, Mother, she's not wounded. She's just fine."

"What?"

"She's fine. That quaint little goldfish you put in her … Fins … patched her right up."

"Fins? Fins healed her?"

"He did … really, Mother, you should have more faith in your creations, after all, look at me! You made me very well, and you made Fins well too. He knows everything Ennez the Samaritan knows, after all, and he did his job. He saved the Countess of Blanchefort … and her son too, though the Black Hats sought to expel him."

"What happened?"

"I … interrupted them. All she needs now is rest and, possibly, a few hearty meals to get her strength up. She will, however, be rather sore for awhile."

Torrijayne walked up to Syg and took a good hard look. "So, this is Sygillis of Metatron, is it? A redhead … it figures. I've been waiting to kill her for years."

Ki clapped Torri on the shoulder. "That was in another life, Torri. She's a good friend, and the loving wife of my best friend. She's not what she was, just like you. She's not a Black Hat anymore. You'll see."

Torri looked at the floor and turned. "Yeah, yeah, we'll see ..."

Johnnie spoke up. "Well, Torri, if there's going to be a fight, my money's on the new one here."

"Shut up, Johnnie!"

Poe and Kilos cleaned Syg off. "Yuck," she said. "Carahil, why didn't you just stick her in that book of yours like you did the Hulgismen? Would have been a lot less slimy."

"I couldn't put her in my book. Her Silver Tech messes it up. I'm still working on that problem. So, it was 'down the hatch' with her."

Kilos, mindful of the slime, listened for her breath: it was thin and shallow, but it was there and it was steady. "Sounds good, she's ok, Lady Poe. She's ok."

Poe wiped a few tears away. "Thank Creation." She was overwhelmed for a moment—her little Silver tech familiar saved Syg's life after all.

"I don't like the look of your eyes, Lady Poe. Let me see," Kilos said. Poe allowed Ki to examine her eyes: swollen, badly bruised, her eye whites were bloody.

Peter sat next to Ki. "If I may?" Kilos moved aside and Peter examined her. "I am no Hospitaler, but I am skilled at field triage. Hmmm, she's bleeding inside. She'll need a Hospitaler soon. Can you see clearly, my Lady?"

Poe blinked. "No … no… a little blurry. I'm all right."

Peter continued to examine her face. "How could someone do this to such a beautiful lady?" he said, and she blushed. He reached into his duster and pulled out a small bag. Reaching into the bag, he retrieved a folded cloth which had a small quantity of pinkish salve smeared within. He took a dab of the salve and massaged it carefully into her face near her eyes.

Poe closed her eyes, enjoying his attention. "You have a healer's touch, good sir," she said.

"You're too kind, my lady."

"What is your name, sir, if I may ask?"

"Peter, Lord of Ruthven."

"Lord Ruthven then," she said happily. "My name is Lady Poe of Blanchefort, and I am pleased to have met you. I'm sorry, I wish I was more presentable."

Peter laughed. "You look just fine to me, my lady." As he worked, he introduced his brothers. "If I may, that fellow holding the gun over there is my brother, John, and the studious-looking man is my eldest brother, Sage."

Sage tipped his hat, and Poe gave a small, smiling nod.

Peter continued. "The elegant lady over there is Madame Torrijayne of Waam …"

"Formerly of Waam," she corrected, looking at Poe with a smile.

"… yes, formerly of Waam," Peter added. "And, last but not least, the noble fellow flying the ship is my Lord Fallsworth, the Duke of Oyln."

Poe gasped. "Oh my, the Great Duke of Esther, I am honored and pleased to be in your presence. I wish to offer my thanks for your timely arrival, and, certainly my brother, the Lord of Blanchefort, shall be willing to offer you a fitting recompense for …"

Torri sat down next to her. "We're not taking your money, Lady Poe. Ki said that you were a fine lady, and I can see that. I feel I like you already."

"Told you you'd like her," Kilos added, re-magging her SK.

Torri clapped her on the shoulder and examined her face. She whistled. "That is a whale of a Shadowmark you have there." Poe felt a little shy and lifted a hand to cover it. Her Shadowmark was clearly a great deal larger than either Torri's or Syg's.

"No need to feel bashful or anything," Torri said smiling. "I've no idea what a big Shadowmark means, but, obviously, you know what you're doing with Shadow tech. I'm told you made that guy Carahil in a fountain. Is that true?"

"Yes," Poe said. "Yes it is."

Torri smiled and shook her head.

Peter stopped rubbing her face. "There, the salve is a mild blood restrictor and will stem the bleeding for a time."

Carahil looked at Peter's work and seemed to approve. His book appeared and he scratched a few things in. It vanished.

"Thank you, my lord," Poe said touching his shoulder. "I feel much better."

"Please, Lady Poe, call me Peter."

Poe smiled. "Peter then, thank you, sir. Please, could you look at Syg also? I am much better now."

Peter slid over to Syg and took a look. Poe scooted in next to him. "What's this gelatinous material?" he asked noting the slime covering Syg.

Carahil blushed a little. "Well, she was in my stomach after all. I'm a Silver tech totem, but I do have a stomach, you know."

"She was wounded in the chest," Poe added.

He moved her gown aside and there, under her ribs, was a large but perfectly healed wound. "She … appears to be healed, as Mr. Carahil said."

Sage moved in to have a look. He touched the wound, trying to pull it open. It held firm. He turned to Poe. "My Lady, you did this … with a fish? Did I hear that correctly?"

Poe shrugged. "I suppose … Fins, a little Silver tech familiar I used to make for my gentleman's nephews who were always hurting themselves."

"Can I see one?"

Carahil loped up to Poe. "She is empty now, sir. See, Mother, I told you … the countess is fine. He nuzzled her face with his whiskers.

The Duke rolled the ship and power dived it down fast. "Boys, let's make this quick. Thirty seconds and we'll be on the ground."

Screaming down to the surface, the *Goshawk* broke the unsettled clouds, and there, parked on the undulating, rolling ground were three black ships—slightly smaller versions of the one they were in. The Duke hit the landers and the ship jerked up as the skids hit the ground. "Let's go, hurry up!"

The Ruthvens hopped out and headed to their ships. Overhead, the sky was turbid, angry.

Peter stood. "Your pardon, Lady Poe, I must to my ship."

"Oh, yes sir, thank you. And, Peter, please be careful."

"I will, ma'am."

Poe watched him as he ran to his vessel.

John of Ruthven turned to Kilos. "Want to come with me, Ki? I've got room for two."

She smiled. "No, no, Johnnie, thanks. I want to stay here with Poe and Syg. Watch it out there, ok?"

"I will." He tipped his hat and mounted his ship. A few moments later all four ships were blasting skyward.

In the cockpit the Duke was busy hitting switches. "Torri, dear, please set a Mode 4, will you?"

"Mode 4!" she repeated. "Ok! Why are we doing this?"

"Mode 4 will ease our transition from atmosphere to low-orbit."

"Oh."

The Duke looked at his screens and gasped. "We are in deep, deep trouble. Carahil, I thought you said this was going to be easy!!"

"It was easy … I thought it's been easy so far."

"Torri, are you sure you can't Cloak us?"

"No, I'm sorry, Fall—they've got it knocked. They have my key! I can't Paint a Cloak if they know my key."

The sensor was rapidly filling with incoming blips.

"Then we're going to have to run for it. Everybody strap in!!"

Torri looked crestfallen and touched the Duke's shoulder. "I'm sorry, Fall."

"Not your fault, dear. It's my fault, for getting us into this, for listening to that silver trouser-toucher back there!!"

"Actually," Carahil said from the back, "I've never touched a pair of trousers in my life. But, don't worry, I'm certain that you, sir Duke, with your fine illegal vessel here, is more than up to the job."

The Duke, holding his controls looked back. "I keep hearing how you are supposed to be this mighty Silver force of good. I've not seen much out of you, up to this point, aside from the slightly disgusting rescue of the Countess of Blanchefort."

"She's disgusting, all right," Torri said.

Carahil picked up his whiskers a bit. "Well, you've not needed me so far, have you? You're doing fine. Remember … he who does for himself, empowers the gods. Balance, Duke, balance, that's the key."

"Then why have gods?" Torrijayne asked buckling her seatbelt.

Carahil opened his mouth to answer, but found he didn't have a good witty reply. He closed his mouth and stayed quiet.

Kilos looked out the window. Outside, pursuing, was a dark cloud of black ships following them at the edge of night—more than she could count.

7—An Alleged Pirate

One of Davage's initial thoughts about Lt. Verlin, this attractive Lady of House Hobby, was whether or not she didn't mind getting a little dirty. The test with the SK in his office proved she was capable with her hands, but this display: coat off, sleeves rolled up, turning tools under the open panel of the read-data station, was some handy work. She had been under there about twenty minutes, pulling out cabling, re-routing this and re-centering that. The main sensor was coming on and going back off at an alarming rate. The Ops crewman and the Missive stood there shaking their heads. Larsen brought her a cup of coffee which she thankfully accepted.

Several B-Venture X-2 modules had been brought to the bridge from engineering. These unwieldy consoles were normally used to calculate Stellar Mach jumps, a process that required reams of calculated data in order to be performed safely. Any *Straylight* normally used about seventy of them strung together in the bowels of the ship to get the data out in a timely fashion. These units were hot spares from the reserves. Lt. Larsen was busy stringing them together and powering them up from extra leads at the Missive's station.

Soon, Verlin emerged and, with Larsen's help, connected the read-data board to the units. Cleaning off her hands, she punched a few buttons. "Now, Captain, we should have enough scanning and processing power to …"

The lights on the bridge flickered and the holo-cone went black.

Cursing in her Howell accent, Verlin got back under the panel, Lt. Larsen kneeling down with her. They bandied back and forth for a bit, and then the holo-cone came back to life.

Verlin stood back up. "I'm sorry about that, Captain." She began pressing buttons, Larsen watching and offering suggestions. "Now, we will be able to follow the thin Shadow tech trail at speed, and our sensor range will be temporarily tripled."

Davage was impressed. “I see, and well done. Crewman Sasai,” he said turning to her. “Do you have a fix on the trail?”

“I do, sir,” she said. “It’s faint but readable, and at speed.”

“Please forward to the Helm. Lay in a pursuit course, winding for maximum possible speed.”

“Aye, sir.”

“Lt’s Verlin and Larsen, again I am impressed—pity I cannot have two first officers. Lt. Verlin, will you please man the navigator’s position and Lt. Larsen, will you please deep scan ahead for the enemy vessel. I want to know the moment it comes into scope.”

* * * * *

A short time later, Syg opened her eyes. She tried to rise and found her chest was very painful, too painful to sit up. Looking around, she saw a smiling but rather swollen Poe sitting next to her, holding her hand. Also there was Kilos—Kilos??

“Ki …?” she said weakly. “Is that you? Poe? What’s going on …”

She saw Carahil nearby. “Carahil too?”

Carahil twitched his whiskers. “Welcome awake, my countess.” He nuzzled her cheek.

“Still mad at you over the pie thing …”

“I’m glad you’re still with us to be mad at me,” he replied.

Ki smiled, unbuckled and slid toward her. “It’s me, Syg. How’re you feeling?”

“I’m fine. Where did you … where did everybody come from?”

“It’s a long story. I’ll tell you later,” Ki said.

Syg squinted. “Poe, your face … are you all right?”

“I’m better now, seeing you awake, hearing your voice. I was so worried about you, Syg.”

Syg looked around and tried to sit up again. “Dav … where is he?” she said rustling a little. “Why isn’t he here? I want to see him … I want to see him.”

“You’re on a ship, just not the *Seeker*. We’re trying to link up with it. Again, it’s a long story.”

Torrijayne unstrapped from her seat, kissed the Duke and slid out of her chair. She leaned against the bulkhead and looked down.

“Hiya’, Syg!” she said cheerfully.

“Not now,” Ki said, sensing pending trouble.

Syg strained to look at her. "Do I know you, Madame?" Syg noted the Shadowmark on her face.

Torri smiled in a toothy fashion. "You sure do."

Syg rustled about. "Your pardon, please. I cannot recall your face, which follows seeing how you once were a Black Hat."

"That's right … you've never seen my face, and I've never seen yours, until now. Let me help you out. My name's Torri … Torrijayne of Waam."

Syg's eyes flared, and she struggled to sit up, despite the pain. "Torrijayne of Waam? The Painter? The Painter I hate?"

"The same … and right back at you. For the sake of my Duke, I'm trying to be civil."

"And, for the sake of my friends, and my sister-in-law, and my lord, I'm doing the same, though if you want to fight in private, I'll meet you anytime, anywhere."

"Really? How about right now?"

Ki stood up and Poe, alarmed, put her arms around Syg in a defensive fashion.

"Ladies, please," Ki said. "Look, I'm certainly not one to talk, about holding grudges and things, but anything that happened between you whilst you were Black Hats best ought to be forgotten."

"She tried to kill me once …" Torri said.

"After you left me to die on the field!"

"Yeah, well big deal! You put my temple to the ground in Waam—with me still inside!"

"And you Painted me into a death-illusion!"

Ki got between them. "If you two have a score to settle, that was in another life, when you were Black Hats, but you both have moved on. Can't we call it even?"

"We cannot," Torri said. "I want her blood!" she said in an ugly Black Hat voice. She looked back at the Duke and blushed, ashamed that he had heard that.

"The moment I'm better, we're going to settle this once and for all, Torrijayne of Waam. For the sake of my lord, whose example governs everything I do, I'll not kill you for he shan't approve. I'll just give you the best beating of your life. I'm going to distress that pretty face of yours and pull out some of that black hair."

"Fine, 'Syg'... let's mix. I'm going to break my fist all over your face, carrot-top! I've been waiting for this for years."

"As have I!"

The Duke looked back. "Torri, that's enough. Let her be, will you?"

Torrijayne turned and sat back down next to the Duke. She sat there and stewed.

Poe knelt down over Syg. "Syg, I'm going to tell Dav about this when I see him. You're not going to be fighting anyone. That is not something a proper countess does."

"Poe, don't be an old lady, will you—this is between me and her, countess or not. And don't tell Dav, either. I'll tell him myself, for Creation's sake."

Syg squeezed her hand. "Poe … I owe you my life. Me and Dav … and our son, we owe you everything."

She laughed. "You're my sister, Syg. I'd do anything for you. I'm glad my silly little Silver tech fish was able to heal you. I'm astonished actually."

"There's nothing silly about him. The things you can create—wondrous, simply wondrous. I couldn't do what you did. I can't think of many Black Hat's who could have done it either. You are a lot more powerful than you give yourself credit for."

Poe, holding Syg's hand, looked down at the floor. "Then, I guess I'll make a whole bunch more, set them loose in the Telmus ponds and streams … my future nephews and nieces will need them no doubt. I'll expect many of them … the castle, the Grove laughing and bursting with sounds and life. I can't wait."

Syg smiled, thinking about her son and the many children that were to follow. "Nor can I."

Poe beamed and stroked Syg's cheek. "You mentioned planning a party for Dav. I'm going to hold you to that Syg, I've already got a bunch of ideas that I'd like to share with you. And don't tell Pardock about it … she'll try to boss in."

"I won't, as long as you promise to consider allowing Lord Probert to be your escort."

Poe laughed. "Deal."

* * * * *

All this talk of Silver tech reminded Ki of something. She got Tweeter out—he just sat in her hand. He looked uncharacteristically tired and sluggish. One of his silver wings hung limply to the floor. He could barely stand on his little silver feet.

"Pardon, Lady Poe, Tweeter here seems to be sick, can you help him?"

Torri, interested, watched.

Poe looked at the tiny silver bird in Ki's hand. "He's only got an hour or two left, Lt. Do you want me to get rid of him for you?"

Ki was alarmed. "No, no—is there anything you can do for him? This little guy saved my life. I don't remember exactly what happened in those dark tunnels, but I do know that he was right there with me … he guarded my sanity, and he got me out. Whatever was in there, he got me past it. I was hoping he'd last forever. He's my good luck charm."

"He's timed, Lt. A Tweeter will only last for a few days by design. I can make you a brand new one if you like once I've charged up a bit—he'll be exactly the same."

She shook her head. "No, no … this one—me and this little guy have been through a lot together. This one, Lady Poe, please, he's important to me. Can you do anything for him?"

Poe thought a moment, then stretched out her arm and waved her fingers. She then touched Tweeter's little silver head, and then touched Ki's cheek, and suddenly Tweeter burst with light and was flush with new energy. He hopped onto her shoulder and chirped just like normal, fluttering his wings.

Torri, watching, sucked in her breath. Syg did too. Incredible.

"There, Lt., now as long as you live, he'll live."

Ki beamed and rubbed Tweeter's tiny silver head, all smiles. "Thanks, Lady Poe! Thanks a lot! I can't tell you what this means to me! Hear that, Tweets—it's you and me for the duration!"

He chirped.

Syg painfully lay back down. "Any thoughts on when we'll link back up with Dav and the *Seeker*?"

"We still have to find the *Seeker*," Ki said, Tweeter jumping around on her

shoulder.

There was an alarm bell from the cockpit.

"We might not be linking up with anybody! We're in bad shape!" the Duke cried.

Ki stood up. "What is it?"

"Our friends are back, in force, and they are gaining on us."

"Can we hold our own? Can we match speed?"

"We can, but what about the opposing force of ships coming in at 9pm? We're about to run head-long into them! Torri, we need that Cloak!"

* * * * *

"You have something, Lt.?" Davage asked.

"Yes sir!" Larsen said. On the cone, through the enhanced sensors, a blip popped up, followed by hundreds of other blips.

"Sir, we are detecting what appears to be a League ship being pursued by a force of unknown vessels. Actually, it's four ships flying in a tight combat box."

"Heading?"

"2pm mark 5am of Heron. They're heading in this direction."

"Can we identify these League vessels?"

Larsen spoke up. "They are not Fleet vessels, sir, but their configuration appears to be League. The lead ship is flying no colors or tax ID. It is, however, broadcasting a four-point encryption packet, probably for the purposes of navigation between the four ships. I recall seeing this particular encryption in the latest call sheet of suspected pirating vessels in and around the League. Sir, if I am remembering correctly, it is thought to be used by the Duke of Oyln."

"The Duke of Oyln?"

"Allegedly, sir, yes."

Verlin spoke up. "And that's not all, sir. We are detecting an opposing force of unidentified vessels 9pm of 4am, bearing in on his position. He'll be engaged any minute, sir!"

"Composition?"

"Over a hundred vessels—that's what he's got in front of him."

Davage rubbed his chin. "What's a rootless pirate like the Duke of Oyln doing out here in all of this? Probably running a load of something and got ambushed, that's what I'll wager."

"Possibly, sir, and again his current status is: 'alleged pirate'."

"Orders, sir?" Larsen asked.

Davage thought a moment. He walked to the front of the bridge.

Syg, he couldn't lose her trail. "Lt., should we divert to assist the Duke, will we be able to re-acquire the Black Ship's trail?"

"Unknown sir, it is rapidly dissipating."

"Can we lock in and map ahead?"

"We are at our horizon, sir. No further mapping is possible, save continuing on."

"I see."

Damn the Duke, he got himself into this, let him get himself out.

"Sir, your orders please," Larsen repeated.

Duty calls—a League citizen's about to be cut to pieces between two hostile forces.

Duty be damned, his countess is out there.

He remembered Admiral Scy. He remembered his Pledge.

Defend life.

Protect the League and its citizens wherever they may be, whomever they may be.

Syg was there, she listened to him take the Pledge.

He took a deep breath. "Beat to quarters! Navigation, mark this position and then set course to intercept League vessels, maximum possible speed! The Duke of Oyln might be a bloody alleged pirate, but he's a League citizen. We'll save him, then arrest him, and resume our search for Countess Blanchefort."

Davage unsaddled his CARG as the claxons went off and the crew jostled into position.

"Prepare for battle!"

* * * * *

Torri looked miserable in her chair. "I told you, Fall ... they know who I am and they know my key!" she said pointing to her Shadowmark. "They'll use it to tear my Cloak right back down again."

"What are you talking about?" Ki demanded.

"Every Shadow tech female has a key. Each Shadowmark is unique, rather like a fingerprint, and that is her key. If one's key is known, then it can be used to partially undo their Shadow tech creations, Painted illusions included."

Sage's voice crackled in over the intercom. "We're about to be engaged from our right, 9pm and closing fast!"

"I see them, I see them!" the Duke said.

Torri rubbed her forehead. "Wait … wait. They have my key, and that's a fact, but … but, if I put enough power into the Cloak, they won't be able to drop it right away, it'll take time!"

She got out of her chair and went to the cargo door. "Raise containment, please," she said. There was a hum and she opened the door, open space whizzing by on the other side of the field. "Lady Poe, I need your help."

Poe stood. "What, my help? I'm so low … they drained me. I need a few hours."

"Any little bit will help, please."

Poe, walking on her painful feet, made her way to Torri's side.

Johnnie's voice cracked in through the Com. "They're on us, Fall! No, good running, I'm tired of running! Let's Badger!!"

"Johnnie, keep your throttles pegged, and stay on course!"

Through the open door, they could see Johnnie's *Goshawk* open its guns and bank hard, the computerized thrusters on his ship configured to mimic in-atmosphere flight.

The Duke shook his head and opened his Sar-Beams. "Everybody hang on!"

He then banked into the swirling black masses, guns squealing. Peter and Sage followed. Soon the scene was full of swirling black ships and barreling *Goshawks.*

Carahil loped up to the front. "Duke if you see any large, greasy-looking black spheres emanating from the enemy ships … you're going to want to avoid those at all costs."

"You!" the Duke roared skidding the ship into a savage roll. "Are you going to do anything? Are you going to help out or are you just going to sit there and do nothing but suck up our air!"

"Honestly, Duke, I'm not breathing …"

"Are you going to help us or not?"

"Are you asking?"

"Yes—I am! Get out there and help us! Do something! Destroy some ships!! Kill somebody!!"

Carahil rose up and clapped his flippers together. "Ok," he said happily, and then loped away.

The Duke looked around and rolled the ship, blasting his SAR-beams. "What did you do? Hey, what did you do?"

"Duke!" came Sage's voice over the Com, "my chronometer just jumped!"

"Mine too!" Peter cried. "Creation—lances! We're going to be swamped!"

Over at the open cargo bay door, Torrijayne had painted a large arcane symbol out in front of the Duke's, rolling tumbling ship.

Outside, ships, black spheres, red Sar-Beams, and lances of deadly Shadow tech mingled.

The Com was electric with callouts.

"Roll Peter, roll!"

"Hit, good hit!"

"For Creation's sake, get out of my way!"

"Watch where you're shooting, Johnnie!"

"Sage, you're skidding, you're skidding!! The bar, Sage, kick the bar!!"

"Watch the sphere, watch the sphere!"

"That's it, Johnnie, Johnnie boy!!"

Torri's key stood in place, matching the ship's movements. "All right, there it is. Lady Poe, give me your hand."

Torri took Poe's hand and the symbol immediately got brighter."

"Good, good," Torri said. "More is needed, Poe, more power!"

"I'm trying … I'm so low. They drained me!"

Peter called out. "Duke, there's another ship entering the theatre! It's a Fleet vessel, *Straylight*-class, flying the colors MFV *Seeker*."

"I never thought I'd be so glad to see one of those!" Johnnie shouted.

"That's our ship! That Dav's ship!' Ki cried.

With a crash of light, the huge *Seeker* blasted into the clogged, chaotic theatre, its main sensor searching about like a Cyclops eye. Banking its wings, it waded into the roiling mass of ships, canister and Battleshot batteries erupting. The weight of its massive firepower cleared large areas of Shadow tech ships at a time, but, as always, they didn't stay down, they stretched, broke apart, reformed and attacked again. The *Goshawk* ships used the *Seeker's* mass as a screen.

"Torri! Where's my Cloak?"

"Almost, almost—nearly there, Lady Poe!"

Poe panted and wheezed with the strain. "I've nothing left to give!"

"No … no … not enough! Not enough!!"

As Torri and Poe struggled, a small hand joined theirs.

Syg. Leaning against Poe, she laced her fingers in with theirs.

"Sit back down, bitch!" Torri said in any ugly voice.

"Make me—whore!" she said in an equally ugly voice adding her power to their combined effort, leaning against Poe to stand.

They were speaking with their Black Hat voices, and it was hideous to hear.

Outside, Torri's key went to white light.

"Wait!" Kilos cried. "What about the *Seeker*, we need to Cloak her too!"

"Ki?" Torri cried. "Cloak a monster ship like that … we still don't have enough power to Cloak ourselves … even with this bitch hanging on here!"

"Watch it! That's my lord out there risking his life, and he gets Cloaked too … or you die right where you stand!!" Syg said.

"Your Lord," Torri spat. "Hitching his wagon up to a bimbo like you—that's his loss!"

Syg and Torri started squeezing hands—hard. They relentlessly stared at each other. Poe, her hand caught in the middle, winced in pain. "Ladies … I …"

Carahil loped up to them. "Here, the 'Trouser-toucher' wants to help out." He lifted his flippers, and began tickling Lady Poe about the waist. Astonished at first, Poe then began uncontrollably laughing. "Carahil, what are you—a, hahahahhahahahaaha!" Suddenly, Torri's key expanded in white hot energy and disappeared.

"That's it, that's got it, we're Cloaked—yes, the *Seeker* too."

The Duke rammed his sticks. "Johnnie, Peter, Sage, pull up hard to 1pm and stop firing!"

Ki sat down next to the Duke. "Duke, Duke, we need to reach the Com on the *Seeker*, and let them know what's going on!"

"I'm doing that now. Good Creation … a Fleet vessel and here I am with my trousers dropped."

Syg and Torri continued their hand-squeezing duel. The only one who seemed to be suffering was Poe. "Ladies … you're breaking … my hand," she piped.

"Too bad it's not your neck—Syg," Torri said in her Black Hat voice. "That lord of yours must either be blind or half-stupid to shack up with—"

Suddenly Syg let go, hauled off, and slapped Torri hard across the face. She flew back a bit, recovered then charged Syg. A moment later, they were arm-in-arm. They slammed against a bulkhead, grappling for punching room, kicking room. In a flurry they twisted down to the floor. One of Torri's Macco boots flew off in the process.

"Stop it!" Poe shrieked, pawing at them in tears. "Stop fighting!"

Ki waded in and moved Poe aside. "Break it up!" she yelled, well practiced at stopping fights from her early Marine days. She just about had them separated when strands of Silver and Shadow tech began coming out. They were roping each other.

Carahil stepped in and stopped them, wrapping them both up in Silver tech until they cooled off. Syg, in worn-out shape to start with, was hardly able to move after the ill-thought out fight.

8—The Duke's Cargo

Under Torri's Cloak, the Duke's *Goshawks* moved in station around the *Seeker*, like bumblebees swarming around a huge swan—tiny black vessels around a huge white one.

The Ruthven's smaller *Goshawks* were just small enough to enter Bays 5, 6 and 7. The larger one, the Duke's personal ship, was forced to hard dock at the front of the vessel.

Captain Davage, an orderly, and a squadron of Marines awaited the Duke's disembarkment. The orderly held a pad filled with charges a mile long that were to be read to the Duke immediately. Then, he was to be taken to the brig and locked up. The acting first officers, Verlin and Larsen, were doing the same thing in the Ripcar bays with the small *Goshawk* ships. Ennez the Hospitaler came down with the captain to see if any required medical attention on the Duke's ship.

To rescue the Duke, he had risked his ship and put the search for his countess on hold. He wondered if the Black Ship's track could be picked back up. And, for that, the Duke was headed to the brig.

The docking doors opened and out came the Duke: tall, about as tall as Davage, broad-shouldered and stocky in the Esther fashion. He was blonde-headed, attired in his usual black duster and triangle hat. His pipe smoked in a lazy fashion.

He looked around, at the captain, at the Marines. "All these Marines, Captain … oh, I am sorry." He quickly snuffed his pipe out. "I'd forgotten, no tobacco on Fleet vessels. I'll make a note to remember that."

Davage raised an eyebrow. "Herv," he said to the orderly, "please add a fine for smoking aboard a Fleet ship to the Duke's lengthy list."

"Aye, sir."

"Thank you."

The Duke looked around and offered greetings. "Lord Fallsworth, Duke of Oyln, Esther," he said tipping his hat.

Davage replied in kind. "Davage, Lord of Blanchefort, captain of the ship. Vith."

The Duke smiled. "Ah, Vith, I see. Oh, you're welcome for the Cloak, Captain. Think nothing of it."

"And you're welcome for our clearing the area and taking most of the heat for you, Duke," Davage shot back. "Now, let's to it, shall we? Duke, I am relieved to see you unharmed after such a conflagration. Will you please hand over all of your weapons to the Marine Sgt.?"

"Of course." The Duke then began the lengthy process of handing his small arsenal to the Marine. Davage and the orderly, Herv, stood by patiently as he did so, weapon after weapon coming out of the duster. Davage noted with a raised eyebrow the FENNISTER, the BAZU, and the brace full of RED HAW.

Finally he was done.

"How about the scarf at your neck, please. I know a House Ruthven SAPP when I see it."

"Ah yes," the Duke said handing over the scarf. "Well spotted. You know your LosCapricos weapons."

Davage shrugged. "Indeed I do. Lord Fallsworth, Duke of Oyln, I, Captain Davage of the Main Fleet vessel *Seeker,* Lord of Blanchefort, do hereby remand you into Fleet custody, effective as of this moment. Herv, please make a note."

"Aye, sir."

"Thank you."

Again the Duke smiled. "And, the charges, sir Captain?"

"Oh, the charges, the charges indeed. Since we've not all day to hear them all at length, I'll give you the short list: Piracy, sir. The reception of both stolen and illegal goods. The pandering of both stolen and illegal goods, and the sale of goods determined to be classified as contraband by the League Duties Ministry to both enemy and domestic parties. Oh, dear me, and I am afraid I must add: flying aloft in space in a private yacht that is not only armed with fixed cassagrain weaponry, but, according to our scans, is brimming with Xaphan and Ming Moorland technology. You also were not flying your legible colors or your current tax permit as is required of all civilians. Herv, please add those charges to the list as well."

"Aye, sir."

"Thank you."

Davage continued. "My acting first officers, Larsen and Verlin, are performing a similar 'service' for your crew docked in the bays at the rear of the ship."

"Oh good … I was hoping the Ruthvens weren't lonely right now."

The Duke held out his arms in a dramatic fashion. "Well, sir, you got me fair and square. I suppose I couldn't go forever without getting bagged by the Fleet. I must say, it is a bit of a relief."

"I am glad you feel that way, and furthermore, I am glad nobody was hurt in the process. And, off the record, I'll mention that you flew well in those illegal vessels of yours. Yes, quite well."

"Thank you for saying, Captain. Also, I do have a final cargo aboard my 'illegal' ship here … one that I would like to remand into your custody immediately."

"I see. You wish to hand over these goods willingly, without forcing my Marines to search for them, or myself having to Sight your vessel?"

"The Sight? I didn't think the Sight existed. There is no Sight in the Estherlands."

"There is in the Vithlands."

The Duke appeared impressed. "Well, no need to strain yourself, Captain. I willingly surrender my cargo to you."

"Herv, please note that the Duke was most forthcoming and cooperative at the time of his arrest, and that I, as his arresting official, was very appreciative and wish it noted for reading during his pending arraignment."

"Aye, sir."

"Thank you."

The Duke stepped aside. "Before I hand over my cargo, I wish to introduce you to my betrothed …"

A vivacious black-haired woman came bouncing out of the hatch, and snuggled next to the Duke. Davage instantly noticed the Shadowmark on her smiling face.

"Torrijayne of Waam. Soon to be my duchess."

"A … Black Hat?" Davage said in shock.

"Yeah …" Torri said sheepishly. She looked at Davage. "Wow, he's handsome!! How the heck did what's-her-name end up with such a good-looking guy?"

"What?" the Duke said.

"Well, he is … He's not you though, Fall, my big snuggy-bear!" she said pinching his cheek.

Davage tipped his hat to Torri, seeing a lot of Syg in her.

Syg …

"Madame, I congratulate you on your upcoming union to the House of Oyln, and I swear I will do my best to ensure you receive the maximum visitation privileges at whatever correctional facility the Duke is incarcerated after his trial and conviction."

"Thanks!" she said happily. "Did you hear that, Fall, I'm going to get to visit you in the slammer all the time. I can't wait!"

The Duke smiled. "Ohhh … the conjugal visits we shall indulge in."

Torri winked and purred loudly.

"Ah," the Duke said. "Now for the cargo I promised. Here comes part of it now."

Someone tall was coming through the hatch.

"May I please re-introduce you, good captain, to a friend of yours, so I'm told. The incomparable Madame Kilos of Tusck."

Ki came through the hatch, still in her now well-used dress and boots, her holstered SK strapped to her leg, Lady Poe's Tweeter sitting spritely on her shoulder.

They looked at each other for a moment, Davage in disbelief, then they embraced.

"Ki, what in the name of Creation are you doing out here? And, where did you get that SK from? Could that be the meaning behind the odd note I found on my desk the other day: 'IOU one SK, signed –C'?"

Ki pulled away from him. "Forgive me, Dav … forgive me for what I've done. I was feeling jealous … of you and Syg. I wanted you to beg me to stay. I did—I was stupid and childish. Being here with you and Syg means everything to me. I want to come back. I want to come home …"

"Ki, you quit the Marines—it's done. I can't just make you a Marine again."

Tweeter jumped off of Ki's shoulder, and landed on Davage's hat.

Ki looked at the floor, miserable. "Dav … please don't turn me away, please … you don't know what I've been through." She was beginning to get misty. Davage was open-mouthed in shock at such a display from Ki.

"Ki, what do you want me to do? You quit your job!"

Ki stood there, eyes watering. "… don't turn me away …" She clutched her stomach and bent over a little, as if she was either going to pass out or get sick.

He gently patted her on the back. He thought a moment. Tweeter chirped. "Herv, please note ship's log, Captain's entry: incidental. As of this moment, I, Davage, Lord of Blanchefort, captain of the Main Fleet Vessel *Seeker*, have received in person, reviewed, and accepted the petition of Madame Kilos of Tusck … to gain immediate and furtive admittance to the Stellar Fleet, effective: immediate, rank: crewman, status: active. Current venue of assignment: Main Fleet Vessel *Seeker*. Please note, all required paperwork, signed documents and oaths required for Crewman Kilos' admittance shall be accomplished at Fleet immediately upon our return to Kana. Furthermore, given Crewman Kilos' vast previous service in good standing as an officer with the esteemed 12th Stellar Marines, I, Davage, Lord of Blanchefort, captain of the Main Fleet Vessel *Seeker*, as of this moment, do hereby assign to Fleet Crewman Kilos immediate field promotion to … Full Lieutenant with all the responsibilities and privileges so entailed. Let it so be written, and let it so be carried out."

"So noted and witnessed, sir," Herv said, working the pad at a furious pace.

Ki stood there dizzy, not knowing what to say. She wiped her eyes.

Davage winked at her. "Congratulations and welcome to the Fleet, Lt. Kilos. I will excuse you being out of uniform for the time being, and I don't envy you the paperwork you'll have to fill out, and the long line of Admirals you'll have to oath to once we return to Fleet."

Davage reached up a gave Tweeter a pat. He took wing and settled back on Ki's shoulder.

"So … it's that easy? Just like that, I'm an officer in the Fleet? I remember years ago, I wanted to join the Fleet but I couldn't because I couldn't get a Letter of Recommendation from Lord Pittsfield."

"Captain's privilege—you've friends in the right places. And, no, it's not just that easy, Ki: you've oaths to take, paperwork to fill out—and we know how you excel at paperwork. I had to do a lot of lip-flapping just now, and Herv here had to work her fingers red typing in my log notes. Finally you've to be fitted for your uniforms. No off-the-rack in the Fleet, it's all tailored. Also, you'll have to turn in that SK and kit out with a MiMs."

"MiMs ..." Ki said blankly.

"Yes, MiMs. Not much of a gun in comparison, but they do come in a fine selection of colors, if that's any consolation for you."

Ki looked like she was going to faint.

"You all right, Ki?" Davage asked, smiling.

"No ... Dav ..."

Torri clapped. "Congratulations, Ki, I mean, lieutenant. You should have heard her, Captain, moaning about having to wear a dress all the time."

"I can imagine."

Numb, Ki stepped aside, leaning on Davage a little, still contemplating her situation.

Davage turned to the Duke. "I will look forward to hearing how Lt. Kilos ended up in your charge, sir, but, in the meantime, you have my gratitude for keeping her safe."

"It was my pleasure, Captain. She's certainly a heck of a lady, and a dead shot to boot. I'd hoped she would have wanted to become a Goshawk and fly in style with us."

"A dead shot? You've been in a shootout together, I take it?"

"Indeed we have—she'll tell you all about it later. Oh, and to continue the 'unloading' of my cargo."

"There's more?" Davage asked.

"Indeed."

Lady Poe came out of the hatch, with Carahil at her side, ever dutiful. Davage's jaw hit the floor. "Lady Poe ... Carahil? How did you two ..."

He saw her blackened, swollen face and her bandaged feet. He took her by the shoulders. "My lady, what has happened? Who did this to you?" His glance shot to the Duke.

"I'm all right, Dav, and it wasn't the Duke. The Duke, and his friends, and Lt. Kilos saved my life. It was a crazed, blue-haired girl who did it."

Davage thought for a moment. "Blue-haired ... Vroc, Princess Vroc did this?"

"I guess, when Lt. Kilos gets to explain how she ended up here with us, then so too can Lady Poe. It'll be like a big cookout …" Torri said in her bright, sunny voice.

Ennez came forward and scanned Poe's swollen face. "Lots of bone bruising. I'm concerned about her eyes, Dav. I'll want to get her to my dispensary right away for treatment."

"Yes, yes." Davage embraced and kissed her on the cheek. "Poe, you go with Ennez and he'll take good care of you; then later, when you're refreshed, I'll want to know what has happened here."

Davage turned to the orderly. "Herv, we'll need immediate quarters for Lady Blanchefort—oh, and for Madame Torrijayne as well. Please make sure they are accommodated in the best we have to offer."

"Aye, sir."

"Thank you."

Carahil looked up with his silver face. "It is good to see you, Lord Blanchefort."

"And you, Carahil. If I were to guess, I would to say that you are, at least partially, responsible for this unusual development, yes?"

"Yes, my lord … well spotted."

"Well then, I suppose you will be joining Ki and Poe later in sorting this mess out—the 'cookout' as Madame Torrijayne put it. Herv, Carahil will also be requiring quarters."

"Aye, sir."

"Thank you."

"How about quarters for me, Captain?" the Duke said brightly.

"The brig, sir, shall be your quarters. It appears that I owe you much in all of this, for my friend, my sister, and Carahil here, and I am not unmindful of that. Still, your arrest is in progress and I've no choice but to …"

Ki, recovering from her shock of being a new Fleet officer, spoke up. "He's not done, Dav."

"What, there's more? Who's to come out next, Countess Pardock, Dear Sadric, my late father … an Elder perhaps?"

"You better brace yourself," Ki said.

Kilos and the Duke went into the ship. A moment later they came out bearing a small stretcher. Syg lay on it, half asleep. She looked dazed and slightly out of her head until she saw Davage, then she was all smiles. Her green eyes lit up.

Davage, upon seeing her, choked and fell to his knees.

"hey, love … hey …" she whispered reaching up for him and taking his face into her hands.

Davage, usually very tight about public decorum regarding his countess, forgot all about it. He hugged her and kissed her hand. Syg was battered, dirty, and slightly slimy, but safe and very much alive. "Syg …" he whispered. "Is it true … is it you?" He said it over and over again.

"Yes … love, it's me. It's me … my lord … my beloved Davage …"

"Are you wounded? Are you hurt? Ennez!"

"I'm fine, Dav, I'm fine … Poe, she saved me. She saved me and our son."

Davage Sighted her—remembering the Syg monster on the bridge. There she was, basking in his Sight, not recoiling from it as the monster did. There was evidence of a recent severe cutting trauma to her chest and left lung—all repaired and healed. Also, there was their son, in her womb, a tiny nut ready to begin sprouting.

His countess … his Syg.

She should begin showing in a few months.

"Ennez, take the countess to the dispensary please for a complete examination."

"No, Dav … no, I'm fine."

"No arguments, countess, I'll be there soon."

A pair of Marines took the stretcher, and they went down the hallway with Ennez and Lady Poe.

Davage stood there a moment. He turned to the Marine Sgt. "Sgt., please take the Duke's weapons and store them for safe keeping where they may be returned to him later," he said.

"Aye, sir."

"Marines," Davage said. "Thank you. You are dismissed."

The Marines turned and marched down the hall.

Davage turned to Herv.

"Sir?"

"Please delete all charges pertaining to the Duke of Oyln, and issue him quarters."

"He'll be staying with me," Torrijayne said. "But you'll need to set something aside for the Ruthvens—there's three of them."

"Herv, please ensure the Madame Torrijayne's quarters are commodious enough for two, and three more for the Duke's comrades. Oh, and Lt. Kilos is going to need her billet back."

"Aye, sir."

"Thank you."

Herv tapped the pad.

Davage, trembling slightly, took off his hat, and bowed on one knee, arms outstretched.

"To you, Duke of Oyln, I owe thanks for all that I hold dear. For the lives of my friend, my sister, Carahil … and for the safe return of my beloved countess. I am Vith as you previously noted, and Vith pay our debts."

The Duke smiled. "Don't thank me, thank this fine fellow Carahil here. He is the master of it all."

"He is," Torrijayne said. "And you won't believe what he'll have to tell you … at the cookout. When's that going to be … I'm hungry."

Davage looked up and gave Carahil a pat on the head. "You little prankster you … Indeed, I'll look forward to these revelations—but later, I'm in no fit state to hear them now."

"I am thinking you'll want to your countess's side at once," Carahil said.

"That's where I am headed. Herv, please show the Duke and Madame Torrijayne to their quarters, and see that they are served lunch. Come on, Carahil, let's see how everybody's doing."

"Dav," Ki said trotting at his side. "What about my uniforms?"

* * * * *

Davage sat with a coffee in the tiny dispensary. Syg lay asleep next to him on the bed, holding his hand. Poe sat on the other bed, Ennez tending to her face.

Ki was at the ship's tailoring shop getting fitted for her Fleet uniforms. As soon as she found out for certain that Syg was all right, she went straight to the tailor's shop. She loved wearing a uniform, Davage thought. Too bad she won't get them any time soon, Fleet uniforms are hand-made on Kana. Some of the fine fabrics used in their making came from his own factories in Blanchefort village.

"You sure Syg's all right, Ennez?" he asked.

He turned from Poe and looked at his scanner. "She is. She's bled out a little, but other than that, she's patched and fully healed. No sign of disease or blood poisoning, and your son is doing fine. She's going to be sore and she'll need rest, though. It's a good thing she can manage pain as well as she does, as she was in quite a bit of it." His scanner was trained on Syg's chest. Through it, her innards could be clearly seen.

"Remarkable." Ennez zoomed the scanner in. "There's also this thing I was wanting to ask you about, Lady Poe."

She looked at the screen. There, printed in silver on Syg's ribs in a lilting script was:

FIXED BY FINS

"Can you tell me what that's supposed to be, please?" Ennez asked.

Poe laughed. "Oh! Oh, I forgot all about that. I added that to Fins for fun ... the kids just seemed to love it. They'd proudly show it off like a badge. It'll go away eventually."

Ennez shook his head. "I recall and odd session one evening where you pulled knowledge from my head as Silver tech, though I wasn't fully briefed on what you were up to—I recall being a tad drunk at the time and didn't think to ask. Is this the end result of that session?"

"Yes."

Ennez was impressed. "Hmmm, I see. Where is this Silver tech creature? May I examine it?"

"He's gone," Poe said. "It takes a lot of energy to repair wounds on living tissue, so, as he repairs the damage, Fins incorporates himself into the repair. The only thing left of him is this little message."

"I must admit, I'm fascinated. Could you, by chance, create another one?" Ennez asked.

"Certainly, sir, I think I'm recharged enough to make one," Poe said excitedly and she began moving her fingers around, silver forming in front of her.

Davage turned to Poe, sitting in the other bed, her feet wrapped up. Carahil sat next to her on the floor. His large book was open in front of him. He was scribbling something in with a marker in his teeth. "Poe ... I owe you ..."

She waved him off. "Dav, I think of Syg as my sister—I love her. I'm grateful Fins was able to do such a good job. I'm astonished, actually."

Poe looked at Davage as she worked her fingers. "She loves you, Dav. All she could think about was you … how she thought she would never see you again. You mean everything to her."

"When we get home, you'll need to seed the ponds with Fins."

Poe smiled. "I was already planning to."

Davage looked at the ugly swellings on Poe's face. "I'm going to get her, Poe. Princess Vroc, I'm going to get her for this; for what she did to you, for what she did to Syg. My patience only goes so far. Either she's coming in to face justice, or she's going to die."

Poe finished, a happy, silver goldfish, big-eyed and bright sat in her palm. She gave it to Davage, who looked at it with wonder. "I owe you and yours, buddy," he said.

Fins blinked up at him.

"He's ready, Ennez, just keep him in a bowl of water, and he'll last a long time."

Ennez fetched a clear tankard, and Davage plopped Fins in, where he swam around.

The Com's voice came down. "Sir … message for you, marked black."

"Black? I'll take it here, Com."

Davage opened Ennez's terminal, and up popped Hezru, King of Xandarr. He was sitting near to the screen, holding a cat in his tubby arms. Carahil put his book away and moved into position where he could watch.

"I see my daughter has done her work—I warned you not to underestimate her, did I not?" he said. His voice had lost that jolly, beefy aspect. Now, his tone was dark and sinister.

"I am going to find your daughter and arrest her, King. I hope she chooses to put up a fight, so that I can kill her in good conscience."

"Not very noble of you, Captain."

"She attacked and injured my sister … a person who has never harmed a soul in her life. She abducted and nearly killed my countess, and she has endangered my crew. She has much to account for, and so do you."

"Me … what have I done?" Hezru said smiling.

"You provoked this, encouraged this, set this into motion—and all to line your filthy pockets. You are wholly to blame, and I am coming for the pair of you, King."

"Are you?"

"I am, and I am going to take you and her into custody. You are going to face League trial for your role in all of this, or you are going to die. How many more Xandarr children am I to face?"

King Hezru grinned a chubby grin, his face filling the screen. "You know where I am, Captain, I am not hard to find … come and get me, if you dare."

The cat he was holding hissed.

He screened off.

"Misanthrope," Davage said. "If he thinks he's to escape my anger he's—"

Davage noticed Carahil sitting there on the floor looking up at the now black terminal screen. He had an odd and rather serious expression on his face, which, for the normally jovial Carahil, was quite striking. "Carahil?" he asked.

"Pardon me, my lord," he said and vanished without another word.

9—The Celestial Arborium

The initial shock of seeing Ki, Lady Poe, Carahil, and finally Syg had worn off and Davage felt like celebrating. They had a day before they reached Xandarr, and he ordered the ship's chef, Lord Ottoman, to prepare a huge pig roast, complete with flowing narva and grog for the whole crew to enjoy in their off-shift time. With all that good food and drink, the mess was filled with song and fellowship, just like in the old days after a huge victorious battle with the Xaphans. Davage sat at a large table with his guests and his sister—Larsen and Verlin were on the bridge, Verlin at the navigator's position, Larsen in command. Davage made sure to save them some choice cuts for when they came off shift.

He had to admit he liked the Duke, Torrijayne and his men. Torri reminded him a lot of Bethrael of Moane; very pretty, very friendly and fun-spirited. She was easy to know. Still, he noticed whenever she and Syg locked eyes, her smiled faded into a scowl. Syg and Torri did not appear to like each other at all. Probably had issues from their Black Hat days. Syg had told him that she had many Black Hat enemies, and clearly Torrijayne of Waam was one of them. He hoped they could put whatever it was behind them.

Syg was too sore and weak to pay Torrijayne any mind. She quietly sat next to Davage in a white gown, leaning against him a little. She didn't set her hair, as she normally did when wearing her gowns. It lay long, wavy and red at her back. Davage helped Syg cut her food. Beneath the table, they held hands when they could.

Nearby, Ki was hoisting a mug of narva, and singing war songs with several of her Marine friends and John of Ruthven; apparently he was a drinking kindred spirit. Tweeter, glowing, wings flapping, fluttered as if in time with the song. Davage couldn't help but notice that "Little Johnnie" had eyes for Ki, and, oddly, Ki didn't appear to be dismissing him totally. That was very unusual for Ki who, normally, was very, very married. Mugs aloft, they leaned against each other in a flirty sort of manner as they sang.

He noticed Poe, face swollen, was sitting off a few chairs down by herself with her food. She had always eaten alone, going back to the days when she was infirm with her undiagnosed Shadow tech sickness. A spell was always a possibility. She hadn't wanted to attend the feast at all. He had to make up some sort of important-sounding story that it was Fleet tradition that those wounded in battle were expected to attend a celebratory feast, which Poe bought without question. Davage was about to call her over to sit with him when Peter of Ruthven, holding his plate, walked up and asked if he could join her. While standing in line to get his food, Davage had noticed Peter exchange a quick glance with Poe, and now there he was sitting with her engaging in pleasant conversation. Real charmers these Ruthvens appeared to be.

Carahil was oddly absent.

* * * * *

It was like nothing Poe had ever experienced before.

She had wanted to eat alone in her room. Her face was a blackened, puffy mess, her feet were bandaged and too swollen to wear proper shoes, and, most importantly, her gown was stale and stained. It was important for a Great House lady to wear a proper gown, befitting and honoring her House. Of course she could create a gown using Silver tech, she could do it in a quick second, and it would look smashing as well, but that wasn't proper. That wasn't a thing a lady did. A Blanchefort gown was supposed to be created by Elder hands using approved fabrics and threads, made on Blanchefort looms. To simply conjure one up out of thin air, why, it would be a slap on her House's face. It was ridiculous for her to even consider such a thing.

So, she wanted take dinner alone in her room, or possibly with Carahil, though he was missing at the moment. Dav and Syg had come in and demanded that she eat with them. They said they were having a celebration—for everyone's safe return, and Dav wanted her to come and join them in the mess. They said everyone was asking about her.

"I'm not in a proper fashion, and my gown is unacceptable," she said.

Dav, though, said that nobody expected her to be ballroom ready. They knew she'd been through a terrible ordeal. They understood that she was recovering from wounds dealt to her by a cruel and implacable foe.

"I do not wish people to see me like this," she insisted.

Dav then told her that it was a Fleet tradition, after a battle, to have a feast, and, he added, that those wounded in battle were given a special place of honor and were expected, if able-bodied, to attend. He said to choose to not attend would be dishonoring hundreds of years of Fleet tradition.

"Oh, well, in that case," Poe said. So, cleaning herself up as best she could, she joined Dav and Syg in the mess.

She sat through the meal, trying to blend in. The crew was noisy and festive and, passing by, they wished her well with raised mugs. Lt. Kilos was singing some sort of fighting song nearby and Poe listened, quietly humming along with the tune. After a little longer, she wished to excuse herself and go back to her room.

Standing in line with his plate to get a helping of pork, was Lord Peter—the nice fellow she had met earlier. He was a touch shorter than she was; Blancheforts being taller than most, and wore a long, black coat with a white linen shirt. He had a black pair of pants tucked into Esther-style boots. His hair was sandy and cut short. Esthers generally didn't wear their hair long in a tail like Vith, Zenons and Remnaths did.

She remembered his hands; so skilled, so soothing. She hoped he would look her way so that she could acknowledge his kindness with a courtly nod. But no—he was a Ruthven, a bound House Minor, and was badly outranked in the scheme of things by the House of Blanchefort. Proper etiquette demanded that he not look at her while she was eating. The League, with its societal rules and decorums, could sometimes be a stuffy thing. She planned to write him a letter thanking him for his attention, and mentioning that his kindness had meant a great deal to her. She then planned to make it known that the House of Blanchefort shan't be offended by a visit. She, using proper channels, wanted to invite him to come to Blanchefort, though, the correct thing for Lord Peter to do would be to graciously decline the offer. House Minors did not mingle with Great Houses, even if invited. It wasn't proper.

She allowed her thoughts to wander, to fantasize. She dreamed of inviting him to come to Blanchefort and bowl with her in their private, hidden alley. She dreamed of showing him her prize pink bowling ball, and, if he didn't have one of his own, she would have one specially made just for him.

Imagine: to enjoy an afternoon of bowling with Peter under the Palantine courtyard; an afternoon of laughing, of listening to the ball rolling down the waxed lane and the clash of the pins falling. Perhaps they could drink lemonade and score their games by hand with pad and pencil. The thought of such an afternoon made her tingle. She tormented her napkin into careless shreds she wanted it so much.

But, it wasn't proper. It wasn't proper …

Peter looked up and turned to her as he waited to get his food. He stared at her. She remembered her swollen, blackened face. She blushed and felt ashamed. She looked away for a moment.

When she looked back up, Peter was still staring at her. He looked at her in an odd way. He looked at her the way she fancied Dav looked at Syg. She felt uplifted by it. No longer was she bruised and blackened in a stale gown; now she was beautiful. Now she was perfect. He made her feel beautiful.

That look. Was that what she was missing all this time, with all those Great Lords looking at her and seeing nothing but the gown and the House behind it; the rank and the status?

Could it be that a mere momentary look across a noisy room finally created in her all the things she had wanted to feel but never managed before?

Do you see me, Peter? Is that possible? Am I beautiful to you?

Peter got his serving and made to sit with his brother Johnnie and Lt. Kilos—the two of them singing away.

He stopped and approached and asked if he could join her. How could this be? This broke any number of rules. What people might say? After a moment of astonishment, she found she didn't care about rules and social constraints anymore. It was just she and Peter—nobody else mattered. Soon, they were lost in conversation, just the two of them.

It was wondrous.

* * * * *

The next morning, with the final approach to Xandarr only hours away, Davage pulled everybody into the conference room. Now it was time to hear how all this had come to be.

He listened to Ki talk about Carahil and the Hazards of the Old Ones, how she didn't recall what she saw or did in there, and how the Duke, again at Carahil's planning, was there to pick her up.

He listened to his sister talk about her abduction, and he got angry as she told her story—his kind, gentle sister being put through such an ordeal. He watched as his sister and Lord Peter made eyes at each other.

He listened to the Duke talk about picking Ki up, and then taking a detour at Carahil's insistence to an uncharted planet, which turned out to be a Black Hat stronghold. And there they freed Syg and Poe.

With the exception of Lady Poe's abduction and Syg's capture, everything appeared to have a central, common thread: Carahil.

"Well," Davage said, "all we need is Carahil here to explain a few things."

The door to the conference room opened, and in came Carahil. "Am I late?" he asked.

"Where've you been?" Ki asked.

"You're right on time, actually," Davage said. "So, Carahil, what is all of this? What is going on?"

Carahil hopped up onto a chair and paused for dramatic effect. "Of course you know I am an Elemental Spirit, and soon to be a member of the Celestial Arborium, yes?"

"The what?" Davage asked.

"The Celestial Arborium. It's basically a fraternity of insanely powerful, ridiculously good-looking Elemental Spirits who are charged with maintaining order and balance. I am simply its latest recruit though I've not fully joined as of yet. They said they'd do anything if I'd only join."

"You know, you're good looking, but not that good looking," Torri said, smiling.

Poe chimed in. "Carahil … I made you in a fountain."

"Yes you did, Mother. Surprise—you created an Elemental Spirit, and the Arborium thanks you for that. Such grace and beauty could not possibly go unnoticed, and not be asked to join. If I may—it was a no-brainer."

"No-brainer, huh?" Ki rolled her eyes. "Carahil, you simply cannot get enough of yourself, you know that, yes?"

"I know. But, though it pains me to say it, enough about me—let us cut to the matter at hand. I saw something some time ago … I saw a terrible event that was to happen in the near future. I have taken steps to subvert this event. That is what the Celestial Arborium does. We monitor the universe and strive to maintain order and balance."

"What is it? What is this event?" Davage asked.

"I saw death … I saw people screaming, people dying. I couldn't allow it to happen. I had to take steps, but I had to do it the proper way. Maintaining balance is an exacting thing … thus, here we are."

"What do you mean you had to take steps? What sort of steps did you take, Carahil?" Ki said, a bit of anger forming in her voice.

"A push here, a shove there … an improvised speech or two."

Ki's huge brown eyes began to twitch in growing fury. His book appeared in a flash and he consulted it for a moment. The book then vanished and a vase of interesting alien flowers suddenly appeared in front of her. "Flowers, Lt.?" he proffered.

"Oh," Torrijayne cried. "Those are neat! Can I see?"

Ki, not releasing Carahil from her gaze, picked up the vase and set it down in front of Torri. "Carahil … I am going to ask you a question, and you better answer carefully, otherwise you might end up with a hole in your head. Did you have anything to do with me quitting the Marines? Did you make me do something I otherwise wouldn't have done?"

"You did that yourself, Lt., as we have touched upon earlier. Certainly, however, my proximity didn't hinder matters."

"I ought to pop you one! You ruined my life!!"

"I needed you with me … I required your help, and you performed better than I could have ever asked for. I don't see why you're so mad, it all worked out fine in the end."

Carahil looked down and twitched his whiskers. "My only regret is that I had to allow my Mother to suffer … for I needed her too."

"That's why you didn't come?" Poe asked.

"Yes, Mother, and I am sorry. I kept an eye on you though. I would never let any harm come to you."

"Well, I'm happy," Torrijayne said. "You brought me to my Duke."

"I'm glad to have helped."

Ki was mad. "I don't ever see you doing a whole lot of anything, 'oh beautiful warrior you'," she said.

"There are cosmic rules—rules that must be followed. We, as Elemental Spirits, follow the rules to the letter. We must set the stage to allow others to do for themselves, to give a nudge, provide leadership and inspire. If I were to simply 'sling it around', then that's when the trouble starts. That's when it hits the fan. That's when you fall into the Windage of Kind and become a demon—and I do not wish to become a demon."

"Are you barking mad?" Ki asked, the anger clear in her voice.

"No, I am not barking mad, Lt." Carahil shuffled uncomfortably. "The prime tenet of the Celestial Arborium is balance, Lt. Here's what it is—the universe exists in a state of balance. Something happens over here, another offsetting thing happens over there. Give, take, push, pull—everything's in balance, get it? We can see things that you cannot. Sometimes we lend our aid. Sometimes we see things we don't like and try to take steps to prevent the undesired thing from happening. The problem is balance. If we intercede too much, then balance is upset and the cosmic scales go haywire."

"I'm going to bash you over the head with these scales in a second, here," Ki yelled. "Speak plainly or shut up!"

"Look, if I wanted, I could easily tip the scales of balance any way I so chose to. But, if there's no weight on the scales, then as soon as I let go, the scales will swing wildly in the other direction—and whatever happens then is unknown. Chaos prevails."

"You're pissing me way off," Kilos roared.

Carahil continued. "Let me dummy this down for you, Ki. What I'm saying is, I can save you from the bus that's about to hit you today, but I can't save you from the piano that's going to fall on you tomorrow. I just can't."

"What bus?" Ki said, smoking mad.

"A bus and a piano! I'm trying to make a metaphorical example, Ki, for Creation's sake! Without the proper weight on the scales, if I save you from the bus, then that falling piano is going to get you sooner or later—that's balance swinging back in the other direction. Then you're dead and I'm in the Windage becoming a demon for my troubles, sucking the Universe's hind-wind. Just like Maiax. He really swung the balance, he had his foot on those scales for years, and look what happened—all those poor people who counted on him, dead, and in not a very pleasant way, either. You have to turn your back sooner or later, and that's when the Universe jumps up and bags you in the rear."

"You're going to get bagged in the rear, all right!" Ki looked like she was going to start cussing, but Syg cut her off.

"Who's Maiax?" Syg asked.

"Maiax, countess, is a demonic Elemental Spirit once worshiped by the extinct House of Bodice," Sage said. "Maiax deceived the House of Bodice and led them to their extinction three thousand years ago."

"He's the guy who's been leaving us messages, Syg. 'M' for Maiax," Ki added.

Sage continued. "That is a very common theme in various mythologies; those who dally too much with Elemental Spirits end up dying in a cataclysmic fashion. The Bodice is one, the Xaphan space station Zall 88 from antiquity is another example. They worshipped a feline goddess and were led to their downfall. Mabsornath was her name, if I recall my reading."

"Mabsornath?" Davage said. "Isn't Mabsornath a Xandarrian deity?"

"They incorporated her into their pantheon of gods after they destroyed Zall 88," Sage said. "The reason the House of Xandarr sacked Zall 88 was to steal their knowledge. After they'd put all aboard to the sword and discovered they couldn't understand the knowledge and wonders that were there, they destroyed everything in spite and turned their benevolent goddess Mabsornath into a cursed demon of pestilence. Again, the Elemental Spirit connection tends to be a deadly one."

"Yes well, Lord Ruthven," Carahil said, "scribes, it seems, usually like to write about horrible things for shock value and fail to jot down the good stuff that happens. Too mundane, I suppose. Elemental

Spirits who follow the rules are a positive thing, but are generally unsung in the histories. It's the ones who mess up that you remember. The Bodice, Zall 88: who could forget such tragedies? And, to clear the record, I think Maiax might have gotten a bit of a bad rap over the years. Did he truly intend to lead the Bodice to their death as the scribes so dramatically say, or, did he simply make a mistake? Did he, in his adoration, upset the balance? I think Maiax truly loved the Bodice. The fate of the Bodice is precisely is what I'm trying to avoid here."

"So then, why's he leaving us all these nasty notes?" Ki asked.

"He isn't, Ki. Wrong 'M'."

Sage continued. "I believe I understand what you're saying, Mr. Carahil, and it holds with various ancient doctrines of cosmic equilibrium. So then, to further illustrate your metaphorical point, you, from your lofty cosmic perch, can see that, for instance, Captain Davage is going to soon be killed by a passing bus. You wish to save the captain, but cannot do so directly, because cosmic balance has predetermined that he is to die. To proceed anyway will consign him to an even worse fate, your 'falling piano' metaphor, and cause you to become a demon for your efforts," Sage said.

"Yes, yes!" Carahil clapped his flippers together.

"You spoke of adding 'weight' to the cosmic scales of balance, and I am assuming that when the scales are properly weighted, then miracles can happen—fates can be changed. So then, how does one apply the proper weight to the scales of balance and prevent such a calamity?"

"I was waiting for somebody to ask me that!" Carahil cheered. "You put the weight there yourself, Lord Ruthven. You, by your actions, by your decisions, by your courage and your free will, apply weight to the cosmic balance. If I can get you to willingly take steps to save Captain Davage from the passing bus, possibly endangering yourself in the process, then your actions will properly weigh the scales. You will have armed the gods. And, best of all, if you put enough weight on the scales, you'll give me a little wiggle room to really do something spectacular. Thusly armed, I can then move the scales of balance about all I want. I can save Captain Davage from the bus. I can slow it down, I can stop it cold. I can make it disappear or turn it into spun sugar, and there won't be a falling piano waiting for him tomorrow. Tomorrow will just be another day."

He looked around at the faces at the table. Sage seemed to fully understand, but the rest were rather perplexed. "Ki," he said somewhat hurt, "are you mad at me?"

"Yep."

"These flowers are cool!" Torri said, sticking one into her hair. "Where did you get these?"

"Look, I'm sorry I—"

"Carahil," Davage said interrupting, "Ki will get over it, as you said, things appear to have worked themselves out. Now, you obviously have gone to great lengths to bring us together—obviously, as you put it, there is a 'bus' waiting to run over somebody that you want us to try and prevent—yes? So here we are. Why don't you simply tell us what is going on? What did you see? Who's going to get hit by this cosmic bus you talk about?"

"I … really can't say more than I already have."

"Why?"

"Because, Captain … if I were to do that, you will stop doing and start waiting; waiting for me to take action, waiting for me to save the day. That cannot be. As I just pointed out, I am powerless until so empowered. I need the weight on the scales to act, to receive my arms. I can be great only if you are great first, that is the first rule of balance—to arm the gods by force of deed under free will."

"Oh yeah," Ki said, "who made up that stupid rule?"

"The Universe did."

"Yeah, right!"

Davage shrugged. "Look, Carahil, I appreciate what you are saying, and I believe that you truly do wish to help, to prevent some sort of disaster from happening. Look at the lengths to which you have gone. It would be helpful if you simply told us what and where. Where is this metaphorical bus, and who is it heading for?"

"Again, I'd rather you tackle it headlong and …"

"Can you give us a hint? Can you do that?" Poe asked.

"A hint??"

"Sure, certainly some cryptic, devilishly well-crafted hint to keep us guessing would be allowed."

Carahil's whiskers pricked up. "A hint? Well I don't know. I do have gifts, though! Presents; something for everybody!" His book appeared again, and he began nosing through the pages. "Let's see. Ah! Here they are."

Small boxes of white cardboard shot out of the pages of the book and came to rest in front of each person sitting at the table. Each box had a pastel-colored bow.

Syg stood and backed away from hers. "Do not open those! He's going to hit you square with a pie!"

Carahil laughed. "I promise, my countess, there are no pies in the boxes. I really do want to give each of you a gift. Now, before you open them I need to give you a quick warning. I feel I can do that. The House of Xandarr, it's—"

FOOM!!

There was a flash. Carahil looked to his left, startled.

FOOM!!

There was another flash, and he vanished.

Everyone seated at the table looked around, at Carahil's now empty seat.

Poe shook her head and laughed. "All right, Carahil … very impressive, now, where are you?"

Nothing, his chair remained empty. Just his book and his gifts remained on the table.

Syg weakly leaned over. "Maybe he's invisible."

Davage lit his Sight and looked around.

Nothing. Carahil's seat was certainly empty. He looked around the room to see if Carahil was hiding somewhere.

He didn't see Carahil, but he did see something else. He saw, crawling on the ceiling no less, near Carahil's seat, a strange skeletal figure. It was man-shaped, thin, with overly long arms and legs, its clothes were stylish, if a little garish. Its face was strange, puckered, withered, painted and topped with a huge brown wig. Its coattails hung down toward the floor like a pair of icicles.

In its freehand, it fiddled with some sort of compact control device. The other hand was held to the ceiling, like a fly. He saw a fading bit of energy surrounding Carahil's chair.

"Do you see, Carahil?" Syg asked.

"No, no … but I see a rather disturbing ghost."

"A ghost?"

"Yes, stuck to the ceiling, just there." Davage pointed up.

The "Ghost" appeared shocked that Davage could see it. It put away its control device, jumped down to the floor, and exited the room through the door.

Davage Sighted it as it went. It was standing out in the hallway where it vanished in a flash.

Carahil's book lifted off the table by itself, and opened. The gifts sitting on the table were quickly pulled back into its interior. It closed.

The book then vanished.

* * * * *

Davage and Ki sat at the conference table. Lts Verlin and Larsen were also there. They appeared a bit disappointed with the presence of Kilos.

Kilos, usually a fairly quiet person, chattered without pause about her new appointment to the Fleet.

"I'm all fitted, Dav—it was marvelous. We never got more than simple alterations in the Marines. How long before they're ready?"

"Not until we arrive back home, they will be waiting for you at Fleet."

"By the Elders … I'm going to bust!"

Verlin and Larsen looked at each other and shook their heads.

"And, Dav … the tailor asked me what I wanted for my 'Design'. I wasn't sure what he was talking about, so I said I'd get back to him. What was he talking about?"

Davage smiled. "Lt. Larsen, please explain the Design to Lt. Kilos."

"The Design is a small, unique device, embroiderment, or other small addition to your uniform. It's a Fleet tradition, it's just a small alteration to your uniform that is personal to you. Nothing overly noticeable or out of sorts, just a small touch all your own."

Ki was ecstatic. "Really? Dav, what's yours, if I may ask?"

"Mine is an extra button hole and button. I added it long ago. I had hoped that one day, it might be filled by …"

Syg came into the room, slowly. She was a little bent over.

"Filled by what?" she said sitting down next to Davage. "Oh, you're talking about the button hole aren't you? Go ahead, Captain, tell her what the button hole was for. Tell her."

Davage continued. "… Filled by Princess Marilith, as a symbol of my love for her. If, somehow, we were ever to be joined, then she would add a button and loop it through."

"Yes, well," Syg said proudly, "that button hole got looped through sure enough, but not by her. Go ahead, Ki, take a look."

Ki leaned over the table. The lowest button on his coat was not a real one, it was an extra—she had never noticed it before. The button was even different—all the real ones were embossed with the Fleet crest. Dav's fake button was engraved with an intertwined D and S.

"Yep," Syg said happily. "I put that button there—take that, Princess Marilith. I had to use Silver tech though … I can't sew, though I'm taking lessons."

"Dav, I never knew that!" Ki said excited. "Oh, I know what I want mine to be!"

"Well, enough about that. I wanted to discuss the first officer's position that is currently open here on the *Seeker*."

Verlin and Larsen shifted in their seats uncomfortably.

"I wanted to make it clear to all present … that the competition continues."

Syg's jaw hit the floor.

"WHAAAAT!" Kilos roared.

"Ki, these two fine officers have come a long way to compete for your job … which you vacated. They have performed brilliantly, and I am not going to dismiss them out of turn."

They both smiled.

"Dav … it's me. It's Kilos. I'm back! Besides, it was all Carahil's fault."

"Don't blame Carahil, Ki. And, obviously, you have the inside track, however, these people have impressed me greatly, and I will not look down on them by summarily re-instating you. The competition continues."

"No, no, no … Dav, the competition is over!" Ki said, getting her temper and her insubordination up.

"No, Ki, it is not," Dav said patiently.

"DAV…" Ki said at a shout, ready to give him a good tongue lashing.

Verlin cut her off. “Lt.,” she said in her proper Howell accent, “the captain has said the competition continues, and I suggest you prepare to compete to your best, as I intend to compete as best I can.”

Ki turned to Verlin and spoke in an ugly, condescending way. “I … suggest … Lt., that you sit there and be quiet … *Marine*.”

Davage rolled his eyes. “Good Creation Ki, this must be a record. You've been in the Fleet for approximately a day, and you're already talking down to the Marines.”

Verlin reached into her coat and pulled out a folded handkerchief. She rubbed it on her neck then slid the cloth to Kilos. “That, Lt., is called perfume. I entreat you to try it some time.”

Ki looked at the handkerchief, her large brown eyes flaring with rage.

Syg settled into her seat, thoroughly enjoying this confrontation. She remembered this sort of thing well, Ki could be an intimidating person, and it usually took one or two fist-skinning sessions with her before her nasty bearing changed. To her credit, Verlin showed no signs of backing down.

Ki pushed her chair back and made to stand up.

Davage intervened. “Keep your seat, Ki. In any event, however this plays out, the two who do not get the job will leave here with an armload of glowing recommendations from me that will, with luck, open the door to any duty or ship you choose to go to.”

“Thank you, sir,” Larsen said, feeling a bit better.

“Thank you, sir,” Verlin said. “However, after experiencing your skill of command first hand, I have my heart set on this job, Captain. I wish to be your first officer, sir. I wish to serve you, and intend to prove my worth.”

Kilos shot Verlin a deadly look. “Is that a fact? You, Lt., you're with the 53rd, correct?”

“That is correct, Lt.”

“The 53rd is a science and weather outfit.”

“And what of it?”

“*And what of it??*” Ki said, mocking Verlin's Howell accent. “The 53rd is not even a real Marine disposition. The only thing you've ever fought is a cold front and a rain squall.”

Verlin stood up. “Care to find out how much of a Marine I am, Lt.?”

Kilos stood up. "Ladies, sit down," Davage said firmly.

They did, still eyeing each other.

"Ki, that was uncalled for. Lt. Verlin has done herself, her House, and her unit proud, and I am honored to have served with her. Again, this competition continues, and if you want this job, Lt. Kilos, I suggest you look to it and show these two fine officers the proper respect."

Ki stewed. "I'm sorry, Dav."

"It's not me you should be apologizing to, Ki."

Kilos turned to Verlin. "Lt., I'm sorry that you are assigned to a science and weather detachment ..."

Verlin flew out of her seat and tackled Ki, and before another moment had passed they were locked up into a tight rolling fight: Ki trying to punch and Verlin seizing her by the hair. Being such tall, strong women, it took Davage, Ennez and Larsen a great difficulty to separate them, Syg too weak to help. Eventually, Davage had them standing side by side at attention, Ki's hair a tangled, stretched bail of straw.

"I am heartily disappointed in the pair of you. If you two have an issue with each other, you may work it out on your own time in the gym, am I understood?"

"Yes sir!" Verlin said.

"I was attacked, Dav! Just now!" Kilos said.

"After you all but spat in her face, Ki. You had that coming to you, and you know it! Now, I'm willing to forget this happened here today, but if I have to separate you two again, you both will be spending time in the brig! Understood?"

"Yes sir, Dav ... and you can bet, Lt., you and I will be sorting this out later," Ki said in a nasty, threatening tone.

"Look forward to it."

"Now, may we proceed with the briefing?"

"Yes, sir, and I'm sorry," Verlin said again.

Ki fumed.

Everybody sat down, and Davage proceeded. "We have set course for the planet Xandarr. Our mission there is to apprehend King Hezru of Xandarr and, if possible his daughter Princess Vroc. Of course it is quite unusual for a League Fleet vessel to take into custody the sovereign king of a Xaphan world, but he has admitted to sponsoring, training and setting loose a terrorist whose only purpose is to fight and kill in League space. We must stop both he and his daughter before any League citizens may be hurt or killed in the process."

Davage hit a button and a map of Xandarr Keep came up in a floating 3-D display.

"I anticipate resistance. Here it is. Xandarr Keep is a large, sprawling estate set in a dry valley in the middle of a small village. There, to the west of the Keep is the River Torr—pretty much the main source of water on Xandarr. A direct assault and quelling operation might be difficult given the complexity of the Keep and its proximity to a sizable civilian population. I will expect, upon our arrival, thoughts and plans as to our method of attack."

Davage turned to Ennez. "How is my navigator?"

"He'll live, but he's out of commission for the time being."

Davage thought a moment. "Lt. Verlin, will you please continue to man the navigator's position for now?"

"Aye, sir."

"Thank you, Lt. Now, I needn't remind everybody present that, although Xandarr is fairly near to the League border, we are nevertheless in enemy territory … we could be attacked by anything at any time. I want everyone looking sharp and on edge."

10—Xandarr Keep

As the *Seeker* came thundering into the theatre, the planet Xandarr loomed ahead. It was a colorful, garish planet, livid with purples, greens and dark browns. Around it, arranged in a gallery, were seven moons of various colors and the occasional satellite.

Lt. Larsen stood at the Ops station, tapping buttons. Lt. Verlin sat at navigation. All of the various sensors and gear she had installed were pushed aside to make room for her long legs. These two, vying for Kilo's job had only been aboard for a short time, but, given what they'd all been through, they seemed like old friends. They were both admirable people. Davage also thought he'd caught them looking twice at each other.

Ki stood near Davage. Without her uniforms, she was wearing, of all things, one of Syg's beloved Hospitaler bodysuits. But, instead of just going shoeless as Syg always did, Ki had on a pair of tall black Brusards—she having forgotten that she had a pair at the tailor's for repair before her departure. Her SK was holstered at her left and Tweeter, small, glowing silver, sat on her shoulder, chugging with energy. Davage could tell she felt a little ridiculous in the tight outfit, but it was better than the dress which she hated. It galled her that she had to wait for her uniforms.

He had a thought to tease her, but thought better of it.

Davage looked at Syg, sitting in his chair in a green Blanchefort gown. She was battered, but unbroken. She glanced back at him and smiled.

<*Are you certain you don't want to go back to the dispensary, darling?*> he asked her silently.

<*Positive. I'm not letting you out of my sight, love.*>

<*And Ennez approved of you being here on the bridge?*>

<*Yes, yes … I was 'FIXED BY FINS', remember?*>

She winked at him.

Davage stared at the image of Xandarr on the screen, getting larger by the moment.

"Com," he said, "send to Hezru, King of Xandarr, that we are here to take both he and his daughter into custody. Tell him we appreciate his station and wish to not make a great scene if possible. We wish him to come quietly, but are prepared to take further steps if necessary."

"Aye, sir. No response."

"Do we have any contacts?"

"No, sir," Sasai said. "The sky is clear."

"Lt. Larsen, bring up a positional map of Xandarr Keep."

Larsen tapped a few keys and a display of the large castle appeared on the cone. It was a huge, sprawling complex.

"What is the state of Xandarr's militia?" Davage asked.

Larsen answered. "The current militia strength of Xandarr consists of a few ground-based light infantry units. They do not currently have a stellar force of note—the previous one was seized by the Black Hats."

"Good, good. Lt.," Davage said to Larsen, "I'm thinking we should Arrow Shot down southwest of the Keep grounds, adjacent to the River Torr, and take the central courtyard there."

"My thoughts as well, sir."

Davage turned to Verlin sitting at navigation. "Lt. Verlin, opinion."

"I think we should, in addition to taking the central courtyard, deploy a squadron on the flat plain to the east of the Keep. There they could blunt any attack from the north, and be available to cut off any escape attempts by the King, either overland, through the air or waterborne."

Davage thought for a moment. "I agree. Lt. Kilos, your thoughts."

"I advise caution, Dav. I've heard of a vast network of tunnels under Xandarr Keep. Obviously Xandarr does not have the force to deal with a ship like the *Seeker* directly, but, should he go to ground, he could hold us off indefinitely."

"Your husband tell you that?"

"Yep."

"I've also heard of these tunnels, Captain," Verlin said, getting a dirty look from Ki. Verlin returned the dirty look and then some.

Davage stared at the map. "Do we know where Carahil might be?"

"He's not turned up, Captain," Syg said from her chair.

"Always the vanishing, always the popping up at the last possible moment, with him. He mentioned something about the House of Xandarr right before he vanished. Well, we mere mortals will have to proceed on our own I suppose. Let's get posted." He thought a moment. "Lt… Verlin, please assume command of the bridge. Lt. Larsen and Lt. Kilos, you two are to the shore with me. Com, please ask Samaritan Ennez to join us."

Davage headed for the lift, as did Ki. Larsen grabbed his hat and followed. Syg slowly stood.

<Dav, I need to change first. I'm not ruining another gown.>

<You're not coming, Syg. You're stay here with Poe.>

<The hell I am. I'm not letting you go again, so, if you'd like to fight about this right now in front of all these people, I'd be glad to accommodate you.>

They got into the lift. Syg, eyes tired and baggy, body sore and beaten up, stared at Davage relentlessly.

"Meet us in Bay 3," Davage said to Ki and Larsen. "We'll be there in a moment."

Syg smiled—she loved winning fights with Dav. They exited the lift and went to their quarters. In a flash, Syg changed into her bodysuit and rolled-up blue shawl. Davage picked her up and held her close. "Syg, you need to recover."

"I'll recover on the planet surface. I'm staying at your side. You'll need me."

"Of course I need you … I need you safe and sound."

"There's no such place right now, not until this is over. On the planet or up here … it makes no difference."

Davage set her down, and she put on a pair of sandals. "Are you sure our Lord Kabyl's all right?"

"I cocooned him in Silver tech. He's the only part of me that doesn't hurt right now. The Black Hats weren't going to harm our child."

They walked out the door. "So, I guess it's going to be Lord Kabyl after all," she said. "I've gotten used to it."

"Excellent. I knew you'd see it my way."

She reached up and kissed him, and they entered a Lift.

A short time later they entered Bay 3. Lt. Larsen, Ki and Ennez were loading a ripcar. They all climbed in, Davage lit containment, and they shot out of the Bay into space. Ahead of them, several Arrow Shot loaded with Marines and Sisters were already entering the atmosphere.

11—The Circle

The hum of equipment was loud and droning.

Carahil opened his eyes and looked around. He was in a large antiseptic room. Huge, latticed machines were huddled here and there, large monitors, status displays, power equipment, and massive computing machines made a craggy, artificial canyon that he was smack in the middle of.

He was lying on a flat, metal floor. If he had been subject to baser things, like being hot and cold, the metal floor might have chilled him to the bone. He was encircled by an arcane drawing in chalk—an odd sort of juxtaposition: the modern machinery all around, and the arcane magical symbol drawn on the floor with him in the center of it. He had to laugh.

He didn't quite remember what had happened. He was on the *Seeker*, he was just about ready to spill his guts regarding his vision, and then, 'poof!', here he was.

Carahil really hadn't wanted to say too much about it anyway—when the gods flapped their gums, that's when things got really, really bad. That's when people stopped doing and started waiting.

The circle he was contained in was nothing more than chalk, mixed with rice and salt. He could, if he wanted to go renegade, pass over it, no big deal.

But, as in all things, there are rules. Rules about this, rules about that. Rules he had to follow. The Celestial Arborium was an exacting thing. The rules stated clearly that, if some fool was able to encircle him with a mixture of chalk, rice and salt, then, he'd just have to sit there and wait until it was broken ... unless he wanted to become a demon and go to the Windage.

Gahh!!

As he looked around, he noticed several robed Science Ministry types standing about, holding pads and clip boards beyond the perimeter of the circle. They saw he was awake and noted it in their pads. They approached, smiling.

"Good morning," one of them said. "How are you feeling?"

Carahil didn't reply.

The Science-types looked at him and made more notes. "Can you understand us?"

Again, Carahil didn't reply.

"If you can understand us, please make that fact known."

Carahil, feeling mischievous, lifted a flipper.

"Harken, it raises a fore-appendage. Note the time."

"4:14am: the silver creature raised its right front appendage."

"What does that mean, do you think?"

"Did it understand us?"

"Perhaps it needs to pass a stool."

The scientists hammered their pads. "Do-You-need-to-Pass-A-Stool?" one said slowly.

Carahil excitedly nodded his head.

"Remarkable!" they exclaimed. "Well, then, shall we let it outside to evacuate?"

"Indeed, before it fouls the lab."

Carahil couldn't believe it, they were about to break the circle.

A cracked, high-pitched voice came raining down from above.

"Stop, right where you are, you Shoe-Sucking Cesspools!"

The Scientists froze.

"I have labored at great expense to secure this Imp, and you Lunch-Box Luggers and Three-Ulcer Urchins were seconds away from freeing it!"

A wigged man in knee-britches, leggings and a regal coat stood on the catwalk overlooking the lab floor.

It was Hershey, Lord of Milton. Spidery on long, thin legs and arms, he stood there looking down, slightly swaying. "Welcome, Imp," he said in a mocking voice. "I trust you are comfortable. I entreat you to consider yourself my guest. It appears you have access to knowledge and secrets that I want. You'll either hand over this knowledge and these secrets, or, I shall have need to get rough with you. I shall have access to all your secrets, even if I have to vivisect them out of you."

"My Lord," one of the scientists said, "we have not determined if this creature understands the common vernacular."

"Of course he can understand you, you simpering, smock-wearing stocking-stuffer!!" Milton roared. "They say every scientist eventually wears a silly hat—well go and get yours!"

The scientists returned to writing in their pads.

"So, Imp, you meddling Fish-farter, first I am going to have to deal with your friends—that duster-wearing dunderhead, and his seductive, Shadow-tech slinging strumpet! They have but hours to live! That's right! Danny Duke and Sally Shadow tech are going to die! Your pardon if that distresses you."

Lord Milton gesticulated wildly as he spoke. The lighting from above caused his shadow to come down from a number of angles. His shadow had many heads and many waving arms.

"My Lord," one of the scientists said. "I do not believe that insulting or frightening the creature will be at all productive."

"Quiet, you robe-wearing, pad-carrying, number-crunching numb-nuts!!" Milton shouted. "I am paying you max-coin to record and gather data, not to comment on my interrogation techniques!! Why don't you go and punch a button somewhere!!"

Milton, apparently satisfied with his tirade, turned and made to leave.

He stopped suddenly. "Oh, Imp, by the by, I've have something I've been wanting to give you! Consider it a gift …"

A brown cascade of feces and rotten fish came down from above, coating not only Carahil, but the scientists as well.

Milton, holding a rusty pail, rocked with delight. "Oh my, oh my! It appears that you are covered in filth, turd-noggin!! Ha! That felt good!"

Milton threw the pail down and stormed away.

Carahil, covered in poop, twitched his whiskers. He had to admit, Lord Milton had style.

12—Alone in the Great Hall

Davage helped Syg off the ripcar; it was a long drop for her. She looked so tired. She needed sleep.

Larsen jumped down and signaled the *Seeker* that they were on the ground with his holo-mon. Ki got out of the ripcar and looked around.

The huge Keep, the dusty village, the mountains in the purple distance—it was Xandarr all right. Nearby, the Arrow Shot transports stuck out of the ground like red mushrooms. The Marines and Sisters were already deployed and ready for anything.

They made their way into the outer holds of Xandarr Keep. The structure itself was a magnificent brass color, but in the purple light of mid-day, it looked rather green. It was a high-domed, bony-looking, brass-covered structure. The climate in this region of the planet was very dry and mild, and the Keep was very open to the elements. The whole thing resembled a pile of children's blocks arranged in a vague anthropomorphic fortress shape, with a huge turnip sitting on top for a dome.

Larsen received a silent message on his holo-mon. The Marines had secured the first three levels of the Keep. They had encountered no resistance.

Empty courtyards and passages, decorated walls and the occasional wide-open battlement, the whole Keep was ominously quiet. Davage and Larsen treated with the Marine Lt. who updated them on the situation, and continued into the interior of the Keep.

"I don't like it, Dav. Where is everybody? Where are the guards?" Ki said.

"Probably to ground, like you mentioned earlier."

With Ennez and Larsen ahead, Syg, in near exhaustion, leaned against Davage and took his hand.

"You need rest, Syg. You should have stayed on the ship. I should have insisted."

"I'll be fine, love."

"You were nearly run-through."

She began to cry. "I'm staying with you Dav …"

Continuing on, the Keep was a confusion of courtyards, passages and open-air halls. Everything was carved stone and beaten brass inlaid with mosaics. Davage imagined the droning of stringed Xandarr instruments drifting on the wind. The instruments Princess Marilith used to love to play.

The whole place was empty of life; an ornate shell. The music once filling these halls was silenced.

"Dav," Ennez said waving his scanner around. "I'm detecting energy fluctuations ahead."

Larsen got his GREAT DORE out. Davage unsaddled his CARG. Ki pulled her SK and cocked it. Tweeter fluttered on her shoulder.

Ahead, they entered into a huge, open air hall at least a hundred yards long. The hall had a beaten copper and brass ceiling, decorated in hammered pictograms and enameled lettering. The House of Xandarr was of Vith roots, however, their architectural style was completely un-Vithlike. The eastern and southern corners of the hall were walled and led into the interior of the Keep. The walls were lined with large, colorful pillows and rugs, and man-sized brass decanters and smokers. The north and western sides of the hall were open to the elements, the view outside obstructed only by the occasional, decorated pillar. A huge feasting table at least twenty yards long, and done up in the lacy Xandarr style, sat in the center of the room. Beyond, through the open northern part of the hall, soft mountains and valleys lolled in the distance. The hall smelled faintly of old incense and fancy cooking spices.

Lt. Larsen's holo-mon around his neck blinked. The holo-mon was connected to Missive aboard the ship and allowed him to see and hear everything they did. It also connected him to the Marine Commander. Davage, as a Gifted Vith, detested such things and left its technological wonders to others. Larsen began speaking into the air, having a conversation with the airborne Missive.

Davage recognized this room. Here is where he had spoken to King Hezru. They had sat at this very table. Here, he had seen Princess Vroc for the first time.

"Sir," Larsen said. "The Marines report the Keep grounds are secure."

"Did they encounter any of the Xandarr clan? Did they encounter anybody at all?"

"No, sir, they did not. The Keep is abandoned."

Something wasn't right. Carahil's undelivered warning entered his mind. "Syg, are you detecting anything?"

"No, no …" she said looking around.

Davage slowly walked the room. The pillows, the finery, the mountains in the distance. He wondered how many meals Marilith had eaten here; how many discussions about him had taken place in this very spot.

Abandoned. Lonely.

"Ennez are you detecting anything?"

Ennez moved the scanner about. "No, not a thing. I was previously, but no longer."

"I don't like it, Dav, there is no way this whole Keep can be abandoned. We're about to be hit!" Ki said. She looked to Tweeter sitting on her shoulder. "Tweeter, if there's anybody Cloaked or otherwise hiding in this room, point them out."

Tweeter took wing and settled on one of the chairs at the table.

"What's that mean?" Ennez asked.

"I don't know!" Ki said checking underneath the table.

She whirled about in her black bodysuit looking this way and that. Davage still wasn't used to seeing her in it. He couldn't wait to see her for the first time in her Fleet uniform. He was sure she'll look stunning.

Ki examined the chair Tweeter was sitting on. She felt about, lifted and set it down testing its weight. "I can't tell anything."

"Are the Sisters detecting anything, Ki?" Davage asked.

"Nope."

"Lt. Larsen, anything happening in orbit?"

Larsen consulted with the Missive. "No sir. Nothing. Nothing on long range either."

Ki was puzzled. "Dav—what are these?"

Sitting on the seats of the nearest four chairs at the great table were small white boxes topped with a pastel-colored bows of orange, blue, pink and green. The boxes sat there innocently.

"Those look like Carahil's gift boxes from the other day," Davage said.

Ki pulled the box, orange-bowed, off the chair and placed it on the tabletop.

"Be careful!" Syg cried. "I know there's a pie waiting to come out of that box."

Ki gathered the rest of the boxes and lined them up at the end of the table. Syg was dubious and skeptical. Davage leaned down and Sighted them. "I don't see any pies in these boxes," he said.

"Then what's in them?" Syg demanded.

"Something small, in bags."

Ki snorted and opened the first box. She reached in and pulled out a small linen bag. She tested the bag in her hand. "Feels like a bag full of marbles."

She un-did the string and dumped the bag out into her palm. Small silver objects tumbled out. The others gathered around to get a better look.

"They look like little Carahils," she said. Sitting in her hand was a small pile of silver figurines all in the shape of a smiling Carahil. "What are these, do you wonder?" she asked.

They reached in and took several each. The figurines were about an inch high and two inches long. They had a very rubbery, semi-squashy feel to them. Davage squeezed his about the mid section and it made a shrill noise, like a child's toy with a squeaker.

"T-K …!" it squeaked. "T-K …!"

"That's damn peculiar," he said.

Ennez went to the remaining boxes and opened them. In the other boxes were bags containing similar figurines, all depicting tiny Carahils, though they were molded in different poses, rather like collectible toys from a vending machine. They were colored: black, white and a speckled one of black, silver and white.

"Creation, he fancies himself, doesn't he?" Ki cried picking up a white one. "Hey, that's a neat one," she said commenting on a speckled one in Syg's hand.

Ennez picked up a black one. "I wonder," he said, squeezing it as Davage had done. The figurine made a wheezing "Point! Point!" sound. "These rather remind me of those odd animal trinkets used by the Fanatics of Nalls to absorb the potency of various Black Hat Gifts. Do you recall those?"

"I do," Davage said. "Very handy accessories, if I recall."

"The Sisters have managed to replicate them. I've seen them myself at Twilight 4, and they work pretty well. The Sisters are calling them 'Nall tech', after the Fanatics of Nalls. They are still in the trial and testing phase though. You know the Sisters, trying to be thorough."

Syg squeezed the speckled one she was holding. "Sten! Sten!" it squeaked.

"It could be that the Silver figurine absorbs TK, the black: the Point, and the speckleds: the Sten," Ennez said.

Ki squeezed the white one she was holding. "Shadow tech!" it squeaked.

"We aren't seriously thinking these trinkets will do something worthwhile, are we?" Syg asked.

"Can't hurt," Ennez said as he began separating the figurines into equally mixed piles.

"Obviously, Carahil expects us to run into a whole lot of Black Hats down here. Perhaps that's what he was hoping to warn us about. The Sisters have detected nothing, Ki?"

"Not a thing."

Davage lit his Sight. As usual, Syg watched him, mouth open. The room appeared normal. He adjusted, passing his Sight through various spectrums and prisms not really sure what he was looking for. He could see the energized holographic bits floating around Larsen from the holo-mon. He could even make out a mass of bits in the long-coated shape of the Missive standing next to him. He panned around, taking it all in. All appeared normal—it was just a big, pretty, abandoned room.

"Do you see anything?" Ki asked?

"No … all looks clear."

Ennez came to him and offered a small pile of variously colored Carahil figurines. Davage took them and put them into his coat pocket where they tumbled to the bottom. Ennez did the same for the others. Ki took hers and was dismayed. "Hey Syg, where am I going to put these? I don't have any pockets!"

Syg laughed as she slid hers into her shawl. "That's why I wear a shawl, for pockets."

Ki, red-faced, stuck hers into her holster.

As Davage Sighted the room, he noticed the chair Tweeter was sitting on. The shadow it cast in his light was facing the wrong direction.

"Wait," he said. "This room is a Painted illusion. A good one, too."

"Are you sure, I'm not feeling anything," Syg said.

"Positive." He strained and concentrated. A Painted illusion could be devilishly difficult to pull apart. It was like a puzzle, each piece inter-locking and attached to the next. Slowly, bit by bit, he pulled the illusion apart.

Finally, he was seeing the room as it really was. Everything was pretty much where it was in the illusion, except things were more tossed about and neglected; more weather-beaten and dusty. The elements were starting to take hold. Grit and sand coated the floor.

Davage looked at the table. "Good Creation!" he gasped.

There, sitting in the lavish chairs, was the House of Xandarr.

All of them.

They were sitting there: still, silent, propped up … dead. All of them long dead. Their grimacing withered faces were dry and peeling strips of brittle, parchment-like flesh. Many of them had been picked at by birds. Their garments of light veils were ragged and torn, faded, and, in some cases, were missing all together. Some of their corpses were quite nude. All of their faces were pained. Their tongues stuck out, as if they had been strangled. Their blue hair was straw-like and messy around their heads.

Even the stench of their decay was covered up and Painted out in illusion.

Davage was horrified. What had he spoken to not two days past? Carahil knew it. He realized they were all in deep trouble.

"Larsen," he said. "Send to the Marines, I want an immediate abort! This whole Keep … it's snared and Painted."

He began communicating to the Marines via the holo-mon.

"What? What do you see, Dav?" Syg asked.

"I see the House of Xandarr. They're all here, at the table: dead, murdered by the look of it. Been dead for a while."

Ki was jubilant. "Aha! You see, Tweeter—never wrong!"

Ennez approached the table and scanned. "I'm not getting anything."

"It's in deep Paint."

Ki inspected the apparently empty chair, feeling nothing. "Where's the King?"

"Right in that very chair—you have your fingers in his mouth."

Ki lurched back, disgusted, hands in the air. "Oh Feature!" she cried. "But you just recently spoke to King Hezru … twice, right?"

"Obviously, I was speaking to a Painted illusion or some other sort of construct. We've been lured here. Somebody's scragged this whole area, and we just walked right into it."

Davage looked at Ennez's scanner. He could see Shadow tech Traps—StT's—all over it, working their way up his arm. "Your scanner, it's snared with StT's, Ennez. Drop it!"

"Why am I not detecting it?" Syg asked.

"The Black Hats have somehow modified Shadow tech. It doesn't react like it once did. It looks different. Even the Sisters appear to not be able to detect it."

Davage looked over Larsen's holo-mon at his neck. It was covered in StT's as well.

"Lt., your holo-mon, take it off… it's crawling with Shadow tech."

Quickly he reached up and unclasped the holo-mon, allowing it to fall to the floor. He stepped away and expanded his GREAT DORE.

Ki spun around, holding her SK at the ready. "How could they have snared our equipment so fast?"

"Must have set to it the moment we landed. They wanted us in deep before tipping their hand."

Syg got next to Davage and lofted a blob of Silver tech. In a moment she had a perfect miniature replica of the *Seeker* floating about, ready for action. Her Silver tech familiar was a marvel. She could see what it saw from the heights, and it could unload a withering wall of firepower should it be needed.

"Captain, are you certain the entire House of Xandarr is here?" Larsen asked.

Davage examined the table again. "There's the king, and there's his queen, Xanthipe," he said pointing. "And then, farther down, are ten smaller bodies—their children."

"Including Princess Vroc?"

Davage pointed. "She's down there, third chair from the end."

Larsen and Ki stared at the apparently empty chairs. "Who then were we fighting on the black ship, sir?" he asked. "Who nearly killed the countess?"

"I don't know." He took a few steps further to more closely examine Vroc's tiny corpse, when he saw something. "Everybody back away from the table, now!"

They all backed away. "What do you see?" Syg asked.

"I see StT's, hundreds of them, crawling on the tabletop. Crawling on the bodies ..."

"I can handle them, Dav," Syg said. She brought her *Seeker* familiar around and lit up its tiny main sensor. It threw a powerful beam of silvery light that moved across the tabletop and chairs in a bright, roving spotlight. "I've modified my familiar to dissolve StT's—handy ability to have. Poe's not the only one who can do neat things with her familiars. Now, all I need to do is get it to expand in size so we can ride in it. Poe might have to help me with that."

Davage saw the vaguely cockroach-shaped StT's withering under Syg's silver light. "It's working, Syg. Give the table another few passes and it should be clear."

As the tiny *Seeker* moved its spotlight up and down the table, Larsen picked up his holo-mon, but it was melted. The StT had destroyed it. Syg then illuminated everybody in her familiar's spotlight one at a time to destroy any StT's that might be on their bodies.

"Syg, now send your *Seeker* over to the Marines. Let them know that we need to abort immediately. The Keep is lost in snare. Ki, reach the Sisters and give them an update as well."

Syg began moving the *Seeker* … in the wrong direction. Everything was distorted in the Paint. All of their eyes, except for Davage's, were betraying them.

"No, that's the wrong way. Let me guide you." With Davage guiding her, she sent her *Seeker* to the Marine formations down below. Ki, using telepathy, contacted the Sisters, and informed them of the situation.

13—The Shadow tech Conspiracy

<*So, what do you think, Father?*> Davage heard a voice say in his thoughts.

He turned. In his Sight, he could see Princess Vroc standing there at the far end of the room, deep in illusion and very much alive.

The chair where she had previously been sitting was now empty. She looked off-color, like an ancient photographic negative. Her left arm was wrapped, badly mangled from Syg's Silver tech blast.

"Princess, what have you done?"

The Princess walked up to the table and giggled. <*What have I done, Father? Isn't it obvious?*>

"Who are you talking to, Dav?" Syg asked whirling around.

"It's Princess Vroc—she wasn't dead!"

Her expression was exaggerated, strange, as if she wasn't all there. Her long, sleepy eyes twitched. Her sanity was questionable.

"When, Princess? When did you kill your family?"

<*Several years ago …*> Princess Vroc said. <*I fell upon them as they slept. I strangled them one after the other. I took my time too. I wanted their dying to last. They're not dead though … I still hear them talking to me … laughing at me…* >

"Why, Princess? Your family …"

Larsen and Ennez stood with their weapons at the ready. Syg held onto Dav, not liking this situation one bit. Ki stood close by, covering their rear, against enemies she could not see or hear.

She swallowed, and held her SK tight. "Tweeter," she said, "get in my holster."

Dutifully, Tweeter flew into her holster and didn't come out.

The Great Table (*Carol Phillips*)

<*My family hates me!*> Vroc said. <*They've always hated me! They hate me because I tried to kill them. You heard the illusions—they spoke truthfully. I am the eleventh daughter … the unlucky daughter. The worthless daughter!! All of Xandarr hates me.*>

She paused a moment and pawed at her head. <*You bound me into prostitution when I was a mere child, and when I failed at that, you sold my flesh to a meat market. I hung from a hook, Father, plied with drugs to keep me quiet and fresh. And I hung on that hook … waiting to be bought and eaten. That's when they came … the Black Hats. The one with eyes like a cat got me off that hook. They wanted revenge on Xandarr, for Marilith's folly … they wanted Xandarr's blood, and what better way to get than with the help of the eleventh daughter? They took me back, and made me mighty. That's when I did it. That's when I tried to kill them all!! They're hiding from me, and I miss them … I miss you too, Father.*>

"So, now what? What is next, Princess?"

<*The Black Hats … are very angry. They … hate … everybody. They are going to kill this whole planet … nothing will live, nothing will crawl. They wish to show any who have the courage to look what happens to those who cross the Black Hats. The Black Hats wanted your harlot, Father, and your sister … but they were afraid of you, afraid of your light. I was to bring you here so they could have you, trussed up and dead. It was so easy—you are so predictable. I can take you away, Father, but your harlot and your sister and your vessel are all to die here. I can protect you, Father, but the Black Hats demand their blood and I am going to give it to them. It's for the best. Don't try to stop me … you'll only make it worse.*>

She drew her BEREN, and approached Larsen with a diabolical look on her face.

"Lt., back away to your left!" Davage shouted. "Everybody get behind me!" he shouted raising his CARG to the guard position.

Larsen began moving, and, quick as lightning, Vroc sprung, bringing her BEREN around to apply a killing stroke. Davage jumped between Vroc and Larsen, his CARG blunting her attack.

"Princess, there is still time to stop this, to end this!! You needn't walk this road. Let us help you!"

<*Oh, but I must,*> the Princess said. <*Have you ever hung from a meat hook, Father? Knowing your whole life was worth nothing more than the savor of your own flesh? YOU HUNG ME ON A HOOK … WHY FATHER … WHY!!! I HATE YOU!! I FORGIVE YOU!!*>

The Princess, slavering, started moving toward Syg.

"Princess, you were treated terribly—I acknowledge that. No daughter is unlucky, no daughter is worthless. But, that does not give you lease to commit murder. Please, come with us and end this now. We will help you."

Vroc brandished her BEREN and sprung at Syg. Davage flashed his CARG and engaged Vroc, the black, negative image of her BEREN appearing clearly in his Sight. The CARG and BEREN met and held.

"Dav, what is going on?" Syg cried.

"Syg! Back away, get away!" he yelled.

Ki hammered her SK, and fired in the direction where she thought the Princess might be.

The blast sailed over her head. She giggled. <*You missed ...*>

"Dav, tell me where she is! Guide me!" she shouted. She looked to her holster. "Tweeter! Princess Vroc is here under Cloak—point her out!"

Tweeter launched out of her holster and, after a moment, was fluttering over an area right in front of Davage. Ki moved to get into a good firing position. She was going to put an end to her right here and now.

Vroc looked at the fluttering silver bird. <*There's a demon, father, I'll send it away.*> And, with two quick movements of her BEREN, she had Tweeter in three pieces, the oddly-sized chunks flapping to the floor, spinning in a death dance, where they went over the side to the courtyards below.

"TWEETER!" Ki cried in dismay. "YOU'RE GOING TO DIE, BITCH!" she slavered.

Grinning, Vroc turned her blade to Ki and sent it streaking toward her throat. Davage quickly met it.

As Davage and the Princess crossed weapons, he saw, out of the corner of his eye, a dark figure sneaking up on Lt. Larsen.

"Duck, Lt., duck!!" he cried. "Behind you!"

Larsen swung blindly with his GREAT DORE, bisecting the figure—a Black Hat. She fell.

Davage took his eye off the Princess for a moment, and she put a massive left cross into his cheek—full strength. An incredible punch from such a tiny girl. He staggered a bit, then parried the BEREN again, just in time to see another figure sneaking up on Kilos.

Black Hats were climbing up into the great hall from below.

"Ki, duck … duck!"

Kilos hit the deck and fired her SK … again in the wrong direction.

The figure rose over her and raised an ugly set of black claws into the air.

Davage tried to disengage and come to her aid, and the Princess again walloped him, sending him toppling. "Behind you!" he shouted, his mouth full of blood. "Ki!"

Larsen whirled and threw his GREAT DORE. Energized, it sailed over Ki's head, and buried itself in the Black Hat's chest, knocking her off the edge of the hall into the courtyards below.

Davage, standing, watching the skewered Black Hat go over the side, was just barely able to parry the Princess yet again … his CARG just stopping her deadly BEREN from entering his throat.

They whirled and went at it, the Princess's light, fast BEREN against his large heavy CARG. This was a situation Davage wasn't used to. He could normally move his CARG fast enough to quickly end any sword-fight he got into—but this Princess Vroc was a whole different thing. She was a master, and was devilishly fast. She was clearly the best swordsman he'd ever faced.

And she was obviously out of her mind, fighting with a lunatic's skill.

As they crossed weapons Syg and Ki fired into the air where they thought the Princess might be. "Dav! Guide me! Where is she? Where is she!" Ki shouted, her SK smoking.

Carefree, almost joyously, Vroc evaded the shots and blasts, still fully able to press Davage with her lightning fast BEREN.

Davage caught sight of a figure creeping up on Larsen again. "Larsen, duck!"

Larsen turned around and drew his MiMs. A clawed hand took his head off at a swipe. His spurting body fell headless. A Black Hat Painter. She tittered in delight, waving her Shadow tech claws.

<*You see, I've friends,*> Vroc said. <*This Keep … this whole area is crawling with Black Hats! I'm sorry, Father … your harlot and your friends have to die. Let me kill them, then your ship, and we'll be off.*>

The Black Hat began moving in Syg's direction.

Vroc's skill was incredible, the BEREN moving in a flailing cloud of speed and precision. Davage couldn't concentrate—couldn't focus. "There's a Painter, Syg! A Painter just there! Ennez, Ki, to your right!"

Syg and Ennez looked around. All they could see was Davage in a fight with nobody, and Larsen laying there dead. They were stuck in the illusion.

Davage glanced over to Ennez. The Painter was coming up on him fast, claws at the ready.

"Right in front of you, Ennez!" he shouted. Ennez rolled and moved his jet staff in a flurry.

Amazingly, the Painter deftly avoided the staff. Apparently, she wasn't wearing the Dora shoes.

Ennez opened his pouch and scattered a bunch of the Carahil figurines about on the floor. She reared back exposing a horrid clawed hand.

"Ennez, duck!" Davage said managing to parry a blow from the Princess.

Ennez ducked, and Syg sent a bolt of Silver tech whizzing just above his head, and Ki fired a burst, emptying her magazine. When Davage had a moment to look, he saw the Black Hat Painter laying there, her chest blasted open, shot in the face.

The Princess cursed and drew her Mazan, aiming it at Ki's head. Davage hit the barrel with his CARG just as she fired, chopping it in two. A partial green beam blinked out of the destroyed weapon and scorched Ki's arm. She fell backward with the force of the shot.

In his peripheral vision, he could see more Black Hats coming into the room, some from the door to the east, some climbing up from below, deep in illusion. Without the Sisters, this fight could end in no way but disaster.

"Ennez, get Ki! There are Black Hats entering the hall from the interior door!"

CLANG!

He couldn't concentrate. This Princess was too dangerous, he couldn't focus on the task at hand. She had to be removed from the picture.

He tried a dirty trick. He began to Waft, the usual wind and air forming around him. Vroc, expecting him to Waft somewhere behind her, turned in anticipation. Hardening into Full Strength, Davage stopped the Waft, and right crossed her square in the face. The force of the Full Strength blow broke her cheekbone, and knocked the light, tiny Vroc out of the hall and over the side to the courtyards below. Her BEREN clattered from her hand and spiraled down in some random direction.

Good riddance!!

"Dav, what's our situation?" Ennez said, wheeling around, seeing nothing.

"Grave," Davage said. He ran to Syg's side, and pulled her toward the edge of the hall. "How's your arm, Ki?"

"Wonderful," she said re-magging her SK.

Ennez emptied his pouch, little Carahils scattering all over the floor: some right-side up, some on their side and others resting on their front flippers doing a face plant.

"Should we bail, Dav? Should we hit the courtyards in the lower levels?"

Davage looked over the side; Hulgismen, moving with army ant precision, jostled below along with a solid carpet of crawling StT's.

"The courtyards are full of Hulgismen and Shadow tech Traps!"

At the far end of the Hall, four Black Hats danced into the room. Peeking beneath their robes, he saw they were wearing light slippers—the Dora being dispensed with. They also had little goggles on under their black masks—protection against Dav's Sight.

One Black Hat pulled up, and began Pointing at Syg. A black Carahil figurine nearby began expanding, absorbing the Point energy. Davage drew his MiMs and shot at the Black Hat, aiming for her head. The tiny bullet sparked off of her Sten field. Blast!

The Carahil figurine seemed to come to life as it absorbed the Point energy. After a few moments, it charged forward, reared back and blew a gout of bluish fire that passed through the Sten without resistance. Screaming, the Black Hat was enveloped in flames and spun to the floor. The figurine, barking and fins clapping, then vanished.

Sight—Davage saw a Black Hat sending a killing wave of Shadow tech.

"Syg, we need a shield and fast!"

Syg waved her arm and a thick wall of silver formed in front of them. Crouching behind it, a roaring storm of Shadow tech hit it and passed overhead, invisible and unheard. Several white Carahils consumed the Shadow tech blast like candy, expanded, and attacked the offending Black Hat. Instead of blowing fire, they seized her by the arms and legs and loped out of the room with her in tow.

"What is going on, Dav??" she cried.

Sight—The Sten. They were about to be Boxed-In.

"Sten, Sten!" he cried.

Several speckled Carahils came to life. As with the others, Davage saw them absorb the Sten energy, grow and attack. This time they seized the Black Hat and flew her, legs kicking, out of the room. These Carahil figurines were working wonders.

Sight—another Sten. Davage got speckled Carahils out of his pockets and threw them. The speckles again began growing. Another struggling Black Hat was bodily carried away. Her featureless mask fell away as she was carried out exposing a pretty face and long blue hair.

Sight—Davage sighed.

"Sten, Syg, Sten!!" he cried fishing for more speckled Carahils but finding none. Syg and Ki began desperately digging for figurines.

No Time! With no other option, Davage dropped his CARG, collected the three of them, and Wafted to the other side of the hall just as a large, deadly Sten box appeared where they were. Davage, his heart pounding, blacked out with the effort. The strain of Wafting Ennez, Ki and Syg was overwhelming. The last thing he saw were two standing Black Hats and several more entering the room, along with a hoard of Hulgismen and StT's.

* * * * *

"Dav!" Syg screamed as she knelt down over her fallen husband.

Ennez and Ki stood there gazing at a hall full of Black Hats and Hulgismen that appeared, to them, to be empty and quiet, the only thing giving away the Black Hat's presence: the loping pack of rapidly expanding black, silver and white Carahils on the floor: Points, TKs and Shadow Tech blasts being hurled their way Every so often, the Carahils would charge forward, blow fire or fly out of the room with something invisible held in his jaws.

Ki opened her chamber, and began blasting as Syg, in tears over Davage, put up another Silver tech wall, and struggled to keep it up against the pounding, yet unseen and unheard, Shadow tech waves coming from the other side. Ennez and Ki threw the last of their figurines. The barking noise made by the Carahils filled the hall.

14—Verlin's Hero

Lt. Verlin sat in the captain's chair on the bridge. She was just now getting used to being on the bridge alone, without Captain Davage, and, oddly enough, without Lt. Larsen. She found she liked Larsen, she liked him very much. What a fine gentleman: witty, soft spoken, good at his job, and quite handsome too. How she wished she had a moment to get to know him more personally. Captain Davage as well—he was every bit as first-rate as she had hoped: confident, personable, approachable, easy to follow, easy to love. He was why she had wanted to come to the *Seeker* in the first place, for she had long followed his exploits with interest. With Davage around, she felt empowered. She felt like she could command a whole armada.

Without him, she wasn't quite so confident.

She could certainly do without that Lt. Kilos character, her arrival spoiled everything. She didn't like her at all—didn't know what in Creation the captain saw in her: a rowdy, unruly … Brown. A "Bronzer" Major Westwind, also from Onaris, had called her—not a flattering thing to say. She had hated to make a scene in the conference room, but Kilos had thrown it down, directly challenged her, and right in front of the captain too. She had no choice but to fight her, what should the captain have thought had she not? She'd have proven that she was nothing but a timid lady of Hobby; a whole family of weak, spineless merchants.

She and Kilos will square it up later. She was eager to bounce her Hobby fists off of that Bronzer's face.

She was getting used to the bridge crew as well. She knew the helmsman's name was Saari, a lady of the House of Fallz: blue-haired, stately—of a strong Science Ministry background, yet chose to serve the Fleet. Rather like herself, Lady Saari had bucked tradition. She had strayed from her family's usual path. Saari also appeared to a person who, like her, was extremely confident when Captain Davage was around, but far less so when he was not. Saari was still fairly green, still needing a firm hand. She also knew that with the captain around, he could grab the wheel should things get too out of control—a huge safety net.

The Fore Sensor was manned by Crewman Sasai, a lady of House Cordial, again an old House of Zenon. The Com was Lt. Gervin, a gentleman of House Rickson. The Missive was a stately, if stuffy, man with iron gray hair who spoke often of his pending promotion to Fleet Command: a Lt. Derlith of the House of Cone, a Remnath House and a distant relative of hers. Captain Davage certainly had a commendable crew, a fine crew indeed.

* * * * *

The first time she'd ever seen Davage, Lord of Blanchefort, was eighty years prior, at his wedding.

The failed wedding. The wedding that never happened.

She was just a girl at the time. Her father, Lord Merivel of Hobby, a prosperous and well-regarded merchant of Howell, held the tiny Verlin in his arms; she wearing a child's pink gown in the Hobby fashion. She had a dim memory of seeing the wedding baton passing from her right to left as it made its way to the front of the procession. She remembered all of the hands reaching out to touch it, to send it on its way. She recalled thinking the baton, bronze by tradition, all decorated and gilded in jewels, was pretty. She recalled wanting to play with it.

She remembered the sound of the baton hitting the floor—it was a pleasing, metallic sound, like a struck tuning fork.

And, most vivid of all, she recalled Davage, Lord of Blanchefort, go running past from left to right in his fine wedding attire, weapon at his side, chased closely by a woman in a blue gown.

She remembered his face ... the anguish. His eyes, she clearly remembered his eyes as he passed by. That was the first time she'd ever seen sorrow.

In later years she never forgot those eyes. One lazy afternoon, she asked her mother about that man, that sad lord she remembered seeing as a girl. Her mother, Lady Jana, said he was Davage, Lord of Blanchefort, and that was the famous Wedding that Never Was.

Verlin didn't know where Blanchefort was. Way to the north, her mother commented, where it's cold all the time. Verlin, always having an interest and a good head for geography, went to the library and got out a huge atlas. Wrestling with the book and tracing with her long fingers, she found Blanchefort. There it was, way far to the northwest of Howell where she was, in the northern continent of Vithland. A sea, an angry mountain range and several thousand miles stood between Howell and Blanchefort.

She made a mental note and added Blanchefort to the long list of places she wanted to visit when she was older and able to travel on her own.

That might have been the end of her attention, had, that very afternoon, she spied something in her day's reading that caught her interest.

Unlike her nine sisters, and her many friends, Verlin loved to sit in her father's huge library and read. She read of the Epochs of Time, of fabled places like Emmira, Cammara and Eng. She read of the seven tribes of man. She read stories of the Giants that once roamed Kana and of the Vith heroes who fought them. She read the sad story of the House of Bodice from Hala, a House of farmers who were driven mad by a demon in the shape of an elephant and fled to the Xaphans for relief. The Bodice found no solace with the Xaphans, and were preyed upon by them and made extinct. That was a sad book—one that she didn't want to read again.

Howell having such mild weather, most members of House Hobby spent a great deal of their time outdoors, enjoying the temperate sun. Verlin, however, liked to stay indoors. In the cool, vaulted splendor of the Hobby library, lights dim, the smell of old books, furniture and fabrics thick in the air, she sat for hours and read the daily posts from her favorite terminal. She read by-lines and editorials. She loved staying current on League happenings, but, she generally avoided the lurid headlines and acerbic catty articles dotting the front of the post—one couldn't learn much from those. Rather she liked reading the little items at the end of the posting—those were jewels of information. That's where you kept on top of things. Crisp stories told neatly and succinctly without gloss or social commentary.

That day she found, at the very end of the post, a small notice entitled:

"RENOWNED FLEET HELMSMAN PROMOTED TO LT."

--PROVST (Synthnet): In a movement considered long overdue by the 10th Admiralty, the Stellar Fleet has promoted Master Helmsman Davage, Lord of Blanchefort, to the ranking of Full Lieutenant. Lord Blanchefort, a Helmsman of wide regard, has piloted the Fleet Vessel *Faith* in over forty engagements against the Xaphan Armada, most notably at the Battle of Two-Pitch Nebula, where the *Faith* survived unscathed against a force of ambushing Xaphan *Merci* ships.

As Verlin greedily read the small, non-descript notice, she found herself becoming fascinated by the Lord of Blanchefort … the man with the sad eyes. She began making it a point to look for notices regarding him and collecting them. It was difficult going, sometimes news was scarce, but, every so often, her efforts were rewarded.

"FLEET VESSEL *FAITH* FOILS XAPHAN ATTACK"

--Brindicea, HOBAN (Hoban Royal News Wire): In a daring action over Hoban, a four ship combat formation led by the Main Fleet Vessel Prince Elmo discovered, met, and turned back a Xaphan attempt to abduct the Governor of Brindicea. The surprise ship of note in the day's action was the Faith, a venerable Webber-Class vessel chaired by the retiring Captain Garzamel, Lord of Champion. The Faith, helmed by the well-regarded Lt. Davage, Lord of Blanchefort, blunted the Xaphan attack and turned it back, sinking their flagship Bloodsimple with many prisoners taken. The Governor, Lord Basil of Croatoa, was not harmed in the assault. The Xaphan forces were, according to sources, under the command of Princess Marilith of Xandarr, who was once engaged to Lord Blanchefort.

And so on. She eventually had a whole vid scrapbook detailing Lt. Davage's exploits and career in minute.

Verlin became a real fan of Lt. Davage, following his activities as best she could. Borrowing her brother's telescope, she became familiar with the comings and goings of the Fleet; it was easy to learn those things if one really wanted to, and trained the telescope up to the Fleet docks high overhead. She nearly had a heart attack when, gliding into her viewfinder for the first time one evening, was the *Faith.* She was excited. She felt like a bird watcher who had finally spied that rare, elusive specimen after much searching and dedication. It was an old ship, the *Faith*—the *Webber*-Class being a gangly, ugly design when compared to the brand new, swan-like *Straylights* just coming off of the blocks. But, to Verlin, the *Faith* was beautiful and proud, flowing through space with a grand, graceful movement. She imagined Lt. Davage standing there, the helm wheel firm in his grasp. She wondered if his eyes were still sad.

When her sisters and her friends began concerning themselves with parties, gossip and gentlemen, Verlin, though vaguely interested in gossip, was still mostly interested in the posts, in word of the Lord of Blanchefort. He was like a famous sportsman to her. From Lt. to Commander, to Captain, to Captain of the Main Fleet Vessel *Seeker,* she watched it all through the posts, and through the telescope, for she had seen the beautiful *Seeker* too, soaring up there like a great, white bird.

As Captain Davage's dealings with Princess Marilith of Xandarr became more and more frequent, and more and more spectacular, his notices began a swift migration from the back of the posts to the front, blasted out in huge headlines. She couldn't help but feel somewhat saddened that her intimate, personal relationship with Captain Davage was now the talk of the League and subject of A-List gossip. It didn't seem as pure.

Her family was invited to a grand party in Blanchefort one year and, for a change, Verlin happily agreed to attend with her brothers and sisters. House Hobby had just completed a large business transaction with the House of Blanchefort and, as a courtesy, they were invited to a ball at Castle Blanchefort. Being so far away from Howell, and they being Vith and the Hobbies being of Remnath stock, the two Houses usually didn't interact socially. But, it was a lovely trip, Verlin and her brothers and sisters, all bundled up in their fur-lined cloaks and mufflers, piled into the House transport ship and headed north. Howell being a very temperate place, Blanchefort was brutally cold for them.

What a wonderful place, Blanchefort, tucked up in the breath-taking northern mountains, cold certainly, but pretty with a quaint village by the sea. Their HUGE Vith castle was one of the finest she'd ever been in.

The ball was lavish and full of all that old Vith circumstance expected from a north League Great House, but, as she scanned the endlessly long dinner table and ball room floor, she was terribly disappointed to learn the captain wasn't in attendance, only his father and sister being there. Crestfallen, she sulked the rest of the evening away. The following day, she and her brothers and sisters again bundled up against the cold in their mufflers and cloaks, and made their way through the village to the dock to return home to Howell.

Verlin was sullen and unsocial as she walked, determined to be a mad stick-in-the-mud.

She stopped dead in her tracks.

There, parked in the bay, was the *Seeker*, the captain's ship, and she was certain it hadn't been there yesterday; how could she have missed such a thing? She broke away from her group and went to the dock, pushing through the vendors and passersby, staring at it in wonder. It was so big, so powerful-looking, so … real sitting there in the bay, much different than the flat image she'd seen of it in her telescope viewfinder. As she stumbled, open mouthed with her breath coming out in clouds, she saw, out of the corner of her eye, two Fleet officers sitting at a bench enjoying a modest boxed lunch. One of the officers was an elegant red-headed woman, the other was a tall, regal, blue-haired man: Captain Davage himself!

There he was—her hero.

Star-struck, entombed in her furry cloak and muffler, Verlin made her way to them, giggling, not quite sure what to say.

The captain noticed her, wiped his lips and smiled. "Afternoon, ma'am," he said brightly. He looked her over and laughed. "I mean no disrespect, my lady, but you, standing there all bundled up, rather look like a polar bear."

Verlin just stood there. She noted his eyes, remembering them from when she was young. There they were—they same eyes, only the sadness was gone.

"Certainly you were here for my father's ball yesterday. I hope you enjoyed yourself, and I'm sorry for the cold. One does get used to it after a time."

Again, Verlin just stood there, lost in the moment. The red-head sitting next to him rolled her eyes and looked impatient.

Davage put down his sandwich. "Well, 'Little Bear', is there anything I might assist you with? Are you lost?"

Captain Davage had an easy manner to him, belying his stature, and his fame. He genuinely seemed a decent man. Verlin felt her initial bashfulness fade. She opened her mouth to speak.

The red-headed woman cut her off. "My lady, if you will. The captain is at his lunch, and shan't be disturbed. You'll most likely find your ship in that direction." She pointed to the far end of the dock where a group of House transports awaited.

Stung a bit, feeling she'd terribly shamed herself, she turned and walked away, wishing the ground to swallow her whole.

She heard the captain reproach the woman. "That was very rude, Hath. Ma'am, Ma'am?" he called out, but Verlin just kept walking. She had never felt so humbled.

* * * * *

Verlin was one of the few civilians who knew of the two battles of Mirendra 3 as they happened. Of course in the following days and weeks the Fleet was hailed as conquering heroes; songs were sung, stories told, all glamorous and romanticized. She was one of the few who appreciated how close the League came to falling. She was one of the few who understood the cost. She remembered her heartbreak as she watched the Fleet vessels limp back to dock, some badly battered, others in full tow, others still so badly damaged they were scuttled right there and then. And there were the ships that never came back at all, and there were many of those.

The empty berths, the loss of life. Old friends gone and turned to dust.

The *Seeker?* Where was the *Seeker?*

She scanned around, desperate, where was it … where? Ship after ship in various stages of distress, and no *Seeker.*

Then, after hours of searching, there it was, Captain Davage's ship, blackened, pocked with battle damage but undefeated, unbowed. It flew amid the sad carnage with unmatched grace and beauty.

Verlin had seen enough, she was going to join the Fleet. She wanted to get up there and do her part.

* * * * *

"You want to do what?" Lord Merivel of Hobby asked, incredulous.

Verlin, in her teal Hobby gown sat at the grand table. Hopkirk, her footman stood behind her. "I want to join the Fleet."

Merivel gawked at her. "You must be not feeling well. Hopkirk, check her temperature will you please—perhaps she is addled with some airborne fungal malady. I read, in a fascinating Hospitaler gazette, that the temperature of one's forehead is often telling when determining the presence of infection," he said proudly.

Hopkirk put his hand on her forehead. "Her forehead feels normal to me, my Lord."

Annoyed, Verlin moved his hand aside. "Father, I am fine. I wish to join the Fleet, I wish to make a contribution of some sort. I wish to see the stars."

Merivel put his hand to his chin and thought a moment. "I know," he exclaimed, "what you need is a good husband—someone to help you forget all those lurid posts you love to read. How you sleep sometimes, I'll never know. We'll have a grand ball with you as the Lady of Honor. Gentlemen from all around the League will be at your leave."

"I shall be glad to fall in love and be married some day, father, but first I wish to serve. I wish to join the Fleet."

Lord Merivel glared at her as his plate was filled with a whole steaming roast duck by his footman. "You will not be joining the Fleet. You will be engaged in simple frivolity, you will begin a tapestry, you will fit for more gowns, you will laugh and gossip with your sisters and your friends, you will go to town and spend a vast quantity of my money—you will do things expected of a lady … you will not, however, join the Fleet."

A roast duck flopped down onto her plate with a splat. "We shall see, father, we shall see."

The next day, Verlin made her way to Howell, to the quaint Fleet office there in the town square. It was a lovely day, the birds, the sun, the fountain gurgling happily. Determined, she marched to the steps to the Fleet office ... only to be intercepted by Hopkirk, the Footman, who, forcibly, dragged her home.

She tried again the next day and the next—always Hopkirk popping up from nowhere, always the embarrassing trip home.

Determined, she tried a dirty trick. Knowing that Hopkirk will be compelled to drink her tea or beverage should she breach any of House Hobby's loose dining protocols, Verlin kept violating the house rules. With a sigh, Hopkirk then took her full goblet and drank the contents down. She did it four times at breakfast, then another six times at lunch.

She then went into Howell.

Watching from a bench at a distance, she scanned the area and waited.

Hopkirk emerged from the bushes in front of the Fleet office, in a state of obvious distress. She watched as he could no longer stand it, and trotted off to find a bathroom.

Verlin ran into the office. With a smile, the Lords in the Fleet office listened as Verlin made her pitch to join. The Lords explained that she may certainly join the Fleet, however, she needed to have a signed Letter of Recommendation from the local Lord, or she couldn't join.

No exceptions. Her father was the Local Lord, and there was no possibility of getting him to sign one for her.

Defeated, heartbroken she left the office and allowed the surprised, yet relieved, Hopkirk to take her home.

She tried to forget the Fleet over the next few weeks. She stopped reading the posts, she even stopped looking skyward with her telescope. She started a tapestry, she started following her sisters, and she spent a massive amount of her father's money. They went into Howell one morning to gather gossip, and she followed.

Again the lovely town square, the birds, the fountain, and the now reviled Fleet Office.

But, something was different that day. A colorful red and black ship had set down in an empty lot just off the square.

It was a Marine cutter ship.

They came regularly, about once every few months, trying to interest recruits. Howell, being a stately and land-locked town, usually wasn't very fertile ground for them, but they made regular appearances anyway. Verlin could see the Marines, regal in their handsome red uniforms, setting up their table in the afternoon sun.

Verlin had a thought and, without allowing herself time to fully mull it over in her head, broke away from her sisters and made a direct path to the Marines.

The Marines were clearly astounded when Verlin approached them. They sat there behind their table as their glasses of iced tea sweated in the sun, and stared at her. A tall, young lady of Hobby wanted to join the Marines? They thanked her and tried to send her on her way—her novel prank not really appreciated.

Verlin was steadfast. This was no joke. She wanted to join. If the Fleet was not available to her, then she'd join the Marines. After a bit more talking, one of the Marines went into the ship and emerged a few minutes later with their commander. Smiling, he invited her into the ship, and gave her a brief but lavish tour. He spoke of the Marines mission: to defend the Sisterhood, to serve them and to serve the Fleet. To do the things that needed doing. To serve the League. He thanked her for her interest and showed her out of the ship.

She still wanted to join. She still wanted to be a Marine.

He looked her over: tall, fit, and a Lady of Standing. Hmmm … He bade her take some time and fully think the matter over. He gave her an armful of holo-literature. He said they will return on the morrow, and if she still wished to join, then they will gladly have her.

The next day, as promised, the cutter ship returned. And, as promised Verlin wearing a canary Hobby gown, joined the Stellar Marines.

Her experience was not typical. She was treated like royalty. She was trained at an exclusive camp on Bazz where only the richest, and most favored of recruits went: the sons and daughters of Great Houses. It was a small class—not many lords and ladies joined the Marines. There, she was taught to speak with the Sisters. It was wondrous. She was then, immediately upon her graduation, sent to school at a science facility at Bonham; again the best the Marines had to offer. Though the

Marines had been a second thought, an afterthought, she grew to love the service for all they had given her.

She graduated first in her class and was immediately promoted to P-Lieutenant, or Lieutenant Practical, and assigned to the 53rd Marines, a science and weather forecasting outfit located on the Milford-Paulson shores of Bazz. Her father, at first enraged that she had joined the Marines, sent word at last that he was proud of her, and couldn't wait to see her in person in her uniform. When she got some time off for Nether Day, she went home and her father threw a grand party for her, a lady of Hobby … a celebrated Marine Lt.

* * * * *

Her commander, Major Westwind, a commoner from Fig on Onaris (but a man whom Verlin greatly respected) had called her into his office.

He sat behind his desk and shook his head. "She was a disgrace for Creation's sake, V—a rotten, hot-headed, unknowable bore, who was in jail more often than she was out of it. Then, somehow, this Kilos of Tusck character ends up the first officer aboard the *Seeker*, of all ships. Of course, we all simply suspected that she was … satisfying … the captain. I mean she had no skills to speak of, other than she was a Bronzer from Tusck with a pretty face."

Verlin couldn't believe it. Not Captain Davage. He would do no such thing. "You mean they were having an affair?" she asked.

"That's what we at first thought, but it doesn't appear to be the case in hindsight. I've never been one to particularly dote on the Fleet, but apparently, Captain Davage can make a soldier out of anybody. Lt. Kilos lucked into a very prosperous situation and she made the most of it. Which is why I have asked you here, Lt."

"Sir?"

"Lt. Kilos has quit her post and resigned her commission."

"Why?"

"Unknown. Some of the bigs over at 0-Foxtrot wanted to throw her in prison, but I suppose cooler heads prevailed. She's already out of the Marines, and on her way back to Tusck."

Westwind looked at his hands. "Her stature as first officer on a Main Fleet Vessel was very much liked by Marine Command: it helped recruiting, it helped the Marines in procuring needed supplies from the Fleet. It enhanced our general prestige. And, now that the Bronzer is gone, Command is scrambling, they want her replacement to be a Marine aboard the *Seeker*."

He took a deep breath. "V, I am loath to ask you this, because I do not wish to lose you, but … I want to know if you are up to replacing Lt. Kilos aboard the *Seeker*. We think that you are an ideal candidate. Command is trying to get us an immediate audience with the captain." He paused. "And I know you shall make us proud."

Verlin stood up and went to the window. Outside, was a bright, sunny day, one just like home. A gardener trimmed the grounds. Officers strolled about. She smiled and put her hands on her chest.

"Me … Captain Davage's first officer?"

"I know you've been a fan of his for some time."

"When do we leave?"

Westwind sighed and stood up. "Immediately, if we're to intercept the *Seeker* on her current course."

Verlin took a deep breath, couldn't believe what she was hearing. "I can't wait to meet him at length, to sit in his presence."

Westwind grabbed his Marine cap. "Then I suppose we'll be taking a cutter ship to Heron within the hour. Make haste, go pack your things."

Verlin snapped out of her reverie. "Yes, sir," she said heading to the door.

"And V—I want you to be careful, yes?"

"I'll be sure to present myself in the proper …"

"That's not what I meant. I don't want you to be too disappointed if Captain Davage isn't what you hope he is. Our heroes, V, many times are unable to meet up to the standards that we have set for them. Our heroes often let us down. I just don't want you to be too disappointed if that's the case."

Verlin smiled. "I expect him to be brave and courageous … obviously he is those things and more. I expect him to be a fine captain, apparently he is that—he got the best out of that paid slug Lt. Kilos, didn't he? If he is a kind man, if he is inspirational and true, then that will be a bonus."

* * * * *

The Com began lighting up.

"Lt.," the Com said. "We are getting an immediate evac order from the planet surface."

"Who is sending the order?"

"Captain Davage."

"Very well, Beat to Quarters. Recall the Sisters and Marines, prepare to receive, and set to station. Once we are fully complimented, begin a forced withdrawal to League space."

"Aye, ma'am."

The Missive, Lt. Derlith, turned from his console and spoke. "I must disagree with this evacuation order. I am in contact with Lt. Larsen via ship's holographic-monitor. He is at the captain's side, even now. Clearly there is malfeasance afoot."

"Can you put him on the cone so that I may speak to him?"

"Of course." The Missive pressed a few buttons and Lt. Larsen appeared on the cone.

Verlin smiled. "Lt., is everything all right down there?"

He replied. "It is. The place seems rather quiet."

"I'm so glad to hear that. We've received an evacuation order from Captain Davage. I was about to recall the Marines and Sisters with all speed."

Larsen shrugged. "The captain is right here, would you like to speak to him?"

"I would, thank you."

He leaned over and reached for something. He pulled back Captain Davage's severed head, dangling from his fist by his hair. Larsen's voice became a growl. "You wanted to talk to him, so talk! Here he is—say something! HAHAHAHAHA!!"

Crewman Sasai screamed.

"You're going to be joining him before long, Lt.! You're all going to die here! You're—"

Verlin put her hand to her mouth. "Missive, cut the link! Cut it!"

The Missive cut the connection and the cone went blank. "By Creation! What did we just see?"

"That was a Shadow tech manifestation. I've seen it in the Marines," Verlin said. "StT's can inhabit technological devices, such as a holo-mon, and bend them however they may please. That was an illusion we just saw. Therefore, speed the recall process! We must recover our people as quickly as possible and begin our retreat! We must also reconnect with the captain and his party immediately!"

Sasai leaned over her sensor, puzzled. "Ma'am ..." she said.

"What is it?"

"Ma'am, I am reading a large ring around the planet's equator."

"Xandarr doesn't have a ring," Verlin said.

"I know ... yet, there it is ... it just appeared on my screen moments ago."

Verlin rubbed her chin. "Let's see it."

The holo-cone flipped and, sure enough, a strange black ring encircled the planet. Verlin stared hard at it. It was composed of dark black material, and was sinister to look at. Even at a distance, it appeared to move and throb with purpose and intelligence.

"I don't believe it. This must be another illusion." She marched into the captain's office and looked out the windows. Sure enough there was a huge, ugly ring around Xandarr where one shouldn't be. She rubbed her eyes. Was this an illusion too?

She came back out to the bridge. "What is the composition of this ring?"

Sasai stared into her sensor. "Ma'am," she said, "it's Shadow tech. It's reading the same as that creature in the image of the Countess we fought earlier. I captured the readings."

Verlin had had enough. "This whole planet's a death trap. What is the status of the returning Marines?"

"Five minutes until recovery! Arrow shot on high!" the Ops said.

"And the captain and his party?"

"No response since his evac order."

"Keep trying to raise him. Com, have you been taught the base litanies against Shadow tech illusions?"

"I have," he said.

"Then use them. If you reach the captain it's possible you could be speaking to another Shadow tech illusion. In any case, if, after five minutes, we've not heard anything, we're securing the Marines and Sisters, and going down after him!"

Helmsman Saari spoke up. "Ma'am, at our current course, we will pass through the planetary ring in three minutes. I highly advise steering clear of it."

"Maneuver away from the ring, Helm," she said. "Keep it a wide berth."

Saari moved the wheel … and nothing happened.

"Ma'am!" she cried, in near panic. "The Helm wheel is unresponsive."

Verlin ran to the Helm and moved it. It turned freely, no pressure or resistance.

"What's happened?" Verlin shrieked.

Saari stared wide-eyed at the now useless helm wheel. "I—I don't know, ma'am. It was working fine a few minutes ago."

"Com, send to Commander Mapes. He's to the bridge immediately … priority 1!" Verlin cried.

Ahead, the black ring loomed ever closer, filling the cone with black, waiting to swallow them.

They heard evil singing just then, penetrating the walls of the ship from outside—coming from the ring. The singing leeched into their brains and plucked telepathic notes on their souls.

They heard:

"Witness you the planet Xandarr
*Planet of Sorrow, planet of Sha***M***e.*
*Condemned to de***A***th, despised in name.*
Witness you the **B***lack Hat's wraith and the Black Hat's bane,*
*Flee, curiou***S** *traveler, lest death take you just the same."*

15—The Invisible Enemy

Syg lifted a Silver tech wall. Instantly, it dented and warped with Shadow tech blows on the other side.

Syg closed her fists, reared up over the wall and loosed a Silver tech blast, having no idea what if any damage she had just done. She swept this way and that.

She noticed several of the Carahil figurines continuing to expand—Points, Stens and TKs were being sent their way and they only had seconds. She fished around in her shawl and threw her Carahil figurines. They instantly began growing and coming to life.

TACK, TACK, TACK—CLACK!! Ki's SK emptied.

"Get Dav out of here!" Ennez shouted and, spinning his jet staff, leapt over the Silver tech wall.

"Ennez, get back here!" Ki cried, re-magging her SK.

Syg shook Dav, trying to rouse him. Something clattered into the other side of the wall roughly. Ki crouched down, having no idea what was coming. Holding Dav about the neck, Syg prepared to make her last stand.

A company of Marines in ground transports entered the far end of the hall with all their usual aplomb. They quickly exited their transport and established a defensive formation. With them was a lone Sister, and, with a wave of her hand, the Black Hat's illusion came down in all its various layers. The power of even a single Sister was awesome to behold.

Syg looked around, finally able to see. The hall was a neglected, dusty mess. There was a din of shouting and clanging. The Marines were heavily engaged with the Hulgismen, who were struggling to get to the newly arrived Sister—the "TACK!!, TACK!!" of their SK's filling the hall in a tap dance of death and smoke.

A surge of StT's came at them—the Sister swept them aside, temporarily clearing the hall.

"Captain Davage … fall back!!" the Marines shouted.

She watched a white Carahil figurine grab a Black Hat by the neck and fly her struggling body out of the hall, with several more following.

She saw the table, and the dead bodies Dav had been talking about. "Be safe, love," Syg said kissing him as she cocooned him in Silver tech. She then stood against her wall and prepared to fight.

* * * * *

Ki cocked her SK, then stood up with Syg, blasting the weapon. Of all things, her thoughts were on Tweeter, her little bird now dead. She knew if she got out of this alive, in her first quiet moment, she would grieve for him as if he were a family member or close friend.

* * * * *

Beyond a gaggle of Hulgismen moved about in a chaotic fashion. Gouts of Shadow tech emerged from the back of the hall, only to be displaced by the lone Sister. A Black Hat was TK'ed into the air, squeezed, crushed to death and cast aside. And then another. And another.

The Point: several Marines exploded in a spray.

Another Point; this one got absorbed by a black Carahil figurine. She watched him blow blue flames over the attacking Black Hat and disappear.

Syg squeezed her fists, built up a charge and, with a wave of her arm, blasted aside a mass of Hulgismen. They toppled over gutted in a steaming pile like dead mackerel. She swept the other way, and more Hulgismen fell.

Ki hammered her shots into the mass. She noticed Hulgismen were clambering up over the side from below, trying to get behind them. She turned and gunned them down, sending them falling into the masses below.

Syg expected the Black Hats to disengage at some point; that's how they normally fought. They engaged, did some damage, and withdrew.

This fight was different. The Black Hats seemed crazed, insane. They seemed determined to fight it out to the bitter end.

Syg sent out another *Seeker* familiar. It floated and began firing, blasting holes in the Hulgismen's lines and melting hordes of StT's in its light, but was quickly blown to shreds with multiple Shadow tech blasts. She crashed it into the Black Hats where it exploded, killing at least two of them and probably fifty Hulgismen. More charged in from the interior. These Black Hats were fighting for keeps.

The number of Carahil figurines was rapidly dwindling.

Now that she could see her enemies, she could counter them. A Black Hat tried to send a Sten onto their position. Syg met it with one of her own and held it. "Second from the left, Ki!" she said, and Ki took aim and blasted her head off—the Black Hat wide open. An aimed shot from Ki was as good as dead.

A few more fell that way until the Black Hats stopped trying to Sten and kept them sucked in, saving themselves from Ki's murderous SK.

A wave of StT's came in. Syg met them with a blast of Silver tech, blowing them apart.

More Shadow tech, more Hulgismen. Syg swept them aside—bodies flying, bodies chewed up, silver rending limb from limb. The Hulgismen, single-minded as ever, wanted the Sister, and they charged regardless of the danger. The Marines, their ranks thinned by the endless attack, could no longer stop them, the Hulgismen breached their lines and fell on the Sister and, screaming, she died in a tangle. They held her severed head aloft and fought over it.

The Black Hats then turned their full attention to Syg and Ki. Stuck to the western side of the hall in the center section of the room, they were surrounded. She threw up a large Sten and killed more Hulgismen than she could count in an instant.

One of the Black Hats countered it in a huge clashing spark. Syg dropped it, panting—she was running out of endurance. Even at full strength and health, this fight would have been exhausting, and, weak as she was, Syg knew she was just about done … finished.

Syg couldn't see Ennez in the mass of people—he must be dead, had to be dead. She threw up another Silver tech wall and began tossing small silver tech balls—balls that exploded in a hail of sharp fragments. The balls exploded, Hulgismen went down. A Black Hat, clutching her throat, also went down. Blasts crashed into her wall, she strained to keep it up.

Ki targeted a newly arriving Black Hat and got her right through the eye. She targeted another, but she was Stenned.

"Syg!" she cried. "We can't stay here!"

"Ki, get next to Dav ..." she said weakly.

Ki went to full Auto and emptied another magazine. She then crouched down and got next to Dav.

"Where's Ennez!" Syg screamed.

"Dead!"

Syg lay down, put her arms around the cocooned Davage, and built a Silver tech bubble around the three of them. She waited for the inevitable thud of a Shadow tech blast, which came seconds after she created it. The Silver ball blasted out of the hall and went down several levels into a courtyard below, Hulgismen clamored around it, beating on the warm silver sphere with their filthy hands. StT's crawled over it.

* * * * *

Commander Mapes, accompanied by two of his technicians, charged onto the bridge. They quickly made their way to the helm, the technicians moving in and examining it.

"Sir," one of them shouted, "the Helm appears to be floating!"

"How can that be!" Mapes said.

They opened the back panel, exposing a complex array of connectors and linkages—the Helm wheel being connected to literally thousands of thrusters, levelers and flood ports. It was by far the most delicate piece of equipment on the bridge.

"Sir," the tech said, "the Helm has been completely disconnected!"

The black ring loomed large in the cone. "Commander, we need helm control immediately!" Verlin shouted.

"It'll take hours to reattach everything, and then we'll need days to properly calibrate it!" Mapes replied.

Verlin looked at the cone full of black. "Commander, we have about three minutes!"

16—Under Xandarr Keep

The silver ball came to rest in a courtyard fairly far from the raging hall above. The courtyard was literally crawling with Hulgismen and StT's. They surrounded the sphere, stabbed at it with their Nyked knives, and pounded it with their dirty fists.

The sphere exploded outward in a blast of silver energy, killing many Hulgismen instantly, dismembering and badly wounding a great number more. The rest were thrown high into the air, many out beyond the edge of the courtyard.

Kilos rolled out and took a defensive stance: they were right in the middle of the courtyard. Head on a swivel she looked around. There were a couple of wounded stragglers to the west and she gunned them down. Several bodies that had been thrown into the air landed with a life-ending crash. Everybody else was gone or dead for the moment, but she could hear a great mass of angry shouting coming from nearby.

Syg … in near total exhaustion, wept and shook Davage.

"Dav! Dav! Wake up!" Davage, however, wasn't moving.

Ki grabbed the captain and pulled him up. "Syg, we've got to get to a better position! Help me with him!"

Ki, dragging Davage, started moving him toward the far wall. Syg tried to help her, but, barely able to stand, she was more hindrance than help. Ki, picked the tiny Syg up with one arm and continued with the both of them.

"Ki, I can barely keep my eyes open, I'm going to pass out …" Syg said. "Don't worry about me … get Dav to safety. Drop me, Ki!"

"Shut up!" Ki yelled.

Ki got to the wall, and, arms aching, dropped them. She remagged her SK. "This is it, Syg, my last mag … I've got 25 shots and I'm done."

Syg collapsed to the ground, exhausted.

Lt. Kilos in Xandarr Keep (*Carol Phillips*)

Ki quickly looked around again: dead bodies, sundered limbs everywhere, roaring and shouts coming from all around. Soon, this courtyard will be overrun again. She checked her holster for more Carahil figurines, but they were used up. Heck of a gift they were, she had to admit. Those silly-looking little things held the line until they were able to see what they were fighting. If she survived she'd have to thank him for them later.

She wondered about the StT's—there were thousands upon thousands of them crawling around like cockroaches in the halls above, and each one of them had the ability to either kill, give away their position, poison or tag them. So far, this courtyard seemed strangely devoid of them. Of all the horrors of fighting Shadow tech, StTs were probably the worst, the sneakiest and hardest to spot. She'd probably rather fight a Shadow tech beast or a Hulgismen straight up than wonder if an StT was lurking about. Besides that, they reminded her of bugs, and she didn't like bugs.

No time to wonder over her good fortune. Where could they go? What could they do?

The sky turned black, must be a storm coming in. She glanced up. The sky was full of roiling clouds of Shadow tech, layer after layer rising up to towering heights. Occasional patches of purple shown through along with traveling rays of sunlight. And what was that thing to the south rising up through the breaks in the clouds? Was that a ring, a black ring? Xandarr didn't have a ring. Creation—this place is Scragged Max—no kidding around. The Black Hats had dropped their own Painted illusion and tipped their hand. No more hiding, here they were.

As Ki gazed at the dance of black clogging the sky, a Hulgismen, crawling with StT's, dropped down from above, surprising her. Falling together to the dusty ground, he put his filthy hands on her throat, the StT's running down his arms to get at her.

Feeling the life being squeezed out of her, Ki, lifted her SK and pressed the STUN button; SK standing for STUN/KILL, though Ki rarely ever used the STUN portion. In this instance she had to conserve shots, even in this life-or-death situation.

A fierce blast of air hit the Hulgismen in the neck and he doubled over holding his throat. StT's were all over her. She whirled around, batting them off, hitting the Stun trigger again and again, careful not to get herself with the blasts.

The Hulgismen made a gargling sort of noise. Ki reared up and clubbed him hard over the head with her pistol butt, over and over again until he dropped. The SK had a very hard, knobby butt for just that very purpose. More StT's streamed away from his dead body.

Panting, Ki turned—just in time to get walloped in the face by another Hulgismen. She fell and dropped her gun. The Hulgismen flopped on top of her, reared back and smashed her in the jaw.

Everything began to spin.

He reared back again to finish her off.

Something chirped and light blossomed around the Hulgismen's head.

Tweeter!

He was back in one piece, and was greatly annoying the Hulgismen who pawed at him with his filthy arms, StT's falling away.

Recovering, Ki reached, got her gun, and blew his head off in a spray of gun smoke and ruined flesh.

Ki threw the body aside and Tweeter settled into her hands.

She was overjoyed. "I thought you were a goner, Tweets!" she said, half laughing, half crying. She looked him over—he seemed fine, his Silver tech body completely reformed like nothing had ever happened to it. "I should have known you'd be ok."

She looked around, ready to fight the swarms of StT's that had been crawling over their bodies. They were on the sandy floor of the courtyard, flipped upside down, legs waving feebly. She watched as they slowly dissolved into pockets of ash.

"That's weird," she said casually, fascinated by what she was seeing.

She heard noise—shouting, roaring. Hulgismen, lots of them, on the move. She looked to Tweeter. "We're in sorry shape here, Tweets, can you get us to safety? Someplace safe? Can you do that?"

Tweeter chirped, and flew to the south, settling on a post far off in the distance. He waited for her as usual. Dragging both Dav and Syg, Ki began following him, her faith in the little silver bird now unshakable.

Seeing him reinvigorated her, leant her strength.

As she approached Tweeter's position, she heard an angry mob moving about somewhere in a nearby courtyard behind her. Tweeter took flight and flew through a doorway, turning to the east, Ki following as best she could, her heart pounding from the strain of carrying the dead weight of Dav and Syg.

Tweeter flew into another open courtyard, the dome of the Keep rising high above in the afternoon haze flecked with Shadow tech, looking like a huge, mottled turnip. He settled on a large pot near a far wall about a hundred yards away.

She stopped for a moment to take a breath, when someone touched her from behind. She whirled around, dropping Dav and Syg, and pulling her SK.

"It's me, Ki … it's me!" a torn, bleeding Ennez said, his bloody and dented helmet sitting askew and backwards on his head.

Ki gasped with relief, and threw her arms around him—a rare display of emotion from the normally subdued Kilos. "Ennez, good Creation! What happened to you? We thought you were surely dead!"

"I managed to get through the lines of Hulgismen, and get one of the Black Hats in the head—might have killed her too, I think. A Black Hat was about to Point me, when a white Carahil grabbed her and carried her off. Heck of a thing to see. Then I got locked up with a bunch of Hulgismen, when there was this loud rushing sound and a burst of light—must have been a sweep of Silver tech from Syg—which isn't a fun thing to experience let me tell you. In any event, I got knocked off the side of the courtyard. How's Dav and Syg?"

"Bad. Dav's out cold from that Waft still, and Syg is so exhausted, she can barely stand."

Ennez groaned. He was carrying Dav's CARG … that seventy-pound slab of metal.

"This thing was nearly the death of me," he said pointing to the big dent in his helmet. "I wish I could just drop it, but Dav will probably kill me if I did. Here, you carry it for awhile."

"I don't want it, but don't you dare drop it either. I'll bust you in the chops if you drop it. Come on, we need to keep moving."

"Any thoughts as to where we're going?"

"I've been following Tweeter, so far he's got me through. He's going to lead us somewhere safe until we can reach the ship."

Ki continued to drag Davage, and Ennez, encumbered with Dav's CARG, took Syg. They made their way to the wall where Tweeter was sitting.

"So, now what?" Ennez asked. "You should see all the StT's a few courtyards back."

Ki looked at the wall; tall, not scalable, at least not by her, with about a dozen large earthen pots stacked up against the base. She spun around, looking for anything. "I don't know. I asked him to get us to safety … he's never wrong."

In the distance, they both could hear a great roaring, a mass of angry Hulgismen heading toward them, possibly just a courtyard or two away. Ennez looked up at the sheer wall.

"Ki, I can scale this wall, but I'm pretty sure you can't. Come on, we've got to keep moving."

Ki stared at the wall. "He's brought us here, to this very spot, there must be something."

She had a thought. "Wait!! Tunnels, tunnels, don't you see? The Marines have reports of a maze of them running under Xandarr Keep. There must be a tunnel under this wall, there must be! Help me with these pots!"

They moved the huge earthen pots aside. When they made a space, Tweeter hopped down and vanished through a tiny crack at the bottom of the wall.

The roaring was getting nearer.

Frantically, Ki felt around at the bottom for a switch or lever—anything.

"Maybe there's no access point here, maybe it's just a vent," Ennez said, expecting to see the enemy at any moment.

"No, no there has to be something we can use. He's brought us here for a reason."

She reached into the crack and felt around. A moment later, her fingers found what felt like a small lever. "Here, yes here's a lever, but … I, I can't move it."

"Let me," Ennez said moving Ki out of the way. He jammed Dav's CARG into the crack, found the lever and began hitting it. "It's rooted in there good!"

He continued pounding it. "There … there, it's moving!"

A small, cleverly hidden trapdoor opened. Beneath was Tweeter sitting there, happy and patient as ever. There was some sort of strange, inter-locking symbol painted on the dirty floor near the opening. Ennez and Ki didn't have time to puzzle over it, they quickly put Dav and Syg down into the hole.

The roaring seemed to be just around the corner.

"Hold on!" Ki cried. I'm going to put those pots back!" Straining, she moved the pots back into place as best she could, just in time to see a hoard of Hulgismen and seven Black Hats enter from the far end.

She slid down into the hole and, together with Ennez, closed the trap door.

They could hear the racket of people searching for them above.

"They didn't see you, did they?" Ennez asked.

"I don't think so. See," Ki said whispering, holding Tweeter on her finger, "this little guy is never wrong."

Ennez gave Tweeter's beak a rub. "I don't think Lady Poe realizes how potent her cute little Silver tech creations really are. That Fins thing she made for me … I was examining it in my office. It's a marvel, a work of genius. Such a thing, made in quantity, could revolutionize the Hospitalers. I showed it to one of the Sisters, and she nearly fell out of her headdress."

"I know …"

Ennez inspected the odd painted symbol on the floor, following its lines with his hands. "Ki," he said, "this is a Xaphan Cabalist's symbol."

"Pretty," she said. "Come on, let's get Dav and Syg safe."

They made to move further into the gloom of the tunnel. They crawled through a small space for several feet that opened into a larger chamber, Tweeter's silvery body lighting it up.

There, illuminated in the silver light were dozens if not hundreds of people.

* * * * *

The technicians on the bridge had managed to hook up a few of the leads to the helm wheel. As such, the Helm had basic control of the ship: nose up, nose down, bank left bank right. No AM or PM control whatsoever.

Saari grabbed the wheel and tugged on it—the black material of the ring filling the cone.

"Somebody help me, it's too heavy!" she yelled, the wheel being completely out-of-calibration and too heavy to move.

The techs and Commander Mapes latched onto the wheel, and together the four of them lifted the nose and banked away.

Sasai stared at her sensor. "Lt.! We have multiple objects approaching from the ring! I count one hundred plus!"

"What are they?" Verlin asked.

"Shadow tech vessels, and they are on fast approach!"

* * * * *

He lingered for as long as he could, then he walked away from his body, through the ether.

The Waft had been too much for him—he knew it. He knew he was sacrificing himself for his wife and his friends when he tried it.

There was really no thought in the matter, to offer his life for theirs was an honor and a privilege. So, Captain Davage's soul drifted away from his dead body that Ki, dear Ki, struggled with.

Just drop me, Ki—it's all right. Get yourself to safety.

He went to whatever awaited him and hopefully wait for Syg. He hoped he had long to wait—that she must get through this, raise their son and be a good mother. Then, when she was done, she will join him here, and, hand in hand, go to the lands beyond.

He went a short ways and thought he could see a gallery in the distance, full of loved ones and fallen comrades.

They beckoned to him. He smiled and was eager to join them.

"No, no!!"

Soft arms came around his waist. He turned.

There was Syg.

"What are you doing? Where are you going?"

I'm gone, Syg—I'm done. I'm sorry.

"You're not leaving me, and our son to raise! I lay there on the Black Hat's stone and forced my heart to beat—for you and for our son! I fought to live and you are going to do the same! You are going to endure the fires of hell and toil as we work through this, and you are going to suffer me and my ravings as our son progresses to term. I don't envy you what you are going to suffer with me! You walk toward paradise. I offer you pain and hardship, frustration … and love, with me and our son."

Syg took him by the hand and pulled him back to the sorry scene in Xandarr Keep.

"Come, Dav—we've got work to do. When Paradise calls, we'll go to it together."

Dav's soul and Syg's soul, hand in hand, returned to what awaited them.

Paradise, is where you find it.

17—The King of Xandarr

Davage awoke in a dimly lit, hot, dusty place. The thick air smelled of rotten fabric and cooking spices. Sick to his stomach, he leaned over to wretch, but was able to calm himself. The Waft—just about killed him, Ennez was so big, Kilos too. Even Wafting Syg, tiny as she was …

Syg!! Where was she?

He looked around, and, bundled up in dirty burlap cloth nearby, was Syg, her head resting on a bunch of dusty old sacks. He Sighted, checking her over. She was fine, she was perfectly fine, just exhausted. She should have never come down here. He leaned over and kissed her sleeping face. She stirred a bit, licked her lips and resumed her deep sleep.

His CARG was resting against a near wall, his hat hanging from the X-shaped hilt.

Curled up on the other side of him in her dirty bodysuit and boots, gunbelt wrapped up beside her, was Kilos, again using an assortment of old sacks as a pillow. Her Tweeter sat on a basket nearby, his light filling the chamber with a soft glow. Odd, he recalled seeing Tweeter get sliced into three pieces by Vroc's BEREN.

He didn't see Ennez, he didn't see Larsen. He reached into his coat pocket and felt, at the very bottom, one Carahil figurine remaining. He pulled it out; it was a white one. He gave it a squeeze. "Shadow tech …" it squeaked.

He laughed. "Well done, Carahil, and thank you, wherever you are."

Kilos stirred and rose.

"Hey … Dav, you ok?"

She put her hand on his shoulder. "You all right? You had me worried there."

His pocketed the little figurine. "Fine, Ki … stomach in knots. Where are we?"

"In a tunnel under Xandarr Keep. Ennez and I dragged you and Syg in here. Tweeter found it."

"I thought he was dead, cut in thrice."

"Ha! You think that little blue-haired psycho could put the hurt on Tweeter? Guess again."

"Were we seen coming in here?"

"By the Black Hats, I don't think so … there's a whole lot of them roaming around up there looking for us. There are lots of people in this tunnel and they saw us come in."

"Who are they?"

"Refugees by the look of it. Once they saw we weren't Black Hats or Hulgismen they didn't give us any trouble, and they even offered us some food and water—though it's pretty nasty-looking."

He stood up and stretched, again his stomach was a rickety mess. "Have we contacted the ship, apprised them of our situation?"

"I don't have a communicator, and Lt. Larsen's holo-mon got snared with an StT."

Davage was quiet a moment. "Where is Larsen?" He asked the question, though he already knew the answer.

Ki looked at the dirty floor of the tunnel. "He … he fell, Dav. He fell in the Great Hall."

Davage flopped back down and sighed. "He was entrusted to me, I was to keep him safe and I failed him."

"You gave him every chance to live. Your Sight saved all of us. You did your best, it's not your fault, and it's not his either … he just couldn't react fast enough in an impossible situation. You were right, he seemed a fine fellow, and he saved my life up there. I wish I'd a chance to save his in return."

Davage whirled around suddenly. "Where's Ennez?"

"He's around someplace, Dav, he's fine. Probably exploring the tunnel."

"You're sure?"

"Yes, Mother-Hen. He carried Syg down here, looked her over, and wrapped her up personally. He also carried your CARG, though he wanted to drop it. Thing's heavy. I told him I'd bust him one if he dropped it." She laughed.

Davage cheered a bit, reached out and put his hat back on. "Can you reach the Sisters on the ship?"

"No, I tried earlier. Something's blocking our telepathy, jamming it somehow. Probably all those damn StT's out there doing it."

"The Black Hats. This must be what Carahil was talking about … here's where they're going to have their blood. Probably going to raze Xandarr Keep to the ground and snare it into some sort of ghastly Shadow tech amusement park as a warning to others."

"Here? Xandarr Keep?"

"They hate House Xandarr. In their minds House Xandarr caused their fall from wicked invincibility, because of Princess Marilith and the failed attack on the *Triumph* some years back. Now look, people are facing Black Hats in battle, capturing them … marrying them. The Black Abbess wants the League and the Xaphans to tremble at their name once again, and here is where they're going to get their dark status back. We need to reach the ship either via telepathy, or a com-link. We need a ripcar."

Ki stood up and grabbed him by the arm. "I don't know if we'll be going anywhere soon, Dav. The sky was full of Shadow tech. All in good time, I suppose. Come on, let's look to it and see what's about."

He looked up and Sighted through to the surface. He saw the gallery of Shadow tech in the sky, the army of Hulgismen and the hopeless swarm of StTs roaming about like locusts. He didn't see any in the tunnels, which struck him as odd—normally StT's got into everything. He sucked in his breath. "Well … that is impressive indeed. I've never seen so much Shadow tech in one place. They must have been at work preparing this attack for years—I've never seen so many StT's either. They're probably trying to create an extended desolation zone around the Keep for added effect—as they did in the Gorman-Billson region on Bazz years back. The Sisters had to declare the area uninhabitable because of the swarm of self-replicating StT's placed there."

Davage, weary and feeling sick, stood. He glanced at Syg's tiny sleeping form.

"She'll be fine, Dav … let her sleep."

They were in a small, rough tunnel, poorly cut, lined with sacks of dried fruits, stale salted meats hanging from sticks and wicker baskets full of odds and ends. He could hear people all around. Above, outside, he heard muffled explosions and cries—it sounded like a battle was going on.

He checked Syg one more time, then stood and walked down the length of the tunnel with Ki. They came across a large symbol painted in mushy white dye on the dirty wall. "What's this?" he asked.

"Don't know. I've seen those all over the place."

He waved his hand in front of it. "It's coursing with radiant energy. Its wavelength is a little too short for you to see, but I can see it just fine. It's bright."

"Ennez said it's some kind of Xaphan Cabalist symbol. I don't know what it does. Is it dangerous do you think?"

"Doesn't seem to be—but let's give it a wide berth for the time being."

Ahead was a brighter lit circular chamber. Many people were there, huddled on the floor. There was Ennez, silver-helmeted, standing amid the people. He had his back-up scanner out, checking the ragged refugees over. His usual scanner was worthless and discarded—melted with Shadow tech traps. Many, it appeared, suffered various injuries. Some looked to be in the final stages of pregnancy. There were so many needing looking at.

A tall man, wearing torn Xandarr veils and a dirty blue vest, saw Davage and made his way toward him. The man was skinny and filthy, every inch of him covered with dust.

The two regarded each other for a moment.

"Am I to thank you, sir, for this timely respite?" Davage asked.

The man looked at the floor and shook his head. "We were uncertain how you found your way in here, that entrance is supposed to only be opened from within the tunnels. Still, as you appear to be friendly, you are welcome here. All are welcome."

"For my countess and my crewmen, I thank you."

"No, we should be thanking you … we hadn't hoped to have a League Hospitaler in our midst. Samaritan Ennez has more than repaid us in the service he has offered. The wounded here are many. He also safely delivered several children a short time ago—the irony, to be born on the day Xandarr dies. Our planet is under attack from all quarters by the Black Hats."

"Excuse me, the '*planet*' did you say?"

"Yes."

Davage was taken aback. "Hmmm. We, of course, know that the Black Hats have a particular dislike for House Xandarr, from the failed attack on the *Triumph* authored by Princess Marilith years ago. We thought their anger should stop with the House of Xandarr. We didn't stop to think that—"

"That the Black Hats would murder the whole world? They are, sir, right now, even as we speak. The Black Hats have authored the death of House Xandarr, as I am sure you now know. Now, they turn their attention to the people and all that has been built. They crave the death of every living thing on this planet: man, animal and vegetable."

"Do they know of these tunnels?"

"They do, but, as of yet, cannot gain entrance. They have sought to swamp us out with hoards of StT's, however, we have arcane methods of keeping them out that are quite effective. Here, for now, we are safe."

"Ah, good, good," Davage said looking around. "We shan't tarry here and consume your supplies, as I am certain they are vital. We must to our ship and away. I will, of course, share our supplies with you, to help treat and feed these people as thanks. Please, allow me to introduce myself. I am Davage, Lord of Blanchefort, captain of the Main Fleet Vessel *Seeker*."

"I recognize you," the man said. "I know you well."

"Really? I also have with me Sygillis, Countess of Blanchefort—my wife—and you have already met Samaritan Ennez of the Grand Order of Hospitalers. Finally, this is Lt. Kilos, also of the Stellar Fleet…"

"I'm his first officer," Kilos stated proudly.

Davage glared at her for a moment. "Might I ask your name, sir?"

Again the man looked down and blushed. "… Balor…" he said quietly, as if the sound of his own name bothered him. "… King of Xandarr."

"Balor? If memory serves, Prince Balor was the third eldest House Xandarr heir, after Marilith and Nalfeshnee. I saw Balor's corpse in the great hall not long ago. Princess Vroc killed Prince Balor of Xandarr."

The man shrugged. Slowly he patted the dust out of his hair. Soon, the blueberry hair tint came through—clearly a Xandarr. "She killed my body double, Captain, that night when she came, crazed, weeping so I'm told, and fell on my family. That night I was in the arms of a dirty courtesan in the city, a capricious hobby of mine that my mother frowned upon. I had many capricious hobbies, however, the delights of a weed-infected courtesan were my favorite and more than I could resist. I used a body double to stand for me when I felt the need to go into arms with one. I employed a whole host of them in the village. Obviously, my dallying saved my life. I returned the next morning to a horrific sight, Vroc and Black Hats, everywhere in the Keep … my family … all dead. And I have been on the run ever since, hiding from the spies, the Black Hats. As Vroc arranged their dead bodies in the Great Hall, she noticed my body double; she saw that it was not I. She has pursued me ever since—to seat my dead, strangled body at the table with the rest. She is relentless. She is insane, Captain."

"She seems to think that I am her father."

"She thinks everybody is our father. She loved him very much, yet, for his treatment of her, she hated him even more. And now, that he's dead, by her hand, she cannot bear to be without him. She wants her whole family with her … at the grand table where she was never permitted to sit. The Black Hats have somehow enhanced her skills and her strength, and she has dogged my footsteps ever since I went to ground."

Davage listened and was skeptical. "And, that being the case, why did you not quit the area, go into posh hiding on some Xaphan resort planet?"

Balor continued. A tired-looking, rather homely woman wearing torn garments saddled up next to him.

"I tried to do that, but, being it generally known that the Black Hats craved my flesh, I became social poison. Nobody wanted me. All the doors once wide open were slammed hopelessly shut. I was, essentially, trapped here. I took to the tunnels, to the underground depths beneath the city and the Keep. A miserable maid servant of the Keep, a woman whom I'd never looked at twice, saved me. She brought me down into the tunnels and the people hiding here took me in, though I did not deserve it. And here, in the dust and the mud, scrabbling for food, I have found a home, and a beloved wife, as I married Jemerlin, the servant who saved me. These here in the dark … are my people."

Davage thought he heard Syg stir, he turned to go to her side, Balor following. "Your people? I never thought the House of Xandarr gave much stock to its people."

"Perhaps it took a bit of starving along with my people to help me see what I was. Perhaps it took hiding with them in the dark, stealing food with them, sleeping in the mud with them … for me to shed my family's arrogance and become a Man at last. To become a King at last. I suppose that's what I am now."

Davage knelt down over Syg, she was coughing in her sleep, too much dust on her makeshift pillows. Davage took a handkerchief and wiped her face.

Balor looked down at her. "We had heard that you had taken a Black Hat as a wife. That mark on her face, is that a Black Hat tattoo of some sort? We have never seen one of their faces before."

"It is, though it is not a tattoo, it's her Shadowmark."

"She is very beautiful. You do not fear her … fear her power?"

"I do not. I trust her with my life, and she carries my unborn son. How many people are down here?"

"Thousands. More people arrive at a steady rate, every hour, seeking shelter now that the attack is underway."

A great tremor passed through the tunnels from overhead, sending people scrambling.

Davage lit his Sight and looked up. He saw in the courtyard above a literal army of Hulgismen, black carpets of StT's crawling on the walls, and the occasional Black Hat roaming about.

And that wasn't all.

He saw that Balor had spoken the truth—this attack wasn't just against the House of Xandarr as he first thought. There was Shadow Tech as far as he could see, for miles and miles. The sky was black with it. Farther up, he could see that Xandarr, a ringless planet, now had a copiously huge ring composed of Shadow tech ships circling its equator. He didn't see any tell-tale wreckage, so he knew the *Seeker* was still up there, somewhere, possibly on the other side of the planet.

He'd not thought it possible. The Black Hats were indeed seeking to turn Xandarr into a hopelessly snared, haunted world, ringed with deadly Shadow tech, transforming the entire planet into a huge, spinning metaphor and lesson to all.

And still that wasn't all. Huge Shadow tech beasts, each several miles high, roamed the arid landscape. They looked like massive black spheres supported on a host of thin Shadow tech tentacles. They roared with evil malice. One stood over a town, its tentacles reaching down, scooping up and letting fall back to the ground: people … great masses of doomed Xandarrian people, falling like bits of sand. Opening its huge maw, it popped them in, devouring dozens at a mouthful. Its laughter shook the ground.

Flocks of giant Shadow tech birds followed in the wake of these beasts, pecking at the remainders.

Davage calmed his Sight and looked away, unable to watch any further.

"I am sorry, Balor … King Balor, you are quite correct in your assessment—the surface is hopelessly snared. I've never seen such a thing. I am not unsympathetic to the plight of your people. We will away to our ship and contact the nearest Xaphan stronghold, and inform them that Xandarr is attacked and in need. I will do my best to convince them to come and assist, though I do not know what weight my voice will have, my League voice."

Davage cleared the dust out of Syg's face, still fast asleep. "And again, as I have said, I will leave you as much as I can in the way of supplies when we depart."

Balor sat down on a straw basket near Syg. "In the Keep, Captain, there is a sophisticated communications device—I believe my sister used to use it to contact you in private. On the `morrow, when your countess is better, we will get you there, so that you may pierce the Shadow tech veils and reach your ship. I am certain the device will still function."

Davage was impressed. "So, you wish to help us? You'd endanger yourselves, for us?"

"We will do what must be done … we will get you to the communications device."

"And, in return?"

Balor shrugged. "In return? Should that not be obvious? In return I request you help us. In return I request the Fleet. I am asking you to stand with Xandarr and save it."

"Pardon, sir?"

"Captain, we are under attack … all of us. And there will be none of us left unless we receive immediate aid. We need help … in force. We need the League. With their might, surely we could …"

"Sir, as you know the League will not come," Davage said cutting him off. "This, regrettably, is a Xaphan matter. It must be dealt with by Xaphans. I have told you that I will go to the nearest outpost, possibly

Nalls, possibly Holly, and entreat them that Xandarr is in need. Surely, you've allies among the Great Xaphan Houses who will ..."

"These are Black Hats, Captain! This planet is under the gaze of the Black Abbess, and they are afraid in Nalls and on Holly. The Xaphans will not come, not for the sake of us ... therefore, there is only the League!! I am asking for the League. I am asking for the Fleet ... to come here and fight. Fight with us to save our people."

Ennez arrived in the corridor, followed by a mass of hurt, thankful people. He listened to the conversation unfold.

"Again, King Balor, this is an internal Xaphan matter. The League will not come, and nor should it. There are decorums and mutually understood treatments that the two sides have maintained for centuries. And this, if I may point out, is not the first time two disparate Xaphan factions have come to grips. I recall the horrific tales of the carnage created by the feuding Houses of Grith and Charn—nobody asked the League to intercede in that bloody affair. What of the poor Bodice—massacred by the Charn? I also do not recall being asked to come to the aid of Zall 88 when House Xandarr—your House—obliterated it centuries ago."

"Then perhaps they should have asked. Perhaps my family should have been stopped. And, I will remind you, Captain, that the Grith-Charn dispute, though cruel and a shocking waste of life, was fought with House forces and not laid waste upon the general population of the fiefdom. Yes, yes, we are Xaphans, true enough. We are the enemy—your enemy. We are soaked in blood ..."

Balor waved his hand at the masses of dirty, injured, filthy people. "And just look at them: Xaphan women, Xaphan children, Xaphan infirm, Xaphan infected, Xaphan farmers, and on and on. Yes ... we are Xaphans, but we are Xaphans who have done nothing. All the evil that has been done here has been done by my family, and I will gladly face any pending charges or warrants written for me or any member of my House. I will make amends, I will face those charges. First, however, I am begging you to help us!"

Davage was shocked: a king, a Xaphan king, begging? When had such a thing ever happened? Xaphan kings were prideful, even to their deaths.

"You are begging me, sir?"

"YES, I AM BEGGING YOU!!" he shrieked. "I am the King of Xandarr … and what is a Xandarrian king? An empty throne, a tarnished crown upon a foolish brow? A king is the mouth and the body of his people, a king does what he must for his people! What good are my knees, if not to bend them for my people, what good is my mouth, if not to beg for help? And I, Balor of House Xandarr, King of Xandarr, am on my knees!"

Balor fell to the ground, and Davage quickly pulled him back up. "Get up, sir, please."

"In all those years you fought my sister, I watched, and I laughed at you, mocked you, but I always secretly marveled at your skill, and your goodness. You are Pledged to defend life … you have kept that promise, please, do not forsake it now, do not forsake us. If not you, then there is nobody. If not you … then Xandarr dies and becomes nothing more than a fable, a story to frighten children. But perhaps … perhaps with your help, Xandarr can mean something entirely different. Perhaps Xandarr can be a place of hope, where a King finally saw the worth of his people, and was Man enough swallow his pride and ask for help. Redemption is never too late."

Davage looked around, at the broken, torn people in front of him. "I will consider your request, King of Xandarr, though I can promise nothing."

18—RED HAWs

The *Seeker* wobbled in its orbit. The helm, though now fully reconnected, was hopelessly out of calibration. All around it, Black Ships were everywhere, and it took every bit of strength Saari the helmsman had to keep from hitting them or yawing into the upper atmosphere.

The *Seeker* was safe in a fully Painted Cloak.

On the bridge the Duke of Oyln, his Black Hat consort Torrijayne of Waam, Lady Poe of Blanchefort, the Captain's sister, and the three Ruthven men stood, staring at the holo-cone in muted interest. Technicians continued to work on the helm, trying to restore its delicate touch, though days of exhaustive work will be needed. Commander Mapes had returned to engineering to try and make the crude reconnections a bit more functional.

Lt. Verlin sat in the command chair, and looked with a bit of gut-churning horror at the dark scene outside the ship. She burned to throw the Duke and his lot off of the bridge, with, possibly, the exception of the captain's sister, yet, the Duke of Oyln was a powerful, influential man—even if he was a pirate. And, she had to admit, they were the reason the *Seeker* was still in one piece.

"What is our status," she asked. "How's the Cloak?"

Torrijayne looked back at her and smiled. "It's fine, more than fine, it's great. The Black Hats might have my Key, but they don't have Lady Poe's here. It'll take them years to figure it out and knock it down. The only way they can find us now is by getting us in a darklight, but there's no chance of that."

Poe, shy as usual, blushed. "I did nothing but follow your instructions, Madame Torrijayne."

"Are you kidding?" Torrijayne said. "You saw the crappy one the Sisters tried to throw up and get mashed. This is an awesome Cloak, and I'm going to want to get with you later and discuss some of the things you did. You're a genius!"

Poe smiled and looked at the floor.

Verlin stood and offered her seat to Lady Blanchefort, who graciously accepted it, her feet still a swollen mess. She sat down, but then lurched back up. Sitting in the seat was a white box with a bright magenta bow. It hadn't been there before.

"Where did this come from?" Poe asked picking it up and placing it in her lap.

"That looks like one of the gifts Carahil wanted to give us," Peter said.

Verlin was uninterested. "What is the status of the Captain?" she asked the Com.

"Still no word. He has not responded to our attempts to reach him. Additionally, we are still missing a Sister and her personal company of Marines. All else are accounted for."

"What are our in-atmosphere capabilities?"

Poe lifted the lid and peeked into the box. A fast-moving tide of large, quivering bubbles came out and drifted to the floor, quickly spreading out over the bridge. They were slightly scented like hard candy.

"Lady Blanchefort, please," Verlin said kicking some bubbles away.

"I am so sorry," she said, mortified, closing the lid to the box.

"Crewman," Verlin said to Helmsman Saari, "I await your response."

Saari, distracted by the bubbles, snapped out of it. "Pardon, Lt. In our current state, it is inadvisable to attempt to enter the atmosphere. The Helm is still too slow to respond, and we shall find ourselves quickly out of control," Saari said.

Sage of Ruthven turned to Verlin. "What is wrong with the Helm, Lt.?" he asked.

"That is ship's business, sir," she said in her Howell accent.

There was a brief flash.

"What was that?" Verlin asked.

Everybody looked around.

There was a faint, casual clatter of metal against metal.

"Wait, stop, everybody freeze … DON'T MOVE!!" the Duke cried.

Verlin was startled. For a moment she thought the Duke, a suspected pirate, was forcibly taking over the ship.

"Listen to him … everybody, stay where you are. Don't move, please!" Torri said.

"What is this?" Verlin asked.

The Duke, frozen in place, spoke through a closed mouth. "Do not move, Lt. Do not breathe … all of our lives depend on it."

The bridge crew froze up as commanded, only the clicks and bleeps of equipment indicated that time moved on. The Duke stood near the viewer, Torrijayne at his right, John of Ruthven on his left. Lady Poe, her face and feet bandaged, sat in Davage's chair where Syg usually sat. Lt. Verlin stood leaning over the Ops panel. Helmsman Saari stood in an awkward angle—she had been adjusting her boot. One of the technicians was kneeling against the Helm column unable to see anything. The Missive was in an embarrassing position; his finger was quite close to his nose.

And there were RED HAWs all over the floor, rolling about. They appeared to be Cloaked, however, the bubbles on the floor had gravitated to them en masse. Through the filmy surface of the bubbles, the RED HAW's brassy capsules could clearly be seen.

"Duke, what is going on?" Lady Poe asked through frozen teeth, her eyes whirling around in their sockets. At least she was sitting.

"There are activated RED HAWs on the floor. I count four …"

"Actually, I see six," Torri added.

"And I see a seventh … Lady Poe, do not move a muscle, one is right near your left foot," Johnnie said.

Poe tried to look down. Vaguely, she could feel a cold metal capsule frosted with soapy bubbles nudging her foot through the light bandages. Looking around with her eyes, she could see several more rolling about at various places, a dim red light glowing on each, lit up by the bubbles.

"Where the hell did these come from?" Peter asked

"Don't know," Oyln said. "All of mine are still locked in their brace.

Crewman Saari at the helm was suffering in her awkward position. "Lt., we are in a 15 degree starboard bank, heading toward the planet. I had leaned over to fix my boot when …"

"Do not move that wheel, crewman," Verlin said, still a little unsure what was going on.

The bridge was locked in place, one wrong move, and it would all be over.

* * * * *

When she finally began to stir a short time later, Davage pulled Syg out of her burlap blanket and held her for a bit.

Ennez came up. He'd been busy examining and treating as many refugees as he could. Fungal infections were rampant down here in the tunnels, Ennez had already diagnosed five women with various fungal maladies. Syg, now fully conscious, was parched. Davage felt dubious giving her a drink from the tankard of brownish water given to them by King Balor, but Ennez proclaimed it potable, and Syg greedily drank the whole thing.

Balor returned. "The preparations are in place, we are ready to take you to the communications device."

Giving Syg her shawl and sandals back, they followed Balor down a chain of tunnels that seemed to stretch on without end. At various intervals, the walls of the tunnel were scrawled with strange symbols, which various people refreshed with a simple white dye. "Those symbols are what keep out the StT's," Balor said. "My wife is a Cabalist."

Moving on, they eventually, they reached a hatch and ladder going upward.

"This hatch," Balor said, "goes all the way to the top of Xandarr Keep. It's very tight in there so be careful."

Climbing, they made their way up the ladder, Tweeter lighting the passage up.

Balor was right about the passage being tight. There was barely enough room to allow one to take a step up—their knees kept banging into the rough side of the passage.

At last they made arrived at a small trap door.

"Here," Balor said whispering, "is a doorway leading to the ninth level of Xandarr Keep. Take a look, Captain, and see for yourself."

Davage lit his Sight. Beyond the hatchway, he saw a regal passageway filled with furnishings and ornamentation in the Xandarr style. As usual with Xandarr Keep, one of the sides of the passageway was open to the elements, and he could see down into the levels and courtyards below. The Xandarrian horizon, normally soft purple, was brackish and black in areas with Shadow tech.

"Look to a room near the end of the hallway to your right," Balor said.

Davage looked. In a large, lavishly decorated room, was an elaborate-looking device. Arrayed in front of device were a number of poufs, couches and pillows. Davage thought he recognized them—Marilith once sat on those pillows. A brief pang of nostalgia touched him—he quickly dismissed it.

"I see the device," Davage whispered.

"Is anybody out there?" Syg asked.

Davage looked around. "I see five Black Hats, two in the room in question, three roaming the hallway."

"Hulgismen?" Ki asked.

"Yes … about a hundred. The Black Hats are manning an arcane device that is throwing a beam of ebon light into the sky."

"That's a dark light," Syg said. "They're looking for Cloaked objects."

"How are we going to fight our way through all of that?" Ki asked.

Balor began making his way back down the ladder. "I shall give you the time you need."

"Where are you going?" Davage said.

Balor looked up at him. "You will have the time you need. I pray you sir, do not allow our sacrifice to go wasted. Use the time wisely and … remember what I have asked of you."

"Balor—get back here!" he hissed.

Balor, though, wasn't listening. He continued down the ladder and was gone.

* * * * *

The RED HAW had been the LosCapricos weapon of House Milton for centuries. It was said that the original RED HAW was designed by another, now forgotten House on Onaris, and, to this day, it bore the distinctive swirls and notches indicative of that world. It was said that the Miltons stole its secrets and made it their own, taking it to Kana with them when they settled in the Esther region. Resembling a three inch long brass capsule, it was always considered a potent and undeniably deadly weapon.

When activated, it, upon impact with the ground or a person, burst open, unleashing a long coil of taught wire lengths that undulated around in a death-dealing cloud, sundering virtually anything they touched. The whole ghastly event looked like the sprouting of a hawthorn bush, sped up in time; in fact the ancient name of the weapon was RED HAWTHORN: hawthorn for the plant it resembled, red for the blood it was soaked in after it had done its grim work.

It was a fairly unique LosCapricos weapon. There were of course many that could be timed and thrown, but the RED HAW was one of the few that could be set in place, lurking, waiting for a victim. It was one of the few that could be used for assassinations. LosCapricos weapons were given a special, if undeserved, place in law. Duels could be fought with them, and no punishment was possible. Murder too, for few dared acknowledge that nothing other than true, noble acts could be performed with a legendary Elder-made LosCapricos weapon. The RED HAW, with its lurking, indiscriminant, death-dealing ways, skirted the line, gave many Houses considerable pause.

* * * * *

Seven RED HAWs rolled about on the bridge floor, occasionally knocking into each other as the ship began to buck slightly in the atmosphere, their red lights glowing innocently.

"Don't worry about them hitting each other ... they'll only respond to obvious warm-blooded movement," the Duke said through his teeth.

"Lt.!" Saari cried, stuck in her awkward position. "I—I think I'm going to fall over!"

"Crewman ... relax and clear your mind ... you are not going to fall over," Verlin said softly.

"Yes—yes I am!"

"No you're not ... relax, relax "

Saari looked terrified, her legs started trembling slightly.

"I'm falling!" she said.

She just began to topple over when Torri caught her in a full TK.

"I got you, I got you," she said.

Saari, like a bug stuck in a web struggled minutely. "I—I can't breathe. I can't breathe!" she said.

"Yes you can," Torri said in a soothing voice. "Just relax, I got you. Relax and breathe normal."

Saari relaxed a bit, held in place in Torri's TK.

"How are you doing, crewman?" Verlin asked.

"F-fine," she stammered. "I'm fine ..."

The crew stood there frozen for another few seconds. A warning bell went off—too hot outside.

The bubbles covering the RED HAWs were beginning to pop. Without the bubbles, the devices were Cloaked into full invisibility. One only had a bubble or two left.

"What are we going to do, Fall?" Johnnie hissed. "What are we going to do?"

The Duke sweated. "You remember Midas, Johnnie ... that's what we're going to do. Does anybody have a shot?"

"A shot?" Verlin said. "And how, may I ask, did you re-acquire your weapons, Duke Oyln? I believe the captain confiscated them."

"Trade secret."

"I can Sten in two," Torri said. "The ones over by the Helm.

"I've got a clear shot at one," Peter said. "The one near Lady Poe's chair."

"Remember, Peter, you can't shoot them with a pistol, you need an energy weapon to flash melt it," the Duke said.

"I've got my Hertamer in my duster."

"Good, good. Who else?"

"I—I can get two, I think," Lady Poe said.

"Which ones?"

"The ones near the Lt's legs."

"Are you sure?"

"Yes ... yes ..."

"All right, I've got the one by the lift door square in my sights," the Duke said. "That leaves one more by the viewing screen; the one that's almost invisible."

"I've got a shot at that one," Sage said.

"No, Sage, shut up will you—you can't shoot!" Johnnie cried. "Somebody else take the shot. Damn!"

"I can do it," Verlin said. "I'll take the shot."

"No, you've got an SK, Lt.—that won't do! It has to be an energy weapon." The Duke grimaced. "Come on, we've got one more, by the viewing screen, and from its positioning, it'll kill the Missive, and those two standing by the sensors. Who has a shot?"

"I've got a shot," Johnnie said. "One problem, I think my Hertamer's set to safety.

"What?"

"I don't know, it might be on safety, and it might not. But … I'm pretty sure it is."

The warning bell became a steady claxon. "We are one minute away from melting the outer hull!" Saari said.

"Looks like it's not going to matter one way or the other. Johnnie take the shot."

The crew held their breath a moment, the claxon sounding.

"Everybody ready? All right … on three … Ready? One … two … THREE!!"

Of all people, Poe was the quickest on the draw by far. In a blur, she had her two RED HAWs surrounded in a sphere of Silver tech.

Out came the Duke's Hertamer, and with a FWIIIEEEE!! his RED HAW got melted into an angry lump of slag. Bubbles popped.

Torrijayne dropped her TK, unceremoniously dumping Crewman Saari to the floor, and quickly Boxed-in Stenned two RED HAWs. They blossomed under the invisible Sten, making a somewhat hairy-looking, writhing mass that sparked as the coils touched the field. Saari, laying there on the floor, watched it in horror, a front row seat.

Peter, drew his Hertamer, and with two quick shots melted his—the first shot partially missing, almost getting Lady Poe in the foot.

Johnnie, his hand moving with a practiced motion, drew his Hertamer from his duster.

He aimed and squeezed. The trigger didn't move.

Nothing happened. His safety was on.

The RED HAW, activated and trembled like a jumping bean, and began to make a hideous scream when Poe, with her other hand, surrounded it with a ball of Silver tech. The sphere deformed with the efforts of the bound coils within.

That was it, all were contained. Everybody thanked their Maker.

Claxons!! Burning up!

"Helm, left full wheel! Z plus 600 meters and mark at four!" Verlin shouted.

Saari stiffly stood back up and rammed the wheel with all her strength, the equally stiff tech helping her. Soon, the ship righted and pulled out to safety

"Lady Blanchefort!" Johnnie cried. "I'm in love! Did you see how fast she took her's down."

Poe smiled in her usual shy bearing

Peter approached her. "Lady Poe, that was an impressive display of speed and control." He took her hand and kissed it.

"Thank you, Peter. And thank you for not shooting me in the foot."

19—The Ghost

Verlin stormed into the conference room. The Duke, Torrijayne, the Ruthvens and Lady Poe were taking their seats. Peter offered Poe a chair and properly seated her. He then sat down next to her.

"All right, I want to know what the hell just happened!" Verlin sputtered. Her Howell accent became progressively more pronounced as she got more and more angry.

The Duke opened his duster and unclipped his brace. He set it on the table, pulled out a RED HAW, and handed it to Verlin.

"RED HAW," The Duke said, his regal East Esther accent bearing steady. "It's a LosCapricos weapon, and it's quite deadly, I assure you, Lt. Don't worry about that one, it's not enabled."

Verlin carefully examined it with her long fingers. It was a small brass capsule about three inches in length, its surface was etched with bold-relief; the swirling designs were indicative of the North Pinthrop area of Onaris, which she had come to know in the Marines. It was very heavy for its size, weighing about five pounds.

"I think Carahil helped us," Poe said. "That box I opened was from the other day when he wanted to give us a useful gift. I think if those bubbles hadn't been there we would never have seen them. We might all be dead now."

"Yes, food for thought," Verlin said setting it down on the table. "But, the question remains, how did these things end up on the bridge in the first place, Duke? I should have you thrown in the brig for this."

"For what?" Torri cried, indignant.

"For nearly killing everybody on the bridge with your careless use of these weapons."

"Now, wait a second ..." Torri said, getting angry.

"Let's not be hasty here, Lt.," the Duke said. "I only have five RED HAWs, and, as you can see from the one in front of you and the four remaining in my brace, they're all here. Nobody else carries them."

Verlin was skeptical. "You expect me to believe that?"

Torrijayne stood up. "Yes, Lt., we do. You're an acting first officer competing for Ki's job, trying to impress the captain. I suggest you do a better job of showing a bit of courtesy in the face of a League Duke who has saved this ship on two occasions now."

Verlin picked the RED HAW back up again in frustration. "I'm sorry, you are correct. Then, if I may pose a question, sir, where did they come from?"

Sage rustled in his seat. "Lt., I believe the answer here is clear."

She whirled around to face him. Sage was bookish and studious-looking, not nearly as handsome as his two brothers. "I'm listening," she said. Verlin was trying to sound confident and authoritative. She hoped she wasn't over-doing it.

Sage adjusted himself and began. "There have been several unusual and unexplainable events recently that I have taken note of, this incident being the latest. I believe we have been infiltrated, and are, even at this moment, under attack."

She moved across the table and sat down next to Sage. "Please go on, sir," she said, trying to soften up a bit.

He continued. "Allow me to bring you fully up-to-date Lt., so that my thoughts may present themselves more clearly. Two days ago, we were attacked by a group of toughs as we were in the process of picking up Lt. Kilos in the Tartan-lands of Kana."

"I would hardly call Ellington and his lot, 'toughs'," the Duke said.

"Regardless, they were certainly not an overly skilled or stealthy lot, yet they got the drop on us hard. Where did they come from? I recall no ship in the area as we departed, and I made it a point to look. Also, how did they follow us to the pick-up location at all, as we were under a full painted Cloak?"

"I was wondering about that too," Torri said.

"To continue, yesterday, in this very conference room, Mr. Carahil disappeared right in front of our eyes in a flash."

"Oh, he likes to be mysterious. He'll probably be back right in the nick of time. It makes him feel special," Poe said.

"That may be the case, however, something the captain mentioned at the time gives me pause."

"He said he saw a ghost exiting the room, as I recall," Peter said.

"Correct. And, if the captain's Sight is as good as we have heard it to be, then what did he see, and why should a ghost need to exit through the doorway? I know I saw it open and close by itself. Clearly, the captain saw something, or someone, exiting the room through the door right after Mr. Carahil vanished, and I'll wager it was someone under Cloak who can't Waft."

Verlin stood up and went to the door, looked at it, and thought.

"Lt.?" Sage asked. "What happened with the Helm on the bridge?"

Verlin took a breath and sighed. "The Helm somehow got completely disconnected."

Sage stroked his chin. "Hmmmm ... not something that normally happens by itself. So, we have the toughs on Kana, the disappearance of Mr. Carahil, the ghost, the sabotaging of the Helm and, finally, this most recent near disaster on the bridge. I believe, given all this information, that we are most certainly under attack, and I am convinced the identity of the attacking culprit is obvious."

Sage stopped. Everybody looked around at each other. Verlin smiled, she found she was beginning to like these fellows. "Well, Lord Ruthven, please, disclose the identity."

"The attacking weapon on the bridge was RED HAW, and they were the real thing, as I got a good hard look at them though they were covered with bubbles. The RED HAW is the LosCapricos weapon of House Milton, therefore, the attacker can be only one person: Hershey, Lord of Milton."

"Lord Hershey of Milton? The accountant?" Verlin gasped.

"You mean the scary-looking guy with the wig in the other house?" Torri asked.

"The same. Either he or one of his associates. Ellington and his lot were Lord Milton's personal servants, and, as the captain said he saw a ghost, I am inclined to assume that Lord Milton himself is at work here, as he likes to present himself as a withered old man, and he cannot Waft."

"Sage," the Duke said dryly. "I see where you're going with this, and it makes a great deal of sense, but, you're forgetting one small point: Lord Milton is about 12 light years from here."

Sage stood up and made his way to Poe. "Lady Blanchefort," he said, "I have been told that you wear a wondrous silver medallion, one that calls Mr. Carahil when pressed?"

"Oh, oh yes." Poe pulled her medallion out of her gown. It sparkled on its chain.

"May I, perhaps, see it for a moment?"

She took it off and gave it to Sage. He examined it. "And, all that needs done is to press it and Mr. Carahil comes?"

"Yes, though he doesn't come instantly … he takes his time."

"I see, and have you tried it since his disappearance?"

"Yes, but he hasn't shown up. Sometimes, he takes a while."

Sage showed the medallion to the Duke. "Does this look familiar, Duke?"

"Yes, I used one similar to that once. I called him and he came, and he broke the darkness around Torri."

Torrijayne winked at him.

"What happened to that particular medallion?"

The Duke thought a moment. "I put it back in my drawer in the study—I never saw it again, I was busy with my Lady here."

"I believe Lord Milton has since stolen it, and has discovered its workings, duplicating its functions via technological means. I believe that he is fully able to appear here at his leisure. In fact, he could be here with us even at this moment."

Everybody at the table looked around dubiously.

An orderly came into the conference room. He was holding a small slip of folded paper.

"Lt.," he said. "Message for you."

Verlin took the paper, opened it and read.

"Crewman!" she said. "Where did this come from?"

"It was sitting on the rail by the Ops station. I thought it might be important, so I brought it to you right away."

"What is it, Lt.?" Sage asked.

Verlin ran a hand through her blonde hair. "It says: 'All you Fleet Fart-sniffers and Duke-worshipping Dung-doodlers are about to die!! Signed, Lord Milton.'"

Verlin turned to Sage. "Lord Ruthven, you really think Lord Milton might be here with us, even at this moment?"

"I believe so, yes," he said looking around.

"He can Cloak?"

"Yes, that is the sole Gift available to him, though he can Cloak extremely well."

The Duke shook his head. "Sage, that's not quite correct. Lord Milton can do a lot of things that are Gift-like, without being Gifts, per se."

Verlin looked around the room. "This medallion you believe he's using, how does it work?" she asked.

Sage thought a moment. "Well, it must be …"

There was a BLAM!! Gun smoke filled the conference room. Sage fell out of his seat, holding his chest, blood oozing out of a gushing chest wound.

Torrijayne sprang to his side. "I'm going to Cloak all of …"

BLAM!! She was hit in the arm.

BLAM!! She fell, clutching her throat, a terrible gaping wound near her adam's apple.

"Euugghhh!" she gurgled.

BLAM!! The Duke fell, struggling to right himself, shot to the belly. He weakly drew his Grenville 40 and dropped it.

BLAM!! Someone took a shot at Lady Poe, but, in a blur, she Silver tech'ed the large caliber bullet heading toward her head out of thin air.

Peter drew his Hertamer.

BLAM!!

"Peter!" Poe cried and Silver tech'ed the bullet. It was headed for his skull.

BLAM!! She caught another bullet, heading this time for her throat.

In another lightning move, Poe threw a Silver tech net in the direction of the blasts. There, a man-shaped form appeared under the silver.

Verlin rose and drew her brand-new SK. She flipped to Auto and peppered a long shot at the person there. Bullets bounced off of the Silver tech—an inadvertent shield.

The shape staggered to the door, and went through it.

Crawling, bleeding, the Duke moved to Torri's side, her blue eyes wide with panic, her ruined throat spurting blood.

"Hospitalers to the Bridge Conference room, urgent!!" Verlin shouted. "Com, the *Seeker* has been boarded! I want the Marines to case the entire ship!"

"Who are we looking for?" the Com asked.

"Hershey, Lord of Milton, and he is armed, under Cloak, extremely dangerous and possibly wounded! Call out the Sisters as well, I want a coordinated effort and sound General Quarters to all personnel not currently on duty!"

"Aye, ma'am!"

Torri's life pulsed out into the Duke's hands. Shot in the throat, every beat of her heart led her a bit closer to death. Her throat was a shot-through, bloody disaster. She convulsed, her dimming eyes bulging out of their sockets.

Nearby, Sage was turning a sickening gray color as he bled out, Johnnie and Peter desperately trying to slow the bleeding.

Verlin spun around, seeing two, possibly three people dying right in front of her.

"Hospitalers, status?" she roared, still holding her SK.

Poe knelt down next to Peter and began swirling her fingers. Soon, after several moments, two big-eyed, happy-faced silver fish sat in her hands.

"Here, Peter, quickly. Place Fins on his chest. This other one is for Torri."

"This is Fins? Like what you used to save Countess Blanchefort?" Peter asked looking at the comical, big-eyed fish.

"Yes."

The Duke propped himself up on his elbows and held out his hands. "Please, Lady Poe, I'll put it on her."

Verlin knelt down, and looked at the strange silver fish. "Is this really going to work?" she asked.

"Yes," Poe said with growing confidence, "yes he will. Fins will do his job."

The Duke took Fins into his hands. Fins blinked at him. Quickly, he put the fish on Torri's mangled throat. Fins sat there for a moment in the stream of pulsing blood, then disappeared into the wound with a splash.

Several moments later, Torri stopped convulsing, stopped rasping for breath. As the Duke and Verlin watched, the heart-breaking, collapsed structure of her throat returned to normal, and the ragged wound sealed.

Soon, several words appeared on her neck in a fun, silver script that shimmered in alternating colors: FIXED BY FINS.

Kissing her hand, the Duke could, ever so dimly, feel her squeezing back. She tried to smile, then fell unconscious.

"Johnnie, how's Sage?" the Duke said, beginning to feel real, roaring pain from his wound.

"Ok, he's ok," Johnnie said. "Bullet's out, the bleeding's stopped. It worked, just like Lady Poe said."

Peter and Verlin rolled the Duke over and saw the bloody wound in his belly. Lady Poe's fingers began spinning again. "Your turn, Duke," she said. "And, Madame Torrijayne's arm needs fixing."

The Duke lay there, Lady Poe kneeling next to him. "I am … in your debt … for Torri's life, Sage's life."

She continued working. "If I kept track of such things, I'd say that we are even for getting me out of that horrible place, but since I do not, I am glad I am able to help."

Blood was darkening the floor, both from the Duke and from Torri's arm. In a moment, Poe had two more Fins sitting big-eyed and happy in her hands. She handed one to Peter, who quickly parted the Duke's shirt and placed it on his wound.

"That was a big gun, probably a Inseroth D2a or Dfq," Peter said. He smiled at her. "We'd be dead without you. You, Lady Blanchefort, are an angel."

Poe smiled. She took the other Fins and placed it on Torri's shoulder.

"My whole life, people have been taking care of me, protecting me. It feels good to finally be able to give back when I can."

A moment later, the bullet came skittering out of the Duke's wound, and a bullet literally flew out of Torri's arm like a nugget of dirt from a gopher hole, and the ragged wound sealed. FIXED BY FINS appeared on her arm a few moments later, like a merchant-man's tattoo.

"I'll have to adjust that," Poe said.

"No, no," Peter said. "It's a nice touch. If Torri could speak right now, I'm sure she'd be proud of it."

Verlin, seeing it for herself, still couldn't believe it. The door to the conference room opened and several Hospitalers entered. "The Duke, Lord Sage of Ruthven, and Madame Torrijayne, all to the dispensary now for examination," she said.

"What has happened?" one of them asked.

"Shot, by a large caliber pistol."

Peter picked up one of the bullets. "Yes ... an Inseroth D2a by the looks of it. Very large caliber weapon."

The Hospitalers quickly inspected the three and waved their scanners around. "We don't understand these readings. They all appear to have been shot as you say, but their wounds look to be healed."

"They were given a novel 'field treatment' as we awaited your arrival. Lady Poe of Blanchefort will debrief you later. Now, to the dispensary."

They collected the three and were off, leaving only fresh bloodstains on the carpet.

Verlin, still holding her SK, finally holstered it. "That was smart work, Lady Poe," she said. "Very smart work—if I hadn't seen it for myself I'd not believe it."

She picked up one of the bloody bullets. "And I agree with you, Lord Ruthven, it does appear to be a bullet from an Inseroth D2a." Behind, dug in the wall, was the bloody bullet that had passed through Torri's throat.

"I know my weapons."

"You are very knowledgeable, sir," Poe said as she scooted next to him and put her head on his shoulder. She sighed.

20—Marilith's Communicator

Davage, Syg, Ki and Ennez stood on the ladder in the dark.

"Do you see anything, Dav?" Syg asked.

"Same thing as before. Five Black Hats … lots of Hulgismen." He reached down and yanked on his CARG, which had gotten stuck in the tight quarters.

"So, what are we going to do—just sit here?" Ennez asked.

He looked around. "Well, I suppose we could—"

In an instant, a commotion rose from down below. The Black Hats and Hulgismen went to the edge of the corridor and looked down.

In the lowest courtyard, he saw something, and he was horrified.

Ragged people were running along the wall: men, women—some carrying infants, and they were in a shooting gallery. Black Hats fired Shadow tech blasts at them, Hulgismen charged down from the heights.

"Good Creation!" Davage yelled. "Are they insane?"

The Black Hats on their level, howling and laughing, filtered to the edge of the corridor and began firing Shadow tech at the people below. Hulgismen began leaping down. The two in the communications room exited to join the fun.

Down below the people running against the wall were being blown apart. Men, women, the infected, and wounded fell in a savage gallery of Shadow tech blasts and barbs. Davage, in disbelief, saw people down, people dying, people dead. An infant struggled under the bulk of its fallen mother. He saw the frightened survivors backed into a corner and several Black Hats slowly advancing on their position, savoring the kill.

"We're going!" he roared. "Syg, they're all standing on the edge of the parapet looking to the courtyards below, sweep them down!"

Davage tore through the doorway, followed by Syg, Ennez and Kilos.

Syg, refreshed from her sleep, and feeling much better, sent a huge column of Silver tech roaring down the corridor. The column slammed into the unaware Black Hats and Hulgismen, blowing some apart, sending the rest toppling down in a naked, erratic heap. The passageway was cleared of enemies.

Davage unsaddled his CARG. Lining up a Black Hat far below, he threw his CARG, sending it down in a lopsided, whistling frenzy. It passed through the Black Hat's chest and stuck into the ground.

"Get in there and send word to the ship!" With that he Wafted away and into the chaos below.

He reappeared down in the courtyard, standing in front of the frightened peasants. With MiMs drawn he retrieved his CARG and stood ready, facing the hoards.

Dumbly, blindly, the ragged survivors just stood there, watching him.

The Black Hats raised their arms, and Hulgismen began advancing in earnest.

"BACK!" Davage roared lighting his Sight. "GET BACK!"

Though they were wearing those strange goggles, ostensibly to protect themselves from his Sight, the Black Hats covered their eyes to keep from seeing. They cowered, truly frightened of it—Black Hats were normally fearless. The Hulgismen, naked, illuminated in the golden light stood and stared.

He panned this way and that, lighting them up, the Black Hats trying to avoid his gaze.

The sky blackened.

He looked up.

A looming Shadow tech beast, miles tall, wreathed in passing cloud, towered over the Keep and was sending a giant tentacle down into the courtyard. It was huge.

It blotted out the sky.

* * * * *

Kilos and Ennez ran into the communications room. The near end of the chamber was decorated in the Xandarr fashion, with intricate rugs of lurid colors, dyed veils, and a copious amount of pillows and poufs. At the far end of the room was the machine. It was a huge communications device—it looked like Ming Moorland technology. Very powerful, very expensive.

Ennez and Kilos looked it over. "Wow," he said. "Princess Marilith wasn't fooling around with the stuff, was she?"

"Nope. Ultra-wave … it's an ultra-wave!" Ki said, flipping switches.

"Do you know what you're doing? Can you reach the ship?" Ennez asked watching her adjusting the controls.

"Half a moment."

A soft wave of air filled the room. Ennez, alerted, looked around.

"Here, look here. We're sending, we're sending! The Ultra wave cut through the interference the StT's are creating like nothing."

Ennez activated his gerts and drew his jet staff. "Ki, there's someone in here with us!" he said climbing the walls.

Ki continued keying in the data transmission. "You sure?"

She looked back in time to feel a hard punch go across her face, and then quickly to her stomach—two of the hardest punches she'd ever felt. Ki was a veteran of many, many fights, with the bums in Tusck, the tramps in the Marines, and often with Dav in the gym. Syg too … Syg could hit hard for such a tiny woman, and if she managed to get her legs around you, forget it. But these, these were ruinously hard punches.

Tweeter, sitting on her shoulder took flight and landed on the communications device.

She swung back in response, her fists swishing through the air.

Another massive blow to the gut, and then what felt like a boot heel to the face. Ki went flying. "The Princess, she's in here with us under Cloak!" Ennez roared.

Guessing where the Princess might be, Ennez jumped down and fanned the area with his whirling jet staff. He heard and felt nothing, but thought he saw the staff shudder once or twice, possibly hitting a Cloaked person.

Pow, pow!! His lip opened up, then a crushing blow to the side of his face sent him sprawling. She had to be unarmed, having lost her weapons in the chaos of the battle, otherwise they'd both be dead by now.

Ki went to draw her gun, but it wasn't there. Her SK, now apparently gripped in the hand of a mad Cloaked princess—it too fell into the Cloak as well, the hallmark of a good Paint.

"Ennez!" she cried diving for cover. "Move, keep moving—she's got my SK!!"

Ennez hit his gerts and, moving as only a Hospitaler can, began a fast crawl/run on the wall like a big black and silver gecko.

A throaty high powered slug hit the wall right behind him making a pock mark the size of a small crater.

More craters blossomed behind him as he desperately ran.

Ennez added wings to his feet and tore across the wall. A loud, plaster-destroying auto shot followed him in a dusty trail, sending bits of wall everywhere.

The Cloak was perfect. Ki could see the shots hitting the wall, but could see no indication of where the Princess was standing, heard nothing and she didn't even smell gun smoke, though, no doubt, the room was probably full of it.

The Communications device was peppered with shots. It protested a moment, then Marilith's communicator died in smoke and went quiet. Tweeter again took flight, looking for a safe place to land.

And Ki saw something.

With his silver light filling the room, Ki thought she saw the faintest outline of a small girl holding a huge SK.

Ki lunged, tackling empty air. She rolled to the ground, and began punching, over and over as hard as she could. She had no idea if she was hitting anything, but, after a few swings, her fist got that ragged, chipped around the edges feeling she usually got after being in a fight.

Her SK reappeared and clattered to the floor, apparently dropped from the Princess's hand.

She reared back for a haymaker, and got socked in the jaw. Ki, usually able to take a good punch, was stunned with the force of the blow. Another punch sent her sideways.

She felt something light jump on top of her and start biting her cheek, drawing blood.

In a flurry, Ennez sprang off the wall and sent his Jet staff whirling over Ki's head. A huge blast of wind whistled through the room. The thick smell of gun smoke filled the room as the Cloak dropped.

"She's gone. She Wafted away!" Ki said, her face bleeding.

"You all right, Ki?"

"Yeah..."

"How was she shooting at me? Where's your palm sprander?"

"I took that thing off years ago, Ennez. If you're worth your stuff, you don't get disarmed.

He helped her up, and Tweeter landed on her shoulder. They looked at the shot up communicator.

"Did you get the signal out?"

"Yes, for just a bit, enough to send the Captain's code and ask for a ripcar."

Ennez grabbed the dazed Kilos, exited the room and helped her back into the tunnel hatch.

* * * * *

Davage looked at the gigantic tentacle coming down from the dizzying heights. Such a thing will demolish the entire courtyard, himself, the refugees, Black Hats and all.

He illuminated it in his Sight. It appeared to bubble and smoke. But it didn't stop. It kept coming.

There was a blast of wind. Syg, Wafted down from the heights.

She reached up and sent a huge gout of Silver tech skyward.

"DAV, I'M GOING TO KILL YOU LATER!" Syg roared as she coated the tentacle in silver. "DON'T YOU EVER DO SOMETHING LIKE THAT AGAIN!" she yelled, her eyes alight with green fire.

The creature appeared tentative and confused. It pulled back the silver coated tentacle and looked at it, watching as it began to dissolve. The Silver tech ate through the Shadow tech like acid. Dissolving Shadow tech came down in a foul rainstorm. Syg then threw up a huge silver bubble covering Davage and the refugees.

Davage picked a trembling child up, and gave him to one of the peasants. "Get back into the tunnels!" he said. "All of you!"

He looked around. "Wait!" he said. "You've wounded. Get these wounded to safety."

The refugees stopped. "But ..." one said softly. "They're all dead."

Davage Sighted. "No. Look there, that man is alive. There, that woman needs assistance. Over there, that child. There, there ... and there!" he said pointing with his CARG.

The refugees did as they were told and were astounded, Davage was right, many of the fallen were simply wounded.

The shield recoiled from a powerful explosion from outside. "Dav!" Syg yelled. "Hurry, we've got to get out of here!"

Davage returned to Syg's side and led her toward the tunnel entrance.

"Sorry, Syg," he said. "I couldn't bear to see those people dying just for us … slaughtered."

Her eyes softened as she climbed down. "You scared me to death, love."

He closed the tunnel door behind him and kissed her. "Leave the shield, let them batter it down and they'll find nothing."

Slowly, they advanced into the depths of the tunnel.

* * * * *

Lt. Verlin, Peter of Ruthven and Lady Poe of Blanchefort stood in a lonely section of Deck Six, in the neck of the ship. The Duke, Torrijayne, and Sage were all crowded into the dispensary—each out of danger, but tired and needing rest. Johnnie was in the dispensary with them, on guard in case Lord Milton should try again. A bowl of water containing a school of several Fins sat on the desk if they were needed.

Verlin really didn't know what to do. With the captain gone, with a mad invisible killer on the loose, she was standing in the hallway discussing sensitive ship security matters with two civilians: one a lady of standing who was once infamous for being mentally ill, the other an alleged pirate.

What else was she supposed to do?

She was in command of a ship surrounded by literally thousands of enemies—she had to adapt, be flexible, and use the resources available to her. She guessed that's something the captain would do.

A group of three Sisters stood nearby.

"Here, right here they are detecting an energy flux," Verlin said. "And they are not detecting any additional people on the ship, Cloaked or otherwise. So, that's a relief in any event," she said.

Peter looked at the floor. "I suppose, then, that Lord Milton is no longer aboard the ship, but rather back at his manor in Esther. Sage had mentioned the medallion. The medallion must some type of point to point teleporter. Therefore, in order to make use of it, you will need Medallion A at one end and Medallion B at the other. Is that how it works, Lady Poe?"

"Yes, I suppose so. It just works."

"So, this Medallion B, if true, will have to be around here somewhere," Verlin said.

"And, I'm guessing that it is probably fairly small, and either in one of our ships or on us at this moment."

Peter looked down at himself. "It must be. And, Medallion B has to be Cloaked."

He turned to Lt. Verlin. "Lt., could the Sisters check us for Cloaked items?"

"You needn't ask me, Lord Ruthven. Ask them directly."

The Sisters stood, headdresses bobbing.

"Sisters, could you please do us the honor of scanning us for Cloaked devices?"

The Sisters looked them over.

Lt. Verlin spoke up. "The Sisters say you are not carrying any Cloaked devices. They do say, however, you are armed to the whiskers, which I will be speaking to you and the Duke about later."

"This Medallion B has to be on one of our ships. "Sisters," Peter said, "could we please check our ships for Cloaked devices?"

Verlin spoke up. "They will be delighted."

The Com crackled to life overhead. "Lt., we have just received a signal from the planet surface. It's Captain Davage."

Verlin lit up. "The captain, are we sure?"

"The signal contained his personal code. It's him, there can be no doubt."

"What is his status?"

"He is barricaded in Xandarr Keep. He reports many Black Hats in the area along with several thousand Hulgismen, and several gigantic Shadow tech beasts. He is requesting a ripcar sent down on manual pilot. Once received, he will fly it out to safety."

Verlin shook her head. "Unacceptable. A ripcar, un-armed, will get blasted out of the sky. The *Seeker,* under Cloak and unseen, can at least fight the hoards back long enough to collect the captain and be off. With any luck the lost company will call in whilst we're in route. Com, inform the Helm we are going down and will pick up the captain personally."

"Lt., the Helm reports it is not advisable to enter the planet's atmosphere at this time."

"Com, inform the Helm that her opinion is noted. However, we are going down, and I suggest the Helm set herself to it. Verlin out!"

21—The Demons

The lab was dark, shut down for the night, though it thrummed and moved with mechanical life. Panels blinked and clicked with small, flashing lights and sounds. Ventilators droned with a loud but soothing whoosh of air. The shadows were everywhere, and they seethed with arcane movement.

Dark forms crept through the lab, snaked their way past the offices and machines, past the catwalks, equipment lockers and observation stations, to the center of the room, to the circle, to the silver seal trapped within.

Carahil was asleep, his whiskers twitched slightly. The dark forms settled into the shadows on the circle's perimeter. One dark form, dull red eyes staring, came forward and watched him sleep for a moment.

"Carahil," it finally said. "Carahil, wake up."

Carahil awoke, looked around for a moment wearily, then saw the figure. He shook his head and fluffed his whiskers. "Oh, hello, Mabs," he said. "I was wondering when you'd be by. I figured as much."

The figure, Mabs, shrugged. "I was just curious why you're still stuck in this circle?"

Carahil looked around, noted the others hiding in the darkness. "I know you're all here, come on out and let's be friends." His gaze turned back to the red-eyed creature. "I can't leave the circle, Mabs."

"You can't? Why not … it's nothing but a crude drawing of sand and chalk mixed together on the floor, barely a forth of an inch high. It's not even a perfect circle, it's lop-sided over there. Go ahead … go past it."

"I can't and you know it."

The red eyes blinked. "Why … `fraid you'll become a demon?"

"A demon like you, you mean?"

The eyes came forward into a milky pool of night-light. Mabs was a small cat, tabby in configuration and mackerel in color, complete with a large "M" stamped on her forehead. She was fragile in appearance, though appearances were obviously deceiving. The cat approached the circle and sat.

Her eyes were large and red.

"Yes, a demon like me. A demon like those around you. It's not so bad really, and not so different."

"Your presence is missed in the Windage, Mabs. You're on the wanted roster."

"Are we," she said.

Mabs the cat licked her paws and took a look around. Arranged around the circumference of the circle were numerous trays on wheels. Sitting in the trays were a vast assortment of medical tools: scalpels, knives, saws, hammers and drills. Other trays held larger, more industrial-style tools: laser drills, pneumatic hammers, rock borers and spreaders.

"What is all of this?" Mabs asked.

Carahil looked at the tools and shrugged. His diary appeared in a poof. He nosed through the pages. "Ah, it says right here I'm due to be vivisected tomorrow. Ten bells sharp."

Mabs pricked up her ears. "Oh, sounds frightening. Are you worried?"

"It doesn't say in the book if I should be worried or not. Lord Milton seems to think he'll become privy to all my secrets by cutting me open."

"Does Lord Milton believe there's some sort of instruction manual inside of you?"

"He must. He seems most eager for the vivisection."

Mabs flicked her tail. "Are you going to let them cut you open?"

"Do I have a choice?"

Beyond, in the shadows, there was restless movement.

"Certainly you do," Mabs said. "You don't have to sit there and let them try to cut you open—what rule says that? Show me the rule that says that. I'd never let them cut me open no matter how far I fall. I'd have this silly lab on the ground … I'd have Lord Milton crawling, naked and humbled."

"Then, I suppose that's why you're a demon in the Windage of Kind and I'm not. The rules say we must wait, we must endure them, put up with their silliness, even if they don't know entirely what they're doing. Do any of us really know what we're doing?"

"What do you know of the Windage of Kind? I was there for ages. I can tell you all about it."

"I've been to the Windage," Carahil replied.

"Oh? Why? What business would you have there?"

Carahil smiled. "I came to see you, Mabs."

"It's true," a deep, somewhat congested voice came from the shadows. "I saw him looking in. I tried to tell him to run, but he didn't hear me."

Mabs seemed taken aback a little. "You, came to see me?"

Carahil opened his book and nosed to a page. There was a sketch of the ugly, steamy buildings of the Windage of Kind. Looking out of one of the windows, was a small cat.

Mabs looked at the sketch, stood and pawed at the chalk line. "You made a decision to come see me at the Windage. What other decisions are you ready to make? The Softlings. They really are children, are they not? They are weak, unsure … lost and without direction."

"They can't see what we can see."

"They've decisions that need made …" Mabs said.

"They aren't up to making some of those decisions. They lack information."

"Well, if they won't make them, why not us. Why tie our hands? That's what we say in the Windage."

Carahil looked at the tools in the trays. "Lord Milton's made a decision … he's going to vivisect me."

"I'm not talking about that freak, Carahil."

Carahil raised a silver eyebrow. "And you know the correct decisions to be made, Mabs, do you, regardless of the pain and suffering they create?"

Mabs seemed to grow in size. "Right decisions are sometimes painful, Carahil. How many times does a child fear and hate their parents for the decisions made in their interest? It's all for the best. So, given that, why not cross the line. Why not free yourself, and do what needs doing?"

"I cannot."

The creatures listening in the dark came forward. A red-eyed monkey emerged from the shadows. "All the dying you saw … it's already underway. You could do something, you could stop it," he said. "You want to stop it."

"Hello Barr, I'm glad you're well. I've my friends in place. They will stop it if I am unable to."

A massive elephant appeared, the floor shaking under his huge round feet—again his eyes were a dull glowing red. "Many have already died. The Shadow tech beasts feast in earnest, and there is nobody to save them," he said through his trunk.

"You're here too, Maiax? My friends will face the beasts … they will fight."

A crane stepped forward, feathers shining and pink. "Your Mother is in grave danger."

Carahil's whiskers drooped. "My Mother, Ibilex?"

"She was beaten, chained, and forced to wear the Dora, all while you watched and did nothing."

"I needed her where she was. I …"

"You allowed her to suffer," Mabs said. "She nearly died, alone there in the dark, cold and frightened. She took the medallion she made, and, with trembling hands, she pressed it over and over. She cried out your name and still you didn't come."

A tear came to Carahil's eye. "I needed her where she was. I will make it up to her."

Mabs' eyes grew large. "Then, make her proud … save those people while she watches, cast aside the Shadow tech … cleanse Xandarr."

Carahil looked at the chalk line—a barrier only in his mind, in his soul.

"Save your Mother," Mabs said.

The line stood in front of him. His Mother was on the other side of it. All those people he wanted to save were on the other side too. He turned to his book again.

Mabs spat and seized the book with her tail, sending it spiraling away. "Enough of that stupid book! Cross the line, Carahil."

"And become a monster? Fall into the Windage of Kind? I'd fail her," he said.

Mabs became frustrated. "But you are already a monster, Carahil. You are already a freak!! Do you really think you'll be so different once you cross the line? Will you suddenly be cruel? Will you suddenly be evil? You will still be you … just more free, more wise. More able to help. You will be unchained."

Carahil looked at the line. "That true, Maiax?" he said to the elephant. The elephant looked down at the floor, the light of his eyes glinting off of his curved tusks.

"Cross it!!" Mabs yelled.

So easy, he thought. So easy … He thought of his Mother, smiling, innocent, sitting with him in the Grove, reading stories to him that he already knew but loved to hear anyway.

His Mother, in agony, wailing in the dark.

He moved to the edge.

"Yes, Carahil, cross over and save those people, save your Mother … and join with us."

Carahil glanced at his book. It was open to one of the many sketches of his Mother, Lady Poe. So happy. So proud.

He stopped, thought a moment, then backed away. "And, with good intentions, I'd, through my actions, hurt, maim and slay all those I wanted to save."

"That's not true."

"It is true. How many have you slain, Mabs?"

"Not many."

"Really, not many? Come now, Mabs, tell me about Zall 88. What about that?"

The Cat's face darkened. "Zall 88?"

"That place of peace and enlightenment laid waste—Xaphans tearing the throats out of other Xaphans. You were worshipped there as a goddess."

"That wasn't my fault. I gave them knowledge."

"Of course it wasn't … you couldn't help how it turned out."

"I had nothing to do with what happened. I was trying to help. I was trying to help, Carahil!"

"I know," Carahil said.

He turned to the Elephant. "And you, Maiax, tell me of the Bodice."

"The Bodice?" the elephant named Maiax said.

"Yes, those poor souls, tilling their poisoned land, just wanting to be left in peace. Wanting the drums to stop."

"I tried to save them … The Sisterhood didn't help them, so they turned to me. I tried to save the children. I loved those people. They were good people."

"I know you did. And the only mistake you made was that you tried to do it all for them. You didn't try to help them to save themselves. You didn't weight the scales, and look what happened. They cried out for you, and across the angry cosmos, you couldn't hear them. Now they are extinct, and you—their protector—are turned into a demon wasting away in the Windage."

The elephant named Maiax crashed to the floor of the lab and put the stumps of his large gray legs over his head, trying to shut out the voices of those who had died trusting in him. "I tried to save them … I promised the children. I was their protector," he repeated. "They trusted me …"

The cat's face cringed in sadness. "He didn't mean for that to happen. Why did all those souls have to die? How could we, who are so powerful, have failed so terribly?"

"Because, when you break the rules, everything you do goes bad, goes wrong and all those you labored so hard to protect simply die in a manner you didn't expect. That's balance—like it or not. That's the Frustration of the Gods. That's why the rules are there … to prevent things like Zall 88. To protect good people like the Bodice."

Mabs jumped over the chalk line and nuzzled into Carahil's side. The other demons sat next to the circle and appeared sad too.

"And I came to tempt you, to sway you to become like me, and here I am, looking to you for comfort. Perhaps misery truly does enjoy company."

"Help us, Carahil," they cried.

"You were simply overzealous, and a victim of balance—and it is because of your example that I have labored so hard, to do it the way the Universe wants it. If I am to save the people of Xandarr, I must depend on those whom I have brought to the table to save me first. And should I be successful, should this work, I will go to the Arborium and insist they forgive you. I will insist that you get a second chance. That shall be my price."

22—Medallion B

The Sisters wandered around in the Duke's *Goshawk,* looking this way and that. Lt. Verlin was impatient, she wanted to go to the bridge and supervise the Helm. They will soon be plunging under Cloak into the atmosphere. Soon they will be linking up with Captain Davage.

Verlin stepped through the docking ring into the Duke's larger *Goshawk* ship. She looked around—impressed by its design. She also couldn't help but notice Lady Poe and Lord Peter making eyes at each other. Not the best time to be endeavoring to cultivate a relationship, still, Lady Poe seemed to like Peter, and, Verlin had to admit, this "pirate" was a handsome man and seemed to be a decent, capable fellow.

The Sisters were wandering around the ship, looking this way and that. "Anything, Sisters?" she asked.

They became interested in a spot on the floor near the cargo hold and flooded Verlin with thoughts. "They say there was another energy bloom, similar to the one on Deck Six, that formed right in this area."

One of the Sisters began pointing at the wall outside the cargo hold.

Verlin looked at the wall. "The Sister says there's something here, in a deep, deep Cloak.

The Sister began waving at the wall, looked annoyed, rolled up her sleeves and waved again, and suddenly a gangly, blinking contraption appeared. It was a series of three un-elegant boxes inter-connected with thick, insulated cables. A large hunk of rough-hewn black metal was mounted in front of the boxes and hummed. Several thick power cables tapped into the main ship's power grid.

Peter looked at it and cursed. "Right here under our noses, and stealing our power to boot!" He knelt down to examine it more closely. "Yes, yes … without question, this assemblage is our theoretical Medallion B. It's complex, yet stripped down and functional, clearly the work of the Science Ministry; several members of which Lord Milton is very friendly with. With this device, Lord Milton could come and go pretty much anywhere in the ship with a remote control, as it appears to have a considerable range."

Lady Poe's face, still swollen and bruised, lit up as she watched him examine it.

Verlin stared at the device. "I'll call an engineering team to have it deactivated."

Peter looked back at her, a little annoyed. "No need," he said pulling a set of intricate tools out of his duster and set to work, his mechanical skill readily apparent.

The ship gave a lurch. The Com quickly buzzed in. "Lt., the Helm is requesting your presence on the bridge—immediately."

Verlin sighed. "Lord Ruthven, I cannot jeopardize the lives of two civilians in my charge. I shall call an engineering detachment at once."

"This vessel is not a Fleet asset. It is property of the Duke of Oyln."

"It is also illegal and will be impounded."

"Captain Davage dropped those charges, Lt."

The ship bucked hard. The Com again: "Lt., the Helm again urgently requests your presence on the bridge!"

Verlin looked highly frustrated. "Com, you tell the Helm to roll up her sleeves, plant her feet, and put both hands on that wheel, and if she needs a couple of stout lads to help her out, then we'll do that!"

She turned to Peter. "Well, sir Ruthven, it appears that I do not have time to argue with you on this matter, and it seems you and Lady Poe are making good progress here. I'd like updates as they become available, and, I am sending a squadron of Marines, in case Lord Milton chooses to come back through."

"Certainly, and thank you, Lt.," Poe said before Peter could reply.

Verlin turned to leave. "I better to the bridge before the Helm has a heart attack."

Peter continued what he was doing. "Don't be alarmed … you're going to hear some strange sounds in a moment here."

There was a popping sound, and then a series of trilling musical notes. Verlin looked back and Peter, kneeling in front of the device, was calmly taking a panel off the machine, Poe sitting next to him.

"What's that sound?" she asked.

"Peter, what is going on?" Poe asked.

"Countdown to detonation—this device is booby-trapped."

Verlin thought about what he just said for a moment. "What!" she exclaimed.

Peter appeared perfectly calm. "Yes," he said, "there's a bomb in here … good-sized one too. Got about ten more seconds." Casually he fiddled with the inside of the box.

Verlin's eyes bugged out of her head. "Can you … Are you able to … What's the status of …"

"Should I wrap it up, Peter?" Poe asked, concerned.

"No need." Peter pulled a small module out of the box, and the countdown stopped. "There we are. It's a Dortus 6, every expensive, very dangerous. Hard to spot as well. Your engineering detachment, would, no doubt, have tried a standard ingress, causing an instant detonation."

He tossed it to Verlin, and she caught it in her chest with both hands. "It helps to be a sneaky, underhanded, bottom-dealing pirate sometimes, you know, Lt.?"

Verlin sat down on the hatch ledge. "I don't know if my heart can take this," she said, her Howell accent coming out very thick.

"Never you mind, Lt., it's rendered safe," Peter said.

The ship violently lurched. Somewhat wobbly, Verlin stood and left.

Poe watched Peter begin opening the remaining boxes. "You have such skilled hands, sir."

"I am pleased my feeble skills are to your liking, Lady Poe," he said, his arms buried in the depths of one of the boxes.

Smiling, seizing the moment, she did something she had never done before; not in two hundred years of life. She wrung her hands, took a deep breath, and kissed him on the cheek.

"That … is for being my savior just now."

He stopped and blushed. "If there is thanks to be meted out, Lady Poe, it is I who should be kissing you—those fast hands, those miraculous creations of yours, the lives of my brother, and my Duke, and my future duchess … all thanks to you."

"Well then, Lord Ruthven, I suppose a kiss on the cheek will do nicely as payment, if I may be so bold." Poe smiled and leaned forward, head cocked to one side, awaiting her kiss.

Peter put his tools down, and went to kiss her on the cheek.

She turned her head at the last moment, and they kissed.

23—An Unflyable Ship

The *Seeker* stumbled through the thin air of the upper atmosphere, struggling to stay on course. Saari, the helmsman, mouth pulled back in terror, her blue hair quickly falling out of its clips and barrettes, had a death grip on the wheel. The ship was pulling hard to port, and the nose was bound and determined to sink into a terminal dive. Moving it required more strength than she had, and two crewmen had been assigned to assist her: all three straining against the unbalanced pressures, trying to keep the ship righted. She could see through her helm viewer that there was Shadow tech everywhere outside. There were tiny Shadow tech ships flying in locust-like swarms. The captain had always told her that the Helm was the heart of the ship, that through it, one could feel the forces of space moving all around. She could feel the multitude of dull thuds as the black ships blindly bounced off the Cloaked sides of the ship through the wheel, but the sensations told her nothing, gave her no insight. She also felt the slight magnetic pull of the colossally huge, spherical Shadow tech creatures flying through the air. Again, the information gave her no additional thoughts. All she knew was that the ship, in its current state, was virtually unflyable, and were it not for the Cloak, they should have been devoured some time ago. Saari thanked her Mother's Name that Xandarr was a fairly placid world; any storms or great amount of turbulence and the ship easily might have rolled over and nose-dived into the ground by now.

Verlin stood nearby, holding onto the railing. "Helm, ETA to Xandarr Keep?"

"Five minutes … if we survive."

"Keep to a 'Can-Do' spirit, Helm. Good, good. When we arrive, I want you to locate a suitable spot and stand on station. There we will try to contact the captain either by Com or by Sister, pick him up as quickly as we can, then get our League tails out of here!"

Verlin turned to Sasai at the Fore Sensing position. "Crewman, what are you seeing down there?"

"Shadow tech, Lt., and plenty of it. The ring around the planet is dissipating as the small black vessels making up its composition are beginning to blanket the surface of the planet, flying around randomly, intercepting anything that tries to take off—I saw them swarm a launching transport not long ago. The big ones, those huge Shadow Tech creatures appear to be razing towns and villages to the ground, and, ma'am … they appear to be eating the inhabitants."

"Eating them?"

"Yes, ma'am, by the dozens."

"Ma'am, what should we do?"

"The wires are choked with people crying out for help," the Com added. "Any orders, ma'am?"

Verlin stood there a moment. Everyone looked at her. "I don't know, I really don't. With luck we'll soon have the captain back. We'll fully brief him on our findings, and proceed from there. We all need him back."

The ship began pulling hard to the left, Saari and the two crewman fought to level their flight. Verlin turned to give them a hand. If anybody on the ship wanted the captain back, it was her.

* * * * *

"Well, that's got it, I think," Peter said.

Poe, leaning against him, rested her chin on his shoulder, and peered into the box. It was completely out of character for her to behave so—she was normally so reserved and shy, but, Peter didn't seem to mind, they were all alone and it just felt right.

"This block, this one here, is what controls the system. It then feeds power to these crude pieces of urilium, which vibrate at a super-fast frequency, opening a point-to-point portal."

"Remarkable …" Poe said staring at Peter, putting her arm around him, desperate to kiss him again.

"Now, all I need to do is pull this component here, and the whole thing will be rendered useless."

Peter pulled out a small bit of circuitry. The lights and sounds it was making stopped. It went dead. "So much for Lord Milton."

They stood and began making their way out of the ship, when Poe suddenly stopped and shuddered.

"Lady Poe, anything wrong?"

She stood there. "I can feel it … all around us. Shadow tech. And …"

Her Blanchefort blue eyes grew wide.

"Lady Poe?"

She seized him by the hand and dragged him to the front of the ship. "Peter, Peter come quickly!"

They reached the cockpit and looked out the glass. Outside, Shadow tech in waves and layers, was everywhere. Several thousand feet below, a huge Shadow tech beast, at least three miles high, was at work flattening a town.

"This is it, Peter—this is what Carahil was talking about! This is what he saw! This is what he was trying to stop. Dear Creation, he was trying to save these poor people. Look at it … this whole planet will be laid to waste."

"What can be done?"

"We must find Carahil. He'll do something, he'll stop it."

Through the glass, Shadow tech was everywhere.

"We don't even know where Mr. Carahil is. He vanished."

"Lord Milton must have him. He must be restraining him. Peter, is it possible for us to use the device, this Medallion B, to go to his location?"

"Yes, but …"

"Then we must reactivate it and find Carahil."

Poe pulled Peter back to the silent device.

* * * * *

Using his Sight, Davage helped guide the refugees through the tunnels. The Shadow tech beast above was tearing up the landscape, and occasionally, it lucked into a tunnel, collapsing that run. After a bit, they made it into a fairly safe chamber, where the wounded were laid out.

Looking back with his Sight, Davage found Ki and Ennez, moving about in the tunnels following Tweeter. Syg using telepathy, reached Ki and they were able to assist them to the chamber. Ennez, though tired, began looking at the survivors.

Before long the King of Xandarr appeared. He appeared both sad and angry.

"I thought you understood not to waste our sacrifice. Did you get word to your ship?"

"We did," Ki said, her face a mess after her fight with the princess.

Davage stood. "You set women and children out for slaughter, King. I could not allow that!"

"This is a dark day! If you get to your ship and you do as I have begged, then perhaps other women and children may yet be saved." His face darkened. "My beloved wife was out there, leading the people!"

Davage looked around. "Is she here? Is she safe?"

A tear rolled down Balor's face. "She died up there, Captain … buying you time. Buying all of Xandarr time."

"I'm sorry, King Balor."

There was, high above, a commotion of explosions. Outside, the Shadow tech beasts and Black Hats scattered about were probing the dark skies overhead. They probed the skies with ebon searchlights, a sort of opposite from Davage's Sight. They were looking for something, something they were desperate to find.

Davage had a thought. "No …" he said. "It can't be."

He looked around, Sighting hard. Then, to the north of the ruins of the Keep, he saw the *Seeker* descending from the heights in a deep, fabulously intricate Cloak. "Good Creation, they've brought the ship down for us. It must be badly damaged for it's barely able to fly in a straight line."

"Have they dropped the Cloak, are they able to see it, love?" Syg asked.

"No, Madame Torrijayne must have put up a Painted Cloak, because it's a damn good one—I'm having difficulty seeing it myself, but the Black Hats are looking hard."

"I guess she's good for something," Syg said.

He turned to Kilos. "Ki, can you get in contact with the Sisters?"

Ki closed her eyes and concentrated. "Yes … yes, Dav, I can. They're close enough now."

"Good. Ki, confirm our identity with the Sisters, then tell them to have the ship pass beneath the pinnacle of Xandarr Keep. We will then drop down onto the ship and enter through a hatch. Link up: two hours. We'll need to get a move on."

"Aye, Dav! I'm telling them."

Davage went to Ennez. "Ennez, what's the status of these wounded?"

He shook his head. "Bad Dav, these five here are critical."

"Then they are coming with us. We'll treat them aboard the *Seeker*, then return them home once it is safe to do so. King Balor, we will need people to help us carry them to the Xandarr Keep pinnacle."

The King's face brightened a bit. "You will have them!"

Davage looked around a bit more, trying to become familiar with the landscape.

He saw something. "Oh, dear Creation ..."

"What is it, Dav?" Syg asked.

"I see a huddled group of Black Hats in the levels above near the north wall."

"So? There're lots of Black Hats up there."

"Syg, I recognize some of them from our battle in the great hall. These are the Black Hats that Carahil's figurines carried away." Davage was dumbfounded. "I—I assumed they were carried off and killed, but there they are. It never occurred to me that ..."

"Dav, I'm not following you."

"Syg, Carahil's figurines didn't kill the Black Hats, they freed them. The Black Abbess's darkness has been shattered. I don't know how he managed it, but they're free."

"Oh, that trickster!" Syg said. "Why didn't he just kill them? This isn't a game. The Black Hats up there are playing for keeps."

"I suppose he thought they were worth trying to save, Syg. I mean, with the Point there's no stopping it once started unless the Black Hat is killed, yes? So in that case he had no choice but to kill with the blue fire. But, for the rest, he saved them. Perhaps there's a lesson in that."

"How many do you see out there, Dav?" Ki asked.

"I see ... forty-four to be precise. They are huddled, confused. They appear lost. Some appear to be wounded. One with a head of blue hair is trying to lead them to some extent; to keep them together and guide them to safety. There aren't very many safe places up there. I see Hulgismen on the prowl and a vast flock of Shadow tech birds en route from the west. That flock will pick their bones clean. It'll be on them in minutes! They've nowhere to go! Their death is on the wing!"

"Any StT's?" Syg asked.

"No. There's a Cabalist symbol nearby keeping them away—I can see its light. The leader seems to have realized that something special is in that area and is trying to take advantage of that small protection. But, they're penned in and wide open to attack from above."

"Forty-four Black Hats?" Ki said. "Why don't they just blow that Shadow tech flock and the Hulgismen away?"

"No," Syg answered, "you sort of have to relearn how to do everything once you're freed. That's what I remember. They aren't going to be able to do much in the way of competently defending themselves. Maybe if they had another hour or two to get themselves together perhaps, but ..."

Davage drew his CARG and began down a tunnel. "They don't have an hour."

"Captain, where are you going?" Balor demanded.

"Outside. I'm going to get them in here."

"They're Black Hats, Captain! They have come to kill us!"

"They came here to create mayhem true enough, and have found themselves redeemed instead. You yourself said redemption is always possible, and that has just been proved. Look there, you had to crawl through the mud to cleanse your soul; they had to pass through a fire storm and had the good fortune to encounter a being that cared enough to take the extra step to not kill, but to set them free. Now, they are lost children requiring shelter. I am going up to get them."

"You cannot!" Balor put his hands on Davage's shoulders. "Those Shadow tech birds will pick your bones as clean as theirs."

"Get out of my way."

The people watched as the two squared off. Syg and Ki joined Davage at his side.

"You cannot go up there!" Balor repeated. "You are needed beyond these walls. If there are people needing saving above, and you say they can be trusted, then I'll go! The north wall you said, yes? I will lead them down here. If you fall we are lost. If I fall, then perhaps you'll remember that I died trying to save those in need. That I died speaking you the truth!"

A man stood. "I'll come with you, King. I am not afraid."

"Nor am I. I will come," another said.

"And I!"

Balor and his group set off, and, with Davage watching, soon all forty-four Black Hats were in the tunnels, having been fetched only moments before the Shadow tech flock discovered them. They huddled in a mass: eyes wide, parched mouths lolled open. Ennez treated their wounds; some were quite severe. One had been shot by Ki's SK—and lived! The fifty caliber shell passed right through her side, somehow missing everything breakable or vital. Ki was open-mouthed over the improbability of that one.

"Carahil must have been looking out for you, lady," Ki said as Ennez treated the huge wound. She gazed at him blankly in return. The King and his folk, though initially hesitant, brought them food and drink as the birds screeched overhead, fretting over the warm flesh denied them.

* * * * *

It was the best news Verlin had gotten in a while. The Sisters, calm and collected as usual, explained that they had received a telepathic message from Lt. Kilos with the Captain's Code, instructing them to pass beneath the pinnacle of Xandarr Keep, and that the captain will drop down onto the top of the ship and manually enter. The message also contained news of the missing Marines—that they, and the Sister they defended, had fallen. Terrible news.

But, time for mourning later, first it was time to collect the captain, the countess, Samaritan Ennez and Lt. Kilos.

Kilos ...

Verlin couldn't wait to get that Bronzer in the gym.

Helmsman Saari, her blue hair a fallen disaster, protested. "Ma'am, we cannot maneuver the ship that close to a large, fixed structure on the ground, we'll crash!"

"I don't want to hear it, crewman! That is a direct order from the captain, and he is depending on us to be where we are supposed to be! Turn that wheel and get it done!"

On the cone, the sprawling complex of Xandarr Keep, now a largely fallen ruin, loomed ahead. Four Shadow tech beasts, miles high, roamed the perimeter, digging up the ground, and a drifting cloud of black ships milled about everywhere. Black searchlights panned about looking for them.

The pinnacle of the Keep rose up high off of the ground at least a thousand feet. Large, smooth, onion-shaped, it was a typical Xandarr-style dome. At least it was a fairly open area with lots of places to put the ship.

Ebon streams of dark light moved around all over. The Black Hats were searching for them in earnest. They could not stay here long.

* * * * *

Getting up to the top of the pinnacle was tough going, especially with the wounded, and it was a long, long climb. Every one of them was winded. Toward the top, Davage found a small hatch leading outside. Due to the extreme slope of the exterior of the dome, there wasn't really any place to stand and it was a long way down. Looking around, Davage could see the *Seeker* coming in under Cloak, flying terribly; almost laughably bad. He couldn't see any real damage, so he was at a loss. Perhaps crewman Saari had been hurt or killed, and a stand-in was at the helm, that must be it. He Sighted into the bridge, and there was Saari and several lads holding onto the wheel. Saari's blue hair, passed down from her mother's House Pitcock line, was all over the place, and she appeared to be in an ongoing argument with Lt. Verlin. He noted Verlin's SK was nearly empty—obviously something odd had happened on the ship since he left. In any case, it was painful watching the ship stumble in.

Finally, the frontal section of the ship slid in about a hundred feet below.

"Ki! Ki, tell the Sisters to have them raise the ship about sixty feet. Then, we'll just slide down."

"One sec, Dav," Ki said. "Ok!"

Dutifully, Davage watched the ship rise until it was only about ten feet down. He and Syg climbed out onto the precarious exterior of the dome having no fear of the heights. Their ability to Waft made long falls meaningless. Ki poked her head out of the hatch and, of course, saw and heard nothing below. "You sure it's down there, Dav?" she asked tentatively as Tweeter chirped.

"Come on, Ki ..." he laughed. He pulled her out and lowered her down, but Ki was shaky. All she could see was that she was standing on nothing—such was the total and powerful nature of the Cloak. "Dav!"

she called up, trying to steady herself. "Where do I go? Where's the nearest hatch?"

"To your three o'clock, ten paces."

Tweeter swirled off her shoulder and went to the hatch. Ki turned and followed him. She knelt down. "Am I there?"

"You're there."

Tweeter jumped back onto her shoulder as she felt around with her hands. "No, it's no good. I can't work the access panel if I can't see or feel it."

"Just hold there, Ki, and I'll be down in a moment." They began carefully lowering down the wounded. They then lowered Ennez down.

"Your turn, Syg," Davage said.

She smiled. "I'm going to sleep for a week after this is over, love, and you're going to be there with me the whole time."

"Looking forward to it." He kissed her and lowered her down. He then leaned into the hatch and told the refugees to go back down and hide.

Sirens went off. A hundred black searchlights trained their beams on the huddled people standing on the hull. Having a fixed target to concentrate on, the Black Hats brought down the Cloak, and there was the *Seeker* in all its glory, roaring like a banshee.

Shadow tech ships, monsters and blasts from below began converging on their location and the ship rocked with concentrated Shadow tech hits. Davage jumped down and Ki, now able to see the hatch, had already gotten it open and was lowering the wounded in. A black ship came rolling in from 9:00 pm. Syg reached up and shot it down with Silver tech.

A blast of Shadow Tech rolled into the starboard wing, yawing the ship.

Battleshot batteries from all quarters of the ship opened up in answer, thrumming with impossibly loud reports, not destroying but scattering the black ships and raking the Stenned Black Hats on the ground.

The *Seeker* was trapped, it was a sitting duck. There was no place for it to go.

A towering Shadow tech beast came in and seized the neck of the ship with several tentacles. Syg loosed five blobs of Silver tech which quickly formed into her trusty *Seeker* familiars. In a buzzing cloud of silver missiles and tiny shot, they flew up and engaged the beast, swirling around, the creature pawing at them.

It released the *Seeker* made to destroy these little buzzing hornets, waving its tentacles in a frustrated frenzy.

More Shadow tech blasts came in, slamming into the frontal hull, pinning the ship in. The Black Hats had the *Seeker* right where they wanted her, and they were not going to let her go.

As Davage made to close the hatch, he saw an amazing thing. From the ruins of the Keep, a flare was fired, rising into the turbid sky in a lazy arc. Charging up from hidden shelters, about a hundred motley Xandarr ships leapt into the air to engage the black ships. The sky around Xandarr Keep became a confused furball of spiraling, tumbling, firing vessels.

One of the Xandarr ships strafed a nearby courtyard—Cloaked Black Hats, unprepared and unStenned, died in the firing and the blasts of incoming Shadow tech greatly lessened.

They made a hole. The *Seeker* wobbled out into clearer air. Shadow tech ships closed in from all quarters, only to be engaged by Xandarr ships and Syg's silver familiars.

Davage shut the hatch and headed for the bridge as the ship began fitfully climbing for altitude.

* * * * *

"Captain on the bridge!" Verlin shouted with delight, seeing the lift doors open.

Davage stormed onto the bridge, and headed for the helm with Ki and Syg following. Verlin and Ki eyed each other darkly. "Aft quarter!" he roared.

"Aft quarter, aye!"

The moment his hands touched the helm, he recoiled. "What in the name of Creation has happened to the Helm?"

"Sir," Saari said, "the Helm was sabotaged, and quickly reattached without calibration. The ship is barely flyable."

"Sabotaged? You flew the ship down from the heights of low orbit with the Helm like this?"

"Yes, sir, I did, sir!" Saari said with a touch of pride.

Davage gripped the wheel. "I saw you had several lads helping you out with the wheel in such a state of over-balance, well, no matter. Helm, I want you to pay careful attention to what I am about to do and I want you to remember it—it will serve you well in the years to come."

Saari watched closely in rapt attention. Verlin also stopped what she was doing to watch.

"Through the Helm, the ship speaks to you, Lady Saari—you must listen to what it is saying. Now, I want a fifteen degree nose down, with a port counter flood of nineteen minutes. Engineering, I want ten degree boost to the near starboard thruster bank, and two-quarters yaw, after-pitch!"

After a moment, Davage appeared satisfied. "There, much better."

With that, Davage cranked the wheel and banked the ship hard. Saari and Verlin couldn't believe what they had just seen.

He Sighted through the hull, outside, Shadow tech was flying everywhere. Swarms of Shadow tech ships spewed black spheres, which the Sisters stationed in the ship's tower dispelled and kept at bay.

BOOM! BOOM! Several Black Hats were peppering the *Seeker* with Shadow Tech blasts. He was about to bank away and engulf them with Battleshot when they were lifted into the air and pulled apart—the Sisters from the tower again.

More Black Hats to the south in the ruins of the Keep. Down came Syg's familiars screaming in for the kill. Tiny missiles, silver battleshot. "I just got three of them, Dav!" Syg cried. "Ha, ha! That's right, your Sten doesn't work against my Silver tech, does it? So sorry! Oh Creation—one of them is down! Took a blast in the rear. I've got four left out there."

Davage hauled the *Seeker* around in a hard, sucked in turn. He saw several huge Shadow tech monsters were converging on the remains of Xandarr Keep.

He spun the wheel, avoiding a massive tentacle swing. "Canister Control, fire in two, port quarter!"

Several canisters popped out and exploded at various places in the sphere's head. The Shadow tech stretched and deformed, but regained its previous shape. "There's too much, we can't damage it!"

Sighting, Davage watched Syg's little armada of familiars engage the beast and pepper it with canister and shot. He watched the beast taking damage; little holes of melting Shadow tech formed on its head. It took flight and fled the area, the tiny *Seekers* following in a harassing cloud to finish it off.

Syg stood up. "Silver tech, Dav, Silver tech plows right through it. My familiars are making quick work of these Shadow tech beasts. Ha! Write off another one! He's down! Oh, Feature, I just lost a familiar! Damn Shadow tech birds got it!"

Davage thought a moment. "Syg, do you have enough Silver tech to coat some of our canisters?"

"To what?"

"To coat them in Silver tech. Given your familiar's performance, I'll wager a canister coated in a little Silver tech will be instantly deadly to these creatures."

"Yes, yes, I suppose so," Syg said.

Ki jumped up. "Come on, let's go. We'll start in the Forward Canister bay. I'll show you where it is."

Syg headed to the lift door. She stopped, ran to Davage and kissed him hard on the lips, not caring about decorum at the moment. "I love you," she said heading toward the lift.

Saari stared at the holo-cone in horror. "Captain!" she cried as a blizzard of black spheres loomed ahead—too many for the Sisters to disperse.

* * * * *

In a flash, Poe, Johnnie and Peter appeared in a dark metal corridor. Dizzy, feeling momentarily sick, they clutched their heads and allowed waves of nausea to pass over them. Nearby, a gangly machine similar to the one mounted on the Duke's ship, thrummed against a metal wall: Medallion A no doubt.

Recovering a bit, they drew their weapons: their large buzzing Hertamers. Johnnie also took his SAPP scarf off and hardened it—it coiled about like a snake for a moment then took the shape of a black, arcane sword.

"Now, Lady Poe, please stay close to me," Peter said holding his energy gun.

Johnnie began creeping down the corridor. "Give it a rest, Peter."

Ahead, there was a vigorous commotion. There were sounds of heavy machinery running, and the roars and cries of a large animal drifting up from below.

Cautiously, they made their way to the end of the corridor.

They reached a catwalk overlooking a huge, machine-laden laboratory. Down, far below on the floor of the laboratory, were several Science Ministry officials, most of them holding ropes. One was lugging around a huge laser drill.

They were trying to subdue a silver seal with the ropes. Several discarded ropes lay strewn about, apparently having been bit through. The seal was roaring with displeasure.

"Carahil!!" Poe cried.

The Scientists looked up.

Carahil looked up.

A wry voice came from across the open floor of the lab. "Well now, vinegar-pissers, what have we here?"

Lord Milton, gangly on his overly long legs and huge wig, appeared on the other side of the catwalk opposite them.

"Lord Milton!" Poe said. "I'm assuming you are Lord Milton, we are here to free Carahil, for he is needed on the planet Xandarr. I have hopes that you will not impede us."

"*Vith!*" he screamed in an odd voice. Milton appeared to be frightened of Lady Poe for a moment. Then he rocked with laughter. "You … vehement, Vith-vixen, I was shortly on my way to KILL THE LOT OF YOU on the *Seeker*, but, as you are here, you've saved me, at least for now, a nauseating trip."

"You nearly killed my brother and Torrijayne, and you badly wounded the Duke!" Peter said.

"You mean they're not dead? Oh, dear … and how is that Toe-tapping Temptress, and your Book-Reading, Butt-Wiper of a brother? Perhaps I should have shot him in the face and improved his looks."

"He's better than you're going to be in a moment!" Johnnie said leveling his Hertamer and firing.

FWWEEEII!!

Lord Milton, all arms and legs, ducked with unusual agility and returned fire with his Inseroth.

BLAM!!

Peter formed a shield with his SAPP and the bullet thudded off of it.

FWEEEEII!! Johnny returned fire. Again, Milton ducked, incredibly fast. He brandished his gun. BLAM!! BLAM!!

Peter fell to his knees with the force of the shots against his SAPP shield. "Johnnie, will you take him down! My SAPP's coming apart!"

BLAM!! came another shot. His SAPP collapsed and fell into dusty strips.

BLAM!! Lady Poe stepped forward and caught the bullet out of the air with her lightning fast Silver tech.

"Lord Milton, stop this foolishness right this moment!" Poe said.

Milton gave a devilish smile. "You blonde-headed, bullet-snatching belladonna. You … Vith. That is an interesting trick, I must say. Hmmm …"

Poe raised her arm, and sent a thick stream of Silver tech across the open space of the heights and roped Lord Milton from head to foot.

"Now, sir," she said. "We shall take Carahil and be on our way."

Lord Milton, wrapped up like a piece of silver taffy, laughed. "I cannot allow you to leave … nether you two Ruthven Rumpots, or you, woman—you vile bag of Vith-Vomit. And, for that matter, I cannot allow anyone on the *Seeker* to survive as well. I've an image to maintain."

They began making their way down the stairs. "Lord Milton, I do not wish for any to be harmed here. Please, allow us to free Carahil and depart in peace," Poe repeated.

"Mother!" Carahil cried from below. "Break this circle!"

His eyes widened. "Look out!"

Suddenly: BLAM!! BLAM!! Huge Inseroth shots rained down on them. Lady Poe of Blanchefort, not prepared for the shots, fell, blood seeping from a large chest wound on her left side.

"Lady Poe!" Peter shouted as he dove to her side, shielding her from further blasts.

"Mother!" Carahil cried as he loped against the edge of the circle.

Though he was still all wrapped up, somehow Lord Milton had gotten his Inseroth out of the wrappings, and was brandishing it.

"Oh, you gown-wearing gut-grinder, wake up, will you!!" he shouted. "I suppose you'll simply forget the matter of my attempted murder of pretty much everybody on board the *Seeker*? Let bygones be bygones will we? No, no, you, along with these Ruthven teetotalers are going to die!"

He looked down at the scientists standing there with their ropes.

"Well, you pack of Larry Labcoats, and Billy Button-pushers, don't just stand there—get them!"

The scientists dropped their ropes and advanced on the stairs. Johnnie and Peter leveled their weapons, and quickly shot down two. The remaining four looked at each other and then began running in the opposite direction.

"Oh, you paid traitors, you!" Milton cried. "Take that!"

BLAM!! BLAM!! BLAM!! BLAM!! He gunned them down himself.

Johnnie aimed and hit Lord Milton square in the chest with his Hertamer,

"Ha!" he cried. "If that Blonde-headed Bimbo survives a few minutes more, I'll be sure to thank her for this nice shield she's made around me! Very handy and quite fashionable!" Milton got another arm out of the silver tech wrapping. He held several RED HAWS in his bony fingers, which he began throwing down.

Quickly, Johnnie shot two out of the air and side-glanced a third, which clattered to the far side of the lab and opened up with a wiry whine. It gruesomely cubed the flesh of one of the fallen Scientists.

A fourth came down and Peter shot it out of the air. Milton was enraged. "You finger-wagging, toilet-water drinking …"

Milton didn't get a chance to finish his tirade. Peter quickly trained Lord Milton in his sights and fired, hitting him square in the head where his face exploded in a tattered spray of cooked flesh, shattered bone and a bloody wig. He slumped down in a long armed, leggy, silver-coated heap.

"Good shooting!" Carahil said. "Good Shooting! Now, break the circle and I'll be able to tend to my Mother.

Peter approached the circle looked down at it. It was just a bit of chalk, rice and sand. Peter brushed some aside with his hand.

The chalk didn't budge—it was set like concrete. Frustrated, Peter picked Poe up and, crossing the circle, placed her inside. He whispered into her ear. "*You can't die*," and he kissed her cheek. Carahil began tending her wound.

He returned to the circle. He hit the hard-set substance. He hit it with his fist. He kicked at it. He took his gun and started hammering at it with the butt of his Hertamer.

"Johnnie, help me with this!" Peter yelled, still hammering at it.

As Johnnie made his way to the circle, Lord Milton's gangly, tangled body suddenly came down to the floor of the lab with a crash. It shuddered with the impact and then was still, his large Inseroth pistol dropping out of the limp fingers to the metal floor.

A bit put off, they continued banging away at the circle, making no progress.

"Mr. Carahil, how is Lady Poe?" Peter asked, concerned.

"Fine, she's fine. I have healed her. She simply needs rest. Did you guys get my present?"

"What present?" Johnny asked pounding away at the circle.

"Oh, you mean the bubbles?" Peter said. "Yes, we got that. They were a big help."

"Glad to hear it," he said.

The hard set of the circle was stubborn, resisting their hammering.

"I suggest heat," Carahil said.

Johnnie adjusted his Hertamer. "Get away Peter, will you?" he said irritably. "I don't see why you don't just step across, Mr. Carahil."

Carahil shrugged. "Can't. Those are the rules."

Johnnie fired a long burst at the chalk line. The metal floor beneath began glowing and then melted and sagged. The chalk line stood rigid, resisting the heat.

"Good Creation!!" Johnnie roared.

"I suggest something heavier, like that laser drill over yonder, or how about a good whack from your SAPP?" Carahil said.

"Quiet you!" Johnnie barked. "Will you be quiet!!"

Peter, entered the circle and went to Poe. He checked her wound and saw it was perfectly healed, Poe soundly asleep. He caressed her face and stroked her hair. He kissed her on the cheek. Feeling relieved, he looked back with some humor as Johnnie and Carahil bickered.

He noticed something.

The heap of Lord Milton's body … moved. Headless, it shuddered.

"Ummm, Johnnie …"

"What?" he yelled looking in his direction.

A sickening escape of gas came out of burned-up stump of Lord Milton's neck. His legs began kicking. His buckle shoes jingled and his hands clenched and unclenched.

"What in the name of Creation is this gas-bag doing?" Johnnie cried.

One of Milton's shoes flew off in the commotion.

"Johnnie," Peter said, staring in horror, "does it look to you like this headless body is … growing? Getting bigger?"

"Oh, don't be stupid!" he roared. Johnnie aimed and fired a long burst into the headless, kicking body, catching the ruins of his clothing on fire.

Soon, despite Johnnie's protest, there could be no doubt—Milton's headless, burning body was *growing*, the sounds of charred cloth beginning to stretch and tear clear to the ear. Then, as if to cement the unreal scene, the body—hissing, flaming, growing—sat up with purpose and intent.

Not quite knowing what to make of this, Johnnie lunged at the body and made to put the deadly shaft of his SAPP into its chest.

A thin, dainty—albeit giant-sized— arm shot out from the blackened tatters of his clothes and caught Johnnie about the mid-section. The arm was long, delicate, alabaster … distinctly feminine in appearance. Johnnie looked down at the huge hand encircling his waist—it looked like a gigantic lady's hand. Effortlessly, the hand tightened its grip and Johnnie exhaled with a "wuff!" Johnnie was then thrown head over heels, landing roughly some distance away on the other side of the lab near one of the dead scientists, his SAPP clattering after him.

As Peter and Carahil watched, the headless body stood. Through the empty collar of Lord Milton's burning coat, a head emerged—a female head with long, sticky hair. Peter mused the head was rather pretty, though its eyes were wide and diabolical, so filled with rage and hate.

"Well now," she said with her brand-new mouth. "It appears that we're going to have ourselves an undignified scene here, boys—so, with that in mind, I might as well get comfortable…"

Lord Milton again grew in size; at a faster rate this time. His, or rather, "her" chest burst open, revealing a huge bosom in all its glory; similarly, his rear-end expanded into a rather feminine-looking caboose—a defeated corset spiraled away with a "snap". Then, three pairs of long, thin feminine arms emerged from the ruined waist coat. What was left of Milton's clothing submitted to the burning and the stretching, and disintegrated into a smoking pile at the creature's delicate feet. The monster was apparently quite fireproof as the burning clothing didn't trouble it in the least, didn't even blacken its skin.

There, standing before them was a complete, eight armed, eight breasted hermaphrodite, perfectly formed and goddess-like in her lines and curves, framed dramatically in billowing smoke.

Carahil's book appeared and he scribbled in a few things. "Ok, that's what that was ..." he said. "Sorry, Peter, I should have said something. My bad."

"Lord Milton's Secret" ©2010 Carol Phillips

24—Behold, the Enemy of the Vith

Davage, seeing the spheres, cursed and rammed the wheel hard to port. "Saari, for Creation's sake give me a 42 degree left quarter boost!"

She hit the switches and the *Seeker* underwent a gut-wrenching drop with a sickeningly tight left bank. The bridge crew, accustomed to holding on with Davage at the wheel, really had to hold on for this brutal turn. Lt. Verlin, her arms wrapped around the rail, nearly did a back flip with the movement.

Davage whipped his head around, Sighting this way and that, he saw that the severe turn had been mostly successful, the great bulk of the spheres falling to the rear.

Suddenly, the *Seeker* was seized by one of the Shadow tech beasts, its black tentacle wrapping around the ship's neck. The ship groaned and strained to maintain its bearing. It opened its mouth and created a frothing swarm of black spheres, expanding and death-bringing.

<*We're done, love!*> came Syg's telepathy.

"Dav!" Kilos voice came down over the Com a moment later. "Let them fly! Use the forward bank for now. We're moving on to the other ones."

Straining, Davage pointed the nose at the beast. "Canister Control, loose a four shot burst with a staggered screening blast, forward bay only!"

With the usual thud, four canisters shot out of the front of the ship. Davage Sighted them; they were shining silver.

The canisters exploded in a flash, four explosions packed tightly together; their blasts heavy and energy laden. The blasts decimated the black spheres, popping them in slimy film. The top of the Shadow tech beast's head was ripped off, and the rest of it was quickly dissolving, covered in silver. Shuddering, it released the ship and toppled over like a fallen tree, shaking the ground and stirring the clouds.

Davage clawed back up for altitude. Settling at ten thousand feet, he looked around, seeing endless hoards of black ships and hundreds of giant Shadow tech beasts tearing up the landscape. Far away, he saw Syg's remaining *Seeker* familiars in a swirling battle with a flock of giant Shadow tech birds belching clouds of StT's. The birds were overwhelming Syg's familiars.

The black ships were constantly attacking in mass, but the *Seeker* was faster, and with the Sisters and a steady barrage of flak from its Battleshot batteries, they couldn't get close enough to do any serious damage.

<*What happened, Dav?*> Syg asked. <*Did it work?*>

<*It did, darling, well done.*>

<*We're moving on to another bay, love! I'll let you know when we're done. If you see Poe, have her join us!* >

Verlin approached the Helm. "Captain, we're clear … should we not work our way back to orbit and …"

Davage looked at all the beasts in the distance, ripping up the landscape, scooping up people, devouring them. The black ships and birds were keeping any escaping vessel pinned down. But, peppered in here and there, were Xandarr ships from the Keep, battling to the end.

A whole planet in the slow, violent stages of death.

He thought of Balor, the King. At first he hadn't considered to take him at his word, for surely he was lying or had something up his sleeve. He was a Xandarr. But look, he welcomed them, assisted them, sacrificed his wife, and he saved those forty-four Black Hats without fear or protest. He asked for much in return; he wanted the Fleet to come to this death-house and fight. He asked for the unheard of.

But, he asked, and for the right reasons.

"Com," Davage said, "open a channel to the Fleet on Ultra-wave. To all Pledged vessels—Imperative!! Main Fleet Vessel *Seeker* engaged at planet Xandarr with hostile Black Hat and Shadow tech forces seeking the total annihilation of the general populace, and requests all available vessels to assist in the defeat of these forces at once, per formal request of Balor I, King of Xandarr!! Note—standard canister and Battleshot weaponry ineffective. Must coat all ordinance with Silver tech—which was recently declared a legal substance by the Sisterhood of Light at the Council of Pithnar. To that end, *Seeker* requires immediate and due conscription complete with back pay to the following civilians: Chancellor Bethrael of the Grand Order of Hospitalers, formerly,

Bethrael of Moane, and Lady Suzaraine of Grenville, formerly, Suzaraine of Gulle. They may provide Silver tech in earnest for our weaponry."

Davage paused a moment. "I am aware that Xandarr is a Xaphan world, and those attacked are Xaphans, and the attackers themselves are in fact Xaphans. I am aware that Xaphans often prey upon each other, and I am also aware that it is League policy not to interfere. But, here we are, at this place ... witnessing the horror of it all. The lives lost for no reason. I have seen cruelty here, and death and madness unleashed in quantity. But, I have also seen courage and loyalty and selflessness, and I have been re-taught an important lesson that I never should have forgot—that even an enemy is worth making the effort to save. Here, I have learned that valor is the purview of the common man—be he League or Xaphan. And I put it to you that this action here is nothing less than the genocide of an entire people: a populace of simple villagers and farmers, of innocent women and children. We are Pledged ... Pledged to defend life where life is threatened. Our Pledge makes no distinction to political affiliation or territorial boundaries. Our duty as the Stellar Fleet is not to ferry dignitaries and collect taxes. Our job is to protect life, and to keep our Promise, and I say that right here, on Xandarr, is where the fight is! Right here is where life once again looks to us, the League, for salvation ... and here is where the battle will be won! To me! To me, and let us save these people!"

* * * * *

The strange eight-armed male/female creature that was Lord Milton was tearing up the lab, trying to get at the Ruthvens. They peppered it with hits from their Hertamers, but the shots seemed to do no damage. Its soft, pale skin was both energy resistant and fireproof.

"I'll bet you never thought of something like this happening to you!" Milton said swiping at Peter, his/her eight breasts free from the cruel confines of the girdle used to keep them hidden.

"What in the Name of Creation are you?" Johnnie cried firing with his left hand and was lashing it with the SAPP with his right.

"It's a Haitathe!" Carahil called out from his circle. "It's my bad, I should have figured it out earlier!"

At this point, Milton, seemingly growing with each shot taken, stood about twenty feet tall. It was like an amalgam of three women and one man. Its new face was female. It had three sets of female arms, four sets of female breasts and, yes, three fully developed female nether regions, while it also had one male set of arms and one male genitalia.

If Johnnie was being honest, it actually had a pretty decent figure.

"Milton!" Carahil shouted. "This can only end in one way, and you know it! Stop this now!"

Milton, chasing after Johnnie, walked into one of the fallen scientists. It seized the limp form and ate him in two crunching bites. "Ohhhh!" it cried with its brand new female head. "So good ..."

"This is an Elder curse!" Peter shouted. "Perhaps we can help you to be rid of it."

The creature was joyous as it reached for another dead scientist. "Be rid of it? I, Larry Lunchmeat, am your master—you are my cattle!! I've denied myself for so long. Wearing your clothes, abiding by your laws, contenting myself with your putrid Society—FOR FAR TOO LONG!! I AM FINALLY FREE!!" It took a deep breath. "Oh, Lord Ruthven, I can smell you from here! And you smell delicious!" Milton lunged for him. Peter dove out of the way and shot it in the hand. The shot appeared to have no effect.

Moving with the speed of a demon, it turned and began climbing the walls, sticking like a huge spider. It reached out, one of its arms stretching like rubber, and grabbed Peter about the waist.

Johnnie lunged, trying to get at it with his sword-shaped SAPP. With a lightning-fast hand, Milton swatted him aside.

"So warm ... so tasty ..." Milton opened its new female mouth.

"PUT HIM DOWN!!" came a commanding shout from below.

Lady Poe stood there, her silver-haloed fist pointing square at Milton's back.

Milton smiled and made ready to pop Peter in. "Good lady, you Betty Side-of-Beef you, don't go anywhere ... YOU'RE NEXT!!"

A devastating blast of silver came up and got Milton in the back, its force unstoppable.

Milton crumpled to the floor in a terrible mess, a huge, hollowed-out hole carved in its chest. Peter scrambled away from the ruined carcass. Poe stood there, her hands covering her mouth. "I've ... I've killed it ..." she moaned.

Peter embraced her. "You had no choice, my Lady. Milton gave you no choice. You saved my life." He took her in his arms and led her away.

Johnnie recovered his SAPP and, after several heavy blows, broke the circle.

Carahil came loping out. "Come," he said. "Mother, friends … we've work to do, and there is no time."

They went up the stairs, leaving the heap of arms and legs that was once Lord Milton where it lay.

25—Skies full of Silver

After Davage made his call to the Fleet, the waves filled with chatter. Unfortunately, it wasn't the kind of chatter he was hoping for.

"Captain," the Com cried, hanging onto his console, "Camilla, Baroness of Sorrander, has pledged to plant her lozenge on Xandarr and is en route with her armada of ten Ghome 52 battleships. She has called for her allies on Charn and Midas to help her claim her new fiefdom."

"Have her allies answered her call?"

"Aye, sir, they have, though the forces pledged have not been openly said."

Davage turned the wheel and sighed. Should he somehow survive the Shadow tech nightmare engulfing him, he then could expect a pitched welcome from Camilla and her forces.

More bad news from the Com. "Captain! Lord Chiloe of Zoran has declared the cleansing of Xandarr a momentous occasion and proclaimed the Black Hats heroes. He has vowed to wait until the Black Hats have had their fill of blood, and then he shall occupy Xandarr, plunder its remaining wealth and enslave any who might have survived. He swears to plant his arms on the ruins of Xandarr Keep and has raised a bounty on King Balor's head, alive or dead."

And on and on. The various Xaphan clans were lining up to feast on whatever was left of Xandarr's tortured carcass.

"Captain," Lt. Verlin cried. "With respect, sir—we cannot stand here. Either we shall be consumed by Shadow tech or be overwhelmed by Xaphan forces. This place is lost!"

He spun the wheel and banked away from a pesky flock of Shadow tech birds. Perhaps she was right.

The Com again, more bad news, no doubt.

"Captain, a combat wing of four Privateers of the 5th Fleet under the command of Captain Venville of Salla has answered the call and has sworn to interdict Camilla's armada! He is en route to intercept her even as we speak!"

"Finally, a bit of good news! Captain Venville is a skilled man. What class of vessels does he command?"

"Three sprint-class vessels and a *Woodward*-class scout ship."

" Against ten Ghome 52 battleships? No, no, once this situation here has been attended to, we'll join the captain in space."

The Com again. "Sir, we are receiving a wire out of Bazz that the 47th Marines have been sortied with a squadron of *brigantine* attack ships in addition to a command escort by the *Exody* and *Boxwood*! They are to enter the theater at once!"

"Good, good, the Marines will be of critical assistance to Captain Venville and his Privateers. And the guns of the *Exody* and *Boxwood* should put Camilla to the wind."

A private wire came in. Lt. Verlin tore it off and read the notice. "Captain," she said. "An emergency convocation of the Admiralty has just adjourned at Fleet. After some debate, they agree with your assessment and have declared this engagement a general battle, and, to that end, three fighting armadas are being assembled for immediate launch including five Admirals and three Grand Abbesses of the Sisterhood!"

A General Battle? The Admiralty hadn't declared such a thing since the Second Battle of Mirendra Three. Such a declaration would call for the involvement of the bulk of the serviceable Fleet. "What is the designation of this battle?" he asked, somewhat thunderstruck. He had hoped for a few combat formations, possibly a small armada; but this?

Lt.Verlin looked at the notice. "League Battle XXVIL: Battle of Xandarr."

He gripped the wheel and spun away from a Shadow tech beast. Well, King Balor, you've got your wish. There's going to be a fight here, sure enough.

* * * * *

When Johnnie, Peter and Poe and Carahil re-emerged through the machine, they instantly had to find something and hang on for dear life—the *Seeker* was bucking and rolling like never before. Outside they heard explosions and roaring.

They made their way to the front glass and could see the gut-wrenching gyrations of the ship as it tumbled about. They heard the superstructure of the *Goshawk* twisting and torquing with the movement. Outside was a gallery of soaring black ships, a blackened sky and huge Shadow tech monsters raging about here and there. Being at the very front of the ship, they were feeling the full effect of Davage's bucking. Clearly, Captain Davage wasn't trying to get the *Seeker* out of the area to safety—he was engaged. He was in this fight for keeps, gambling the *Seeker*'s power against a whole world of Shadow tech enemies. They saw a silver canister shoot out and clear a huge hole in the black masses ahead.

"So," Carahil said hopefully, unaffected by the movement, "here we are, on Xandarr … I've no more secrets, no more games to play—this is what I saw in the Telmus Grove. I saw the death of this world and all those on it. And though they be Xaphan, I saw the end of their souls, the silencing of their dreams and all the things they'd ever built smashed to dust … to be remembered as nothing more than poor victims of the Black Hat's wrath. I didn't want it, this responsibility, this burden. But it was given to me, and what was to be done? Was I to forget about them? To turn away and pretend that I didn't know their doom was nigh? No, though they are Xaphans, I didn't care, I was going to save them regardless. A screaming Xaphan and a screaming League citizen sound awfully the same.

"But, Balance says that I can't simply charge in and save them—I can't do that. Balance says that you have to do it—you have to make the effort and put yourself at risk and weight the scales, otherwise, I will consign them to an even worse fate later on. To save these people, I needed to be granted my arms—I needed you. And I've brought you all here, manipulated you, imperiled you, and pushed you to peer deep within yourselves to see what sort of person lies within. I've done this to empower you, to help me stop all of this—to help me save Xandarr, a planet of enemies. I risked everything, gambled everything on the notion that you fine people … would want to save them too. Look at the people below, fighting for their lives. Look at Lord Blanchefort, going nowhere, fighting a whole world of monsters. Now, Mother, Lord Ruthven, I'm asking you—what will you do?"

Another canister, this time hitting one of the huge beasts in the distance. The creature toppled, dropping a mouthful of debris. The debris, on closer inspection, was people, dozens of them.

"What do you need, Mr. Carahil?" Peter asked.

"I need some clear air, I just need a moment, and then it will be all right and I will save Xandarr. I will save these people."

Peter jumped into the pilot's chair and began firing the ship up.

"What are you doing?" Johnnie said.

"You saw it. All those people down there are being killed en masse. I'm uncoupling the ship, and I'm going to get Mr. Carahil his clear air!"

"It's a mess out there, Peter—look at it for Creation's sake! You'll be swamped!"

"I don't care."

"They're just Xaphans!" Johnnie said.

"Yes well, run and hide if you want."

Poe sat down in the seat next to him. "Lady Poe," he said, "you should get to safety."

"I am fine where I am, sir."

Johnnie rolled his eyes. "Peter, you're not going anywhere without me watching your rear. What are you thinking?? Give me a minute to get to my ship and I'll join you."

"You sure, Johnnie?"

"Yeah, I'm sure."

A figure darkened the threshold. "You're in my seat, Peter," the Duke said weakly, holding his side as he limped forward.

"You should be resting, Duke," Peter said.

"You can't fly my ship … it's got a lot more pull than you're used to, you'll auger right into the ground. You head to your ship, and make ready to follow me. Carahil … I heard what you said. You wanted us here, you wanted us engaged; you wanted us to fight. So, here we are … in the thick of it. We're going to fight. Are you ready to do your part at last?"

Carahil twitched his whiskers. "I am. You've all done your best and willingly, and I thank you—the rules have been met. The Balance is weighted. The gods have their arms. As I just told your fine friend here, get me a bit of clear sky and you're going to see something, something you'll never forget."

The Duke tried to smile. "I'll bet. Well you two … get to your ships."

More people came into the ship. It was Sage and Torri, still wearing their dispensary gowns. "Got … room for one more?" Sage asked, a bit unsteadily.

"Sage, you can't fly like this," Peter said.

"Well," he said holding his painfully sore chest, "you say I can't fly anyway, so what's the difference?"

"Torri, get back into bed, please," the Duke said.

"You first …" she said with a hoarse voice as she strapped into the co-pilot's seat, the FIXED BY FINS glittering at her throat.

The Ruthvens and Lady Poe exited. After a few minutes they signaled that they were ready.

"You ready, Torri?" the Duke asked.

She smiled and kissed him. "Yep … let's go," she rasped.

The Duke's *Goshawk* uncoupled from the front end of the *Seeker*. The sky was full of enemies. The Duke swerved this way and that, blasting his Sar-Beams, trying to get clear, to find a bit of open space as the three smaller ships linked up. All around was a hailstorm of movement, the giant *Seeker*, twisting and turning, as agile as a fighter craft, blasting and dispelling everything that got near it. Johnnie Peter and Sage swirled in their ships, firing at everything that moved. Peter's ship one person heavy: Lady Poe sitting at his side.

However this turned out, the Duke was proud: proud of his men, proud of Torri … and proud of himself. Finally—finally, he felt like a whole person. He felt like all the pieces were now in place. He felt fulfilled. He had come unwillingly to Xandarr, only to find himself at last in its Shadow tech-filled skies.

The Duke was amazed at the volume of Xandarr ships in the air. There were transports, cargo ships, old rickety beaners, the occasional hotrod and other assorted ships. If the Black Hats had thought the people of Xandarr were going to allow themselves to die quietly, they were badly mistaken. These people were going to go down swinging. He fired his Sar-Beams, he didn't even have to aim. It was impossible to fire and not hit multiple enemy ships.

The *Seeker*, with Johnny's *Goshawk* nearby like a stinging wasp flashing his SAR-beams, knocked down another Shadow tech beast, which toppled with a massive commotion.

There was a clear spot, a bit of open air. Quickly the Duke flew into it, a wall of black all around like the eye of a hurricane.

He looked back at Carahil and opened the cargo door. "All right, Carahil, you're clear. Let's see what you can do!"

Carahil looked at the open door. "As you wish, sir!" he said throwing himself outside. "AS YOU WISH!!!"

And Carahil floated there in open space for a moment, leisurely surfing on the air as though he didn't have a care at all.

Something began glowing red at his throat.

Suddenly, there were two of him, like big silver tadpoles. Then four, then sixteen.

Dozens of Carahils. Hundreds of Carahils dotted the sky.

Chaos and clashing mediums of Shadow and Silver tech in air. Lances and flame and birds on the wing.

Five Warhawks of the League vanguard roared down and began blasting away, trying to clear space and link up with the Seeker.

A Goshawk, beset upon, spiraled out of control. Engines shot away, Sage of Ruthven fell into a churning cloud of Shadow tech.

Ten Carahils pulled him back out, bearing the stricken ship away. "Not today," the Carahils cried as they beat on the Goshawk's glass with their flippers. "One day your time will come, but not today, for I will not allow it! Not another soul dies here--do you hear that, Universe?? Not another soul!! I can do anything I want today, thanks to you--all of you!! Take to the skies and parade with me, my good friend and fear not the dark! A new day is at hand where we made a miracle happen! Hahaha! Fly! Haha! Fly! Fly!!"

The black ring around Xandarr was replaced, for a short period of time, by a silver one and the sickening Black Hat singing was replaced with trilling, joyous laughter.

* * * * *

Carahil Triumphant *(Carol Phillips)*

The Battle of Xandarr was quite a far-flung melee, spanning from Hoban to Conwell deep in Xaphan space in a number of small to large engagements, the most severe happening at 6am of Two-Pitch Nebula where the Xaphan warlord Mathinazar put up a well-coordinated fight. Elsewhere, the Fleet armadas met and turned back the various Xaphan forces mustered to attack Xandarr. A no-show was Baroness Camilla of Sorrander, who was conspicuously missing from the proceedings, though her allies were met in space and sent away by the Fleet. The quietest theater in the Battle of Xandarr was Xandarr itself. When the massive League armada of two hundred ships arrived, there was not quite as much for them to do as first planned. Most of the planet had been cleared and was rather sedate. On approach they fought a pitched battle with thousands of black Shadow tech ships which they fairly easily routed with Silver tech canisters provided by a busy Bethrael of Moane on the *Exody.* Other than that, the planet was still, as if a massive storm had just been weathered. Every Xandarr city lay in ruins, not a village or hamlet had gone untouched, but, the people were still there. They lived. They had survived to stand on the wreckage and raise their fists into the sky.

The *Seeker*, the *Goshawks* and the defending people of Xandarr had, through valor and deeds, given the gods their arms, and they were saved in a rising sun and a blast of silver.

From the ruins of Xandarr Keep, from the fallen and smoking rubble, a fresh day dawned. A strange assortment of animals milled about the blasted rocks and watched the skies, once clogged with swirling black, return to purple. There was a tabby cat with a long, flicking tail. There was a monkey and a brightly colored crane. Sitting on his huge rump nearby was a gigantic elephant. All of the animals had dull red eyes.

They were more and just animals—they were demons. The cat looked at the skies, closed her eyes for a moment, and when she opened again, they were no longer red, but a soft green. The monkey and crane followed suit—their red eyes changed to normal. As Carahil had promised, they were demons no more. They'd been granted a second chance.

"Thank you, Carahil," the cat, monkey and crane said.

The elephant sat there, his eyes still red. The others approached him. "To be forgiven, Maiax, you first must forgive yourself," Mabs the cat said.

"They're all dead because of me. The children are dead. I promised I'd protect them."

The cat nuzzled his huge gray legs. "Then go to them in the lands beyond, and say you're sorry. The way is open for you now—you needn't be a demon any longer. I'm sure they'll forgive you."

Maiax thought about it. His eyes stayed red.

26—Lord Milton's Secret

"Lord Milton, as I am sure you are all painfully aware of by now, was not an Elder, like us," the Duke said lying in his bed. He was in his quarters, still trying to recover from his gunshot wound, which though perfectly healed, smarted like nothing else. Torri lay at his side asleep in a pair of flower-print pajamas, her arms around him. The FIXED BY FINS still shone on her neck and arm. She smiled as she slept.

Through the window, many *Straylights* flew in formation in low orbit, finishing the cleanup of the Shadow tech ships, and defending Xandarr from raiders who might try to loot its remaining wealth.

Sage was propped up in a nearby chair. He was gingerly eating a bowl of soup that Ennez had given to him. His chest wound was also extremely tender. His whole body hurt.

Peter and Poe stood near Sage. Though Lady Poe had been shot as well, she didn't seem to be suffering any ill-effects. Out of view from everybody else, they held hands.

Davage leaned forward in his chair. "So, no doubt, his condition was part of the 'Secret' that had kept his House in sway all these generations?"

"Yes," the Duke said.

"Was he cursed?" Syg asked as she poured Davage a cup of coffee. "Coffee, Duke?"

"No, no thank you, Countess. He wasn't cursed, you see—that is what he, or rather she, was. It all goes back to the time of the Elders. Of course we all know that the Elders selected the ancestors of the seven tribes to fare the heavens for them, to seek out stars for them to nourish themselves, and, in return they granted the Vith and the tribes the Gifts, youth and health—thus the beginnings of the League. They took our ancestors from wherever, our now lost home world of old, and ventured with them across the cosmos, to Lemmuria, to Emmira, to Cammara and Eng, eventually settling on Kana and Onaris. The Old Tribes and the Vith, however, were not the only race of beings the Elders sought out to fare the stars for them. They chose others as well."

"What?" Davage said. Torri stirred a bit and, smacking her lips, kissed the Duke on the shoulder and continued sleeping.

"Yes. These other beings were called the Haitathe, and, like the Vith, they were brought from far away and deposited on Kana. Like our ancestors, they were to serve the Elders, for what specific purpose I do not know. I suppose the Elders expected everyone to get along and live harmoniously, like beloved pets, however, the Haitathe were strange and fierce and they, from the outset, made war on us and attempted to enslave the heroes of old; the tribe of Vith bearing the heaviest brunt of the attack. We all know the old fanciful stories of giants in the earth, and in the dark places that vexed and tasked the Vith—well, it seems they were not merely stories. The Haitathe were the giants of legend. Additionally the cities of Gamboa and Tyrol and the region of Esther, my home, were once ancient Haitathe cities and strongholds."

"Yes, we all know if the Haitathe of old—a rampant Haitathe adorns our Blanchefort coat-of-arms," Davage said. "I simply thought them a fanciful creature of myth."

"No, not at all. Also, it appears they developed a distinct taste for Vith flesh, and sought to slay and to eat them as cattle. This behavior stunned the Elders ... they hadn't expected such a thing. They deported most of the Haitathe back to their home world, wherever that might be, but a few remained, lost in the mountains and shadowy places of Kana ... always lurking, always hungry. And so the Gifts of the Mind; the Elders sought to protect the Vith from the remaining Haitathe. Armed with these new Gifts, the Vith fought back and thrived under the leadership of Homma of Telmus Falls. But the Haitathe could not be eliminated completely, and they lingered in the shadows always ready to pounce, though, occasionally, they could be tamed to some extent if the proper strength was applied. It is said the original Sisters were the product of Vith-Haitathe offspring as well, and every modern Sister came trace a bit of Haitathe in her lineage somewhere."

Kilos, sitting near Davage, thought about the Sisters with their monstrous heritage and shuddered for some reason.

"And so, Lord Milton?" Davage asked

"Yes. As I said, most of the remaining Haitathe were killed by the Old Vith. Some hid in the mountains and swamps and stayed there.

Others snuck themselves into League Society, hiding in plain sight. Such were the Miltons …"

The Duke swallowed, feeling his throat dry a bit. "Countess, I'm sorry, may I have a cup of coffee after all?"

Syg got the Duke a cup and he drank it, wetting his throat.

"It was the most bizarre creature I've ever seen," Poe said. "A hideous mixture of male and female parts."

"He was actually kind of hot, I thought," Johnnie said. "Just sort of crazed and mean-looking, but still rather hot. Nice body."

"The Haitathe start life as male, and are fairly indistinguishable from a standard Vith male, with the exception of being rather long and tall, and no blue hair. They didn't have Gifts in the strict sense of the word, but they could perform something similar to a Cloak. Their skin, though soft and supple, was tough as nails, and they could stick to walls like a gecko. As they grew and got older, they began growing extra female parts, usually acquiring one complete set every ten or twenty years. It wasn't uncommon for an adult Haitathe to have five pairs of arms, five sets of breasts, five sets of mixed genitalia and so forth. And their head, it seems, wasn't a critical area, for, if they lost their head, a new female head would grow back almost instantly. I have always believed that each female set of parts had it own consciousness, its own soul—and so Lord Milton was continuously hearing many voices in his head, struggling for dominance, and the loudest voice was usually the most evil, the most brutal. Eventually, using their long male organ, they seeded the strongest of their own female parts. They, for lack for better terms, self replicated."

"Why did Lord Milton grow?" Poe asked.

"Again, the Giants of old. The Haitathe, as they exerted themselves, grew in size. Lord Milton was always careful not to over exert himself—as they grew, they became more and more savage. A Haitathe could often grow to twenty feet tall, at which point they were nothing short of a crazed berserker starving for Vith flesh. They shrunk back down as they calmed, but, if they let themselves go too often, they'd become stuck in such a state. There, at full size, their sanity often failed and their taste for Vith flesh increased. For many years, my father was able to control Lord Milton with certain drugs and extracts which calmed his horrific nature, and, though he was a surly character, I believe for much of his youth he was happy as he was—a grumpy accountant. As he aged though, his true nature wasn't to be denied, all those voices in his head no longer silenced. He held my father under his thumb, and when I refused to submit, he began trying to kill me. His constant attempts to murder me got more and more violent and brutal with each attempt."

Davage thought a moment. "How did his family come into your sway?"

The Duke took another sip from his coffee. "My great ancestor, Terfall of Oyln, met and felled a Haitathe in battle centuries ago. The region of Esther, House Oyln's ancient home, was plagued for generations by a creature from the bogs and marshes; a creature that stole children and abducted the unwary or the unwise. The people cried out for the creature, whatever it was, to be killed, and Terfall, at that time bankrupt and down on his luck, answered the call with his FENNISTER. He set out into the marshes to hunt down and slay the beast, hoping such a deed might change his fortunes. And discover it he did—a Haitathe of a fearsome note, and they did battle in the marsh. Terfall, being powerful with the Gifts, subdued the Haitathe, and, weeping, pleading, it begged him to spare its miserable life. She was very beautiful, though obviously monstrous. She promised to help Lord Terfall, that she could assist him in any number of ways: she was strong, could climb sheer walls and cliffs with just her hands, and she had an infallible memory, she never forgot anything. A bargain was struck. Terfall then returned to Esther with its gigantic head, and received a large reward for his supposed deed.

"Several days later, Babala, lord of the little known House of Milton, rolled into town, a strange, gangly, somewhat sinister fellow who, it was said was a down-trodden lord from Onaris hoping to change his situation."

"But what of the House of Milton? One cannot just make up a Great House ... the League Inquisitors and duties collectors would soon discover the truth," Davage said.

"The House of Milton was an old Brown House that migrated from Onaris long ago, trying to hack a new life for themselves out of the marshes surrounding Esther. Unfortunately, as they constructed their mansion, they happened upon the Haitathe, who slaughtered them. When the Haitathe struck into bargain with Lord Terfall, it simply assumed the name of Milton. The Haitathe had access to House

Milton's secret documents, its charters and patents, and it had access to the secret of constructing the RED HAW. Lord Milton 'went to work' for Lord Terfall and became his personal accountant and advisor, making him the first Oyln Duke. The relationship was a prosperous one—Lord Terfall's initial reward windfall was grown into a huge fortune with the help of Lord Milton, whose memory and ability with numbers and calculations was a real plus. Draining the marshes, they 'discovered' Lord Milton's ancient ancestral manor, and the unfinished skeleton of the new manor, and reclaimed it, now standing as the estate of House Oyln. Milton Manor, underneath the Esther veneer, is an ancient Haitathe structure which is why it is so big and out-of-scale. The South Manor, my current residence, is the structure that the original Miltons had attempted to build before they were killed.

"And for generations the relationship was a productive one, the successive Lords of Milton, each a self-replicated offspring of the original Haitathe, behaved themselves and led quite respectable lives, seemingly domesticating into League Society and enjoying its nuances. But, the last few generations became more and more problematic. They became bitter and malcontented. The drugs used to control their appetites began to fail, and they looked to fill their bellies with Vith flesh once again. And so, Hershey of Milton, the worst and most malcontented of the lot. My father, Lord Ursul, was terrified of him, the secret becoming a curse for, should it become known that the House of Oyln had sheltered and aided the Haitathe for centuries … what a ruinous scandal. My father had no idea what to do with the evil fellow. Though he was rotten, he seemed to genuinely enjoy League Society, and had never shown an inkling to consume Vith flesh. Perhaps he himself thought he could control his base nature better than he actually could."

"So, what is to be done?" Davage asked.

The Duke thought a moment. "I shall bury Lord Milton in his ancient ancestral home, and then I am going to raze Oyln Manor to the ground, and rebuild elsewhere, probably somewhere a bit closer to Effington. I've a home to build for my future duchess here, and I don't need those old ghosts interfering with our tomorrows."

The Duke finished his coffee and set his cup down. "So, Captain sir, what is to become of me? What will you do with this secret … and others that I have?"

"There isn't a Great House that doesn't have a thing or two hidden in its closet. My House certainly does. As for your illegal ships, and your illegal activities—I am not aware of you running anything that is harmful, and I am not aware of you going out of your way to hurt anyone in the process. So as far as I'm concerned, what you do or don't do is your concern, and if some tax collector or duties official out there finds his purse short then so be it, and all the better. And, regarding Lord Milton, who's to say these creatures, these Haitathe, don't have the right to try and coexist, to at least try and build a life for themselves? Stories of these creatures abound in old Vith legend. Much of our past is rooted with them, and perhaps we owe them a debt for what has been passed down to us. What do you think, Countess?"

Syg sat down next to Dav. "I say your secret is safe with us, Duke. Let it be buried and done with."

The Duke smiled and lay back in his bed, Torri immediately enveloping him as she slept.

* * * * *

They assembled in a small clearing near the river Torr, the ruins of Xandarr Keep rising in the distance. A simple table had been set up on the grass, and various dishes made by the *Seeker*'s chef, Lord Ottoman, sat on the tabletop waiting to be eaten. All of the principles were there: Captain Davage and his Countess Sygillis, the Duke of Oyln, Torrijayne of Waam, the Ruthvens and Lady Poe of Blanchefort (sitting next to Peter of course), Lt. Kilos and her silver bird Tweeter, and Lt. Verlin. Several of the locals who flew into the sky full of Shadow tech ships were there, as well as a few of the tunnel dwellers whose diversion allowed Kilos and Ennez to get to the communicator. Near the head of the table was Balor, King of Xandarr.

King of a battered and smoking, but unbroken world.

At the head of the table was Carahil. Two baskets were sitting next to him. One was filled with kittens, an exotic strain known as Xandarr Pinks. The other was filled with young puppies; more refugees from the ruins of the Keep.

Balor stood and raised his glass. "Dear friends, here we have assembled this evening, ready to share a wonderful meal by the banks of the Torr. By all rights, I and everybody else on Xandarr should be dead. This was to be the first day of Xandarr's eternity. A black ring should be overhead, ready to pounce on any who might dare approach. But, thanks to you all, thanks to your courage and timely arrival, thanks to your bravery and willingness to sacrifice, we live still. There is no black ring in the sky, and eternity yet awaits. Thanks to you, the people are safe. Today, we give thanks for our deliverance. Today we begin the rest of our lives. And, to the chief author of this happy outcome, to he who saw our deaths and was determined to avert them; to he who did not see enemies dying here, but simply people in need, I offer a special toast."

All at the table stood and raised their glasses.

"To Carahil," Balor said, "Defender of Xandarr."

"To Carahil," everyone at the table repeated.

Carahil's silver face blushed, and he adjusted himself in his seat, preparing to say a few words. "Before I start, I'd like to offer all in attendance a small gift as thanks for what was done here." In front of each person at the table a small box with a festive bow appeared. "It's not much, but it's from the heart. Please everyone, open them."

Syg scowled. "What's in the box, Carahil? I don't trust you."

"Oh please, my countess. This is a solemn occasion of the utmost gravity, and we all—myself included—have matured from this experience. There is a time for everything, and this, certainly, is not a time for levity. Please, accept this humble gift that is from my heart."

"Sounds reasonable to me," Davage said looking at his box.

Everyone then, except for Davage, pulled the lids from their boxes.

Fat pies of cherry, cream, chocolate and custard launched themselves out of the boxes and unerringly found the faces of each person with a sweet slap. They wiped filling from their eyes. Davage sighed and opened his box, getting hit with a cream pie.

Carahil erupted in laughter and beat his flipper against the table top. "I'm sorry! I'm sorry! Please, what's a pie in the face after what we've all been through? Think of it like this: the 'Defender of Xandarr' has just anointed you as the best of people! My favorite people! Hahahahahaha!"

They were shocked for a moment, then Davage began laughing as he wiped cream from Syg's face. Ki too, and then Syg joined. Soon the whole table was caught up in mirth.

Xandarr should be a silent tomb, instead, the banks of the Torr bounded in laughter.

27—The GEORGE WIND

Ki and Syg crawled through the small passageway. It was just a warm up run, Syg had said, though Ki strained and grunted to keep up. To give Ki a mild introduction to castle exploration, Syg had picked an easy run—at least an easy one for her. It started in the near south wing of the castle in the small lavender chapel of Countess Harminard, Dav's great grandmother. The chapel was a last second choice. Syg had planned to take Ki to the northern end of the castle and take an easy tunnel out to the Grove. But, Syg thought she'd seen a ghost coming out of the chapel, so she changed her mind, and sent Ki crawling through the chapel's tunnel. From there, the passage, about two feet high, rambled on at a gentle slope ended in a small chamber once filled with wine.

Syg moved through the small passage like a gopher, completely at home in the tight space. Tweeter bounced along, his light making the need for flashlights moot. Ki followed behind her as best she could, seeing the soles of Syg's feet strain as she crawled. Ki was amazed that a woman who never wore shoes had such clean, soft feet—must be a Black Hat thing.

Syg paused and turned. "Ok Ki, up ahead is a little squeeze. It's not as bad as it looks, just remember to relax and deflate your lungs, then, we'll be in the chamber. Creation, I wish Dav was here with us."

Davage was away at the Fleet, getting Ki's field admittance passed through channels. Tomorrow, Ki will go to Fleet Command in Armenelos, fill out her papers and oath in. She was going to have to stay at Fleet billeting for a few days, as this process wasn't going to be quick. Then, she will get her cherished uniforms at long last.

Illuminated in Tweeter's soft silver glow, she watched Syg's feet disappear into what looked like an impossibly small crack in the stone. After a moment she could see Syg's flashlight lighting up the crack from the other side. "Come on, Ki," she said.

With a chirp, Tweeter hopped through the crack.

Ki crawled up to the crack and, after fumbling around for a moment or two, began pulling herself through, feeling the rough stone jabbing into her belly. After a bit of struggling, she made it into the chamber. Once inside, she found Syg sitting up cross-legged, eating a pastry from her pack. She offered one to Ki, who took it and popped it into her mouth.

"Dav tells me that this place was once used to store illegal wines and spirits, apparently Dav's ancestors couldn't resist fermenting Xaphan choker wines, the cheeky devils. Talk about a skeleton in the closet."

Ki looked around, savoring the feel of the place. It hadn't taken long for Syg's love of crawling around in the dark to rub off on her. The age, the history of the place; she was going to have to bring her husband in here, no doubt he'd find it fascinating.

There were a number of earthen jugs stacked up against one of the walls. Overhead was a small shaft cut through the stone for a dumbwaiter. "What's this?" Ki asked, grabbing one of the jugs.

"Nothing," Syg said innocently.

"Nothing, huh?" Ki said uncorking it. She took a sniff. "Hey!" she exclaimed. She took the jug and tossed it back, taking a few generous swallows. "Syg—this is Morninglow, that good stuff made from Nadine syrup. What's the deal? Dav swore up and down to me he didn't make it here anymore."

"Well, Ki—it's not something we talk about too much, Morninglow is moonshine after all. We signed a treaty with League regulators that we wouldn't distil it any longer. But, the staff appreciates it from time to time, and, for special occasions, you know ..."

Ki tossed back a few more swigs. "Uh-huh … Where's this dumbwaiter go?"

"I don't know," Syg said, blushing.

"Syg, you and Dav owe me about ten of these jugs. My family back on Onaris just loves this stuff. And, I hate to break it to you, but pretty much all the Nadine syrup I take home ends up getting cooked into moonshine anyway, but we can never get it as good as this. Wow!" She took another swig. "You shouldn't have brought me in here, Syg, now the cat's out of the bag."

"I suppose not." Ki corked her jug and found something to scratch her name onto the side. As she scratched, she listened to Syg rattle on. "Did you notice that there were four side passages along the way?"

"Nope," she said scratching her name onto a few more jugs.

"There were—got to keep your eyes open or you'll miss things. We'll head to Countess Harminard's chapel next."

"We were just in her chapel."

"That's the one on the surface, there's a hidden one as well … and it's neat, she was a remarkable woman."

"These chapels always creep me out," Ki said.

"Why?"

"Don't know … they just do."

Syg laughed. "Come on, you big baby, it's not far from here. Follow me."

As Syg began crawling back through the crack, Ki readied herself for the squeeze and turned to collect Tweeter. "Come on, Tweets", she said.

He was sitting on a bundle of cloth at the far end of the chamber. Ki took her appropriated jugs and made to wrap them up in it, worried that the staff would come down in the dumbwaiter and crack into her stash.

She jumped in horror as she threw the cloth aside. "Syg … wait. What's this?"

Syg turned.

Lying in a heap in the back of the chamber was the body of a girl, a villager, formerly hidden by the cloth.

"It's Charlene, one of the cooks," Syg cried.

Ki rolled her small body over and found a jagged wound in her chest. "Murdered," Ki said. "At least a day or two."

"But, I just saw her this morning … in the east wing."

"Then we've a Cloaked intruder roaming around in the castle, and I'll bet I can guess who it is."

"Princess Vroc?'

"Yep, that was my first thought. I figured we'd be hearing from her again after Xandarr."

They tended to the body as best they could. They would be back for her later. They had more pressing issues at the moment.

They emerged from the chapel and made their bustling way to the kitchens. There, the staff was busy as usual, making this and that. They didn't see Charlene anywhere. Syg pulled her Head of Staff aside, and ordered her to quietly get everybody into their rooms and lock their doors—she wanted the hallways cleared.

"Now, we've just got to find her," Syg said. "She could be anywhere in this maze."

Ki had a thought. She took Tweeter off her shoulder and held him in her palm.

"Tweeter, there is a Cloaked intruder in the castle, possibly a female named Princess Vroc of Xandarr. Can you find her for us?"

Tweeter took flight and turned to the north, Syg and Ki following. He flew through several corridors and halls until he passed into one of the Grand Halls leading to the cavernous main ballroom. Far down the hallway they spied someone standing on a tall ladder cleaning the high vault overhead. A bucket, various cleaning supplies and a small wagon covered with a tarp were arranged at the base of the ladder. Tweeter began flapping around the person, who, annoyed, tried to wave him away.

Syg stopped.

Straining to see in the dark, she saw that the maid standing on the ladder was not cleaning, but instead holding some sort of small, square device and was trying to hide it in the crevices of the vault.

Ki looked. "Syg, that's an explosive ..." she said under her breath.

Syg loosed a blast of Silver tech down the hallway. The person, hanging onto the ceiling by her fingertips, coiled her body out of the way and the top of the ladder was blasted out from under her. She hung there for a moment then dropped, landing like a cat. A few small squares of ochre-colored explosives fell out of her pockets and scattered on the floor.

Charging, Syg tried the rope the woman. Jumping about like an acrobat, the woman deftly leapt out of the way. She threw aside her Cloak, and there was Princess Vroc of Xandarr, smiling, tiny ... insane. "Hello!" she said. "You're my father's harlot, are you not?"

She picked up a square of explosive, tapped a button and threw it at Ki. Quickly reacting, Syg surrounded it in a Silver sphere, and there was a muffled explosion within.

The Princess picked up another one and made to enable it, when a leaping Ki tagged her square across the jaw, sending her and the explosive flying. A small controller fell out of her hand—a remote!! With it she could light the whole works.

Hitting the floor, the Princess began clawing for the remote. Ki, landing on top of her, struggled to hold her back—amazed by her strength and tenacity.

"Tweeter!!" she yelled, "get that controller out of here and hide it somewhere!"

Tweeter chirped and, seizing the controller in his tiny silver feet, flew off with it, just barely avoiding Vroc's grasping fingers. Laboring through the air, he flew down the corridor and turned out of sight.

Ki, sitting on top of Vroc, rolled her over and readied to start wailing, when in three quick movements, the Princess kicked her in the thigh, the gut and the face—easily the hardest kicks she'd ever felt.

Syg was red-faced with fury. "GET OUT OF THE WAY, KI!!" she roared, wanting to devastate this pesky Princess. Ki's thigh was dead, numb, and she couldn't move fast enough.

Enraged, Syg made to seize her in a TK.

As before, the Princess Wafted and reappeared to Syg's right. She belted Syg one; she was a master at that tactic, and it was frustratingly effective. Syg couldn't do anything fast enough to keep her from Wafting. Syg dropped to a knee with the force of the blow.

The Princess unsaddled her BEREN and showed it to Syg. "Remember this?" she panted, its thin blade invisible as usual; only its silver hilt glinted in the half-light. "This time you'll die by it."

Syg tried to stand, and the Princes butt-ended her in the nose. She went down on all fours, stunned.

"I was planning on having nice blast here … I was going to blow this whole damned castle apart and watch it burn, but since you've interrupted me, I'll simply kill every living soul here personally, starting with you, harlot!"

Syg, still recovering from the blow, tried to rise, but Vroc pushed her back down with her boot.

She raised the BEREN over her head with both hands. "Goodbye … "

She brought it down in a blur.

CLANG!!

The invisible BEREN, light and rapier-like, crossed the strong heavy shaft of Captain Davage's CARG.

Davage stood there, eyes blazing. "I'm home, Syg," he said quietly.

Vroc's eyes flickered and twitched. She giggled. "Father!! Welcome home … I was just making dinner for you … I hope you like it …" She gave Syg a savage kick to the gut as Ki limped to her side.

"Ki, get Syg out of here, and the clear the castle. Now!" he growled.

"Not a chance!" Syg said, recovering. She was red-faced with rage, and loosed a fast Sten.

Again Vroc Wafted out of the way, reappearing to Syg's right.

The BEREN came whistling, Syg's neck its destination.

CLANG!! Dav's CARG intercepted it at the last second. The princess grinned. Ki tried to engage her, but was floored with a whistling punch to the jaw.

They crossed weapons and fenced for a moment, exchanging positions with the Waft several times. Vroc's skill was incredible. She moved constantly, keeping Davage between herself and Syg, who was burning to kill her with Silver tech.

Vroc, insane or not, was a fighting master.

A Silver tech *Seeker* formed in the air, its miniature Battleshot ports open, ready to fire. It banked, looking for a clear shot. Grinning, the Princess kept moving—Syg couldn't open up without mowing down Dav and Ki as well.

As Davage and Vroc clashed blades, a ladder came whooshing into the back of her legs, knocking her down.

Ki, ever the brawler, had the melted remains of the ladder, and was swinging it around. Recovering quickly, the Princess shrugged off her surprise and went on the attack, swerving through the rungs, toying with Ki. She could put her blade through Ki's neck at her leisure.

Sight—Ki dead, run though with the BEREN.

Vroc managed to get very close to Ki, despite the swinging ladder, and nearly broke her knee-cap with a devastating kick to the right knee. Ki's improvised weapon, instead of helping her was turning into a huge hindrance as Vroc deftly moved around and through it.

The *Seeker* moved around for a clear shot. Vroc maneuvered Ki in front of her, again thwarting its tiny guns. She then kicked Ki in the knee again.

Ki collapsed and in a quick movement, Vroc had her BEREN up in the high guard and was ready to skewer her with it.

This fight could only go badly.

Davage, tackled Vroc, then long Wafted. He had to get Vroc alone. He had to get Syg and Ki out of the picture. This princess was a fighting machine and with Syg and Ki around to use as deadly props and obstacles, he couldn't possibly fight her with any hope of winning.

Poof!!

They reemerged several halls away, Davage barely conscious, slumped to the floor, his heart pounding from the strain. He could barely lift his CARG.

<*DAAVAAGE!*> Syg screamed in his mind in a total panic.

Vroc smiled, and kicked him square in the jaw, sending him flying. "Just the two of us ... how sweet." The two of them were swallowed up in the immensity of the empty hall.

She readied her BEREN and made to gut him with it. At the last moment, the CARG came up and met it, Davage rising weakly to one knee.

Toying with him, Vroc pushed his weapon away and belted him in the jaw, rocking him backwards.

<*WHE...ARE...Y....DA..?? DAV, G...IDE ME!!!*> came Syg, her telepathy broken and halting. Her telepathy only got that way when she was very, very upset—hysterical.

Clashing again, they forced their weapons together making a screech of sparks. "If your goal was to make me hate you—you've succeeded," he rasped, still not fully recovered from the Waft.

"My goal?" the Princess said through clenched teeth. "My goal was to make you love me, Father ... that's all. That's all I wanted! And all I ever got was scorn and contempt! Even the eleventh daughter desires a bit of love from her father!!"

<*..AV, PLE...E!!*>

They circled, their booted footfalls echoing in the huge space. Then, the BEREN, moving in an invisible cloud, the Princess attacked.

Slash, the blade went through his coat and tickled his chest, drawing blood. Davage wheezed for air. The blade chopped down on his wrist penetrating flesh through the thick fabric of his Fleet coat. The blade punctured his shirt, dappled red.

"Princess, your father is dead ... back on Xandarr ... you killed him."

"No I didn't ... NO I DIDN'T!!"

They circled again. Davage readied and, this time he sent the CARG down toward her chest regardless of the cutting snips she applied to him. She tried to parry, but the heavy CARG was simply too massive, and the BEREN's dainty blade bent. The horn of the CARG smashed into her chest, breaking three ribs and tearing open a huge bleeding gash. She recoiled, wheezing for breath. "Good one … Father … " she rasped.

Moving as though nothing had happened, she came again, the BEREN darting with master strokes. This way, that way, feint, feint, slash, stab, he was pressed to his limits. The CARG was simply too heavy for an intense fencing match of this level of fury with a light, quick weapon like the BEREN wielded by a master. If he tried to haul back and apply a killing shot, she laced him with quick, wounding cuts. His saving grace was that, unless she managed to run him through, she couldn't kill him outright with one or two cuts, she'd need a lot. She'd need to take him apart. The bad thing was she was well on her way to doing that, her invisible fluted blade finding its mark again and again. His arms and chest were saturated with red tattered cloth. Soon, very soon, he would be sliced to ribbons. Were it not for his Sight illuminating the blade as an ebon image, he might already be dead.

He needed a different weapon, and he still needed to catch his breath from the Waft.

He had a thought.

He Wafted a bit down the hall.

"Oh … where are you going?" she said calling after him with a maniacal, echoing voice.

"You want me, you may come and get me!"

She Wafted, following him. Davage Wafted again. Again and again they Wafted, making a long circuit through the castle. Fortunately, they encountered nobody along the way, Syg apparently having gotten everybody either out or safely in their rooms.

"You're starting to bore me, Father!"

Finally, at long last he appeared where he wanted: the giant Capricos Hall, the high ceiling fluttering with House banners, the walls lined with ancient LosCapricos weapons. There were hundreds of them, intricate weapons of all kinds. Most of them didn't work, they were simply well-made mock ups.

A few, however, did work. One in particular, worked quite well.

Vroc, holding her BEREN at the ready, looked around. "I like what you've done with the place. I like it a lot."

Davage smiled. "Then, you will love this."

A thin elaborate sword, brass and enameled in black, hopped off the wall on its own accord and began streaking through the air toward Vroc.

She heard it at the last second and turned to parry, her BEREN crossing with the elegant brass sword held by nobody. "What's this?"

"That, Princess, is the GEORGE WIND, the LosCapricos weapon of House Hannover, my mother's House. You say you've been studying me your whole life, then you should know my Mother, Lady Hermilane, taught me to sword fight with the GEORGE WIND when I was a child, well before I learned to use the CARG. The GEORGE WIND floats, it needs no hand to wield it if one knows its lore."

The GEORGE WIND, floating on air, clashed with the BEREN in a flurry of strokes and cuts. Slash, the weapon found its mark, cutting her in the leg. Slash, her left arm was bleeding. Slash, a nick on her face. Davage's control of the ancient weapon was precise.

He sat down at the huge wooden dining table and watched, letting the horn of his CARG rest on the floor. Given pause, he felt his strength returning.

"My mother once chased me through the castle with this very weapon, dancing it at my throat, hacking my clothing to bits. I firmly believed that she'd gone mad and was determined to kill me with it. But no … she just wanted me to become an expert swordsman, and to be creative in a fight. What do you think of it? How do you like it?"

"Fight me like a man!!" she screeched, panting as the GEORGE WIND pressed her to her considerable limits.

"Oh, what's the matter? You were perfectly happy fighting me with my huge cleaver. Don't like fencing with a light sword to match yours, do you?"

Vroc was ripped down the length of her arm, and she winced in pain. She tried to side-step around the GEORGE WIND and engage him when, from the far end of the hall, a small ball of silver light entered.

It was Tweeter, his little wings flapping in a silver flutter. A moment later, the *Seeker* banked into the hall, and a moment after that, Ki came limping in. She stopped and pulled the MT CALM, a wooden club of

House Woolover, off the wall and charged. There was murder in her large brown eyes.

Vroc watched her advance, smiling.

The *Seeker* loosed two tiny silver canisters and Vroc Wafted aside. Davage and Ki also had to jump away as the small explosions blew a hefty piece out of the dining table.

Vroc emerged, ready to take on Davage, the GEORGE WIND, Ki and the *Seeker* all at once.

Syg suddenly appeared from a Waft cloud behind her and ran two long saber-like silver claws through Vroc's tiny mid-section. Vroc arched back and screamed.

"Gotcha', bitch!!" Syg slavered pushing her claws in deeper and deeper.

Reeling, Vroc Wafted and was gone just as Ki closed with her. Syg quickly dispersed her claws and ran to Davage. Seeing his wounds, she began tenderly kissing him.

"She's not getting away!" Davage said lighting his Sight. He looked this way and that, then, he found her in a clearing just beyond the castle perimeter. She was staggering into a hidden ripcar.

Grabbing the GEORGE WIND out of the air, Davage saddled his CARG and Wafted after her.

"Wait, Dav, I'm coming with you! Which way is she? Wait!!" Syg cried, but too late, Davage was gone.

* * * * *

Vroc, shaking, in pain from her cuts and her broken ribs, going into shock from the deadly wounds Syg inflicted on her, slowly lifted the ripcar into the air.

She was frightened. She didn't know what to say to her Father … she'd made a mess of things. He will punish her and call her worthless … his damned eleventh daughter.

Wait … her father was dead. Somebody killed him. Mother too. Dead. Her whole family was dead.

Who could do such a thing?

She did it … she killed them. The Black Hats … they would not be quiet. They wouldn't let her sleep. They said kill them, and she did so she could rest. The Black Hat's monster with cat eyes had pulled her off the meat hook, she owed them. The Black Hats made her strong. Filled her head with knowledge and fighting skill.

She missed her family.

She hated her family.

The Black Hats were speaking to her now.

Kill them … kill everyone.

She looked back at the Castle … she'd have to try a new approach. Maybe a …

Poof!!

Davage Wafted into the shallow cockpit of her ripcar. "This is my ripcar!!" she wailed reaching for her BEREN, shaking off her injuries and moving like lightning. Even wounded and insane, this tiny little girl was incredibly fast and strong, socking Davage several times in the face.

As they jostled about in the ripcar, they barely noticed that the car was heading straight for a high tower—Joliet Tower to be precise. They both barely had time to Waft away as the car smashed against the sturdy red side of the castle.

Down below, they both reappeared, crashing into the steep pinnacle spire of Josephina Tower on the castle's sheer west face, once one of Lady Pardock's favorite towers.

BEREN and GEORGE WIND crossing, they struggled to hold on to the steep, shingled spire. They slid down to the bottom, there being just enough of a rim for them to stand on, a four thousand foot drop looming just beyond. As bits of the destroyed ripcar came smoking down in a shower of debris, they clashed weapons. Davage let go of his small blade and it began dancing, as before, on its own, pressing Vroc, pressing the BEREN, its advantage of invisibility and speed negated.

The wind at this height was a tremendous, blowing gale, threatening to unseat them both off their unsteady perch. Davage's coattails and Vroc's flight jacket flapped.

Vroc became frustrated and, in a lightning move, pinned the GEORGE WIND and drew her thrumming Mazan.

Davage grabbed her wrist and drew his MiMs.

They stood there for a bit in the howling wind, they could feel the slight sway of the tower and four thousand feet of nothing just an inch away.

Vroc discharged her Mazan—an angry rush of green energy pouring out of the solid barrel, thrumming with energy. "Let me go, Father!"

Davage pulled the hammer back on his MiMs, the long barrel going slightly up Vroc's nose. "I am not your father!! For my wife … for my son, I should pull this trigger and put an end to you once and for all!"

Vroc grimaced, and let go of her gun, the Mazan spinning down the sheer face of the tower. "I almost wish you would. Who shall miss House Xandarr's eleventh daughter—a waste of Xaphan skin. You won't miss me, will you Father?"

With a burst of dying strength, she wrenched her hand free and dropped off the rim, her body and hair fading into the distance like a fluffy blue pom-pom.

Davage slung the GEORGE WIND. He dropped off as well and Wafted beneath the falling Vroc, landing a stunning blow to her unsuspecting face.

She Wafted, emerging several yards north, again into a waiting Davage fist.

Again she Wafted, again she got socked. Davage's Sight, his ability to see the near future, what could she do??

He tortured her, all the way down to the bottom, pounding her relentlessly. For all she had done, for Syg's torment, for his sister's agony … for attempting to destroy his home, for all of Xandarr she was going to pay.

They got to the bottom, in the crags near the woods, Vroc emerging from Waft a bleeding, toothless disaster. She skittered into the ground.

She lay there in the dirt and loose rocks, blood coming in broken strings from her mouth, blood pouring from her midsection, little bits of leaves and dirt in her blue hair.

Davage stood over her, tall and terrible.

"And so … what are you waiting for," she said. "… do it. Kill me. Show me no mercy. When have you ever shown me mercy, Father? When did you ever show me a moment's love?"

He looked down at her small, battered body. He threw the GEORGE WIND down and unsaddled his CARG, raising it over his head.

"Do it!! Perhaps, in death, you'll allow me to sit at the table with everyone else for once. KILL ME!!"

The sunset, the birds rustled in the trees and took flight.

* * * * *

The door opened. Light pooled into the dark, stony room. The Waft-proof field, operated at huge expense, hummed slightly as the door swung open.

Three people stood in the doorway: two tall, one much shorter. They entered the room. It was large, clean, with a small frameless bed on the floor in the far corner. Several trays, stale with the remains of partially eaten food, lay on the floor near the door.

In the back corner of the room, a figure huddled against the wall, hiding, shunning the light.

"Here she is," Davage said, "and you're welcome to her."

Vroc crawled on the floor—a mere shell of the magnificent fighter who was nigh unstoppable just weeks earlier.

Davage couldn't kill her. She was mad, insane, and his conscience was at work, not allowing him to proceed with her murder.

Ennez had treated her wounds, and repaired the teeth that Davage had destroyed, but the girl herself was lost in madness, mumbling, speaking to her dead family; afraid of everything. The effects of the Black Hat's strange medicine worn off and gone.

Balor, King of Xandarr, approached the cowering figure. "Vroc …" he said. "Vroc, it is I, Balor … your brother."

The figure stirred and spoke in a halting, broken voice. "I have no brother. All my brothers are dead. I killed them. I killed them. I miss them."

"No, Vroc, I still live, and I am going to take you home. We are eager to have you. We wish to take care of you."

"I have no home. I am the eleventh daughter."

Balor sat down next to her. She cringed for a moment, then huddled up next to him. "I killed you, Balor. I am sorry."

"I know, I know, Vroc. We wish to apologize to you … for all the cruelty that was inflicted, for all the blame that was wrongly placed."

"The eleventh daughter!!" she shrieked.

Balor unwrapped her from her robe, her blueberry hair standing out in the dim light.

"Shhhhh … just a number, Vroc. Just a silly number. It means nothing. Let me take you home."

"May I sit at the table? May I please sit at the table?"

"You may. You may sit with us and share your heart and eat your fill."

He cradled her and, moaning, she settled into his arms. Balor looked up. "Captain, Great Countess, I will take her now, back to Xandarr, and give her there the home she never had. Perhaps, under our care, the spark of her sanity can be recovered. Perhaps, she'll have peace at last."

He picked her up, her trembling body small in his arms, their heads of blueberry hair a matching set. "Imagine, if you will, Captain, always being at fault, everything blamed on you—everything: a bad business transaction, a failed crop, even the weather. There was a failed crop one year, and the people came to my father to demand help. Instead of helping them, he put Vroc on trial for being the cause of the failure. She was barely ten years old, and was standing trial for a bad harvest. She was convicted and suffered a lash from every farmer who'd lost their crop, and the people accepted that as recompense. The eleventh daughter, the bringer of bad luck, had her punishment. Lashed and held in state at ten years of age. And that wasn't the last time my father allowed the people to vent their anger on his "worthless" eleventh daughter. She was tormented, first by her own family, her own people, then by the Black Hats. She couldn't endure … her mind snapped."

Davage looked at the ground. "And then she was tortured by me …" he said quietly, all of his former fury turning to shame. "As we fought … I wanted her to feel all the pain I could inflict upon her."

"You had cause to be angry."

"I am the Lord of Blanchefort. I should be bigger than that."

They walked out of the castle into the usual bright sunshine of the north.

"I have abolished all laws and customs regarding the eleventh daughter back on Xandarr. I was amazed at how rooted the custom was, how engrained, how resistant the people were to let it go. But, upon pain of law, upon my reign, no eleventh daughter will be treated as she was ever again. I swear it."

They approached the King's skycar. Several attendants waited at attention. A small woman got out of the skycar. She was dressed in light Xandarr veils. Her blue hair was ringed and set. Though she was lightly dressed, she seemed to not feel the bone-chilling cold.

The lady was tiny. She was like Princess Marilith in miniature.

"Lord and Countess Blanchefort, please allow me to introduce you to my consort and future queen, Zoladerra of Xandarr. Formerly: Zoladerra of Vain."

The woman bowed in a courtly fashion, the Shadowmark on her face impossible to miss. Around her neck she wore a tiny charm in the shape of a seal embossed with a "1".

Davage tipped his hat and Syg nodded to her. "Your consort, King? A Black Hat? Is she one of the ones you rescued?"

"She is. She was the one trying to lead the group. She is a fine woman, and I am fortunate to have her at my side. And, I'm pleased to say the other forty three are also doing well. They are treasures indeed."

Davage smiled. "Well, hearty congratulations to you both. It appears House Xandarr is destined to always be blue-haired."

"It is certain," Balor said with a chuckle.

"Well then, take your sister home, good King, and, with love, perhaps she might recover and live out her life in peace after all."

"That is my hope."

Gently, Balor gave Vroc's tiny form to the attendants, and they seated her within the skycar; her robed form small and trembling in the seat. Balor turned to Davage and Sygillis and bowed.

"As always, Lord and Countess Blanchefort, I am your humble friend and ally."

Syg smiled. "It seems that the people of Xandarr have their King at long last, and what wonders you will create together, hand in hand. Safe journey to you, Balor, King of Xandarr."

"Blessings be upon you, Great Countess, and may your unborn son be well-favored."

"Speedwell," Davage said.

And with that, Balor, Zoladerra, and the attendants seated themselves in the Skycar, and, moments later it was gone, Davage and Syg watching it climb into the heavens.

28—In Elysium

The place had many names, and meant different things to different people. Some called it Arcadia, a place of sunlit gardens and abundant fruit. Others called it the Land of Leal, the Garden of Irem or the Happy Hunting Grounds.

Some simply called it Heaven.

The people there tended vast fields and grew healthy, abundant crops under warm skies that never darkened. To these people, to simply work the fertile lands with their own hands, to watch their crops grow and to harvest them, was paradise, was everything they had ever wanted.

They were a simple people with simple wants. The House of Bodice, tormented, exterminated, extinct; but, in Elysium, they flourished forever more, safe from the drums and reaching hands that had haunted them. Safe from all who wished them harm.

A large creature with red eyes watched them work from a grove of trees. It sighed and quietly emerged, feeling rather shy.

It was a huge elephant, holding in its trunk a large box wrapped in pink and gold paper.

The elephant stepped forward and watched the Bodice tend the fields. Suddenly, it lost heart and turned to go back the way it came.

It was afraid. It had power untold, and yet it was afraid of the simple people tilling the land.

The people in the fields saw it and stopped what they were doing.

"Maiax!" they said. "Look, it's Maiax!"

Maiax the elephant turned to face them. The people had dropped their tools and trotted toward him, all smiles. They surrounded him, patting his strong, gray flanks with genuine affection. "Where have you been?" the people asked. "We've missed you!"

Maiax gave the package to one of the children. "I failed you," he said. "I was punished." He looked at all of them with his red eyes. "I'm sorry. I'm sorry I couldn't save you."

One of the children opened the box. "Cookies!" they all cried in delight.

The Bodice took Maiax the elephant, a god, by the trunk and led him into the fields with them. "You did your best, and it wasn't your fault. We looked to you for everything, when we should have looked to ourselves. It turned out all right. We've everything we've ever wanted. Join us, Maiax. The only thing we lacked here in paradise … was you."

Maiax threw his head back in joy and gave a loud trumpet. His eyes changed from red to gray—a demon no more. He picked the children up and gently placed them on his back, as he once did. The people he had failed out of kindness, the Bodice, had forgiven him, and, in the end, gotten what they had so desperately wanted in the first place—peace and good lands to till. In Elysium they bore him away to a celebration that would know no end—a god who had, finally, found salvation in the people he loved.

Epilogue

"And so," Davage said in his office, Lt. Verlin and a "newly minted" Lt. Kilos in her brand new Fleet uniform, only hours old, sitting across from him, "I have decided after a considerable bit of debate that you … Lt. Verlin … have won the job of first officer aboard the *Seeker*."

Verlin's mouth opened in surprise and relief, she raised a hand to cover it. "Oh, sir … I am honored and, I swear on my House, I will not disappoint."

Davage smiled. "I am certain you will not. You have stood with this crew, you have fought with them, commanded them, you have earned it—you have done well. My only regret, Lt., is that I will not be here to take advantage of your presence and watch your continued growth."

Verlin was shocked. "You'll not? Then who?"

"That is a matter for the Admiralty. I will be facing Appointment for the captain's chair of the *New Faith*, a new *Triumph*-class beast just coming off the blocks in Provst. It's an ungainly leviathan to be sure, but, as I have been told, time moves on and so too, it seems, must I. Lt., the *Seeker* is getting old. I can feel it in the wheel, I can hear it in the seams as I prowl the decks. I have taken and taken from this proud ship, and she has always come through. But now, I think, it is time for a new direction, a new vision for this grand lady. Perhaps she deserves to take it a bit easier, to bear proud host to an Admiral or two at last."

Verlin looked down and didn't disguise her disappointment.

Davage saw it. "Why so sad, Lt., you have earned this posting, you have made the Marines proud. Whomever is appointed as the *Seeker*'s new captain, they will have a fine first officer waiting for them."

"I was hoping to serve under your command, sir. You have been my personal hero for such a long time, I was hoping to impress you."

"Heroes, Lt., are a dangerous thing. Heroes fail, and they disappoint. If you were wishing to impress me then you have succeeded, a tenfold. You have done yourself, your House and the Marines very proud.

And I shall expect you as a guest in my home often, Lt., for you shall be invited there as you wish. I will look forward to listening to your continued adventures. In this you have earned yourself not only an admiring colleague, but a friend as well."

"You are a great captain, sir. You are everything that I'd hoped you might be and more. If I excelled, it's because you made it easy to do so."

Davage blushed. "That's my job, Lt., to create an environment that is open and inviting, where all are free to be their best. If I am able to cultivate a situation where my crew is at ease to contribute a thought and offer up a deed, then I have done my job."

"You have done your job … very well," Verlin said, wiping a tear away.

Kilos, triumphant in a number of ways, smiled. "Congratulations, Lt. … well done, and well earned."

Verlin turned to her with unvarnished loathing—obviously the issues between them were unresolved. She leaned forward and put her hands to her face.

"Lt. … Lady Verlin, look at me please," Davage said placing his hands on her shoulders.

Verlin looked at him, red-faced.

"Lt., I want to share something with you. On our first meeting, you told me something which touched me very deeply."

"Sir?"

"You had said that you first wanted to serve after witnessing for yourself the aftermath of the Second Battle of Mirendra 3, that you were one of the few people who really understood how close the League came to falling, and the cost that battle exacted. And when you saw the blackened ships and empty berths, you felt great sadness and wanted to, in turn, do your part. After seeing all of that, you wanted to serve. Knowing that we had helped to make safe a fine person such as yourself, and that you, standing there by your telescope, understood and appreciated the magnitude of the effort, the sacrifice … made it all worth it. I just wanted to share that with you."

She took a deep breath and smiled. "Sir, if I may ask, what is to be done with Lt. Larsen's body?"

"On the moon, myself and my countess will take the Dead Man's Walk as is Fleet tradition to Blue Pierce, the domain of Zenon with his remains, so that I may tell them there what a fine son they had, and how I was honored to have served with him."

Davage darkened. "Then, upon bended knee, I shall beg their forgiveness ... for not protecting their son; for not safely bringing him home."

"Sir," Verlin said. "I wish to take that walk with you, not only as a Marine, but as a lady of Hobby ... a lady who was hopeful for their son. He was a fine gentleman."

Davage bowed to her. "Lt., my lady ... I would be so honored."

* * * * *

Syg emerged through a small hole in the stone and rocks. It was extremely dark, yet she moved easily, able to feel her way without needing light. Behind her, in the hole, a light bobbed.

Poe, holding a lantern, came through a moment or two later. The two of them were body suited and dirty from crawling through the narrow passages. Syg, as usual, was barefoot. Poe wore treaded climbing boots.

"How can you do this without shoes on, Syg?"

"Easy. Well, here it is!" she said cheerfully. "We'll throw some ideas around for a bit and then hit the lanes."

Poe stood and waved the lantern around. "Alright," she said.

The room they were in was huge, at least two hundred yards long and a hundred feet high.

"Obviously," Syg said, "we'll need to clear the entry way, we don't need our guests crawling in here for the party, do we? So, Poe, what do you think? You think Dav will like it?"

"I think he'll love it," she said looking up at the impressive ceiling. "I've lived in this castle for over two hundred years, and I never knew this was here. You know more about this old place than I do by far."

Syg sat down on a low Vith pillar and opened her pack. She pulled out two sandwiches and handed one to Poe.

Poe took it and closely examined the walls—the ancient Vith stonework was breathtaking, the ceiling too. "It's marvelous," Poe said. "Marvelous. It'll be a grand event—the talk of the League. One thing though, Syg—Dav hates big League Society functions, and he hates surprises too."

"Well, I suppose he's just going to have to get over it, isn't he? You're starting to rub off on me, Poe—I'm beginning to like parties and balls, and things like that, and why shouldn't I? I've got the most handsome man in the League at my arm. I find that I enjoy all the envious looks that I get, and my bowling average is now over a hundred and climbing. Let the ladies chew on that! I suppose I'm turning Bluer as time passes. I'm going to present this place to my husband as a gift, and I want the whole League there when I do it."

Poe took a bite from her sandwich. "Oh, don't forget, Syg … you promised not to tell Pardock about it. My, she's going to be so mad that she didn't get to help in the planning. I can't wait to see the look on her face."

"What's Pardock's average again?"

"215-230."

"Wow! Really?"

Poe nodded. "Pardock is a heck of a bowler. She does everything well—that's why I want her sitting out the planning of this party."

"I challenged Pardock to another bowling match--only this time I said in clear tones that I didn't think she was woman enough to bowl me naked."

Poe laughed. "And what did she say? No, wait, let me guess. She probably didn't care, right?"

"Right. Said she'd bowl me shod or unshod, fully clothed or naked. She's a trooper."

Syg set her sandwich down and walked up to Poe. "And, don't you forget … you promised to let Milos be your escort. You promised."

Poe looked down at her hands. "Yes, Syg, yes I did. But, I was hoping to …"

"To what?"

"To beg out of that promise."

Syg reseated herself on the stone platform, her feet dangling. "Why?"

Though it was dark, Syg could see Poe was blushing. "Because, I've my heart set on someone else escorting me. Please , I love Milos … I cherish him—but as a friend, as a brother. I tried and I tried, but I just don't have those sorts of feelings for him. I just don't. I really wish that I did, but ..."

Syg smiled. "So … who is this lucky fellow, then?"

"Can't you guess?"

"Is it that Ruthven mechanic, Peter of Ruthven?"

Poe held the lantern to her chest. "Yes … Peter …"

"Why him?"

Poe thought a moment. "I've no idea, really. My heart quickens when I see him. He inhabits my thoughts, my dreams. It's not that he's any more handsome or interesting or rich than the other League Lords I've courted, it's just … I think it's the way he looks at me, how it makes me feel."

"It's often times not possible to explain in logical detail why one person loves another. Are you falling in love with this fellow, this Peter of Ruthven, Poe?"

"Yes … I think so, yes."

Syg hopped off the pillar and walked up to Poe, head and shoulders shorter than she.

"Are you certain?"

"Yes, I am certain."

Syg reached up and put her hands on Poe's slender face, her short blonde hair lit up in the lantern light. "So, you're telling me that I might, one day, have a pirate for a brother-in-law?"

Poe beamed. "Yes, to go along with my Black Hat sister-in-law … and how I love them both."

Syg finished her sandwich. "Then, if Peter makes you happy, who am I to complain." She shook her head. "I suppose this means I'm going to have to settle my dispute with that cheap slut Torrijayne of Waam, since it appears we are going to be seeing more of that bitch around."

Poe was alarmed. "You're … not going to kill her … are you, Syg?"

"She deserves it, she really does, but, as everyone has told me, that was a different Torrijayne in a different place, and everyone appears to like her."

"I like her," Poe said. "I like her very much. In fact, she was asking if she might be invited to visit from time to time, as she wanted to tutor with me, though I don't know what I could possibly teach her." Poe looked quizzically at Syg. "I can invite her, yes?"

Syg smiled. "Sure, Poe, you can invite her to come—it's a big castle, I'm sure our paths won't cross. And I promise, I won't kill her—it seems you and Dav will never forgive me if I did. I'll just have to settle for beating her within an inch of her life once or twice."

"Well, that's a relief … I think."

Syg turned and looked around. "So, for our dedication party, I was thinking of some sort of fall motif, fall is mine and Dav's favorite season …"

Chattering, full of excitement, they tossed ideas around all afternoon in the dark of the great hall.

* * * * *

She walked through the crowded streets of the village. It was nearly dusk. It happened to be a relatively warm evening in the far north, and the people were in the mood to celebrate. The lanterns strung across the rooftops were lit up with a soft glow and the village was set for a party.

Kilos walked alone, heading away from the center of the village. On the morrow, she was heading home to Tusck and her husband for a few weeks. She was eager to see him. She wanted him to look at her in her Fleet uniform. She wanted him to be proud, and she wanted to rest in his arms—husband and wife.

There was one bit of business she needed to take care for first before she left.

Though she strolled casually, she walked with a purpose. She was headed some place in particular. She hoped, once she got to where she was going, that she'd have closure.

She was wearing her brand new, perfectly tailored Fleet uniform. It felt wonderful, the silk shirt, the fine linen pants and felt coat; if she had a bed she could have gone to blissful, comfortable sleep in it. The only thing she had to get used to was the large triangle hat—it was a bit heavier than her old Marine cap. She marveled at her uniform, taking in the detail, the workmanship. She had never really appreciated the embroidery on a Fleet coat before, the symbol of rank, but now she loved it. Her collar was flush with twisting, interlocking ivy—a lieutenant. A Fleet Commander had eagles mixed into the ivy, and a Captain had stars woven in.

It all seemed a dream—it didn't feel real. She hoped her short journey this evening might bring it all home.

Tweeter sat on her shoulder. She had added as her Device, a little pocket placed just on the inside lining of her coat on the right side. The front of the pocket read TWEETER in twisting silver script. She showed it to him and, nimbly, he ducked in and out of it, his little head popping out and looking around.

She arrived at a small grocery, lit up in white light as the azure evening twilight approached. The store was mostly empty of customers. She walked in and picked up a basket, browsing for this and that. A drone of crowd noise from a sporting event played on the Aire-Net by the counter.

The grocer came up from the back of the store, carrying various items to restock his shelves with. He'd had a busy day.

He saw her and smiled. "Good evening, Lieutenant," he said brightly, easily able to recognize her rank. "Is there anything I can help you with?"

Somebody scored—the crowd reacted.

That's it—that's what she wanted to hear. Once, this grocer had inadvertently broken her heart by calling her "Miss." She stood there holding her basket and reveled in being a "Somebody" again—the bad dream truly over. After a moment, she tipped her hat, and smiled from ear to ear. "Good evening to you, sir."

Now, she could get on with her life.

* * * * *

They wound their way through the huge new ship, the smell of fresh materials and framing heavy in the air.

Captain Davage walked arm in arm with his countess through the corridors. Lt. Kilos and a nervous Lord Probert and Lady Branna trailed them. The countess was regal in her yellow Blanchefort gown.

Walking behind them, the Duke of Oyln, Torrijayne of Waam, the Duke's betrothed, and John of Ruthven toured the ship as the captain's special guests. Torrijayne was lovely in her lavender, flower painted Oyln gown.

Lady Poe and Peter of Ruthven had also been part of the contingent, but they had disappeared shortly after boarding the ship.

Syg and Torri had agreed to simply ignore each other, that was as deep as the hatchet was to be buried. They could tolerate each other in public, they could even be civil—but that was it. Put them together in a room by themselves, and before long they would be at it again like angry children, and nobody really wanted to see a countess and duchess-to-be at such an activity.

The countess, her head on a swivel, was taking in everything, every detail. Every so often she stopped and look twice at something—all in attendance anxiously watching her, to see if she reacted in a bad way.

After all, the last time she was on a *Triumph*-class ship, she was tortured by the Fanatics of Nalls and nearly lost her mind. As Davage had told Lord Probert, whether this ship flew or not depended wholly on the countess and her reaction to it.

Lord Probert, in debt to her for saving his life—and because she was his friend, had completely re-designed the interior of the ship. It looked a lot like a *Straylight*—certainly no bad memories there. "How are you, darling?" Captain Davage asked frequently.

"Fine, love," she quietly responded, "Fine," as she looked around.

Lt. Kilos was all smiles, rubbing the sleeves of her lovely new Fleet uniform, looking down at her frilly white shirt, black command sash and holstered gun. Tweeter sat happy on the brim of her blue triangle hat.

"Your new Fleet uniform scratching you, Ki?" he asked.

"Feels like a silk nightgown, Dav. It's great to be in the Fleet. It's great to be your First again."

He looked down at her holstered MiMs—a red one with a little bird engraved into the handle. He smiled. "So, Ki, did you really think you could fool me with this?"

"'Fraid I don't know what you're talking about, Dav," she said blushing.

"Your SK that you're hiding under a Painted Cloak. What, did you get Madame Torrijayne to Cloak it for you to look like a MiMs, is that what you did?"

Torri spoke up from behind. "You can see that, Captain? Wow—you have a hot Sight!"

Ki looked back. "Tattletale." Torri winked at her.

"You're going to have to get rid of that SK, Ki—we use MiMs here in the Fleet, you know that."

Ki, adjusting her hat, was dying for a mirror. "News flash for you, Dav—that's a toy gun."

"No it's not."

"Yes it is."

He winked at her. "Glad to have you back."

John of Ruthven approached and walked beside Ki. "Lt., I was wanting to apologize to you, for my rude behavior upon our initial meeting."

"S'ok, Johnnie. After all we've been through together, what's the big deal?"

"You deserve better, a better treatment. You … you're a fine woman and your husband is a fortunate man."

She smiled and looked down at him, Tweeter dropping down to her shoulder. "Listen, Johnny, I'm married. I'm devoted to my husband—it might seem weird since we're rarely together, but I'm devoted to him none the less."

She leaned down further and whispered into his ear. "But … that doesn't mean that I didn't think about it a little."

Johnnie laughed. "Hey, when next we meet, can you give me a few seconds head start—since we're friends and all?"

"I'll give you a whole country minute, how about that?" She clapped him on the shoulder.

As they made their way down the hallway, a door opened and out came Peter of Ruthven, looking a little rumpled. He was putting his duster on. He saw the procession coming down the hallway and straightened up. "Captain, Countess! My Duke!" he said.

"Lord Ruthven?" Davage said. "Where's Lady Poe?"

The door opened again and a thin stream of Silver tech came flowing out. The stream found Peter and began wrapping around him, stopping at his face, mussing his hair. The end of the stream wandered into his ear.

Poe, also looking a little mussed up, came out of the room. "Peeeeeeter …" she said, "I was getting—oh!"

She saw everybody looking at her. "Oh, Dav, I …"

Syg smiled. "So, Lady Poe, what's going on?"

Poe turned a deep shade of crimson. "Oh, nothing, Countess, nothing. We were simply checking the appointments of a random room here on the ship. I … wanted Peter to … double check and make sure all of the technological accessories were safe for layman's use."

"What!!" Probert roared. He looked at Poe with a bit of anguished longing for a moment, standing there in his buckle shoes. "I assure you, my lady, everything here is safe for use," he said quietly.

"Milos, my friend, I didn't mean to imply …"

Lady Branna elbowed him hard in the ribs. "Never mind this old fart, Lady Poe," Branna said. "I'll throw him into my dungeon if you wish to quiet him down. Isn't that right Milos?"

Probert turned to Branna: small, blue-haired, pretty, his constant foil and intellectual rival. She smiled and touched him on the nose with her finger. "And I would love to have you, Milos," she said quietly.

Probert blushed and Davage laughed. "Carry on, Lady Poe."

They continued past and finally made their way to the Captain's quarters—the place where they will both live, should this turn out. They walked in and the countess looked around. Big, high ceilings, lots of windows—the Provst ship yards brimming with movement in the steamy afternoon sun. She walked up to one of the walls and stared at it.

She stared at it for awhile. Davage walked up beside her. "Anything wrong, darling?"

"Yes …" she said quietly.

They all stood and looked at her.

"This room is too small for us," she said finally. "This wall will have to go."

Lord Probert looked around at the huge room. "You wish a bigger room, my countess?"

"Yes, we will need a proper sitting room to entertain guests."

"Aboard a starship?" Lady Branna asked.

"Yes, one never knows. And, the additional space shall allow me to practice my bowling while aloft in space."

Lady Branna shuffled uncomfortably. "B-bowling, countess, is certainly a … quaint … pursuit."

Syg smiled. "Lady Branna, your average is a 164—very respectable. You bowl quite often, and you know it."

Branna cleared her throat. "Anything else you require?"

"I do not like the color in here."

"What do you prefer?"

"Something in a light, soothing blue … right, love? Ki, what do you think?"

Ki was admiring herself in a mirror, chewing it up. "Huh?" She walked forward and stood next to Syg. "Well, I'd say the color is just fine, but maybe a nice blue might do better."

"And, of course, I'm going to want to decorate it myself."

Davage looked around, not seeing anything wrong with the subtle cream. "Certainly, certainly. So, countess, will you be fine in this vessel … no bad memories?"

Sygillis turned to her Lord and smiled. "Not so long as I have you at my side."

Probert made a few notes. "So, take out the aft transverse wall in the Captain's Quarters, and repaint in blue."

Lady Branna moved next to Probert, taking her place at his side. "Yes, yes, blue. I told you, Milos, a lady always likes a fine shade of blue. Perhaps you'll listen to me next time—you who knows not what a woman wants."

"Harpy …" Probert said under his breath.

"Old troll …" Branna said back.

They looked at each other, which Davage noticed. He smiled—maybe, just maybe Probert and the widow Lady Branna might know happiness after all. They seemed made for each other.

He walked up to Syg and placed his hand on her belly—she was just beginning to show.

Suddenly, Syg's eyes bugged out of her head. She doubled over.

Davage knelt down to her aid at once. "Syg, what is it? What's wrong?"

"Our son … he just kicked me."

Davage was shocked. "Kicked you? Is that possible? Is he developed enough yet to kick?" He was concerned. "We should to the dispensary at once for …"

"No, no, love—I'm fine, our son's fine. I've read about Elder embryos kicking out, not with their feet, but with their minds. It's his Gifts." Her eyes bugged out again. "Oh, you little Blanchefort you. He's really hitting me."

Lady Branna smiled. "Oh, my daughter Saari just about beat me to death, as I recall."

"Too bad she didn't succeed," Probert added, getting a scorching look from Branna.

Syg burst into a smile. Davage put his hand gently on her belly.

He felt a definite rap from within. "That's ... that's our son?"

Syg nodded.

Lord Probert and Lady Branna stepped forward. "It's often a sign of good luck to feel a genuine Gift-Kick," Probert said. "It's a rare thing, indeed."

Syg allowed Probert and Branna to touch her belly and soon they felt it. Syg allowed everyone to have a turn, each getting a little jolt from her belly.

"He hits hard," Ki said, smiling.

"He's going to be a real trooper," the Duke said.

Torrijayne approached. The two regarded each other with skeptical eyes. Silently, they came to a mutual agreement, and, smiling, Torri touched Syg's belly.

There's one. There's another. Torri was astounded and laughed with joy. Though these two women would probably never be friends, the matronly side of them could at least agree they were experiencing something special together.

The tenure of the *New Faith* was off to a great start.

* * * * *

"I did it," the woman said. "Everything that happened is my fault."

A handsome young man sat on a checkered cloth under the bows of a large tree. He had silver eyes that caught the light. Across from him, a slender, green-haired woman in a summer dress sat in a semi-reclined position. She wore a green and black charm at her neck with a large "M" etched on the face. They had been enjoying a simple picnic lunch from a basket.

She gazed at him, wondering what his reaction might be. "Please go on," he said.

After a moment, she looked at her trembling hands and continued. "I was angry, for what House Xandarr did to Zall 88, and for the knowledge that was lost. I adored those people. I gave them everything I had to give: knowledge, enlightenment, and all my love. And I had to watch them die because the Universe turned its back on them. Killed by the House of Xandarr, and, because of them, I fell and had to crawl in that terrible place at the bottom of all things for ages, enduring horror after horror. And then they took my name and twisted it into something despised." She clenched her fists and shook with bitterness. "I wanted revenge!"

She paused again, looking for a reaction. She received none. He sat there on the cloth with his silver eyes. She felt nervous and awkward. She brought a hand to her mouth, as if she wanted to lick it, but instead put her fingers into her green hair.

She continued. "I snuck out of the Windage. It's easy to get into that place, and terribly hard to get out. It took me a long time, crawling on my belly, but I discovered a way through the scalding pipes, and I brought the others with me. Free, with nothing in my soul but hatred, I turned my rage against the House of Xandarr. They turned me into a goddess of destruction, and that's exactly what I was going to become for them. I was going to see them dead!"

She tucked her legs up under her chest and put her head down. "It's funny," she said, "how there are so many Universal rules against the preventing of a pending tragedy, but there doesn't seem to be any against intentionally creating one. In fact, the Universe seems to welcome such a thing, to shutdown in one place and start fresh somewhere else. Wrapped up in my malice, I had a free hand. I prodded the Black Hats, prowling in their secret places. I whispered in their ears. I helped them enhance their Shadow tech and move against Xandarr. I came to Princess Vroc as she dangled on that Burgon hook. I fortified her. I gave them the thought to use her as a hammer against her own people. I thought it was clever and ironic of me to use her."

The wind picked up a little and moved through her green hair. "We've become close, you and I. I cherish what we have shared. For the first time in a long while, I actually care for something again; for you. But first, I wanted you to know what I've done. If there's anything that might be cultivated between us in the future, I wanted the air cleared."

The wind rustled through the branches of the tree. The young man still said nothing. She continued.

"Everything was going as I expected, but then my plot grew and became strange. I watched as the Black Hats prepared to destroy not only the House of Xandarr, but the whole planet along with it. And, if I'm being honest, I really didn't care. All I cared about was my revenge. Zall 88 all over again, and I didn't care."

"And then what?" the man asked.

"And then there was you," she said quickly, "coming to Xandarr's rescue. I think of all the kind like us, only you could have done what was accomplished there. You have something that few of us have: you have a heart, just like Maiax, and I thought he was a one-of-a-kind. You still care. Perhaps it's because you're so young. Perhaps the Universe hasn't beaten it out of you yet, but regardless ..."

She closed her eyes in fond remembrance. "I watched you. I watched you doing all the novel things that you did: choosing your brave warriors, placing them upon the board, and then patiently moving them at the correct time. We figured there was no possible way you could succeed. I then tried to impede your progress a little. I … gave Lord Milton the arcane medallion in the pub. He thought I was some Robber Lord from Planet Fall who smelled of catnip. He thought he was being clever and was stealing it. No, I, in disguise, gave it to him in the hopes that he would be an inconvenience for you. I tried to frighten your warriors with warnings and portents. I even tried to place the Sisters in front of them. I put the Sister who was fond of your Lord Blanchefort into fertility early knowing she would come for him and possibly injure the countess. And I came at that girl you took into the Hazards. I think I might have even killed her too, had you not watched over her."

She winced. "I watched the Sisters tear you apart, putting your immortal life at risk because you believed in that girl. I look at you now, and what you mean to me … I should have helped you, but I felt nothing. I just watched. I see that over and over in my thoughts … I'm so sorry."

"I had faith in my friend," he said. "It never crossed my mind that she would fail."

"Faith … Faith is something I haven't had in a long time. That is truly an elusive thing to have."

The woman was done talking. She had said her peace and they sat in silence. She was embarrassed by her revelation, and crushed by it as well. Taking a saddened breath, she stood and picked up her shoes. She gave him a last look and made to walk away.

"Where are you going, Mabs?" he asked.

She stopped, still holding her shoes.

"The Black Hats were going to attack Xandarr anyway, whether you whispered in their ear or not. You didn't make them angry, they already were that way. You didn't torment the Eleventh Daughter of House Xandarr. You didn't do anything other than bring the inevitable to pass more quickly. Can it be you fell so far, after the tragedy of Zall 88, that you lost every last bit of hope within you, even now?" He held his hand out. "Please, don't go."

She sat back down at the opposite end of the cloth, not looking him in the eye.

"But what about your friends, what I did to them?"

"I knew it was you, Mabs. It didn't take me long to figure it out. I wanted you to see what good people can do. I wanted you to see that it's easy to have faith. Have you heard from Maiax?" he asked.

"I heard that he is doing well," she said quietly. "I heard he found redemption. I'm glad for him—he deserves to be happy."

"He certainly does. And what of you, Mabs? What will it take to redeem you? To make you happy?"

She smiled with her Elder face. "I suppose that depends on you, Carahil. Is there enough faith in your heart for one such as me?"

The young man rummaged around in the basket and pulled out a tin full of cookies. He offered it to her. She scooted a little nearer to him and took one. "There's plenty of faith in my heart for you, Mabs."

She sat there holding her cookie. "You see everything in such an unclouded way. I thought you would be angry with me—hate me."

"Hate you? And how would that make you feel?"

"Sad. Heartbroken. I don't want you to hate me. I want to see what you see. I want to have faith once again. I want to believe in something … like you do."

"Don't be sad. I don't hate you. I care about you too much for that, Mabs."

She laughed a little and took a bite from her cookie. "That's what gets us into trouble. I suppose caring too much is a hazard we of the older folk must face. Everything withers around us eventually. And, I suppose we wither too."

"Caring, and to be cared for, isn't a hazard. It's a gift, a simple joy that is timeless. Look at that tree. I know, somewhere along its length, there are those who care for me, and that gives me a place all my own. There's a place there for you too, with me."

The tree they sat next to was huge, universal in size, its branches stretching out to endlessness. Its branches nurtured and enveloped all. The woman moved across the cloth and sat next to him. "It never occurred to me that this might have a happy ending," she said. "Thank you, for proving me wrong, and for creating something in me that I'd long lost."

"Sometimes having a little faith helps. We deserve a happy ending too."

She leaned her head against his shoulder and took his hand, and together they gazed at the Great Tree.

May all be saved.

Lunch beneath the Great Tree (*Carol Phillips*)